P9-DXL-457

OUTCASTS
OF
ORDER

Tor Books by L. E. Modesitt, Jr.

The Saga of Recluce

The Magic of Recluce
The Towers of the Sunset
The Magic Engineer
The Order War
The Death of Chaos
Fall of Angels
The Chaos Balance
The White Order
Colors of Chaos
Magi'i of Cyador
Scion of Cyador
Wellspring of Chaos
Ordermaster
Natural Ordermage
Mage-Guard of Hamor
Arms-Commander
Cyador's Heirs
Heritage of Cyador
Recluce Tales
The Mongrel Mage
Outcasts of Order

The Corean Chronicles

Legacies
Darknesses
Scepters
Alector's Choice
Cadmian's Choice
Soarer's Choice
The Lord-Protector's Daughter
Lady-Protector

The Imager Portfolio

Imager
Imager's Challenge
Imager's Intrigue
Scholar
Princeps
Imager's Battalion
Antiagon Fire
Rex Regis
Madness in Solidar
Treachery's Tools
Assassin's Price
Endgames (forthcoming)

The Spellsong Cycle

The Soprano Sorceress
The Spellsong War
Darksong Rising
The Shadow Sorceress
Shadowsinger

The Ecolitan Matter

Empire & Ecolitan
(comprising
The Ecolitan Operation
and *The Ecologic Secession*)
Ecolitan Prime
(comprising
The Ecologic Envoy and
The Ecolitan Enigma)

The Ghost Books

Of Tangible Ghosts
The Ghost of the Revelator
Ghost of the White Nights
Ghost of Columbia
(comprising
Of Tangible Ghosts and
The Ghost of the Revelator)

Other Novels

The Forever Hero
(comprising
Dawn for a Distant Earth,
The Silent Warrior, and
In Endless Twilight)
Timegods' World
(comprising
Timediver's Dawn and
The Timegod)
The Hammer of Darkness
The Green Progression
The Parafaith War
Adiamante
Gravity Dreams
The Octagonal Raven
Archform: Beauty
The Ethos Effect
Flash
The Eternity Artifact
The Elysium Commission
Viewpoints Critical
Haze
Empress of Eternity
The One-Eyed Man
Solar Express

L. E. MODESITT, JR.

OUTCASTS
OF
ORDER

TOR

A Tom Doherty Associates Book

NEW YORK

OUTCASTS OF ORDER

Copyright © 2018 by L. E. Modesitt, Jr.

A Tor Book
Published by Tom Doherty Associates
175 Fifth Avenue
New York, NY 10010

www.tor-forge.com

Tor® is a registered trademark of Macmillan Publishing Group, LLC.

The Library of Congress Cataloging-in-Publication Data is available upon request.

ISBN 978-1-250-17255-6 (hardcover)
ISBN 978-1-250-17257-0 (ebook)

Our books may be purchased in bulk for promotional, educational, or business use. Please contact your local bookseller or the Macmillan Corporate and Premium Sales Department at 1-800-221-7945, extension 5442, or by email at MacmillanSpecialMarkets@macmillan.com.

First Edition: June 2018

Printed in the United States of America

0 9 8 7 6 5 4 3 2 1

For Charlie
Who personifies determination . . .

CHARACTERS

Beltur   *Orphaned mage*
Margrena   *Healer*
Jessyla   *Healer, Margrena's daughter*
Klarisia   *Senior healer in Elparta*
Athaal   *Black mage (deceased), partner of Meldryn*
Caradyn   *Black mage*
Cohndar   *Senior black mage*
Felsyn   *Black mage*
Lhadoraak   *Black mage*
Meldryn   *Black mage, baker*
Mharkyn   *Black mage*
Osarus   *City Patrol Mage*
Waensyn   *Black mage, originally from Fenard*
Fhaltar   *Captain, City Patrol*
Jhaldrak   *Councilor for Elparta*
Veroyt   *Chief assistant to Jhaldrak*
Raymandyl   *Council clerk*
Alizant   *Trader in spices*
Barrynt   *Merchant, Axalt*
Jorhan   *Smith*
Johlana   *Consort of Barrynt, sister of Jorhan*

NORTHERN

CANDAR

Gulf of Murr

Gulf of Candar

RECLUCE

EASTERN OCEAN

The WORLD

OCEAN

Gulf of Austra

AUSTRA

Brysta

Valmurl

NORDLA

WESTERN OCEAN

Swartheld

Luba

Cigoerne

AFRIT

Atla

Swarth River

MEROWEY

HAMOR

Gandar
Great Western Ocean
Devalonia
Armat
Diev ruins
Bleyans
Rulyarth
West Cliffs
Suthya
River Sarron
Dosai
High Steppes
Carpa
West Horns
Sarronnyn
Lornth
Jera
Bornt
Sarron
the Ironwoods
Middlevale
Jeryna R.
North Branch
Rohrn
Berlitos
River Sarron
West-Wind
Fenard
Biehl
Jerans
Roof of the World
Gallos
South Branch
Delapra
the Stone Hills
Clynya
Summerdock
Kyphrie
Dellash (Esalia)
Cerlyn
Southwind
Copper Mines
Mildr R.
Southport
Stone Hills
West Horns
Naclos
The Great Forest
Phroan R.
Grasslands
Rybatta
the Empty Lands
High Desert
Diehl

OUTCASTS
OF
ORDER

I

Beltur sat bolt upright in the dark, sweating and shivering, the echo of thunder in his ears so loud that it took a moment before he could hear the pelting of heavy raindrops on the split slate roof. Even so, he first wondered where he was, before realizing he was in his bed in Athaal and Meldryn's house.

Except Athaal is dead . . . because you couldn't save him.

Beltur took a deep breath. He knew, honestly knew, that he'd done everything in his power to try to save Athaal, and it hadn't been enough. It might not have been enough if he'd been almost beside Athaal . . . *or you both might have died.* But he'd been where he'd been, and Athaal had been where he had been, and from fifty yards away Beltur had only been able to contain the chaos of the Gallosian mage, but he hadn't had enough power from that distance to also protect Athaal when the order of Athaal's shields had meshed with the chaos of the Gallosian's shields. He could still see that awful moment when that mixed order and chaos had destroyed both Athaal and the white mage. And nothing was going to change what had already happened.

With that realization, one that he had experienced more mornings than not over the two eightdays that had passed since the defeat of the Gallosian invaders, he slowly rolled into a sitting position with his legs over the side of the bed. Dark as it seemed, he had the feeling that it was close to the time he needed to be up, a feeling reinforced by the odor of baking bread that drifted upstairs from the bakery.

Beltur washed and shaved quickly, pulled on his clothes, except for his tunic, yanked on his boots, and hurried downstairs to the kitchen, where Meldryn had started the fire in the kitchen hearth. As quickly as he could, while being as careful as he could be, he fried some mutton strips, sliced the small melon into strips, and scrambled eggs and cheese.

Then he walked down the side hall that led to the bakery, stopped at the door, and said, "Breakfast is ready."

"I'll be there in a few moments," replied the gray-haired and bearded baker and black mage.

Beltur had only been back in the kitchen long enough to pour the hot cider into mugs and seat himself before Meldryn appeared and sat down at the table. He set a small loaf of bread on the end of the table. "This is for you. You have City Patrol duty today, don't you?"

"The first time since before all the fighting. This eightday, my duty days are threeday and sevenday. Patrol Mage Osarus requested that I be transferred back to patrol duty as soon as possible. He never wanted me to leave."

"He was wrong about that. Without you, things might have been very different."

Beltur couldn't argue about that. Whether, in the end, they would have been better for Athaal and Meldryn was another matter.

Meldryn took a sip of the hot cider. "You know I appreciate your staying and helping."

"It's the very least I could do," replied Beltur, not for the first time. And it was, given that Athaal and Meldryn had taken him in when he'd had to flee Gallos with nothing but the clothes on his back and a handful of coppers in his wallet. Besides, more practically, where else did he have to go? "I don't cook as well as you do." Beltur had almost said "as well as Athaal," but managed to change his words, knowing that Meldryn would still likely choke up at any mention of Athaal. That wasn't surprising, given that the two had been together for more than twenty years.

"I still appreciate it." Meldryn took a bite of the eggs, nodded, and then said, "Is it tomorrow when you go back to work with Jorhan?"

"Just for the day, unless he gets more copper." Beltur didn't want to dwell on that. "Have you talked to Cohndar recently?" He doubted that had happened, but he definitely didn't want to mention Athaal, and he did want to know anything Cohndar might have said, since Cohndar was the senior black mage in Elparta and wasn't exactly the most favorably inclined toward Beltur.

"No. He's been noticeably absent since before the invasion, except when he's had no choice, and he was cool toward . . . us, even then."

"Since Waensyn arrived, really," Beltur pointed out.

"Waensyn's a strong black, but . . ." Meldryn shook his head. "And how he could believe that Jessyla would ever be attracted to him is beyond me. She's much more suited to you, and everyone can see that."

"Except him."

"He's one of those people who only believes what suits him. That makes him very dangerous as far as you're concerned."

Beltur nodded as he took a mouthful of cheesed eggs. He didn't need to be told that, not after he'd heard Waensyn's and Cohndar's maneuverings during the invasion, maneuvering that had led to Beltur being given the most dangerous assignments possible for a mage-officer. *A very temporary mage-officer.* And one quickly returned to nonmilitary status as soon as possible. "I've got to leave early, especially in this rain. I'll need to see Raymandyl at the Council building before I go to the Patrol building."

Meldryn frowned quizzically. "You're still in the same duty period."

"I got a message saying I need to report there first before going to Patrol headquarters."

"They didn't even give you an eightday off after mustering you out."

"No, but they did pay me through the end of this eightday." And at three silvers an eightday, his mustering-out pay had amounted to over two golds, which Beltur could definitely use, especially since he hadn't been able to do any work with Jorhan forging cupridium. Still . . .

"What ever happened to that horse of yours?"

"Slowpoke? I don't know. By the time I was on my feet, Second Recon had left to return to Spidlaria. He wasn't in the stables. I went to look." Beltur had at least wanted a last moment with Slowpoke, especially since he doubted he would have survived without the big gelding. "They must have taken him with them."

"From what you've said, he was something."

"He was." Beltur would have liked to have kept Slowpoke, but he couldn't have afforded to feed him, and the bakery had no stable.

After he and Meldryn finished eating and he quickly cleaned up the kitchen, Beltur went upstairs and donned the mage's black tunic that matched his trousers, then pulled on the visor cap he'd been issued as a mage-officer—since he'd been told he should wear it when he was working with the City Patrol, but only then. He almost forgot his whistle, but pulled the lanyard over his neck and slipped the whistle inside his tunic.

He left the house at slightly after sixth glass, wearing a waterproof that had been Athaal's with the loaf of bread wrapped in cloth inside his tunic. The rain had subsided to a cold drizzle, all too common in mid-to-late fall, Meldryn had told him. He checked his shields, not that they were much use against rain, but he'd only been able to hold a full set of shields in the last eightday or so, given how order-depleted he'd been. Early as it was and with the rain, there were few people out on Bakers Lane. The north wind made the air feel even colder, even when Beltur's back was to it when he climbed up the street to the Council building.

When he stepped inside the door on the north side, he took a moment to shake the rain from the oiled waterproof, then walked toward the desk where Raymandyl usually sat. For a moment, Beltur didn't see the Council clerk, but then the black-haired clerk sat up straight from bending over, retrieving something from the file chests flanking his desk.

"As always, at the last moment," said Raymandyl, smiling, as Beltur stopped in front of the desk.

"I didn't get the message until late yesterday," replied Beltur. "You would have been gone by the time I could have gotten here."

The Council clerk frowned. "I gave the message to the runner on one-day. I'll have to look into that." He gestured to the single straight-backed chair in front of his table desk. "You have to sign some papers, and pick up your medallion."

Beltur had forgotten about the medallion worn by all mages working with the City Patrol and was glad to be reminded, but . . . "Papers?"

"You have to acknowledge that your duty has been extended to end seven eightdays from now."

Beltur frowned as he seated himself. "I thought it was six."

"The Council gave you an extra eightday's pay as a mage-officer."

Beltur almost shrugged. An extra eightday of patrol duty meant another two silvers, and he couldn't work every day with Jorhan in any event. *Assuming he can get hold of more copper.*

"I'll sign whatever you need me to sign."

The clerk handed across the record book. "Sign under the words that say you understand your duty has been extended."

Beltur signed and handed the book back. "Payday is still the same?"

"Starting next eightday for you." The clerk placed his seal beside Beltur's signature.

"Is there anything else I should know?"

"Not yet. I've heard that there's some disagreement about how to pay for all the expenses of the invasion."

"What's the problem?"

"The traders in Spidlaria and Kleth feel that those in Elparta should pay more." The round-faced clerk added, "They don't say it that way. It's something about payment corresponding to benefit. Councilor Jhaldrak's anything but pleased."

"They don't think it wouldn't have cost them far more if the invasion had dragged on or the Gallosians had taken Elparta?"

"They're traders," replied Raymandyl, as if that explained everything. He extended the silver medallion. "Don't forget this."

Beltur took it and slipped it over his neck and inside the waterproof. "Thank you. I'm glad I'm just a poor black mage." He rose from the chair and inclined his head.

"You're likely happier."

"But poorer." Beltur grinned before he turned and made his way toward the door.

Outside the Council building, the cold drizzle still fell, and Beltur couldn't help but wonder how many vendors would actually be at the market square. He walked steadily down the hill and past the north side of the market square on Patrol Street, where, somewhat to his surprise, he saw a number of vendors setting up stalls and carts and tables despite the rain. He glanced to the north, where the sky seemed a little lighter. Or was that his imagination?

He shook his head and kept walking. Five long blocks later, he reached the City Patrol headquarters, roughly halfway between the square and the River Gallos.

He entered by the north door, which led into the duty room. Immediately inside the door was a modest open space. A table desk was set forward of the single other door in the foyer, which opened onto a hallway leading deeper into headquarters. Behind the desk sat the duty patroller, uniformed in Spidlarian blue, as were all patrollers.

While Beltur didn't recognize the duty patroller, the man immediately smiled. "Welcome back, ser."

That surprised Beltur. He didn't recall any of the patrollers calling him "ser" before. "Thank you. I'm glad to be here." Even as he said the words and moved to the side of the desk to sign the duty book, he realized that he was glad to be back. Was that because the worst he ever had to do to someone was to restrain them with shields? While that was likely part of it, he felt that there was more, although he couldn't have said why at that moment.

The patroller eased the ledger-like book toward Beltur, and he dipped the pen lying on the blotter in the inkwell and signed. "Do you know who I'm working with?"

"No one's told me."

A voice behind Beltur said, "Who do you think?"

Beltur turned and couldn't help grinning at the sight of Laevoyt—tall and thin, long-faced with a beakish nose between two pale blue eyes and beneath reddish-blond hair. Even with his dark gray waterproof over his uniform, he still reminded Beltur of a river heron.

"I didn't expect that I'd be working with you again," said Beltur.

"Osarus thought it would be best for a few eightdays. After that, it might change."

Beltur couldn't help but wonder why Osarus had felt that way. Because of Athaal's death . . . or just because it would be easier for Beltur to get back to being a patrol mage? "I'd just as soon it didn't, but we don't have much say in that, do we?"

Laevoyt laughed. "We don't, and we'd better get moving." He turned and headed for the door.

Beltur followed, noting as he stepped onto Patrol Street that the rain seemed lighter. Since Laevoyt didn't speak again, Beltur asked, "Have there been more problems at the market square?"

"I wouldn't know. They had me on the waterfront with Dorryl."

"Is he big and tall?"

"Of course." Laevoyt laughed. "I'd rather be here."

The patroller didn't speak for several moments. "The word is that you saw a lot of action . . . and that, for a while you were in pretty bad shape."

"That's true," replied Beltur, "but the injuries were because of magery. That means . . . well . . . you either die or get well. I was fortunate. Athaal . . . he wasn't." That was an oversimplification that bordered on untruth, but Beltur really didn't want to explain. "Lhadoraak just barely made it. I understand another mage died also, but I never knew who it was."

"We heard about Athaal. He was a good man. Quiet, but good. He'll be missed."

"By more than a few people."

Laevoyt nodded.

"I saw there were a fair number in the market square already," Beltur observed, "even with the rain."

"Rain'll likely let up. Then it'll get colder. But folks will be trying to stock up on things before the snows start in earnest."

"I suppose I ought to show my face and medallion before I raise a concealment." Beltur eased the medallion out from under the waterproof.

"That will make the lightfingers more cautious. The ones with any sense."

By the time the two reached the square, Beltur could see that more people had appeared, both buyers and sellers, although the numbers seemed to be only a little more than half those he'd seen on his patrolling during harvest. While Laevoyt continued east on Patrol Street, Beltur strolled down the edge of the square on West Street, letting both vendors and sellers see him, listening and trying to hear what was said.

". . . mages are back . . ."

". . . good thing, too . . . last sixday . . . and sevenday . . . musta been four cutpurses here in the square . . ."

". . . think it's the young one . . ."

"A mage is a mage."

Beltur winced at the last words, knowing that wasn't so, not that he would have contradicted the old woman, because it was likely better that people in the market square didn't really think about the different levels of ability between mages. When he reached the south end of the square, he raised a concealment and eased into the square itself, trying to sense the flashes of the kind of chaos indicative of cutpurses or lightfingers. Usually there weren't that many attempts at straight smash-and-grab thefts in the market square, because with the crowds, escape for an obvious thief was problematical. Lightfingers were the biggest problem. Even with the two of them patrolling the square, some of the most accomplished lightfingers likely would still make a score.

He moved slowly through the aisles and spaces between stalls and carts, grateful that the drizzle finally dribbled to an end, heading back toward the north side of the square, where those who sold more expensive wares located themselves, unlike the produce sellers, who congregated more on the south side. While he'd been recovering from the effects of the last battle, he'd thought about patrolling the market, and he'd realized that he'd often been looking in the wrong places. The reason the lightfingers were around the stalls that carried more expensive goods wasn't because they wanted to take those goods. It was because that was where those with silvers and golds were most likely to be, and lifting wallets and golds was generally easier than boosting well-watched goods. Also, coins were far less identifiable, which meant that, unless the lifter was caught in the act, wallet in hand, proof of the theft was harder to establish.

Once he neared the tables with the more costly items, he dropped the concealment just so he could get a better impression of the people passing by, since he could only sense people as patterns of order and chaos when he was under a full concealment. Also, he had to admit, he wanted to see what might be available from the silks vendors. He could still recall the intense green shimmersilk scarf he'd once admired and had wanted to buy for Jessyla. He hadn't been able to afford it, and probably still couldn't, not and have enough coins to be able to pay Meldryn and meet other obligations with any certainty.

He pushed those thoughts aside and, as he moved toward the silks stall, kept sensing for trouble. As he passed a table with rings laid out on it, the man behind the table nodded politely. Beltur thought the vendor was the one who had almost lost a valuable ring to a trader's daughter—who had later been released from detention with merely a reprimand. But at least the vendor had gotten the ring back, plus a gold in damages from the trader. Beltur doubted some of the others he and Laevoyt had caught had gotten off that easily, and were still in the workhouse and would be for seasons, if not years, possibly without a hand.

When he reached the silks stall, tended by the same older woman he recalled, he glanced across the array of scarves on display, looking for the one that had caught his eye before. He didn't have to look far, because it caught his eye once more, with the way the colors shifted from pale seafoam green to a deep and rich sylvan green. He smiled as he thought, again, just how perfectly it would suit Jessyla.

"You're still thinking about buying it for her?" asked the vendor with an amused smile.

"I am, but not today."

"It won't be here forever. She might not be, either, if you wait too long to show her how you feel."

"It may not be here forever, that's true, but it's not exactly an inexpensive trifle."

"I told you it was three silvers, just for you, almost a season ago. It still is."

Once more, thinking about just how expensive shimmersilk was, Beltur studied the scarf. "She's a healer."

"She could wear it, then, whenever she wanted."

You wouldn't be where you are without Jessyla. "Thank you. You're right. I'll buy it." Beltur eased three silvers and two coppers from his belt wallet and extended them to the vendor.

"I only said three," she said.

"The silvers are for the scarf. The coppers are for the advice."

As she eased the scarf off the polished wooden rack, she said, "I wish you and the healer the very best, ser." Then she wrapped a small woolen cloth around the scarf and handed it to Beltur.

"Thank you." Beltur paused, then asked, "Will you be here all winter?"

The woman shook her head. "Once the snows stick, you won't see me until spring."

"Then, if I don't talk to you again, I wish you well."

The vendor nodded.

Beltur slipped the wrapped scarf into the inside pocket in his tunic, then turned back toward the stalls and tables with the jewelry.

He was again nearing the man who had nodded to him when he sensed a flicker of chaos to his left. He turned to see a man perhaps ten years older than Beltur himself attired in a dark brown jacket and trousers with a waterproof folded over his arm. Something about the man, as well as a faint aura of chaos, bothered Beltur enough that he fixed his eyes on the other, coldly.

The man met Beltur's gaze. "Have I done something to upset you, ser mage?"

Beltur managed what he hoped was a lazy smile. "Not yet. I do hope you don't. For your sake, not mine."

"I wouldn't think of it."

"You already have. Just don't do it."

Beltur could sense the other's dismay by the swirling of order and chaos.

"I appreciate your solicitousness, ser mage."

"You really don't, but you should. Good day." With that, Beltur drew a concealment around himself, but kept his senses fixed not only on the man in brown, but those around him. The other turned, slowly, seemed to scan the stall beside him, and then moved on. Beltur followed the other as he made his way toward the east side of the square, seemingly browsing as he did so.

Another figure approached the man Beltur had followed. "You weren't gone that long."

From the voice and the patterns of order and chaos, Beltur felt that the newcomer was a woman dressed as a young man.

"They've got a mage on duty. Young one, but he spotted me even before I got set up along the jewelry row."

"How do you know that?"

"He made it clear, and he did it in a way that told everyone else around what he thought I was. Everyone was looking at me. We'll have to try the other market square."

"That's a long walk, and the pickings aren't as good."

"There's only one mage on duty on any day. If he's here, he won't be there."

That wasn't quite true, Beltur knew, because Osarus occasionally patrolled the squares, but it was largely so.

The two turned and walked northward on East Street, clearly headed for the square not all that far from where Jessyla and her mother lived with Margrena's sister. Beltur couldn't do much but let them go, since they hadn't done anything, and might not. *Not today, anyway.*

He had mixed feelings about his encounter with the lightfinger, because if he'd just walked past and out of sight, then doubled back under a concealment, he might have been able to catch the man lifting something—and that would have brought him a token worth two silvers. Somehow, that felt wrong to Beltur, even though it was more than clear that the man was a lifter of some experience and likely would never change.

At ninth glass, according to the routine he and Laevoyt had set up eightdays and eightdays ago, Beltur made his way to the corner of Patrol and West, where Laevoyt was already waiting.

"You haven't whistled for me yet. Losing your touch?" The tall patroller grinned.

"I did manage to scare a lightfinger away from the square." Beltur went on to explain, briefly, what had happened, then said, "I know he was going to lift something, but I didn't feel right about trailing him around."

"I don't know about that, but what if he'd been put there as a decoy for another lightfinger? You could have tailed him all morning, while the others were lifting. Osarus warns us about that every so often."

Beltur nodded, then offered a crooked smile and asked, "So we're really here to catch those who are less skilled?"

"Mostly. The most skillful lightfingers prey on the wealthy. It makes sense. Why risk spending a year or more in the workhouse, or even losing a hand, for a few coppers, or even a few silvers?"

"I hadn't thought of it that way."

"You had enough to learn, and you were doing just fine. Better than a lot of mages much older." Laevoyt gestured toward the square. "We need to get back to work. See you at first glass."

"Until then." Beltur stepped away from the tall patroller, raised a concealment, and headed back toward the tables and stalls with the more expensive goods, wondering if he'd find more traces of the flickering chaos.

For whatever reason, he didn't, and he made his way through the square, dropping the concealment as he went down the produce rows, which seemed largely to feature, unsurprisingly, either late-season crops, such as heavy apples, or root crops, although he did see some beans, but then he remembered that some growers planted beans for late harvests.

Despite the chill in the air, which had lessened somewhat as noon approached, Beltur was still thirsty as he made his way to the single ale cart, located, as always, halfway between the north and south sides of the square on West Street.

The clean-shaven and stocky Fosset watched as Beltur approached, then said cheerfully, "So you're back from the fighting." He took a small mug off the wooden rack. His black curly hair was still damp and plastered against his skull.

"They didn't seem to want me any longer than they had to have me," replied Beltur, taking out his loaf of bread. "I could really use a mug of your ale. The ale I got with the company I was assigned to wasn't all that good."

"That's because the Council only buys the cheapest stuff." Fosset filled the mug and handed it to Beltur, a single small mug on each Patrol day being the only free perquisite allowed to patrollers and mages working the market square.

"And your uncle isn't about to brew something that bad?" Beltur took a mouthful of bread and followed it with a swallow of the ale, a smooth solid medium dark brew, better than most, and definitely welcome.

"Not for as little as he'd get for it."

Beltur nodded. "Meldryn had that problem baking bread to supply to the troopers."

"How's he doing? I heard about Athaal. Didn't seem right."

"He's still upset, but he's keeping the bakery going. I help as I can. He and Athaal took me in when I fled Gallos and barely had a handful of coppers. I think I might have told you that."

"Not my type, but they're good people."

"In that fashion, Athaal wasn't mine, either, but neither had eyes for anyone else."

"There's a lot to be said for that. I should have followed that path sooner." Fosset shook his head. "You consorted?"

"No." Beltur smiled sheepishly. "There is a healer, though."

"Good for you."

"Fosset! Stop jawing and draw me a large one. Begging your pardon, ser mage," added the short and stocky graybeard who approached the cart.

"I wouldn't want to keep a man from slaking his thirst." Beltur smiled politely. He thought he'd seen the older man before, probably asking for an ale from Fosset, but wasn't entirely certain.

When Fosset turned to draw a large mug of ale, Beltur ate more of the bread, and then sipped more ale, trying to space it with the mouthfuls of bread. When he finished, he had to wait for several moments until Fosset finished with another customer before he returned the mug.

"Thank you. Much appreciated."

"Any day, ser mage."

Some time after meeting Laevoyt at the first glass of the afternoon and then returning to the square, Beltur made his way along the jewelry row again, once more not under a concealment.

"Why didn't you take in that lightfinger?" asked the man who had nodded to Beltur earlier. "You made it pretty clear what he is."

"He hadn't done anything. I can't have the City Patrol take someone in for what he's thinking. I have to catch him in the act, the way I did with that ring that was switched on you."

"You were that mage?" The vendor frowned.

"I was that mage. You got the ring back and a gold in damages."

"That doesn't happen all that often. I just thought . . . you were younger." The vendor shook his head.

I was, in too many ways. "I was new to Elparta then." Beltur smiled. "I suppose I still am."

"Thank you. I got a good look at the lightfinger, anyway. So did several others. It might help."

And it might not. "I hope so." Beltur nodded and continued on.

Although Beltur varied being concealed and being visible, while he did occasionally sense flickers of chaos, the rest of his duty time was uneventful, and at fourth glass, he and Laevoyt walked back along Patrol Street toward headquarters.

"It didn't seem as though there were as many shoppers or possible thieves around today."

"There weren't. It'll be worse on sevenday. That's if it doesn't rain or snow."

Beltur glanced northward, but the sky was clear.

"We're getting to that time of year when northeasters are more frequent. Just hope you're not on duty when one hits."

"One hit during harvest. It was pitch dark."

"That was a mild one."

"Then I definitely don't want to be on duty when one hits."

Once they reached headquarters, Beltur signed out and said goodbye to Laevoyt, then hurried out and up Patrol Street to Bakers Lane, where he walked swiftly north until he reached the corner with Crossed Lane—and Meldryn's house and bakery.

As he was about to open the door, he could sense someone else in the house, in the front parlor, in fact, where neither Meldryn nor Athaal ever sat unless they had company. Beltur paused, then nodded as he sensed the blackness that signified another mage or possibly a healer, although, if the other person happened to be a healer, it couldn't be either Margrena or Jessyla, because Beltur would have recognized the order/chaos pattern of either. Since he was curious as well as wary, he completely shielded himself from another mage sensing him and then raised a concealment before easing the front door open just enough to slip inside before he closed it as quietly as possible.

Then he just stood there, listening.

"Cohndar and Waensyn insist he's not a true black mage." Meldryn's voice was low. "He's got strong shields, and the skill to handle the tiniest bits of order and chaos."

"I understand that. Even Waensyn will grant that. His concern is that while Beltur may be a good man and a strong mage, he's neither fish nor fowl."

"Why is that a problem? He risked his life for all of us more than once."

"Ah . . . you . . . and, well . . . Athaal as well . . . you've always tried to help people like some collect stray dogs. Beltur's not a lapdog nor a guard dog. He's a talented and well-meaning mongrel. Mongrels are unpredictable."

"You sound like Cohndar."

"I just don't want to see the blacks here divided. We have enough trouble with the Council as it is."

"So what does Cohndar want? To throw him out into the winter?"

"I don't know. I know that Cohndar has met with most of the other blacks . . ."

"And they asked you to bring the matter to my attention."

"It's for his own good."

"I like the way Cohndar and his friends are willing to define Beltur's own good in a way that makes them comfortable." Meldryn's voice was wry. "I should think you'd be happy to have another strong black on our side."

"I am. But I don't want to see us split."

"Why should Beltur be a problem? He's never done anything—"

"Waensyn would disagree. He finds Beltur most arrogant."

"Why? Because Beltur politely told him that he was full of sowshit? Because Beltur defended the man who raised him when he was orphaned? All that told me far more about Waensyn than I ever wanted to know." While Meldryn's voice was level, Beltur could sense the anger behind him, and likely the other mage could as well. "Or is it because the young healer prefers an honest, talented, and forthright young mage to a slimy snake like Waensyn?"

"Waensyn didn't mention anything like that."

"Talk to Margrena about it."

"Talking to everyone would just do more to split us."

"I didn't say everyone. I said Margrena."

"Waensyn claims she is also tainted because of her ties to the whites in Gallos."

"She's as black as black can be, and Beltur is black in the best of all possible ways," said Meldryn firmly.

"Will you let me judge for myself?" replied the mage that Beltur could not identify.

"You will, anyway, I think."

Beltur decided it was time to make an entrance. He eased open the door silently, then closed it firmly and loudly, dropping his concealment and chaos/order shield as he did. "Meldryn! I'm back!"

"I'm in the parlor," Meldryn replied loudly.

Beltur hung the waterproof on one of the pegs behind the door and then walked to the archway on his left, which offered the entrance to the parlor from the hallway leading off the small front foyer.

Meldryn rose from his usual armchair and gestured to the older man in black seated on the settee. "Beltur, I don't believe you've ever met Felsyn. Felsyn, this is Beltur."

"I've heard a great deal about you, ser, but I've never had the pleasure." The older mage didn't look the way that Beltur had pictured him at all. He'd thought to see a wizened old man with tangled white hair, instead of a trim-looking older man with sparse but short-cut gray hair, a round face, and muddy brown eyes.

"I've seldom found that I've brought much pleasure to most other mages," replied Felsyn without rising. "My tongue is too often sharper than my wits."

"I've heard otherwise," said Beltur. "I know Lhadoraak speaks most highly of you, and Athaal and Meldryn certainly respect your knowledge and understanding of magery. I'm certain there are others who do as well, but since I haven't met them yet, I won't try to speak for them."

"Please sit down, both of you," said Felsyn.

Beltur took the straight-backed chair and waited.

"I understand that your uncle was a white in Gallos."

"Yes, ser. He raised me from the time I was nine. My mother and her family, all except my uncle, died of a flux when I was very small. My father died of the green flux when I was nine."

"Were you ever a white?"

"My uncle tried to make me one. I wasn't any good at it. I really didn't learn how to be a mage until Margrena's daughter made the comment that I was really a black. That only happened a few days before Arms-Mage Wyath and his men killed my uncle. He held them off so that I could escape. I didn't want to leave him, but he insisted. He said that my mother would never forgive him if he let anything happen to me." Beltur then described what had happened in the audience chamber in the adjoining room when six white mages and the archers with iron-tipped arrows had attacked the two of them.

Felsyn nodded slowly. "I had heard of that. Did you ever kill anyone in Gallos?"

"No, ser. I did shield some guards to help my uncle when he took me to Analeria . . ." Beltur went on to explain the mission to scout out the plains raiders and how they had been attacked three times by raider bands.

"You never initiated an attack against these plains people?"

"No, ser. All the times, they attacked us first. We didn't even ride toward them."

"Your uncle. Why did Wyath have him killed?"

"I don't know. I would judge that it was because he didn't agree with Wyath, but he never did anything against the Arms-Mage, and I never heard him say anything against Wyath except that he felt Wyath didn't like anyone who didn't agree completely with him."

"How did you end up here in Elparta?"

"I didn't dare return to my uncle's house when I thought all the whites were looking for me. The only people I thought I could trust were Margrena and Jessyla. I went to their house, and Athaal was there. He and the healer thought I should go with Athaal to Elparta."

"You didn't ask them first?"

"No, ser. I really didn't know what to do. I was just looking for a safe place to figure out what I could do next. They were the ones who suggested I come to Elparta." Beltur wondered why Felsyn was asking questions about something that surely he'd heard about. Was it just because he wanted to hear for himself? Or hadn't anyone told him?

Felsyn turned abruptly to Meldryn. "Is that what Athaal said?"

Meldryn smiled wryly. "Yes. In fact, he said that Beltur was so distraught and confused that someone had to help him. He also wasn't terribly pleased that Beltur's uncle hadn't wanted to acknowledge that Beltur was a black."

Felsyn shook his head. "I've heard enough. I don't know why Cohndar and Waensyn are so concerned, but I wouldn't worry about it." He rose slowly, then shook his shoulders, as if trying to loosen them. Finally, he looked at Beltur, who had also stood. "As Meldryn has said, you're as black as any in Elparta, and that's what I'll say. I've taken enough of your time, and I need to be heading home."

"Would you like—" Beltur began.

"You're kind, but I'm not that old. Not yet. If I can't walk four blocks . . ." The older mage walked to the foyer, followed by Meldryn and Beltur.

After closing the door behind Felsyn, Meldryn gestured toward the parlor, and once they were both seated, he turned to Beltur. "How much did you hear before you made your appearance?"

"I thought I was shielded."

"You were. But I heard the door click. Felsyn didn't. His hearing isn't quite what it once was."

"He was saying something about Cohndar and Waensyn saying I wasn't a true black."

Meldryn nodded. "Then you overheard most of the important parts. Before that we were mostly talking pleasantries. He said he came to see how I was doing . . . because of Athaal. That clearly wasn't really what was on his mind. Or not all of it."

"What do you think was on his mind besides Athaal?" Beltur had his own ideas about that, but he wanted to hear what Meldryn had to say.

"I think Cohndar has been trying to influence him. Felsyn doesn't like that."

"Why won't Waensyn and Cohndar leave me alone?"

"Because Waensyn wants Jessyla, obviously, and he's spent eightdays flattering Cohndar, who's always been susceptible to flattery."

"So what should I do now?"

"We should have dinner. Felsyn is most likely on your side, and certainly Lhadoraak is, and we can't do anything more at the moment." Meldryn smiled. "I did make a meat pie."

Dinner sounded very good to Beltur after a long chilly day.

II

On fourday morning, Beltur still got up early, earlier than he had risen before he'd become a mage-officer. That was because Athaal had been the one to rise early and fix breakfast, and with Meldryn now fixing dinner, Beltur felt he should do as much as he could, even if he wasn't quite the cook Athaal had been. Meldryn had already offered a few suggestions, such as adding diced shallots to the cheesed eggs, and Beltur had no doubt that he'd end up a better cook just by listening to Meldryn.

After cleaning up, he was just about to leave to meet with Jorhan, hoping that the smith had been able to locate some copper, when Laranya arrived. She hadn't come on threeday, since Athaal and Meldryn had agreed that she didn't have to come when it rained, largely because rain made her son's ailments even worse.

"How is Nykail this morning?"

"He's better than yesterday. My mother is with him." Laranya glanced past Beltur toward the kitchen.

"It's not quite as bad as yesterday. There are only fragments of cheesed eggs everywhere, and a burned shallot or two." Beltur doubted there was either, but if there happened to be, Laranya would certainly find it.

Laranya shook her head, sadly, then said with mock gravity, "Someday you will learn to cook and clean. Perhaps when I am old and gray."

"If I'm fortunate." Beltur grinned, then slipped past her and stepped outside into a chill wind. While he wasn't that uncomfortable in his old black wool tunic, if it got much colder, he'd need to get a heavy overcoat. *And there's no doubt it's going to get much colder.*

He walked east on Crossed Lane until he came to the east wall road, and then walked south along the wall until he came to the southeast gate, where he passed the guards, one of whom nodded at him, and then headed east along the road that eventually led to Axalt, the mountain town and small land that controlled the only usable pass through the Easthorns in the northern third of all Candar. He wasn't going that far, just to the smithy owned by Jorhan.

Beltur smiled wryly, recalling when Athaal had taken him to meet the smith. Athaal had said that it was only about a kay beyond the gate, and Beltur had begun to wonder about that as the two of them had walked past plots with small cots, one woodlot, and several stretches of rocky pastures before reaching a short stone lane leading up to a graystone house. While the smithy wasn't the more than two kays Beltur had originally thought, it was close to a kay and a half from the gate.

When he turned up the lane, Beltur saw that a line of smoke rose from the chimney of the smithy—a small stone outbuilding with a split slate roof, just like the main house and the small barn that held Jorhan's single horse and cart. The smoke suggested that Jorhan had obtained more copper. Beltur certainly hoped so.

The door to the smithy was ajar, another sign that the weather had turned, since during harvest and early fall Jorhan had kept it wide open. Beltur opened it and stepped inside, then eased the door back to where it had been, enjoying the comparative warmth of the smithy.

The short and muscular smith turned from the workbench where he was working on a mold for casting. "You're a mite early this morning."

"I must have walked faster because of the chill."

"Chill? It's just bracing out."

Beltur caught the glint in Jorhan's gray eyes and laughed. "A little more than bracing, I think, but nothing compared to what I can expect. Or so I've been told. You got more copper, I take it?" When Beltur had met with Jorhan on the previous fiveday, the smith had told him to return on fourday, after he dealt with the Council about the copper and tin they'd supplied.

"Enough for today. I won't get more until sixday morning. Barrynt's bringing me some from Axalt. Tin, too."

"Barrynt?" Beltur hadn't heard that name before.

"My sister Johlana's consort."

"Oh, the one who's a merchant in Axalt. You've mentioned him before, but never by name."

"He's a good man. Doesn't trade metals, but he knows those who do, and he's lined up ten stones' worth of copper. Sent me a message with one of his friends telling me that."

"What ever happened to the copper the Council sent?"

"The Council took back what we hadn't forged. Right after we talked." Jorhan offered a crooked smile. "Not all of it."

"So you need to have copper bought elsewhere?"

"You've got it. Council'd be on me like ticks on a dog in midsummer if they thought I'd kept even a digit of what we hadn't forged into blades. They can't suffer the slightest bit of copper helping a poor smith. They wouldn't even sell it to me. Not unless I paid double the worth."

Beltur couldn't help but wonder who might be behind that. Cohndar? Or just trader greed? "So if there's no copper . . . ?"

"I have some left from before. Made sure the Council knew I had it. Showed them the bill of lading. Bastards even weighed it. You'd think they were from Worrak." Jorhan snorted.

Worrak? For a moment, Beltur didn't understand before he realized that Jorhan was comparing the Council to the pirates who effectively controlled that port city.

"There's enough copper left for some candelabra and some small pieces, plus a pair of mirrors. That's what I figure, anyway. We'll cast what we can today, and I'll do the finish work tomorrow, and then we should be able to do some blades on sixday. That trader from Lydiar wants more."

"The one who took three of them?"

"That's him." Jorhan gestured toward the small hearth. "Might as well get started."

Beltur took off the older tunic he wore when he came to the smithy and hung it on one of the wall pegs, then walked over to the hearth bellows. "What's the first melt for?"

"We'll start with a candelabrum."

Beltur began to pump the bellows, and by little more than a fifth of a glass later, Jorhan used his tongs to lift the stoneware crucible from the forge and carefully poured the bronze mix—a mix with far less tin than regular bronze—into the mold.

After blotting his forehead, Beltur began to concentrate on creating within the hot metal the fine layers of order lattices that held chaos locked within that order. Once the lattices were in place and all linked together, he had to hold them until the metal was solid enough that the bronze and the ordered chaos were one. Then he rested while Jorhan readied the next mold.

After drinking a mug of Jorhan's bitter ale, Beltur said, "You really didn't say much when I asked about how you managed during the invasion. The company I was with rode past here, and I saw a trail of smoke from the smithy, but everything was shuttered tight. Did the Gallosians bother you?"

"No. There was only one bunch, and they didn't stay long."

"We attacked them, but we didn't have enough men to stop them. They withdrew when the main forces kept them from getting any support." That wasn't the entire story, but Beltur didn't want to explain more.

"Could have been a lot worse, like I said before."

"I thought you were thinking of going to Axalt."

"Didn't see much point after that one bunch left. If they couldn't stick around, I figured it wouldn't be long before it was all over. Shame about Athaal. He was a good man. I doubt that there was a mean bone in his body. That might have been his problem. Takes either anger or meanness if you want to win a fight. Not too much of either, though. Otherwise you get carried away and get beaten or killed."

"That sounds like experience."

Jorhan shook his head. "I just got that from watching over the years. You've been the one doing the fighting. You think I'm wrong?"

Beltur hadn't thought of it in quite that way, and although he hadn't, he certainly felt anger against the Prefect and Arms-Mage Wyath. But he hadn't really been aware of that anger during the fighting. *But you certainly felt strongly.* "No, I think you're right . . . except I think other strong feelings come into it."

"Sounds like you had a knack for it."

Beltur couldn't help but think about the captain's words, saying that Beltur would make a good officer. "The captain thought so. I'm not so sure. I probably wouldn't have made it without Slowpoke."

"That's the big gelding you rode."

Beltur nodded. "Wish I could have kept him, but what use does a poor mage have for a big horse. Besides, he was already gone with the company by the time I recovered."

"Happens that way, sometimes. You ready to heat the next mix?"

Beltur nodded and moved to the bellows.

By the fourth glass of the afternoon, Beltur was definitely feeling tired . . . and very out of shape for working the bellows and concentrating on chaos and order. But the two of them had cast two sets of candelabra and two mirrors. Before donning his tunic, Beltur washed up, then waited for Jorhan to return from the house.

"How early on sixday?" asked Beltur once the smith appeared.

"The usual." Jorhan grinned. "Even if the copper's not here, it will be soon enough that the Council won't be able to tell." He extended a single

silver. "This is for the day's work. After I get what the Council owes me, you'll get the piecework pay. Maybe sooner, but I have to pay Barrynt on delivery."

"I understand." Beltur did all too well. He hadn't received any pay for the time he'd spent as a mage-officer until he was mustered out, despite the Council's promises to pay, which had meant going for half a season without any coins coming in. Meldryn had experienced similar problems in being paid for the bread he'd baked as well. But then, traders wanted to be paid, but often delayed paying as long as they could, from what Beltur had seen. "I'll see you on sixday."

The air seemed colder as Beltur walked back along the east road toward Elparta. He hurried, because he wanted to see Jessyla and Margrena before heading back home, Meldryn's house being the closest thing to home he was likely to have for some time.

He couldn't help smiling when he caught sight of the two-story dwelling with the narrow green lintel above the door. That was the only sign that the house held healers, although it actually belonged to Grenara, Margrena's much older sister, who did very little healing anymore, but Grenara had taken in Margrena and her daughter after the two had fled Gallos when the Prefect's arms-mage had attempted to destroy all mages in Gallos who opposed him.

He had barely knocked on the door when the red-haired, green-eyed Jessyla opened it. "I thought it might be you."

"Thought or hoped?" Beltur smiled, taking in just how good she looked in the green of a healer, and mentally comparing the green to the shades in the scarf.

"Both. Do come in." She stepped back and opened the door wide. "You're wearing the old tunic."

Beltur stepped into the front room that also served as the parlor. "I was working today."

"You're all right with working, now?"

"I'm back on duty with the City Patrol. That happened on threeday. It does mean I'll get paid, at least for another seven eightdays." Beltur shrugged as he stood by one of the backed benches in the parlor.

A voice came from the back of the house. "Jessyla?"

"Mother, it's Beltur."

"I'll be there in a moment."

Beltur glanced around the small room. "Your aunt's not here?"

"Auntie's visiting her friend Almaya. I'm sure she won't mind missing your visit."

As Margrena, several digits shorter than her daughter and blond, entered the parlor, she glanced at her daughter, then shook her head.

"She won't," said Jessyla. "But she has admitted that you're a better mage than she thought. She'll never tell you that."

"Not any time soon," added Margrena. "Can you stay?" She gestured toward the bench facing the door into the kitchen.

"Only for a little bit," replied Beltur, moving to the bench, but waiting for the two to seat themselves before he sat down. His eyes went to the feline sitting on the third step of the narrow staircase to the upper level. Growler was a large cat, with intense blue eyes, a tan body, and black-striped legs and tail, a tail that appeared excessively long to Beltur. "Growler didn't run off."

"You moved away from him," said Jessyla.

"Hello there, Growler." Beltur tried to project a sense of order, of all being well.

Growler ignored the pleasantry and began to groom himself.

"One of the reasons I came was to report to the healer who saved my life twice." Beltur smiled ruefully at Margrena.

"Your order/chaos balance appears a little low, but Jessyla could have told you that."

"Some of that's because I was working with Jorhan today. I haven't been working that hard in eightdays."

"You still need to be careful," said Margrena.

Jessyla nodded emphatically.

"You said one reason," said the older healer. "Why else?"

"I'd like to accompany you two tomorrow in your healing . . ."

Margrena raised her eyebrows. "Why? I thought you were working with Jorhan."

"I am, but he won't get any more copper until sixday. I've been reading more in *On Healing*—the book by Leantor—but reading's not the same as doing, and I really need to observe trained healers actually healing. Also . . ." Beltur looked to Jessyla. "You did say I should accompany you someday . . ."

Margrena looked sideways at her daughter.

"I did, Mother."

"That doesn't explain why you want to accompany us. It shouldn't be just for Jessyla's company."

"It's not that. I've been forced by circumstances to do healing. If that happens again, I'd like to know more."

"You've had to do more than the boy with the brain chaos?" asked Jessyla.

"I had to help heal troopers who were injured." Only one really, and a Gallosian at that, but he'd felt almost useless in dealing with a broken leg. "I'd rather learn than just help Meldryn, especially since I'm more likely to be in the way than useful in the bakery. If you prefer, I'll only accompany you, or even Grenara."

For several moments, Margrena said nothing. Then she looked to Jessyla.

"He's being truthful," replied her daughter.

"Why now, though?" asked Margrena.

"I have the time, and too often anything I've put off . . . well, it's turned out that I wish I hadn't."

"We'll try it," the healer conceded. "We leave here at about half before seventh glass."

"I'll be here." Beltur looked at Jessyla. "You don't have to tell me. I will wear my good black tunic."

Jessyla shut her mouth.

Margrena laughed. "I wish your aunt could see the expression on your face."

"Don't you dare tell her."

Margrena looked to Beltur. "What do you think? Should I?" Then she smiled. "Don't answer."

"You'd best answer," replied Jessyla.

"I don't think you should tell Grenara, that is, unless Jessyla . . . well . . ." Beltur grinned.

"You two are impossible."

"Difficult at times, clueless at other times," replied Beltur, "but not impossible." He stood. "Much as I would rather be here, I do need to get back to the bakery. Today was a long day, and I suspect tomorrow will also be long."

"If you weren't . . ." Jessyla shook her head.

"You can see him out," said Margrena, standing and moving toward the kitchen.

Jessyla stood, but made no move toward the door.

"I do have to go," Beltur said. "I'm not used to working as hard as I did today. I think you can tell that." He paused. "And I smell like I've worked that hard."

Jessyla took his hands, then wrapped her arms around him. "You think I care about that?"

Beltur embraced her . . . carefully, although he thought he'd gotten the grime off his hands.

After a time, Jessyla released him. "You do need to go. Make sure you shield yourself on the way home."

"I always do." Beltur squeezed her hands before letting go. "I'll see you in the morning. Half before seventh glass."

Jessyla moved to the door and opened it.

Beltur brushed her cheek with his hand, then stepped outside. "Until tomorrow."

He could feel her eyes on him as he walked toward the corner and Bakers Lane.

III

After fixing, eating, and cleaning up breakfast on fiveday morning, Beltur donned his new black tunic, then slipped the solid silver patrol medallion over his head and tucked it inside his tunic, since he didn't want to leave it behind, not when losing it would cost him half a gold. Then he made sure he had the woolen-wrapped shimmersilk scarf safely in the inner pocket of the tunic before making his way downstairs and out into a morning that was clear but with cold gusty winds, suggesting a storm might be coming. By the time he reached the door of Grenara's house, his hands were chill, and he realized that he was going to need a pair of gloves, and fairly soon. He'd never had to worry about gloves in Fenard, but then Fenard had never gotten as cold as Elparta did.

Jessyla opened the door just before he was about to knock. "Come in. It will be just a moment before Mother's ready."

"Good." Beltur eased out the wool-wrapped package as soon as she closed the door. "This is for you."

She looked at the drab cloth doubtfully as she took it.

"It's what's inside. Go ahead."

Jessyla unfolded the cloth. Her mouth opened when she saw the green silk. "Beltur!"

"Try it on." Beltur just hoped it looked as good on her as he'd thought it would.

"I . . . I don't know. You shouldn't have."

"I've been looking at that scarf almost since the first days I came to Elparta. I decided that waiting to buy it wasn't a good idea."

"What wasn't a good idea?" asked Margrena as she came down the narrow steps.

"Not buying the scarf she's wearing." Beltur stepped back so that Margrena could see.

"*Not* buying it?" Margrena raised her eyebrows as she looked at Beltur. "It's beautiful."

"There are times not to be completely practical," Beltur said.

"I'm glad you said 'completely,'" replied Margrena.

"How does it look?" asked Jessyla.

"Absolutely beautiful on you," declared Beltur.

"You would say that," Jessyla turned. "Mother?"

"It's gorgeous. Especially on you." Margrena offered a quirky smile. "There is one problem. Beautiful as it is, it's totally unsuited to wearing today."

"I'll put it away upstairs in a safe place. I won't be long."

As soon as Jessyla headed up the staircase, Margrena asked, "Do you think that was wise?"

"Not completely practical, as I said, but it expresses what I feel and what I owe her . . . and you, but I could only afford one."

"You really couldn't afford that. What was it? Half a gold, at least."

"The vendor took pity on me. I've been looking at it for a season."

Margrena shook her head. "At your age, that's patience."

"I'm not so sure that I wasn't too patient."

"You thought about getting it before the fighting?"

"I didn't. I should have. I was fortunate."

"Fortunate about what?" asked Jessyla as she hurried down the steps.

"Fortunate that I was finally able to get the scarf for you," replied Beltur with a smile.

Jessyla shook her head. "*That* wasn't what you were talking about."

"I can't keep much from you."

"You shouldn't."

"We do need to be going," suggested Margrena. "You two will figure it out, I'm certain." She moved toward the door.

This time it was Jessyla who shook her head.

Beltur managed not to smile as he followed Jessyla, then waited for Margrena as she locked the door. Once they were on the street, heading west, he asked, "Where do you begin?"

"Where we always do, at the Council Healing House," replied Margrena. "It's two blocks from the northwest market square. It won't be exciting."

"Usually, it's not," said Jessyla.

Margrena glanced sideways, then continued, "Most of the time, it's cuts or scrapes with wound chaos, sometimes a broken bone."

"What about fluxes?"

"We don't see many of those. There's usually not much a healer can do besides telling people what to drink and eat, and what not to, because the chaos is in such small specks and spread through the entire body."

Beltur frowned. "If you could reduce some of that chaos, would it help?"

"It might, but the effort might also take a toll on the healer. A flux isn't like a wound, where most of the chaos is concentrated around one spot. The chaos specks in a flux are so small I can barely sense them. Grenara could when she was younger, she says, and Jessyla can, but there are hundreds upon hundreds upon hundreds of them."

Although Beltur wondered about that, he recalled how hard it had been to eliminate all the chaos from Claudyt's grandson's head—and all that chaos had been in one small spot. As he walked beside the two, a gust of especially cold wind reminded him again that he needed to do something about getting an overcoat or warm cloak—and some gloves.

"There's the Council Healing House," said Jessyla after a time, pointing at the building on the next corner.

The building was just a two-story graystone oblong, with narrow windows. The shutters, the window trim, and the doors were painted blue, and some of that paint was peeling from the shutters. Beltur noticed that there were at least five chimneys, but despite the chill, only one showed a trace of smoke.

Even before the three reached the main door, Beltur could sense the excess chaos, well beyond the normal pattern. When he opened the door for the other two, he felt almost assaulted by that chaos as he stepped into the foyer, floored in wide planks that had been obviously scrubbed into a worn whiteness.

"If you come often, you'll get used to it," said Margrena, taking in Beltur's involuntary reaction.

"I haven't yet," added Jessyla.

"Perhaps I should have said that you'll accept it as necessary," replied Margrena dryly. "No one will mind that you're here, Beltur, but I should introduce you to Klarisia. She's the senior healer in Elparta for the Council."

"Just like Cohndar is the senior mage?" Beltur tried to keep the sardonicism he felt about Cohndar out of his voice.

"I've only met the senior mage in passing, but I think you'll find Klarisia more to your liking." Margrena led the way to the first doorway on the left, stepping into the chamber beyond.

Two other healers stood there, one tall and thin, her hair jet black, likely some fifteen years older than Beltur. The other was about Margrena's height, blond, and appeared only a few years older than Jessyla. The older healer looked to Margrena and Beltur.

"Klarisia, Beltur will be accompanying us. He was forced into doing healing during the fighting, and will be spending some time, I suspect, on and off, learning more about the basics."

Klarisia offered a wide and warm smile. "You must be Athaal's friend. I've heard about you. Felsyn told me about what you did for Claudyt's grandson."

"That's why I'm here," replied Beltur. "I did what I thought was necessary, but I have the feeling I was very fortunate that I judged correctly when I didn't know as much as I should."

"We're glad to have you here." The dark-haired healer looked to Margrena. "If you would begin with the children's room. With the cold, there are already several mothers and children there." She gestured to a small basket on the side table. "That's what we have today. There are more cloths and spirits, but not much else."

Jessyla stepped forward and took the basket by the arched handle.

Beltur sensed that whatever was in the basket had been lightly dusted with order.

"We'll start there." Margrena turned. Beltur and Jessyla followed her into the hallway.

Klarisia was already back talking to the other healer. "As I was saying, there's only so much you can do with the older ones . . ."

Beltur looked at the basket, taking in the folded squares of clean cloth, two corked bottles, and a jar with a large cork.

"Those are the basic supplies, except for poultices or splints and the like."

"What about debriding a wound?"

"All healers have their own knives and tweezers. The clear spirits in the bottles will clean them."

"Are there separate rooms for older people?"

"One for children and one for anyone else," said Margrena. "The more seriously ill are on pallet beds up on the second level. If we're needed up there, a runner will come and get us. Otherwise, we'll go up after we finish with the children."

When the three entered the children's room—a space little more than four yards square—there were three women, each with a child, each sitting on a different wooden backless bench. On the first bench sat a woman and a girl who could not be more than six or seven. The second held a woman and a boy who might be ten. He cradled an arm that Beltur sensed immediately was broken. The third held a woman and two children.

Margrena moved toward the woman with the small girl. "How can we help your daughter?"

The woman eased a patched woolen cloak off the girl, then lifted the girl's shirt to reveal purplish welts across her back. At the end of the top welt, just above her shoulder blade, was an angry pustule almost a digit wide and as long as half Beltur's palm. Greenish pus oozed from both ends of the narrow oblong.

Beltur immediately sensed the orangish-red chaos in the center of the pustule, surrounded by a white chaos mist, and a dull gray at the edges. "The dull gray?" he murmured.

"That's where her body fought off the wound chaos."

"The wound chaos in the center is stronger. I could do something . . ."

"Not yet. You need to save your order for what's necessary." Margrena turned to Jessyla. "You can start."

The girl's mother watched nervously as Jessyla took a small folded cloth from the basket and began to gently wipe away the pus, working from the outside toward the suppurating center. Then Jessyla took a small bottle from the basket, uncorking it and pouring a little of the liquid on the girl's skin, before using a clean part of the cloth to clean away the crust and pus. The child winced and whimpered, but held still as the young healer cleaned the wound.

Finally, Jessyla looked to Margrena. "Unless you want to cut . . ."

Margrena shook her head. "Since Beltur's here . . ." In turn, she looked to him.

Beltur used his senses to study the wound, then began to gather free order, not order from himself, deliberately moving one small piece at a time to the wound, until the orangish red was gone, and the entire wound felt grayish.

Margrena looked to Jessyla. "You'll need to clean it again."

Jessyla did so.

Then the older healer took out her knife and used a cloth dampened with spirits to clean it before making the narrowest of cuts across the center of the welt. Then using the spirits-dampened cloth, she gently worked out more greenish pus.

When she finished and dressed the wound, Beltur added a touch of order.

Margrena turned to the mother. "Keep the wound clean. If she does not get better in two days, bring her back."

"Thank you, Healers." The woman nodded.

Beltur watched as the two left the small room, wondering what the girl possibly could have done to deserve being beaten with what had to have been a belt—using the buckle end—and knowing that it couldn't have been the child's fault.

Margrena turned to the woman with the boy on the adjacent bench.

"He fell off the front step running out the door," said the thin, almost gaunt woman in a patched gray cloak and equally faded trousers. "He put his hands out."

Beltur managed not to react to the falsehood, indicated first by the chaos swirls around her as she talked and by the splotches of fuzzy white in more than a few places on the boy's arms, back, and chest.

"His arm is broken," said Margrena kindly. She looked to Jessyla. "See if there's any knitbone left. We'll also need some heavy cloth and splinting reeds."

Jessyla—almost stone-faced—handed the basket to Beltur and headed for the door.

"Beltur," said the older healer, "is there any deeper chaos around where the bone is broken?"

"There's a little, but it's not bad." *Not nearly as bad as that in the girl's wound.*

"Good." Margrena looked to the boy. "We have to set the bone in your arm so that it will heal properly. That means we have to line up both ends of the bone. When we do that it will hurt some. Then we will splint your arm. That means we'll wrap it tightly so that the bones do not move and will grow back together again. Do you understand?"

"Yes, Healer."

"Beltur, you hold the boy's elbow and the upper part of the lower arm."

Beltur frowned. "You want his arm to remain unmoving, I take it."

Margrena looked almost annoyed. "Of course."

"I think it would be better if I encased it in a shield. That way nothing at all will move." Beltur pointed. "The shield will end there. Is that how much you need to work with?"

"A little more."

Beltur nodded, then anchored the shield to the floor, then formed it tightly around the boy's upper arm, elbow, and perhaps four digits below the elbow. "His arm and elbow won't move. Any time."

"OHHH!" The boy's body twisted, but neither arm nor elbow budged as Margrena moved the bones back into line, then continued to hold the arm.

"I can shield the entire lower arm, now," said Beltur, slowly extending the shield down. "Just move your fingers back as you feel the shield."

In moments, the healer's hands were free. She looked to Beltur. "I wouldn't have thought of that. How long can you hold that?"

"Something that small? Glasses, most likely. I can certainly hold it until Jessyla returns. When you start to splint it, I can make the shield thin and against his skin."

"That might not work, totally. I'm going to surround the skin around the break with a knitbone poultice."

"I can just move the shield so that the part where you put the poultice is unshielded."

"We'll see."

Jessyla hurried back into the room carrying both thick and thin reeds, a large jar, and a spool of canvas or heavy cloth a handspread wide. "They do have knitbone."

"Good."

Beltur just watched and adjusted the shield around the boy's arm as Margrena let Jessyla apply the poultice to the area around the break in the arm. Then Jessyla held the thicker reeds in place as Margrena lashed them together with the thinner ones, and then wrapped the reeds in the canvas. After that, Beltur added a trace of free order to the point where the bones met.

Margrena turned to the mother. "The canvas and reeds should stay in place for at least four eightdays, even if his arm does not hurt. If there's any foulness bring him back here immediately. He's not to carry anything with that arm or hand for four eightdays, either."

"His father will not be pleased that he cannot work."

"If his father wants a son who is either one-armed or dead, he may put him to work." Margrena's tone was icy. "He should not have let his son fall."

The woman looked down. "Yes, Healer."

Beltur looked around, only to discover that the woman with the two girls was gone, but he said nothing as mother and son slowly walked from the room.

"It would have been better to set that in plaster," said Margrena, "but we're short of plaster, and she likely wouldn't have come back to have a cast removed properly."

"He didn't fall," said Beltur. "He had that white chaos fuzziness in too many places. He was likely beaten with a stick or rod and held up his arm to keep from being hit more."

"We've seen more than a few of those," said Jessyla. "If I could—"

"You can't, and you shouldn't even speak like that here," interrupted Margrena. "If word got out, some men wouldn't allow their women—most of them who come aren't really even consorted—to bring the children."

"It's not right," murmured Jessyla, not quite under her breath.

"Sometimes, we just have to do the best we can."

Sometimes? From what Beltur had seen over the past seasons, it was most of the time, but he only said, "The other woman just left."

"There wasn't anything wrong with her or the children, except that they were cold and hungry. Some of the street women know that they can bring in children and just wait. They get warm, and then they leave."

Beltur frowned. The Council Healing House wasn't all that warm, if certainly warmer than the streets, especially with the wind gusting the way it had been that morning.

"Klarisia doesn't say much so long as they don't linger. After all, it is a form of healing, and one that doesn't impose too much on the healers."

At that moment a young woman, little more than a girl to Beltur's eyes, half walked, half staggered into the room. ". . . need help . . ."

Beltur just looked for an instant.

Margrena didn't, but rushed toward the woman.

As she did, Beltur saw the darkness of blood just below her shoulder, and he immediately followed Margrena, who had helped the woman into a sitting position and was examining her.

"Cloths!"

Jessyla grabbed the basket, arriving beside her mother just as Beltur did, and then handed one of the folded cloths to Margrena.

The young woman was swaying where she sat.

The door from the street opened, and a stocky man in brown charged into the room. "Where's the bitch? I'll kill her." In his hand was a bloody knife, but Beltur also noticed blood on his other sleeve as he headed toward the healers.

Without much thought, Beltur snapped a containment around the intruder, stopping him in midstep. Then he glanced toward the still-open door, but no one seemed to be following the man in brown. So Beltur walked to the door and closed it, shutting off the gusts of cold air that had accompanied the knife wielder.

"She stole my wallet and then tried to slice me up!" protested the man. "You can't do this to me. A man's got a right to protect himself. You can't do this."

Beltur pulled out the patrol medallion.

The man's mouth stopped moving.

Beltur loosened the containment. "Drop the knife."

The knife fell to the floor. Beltur shifted the containment so that the knife was outside the shield, then kicked it away from the intruder. He further loosened the containment. "Show me where she slashed you."

There was a long shallow slash across the top of the man's forearm, one that looked to be deep in places, and there was more than a little blood.

"What are you going to do? Let me bleed to death?"

"That wouldn't serve any purpose." Beltur walked over to the bench where the basket sat and took out the other bottle of clear spirits, and two folded cloths. Then he picked up the spool of canvas and walked back to where the man stood. "I'm going to release your arm and take care of the wound." Beltur did just that and used one cloth and spirits to clean the slash. Then he used the other cloth as a dressing and wound a length of canvas—cut easily with the cupridium knife that Jorhan had forged for him—around the wound, tying it in place with canvas strips.

"That should take care of the wound and the bleeding."

"You're just going to leave me here?"

"No. We're going for a walk." Beltur turned to Margrena. "I'll be back as soon as I can."

"We'll likely be upstairs by then."

Beltur turned to the man. "I'm going to release the containment. You and I are going to walk out the door. You try anything else, and you'll be very sorry—that's if you survive to feel anything." That was another overstatement, but not by too much.

When Beltur released the containment, he was ready to impose it again, but the man did not move.

"Go ahead. Walk to the door."

Beltur didn't say anything else until the two of them were outside in the cold and gusting wind. "You got sliced. She got sliced. Neither one of you should have been doing what you did. I could walk you to Patrol headquarters, and you'd spend at least a year at the workhouse. That's if you're fortunate. I've bound up that slash. It should heal if you keep it clean. She may not even live." The girl probably would, but with all the blood, the man would likely believe that. "Even if she does, she won't be using that little knife any time soon. And you might just want to be a little more careful about approaching women. So let's just say that I escort you down the street. You don't get the knife back, and you don't go to the workhouse."

"I got robbed and slashed."

"You almost killed her. You're getting off easily. Do you really want to face a Council magistrate?"

"If that's so, why are you letting me go?"

"Partly because you were the victim, and partly because sending you both to the workhouse wouldn't do either of you much good. If you think I'm wrong, we can just keep walking to the City Patrol."

"If it's just the same to you, Mage, I'll accept your offer."

"You're being very wise. Keep walking. I'll be watching."

Once the other was a good block away, Beltur made his way back into the building, found a staircase, and climbed to the second level. He saw Margrena and walked to join her.

Margrena glanced around, then said, "The girl's in a small chamber. She'll be here for at least a few days. She wouldn't last a night on the streets. We had to get help carrying her up here. Jessyla's settling her down. I thought it might be better that way."

Beltur understood what the older healer wasn't saying and why she wanted to be the one to meet Beltur, rather than Jessyla. "She doesn't have any place else to go?"

"Not that she'll admit. Either she doesn't or she'll be beaten or worse if she does."

"How often does something like this happen?"

"Every eightday, except most of the women don't live, and no one knows who the men even are."

"Do you think this girl will learn anything?"

"She might learn, but it likely won't change much in her life."

Beltur couldn't help recalling one of the lifter girls he'd sent to the workhouse. She'd screamed at him that the one thing she learned from going to the workhouse was that the only thing a poor woman was allowed to sell was her body, and that stealing was more honest.

At that moment, Jessyla came out of a doorway and walked to join them. "I thought you'd be much longer. Isn't Patrol headquarters by the east market square?"

"It is. I didn't go that far."

"You *let* him go?" Jessyla's voice was filled with outrage. "How could you? How could you?"

"How could I not?" countered Beltur. "If I took him in to the City Patrol, he'd say that she knifed him. She'd be sent to the workhouse, and she's in no shape to hide or run. I'd be reprimanded, or worse, for not bringing her in, and then they'd come here for her. Using a knife, theft, and assault while soliciting . . . do you think she'd survive the workhouse?"

Jessyla looked at Beltur, openmouthed. "They'd do that?"

"Unless she were a trader's daughter," he replied sardonically, "and I think it's fair to say that she's not."

The younger healer looked to her mother.

"Beltur's right, dear. It's better for everyone this way. Except maybe Beltur. If you say anything . . ."

"That's horrible!"

"Sometimes . . . life is," replied Margrena. "Now . . . we're needed at the end of the hall."

Jessyla winced.

"What's there?" asked Beltur.

"The old men are," replied Margrena. "It's not Jessyla's favorite healing duty."

"You'll see why," said Jessyla in a low voice.

Beltur got the impression that he needed to see why she felt that way. "Lead on."

Margrena walked almost to the east end of the corridor and then stepped through a doorway, pushing the door all the way open. Jessyla entered next, followed by Beltur. There were four pallet beds in the room, lined up against the far wall.

"Oh . . . it's the pretty healer!" came from one of the men, delivered in a cracked raspy tone, but Beltur didn't see which of the three men propped up in their beds had spoken.

"And we brought a mage today," said Jessyla in the falsely sweet tone that grated on Beltur.

"Ohhh . . ." groaned the bald and wrinkled-faced man in the bed on the far right, offering a smile that was more like a grimace.

Beltur could immediately sense that both his order and chaos levels were low, so low that had the man not spoken and smiled, Beltur might have thought that he was dying. More sensing revealed that the man had no feet, and likely had not had for some time.

Jessyla moved toward the man who had groaned, but stopped just out of arm's reach. "You're looking better today."

"Is that all you can say, Healer?"

Jessyla smiled. "Would you want me to say that you're looking worse?" She turned to the man in the next bed, with wispy white hair and rheumy eyes that remained fixed, as if looking into the distance. "How are you today?"

There was no response, although Beltur could tell that the man's order and chaos levels were higher, if only slightly, than those of the first man, but there were hundreds of tiny points of patterned order and chaos within his head.

"Hartyn's not home today," said the third man, whose voice confirmed that he had been the one who had greeted Jessyla. "He's not home often anymore."

Margrena moved closer to the unresponsive man, touched the top of his head, for an instant, then looked to Beltur.

"I can sense it."

She nodded.

The third man appeared to be slightly younger than the first two, but his right arm was twisted and gnarled, and the left side of his face was a mass of old scars. He was missing his left eye. Beltur could sense pockets and strands of orangish-white chaos everywhere in his body, especially across his chest and in his lungs, strands so interwoven with order that Beltur could see that nothing he or any healer could do would change the inevitable, which was likely not to be that long in coming.

"So how long do I have, pretty healer?" asked the chaos-ridden man, looking at Jessyla.

"Long enough to tease me for a while," Jessyla replied with a smile, reaching down and touching his twisted shoulder for an instant, and providing a tiny bit of order and comfort.

Beltur could easily sense the order/chaos conflict that even Jessyla's slight evasion of the truth created within her.

The man tried to speak, but burst into a paroxysm of coughing that brought up blood-tinged yellow-green phlegm into the soiled cloth he held in his good hand.

Beltur moved forward and touched his chest, using just a little order to calm and remove part of the sickness chaos.

After the man cleared his throat, he said, "Thought you were a mage."

"I am," replied Beltur. "I can do a few things like a healer. You need to rest for a few moments." He turned to the fourth pallet bed, where Margrena and Jessyla just stood.

The fourth man was dead, but there were a few lingering bits of order and more of chaos.

"He died less than a glass ago," said Beltur quietly to Margrena. Lowering his voice even more, he added, "You knew, didn't you?"

The older healer nodded, then drew the blanket over the man's sunken face. "We'll go downstairs and let Klarisia know. Then we'll see if she needs help in the main receiving room."

Once the three were outside in the corridor, Jessyla turned to Beltur, a questioning expression on her face.

"You're about the only cheerful sight they'll likely see all day," Beltur said.

"I know." Jessyla sighed. "But they're still thinking of . . ." She shook her head.

Beltur just nodded.

"Did you do that one any favor?" asked Margrena.

"It was only a tiny amount of order. It won't change anything, I think, but he'll feel a little better for a while." Even so, Beltur had to wonder, as he accompanied the two to the staircase and back down to another chamber on the main floor, one with at least fifteen people sitting on benches.

The sense of sickness and chaos was everywhere. Beltur managed not to swallow as he stood back and waited while Margrena spoke a few words to Klarisia before rejoining Beltur and Jessyla. "We're to take over here, starting with those on the bench at the east end. Beltur, if you and Jessyla would help that woman with the chaos-ridden boil on her shoulder." Margrena's words were not a question.

For a moment, Beltur wondered why anyone with just a boil was even at the Council Healing House—until Jessyla eased away the woman's grayed shirt, and he saw an inflamed and pus-filled circle the size of his palm just above her right shoulder blade, with reddish streaks radiating away from the circle. He eased his own cupridium knife from its sheath and dusted it with order, then showed it to Jessyla. "It might be better to use this."

Jessyla's eyes widened.

"It's cupridium, Jorhan forged it for me. It's very sharp."

"After I clean away the outside."

Beltur nodded and watched, finally handing the knife to Jessyla.

As Jessyla took the knife, the heavyset woman looked up. "You won't hurt me, Healer?"

"It will hurt some," Jessyla replied, "but not nearly as much as if we don't open it and clean it out."

"You healers always say that."

"And it's always true," replied Beltur.

"Usually," said Jessyla, "but it won't heal if I don't clean out the chaos inside."

Beltur just observed as she trimmed the edges around the eruption, then cut a little bit farther, before handing the knife to Beltur to clean while she used more of the clear spirits. Then he handed the knife back to her.

After a time, she looked to Beltur. "That's all I'd like to do, but . . ."

Beltur thought he understood, because there were threads of chaos wound into the muscle below. "See if you can sense what I'm going to try." He concentrated on moving bits of free order into the threads of chaos, trying to make certain that he was using free order and not his own personal order, since the only point of using the order was to destroy wound chaos, not to strengthen or heal the muscle.

Bit by bit he destroyed the wound chaos, and although it took more than a fifth of a glass, he didn't feel worn out or light-headed when he finished. At least, he didn't think he did.

After Jessyla dressed the wound and the two stepped away, she cleaned the knife with the clear spirits and handed it back to Beltur. "Thank you. That made it easier."

Beltur took the knife and again dusted it with order before sheathing it.

For the rest of the day, Beltur accompanied the two, helping where he could, but watching more than anything.

Slightly after fourth glass, Margrena gestured to Beltur. "We're done for the day."

Beltur could see two other older women sitting on a bench in the corner.

The older healer followed Beltur's eyes. "They won't allow anyone but Klarisia or Adyla to heal them. One of them will be here shortly."

Beltur didn't argue, but followed the two back to the first chamber, where he had been introduced to Klarisia. Jessyla set down the basket, which had only one cloth left and only a bit of spirits in one of the two bottles, even though she had refilled the basket with cloths several times over the course of the day.

"Your two are waiting for you," Margrena told the head healer.

"They always do. You two will be here tomorrow?"

Margrena nodded.

In turn, Klarisia handed a cloth pouch that clinked slightly to Margrena, who inclined her head.

Then the three left the chamber. Beltur didn't say anything until they were outside, heading west through a wind even more biting than it had been in the morning. "Thank you for letting me accompany you."

"What did you learn?" asked Margrena.

"More about cleaning and dressing wounds and setting bones, and that I'd rather not set any bones unless there isn't someone more experienced around."

"Are you coming with us tomorrow?" Margrena grinned.

"I'm forging cupridium tomorrow, and then doing my City Patrol duty on sevenday. Would you mind if I came by the house on eightday afternoon?"

"Please do," said Jessyla quickly.

"I do think I should follow you both more, but it will have to be when I have a day off."

"That's an interesting change in wording," said Margrena. "Before, you wanted to accompany us. Now, you think you should."

"Mother."

Beltur kept his smile to himself. "I should because there's so much I need to know, but I want to see you both on eightday."

"Can you stop for a bit now?" asked Jessyla.

"I think I'd best not. Today was work, and tomorrow will be as well."

Margrena just nodded, but Beltur had the sense she appreciated his words.

At the door to Grenara's small house, Jessyla turned to Beltur and took his hands. "Eightday. You promised."

Beltur smiled. "Eightday. I did. I wouldn't miss seeing you for anything."

"Good." She leaned forward and brushed his cheek with her lips. "Until then. And thank you so much for the scarf. It's beautiful."

"You deserve it." *And more.* He waited until she closed the door before he turned and began the walk back home. When he reached the bakery, he was almost as tired as when he spent an entire day working with Jorhan.

Meldryn was in the kitchen. "How did the healing go?"

"I learned some things about healing. I also learned more about Elparta." Beltur filled two mugs with the dark ale and set them on the kitchen table.

"Such as?"

"Can women own property or operate shops? Could they run a bakery? As I recall," Beltur said, thinking of his first days when Athaal had described all the bakeries on Bakers Lane, "all the bakeries are run by men."

"Not all of them. Saelyna is less than two blocks west of here, and she bakes in the style of southern Hydlen. That's why her place is called the Pirates' Pastries." Meldryn paused, then added, "She's the only one."

"Does Celinya have the only tailoring shop operated by a woman?"

"She's a seamstress, properly speaking, but she's the only one I know who doesn't work for a tailor." Meldryn smiled wryly. "You have a good point. I don't know of any law or rule that forbids women from owning property or having shops or anything, or even being traders, but there aren't many. That's because anyone who does business has to put up a bond. For small shops, it's not much. From five to ten golds, depending on the size of the space."

"Who holds the bond? The Council?"

"Who else? Are you ready to eat?"

"More than ready." Beltur eyed the hot meat pie on the platter. "More than ready."

IV

Beltur didn't wake up shivering on sixday morning, at least not until he climbed out from under his blankets and his bare feet touched the floor. He hurried to wash and dress, although the wash water felt ice cold, and he was more than glad to step into the warmth of the empty kitchen, where he immediately set to fixing breakfast over the hearth fire. He glanced out the window. While he didn't see either rain or snow, he did hear the low moaning of the wind.

You can't put off getting a winter coat and gloves any longer. He pushed that thought aside and concentrated on making sure the small bit of tallow in the heavy cast-iron pot had spread evenly before he began scrambling the eggs and then adding the cheese, saving a little of the egg mixture for the egg toast, to be made from several slices of stale bread.

Meldryn arrived from the bakery just as Beltur was about to put the cheesed eggs and egg toast on the platter. "That looks like a solid breakfast."

"It would be better if we had melon slices, but I haven't been near the market when anyone had any late melons."

Meldryn sat down at the kitchen table. "There might be a few." His tone was dubious.

"I can hope," said Beltur dryly as he set a platter in front of the older man, then put one at his own place and sat down. He was warm enough that the dark ale tasted good.

Meldryn ate several bites before speaking. "Your cooking's gotten better."

"I've had some good instruction. Before I came here, it was all by guess." Beltur still knew his cooking wasn't as good as Meldryn's or as good as Athaal's had been.

He waited until Meldryn had finished eating, not that the older mage took very long, before he asked, "Where might I be able to get an overcoat and a pair of gloves?"

Meldryn smiled. "Ask and you shall receive."

"I couldn't—"

"You can and should, but there's a better solution than what you think. Just wait."

Beltur didn't stand and wait. Instead, he started cleaning up the kitchen because he needed to get to Jorhan's by seventh glass. He didn't get all that far because Meldryn returned almost immediately, carrying a heavy long and dark brown coat.

"This coat belonged to Athaal's father. He was bigger than Athaal, about your size. Athaal never wore it. He said it was too big for him. There's no one else who'd want it. No one else will ever wear it, and it shouldn't go to waste."

"No one else? Athaal said his father disappeared when his ship was lost coming back from Hamor. He never mentioned any brothers or sisters."

"He has a brother and a sister in Spidlaria. When we got together, they cut him off."

"But . . ."

"Athaal would rather that you have it . . . and the gloves." Meldryn held up a pair of dark brown leather gloves. "You'll freeze to death once winter hits if you don't have a good coat."

"You're sure?"

"Lhadoraak told me you did everything you could to try to save Athaal . . . and that's why you almost died. No one could have asked more." After a pause, Meldryn added, his voice mock-plaintive, "Besides, you'll freeze to death, and if you don't accept the coat, it will be my fault."

Beltur shook his head. "You do that guilty voice worse than I do. I'll accept the coat—with appreciation."

"Good." Meldryn smiled. "Now . . . I need to get back to the bakery."

"Go," replied Beltur warmly, hoping nothing had burned.

After setting the coat across one of the chairs, Beltur went to work cleaning up breakfast and the kitchen, then hurried upstairs to wash and don the older tunic he wore for working at the smithy. Before all that long, he was back downstairs, had put on the coat and gloves, and was walking east on Crossed Lane to the eastern wall street, and south on that to the southeast gate. The wind was definitely the coldest he'd felt since coming to Elparta, especially when it gusted through the city streets.

As he stepped through the northeast gate and onto the road to Axalt, he looked to the northeast, wondering if there were any storms coming, but the sky was clear, although an almost leaden greenish blue. By the time he reached the smithy, his ears felt frozen, and he was more than glad for the warmth inside the small stone structure when he hung up the coat and his tunic on the wooden wall pegs.

"Feels like a storm coming," offered Jorhan from where he stood by one of the benches.

"A northeaster?"

The smith shook his head. "Doesn't feel that way."

"What are we working on today?"

"We'll start off casting one blade, then a mirror. I just hope Barrynt gets here before the storm. You didn't see anyone on the road to the east, did you?"

"No." Beltur hadn't sensed anyone, either, and since the road curved somewhat east of the smithy, he could sense farther than he could see.

"Well . . . we won't get any smithing done standing around."

Beltur smiled and moved toward the bellows.

Well before ninth glass, they had poured the melt into the mold for one straight-sword, and Beltur had laid down the fine mesh-like net of chaos bounded by order in the hot bronze and held it until the bronze had solidified enough so that the pattern held.

Next came heating and pouring the melt for an intricate mirror.

Beltur had just stepped away from the mold after setting the chaos/order mesh when someone pounded on the door to the smithy.

Jorhan immediately hurried to the door and opened it to reveal a man in a long tan leather coat. "Barrynt! I was a mite worried that you might run afoul of a storm."

The trader was broad-shouldered and a digit or two shorter than Beltur, and he smiled broadly and warmly at Jorhan as he stepped into the smithy. "Wind or no wind, I said I'd get you your copper and tin. Besides, Johlana wouldn't have it any other way."

"Always a man of your word." Jorhan closed the door and half turned. "This is Beltur. He's the mage I wrote you about."

Barrynt stepped forward, still smiling. "It's good to meet you. I understand you've helped Jorhan a great deal."

"He's helped me even more, I suspect," returned Beltur.

"I wouldn't be able to smith for long without Beltur," said Jorhan.

"If you don't mind, we can talk while we unload your copper," said Barrynt. "I can see clouds to the northeast, and I'd like to get the rest of my goods into the warehouse in Elparta before the storm hits full."

"Everything else is going to Elparta?" asked Jorhan.

"Most of it's bolts of woolens from Montgren." Barrynt grinned. "I got word that woolen prices were higher here. Something about having to uniform a lot of men." He opened the smithy door and gestured toward the wagon down at the foot of the lane. "I hope you don't mind, but it'd take a lot of time to get the wagon up here and then back down."

"I'm just glad you arrived when you did. Council's been giving me trouble."

"You're always welcome in Axalt. Johlana'd be more than happy to have you there." Barrynt looked to Beltur. "You, too, Mage. Axalt could use a good mage." With that, the merchant turned and walked briskly toward the wagon.

Although Barrynt had voiced what could have been pleasantries, Beltur had sensed that the invitation to Axalt had been genuine, not only for Jorhan, but also for Beltur, not that Beltur had any intention of leaving Elparta, especially given Jessyla's presence in Elparta.

With a half smile, Beltur hurried from the smithy and followed Jorhan down the lane. By the time he reached the open tailgate of the high-sided and covered wagon, he was beginning to shiver.

Barrynt pointed to the ingots stacked on the wagon bed and nodded to Jorhan. "You've got more copper than you asked for. The only ingots I could get were from Lydiar, and they're a stone's weight each. I figured you'd rather have more than less. So there are fifteen copper ingots and three tin."

"That's . . ." Jorhan broke off his words, then said, "Thank you."

Barrynt glanced to the northeast. "We'd best get all this offloaded."

Beltur followed the merchant's eyes. The clouds moving over the horizon were definitely dark and ominous. Then he looked at the ingots. Each was roughly twelve digits long, nine wide, and five high.

Jorhan loaded Beltur with three of them. "Set them on the floor next to the far bench."

Beltur nodded and started back up the lane. The three stones' worth of ingots didn't seem all that heavy when he started out, but his fingers felt like they were close to freezing by the time he eased the ingots onto the smithy floor. He didn't want to get his new coat filthy, but he did put on the gloves before he headed back down to the wagon, drawn by two imposing dray horses. Accompanying the wagon were two mounted guards.

Despite the gloves, after five more trips, Beltur's hands were cold, his fingers close to cramping, and he was definitely shivering as he stood by the forge, trying to warm up.

Barrynt returned to the smithy carrying a wooden crate. "What's in here is from Johlana. She said not to go through all the pearapple preserves first."

Jorhan laughed. "She would." After a moment, he added, "I appreciate the copper."

"It worked out well for us both," returned the merchant. "I wouldn't have been looking for something otherwise, and come up with the wool. Once we're settled in Elparta, I'll be out to see you. But not until the roads clear."

"I'll be here."

"Until I can persuade you to come to Axalt." Barrynt smiled, then turned toward the door.

Jorhan moved to join him, and the two walked down toward the waiting wagon. Beltur closed the smithy door and walked back to the forge, where he added more coal and then continued to warm himself.

Before that long, Jorhan returned, closing the door quickly and walking over to the forge. "He's a good man, Barrynt is. He would have brought the copper even if he hadn't found something to sell in Elparta."

Beltur nodded, thinking that Barrynt seemed far more likable and straightforward than those of traders' families he'd met so far in Elparta. "You said Barrynt was a merchant, not a trader. Is there a difference?"

"In Axalt, everyone in trade is a merchant. In Elparta, the largest and most prosperous are traders, the rest merchants. Barrynt might be considered a lesser trader if he lived here, but his family goes way back in Axalt. Johlana's much happier there."

"How did they meet?"

"He needed some copperwork done, quick-like, before he headed back to Axalt. Old Paeltyr sent him to me. Never saw such a forlorn fellow."

"Forlorn?" That didn't square with what Beltur had seen.

"He'd lost his consort and a daughter to the red flux while he was traveling and trading. Johlana tried to cheer him up." Jorhan grinned. "He must have liked that. He kept coming back. Took two years, but he finally asked her." The smith looked toward the forge. "You want to work the bellows so we can heat up a new melt?" He smiled happily. "We've still got two more straight-swords to cast."

"I can do that."

Some four glasses later, Beltur took a deep breath once he was certain that the order/chaos mesh was firmly set in the bronze held in the mold of the second straight-sword, then stepped away and just stood there.

As he blotted his forehead, he remembered what he'd meant to tell Jorhan. "There's something you should know. The knife you finished for me . . . well, it's especially useful when I've helped the healers."

"It is?"

Beltur nodded. "That's because it doesn't favor order or chaos."

"That's something to keep in mind." Jorhan frowned. "Healers really can't afford knives like that, though."

"No . . . but wealthy traders who employ healers can."

"That's a thought. Thank you."

"Thank you." In thinking about the knife, Beltur realized something else. "You know, we've cast at least a half score of mirrors, and I've never seen one that you've finished."

"Oh . . . I suppose you haven't. I'll get your pay and bring back the one we did on fourday."

Beltur donned his old tunic, but not the heavy overcoat. He only had to wait a short time before Jorhan returned.

"Here you are." The smith handed over four silvers. "Now that we've got the copper, you're getting the rate for piecework. I still owe you a gold and more, but that will have to wait until the Lydian pays me."

"Thank you." Beltur slipped the silvers into his belt wallet, then took, almost gingerly, the finished mirror that Jorhan extended, examining the graceful raised and chased scrollwork on the back and along the handle, and then studying the silvery polished oval of the face of the mirror. "It's beautiful."

"The cupridium comes out more silver than the bronze, and that makes the reflection seem sharper."

"I think that has to do with your finish work."

Jorhan smiled. "It took me a long time to learn how to do it right, but the same work shows up better in cupridium."

"What will you get for that?" As he handed the mirror back to the smith, Beltur wished he could have bought such a mirror for Jessyla.

"If I sold it, it might bring three golds, certainly two. But this one is for Johlana. She has a bronze mirror, but nothing this fine. I'll give it to Barrynt to take back when he returns."

Beltur nodded. Jorhan had said more than once that the small items forged in cupridium and finished artfully paid well, besides taking less copper. "You know I have City Patrol duty tomorrow."

"I do, but there's enough finish work here to keep me busy until one-day. I'll see you then. That's if the road is clear enough for you to get here."

"Does the snow get that deep with one storm?"

"Not usually, and not this early. It has happened. I don't envy you if you have to patrol tomorrow."

"I can always hope it's not too deep."

"I'll keep good thoughts for you."

"Thank you. I can always use them." Beltur donned the overcoat and then pulled on the gloves. After a nod to the smith, he stepped out of the smithy and into the wind, blowing harder and colder than before under a sky covered with thick and dark clouds. Scattered snowflakes whipped past his face as he strode down the lane toward the road.

By the time he reached the city gate, the snowflakes were falling more heavily, and a thin layer of snow was beginning to accumulate in places sheltered from the wind. Beltur had absolutely no doubts that the question wasn't whether there would be snow across Elparta in the morning, but only how deep it would be.

He turned onto the wall road heading north and kept walking.

V

When Beltur woke on sevenday, his room was even colder than it had been the previous morning, but by the time he finished fixing breakfast, the kitchen seemed warmer than it had been on sixday, perhaps because Meldryn had closed all the shutters the afternoon before, even before Beltur had gotten back from the smithy.

As soon as Meldryn sat down at the table, he said, "Did you see the loaf I left for you?"

"I did, thank you."

"I also left a scarf on the chair in the parlor. You'll need it to keep your ears from freezing. I think it was Duardyn's, but I'm not sure. He died two years ago, and there wasn't anyone to return it to. We kept it because you never know when you might need a spare."

"Thank you. My ears almost froze coming home." Beltur set a platter in front of Meldryn, with his effort at an omelet.

"I know. I could tell when you came in. It didn't get this cold in Fenard, I take it?"

"Not that I can remember." Beltur took his seat and immediately began to eat, thinking that he could have used more salt and a touch of something else in the eggs, but what he wasn't certain.

"This is good."

"It could be better. What spice might help?"

"Tarragon or sage, but not too much. There are dried bundles of each in the spice drawers."

"Thank you. I'll keep that in mind for the next time."

They both ate quickly. Then Meldryn hurried back to the bakery, and Beltur cleaned up, carefully, because he doubted that Laranya would be coming, then donned his good tunic and his visored cap, overcoat, and gloves, belatedly remembering the dark blue scarf Meldryn had laid out.

When Beltur opened the front door to leave for Patrol headquarters, the light outside was so bright he couldn't see anything, and the first breath he took almost hurt because the air was so cold. He immediately wrapped the scarf across his mouth and nose. After a moment, he could see—if he squinted—and he realized that the brightness came from the reflection of the sun off the snow. He was relieved to see that the snowfall totaled perhaps thirteen digits at most, not even a full cubit.

He immediately walked along the path Meldryn must have cleared so that people could reach the door of the bakery more easily until he could get across Crossed Lane to the east side of Bakers Lane—shaded by the buildings where the snow glare was less intense. As early as it was, many people had already swept or shoveled paths away from doors and along the sides of the streets and lanes. Even so, he was careful where he placed his boots, especially after slipping and almost falling when he stepped on a patch of ice covered by the fine dry snow.

He reached City Patrol headquarters less than a quint before seventh glass. Laevoyt was already there, waiting, and Beltur signed in quickly, then remembered to ease the patrol medallion out from under his tunic and to adjust the chain so it was clearly visible.

"Good thing you've got a heavy coat," offered the tall patroller as Beltur approached.

Beltur noticed that Laevoyt wore a heavy jacket that only reached midway to his knees, with wool the same color as the patroller's uniform, then said, "It's a legacy of sorts, from Athaal's family. His father's. Too big for Athaal."

"You're fortunate."

"I am," replied Beltur, following Laevoyt out onto Patrol Street, which was already cleared all the way to the square. "Will there be many at the square?"

"Some. Most will wait until close to noon."

Beltur gestured. "I was surprised to find Patrol Street cleared."

"That's done by the young fellows from one of the workhouses. They clear the market squares and some of the main streets. The snow goes into the river. Or onto it when it freezes over."

"They must start early."

"Around fourth glass, I think."

Beltur shivered at the thought of shoveling snow in the cold darkness before dawn.

"The young ones want to do it. They get a copper a day for it. It's one of the few ways they can get coins. Not a bad trade. They get coins, and the Council gets the snow cleared. When the snow is more than knee-deep they get two coppers."

Somehow, that bothered Beltur even more. "What can they spend them on?"

"Extra food, or they can give them to their families when they visit. That's only on every other sevenday."

As they neared the market square, Beltur could see a scattering of vendors, little more than a score, spaced apart on the cold pavement. In places, lines of white, either ice or snow, showed either cracks in the pavement or deeper grooves between stones. He also saw patches of ice glistening in the winter light. There weren't many sellers of the more expensive wares, except for two carts that appeared to be selling woolen blankets, cloaks, and coats. There were several carts selling potatoes, as well as root vegetables like carrots, parsnips, and turnips.

"Is there any reason to hold a concealment?" Beltur didn't see much point in that, but it might be that he was missing something.

"Not until there are more people around . . . or if you want to practice."

Beltur could detect a hint of humor in the other's voice. "I think I'll pass for now. I see enough ice that I don't feel like taking a fall."

For the first glass that Beltur walked around the square, he didn't see more than a handful of buyers, and all of them frequented the produce carts. Another vendor arrived and set up a stall selling what seemed to be heavy flat cakes of some sort. Since there were few people about, and since Beltur could sense no chaos flickers, he made his way toward the table.

"Best nutbread anywhere," declared the square-faced older woman.

Beltur looked at the flat oval cakes, shaded from tan to light brown, which appeared less than appetizing. "What are they?"

"Acorn cakes. They'll keep for a season, and they're good travel bread. Three for a copper."

"I won't be traveling any time soon, but that's good to know. I've never seen anyone else selling them."

"Two reasons. They're winter food, and this wasn't a mast year."

Beltur hadn't the faintest idea what she meant by a mast year.

That must have showed on his face, because the woman smiled and added, "Those are the years when all the oaks provide enormous numbers of acorns. I'm willing to do the work in a year when the trees don't mast."

"Thank you." Beltur nodded and made his way toward the west side of the square, where he turned and studied the scattered groups of sellers.

He'd been looking for a time and had just started moving north when he saw a figure clad in a bulky woolen coat, or perhaps the woman herself was bulky, walking along Patrol Street, eying the square, her eyes clearly taking in Laevoyt's tall figure. She stopped and scanned the square, and her eyes came to rest on Beltur. Then she turned and continued walking, leaving the square behind.

While Beltur hadn't sensed any chaos flickers, he had to wonder if she'd been assessing the possibility of making off with something—either coins or something else—and whether she might be back later when there might be more buyers and possibly more vendors.

Just before ninth glass, as he walked up West Street, he saw a horse-drawn cart appear and recognized Fosset, except that the ale seller's cart looked somehow different. So he angled his steps that way.

The ale seller turned from unhitching the cart and watching the teamster walk the horse back in the direction of the Traders' Rest and raised a gloved hand in greeting. "Mage."

Beltur eyed the two braziers on the cart. "You're not selling hot ale?"

"Mulled wine and hot cider. You get a small one, same as always."

"I'll take the hot cider . . . but later, when I'm really cold."

Fosset laughed. "You sound like all the other patrollers and mages. Never seen one of you taking the mulled wine."

"I can't tell you why," admitted Beltur. "I didn't even know you switched to hot cider and mulled wine."

"More folks want it when it's cold. Besides, the cider's cheaper. Leastwise, it is most years."

Beltur sensed a flash of chaos. "I'll be back later." He turned toward the middle of the square, where he saw two women, bundled in coats that looked like they had been quilted out of pieces of mismatched blankets. The two were moving toward the woman who sold the acorn cakes.

Then both of them grabbed cakes from the table and turned to run. Beltur immediately clamped containments around the two, something he wouldn't have been able to do if there had been more vendors and buyers in the square. Then he fumbled out his whistle and blew on it, three short blasts, as he hurried toward the table.

Neither woman tried to flee or struggle against the two shield containments. Both just stood there, held in place, and began to eat the acorn cakes they had taken.

Beltur had just barely reached the two captives when Laevoyt, coming from the east side of the square, joined him.

"They tried to grab acorn cakes?" Laevoyt's voice was resigned.

"They did indeed," declared the seller. "Would have gotten clean away if it hadn't of been for the mage."

The patroller shook his head, then looked to the woman closest to him. "Things are that bad, are they, Vesthya?"

"What else could we do?"

"If we take you in again, you'll likely lose a hand."

"Better'n dying on the street."

Laevoyt turned to the second woman, even older-looking than the first. "And you? Why?"

Beltur almost swallowed as he realized the second woman was already one-handed.

"You know as well as I."

Again, Beltur was surprised, this time by how well-spoken the older and gaunt white-haired woman was.

Laevoyt shook his head once more as he took out the chains and leather collars, then nodded to Beltur, who released the shield around the first woman while the tall patroller collared and chained her. The two repeated the process with the second.

Then Laevoyt said, "Start walking. You know where."

Neither woman spoke during the time it took to cover the five blocks back to Patrol headquarters.

The duty patroller looked up as he saw Laevoyt, Beltur, and the two captives. His expression seemed half despairing and half resentful. Beltur could sense the mixed emotions through the swirl of order and chaos.

"Petty theft," said Laevoyt. "As small as you can get. Each of them stole a copper's worth of acorn cakes. Less than that. Cakes were three for a copper. They each stole and ate one cake."

The duty patroller took both names and wrote them into the duty log, along with the offenses. Beltur and Laevoyt waited until one of the duty gaolers appeared and took the two deeper into the building.

Without speaking, the duty patroller handed Laevoyt two more sets of collars and chains, and the tall patroller accepted them, also without speaking.

Beltur said nothing either, not until he and Laevoyt were outside and walking back east on Patrol Street. "Should I have let them go? Or just pretended I didn't see them?"

"You can't do that. They'd just keep doing it until whoever was patrolling caught them and took them in. That hurts the vendors."

"But . . . it's almost a form of . . ." Beltur didn't even have a word for it. "They're forcing patrollers to do something that's not . . . somehow it doesn't seem right."

"It's not right. They don't have even coppers, and they're hungry. They'll starve or freeze if they stay on the streets. If we paid for the cakes, they'd do it again when they got really hungry, and some other patroller would have to take them in or feel guilty and pay for their cakes, and that could go on and on."

"Does that happen a lot?"

"More than any patroller would like. It's not like patrollers are paid that much anyway. You can't pay for all of them who need food, and if you start choosing, then you feel guilty for those you can't help."

Beltur nodded. He could see that. "One of them was well-spoken."

"Most likely she was once a trader's mistress or the daughter of a merchant who fell on hard times. There are always a few like that. Most of the street women are just poor bawds who lost their looks and health."

"I haven't seen many men like that."

"They die younger."

Beltur was still thinking about all that when the chimes rang out midday, and he made his way to Fosset's cart, where he gratefully accepted the small mug of hot cider, and then ate his bread, interspersing mouthfuls with sips of the cider that cooled more quickly than he would have liked, but still letting the remaining heat from the hot cider wreath his face. When he finished, he returned the mug. "Thank you."

"My pleasure, Mage."

A little before first glass, Beltur began to notice more and more women, usually dressed shabbily, making their way to the stall of the woman selling acorn cakes. None of them attempted to steal the cakes. As he continued to patrol the square, he kept watching, but the stall had a continuing number of customers, and by third glass, the seller appeared to be sold out and was packing everything into the handcart that she pushed slowly eastward on Patrol Street.

By fourth glass the square was almost empty, and the wind had begun to blow, cold and bitter, if under a clear sky.

As Beltur and Laevoyt left the square, the patroller handed Beltur two leather tokens. "Before I forget, you get these."

"Thank you. I feel guilty—"

"Don't. We get paid for doing what the Council directs."

Still . . . But Beltur didn't say anything more, even if he did feel slightly guilty.

He was more than glad to leave the square with Laevoyt, sign out at the duty desk, and walk north through the wind toward a house he knew would be warm. Even so, he still worried over the two women. Laevoyt and the duty patroller had both been unhappy, and that suggested that what Laevoyt had said was true . . . and that bothered Beltur. More than a little, but he kept walking . . . and thinking.

VI

Beltur slept late on eightday, partly because he was tired, and because he didn't want to get up when it was both dark and cold. When he finally did get up, the house was warmer, doubtless because Meldryn had started a fire in the kitchen hearth. When Beltur came downstairs, after washing and shaving with water bone-chillingly cold, the older mage was seated at the kitchen table sipping hot cider.

"There's more cider in the small kettle on the hearth, and a platter in the warming stove."

"Thank you," replied Beltur. "I do appreciate it. And thank you for leaving the meat pie last night." He took a mug from the cupboard and headed toward the copper kettle.

"Felsyn came by and asked me to join him at the Traders' Rest. It was worth the walk in the cold."

"What was? The dinner?"

"What he said. He's worried about what Cohndar and Waensyn are trying to do."

Beltur frowned as he filled the mug. "I don't like the sound of that." He set the mug on the table, then slipped his hand into the oven mitt, basically an old glove wound with strips of cloth, and used the mitt to open the iron hearth oven and extract the platter of egg toast and ham strips, which he then carried to the kitchen table, where he sat down and slipped off the mitt.

"They've decided that we have to be more organized. They're saying that the attempted invasion by the Prefect was a warning of what could happen again if we don't have something like a council of mages here in Spidlar."

"With Cohndar as the head, and Waensyn as his second-in-command?"

"According to Felsyn, neither Cohndar nor Waensyn has said who might head such a council."

"As if they had to." Beltur snorted and then drizzled the pearapple syrup over the egg toast. "Would the Spidlarian Council have to agree to a magely council?"

"Felsyn says they wouldn't have to. But I can't see Cohndar trying something like that without Council approval."

"What about other black mages? Wouldn't they have to agree?"

"I'd judge so, but I haven't heard anything. We'll just have to see."

Beltur didn't like the sound of a magely council, not after what had happened in Gallos after Wyath had become the head mage, but he didn't see what he could do about something that was only being talked about. "What can you tell me about acorn cakes?"

"They're not cakes, but bread. They're not to my taste. Even with all the leaching of the tannins, they taste bitter to me. They're good for traveling or for the very poor. You can live on them and water for a long time and not suffer. Why do you ask?"

"Yesterday when I was on patrol duty, two women tried to steal some . . ." Beltur went on to explain what had happened. "It all bothered me."

Meldryn nodded slowly. "It's sad that there's no place for women like that. Felsyn tried to persuade Councilor Jhaldrak to have the Council buy an old warehouse for nightly shelter. Jhaldrak told him that the Council was opposed to supporting those who'd made poor choices in life. So I give what day-old bread that there is to the Council Healing House. They send a runner every morning around eighth glass."

Beltur almost blurted "You do?" before realizing that was exactly what he should have expected. But then, Meldryn and Athaal hadn't ever struck him as men who boasted of their kindness and charity, and they'd gone out of their way to help him. "One woman and her children slipped in there the other day when I was helping Grenara and Jessyla."

"You mentioned that. Klarisia does what she can, but she has to be careful. The Council warned her that if she allowed those who weren't truly sick to stay there, they'd close the healing house." Meldryn shook his head. "What are you planning to do today? Besides visiting a certain healer?"

"Not much beyond that. Is there anything you need help with?"

The gray-bearded mage laughed. "Not now. Today's a good day to read in front of the hearth. I do happen to have some meat pies and a loaf that you can take, though."

Beltur grinned. "You just 'happened' to have them?"

Meldryn smiled. "Just happened. When Farodyn brought the meat yesterday, I bargained for a little extra. He was in a good mood."

"I don't suppose a special pastry had anything to do with it, did it?"

"Well..."

"Thank you. I know they'll appreciate it. I won't be going for a while."

"It'll be cold by late afternoon."

"So I ought to go earlier and leave earlier?"

"It wouldn't hurt."

"Would you mind if I read in the parlor until it's time to go?"

"Not at all, just so long as you don't talk to yourself while you do."

Once Beltur finished eating and cleaning the kitchen, he washed up and then put on his good tunic before settling into the other armchair, trying not to disturb Meldryn, who was settled in his favorite chair, appreciating the warmth from the parlor side of the double hearth.

He read for a little less than a glass in Leantor's *On Healing*, especially studying the drawings that showed anatomy, trying to reconcile the drawings with what he could sense about people and what he'd seen at the healing house. When he thought he'd read enough, he turned to the other book that had half attracted him—*Considerations on the Nature of Man* by Heldry of Lydiar, most likely the duke thought of as Heldry the Mad, although Beltur hadn't seen or read anything that connected the writer to that old tale. *But how many Heldrys from Lydiar could there be, especially ones writing about matters to consider when ruling?*

Much of what Heldry wrote seemed like little more than common sense, but Beltur found himself being surprised enough to reread a section.

> ... do not ever attempt to convince another about anything by the use of facts or logic. A stupid man will not be swayed by facts. An intelligent man already knows those facts, and if he does not agree with you, he either has more accurate information than you do or his personal beliefs prevent him from accepting what you know to be true. In either case, insisting on pressing facts and logic on him will only strengthen his beliefs that he is correct and you are not. A gentle question, politely framed, can help determine the basis for his firmness and what course of action may be required of a ruler. If you believe he is indeed in error, first question yourself and whether through your own desires you are seeing what you wish to believe ...

Beltur lowered the book, thinking. From what he had observed, most of those in power would not have even entertained what Heldry had set forth. *But how can you honestly determine how much your desires affect the way you see matters?*

He was still thinking about it when he left the house just after first glass, carrying a covered basket with all that Meldryn had sent. While the sky was clear, the air felt colder than it had on sevenday, and he was more than glad for the coat, gloves, and scarf that Meldryn had given him.

When he reached Grenara's house, Jessyla opened the door almost instantly. She was smiling warmly. "I knew it had to be you."

Beltur noticed immediately that she wore the green shimmersilk scarf, but replied, "Because no one else would be trudging through the snow and cold?" He lifted the basket. "And bringing good things?"

"You and Meldryn shouldn't have." She stepped back to let Beltur enter before quickly closing the door.

"The scarf looks good on you."

"I like it, and I did think you might be coming."

Beltur thought Jessyla might have blushed.

"That's a warm coat," observed Margrena from where she stood in the doorway between the parlor and the kitchen.

"It came from Athaal's family. Athaal never wore it because it was too big for him. I'm fortunate no one else in Athaal's family wanted it."

"They pretty much ignored him, and it was their loss. People can be cruel when there's no good reason at all." Margrena shook her head.

Beltur stepped forward and handed her the basket. "I'll need to take the basket back, but everything in it is for the three of you."

In turn, Margrena extended the basket to Jessyla. "If you'd take it to the kitchen. You and Grenara can put everything away."

As she took the basket, Jessyla offered a smile Beltur could only have described as wicked. "I'll take care of that, Mother." She turned and hurried into the kitchen.

Even before Beltur had his coat off and had hung it on the wall peg by the door, he could hear Jessyla's cheerful words.

"Auntie! Look at everything that Beltur brought!"

Margrena smiled, but the smile faded immediately. "I also need a word with you. On sixday, Waensyn stopped by the Council Healing House. He was coolly polite. He didn't even pretend. Not much. He expressed his desire to consort Jessyla, and he told me that her life with him would be far better than with a mongrel mage like you."

"He used those words?"

Margrena nodded. "Then on sevenday, Cohndar came by the Council Healing House and suggested that Waensyn would be an excellent consort for Jessyla. He also said that a good daughter in Elparta abided by her mother's wishes and looked beyond mere infatuation."

Doesn't Jessyla get a say? Not in Elparta, it was beginning to appear to Beltur, and from what he recalled of Fenard, most families there at least tried to take a daughter's wishes into consideration. Then again, the nefarious duo might just have been overstating Elpartan customs.

"That sounds like they're overstating things."

"Not totally, I fear. Klarisia mentioned something about the importance of a 'prosperous match' for a healer because we don't get paid what we're worth."

"Did you tell Jessyla?"

"No. What good would that have done, except to make her furious? I did tell her that she's attractive and talented, and that it wouldn't be long before there would likely be some blacks, besides you, who would be making advances. She told me that you were the only one she was interested in."

"She's the only one—"

"That's obvious, for both of you. You two need more time with each other, but I wanted you to know what that pair is up to. You should talk things over with Meldryn. He's got a good head on his shoulders."

"Who does?" asked Jessyla, returning from the kitchen, still smiling.

"Meldryn," replied Margrena.

"That sounds like more problems." Jessyla looked to Beltur.

"Cohndar and Waensyn are talking about creating a council of mages here in Spidlar," said Beltur. "I have the feeling they might want to head it."

"Of course," replied Jessyla.

"I'll leave you two for a bit," said Margrena. "Grenara and I will look over what you brought, Beltur, and I'll fix some hot cider."

"Thank you, Mother."

Once Margrena had left the front room, Beltur murmured, "You were wicked."

"I liked every moment of it. She deserved it." Jessyla gestured toward the bench closest to the two-sided hearth. "We could sit down."

"We could," admitted Beltur, putting his arms around her. "In a moment."

In fact, it was several moments before Jessyla released him, and the two did sit next to each other.

"Did you have to patrol yesterday?"

"I did." Beltur then told about the two older women, ending with, "I had no idea what would happen when I stopped them. Laevoyt and the duty patroller weren't happy, either, but Laevoyt pointed out that we had to do something because, otherwise, the vendors, who aren't well-off, either, would suffer."

"That's terrible."

Beltur nodded. "What would you have done?"

Jessyla did not answer for several moments. "I don't know. You have a duty to protect the sellers. Especially an older woman who is only making coppers, and not silvers." After a pause, she added, "I suppose I'd do what you did. I wouldn't like it. You didn't, either, I can tell."

"No. I didn't. I also thought about what your mother said about the poor women who sneak into the Council Healing House just to get warm."

"I think Klarisia sometimes feeds them, but only when there's extra food and not when anyone is around."

"Meldryn told me that Klarisia doesn't get enough golds from the Council, and that's why she can't pay healers all that much."

"She's said that there would never be enough golds to help all those who need it."

"She could be right about that."

"Could be? How can you—" Jessyla broke off her words. "I'm sorry. It's just that when you see so many who are hurt and hungry . . ."

"I never denied that there are scores and scores who need food and shelter," replied Beltur. "I was thinking about how much the traders have and . . ." He shook his head.

"Oh . . . you think they could spare more golds for the poor."

"I don't have any doubts of that. I just don't know whether it would be enough."

"You're being more practical than I am."

Beltur couldn't help but think that, if he'd been that practical, he never would have given her the scarf.

"You don't think of yourself as practical?" asked Jessyla.

"Sometimes, I try to be practical, and sometimes I'm not so sure."

"That shows that you're honest."

"I try at that, too."

"Oh . . . don't be so insufferably modest. Accept a compliment."

Beltur found himself flushing.

Jessyla smiled broadly, then leaned forward and brushed his cheek with her lips, but only for a moment.

Beltur wished the moment had lasted quite a bit longer, but, with her mother and aunt in the next room . . . He tried to come up with something to say. "Do you go to the healing house every day except eightday?"

Jessyla shook her head. "Just four days out of eight."

"And you each get half a silver a day?"

She nodded. "It's enough."

Barely . . . if they're fortunate. "You'd think that some of the traders would need healers."

"The larger trading houses do have healers. Right now, Mother says, none of them need another healer."

"You have some doubts about that?"

"We're outlanders, just as you are. Even Auntie is considered an outlander, although she's lived here for over thirty years."

"Why did she come here?"

"She fell in love with a black mage. He traveled to Fenard often. I think he did the same sort of thing that Athaal did, traveling and trading for the Council. He was much older, and widowed, but they consorted. He died before I was born. He didn't have any children, either by his first consort or by Auntie. He left her the house and a few golds. She's been very careful."

Beltur nodded. "She's had to be."

"You've never said that much about your father, except that he was a scrivener. What was he like? What did he look like?"

"I was only nine . . . but he had brown hair, and Uncle said his eyes were hazel and he was broad-shouldered for a scrivener. He also had a big nose."

"Your nose definitely isn't large. You must have gotten it from your mother."

"Not from him, thank order."

"What else can you tell me about him? Did he read to you a lot? Since he was a scrivener . . ."

"He did, sometimes . . ."

Beltur kept answering Jessyla's questions for some time, possibly a glass, until Margrena appeared in the doorway to the kitchen. "Since you're here, Beltur, and since you brought enough for supper," she said with a smile, "we thought we'd fix it a little earlier so that you could enjoy it with us."

Beltur sensed a certain dismay from Jessyla. *Because that means you'll have to leave earlier? Or that we get less time together? Both?* He managed a warm smile. "Thank you. I appreciate the thoughtfulness, but you really didn't have to go to all that trouble."

"How could we not, when you've been so generous?"

Those words, Beltur felt, were completely honest. He stood, trying not to seem reluctant.

Jessyla rose from the bench, definitely reluctantly.

Margrena looked hard at Jessyla.

"Yes, Mother."

Beltur followed the two into the kitchen. On the table, in addition to the bread and one of the meat pies that Beltur had brought, there was a dish that held what looked to be a turnip and potato cheese casserole, as well as four mugs of hot cider.

"Please sit down." Grenara turned to Beltur. "I have to say that you do try to make yourself welcome and never a burden, and that's an excellent trait."

"Thank you. I do try." Beltur was definitely surprised, since those words were among the warmest he'd ever received from Jessyla's aunt. He waited until the others were seated before he did the same.

Once he was seated, he was careful to take only a modest serving of the meat pie, since he really wanted most of it to go to Jessyla and Margrena . . . and even Grenara, even if there were two others that he'd brought. He wasn't certain about the casserole, but he took enough of a serving, just enough, so that Margrena didn't think he was avoiding it, and he began with a mouthful of it, thinking that, if it tasted terrible, he could space it out between bites of bread and meat pie, and sips of the cider. That wasn't necessary, as the casserole was pleasant, if rather bland.

"Did you have City Patrol duty yesterday?" asked Margrena. "Even with all the snow?"

"The square was clear. They pay the young men in the workhouses to clear it."

"A good use of the Council's coppers," said Grenara. "Unlike some."

"What were you thinking of?" asked Margrena.

"The golds they spent to refurbish the quarters the other councilors use when they come to Elparta. They're only here a few eightdays out of the year."

"When did that happen?" Jessyla asked.

"Last year. And before that, they increased what they paid the tariff inspectors. They said it was so they wouldn't take bribes. I'd wager they do anyway."

"We can't do much about either," observed Margrena. "We might as well talk about something else."

"I can do that," said Grenara, her tone not quite casual, as she looked to Beltur. "I heard that you used a cupridium knife on fiveday. How could a poor mage like you ever afford something like that?"

Beltur could sense Jessyla's reaction, but he just smiled. "I couldn't. Jorhan forged it especially for me. I just thought it was one of several we'd done for a Lydian trader. I almost never see what we cast after Jorhan does the finish work. That's because he does that when I'm not there." He stood and eased the knife out of its sheath, then handed it to the oldest healer before reseating himself. "He even forged the nameplate to insert into the grip. It's a little darker bronze because he did that out of bronze and not cupridium so that it would be a surprise."

Grenara couldn't quite conceal her dismay. "Why would he do all that?"

"Because he couldn't pay me what he'd agreed when we were forging blades for the Council and because the cupridium candelabra, mirrors, platters, and blades we forged allowed him to pay off his debts to various traders."

"You worked for a time for less pay, then?" asked Margrena.

"Neither of us would be making coins, otherwise." Beltur reclaimed the knife from Grenara before handing it to Margrena.

Margrena studied the blade for a time. "It's beautiful. Any healer would love to have a knife like that." She returned it with a smile.

"I was completely surprised." Beltur slipped the knife back into its sheath. "And I'm well aware that I'm fortunate to have it."

"You earned it," said Jessyla firmly.

"Yes, you did," agreed Margrena. "What do you think about the weather here in Elparta?"

"It's cold, much colder than in Fenard." Beltur understood that the rest of the conversation was going to be about pleasantries.

Almost a glass later, Margrena said, "Given how cold it's getting, we'd best not keep you."

Beltur understood. "That's true, but I did enjoy the dinner and the company, and I appreciate your including me." He stood and stepped back from the table, surreptitiously easing two silvers from his wallet into his hand.

"You can see Beltur out, Jessyla. We'll clean up."

"Thank you." Jessyla offered a smile she didn't feel and stood, moving toward the front room.

"And don't forget Meldryn's basket."

Jessyla immediately turned and picked up the basket, her movements swift and not quite angry.

Beltur followed her, and once they stood near the front door, Jessyla set the basket on the floor, slipped her arms around him, and murmured, "She's not being fair. We don't get to see each other that often."

"It's as fair as she feels she can be," replied Beltur, his voice low. "It is Grenara's house."

"I know. I don't have to like it."

For a time, they held each other. Then, as they separated, he slipped the silvers into her hand.

"Beltur . . ." Her voice was low.

"I can do this," he murmured. "I won't have you and your mother not having enough food." He managed a smile. "Especially when I end up eating too much of what I brought."

"You didn't eat that much."

"I ate enough." He stepped back and took his coat off the wall peg, putting it on and then wrapping the scarf around his neck. "I did enjoy the afternoon. With you, I always do."

"I enjoy any time with you. I still wish you could stay longer."

"So do I." *But I'm not about to displease your mother and aunt, not when both of us need their goodwill . . . or at least not their opposition.* He smiled. "If Jorhan can't use me later in the eightday, I may come and spend some more time healing."

"That means you won't be making coins."

"If I'm not earning, at least I'll be learning." Beltur pulled on his gloves.

"Rhymes, yet." Jessyla shook her head.

He grinned, then put his arms around her again. "Sometimes . . . words have to do."

At that, she turned her head and kissed him, on the lips, for a long moment, before saying, "Sometimes . . . words aren't enough."

Finally, Jessyla handed him the basket and opened the door. "Please be careful."

"I will. You, too."

Chill air swept past the two as Beltur stepped out into the gusty wind. After a last look back at Jessyla as she closed the door, Beltur turned and began to walk toward Bakers Lane, the wind at his back.

By the time he reached home, his ears were nearly frozen, and he was more than glad for the warmth that greeted him once he stood in the small front hall and set down the basket before taking off his coat, scarf, and gloves.

"Have you eaten?" asked Meldryn from the front parlor.

"I have," replied Beltur, standing in the archway. "They insisted on having an early supper with some of what you sent."

The older mage smiled. "I thought that might happen. I ate just a while ago. Did you have an enjoyable afternoon?"

"For the most part, I did."

"Grenara was her usual charming self, then?" Meldryn's mild, but deep and mellow, voice bore only the slightest trace of the sardonic.

"Grenara wasn't that bad. Margrena told me that both Waensyn and Cohndar have been suggesting that it would be best for Jessyla to consort Waensyn."

"Best for Waensyn, no doubt."

"But even Klarisia was hinting it might be a good idea."

"That's because she needs Cohndar's backing to keep the Council's support of the healing house. She barely gets enough from the Council as it is. If she only hinted, she doesn't like the idea at all, but she feels that she has to be able to tell Cohndar she pushed the idea to Margrena."

"That explains a few things. I wondered why Margrena and Jessyla were paid so little."

"The Council doesn't like to spend coins on those who don't make them golds. They only support the healing house because Klarisia showed them that she healed laborers and dockworkers and their consorts and children, and that meant they missed less work."

Beltur nodded. He couldn't say that he was exactly surprised.

"You're working with Jorhan tomorrow?"

"I am. I probably won't be working with him every day that I could. The casting takes less time than the finish work. That's just a guess, though."

"You're already not working with him three days out of eight."

"I could stand to learn a bit more about healing."

"If Jorhan doesn't need you every day, you might talk to Veroyt about doing some work for the Council."

"That's a good idea." Beltur nodded, knowing that was as close as Meldryn was going to get to saying that the Council might need to replace Athaal in inspecting piers and wharves. "After I talk to Jorhan tomorrow, I'll know better how often he'll need me."

"Don't wait too long."

"I won't, but do you really think Waensyn would lower himself to inspecting piers?"

Meldryn chuckled. "Probably not, but he might need the coins."

"Do you know what he's been doing?"

"I heard he offered his services to some of the larger traders, detecting chaos, spoilage, and those sorts of things in their warehouses and wagons. Cohndar recommended him."

"Then it's likely that some of them will use his services and pay for them." Beltur frowned. "I never said much about it before, but shouldn't there be other services blacks could do that bring in more coins?"

"You haven't thought about it because you were raised to be a white, and since you came here, you've been doing anything you could to earn coppers and silvers." Meldryn closed the volume he had been reading, slipping a leather bookmark in place. "Athaal . . . and I talked about it a great deal. The essence of order is to strengthen, or to protect, or to detect chaos flaws. Those with coins will pay more for destruction that they can control than for protection. They'll pay more for the object than its protection. You and Jorhan get coins because of the objects you create, not because of the order-confined chaos that you instill in the cupridium."

"Then there ought to be a market for a black iron, shouldn't there?"

"I'm told that working black iron is even harder than cupridium, that it almost never works unless the smith is a mage as well as a smith."

Beltur had to think about that for a moment, then nodded. "That's why you're successful as a baker. Your understanding and control of order makes your bread and cakes enough better that people are willing to pay a bit more."

Meldryn nodded. "Exactly. That means that for a black to make a good living requires that he be not only a good mage, but good at something else."

"Are you saying that I ought to learn more about smithing?"

"You're already learning, aren't you?"

"I've seen what Jorhan does, but that's not the same as doing it."

"It's a start, I'd think."

"You're right." Beltur nodded. "Do you mind if I read here for a while?"

"Be my guest." Meldryn smiled.

After returning the basket to the bakery, Beltur retrieved *Considerations on the Nature of Man* and settled into the other armchair.

VII

Oneday was sunny, and markedly warmer than either sevenday or eightday, but still cold enough that ice and snow remained unmelted. Even so, walking from the bakery to the smithy was almost pleasant by comparison to previous days, but only because Beltur was wearing coat, gloves, and scarf.

Jorhan was, as usual, already working in the smithy when Beltur arrived.

"What are we casting today?"

"Two more straight-swords for the Lydian, and a matched set of platters and candelabra for Barrynt. He's acting for a merchant out of Sligo. He told me about those last night. Had to work late on the molds."

"He hasn't left Elparta yet?" Beltur took off his coat, scarf, and gloves, and hung the coat on the wall peg, then stripped off his tunic and put it on the next peg.

"He says that by midday tomorrow, it will be much warmer, and he'll have at least a few days before another storm comes. The mold for the first blade is just about heated enough."

Beltur moved toward the bellows, where he began to pump as Jorhan adjusted the position of the stone crucible.

Later, once Jorhan had poured the bronze into the mold and Beltur had set the order/chaos net into the metal that would harden as cupridium, Beltur blotted his forehead and said, "How much work-hardening is necessary for a blade?"

"As much as it takes. Why?"

"I just wondered. You do all that when I'm not here, but from what you've said, it takes a lot of time."

Jorhan shrugged. "The cast cupridium is hard enough for platters, mirrors, and the like without much work-hardening. It sometimes takes a fair amount of polishing, more than bronze because the cupridium is so much harder. The chasing I do for decoration adds some hardness to the surface. Polishing the mirror surface gives an even harder thin outer surface."

"How do you know how much to work-harden which parts of the blade?"

"You need to have a harder edge to the blade. That's why I fuller it a bit. I can't fuller cupridium that much. Otherwise the edge splits away in a layer the way it happened to those first pieces we tried . . ." After a pause, the smith asked, "Why do you want to know?"

"I thought that if I knew I might be able to make things better. I might be able to adjust the order/chaos net better."

"You're doing just fine as it is. Sometimes, trying to make perfect something that's already really good ruins it. Besides, nothing's perfect. No matter how hard we try, there'll always be tiny little things that we could have done better. No, making strong, good, honest blades or platters or mirrors that are simple and beautiful day after day will do more for us and for those who need what we forge than a perfect blade or candelabrum once an eightday." The smith turned toward the forge. "This second mold is hot enough."

Beltur moved back to the bellows.

Although Jorhan hadn't asked, Beltur stayed at the smithy for almost a glass longer, turning the grinding and polishing wheels, because it was clear that the smith worried about finishing the platters and candelabra before Barrynt left to return to Axalt.

Once the second candelabrum was polished, Jorhan turned to Beltur. "I can finish the platters. You need to head home before the wind picks up."

"You're sure?"

"That I am."

While Beltur cooled down, Jorhan left the smithy, returning shortly, and handing Beltur two silvers. "By next twoday, I'll be able to give you the back pay I've owed you. The Council still hasn't paid, but a Traders' Council acts like traders and pays everyone as late as they can. But twoday's when the Lydian will be here for his blades. Might be a day sooner or later, but around then."

"Thank you." Beltur took the silvers, slipped on his tunic, then his coat, gloves, and scarf.

"My thanks to you. I appreciate your staying late today. If I know Barrynt, he'll likely be here earlier than he said tomorrow."

"He strikes me as a good man."

"He's been good to me and especially to Johlana. He doesn't have trouble trading here, either. For now, anyway."

That raised a question that Beltur had wondered about. "How does the Council collect tariffs on goods from Axalt?"

"There aren't any to speak of, except on weapons, and that's usually ignored. The Viscount has a fort on the east side of the pass. That's where he collects tariffs on goods coming into Certis, and Axalt has a post there for goods coming into Axalt. If they're destined for Spidlar, part of the tariff goes to the Council."

Beltur recalled that Veroyt, Councilor Jhaldrak's assistant, had quoted tariffs on blades. *But then he probably wasn't about to mention to the councilor that they were seldom paid.* "The Council trusts Axalt on that?"

"It's not a matter of trust. There once was a tariff post at the west end of the pass. It cost more to collect the tariffs than the Council got back, and a lot of the tariff fees disappeared. Some might have ended up in Axalt, but no one's ever been successful in attacking them."

"And this way the Council gets something."

"The traders also get to send goods to Axalt without tariffs, and Axalt sends things here without tariffs."

"Tomorrow, then?"

"Tomorrow," affirmed the smith.

Beltur stepped out into the late, late afternoon chill and headed down the lane.

His eyebrows felt frosted by the time he stepped through the northeast gate, and his feet, even inside his boots, were definitely chilled when he reached the corner of Bakers Lane and Crossed Lane. He was more than glad for the warmth of the house and the smell of baked goods when he closed the front door and took off the heavy coat.

Meldryn was in the kitchen, rising from the table as Beltur entered. "You're late."

"I didn't know I would be. We had to cast more than Jorhan planned. He got a late order from his sister's consort. I stayed an extra glass to help with the grinding and polishing." Beltur offered a crooked smile. "Someone did suggest that I needed to learn more."

"You do take things to heart. Get the ale, and I'll serve."

"That sounds good."

"You don't even know what we're having."

"If you fixed it, I don't have to worry." Beltur took the mugs from the cupboard and then went to the small keg, where he filled one mug and then the other before setting them on the table and sitting down. "How did it go for you today?"

"Slow. Like most onedays, but not as bad as some. The good thing is that I judged right. Not too much left. That's why we're having a fowl pie." Meldryn set two platters on the table and seated himself.

"Oh?"

"Farodyn asked if I'd take a capon in trade for a molasses potato pie. I did, and I made three fowl pies. I usually can sell some on twoday or threeday, but this one is for us." Meldryn smiled.

"I'm glad of that, but . . ."

"Everything's fine. Veroyt said he'd bring what the Council owes me threeday morning."

"They must pay everything on twoday."

"Mostly."

Beltur took a bite of the warm meat pie, enjoying the combination of meat and root vegetables in the flavorful filling, combined with the thick but flaky crust. "This is good."

"I thought so. Have you heard anything interesting?"

Beltur thought, then said, "You might already know this. Jessyla told me that Grenara had consorted a black and that she'd inherited the house when he died . . ."

"She did. Her consort was Ghelhan. He mostly inspected boats and their cargoes."

"Inspected boat cargoes?"

"Both boats and cargoes," Meldryn repeated mildly. "He could tell if the boats had hidden compartments or goods stashed where inspectors couldn't find them. That's what Lhadoraak does now. Ghelhan could also sense where hulls were weak long before the weaknesses were dangerous."

"If the Council paid him the way they do for other things . . ."

"They did. The Council is not notably generous to blacks, except in the case of invasions that threaten their trade." The last words carried more than a trace of irony. "Then they pay more, but still less than the worth of the service."

"So how did Ghelhan come by a house? I mean, from what you've said, it took a long time and two of you to come to own this house."

"You're right. It did take time. Ghelhan was more fortunate. The house was a wedding gift from the father of his first consort. That was Trader Viltaar, the elder. Ghelhan inspected all of his boats and cargoes and got a stipend for doing that. Viltaar had more than a few daughters, and there weren't enough traders' sons for them to consort. He felt that she wouldn't suffer unduly as a mage's consort, provided she had a decent house, and he could also get the Council to offer some additional work to Ghelhan."

"Does Lhadoraak do that now?"

"No. The Council insisted that another mage do that. They said it wasn't right for the same man to do both. Right now, that's Mharkyn. He obviously doesn't make much at the moment. You haven't met Mharkyn, have you?"

"No. You've mentioned him, though." Beltur paused. "How much would a house like Grenara's cost to buy . . . these days?"

Meldryn laughed. "I can tell what you have in mind."

Beltur flushed. "Well . . . someday I will consort, and it wouldn't hurt to know."

"Grenara's house? I haven't seen it."

"Kitchen and parlor on the lower level, and two rooms plus a small washroom on the upper."

"Depending on where a house like that is located and its condition, you might be able to buy one for twenty golds. That's about as little as you could expect for anywhere that you'd wish to live. If you're fortunate, you could rent a house like that for half a silver a eightday."

Beltur couldn't say he was surprised. He might have, all told, close to four golds in silvers to his name. That suggested that even saving every spare silver, it would be years before he could buy anything. Renting, however . . .

After a moment, he said, "You two must have worked very hard and saved every copper."

"It took us ten years."

Beltur could believe that.

"Right now, you're earning more than we did."

"That's for now," Beltur pointed out. "I worry about how long people will be willing to pay for cupridium, especially in Elparta or even in Spidlar."

"If you and Jorhan are the only ones forging it, you might be able to do well for years. But you'd best be careful, because when you sell to merchants who sell elsewhere, you'll get larger sums far less frequently."

"I think Jorhan's already had that problem." Beltur didn't know that for certain, but he did know that the smith had owed a fair amount before Beltur had arrived.

Meldryn just nodded, then said, "There is a small pearapple tart. Enough for two."

Beltur couldn't help smiling.

VIII

Twoday morning was sunny again, but warm enough that Beltur did not have to wrap the scarf around his ears and across his nose on the walk to the smithy, at least not until the last kay. He actually arrived before seventh glass. Jorhan was already at work on the polishing wheel, putting a last finish on the cupridium set for Barrynt.

After taking off his outerwear and tunic, Beltur immediately took over using the foot pedal to turn the wheel. "You've been here since dawn?"

"Not that long. A glass or so. I needed light to see where I had to touch up the finish."

A glass or so later, when Jorhan was satisfied and had laid out the set on the workbench, Beltur took his place at the bellows.

"Now look at the melt," said Jorhan. "Don't ever let it get to a whitish color. That means you've overheated it."

Surprised as he was at what Jorhan volunteered, Beltur just nodded and kept pumping the bellows and listening as the smith continued his explanations.

Some time later, Jorhan poured the bronze-like metal into the mold for another straight-sword, and Beltur created and held the order/chaos net in place as the metal cooled. Just as Beltur felt it was nearing the time when he could release his concentration, there was a rapping on the smithy door.

"I'll get it," said Jorhan. "Don't want you to spoil the set on this one."

Although Beltur hadn't done that except at the very beginning, when he was feeling his way, he kept concentrating, forcing himself to just hold the complex pattern in place, although he knew that the caller had to be Barrynt from what he overheard.

". . . don't mind that I'm a bit early . . ."

"You've never been late. The cupridium set's laid out on the workbench, the back one away from the forge. Don't mind Beltur, he's working on making certain his order/chaos pattern sets right in the bronze."

"How hard is that?" asked the merchant, his tone cautiously curious rather than sardonic or sarcastic.

"Hard enough that he's more tired than I am by the end of the day."

Jorhan laughed. "Part of that is that he also acts as my striker, but even when he doesn't he's sweat-soaked by then."

"Like many things, magery is harder than it appears, then."

"More dangerous, too. Half the mages fighting in the invasion ended up dead."

Although that number was close to what Beltur thought it might be, he had never mentioned anything like that to Jorhan, and he wondered where the smith had heard about the mage casualties.

"Here's what you ordered."

There was a long lull in the conversation before Barrynt spoke again. "These are better than Zaethyr deserves, better than he paid for, but I'll have to honor the price I offered him. I won't change terms the way some do, like Emlyn."

"Ask him for a favor in return," suggested Jorhan. "That way he can boast that he got them for less by offering the favor, and if you get other orders, you can charge more, or garner more favors."

"You talk like a merchant, Jorhan."

"I'm no merchant. I can talk louder with friends and family, but I don't do so well when I'm talking for myself. You know that as well as anyone."

This time, Barrynt laughed. "That's why you ought to come to Axalt."

"I'm not ready to put away my hammers."

"You wouldn't have to."

"I'd have to pay for coal."

"You could afford to."

As the two continued to banter, Beltur could finally feel that the order/chaos net was firmly set. Even so, he waited for a time longer before he finally released his hold on the pattern . . . and took a deep breath, then blotted his forehead.

Jorhan broke off whatever he was saying and looked to Beltur. "You finished there?"

"It's set, but don't hit the mold or move it for a while." Those words weren't really directed at the smith, but to the merchant.

"Do most mages work as hard as you do?" asked Barrynt.

"Not from what I've seen," replied Jorhan before Beltur could reply. "Beltur works long days here and two days an eightday as a City Patrol mage."

"Meldryn works long days, too. He's up before I am."

"Meldryn?" asked Barrynt quizzically.

"He's both a black mage and a baker. I live in his house, and I pay for the lodging. His partner was one of the mages killed in fighting back the invasion."

"I thought I told you that," added Jorhan. "Beltur barely escaped from Gallos. His family was all killed, and he almost was. Athaal and Meldryn took him in while he was getting on his feet."

"If Athaal hadn't introduced me to Jorhan, I'd be in very poor shape."

"So would I," replied the smith dryly.

"You don't have a consort?" asked Barrynt.

Beltur understood the question that hadn't been asked. "I've been seeing a healer. She lives with her mother and her aunt. I'm hoping, once I save more silvers. But she and her mother are likely worse off than I am. They had to flee Gallos, too."

Barrynt nodded. "No wonder you're working so hard."

"She's worth working for," replied Beltur with a smile.

"Just from your expression I can see that."

"We'd best not spend any more time jawing," said Jorhan, looking to Barrynt. "We'll just delay you, and I don't want Johlana blaming me if you get caught in a storm."

"She'd never blame you," replied Barrynt genially. "She'd tell me that it was my fault, and that I know better. But there's little sense in tempting fate or the weather. I've got a case in the wagon, and some clean rags to pack up the cupridium. I'll be right back."

After Barrynt hurried out, Jorhan looked at Beltur and grinned. "You sly demon. You never said anything about a healer."

"Ah . . . well, not many people know, and there's an older black who's trying to insist she consort him. She doesn't want that, and I don't, either."

"You've got good reasons to work hard. She'd be a fool to choose another."

"She doesn't want that. Neither does her mother, but they don't have much because they had to flee Gallos as well."

"Coins don't make a good match, but a good match gets stronger when you're earning coins."

At that moment, Barrynt returned with a wooden box that he carried straight to the rear workbench.

Jorhan looked to Beltur. "We'll talk more about that later." He moved to the workbench and helped Barrynt wrap and pack the cupridium pieces.

In a fraction of a glass, the candelabra and platters vanished into the box, and Barrynt stood by the smithy door. "Just remember, both of you, what I said."

Beltur could sense the honesty behind the statement.

"I'll walk you down to the wagon," said Jorhan, heading toward the smithy door. "Add some coal to the forge, would you, Beltur?"

The door closed behind the two, and Beltur took the short shovel and carefully added coal to the fire, trying to replicate the pattern that Jorhan used.

The smith was shivering by the time he returned and stood in front of the forge. "Had to take two kegs to the house. Wine and ale. He's a good man. Always brings a little extra. Couldn't ask for a better consort for Johlana. He'd face the black angels for her . . . or for their children. I wouldn't want to be the one who angered him that way."

"I got the feeling from what he said about not changing terms."

"He's a man of his word. Always has been." Jorhan paused, then looked directly at Beltur. "Hope you don't mind my saying so, but there's no perfect time to ask a woman to consort. Black angels, there's no perfect time for anything." The smith offered a grimace. "There can be a wrong time and a wrong way. I know that. Menara turned me down when I came calling fresh from the smithy. Said I needed to come clean. Never forgot that."

"She didn't turn you down outright, then?"

"No, but I got in the habit of washing a lot more."

Beltur couldn't help smiling.

"Best we get on with it," said Jorhan, moving toward the forge. "We could cast and finish all winter, but once the roads close down, there won't be many buyers."

Beltur moved to the bellows.

The remainder of the day was spent casting daggers and an ornate vase, which Jorhan explained by saying, "We need to have a few different things for the outlanders."

Right at fourth glass, after getting paid, Beltur hurried off because he wanted to get to the Council building before Raymandyl left for the day.

Even so, it appeared as though the clerk was tidying up prior to leaving when Beltur rushed through the door and toward his table desk. "You cut it close again, I see." The dark-haired clerk offered a friendly smile.

"I've been working with Jorhan. We had to get some pieces ready for different traders."

"You do seem to keep busy."

"That's what happens when you arrive in a new city copperless."

"I doubt you're that copperless now." Raymandyl opened the pay ledger, made a notation, and turned the ledger so that Beltur could sign it. Then he set two silvers on the desk.

Beltur picked them up and slipped them into his wallet. "Not now, but I haven't forgotten owing Athaal and Meldryn so much." He then took out the two tokens, the ones he still felt slightly guilty about, and passed them to the clerk. "I've also got these."

"I don't see many of these once it snows."

"I almost wish you didn't see these."

"Street folks stealing food?"

Beltur nodded. "I didn't realize that was going to be a problem."

"It's been a problem for years. Likely always will be. There's no easy way to deal with it." Raymandyl took out the second ledger, opened it, made the entry, had Beltur sign, then applied his seal. After that, he handed over four more silvers. "There you are."

"Thank you."

"Don't spend them all in the same place. They'll be harder to come by in the eightdays ahead."

"I got that impression from Laevoyt."

"He's a good man. A good patroller as well."

"Did you ever find out why your message to me didn't get delivered on time?" Beltur grinned.

Raymandyl didn't. "I never got a straight answer. One runner said he'd been told to give it to another. The first swore he gave it to the second. The second said he never got it. I don't think either was telling the truth. That bothers me, but I can't do much about it."

It bothered Beltur as well, but he wasn't about to say so. "Sometimes, those things happen. I'll see you in another eightday."

"Just keep warm."

"I'll do my best." Beltur offered a pleasant smile, then turned and left the Council building, heading back to the house and bakery, with more silvers to put in the small iron strongbox he had bought after he'd recovered from his injuries.

IX

When Beltur set out for Patrol headquarters on threeday, he definitely needed his heavy coat, gloves, and scarf. While the green-blue sky was bright and clear, a north wind chilled any exposed skin. Despite the chill, when Beltur and Laevoyt reached the market square, there were already sellers there, including the woman selling acorn cakes and several others selling heavy woolen blankets and coats, and a number of carts with potatoes and other root vegetables.

There weren't any flashes of chaos, and not any sign of cutpurses or lightfingers. Fosset only had his cart there from ninth glass to second glass, but Beltur was more than glad for the hot cider by the time the city chimes rang out the first glass of the afternoon. Those who came to buy straggled in, most of them between ninth glass and third glass, although there were still a few buyers and sellers when Beltur and Laevoyt left the square and began their walk back to Patrol headquarters. In short, Beltur's entire duty was uneventful and cold.

Fourday morning was only slightly warmer than threeday morning, but the walk to Jorhan's was far longer than the walk to Patrol headquarters and the market square, and that meant that Beltur arrived at the smithy more than ready for the warmth of the forge. On fourday and on fiveday, Jorhan and Beltur worked long, so that Beltur didn't get back to the bakery until almost sixth glass. Yet Jorhan was hard at work when Beltur arrived and continued forging, grinding, or polishing after Beltur departed.

When Beltur arrived at the smithy on sixday and took off his outerwear, Jorhan immediately said, "No casting today. I'll need your help with the grinding and polishing wheels. The Lydian will be here between second and third glass. He won't be traveling back to Elparta again until after the roads clear and the ice melts."

"Sometime in spring?"

"The roads are seldom clear until the second or third eightday of spring."

Beltur looked at Jorhan, seeing the dark circles under the smith's bloodshot eyes. "How late did you work last night?"

"Until I couldn't."

Meaning that this is his last chance for a good sale for more than a season. Beltur walked toward the wheels. "Polishing or grinding?"

"Polishing."

By a little after noon, the two finished the polishing and finish work, and Jorhan began to lay out the four straight-swords, a single sabre, two sets of candelabra, three daggers with simple leather sheaths, and two platters.

"Will he buy all of it?" asked Beltur.

"He asked for the straight-swords and sabre and one dagger and a set of candelabra. Even if that's all he takes, we'll be in much better shape."

Left unsaid was the fact that, in all likelihood, Jorhan would be able to come up with Beltur's back pay, even if the Council took longer to pay the smith.

Once Jorhan was satisfied, he turned to Beltur. "I have two molds for mirrors."

"Who wants mirrors?"

"No one that I know, but the mirrors take less metal and require more artistry and finishing, and from here on until spring, we won't likely get much more copper, and I'll have more time than bronze."

Beltur nodded. What the smith said made sense. It also suggested that Beltur's earnings would decrease considerably in the next season and a half, especially after his City Patrol duty was over at the end of the second eightday of Winter.

He walked over to the forge, added coal in the way that Jorhan preferred, and then began to pump the bellows.

Almost two glasses later, after the two finished casting the second mirror, Beltur finally walked away from the cooling mold, having made certain that his order/chaos net was firmly set. He blotted his forehead and took a deep breath.

At the knock on the smithy door, Jorhan hurried forward and opened it. "Come in, Trader Harfyl."

The trader stepped into the smithy. He was tall and slender, so wiry that he looked underfed, with watery blue eyes and a narrow pale face under white-blond hair. He wore a light brown coat with a matching cap and scarf, and dark brown leather gloves of the same color as his calf-high boots. Beltur didn't sense anything unusual about his patterns of order or chaos.

Two men in bulky brown leather jackets followed the trader into the smithy. One carried a wooden box about three cubits long, and perhaps two wide. The other, empty-handed, closed the smithy door. Beltur immediately sensed something different about the sheathed swords worn by the guards, a darkness permeating the blades. *Black iron?*

"What do you have for me, Smith?"

At least that was what Beltur thought the trader said in his heavily accented voice, an accent he had heard once or twice, but had not realized was that of Lydiar.

"I've laid it all out on the workbench. What you ordered is there, along with several other pieces."

"What I ordered is what I need."

"All that is there," replied Jorhan. "If you don't care for the other pieces, then someone else will. I thought that you should have the first chance at them."

"We shall see." The trader followed the smith to the workbench.

The two guards remained just inside the smithy door, with the wooden box on the floor between them, its top firmly in place.

The Lydian looked over the workbench, then lifted the straight-sword closest to the end, examined it closely, then used it in a set of movements or exercises. When he finished with the movements, he took out a small disk and ran it over the blade, but the disk left no mark. He repeated the same process with each of the swords, the sabre, and the three daggers, and then studied the other pieces in much the same fashion before setting down the last platter and turning back to Jorhan. "I cannot believe you have amassed such a collection."

"I didn't amass it. We forged it."

"Where is the mage?" asked the trader. "It takes a mage and a smith to forge cupridium."

Jorhan looked puzzled for a moment. "What does that—"

"The mage? Where is he?"

"I'm right here," declared Beltur.

"You? A mage?" The trader laughed. "A striker as a mage?" Before Beltur could say more, the trader gestured to the guards and said, "Seize him!"

Beltur immediately threw containments around both the trader and the guards, all of whom looked completely stunned to find themselves trapped.

"Beltur may not look it, but he was the arms-mage most powerful and effective in defeating the Gallosians," said Jorhan, looking to the trader. "Is that enough proof of magery?"

The Lydian offered a wry smile. "It is indeed. That is even more surprising than coming across the largest assemblage of cupridium blades and other wares that anyone has seen in Candar in centuries. Who would have thought that a country smith and a ragged mage would have created such beauty?" He paused. "I had to know. If you will release me, I will pay you for all that is on the bench. Four golds for each sword, three for the sabre, two for each dagger, one for each candelabrum and platter."

Beltur could not sense any swirls of chaos that suggested dishonesty or deception, nor anything like a shield . . . and, somehow, that bothered him.

"Four for the sabre and two for the large platter," answered Jorhan.

"Agreed."

Beltur released the trader, but not the guards.

The trader seemed not to notice that Beltur had not released his men. From somewhere under the coat, he produced a leather wallet from which he counted out the golds, thirty-five of them, laying the coins on the workbench. "The two extra golds are because I doubted you, and I wish that you would think kindly of me when I return in the spring."

"I think we can manage that." Jorhan took the golds and placed them in his own wallet, stepping away from the workbench and moving over beside Beltur.

Beltur enlarged his shields to include Jorhan and then released the two guards.

"Use the soft cloths in the box to wrap everything," the trader directed the two, before turning back to face Jorhan and Beltur. "Are there other items you forge?"

"We've done a few hand mirrors."

"Those would sell well if they are not too costly."

"Three golds," replied Jorhan. "The chasing and decorative work on the mirrors and the need for a perfect reflecting surface takes more time."

"Three golds," agreed the trader, "provided that each mirror is different."

"We can do that." The trader returned his attention to the guards and the wooden box they had carried over to the back workbench. "Use the padded strips to separate the blades and cover them with the old quilt."

Once everything was in the box, one of the guards affixed two locks, and the two carried the box out of the smithy.

Only then did Trader Harfyl turn back to Jorhan. "I will see you in the spring, and I look forward to discovering what else you have created. Several blades would not be amiss."

"We will look forward to your return."

"Again, I will offer my apologies for doubting you, Smith, but I trust you understand just how surprised and concerned I was to see what you offered."

"I understand your caution," replied Jorhan.

"And to you, Mage, I also apologize. I realize that I am most fortunate that you are a black."

"I accept your apology and wish you well on your journey."

"Thank you." Harfyl nodded politely, then turned and hurried out of the smithy.

Jorhan and Beltur followed as far as the door. From there they watched as three guards and Harfyl mounted their horses, and the fourth guard climbed up onto the seat of the small wagon, in which were loaded kegs, barrels, and bundles.

Once the four were out of sight, Jorhan closed the smithy door. "I didn't expect that."

"Do you think he thought you'd found the earlier blades you sold him?"

"He wasn't sure. Part of it might be that."

"So he would have stolen them if you'd found them, but he was willing to pay if we forged them?"

"If we'd found or stolen them, he saw no reason to pay us. If we forged them, then he wants as much as we can supply."

"That doesn't speak any more highly of the Lydian traders than those in Elparta," said Beltur dryly.

"A trader is a trader. Most of them, anyway. There aren't many like Barrynt."

Beltur had definitely gained that impression. "Harfyl must be well-off. He just counted out thirty-five golds. There must have been fifty or a hundred in his wallet."

"He had four guards that travel with him, and he rented the wagon and the horses."

"How did you know that?"

"He told me the last time that he rented wagons and mounts, because it cost less."

"But carrying a hundred golds?"

"Did you see the coat he wore?" asked Jorhan. "It was made of the fine brown wool, the soft kind that comes from the undercoat of midland goats. The coat itself likely cost two golds."

Beltur had heard of that wool, and that, supposedly, a thin coat of that wool was warmer than a thick coat made from sheep's wool.

"I think we can take the rest of the day off," said Jorhan. "Once I pay you." After taking out his belt wallet, he counted out ten golds and handed them to Beltur. "This time I can pay you what you deserve."

Beltur managed not to look stunned as he took them and put them into his belt wallet, making certain that it was securely fastened. He'd certainly hoped for more than the two golds or so that Jorhan had promised him. *But ten golds?*

"You're getting a bit less than half after the cost of the metal and everything else. Fair's fair." The smith offered a crooked smile that held a trace of sadness. "Best you make it last. We'll be fortunate to sell a blade or two and a few candlesticks or platters for the rest of the fall and all of winter."

"That little?"

"Traders in Elparta won't buy that much. Those who can spare the golds likely already have what they want and need, and they won't buy to sell elsewhere until spring because they'll have trouble getting trading goods to their ships in Spidlaria."

"The river won't freeze that soon, will it?"

"By the second eightday of Winter, it will start to freeze over, and the water levels will start to drop because the Easthorns will be getting snow and not rain."

Beltur hadn't thought about that.

"I'd hoped he'd take it all, but you never know."

"He really would have taken it? Just like that?" Harfyl's acts and abrupt about-face still bothered Beltur, more than a little.

"Most likely. Traders stick together." Jorhan grinned. "That's another reason why I wanted you here when he came. He's as smooth as lard, and I have a hard time trusting anyone that smooth."

"But . . ."

"It's not a good idea to trust anyone who has that kind of golds to spend unless you've got something to hold over them. You're all I've got against someone like that. Most Elpartan traders won't buy that much, and we needed someone who would. But all the mages who do City Patrol duty could handle a trader, and after I heard what you did against the Prefect's army, I figured that Harfyl couldn't come up with anything you couldn't handle. That's another reason for your share."

"I think I'd better be here anytime he comes."

"I hadn't thought otherwise." Jorhan smiled. "Now . . . head on out. I'll see you on oneday. Don't spend it all on your healer. A little, but not all."

"I'll be careful. I've been short of coins long enough not to want to repeat the experience." Beltur slipped on his tunic, then his scarf and gloves.

When Beltur headed down the lane a short time later, he was still a little stunned, both by Harfyl's blatant attempt to steal the blades and

other items, and then the casual dismissal of that effort followed by the
willingness to pay extra golds, as if the golds resolved the matter of trust.
*Is that the way all of them do business? Or did Jorhan need to deal with Harfyl
to get enough golds to pay off everything and not rely on the Council?*

Beltur shook his head. On the one hand, he could hardly believe that
he had accumulated over fifteen golds with what he had just received and
what he'd made earlier from Jorhan and the City Patrol. He'd earned more
silvers since he'd come to Elparta than he'd seen in his entire life, and he'd
never actually held a gold coin before. *But you won't see more golds like that
for almost two seasons.* And that meant it would likely take several years, if
not longer, to buy even a small house . . . and if he used the golds he had
to rent a house, it would be just that much longer before he could buy one.

Still . . . he couldn't say he was coinless. At that thought, he smiled as
he hurried through the chill afternoon back toward the bakery.

X

By midday on eightday, Beltur was having trouble concentrating on Leantor and his tome *On Healing,* finding himself reading the same paragraph
for the third time. Finally, after struggling through another few handfuls
of pages, he lowered the book and just sat there.

Meldryn rose from his armchair in the front parlor and opened one of
the inside shutters that helped keep down the chill from the single icy pane
of the small window. "It looks like we've got dark clouds coming in. I
thought I felt something. If you're going to see the young woman . . ."

"I should go early, like last eightday."

"It wouldn't be a bad idea. I've got a basket ready for you in the bakery."

"Meldryn . . . you didn't have—"

"You didn't have to lug two stones of potatoes all the way back after
working all day, and you certainly didn't have to get that honey for me."
Meldryn closed the inside shutter. "Besides, I like them, too, and they need
help. You've been slipping her coins, haven't you?"

"How did you know?"

Meldryn smiled. "I didn't. I thought it likely. Healers never earn enough.
That's why some of the women healers end up as consorts to the younger
sons of traders. The son gets a consort who's acceptable, without tying the

trader into another trading family in an alliance that might not be advan-
tageous or might conflict with other familial consortings, and the trader
gets a healer who's nearly always available. Traders like that sort of conve-
nience." The older mage's last words were heavily sardonic.

"That was how Grenara got the house, you said." Beltur closed the
book, then stood.

"And Viltaar the younger was anything but pleased with that."

"But why? It's a small house. It can't be worth more than . . . what . . .
twenty golds?"

"He felt it had belonged to his sister and that it should have come back
to the family when Ghelhan died rather than going to Ghelhan's second
consort."

"So he would have just pushed her out on the street?"

"That, or charged her rent."

"For the house she'd lived in for years?"

"You're surprised? Viltaar's a trader. Not one of the larger houses, to be
sure, but definitely a trader."

Beltur didn't want to believe that, correct as he suspected Meldryn was.

"Go get yourself ready to go. I'll get the basket from the bakery."

By the time Beltur was bundled up in his heavy coat, with scarf in
place and gloves on, Meldryn had returned with the basket.

"Three loaves of bread, two large meat pies, and an assortment of pastries. Just ones made with the black sweet syrup, though."

"I appreciate that, and they will as well. Thank you." Beltur took the
basket and set out into the graying early afternoon. Although there had
been no more snow since late on sevenday, the wind swirled patches of
what there was into piles at the base of walls or in corners, leaving the streets
relatively clear, not that there had been much new snow there.

There were few people out, and most were hurrying toward whatever
their destination might be. Beltur looked northward. The darker and heavier
clouds were definitely advancing toward the city. He was about to turn off
of Bakers Lane onto Crafters Way when Jessyla appeared almost in front
of him.

He stopped short. "What are you doing here?"

"I thought you'd be coming, and I didn't want you to be surprised."

"Surprised by what?"

"Cohndar is at the house talking to Mother and Auntie."

Beltur had a very good idea what the subject might be, but that raised
another question. "Why aren't you there?"

"Cohndar said that he wished to talk privately with them. Besides, I know what he's doing, and so do you." Jessyla looked directly at Beltur. "Or do I have to spell it out for you?"

"He's most likely pointing out how remunerative a match with the noble and well-connected black mage Waensyn would be for you and your family."

"How long have you known this? Why didn't you tell me?" There was an edge to Jessyla's voice and scarcely concealed anger behind it.

"I've known Waensyn wanted you practically since he arrived in Elparta. I overheard conversations that suggested he and Cohndar wanted me out of the way. What else could his visit be about?"

The hardness largely vanished from her face. "You could have told me."

"I thought you knew all that from the time when you said that they were trying to kill me."

"You're still hiding a little something."

"Not much. Your mother told me that Cohndar was hinting along the same line."

"And she didn't tell me?"

"She said that you'd be furious, and that she didn't want to get you upset." Beltur smiled wryly, knowing as he did so that she couldn't see the expression, except in his eyes, given that his mouth was partly concealed by the heavy scarf. "I had the feeling she didn't want me to tell you, but I can't not tell you . . . since you've asked."

"You won't lie to me, then?"

"No. I never have. It's possible I may not have said everything or not said something clearly, but I've tried never to deceive you."

Abruptly, she smiled. "Good. Now, we can go back to the house."

"What do you intend to do?"

"See what the most dishonorably honorable Cohndar will say . . . or not say."

Another thought occurred to Beltur. "Just how did you know I'd be coming about now?"

"You always come when you can, and I just felt that it would be about now."

"I did bring a few things."

"I can see that." Jessyla dropped her eyes for a moment.

"Oh?"

"Auntie says you're trying to bribe your way into my affections and into Mother accepting you."

"I care about you."

"I know. So does Mother. Auntie . . . she worries."

"Because she consorted for love, and her consort's brother tried to take even her house from her?"

"How did you know that?"

"Meldryn told me. He and Athaal helped her on some healing. He might have found out then." Beltur noticed that Jessyla was shivering, and that her jacket wasn't all that warm-looking. "We need to get you back where it's warmer."

"It's not all that warm in the house."

"I'm sure it's warmer than out here." Beltur took her arm and started down Crafters Lane toward Grenara's small house.

"Cohndar's an evil old man."

"He's set in his ways."

"They aren't good ways."

Beltur agreed with that, but saw no point in saying that aloud. "We need to get you where you're not shivering."

"You're changing the subject. Why won't you admit he's evil?"

"I don't see much point in it, not when he has so much influence over the way most black mages in Elparta feel."

"That's cowardly. I thought better of you."

"If not wanting to get exiled from Elparta with winter coming on is cowardly, then I'm cowardly. I'd rather oppose him less obviously."

"You're a stronger mage than he is."

"That doesn't earn me any silvers, and my duty with the City Patrol ends in the first eightday or so of Winter. I can't ask more of Meldryn, not when he's lost Athaal and the silvers he brought in." *And I won't be able to keep helping you and your mother if Cohndar makes it harder for me to earn coins.*

"I still don't like it." Jessyla stopped before the closed front door.

"Do you think I do?" countered Beltur.

"Oh . . . Beltur . . ." She shook her head, just standing there for several moments before opening the door.

The front room was empty, but as Beltur followed Jessyla inside and closed the door, he sensed that there were three people in the kitchen. He handed the basket to Jessyla so that he could take off his coat, gloves, and scarf. "You might put that in the far corner for now," he murmured.

"You're so cautious."

"There are times caution is a good idea."

Jessyla crossed the room and set the basket in the corner, then returned to stand next to Beltur.

"Jessyla? Is that you?"

"Yes, Mother. Beltur's here."

"I didn't hear anyone knock," called Grenara.

"That's because I saw him coming."

"Just settle yourselves there," said Margrena. "We'll be out in a moment."

"Yes, Mother," replied Jessyla in a tone that was definitely falsely sweet. "Thank you."

Beltur didn't bother to hide the almost inadvertent wince.

"I wasn't nasty," Jessyla whispered.

"Just sweet-nasty," Beltur murmured back.

Jessyla mock-glared at him in return.

Beltur managed not to laugh, but pointed toward the hearth, thinking about how she had shivered. Jessyla shook her head.

So they waited, standing there and not speaking, for perhaps a tenth of a glass before Margrena opened the kitchen door and walked into the front room followed by Cohndar.

The white-haired mage had loosened his heavy black overcoat, but not taken it off, and his black scarf was draped around his shoulders and hung down over the front of his coat on both sides. "Good afternoon, young Beltur."

"Good afternoon to you, ser."

"Are you still working with that smith?" Cohndar's tone was casual, almost bland.

"I am, ser."

"He'll only be able to sell so much cupridium here in Elparta, you know, and not that much more to traders in Kleth or Spidlaria."

"Some have said that might be a problem, but there don't seem to be any other smiths forging cupridium anywhere else in Candar. Do you know of any?"

"Trade is scarcely my business, Beltur. I do know that very expensive goods have few buyers."

"So what are you suggesting?" Beltur asked calmly.

"I'm suggesting nothing. I'm merely observing."

"Then I'll be careful to keep your observation in mind." Beltur inclined his head, just slightly, and stepped back, as if to clear the way to the door.

Cohndar turned toward Margrena. "I do hope you'll consider what I suggested most carefully."

"It's wise to give anything suggested by such a well-known senior mage careful thought, and I will do so."

"Very careful thought," said Cohndar strongly but pleasantly.

"I will." Margrena's smile was pleasant, but not particularly warm as she escorted the older mage to the door.

Once Cohndar had departed and Margrena had closed the door, Beltur walked to the far side of the front room, reclaimed the basket, then presented it to Margrena.

"You are making a habit of this, Beltur," she replied.

"I'm just doing my best to repay your kindness and past support," he replied.

"Cohndar would suggest that you're trying to gain favor with me." A hint of a smile appeared at the corners of her mouth.

"He's done more than suggest, I'm sure," said Jessyla.

"I need to listen to him. That doesn't mean I have to agree with him. Besides," Margrena went on, her voice turning wry, "since you won't agree to his suggestion, I need to be as polite as possible for as long as possible."

"I couldn't live for a moment with that serpent Waensyn."

"You're acting as though no one else matters," interjected Grenara.

"You got to consort someone you loved," returned Jessyla. "Why shouldn't I?"

"That's not something we'll discuss at the moment," declared Margrena firmly. "You're too young to be consorted to anyone right now, especially since you're a healer. Healers need more time to learn about healing before they have to deal with the complexities of consorts and households."

"Waensyn doesn't think so," pointed out Jessyla.

"But I do, and I am your mother." She turned to Beltur. "Since you were so kind as to bring gifts, and since there are several meat pies—"

"And some special pastries," interjected Beltur.

"You should stay for an early supper."

"Thank you. I'd like that very much."

Margrena lifted the basket slightly. "I'll take this, and you two can sit here while Grenara and I see what we can do about supper." She turned, gestured to Grenara, and the two reentered the kitchen, but the door remained open.

Beltur gestured to the padded bench nearest the hearth.

This time, Jessyla did move and seated herself.

Beltur sat beside her.

"Cohndar was as much as telling you that no one will buy much more cupridium from Jorhan. How can he say that?"

"Because there's some truth in what he says. Traders in Elparta and the

Council won't sell copper and cupridium to Jorhan. He had to get his last supplies of copper and tin from Axalt. His sister's consort—he's a merchant there—brought them on his last trading visit the sixday before last. Once the snows come and close the Axalt road . . ." Beltur shook his head.

"That's awful. You said he had trouble getting copper, but you didn't say why."

"I think Jorhan's had problems all along. He sort of hinted that he's always had to pay more for metal. He owed some traders for metal when we started working together. Almost all the cupridium blades and pieces we've sold have gone to outlanders, but the Council's armorer here in Elparta said that the blades he saw were as good as the best anywhere."

"That sounds like they're trying to ruin him."

"I think it's more that they want everything under their control."

"Like Cohndar."

"I'm not sure he has that much choice."

"That's not what I meant."

"I know, but it's still true. Black mages really don't have that much power. People fear whites because they can use chaos to destroy things . . . and people. Most blacks don't think that way, and it's harder to use order as a weapon." But not impossible, as Beltur well knew. "Even in Gallos, the whites need the Prefect's golds, because chaos can't be used to preserve or strengthen things. That means that in Spidlar, the blacks and healers need the golds of the Council and the traders."

"Healers more than blacks."

"I found out that you make more than most city patrollers."

"How do they live?"

"Poorly, I'd judge."

Jessyla turned to face Beltur directly. "What are *we* going to do?"

"Wait and save up silvers." *Your mother won't let us consort any time soon, and I wouldn't want to until we know we can afford it.*

"Is everything about coins?"

"Everything that we need to live costs something, some way."

"How can you be so calm about it?"

"Calm isn't happy. And getting angry at the Council and all the traders won't help." After a pause, Beltur said quietly, "Tell me about what you've done in healing this eightday and how you did it. If you would."

Jessyla looked away for several moments.

Beltur waited. He had a strong feeling that the rest of the afternoon would not be going the way he had hoped.

"Is that the way you want it to be?" she finally asked, slowly turning her head back to him.

"No. But until we have more coins, I don't see matters changing." He hesitated, then asked, "Am I missing something? Is there something I could be doing that I'm not?"

"I don't want to be a matter of coins, Beltur."

"You don't have to tell me that. I know. It's just that . . . you deserve not to be worrying about . . . well . . . everything."

A faint smile appeared. "You've tried hard to make things easier. I appreciate that more than you know. But how long . . . how long will we be wondering whether we have enough?"

"Waiting another season or two shouldn't change anything at all," said Margrena from the doorway as she carried two mugs of hot cider into the front room, where she offered one to Beltur and the second to Jessyla.

"You were listening," accused Jessyla.

"That's sometimes part of being a mother, as I hope you'll find out . . . when the time is right. I'm glad you two are talking seriously." Margrena straightened and smiled, almost enigmatically.

"Mother . . ."

"Beltur," Margrena continued, not looking at her daughter. "You can be too serious. She understands." With that she turned and walked back into the kitchen.

Beltur looked at Jessyla, then shook his head ruefully. "You're both right."

Jessyla slowly smiled.

XI

When Beltur left the house on oneday, the snow was calf-deep and still falling. Wading through the snow that had not been cleared off Bakers Lane, or any streets, slowed Beltur, and it was well after seventh glass when Beltur arrived at the smithy. Surprisingly, the air didn't feel as cold as it had on eightday.

When Beltur stepped into the smithy and closed the door, Jorhan looked up from the workbench. "Took you a little longer today."

"None of the streets were clear. Not yet anyway."

"They won't be. This kind of snow could go on for more than a day."

Beltur stamped his boots and then shook the snow off his coat before hanging it on the wooden wall peg, along with the scarf. "What do you want me to work on?"

"We'll start with a hand mirror. It's more elaborate than the ones we've done before. Once that's done, we'll do two candelabra, also more detailed."

"So you can stretch out the copper?"

"Better artistry takes more time. Especially in making the molds. Right now, it's looking like we're going to have more time than copper."

"Do you know why no one here will sell to you?"

"I can guess. Barrynt heard something when he was here. Someone told him that a trader named Alizant had discovered how valuable cupridium is. This Alizant declared that he was going to be the one who did all the trading in cupridium in Elparta. Before long, he'll send someone to suggest we sell to him at half what we're getting. Maybe less. He might wait until we've run through the copper Barrynt sent."

Beltur swallowed. "That might be my fault."

"How could it be your fault? Do you know this Alizant?"

"No. But one of the undercaptains I served with was Alizant's youngest son. He was surprised to know how much a cupridium blade would bring. I had no idea . . ."

"Is he still an undercaptain? Or is he now a trader with his father?"

"He was killed in one of the battles along the river. He must have told his father or one of his brothers before he died. I'm sorry. I didn't think that . . ." Beltur shook his head.

"There's no sense blaming yourself. This Alizant or another trader would have gotten around to trying to force us to work through him sooner or later."

"It wouldn't have been quite so soon."

"That ice already froze. Besides, there isn't that much copper anywhere in Elparta at the moment, and with winter closing in, there likely won't be any more soon. We might as well get to work on the mirror. The mold's just about ready."

Beltur moved to the bellows. *How could you have known that Alizant would do that?* After a moment, he wanted to shake his head. *After what you've seen about the traders, you should have realized that was bound to happen. But it would have happened later if you hadn't told Zandyr.* Possibly seasons later, after Jorhan and Beltur had forged and sold more blades, platters, and mirrors . . . and earned more silvers.

Three glasses later, after Beltur had finished setting the order/chaos web in the two candelabra, Jorhan went to the smithy door, opened it, and looked out before closing it and walking back to where Beltur stood beside the workbench. "The snow's close to knee-deep. The way it's falling, you ought to be heading back to your place." The smith handed over a silver. "The same as before? The rest when I sell them?"

"That's fine." Beltur paused. "When do you want me next?"

"Snow will be deep tomorrow."

"I'll still have City Patrol duty on threeday. What about fourday?"

"Fiveday might be better," said Jorhan slowly. "Could be a long winter."

Beltur nodded. "Then I'll be here on fiveday."

"Unless we get more snow, and it's waist-deep. Not likely this early, but it could happen."

"I'll keep that in mind." Beltur walked to where his coat and scarf hung and donned them. With a parting nod to the smith, he opened the door and stepped out into the fast-falling snow, closing the door behind him and walking down the lane. The snow crunched under his boots, and he realized that it was colder, much colder, than it had been early that morning.

He kept moving, glad for both the scarf and the gloves. When he reached the road, he saw that a rider had passed by recently, and he immediately followed in the horse's tracks, although the snow was still calf-deep there, as opposed to knee-deep. When he finally reached the northeast gate and entered the city, he was glad to see that half of the east wall street had been shoveled or swept sometime earlier, but not within the last glass or so, since the snow was ankle-deep. That made walking easier. For the next five blocks, the snow on the right side of the street became less and less deep. Peering through the snow, he finally saw why. A block or so ahead of him, men with broad shovels were at work clearing the snow and piling it on the west side of the street.

At the next cross lane, Beltur turned west and walked through the much deeper snow to Bakers Lane, where he turned north. By the time he reached Crossed Lane and the bakery, his legs were feeling tired.

He'd no more entered the house and closed the door behind himself when Margrena appeared. Beltur just looked for a moment before he said, "What's wrong?"

"Nothing's wrong here, or with Jessyla. Meldryn said he thought you'd be back early with this snow. I'm glad you are. Lhadoraak's daughter Taelya's taken a sudden turn for the worse."

"I thought Athaal and your sister—"

"So did I, but she's gotten weaker and so tired she can hardly move.

There's no sign of any flux, and she doesn't have a fever. Meldryn and I thought you might be able to sense more than we can. Felsyn has a fever, and he's not doing well, either. So he can't help. You're the only one we could think of."

"Athaal told me what you were able to do with Claudyt's grandson," added Meldryn as he entered the front hall from the corridor that led to the bakery. "I told Lhadoraak I thought you should come with me and Margrena."

"Didn't you and Athaal and Grenara help her before?"

Meldryn shook his head. "Athaal did it all, along with Grenara. I couldn't do what Athaal did, and Grenara no longer has the touch needed. Athaal told me you had even greater ability than he did in sensing and manipulating small bits of order and chaos."

"What about Jessyla?" Beltur looked to Margrena.

"She'll be a better healer than I am in time, but she's too impatient, and . . ."

Beltur just kept looking at Margrena.

"She's likely to be too rash, especially . . ."

"If I'm there?" asked Beltur.

"I didn't say that."

"But it might have occurred to you."

"We need to go, before the snow gets any deeper," said Meldryn.

"This is serious, then, if it can't wait," suggested Beltur.

"I fear that." Margrena reached for the threadbare brown wool coat on the peg between Beltur's and Meldryn's.

In moments, all three were walking north on Crossed Lane.

Beltur couldn't help but worry about what might be wrong with Taelya, and he wished he'd been able to spend more time with Margrena and Jessyla doing healing. "Can you tell me any more about Taelya?"

"No," replied Margrena. "That's the problem. You'll see."

All in all, it took them almost a quarter glass of trudging through the snow to cover some five blocks before Meldryn gestured and said, "The door with the black lintel."

Lhadoraak's dwelling was a two-story structure even narrower than Grenara's house, Beltur thought. Even the front window to the right of the door seemed smaller.

Almost as soon as Meldryn knocked, the door opened.

Lhadoraak gestured for the three to enter, then quickly closed the door. "Tulya and I appreciate all of you coming, especially in this weather."

He smiled warmly, if almost apologetically. He was actually a few digits taller than Beltur, something that Beltur hadn't really noticed before, possibly because the blond mage was more slender.

"Where is Taelya?" asked Margrena as she took off her coat.

"In the parlor, in front of the hearth. She started shivering after you left."

While the house was cool, it wasn't frigid, not even as cold as Grenara's dwelling had been on eightday. Since the wall pegs were all taken, Beltur laid his coat on the small bench just inside the door, then followed the others down the hallway really too tight for two people abreast at the same time.

Lhadoraak stopped just short of the archway into the parlor and beckoned to the sandy-haired woman standing to one side of the bench in front of the hearth. She immediately walked to the archway, cramped as it was with the other four standing there.

"Dear," began Lhadoraak, "this is Beltur. Margrena thought he might be able to help."

Tulya inclined her head to Beltur. "I'm pleased to meet you. I've heard much about you."

Beltur nodded in return. "Can you tell me how you both noticed the change in Taelya?"

"She's getting weaker by the day," said Tulya in a low voice, "and she's not quite herself. I can't explain it, but she's not."

"That's why I started trying to sense if there was something wrong with her order/chaos balance," added Lhadoraak. "It's balanced, but it's lower than it has been."

"The way it was before?" asked Meldryn.

"It might be lower," said Lhadoraak.

"How old is Taelya?" Beltur asked.

"She's seven," replied Lhadoraak.

"She's small for her age," added Tulya quickly.

Beltur looked past Tulya to where Taelya sat on the bench facing the hearth, seemingly indifferent to the adults in the archway. From what Beltur could see and sense, Taelya was blond and fine-featured, like her father. Unlike him, or her mother, she appeared tiny, far smaller than Beltur felt she should be. *And she should have turned and shown some interest in the adults talking in the hallway.* "I should meet her, then." Beltur really didn't know what else to say, not until he got closer to her and could sense—or not sense—something.

Tulya offered a discomfited smile. "I suppose you should." She turned and walked toward the bench.

Beltur followed, but stopped short of the bench, studying the small girl.

"Taelya, this is Beltur. He was one of the mages who saved your father in the last battle."

Beltur smiled at Taelya.

The girl did not smile back.

Beltur could see the dark circles under her eyes, green eyes that were not bloodshot, but almost dull, in a way. He immediately reached out to sense what he could about her. The overall pattern of order and chaos appeared balanced, as her father had said. At first, Beltur sensed nothing that seemed odd, but he had the feeling that he was missing something. He kept searching, concentrating on her head. There he found a pinpoint of something different, a tiny almost crystal-like bit of order, surrounding a larger, but somehow compressed, bit of chaos. Focusing his concentration more tightly, he could sense that chaos wasn't wound chaos or outside free chaos, but the healthy chaos manifested by all living things. He'd never sensed anything like order confining healthy chaos before. There was also the hint of a link or a filament that led him to another, identical order/chaos structure. He tried to sense deeper, this time concentrating on the order containment. In moments, he realized that the tiny structures were more like shields, and that the scores of them throughout Taelya's small body were all connected by fine filaments, and the combination of the miniature shields around chaos reminded him of the way in which he used order and chaos in the casting and forging of cupridium.

If those order structures are capturing or containing healthy chaos . . . that might be why she's so weak. Beltur almost shook his head, but did not. Instead, he turned to Tulya. "Hold still for a moment, please."

Seeing the frown on Lhadoraak's face, he added, "I want to compare something." After studying Tulya with his senses, and then Margrena, he was convinced that the almost imperceptible shields and filaments were unique to Taelya. He looked back to the girl, who by all rights should have been far taller than she was. "Do you feel more tired than you used to?"

Taelya nodded.

"Did this happen just in the last few days?"

"I think so."

Beltur just stood there. If he tried to explain in detail, would any of the others even believe him?

"Can you do anything?" asked Margrena.

Beltur turned and walked back into the hallway. The other adults followed. Once the four were gathered facing him, he said, "Some of her own order is choking off her healthy chaos. It's keeping her from growing, I think."

Tulya's look was of incomprehension, while Margrena and Lhadoraak frowned.

Meldryn nodded slowly. "I can't sense that, but it would make sense." He looked to Lhadoraak. "Beltur can sense order and chaos in the tiniest amounts, even smaller bits than Athaal could."

"Can you do anything about it?" Tulya finally asked.

"I can try."

"That doesn't . . ." began Lhadoraak, breaking off his words as he looked at Margrena. "What do you think?"

"She'll continue to get worse if something isn't done. It should be done soon."

After several moments, the other four adults looked at Beltur.

"I *think* I can undo the order locks in her body. At least some of them. That should help, but I don't *know* that it will. I've never done anything like that before."

"Has anyone?" asked Lhadoraak.

"Beltur did something like that before," said Meldryn. "With Claudyt's grandson. It worked."

Beltur decided against mentioning that he hadn't been able to undo all the damage caused by the brain chaos.

"How . . . ?" began Lhadoraak.

"Taelya should be lying down, and I'll need to sit down on something close to her. It might take a little while." That was a guess on Beltur's part, but he remembered passing out after dealing with Claudyt's grandson.

"You don't need to be alone with her?" asked Tulya, warily.

Beltur almost laughed. "No. It would be better if everyone's with us. You could even hold her, if you want."

In a few moments, Taelya was stretched out on the padded parlor bench, her head on her mother's lap. Beltur sat on a straight-backed chair beside her.

"Will this hurt?" asked Taelya.

"It shouldn't," replied Beltur, hoping that would be so.

He immediately concentrated on the first and largest mini-shield, the one seemingly at the back of her head, trying to figure out the easiest way to unlock it. He tried manipulating a tiny bit of free order. But the tiny shield just incorporated the new order and tightened its grip on the healthy chaos. Nor did using a bit of his own healthy chaos work. Finally, he used two bits of free chaos linked to one bit of free order . . . and the shield dissolved. From what Beltur could tell, all three bits vanished, and the order bits in the mini-shield dispersed back into the area around where the tiny shield had been, as did the healthy chaos.

Then came the tedious work of tracing down each of the tiny shields in Taelya's body. After more than three score, Beltur lost count. When he finished, his eyes were burning and his skull was throbbing.

He blinked, then shook his head.

"Are you all right?" asked Margrena.

"Nothing that a little ale won't help." His voice was somehow hoarse, possibly because his throat felt dry. "How long did that take?"

"Over a glass," said Lhadoraak.

Beltur looked at Taelya, who was yawning.

"I fell asleep. Everyone was so quiet." She looked at Beltur. "You were right. It didn't hurt."

"How do you feel now, Taelya?" asked Meldryn.

"Better. I don't feel so tired."

"That might be the nap," said Tulya. "She hasn't slept that well in the past eightday."

"Her order/chaos balance is a bit higher," ventured Lhadoraak.

"Is that good, Father?" asked Taelya as she sat up.

Abruptly feeling dizzy, Beltur lowered his head, trying not to sway in the chair.

"Beltur needs a mug of ale," said Meldryn. "And some bread or something to eat."

"I'll get it." Tulya stood and turned toward the rear of the house.

"You don't feel good, now, do you?" Taelya asked Beltur.

"I'm a little dizzy." In fact, he was more than a little dizzy and faint, so much so that he lost track of what the others around him were saying.

Then Tulya reappeared and eased a mug into his hands. "Here you are. I'll be back with some bread in a moment."

Holding the heavy earthenware mug carefully in both hands, Beltur sipped the dark ale slowly. He almost didn't notice when Tulya reappeared with a small basket of bread that she set on the side table, but he set down the mug on the table and took several bites of the crusty bread before having more ale.

Finally, he said, "I should have had something to eat after I got back. I just wasn't thinking that I'd be working with order and chaos."

"What exactly did you do?" asked Lhadoraak. "I couldn't sense anything."

"I sensed tiny flows of order and chaos," said Meldryn.

Margrena nodded at that.

Tulya turned and leaned forward, as did Margrena.

"There were tiny order shields all through Taelya that were capturing and limiting the healthy chaos of the body. I just had to take them apart, one by one."

"How many?" asked Margrena.

"I lost track after three or four score."

"What happened to the order in the shields? And the chaos?" asked Lhadoraak.

"So far as I can tell, it was absorbed back into her body. There's no sign of it or any wound chaos."

Both the other mages clearly concentrated on Taelya for several moments.

After a time, Lhadoraak and Meldryn exchanged glances, and Meldryn said, "I can't sense anything chaotic."

Beltur abruptly realized that he had eaten all of the half loaf of bread Tulya had brought him, and that the mug was empty. "Oh . . . I'm sorry. I didn't mean to eat it all."

"You needed it," replied Tulya.

Margrena glanced toward the door, but before Beltur could say anything, Meldryn did.

"How are you feeling, Beltur?"

"I'm all right now."

"Then we should be going before the snow gets any deeper."

Beltur stood immediately, if carefully, but he seemed to be fine. He'd even regained his shields, without even thinking about it. Then he looked down at Taelya. "You are feeling better, aren't you?"

"A little."

"Good. It will take some time before you're completely well again." Beltur smiled.

A hint of a smile appeared for an instant on the girl's face, before she turned and said, "I'm hungry, Mother."

Beltur could not only see but sense Tulya's relief. "I'm just guessing, but I think that Taelya is going to be very hungry for a while." He didn't say what else he suspected.

"I'll see you out," said Lhadoraak, leading the way to the door, where he turned to Beltur. "I can't thank you enough. She's already looking better."

"I did what I could. I don't think it will come back, but I don't know. I've never seen or sensed anything like it." *And that's certainly true.*

"You've never thought about being a healer?"

"I'm not a healer, Lhadoraak. Margrena can tell you that. I can do some things, and I can sometimes help healers, but there's too much I don't know."

The snow was still falling heavily as the three left Lhadoraak's dwelling. When they reached the corner, Meldryn turned to Beltur. "Why don't you escort Margrena back to her place? I need to get back to the bakery."

"I can escort myself," returned the healer.

"In this weather, it's not that safe. Humor me, and let Beltur escort you."

"As long as you admit that I'd be fine."

"I'll admit anything so long as Beltur goes with you."

Margrena laughed softly behind her scarf. "Then we'd best start walking, Beltur."

The two of them walked perhaps fifty yards through the snow before she asked, "What didn't you tell Lhadoraak?"

"You're as bad as Jessyla," said Beltur, smiling under his scarf.

"Where do you think she got that from? What didn't you tell him?"

"I think she's going to be a mage, and most likely she'll incline toward the white side."

"Are you sure?"

"It's just a feeling, but when I released all that order and chaos, the pattern was closer to what I used to sense with the whites in Fenard. It isn't obvious now, but . . ."

"It isn't even noticeable to anyone but you right now. I didn't sense any of that. I don't think Meldryn or Lhadoraak did, either."

Beltur shrugged. "That's only what I sense."

"From what I've seen, I'm not about to argue. You're likely right, and she's just about at the age where magely talent becomes apparent." After a moment, she asked, "When did you know you were a mage?"

"When Uncle told me so. I was around eleven or so, but I was late. I'd never thought I would be, not when I saw everything he could do. I'd tried to throw chaos or light fires, and couldn't."

"That's not surprising. You were a black."

"But I really didn't know anything about what blacks did."

"Your uncle didn't do you any favors that way."

"Maybe not, but he gave me some training and kept me fed and healthy."

"He must have cared a great deal for your mother."

"He did, but I didn't realize that until later." *Especially after he insisted that I escape from the Arms-Mage because Mother would never forgive him if he didn't save me.*

"Sometimes, children are slow to learn," said Margrena dryly.

A gust of wind hit Beltur with the force of a blow, and the snow felt like liquid ice on Beltur's exposed forehead. Neither spoke more until they neared Crafters Lane.

"I never thought I'd be plowing through snow this deep," said Margrena, clearly breathing harder as the two stopped in front of the door to her sister's house.

"Neither did I."

Margrena opened the door, and they both entered. Margrena quickly closed the door.

Jessyla rose from where she had been reading before the hearth. "I'm glad you're back. The snow is getting really deep."

"It's falling even more heavily than it was earlier," said Margrena.

"It won't stop any time soon," predicted Grenara, standing in the doorway from the kitchen, almost as if she were glad to deliver such a verdict. "You probably should be heading back to your own place, Beltur."

"Let him warm up for a little while," said Jessyla. "It's cold out there."

"You're both right," replied Beltur. "I really would like to warm up, but I shouldn't stay long."

"Go over and stand in front of the hearth," suggested Margrena. "I'll get us all something warm to drink."

Beltur took off his coat and scarf and hung them on a wall peg, then walked to the hearth, where there were actually coals—from coal—burning.

Jessyla slipped up beside him and murmured, "I used one of the silvers you gave me to buy Auntie some coal. Thank you."

"How are you doing?"

"We're doing all right."

"For now?"

"For now. And don't reach for your wallet. I just like having you here, even if you can't stay for long."

Beltur almost said something to the effect that she should let him know if she needed anything, but realized that neither Jessyla nor Margrena would ever ask or even hint along those lines. "I'm glad to be here, even if it's only for a little while."

Jessyla reached out and took his right hand in her left. "So am I."

All too soon, Beltur was donning his coat and wrapping his scarf around his ears and across his nose and mouth.

"Just be careful," admonished Jessyla as she opened the door.

"I will."

He stepped outside, looking back quickly before she closed the door, and then began to walk through the snow that was more than knee-deep in most places, snow that now fell so heavily that Beltur could barely see more than five yards away—and he could order-sense even less than that. He just concentrated on putting one boot in front of the other as he struggled southward along Bakers Lane, glad that the light but chill wind and the snow were at his back.

He'd traveled three blocks or so, his boots crunching on the snow that squeaked where it had been packed down earlier, still thinking about Jessyla and how and when he could help her, when he was suddenly jolted by a blow to his shields as two men ran into him. Both carried lengths of wood that might have been firewood.

He straightened and turned, but barely got more than a glimpse of two men clad in what seemed to be layers of rags, before they were backing away.

"Sowshit and demons . . . just our luck . . . pick a frigging mage . . ."

Then the two were threshing their way through the snow and down an alleyway that Beltur hadn't even seen.

He thought about chasing the two for a moment before shaking his head. He doubted he could get close enough to them running through the deep snow, and with the snow falling as fast as it was, he knew he couldn't hold as many containments as he usually could, and certainly not at a distance. *Besides, what would be the point? Just to make their life even more miserable?*

He paused, wondering if he was just rationalizing, but he realized it no longer made a difference, since he'd never be able to catch them, let alone find where they had gone, not with the snow falling as heavily as it was.

For the rest of the way back, he saw only a handful of people through the curtain of snow.

Once he reached the front of the house, Beltur stamped his boots on the single stone step and brushed off as much snow as he could before opening the door and stepping inside. After carefully brushing the rest of the snow off his scarf and coat, he hung them up so that any spots that were wet from melting snow he hadn't been able to remove would dry. Then he started toward the kitchen, but when he saw that Meldryn wasn't there he retraced his steps and took the corridor to the bakery.

The grayed older mage turned from his worktable. "I'm glad you're back. I have the feeling that the snow isn't going to let up any time soon."

"It's getting heavier. I only stopped for a bit at Grenara's, enough to drink a mug of spiced cider and warm up. Can I do anything?"

"I didn't have a chance to clean the side oven on the left. If you wouldn't mind working on it . . ."

"I can do that." Beltur paused, noticing that Meldryn was working on what looked to be filling for meat pies. "Will you have any customers with all this snow?"

"I'll likely have more tomorrow. I don't know why, but it's always been that way after a heavy snow. Not rain, just snow."

"Where did you get the extra meat?"

"I asked for it when Farodyn came by earlier. He had extra because some of the others didn't want it. He was happy to give me a good price for it. In the cold cellar below, what I don't use will keep for a while." Meldryn smiled. "When it snows, it often works out that way."

"Maybe you have more customers because the other bakers aren't open when it snows this hard."

"That could be."

Beltur almost shook his head, before he went to get the scrapers. He took one of the bladed ones, and one of the pointed ones, then found one of the oven mitts made of rags and opened the oven. He was about to start scraping when Meldryn added, "Felsyn died while we were at Lhadoraak's. Mharkyn came by. He didn't stay long because of the snow, but he said that you and I should know."

Beltur stopped. "How did that happen? He was old, but he didn't seem that frail."

"Mharkyn didn't know."

A second thought occurred to Beltur. "I can see why you ought to know, but why did Mharkyn think I should know?"

"I asked him that as well. He just said that things might change with Felsyn's death. I tried to pin him down, but he wouldn't say more."

"I don't like the sound of that, especially now."

"Neither do I, but why did you say especially now?"

"Because . . ." Beltur paused. How could he explain without it sounding like Trader Alizant was after him? "Just this morning Jorhan told me something he'd learned a few days ago. I've told you about the trouble he's had getting copper and tin and that the last batch came all the way from Axalt with his sister's consort. Well, Barrynt told him that Trader Alizant intended to take over all the trading in cupridium in Elparta . . ." Beltur went on to explain, ending with, "That's likely why Jorhan can't get any more copper and tin, and why he probably won't unless he agrees to sell what we cast and forge through the trader."

Meldryn shook his head. "The trader's a slick bastard. There's no way Jorhan will likely be able to get more copper and tin from Axalt or any-where else until late spring, and from what you've said, he hasn't saved up that much in silvers."

"And I'll only get paid by the City Patrol until a little after the turn of Winter."

"You've been pretty careful with your coins, though, haven't you?"

"I have. I've got enough to last through the winter." *And likely spring as well.* "And I can still pay you, but after that, then what?"

"I can't see that the trader will take everything," Meldryn pointed out. "He doesn't make any coins himself if you and Jorhan don't get enough to pay for materials and food."

"I don't like it," said Beltur. "It's as though just as I find a way to sup-port myself the traders come in and want to take most of what we make."

"Traders have a habit of doing that."

"Is there anything we can do?"

"Aren't you worrying too much right now?" asked Meldryn. "All you know is what this merchant from Axalt told Jorhan. It might not even be true."

"Everything else Barrynt said was true," Beltur pointed out.

"Even if it is true, this trader Alizant hasn't done anything yet, and you don't know what he'll do and if he does how much it will cost you and Jorhan. Right now, all you can do is to be careful with the coins you have and try to think out how you could deal with the problem if it comes to that."

Beltur had to admit that what Meldryn said made sense, but he had no doubts that Alizant would do what Jorhan thought he would and that the trader would take as much as he possibly could. *But you do have some time to think it over.*

He picked up the scrapers and turned back to the oven. He did owe Meldryn more than he'd likely ever be able to repay.

XII

The snow was still falling on twoday morning, and while it seemed slightly lighter, what had already fallen came to midthigh. Beltur was just as glad that he didn't have work at the smithy, since trudging through snow that deep would likely have taken a good glass each way.

Instead, after cleaning the kitchen, he swept and cleaned the rest of the house, if quickly, since it was clear that Laranya would not be coming. When he finished, he went to help Meldryn in the bakery.

"What can I do?" he asked.

"Shovel the snow away from the bakery door and then start clearing the pavement next to the wall on both sides of the corner. Don't do more than two yards out from the wall."

"Where should I pile the snow?"

"In the alley off Bakers Lane."

With those instructions, Beltur set to work. More than a glass later, he finally finished the strip that Meldryn had described, although he knew he'd have to keep shoveling periodically in order to keep the stones relatively clear.

When he stepped back inside and told Meldryn that, the older man smiled. "You'll likely only have to do that twice."

Beltur had his doubts, but he nodded, glad to be back inside and out of the snow and cold.

Very few customers came all that early, but as the snow lightened in midmorning, and after Beltur had cleared the additional accumulation of snow, more appeared, and by noon, when the sky cleared, and the sun appeared, and Beltur cleared the remaining snow and then swept the pavement clean along the cleared stretch, there was a steady flow of people wanting bread and the extra meat pies that Meldryn had made the afternoon and evening before.

By the time Meldryn closed in the late afternoon and began to make up more meat pies for sale on threeday, there were but two meat pies remaining. Beltur went back to cleaning ovens. When he finished and the two repaired to the house kitchen, he had no trouble eating half of one of the large meat pies.

Nor did he have any trouble falling asleep.

Threeday dawned clear and much colder than twoday had been. Sometime in the evening or the early morning, the young men from the workhouse had cleared a narrow way along Bakers Lane, for which Beltur was grateful, especially given the cold. Even with his visor cap, scarf, gloves, and heavy coat, by the time he reached City Patrol headquarters he could feel the chill creeping through his outerwear. He'd also seen that perhaps a fifth of the market square had been cleared, roughly the northwest corner, although he hadn't seen any sellers setting up on the bare stone pavement.

Laevoyt was already in the duty room when Beltur entered. He smiled crookedly at Beltur. "Cold enough for you?"

"It's colder than anything I've been through before," Beltur admitted, moving to the table desk where he signed the duty book. Then he walked over to Laevoyt. "I take it that this is warm for winter?"

Laevoyt grinned. "Not really. It doesn't get much colder than this. The thing is that once winter really sets in it doesn't get any warmer. In a few days it will warm up. Not above freezing, but warmer than this. Did I see you clearing snow yesterday, outside the bakery on the corner of Crossed Lane and Bakers Lane?"

"I was."

"I thought you were working for a smith."

"I am, but there's not as much work right now. So I was giving Meldryn a hand."

"You're not sore, are you?"

"No. Why?"

"That smithing must be hard work, then."

"We're still on duty at the market square?"

"After we take a stroll down River Street. There likely won't be anyone at the square until a bit before ninth glass." Laevoyt headed for the door.

Beltur followed, wishing he'd had a few more moments to warm up in the duty room.

Once they were outside, Laevoyt turned west on Patrol Street.

"What are we looking for?" asked Beltur.

"Broken shutters, doors that look caved in. When it gets this cold, some of the street types will do anything to get warm."

"Except go to the workhouses?"

"Most of them die if they go there."

"Why?"

"Because they can't or won't work, and anyone who doesn't work doesn't get fed."

"Even if they can't work?"

"Beltur . . . we can't solve all the problems in Elparta. Most of the men who won't work chose not to. They thought street begging or scrounging and summer would last forever. Or they felt that what work there was happened to be beneath them. Over the next few eightdays or so, the street crews will be loading frozen bodies onto refuse carts."

"They don't dump those in the river, do they?"

"No. That's against the law. They burn them in the furnaces that heat the workhouses. Hypocausts, I think they call them."

His face largely hidden by the scarf, Beltur winced, but he kept walking. When his boots came down where there was snow, the snow squeaked. Before today, he'd never heard that before.

Before that long, they reached the end of Patrol Street, where it intersected River Street, which fronted on the river, with only river walls between the street and the river itself. The half of River Street closest to the river was cleared as well as the three yards of stone walkway between the street and the river wall. Beltur noted that the solid floodgates were in place at the foot of each pier, so that the yard-and-a-half river wall was unbroken from the south city wall to the north wall. Beltur guessed that there was some law that required the gates to be in place once the snow remained. *The Council seems to have laws for everything.*

Beltur moved closer to the river wall and glanced down. Ice coated the stone beginning just above the water level and extending up a yard or so. The western bank of the river also showed jagged and intermittent ice between the rocks and sand exposed by the lower fall water levels. "When does the river freeze over?"

"Most years, it's solid by the second eightday of Winter. If we get a really cold winter, it could freeze earlier," said Laevoyt. "Keep an eye out on the warehouses along here. Some of the down-and-out loaders try to get inside and live there."

"Do you have trouble with the inns?"

"There's some most every night, but not at this time of day."

The two walked another two blocks. Much farther ahead, Beltur could see several wagons and the men from the workhouses shoveling snow from the wagons over the river wall and into the water.

Then, from a doorway some thirty yards ahead of them, on the side away from the river, a man in a ragged cloak appeared and walked quickly along the cleared side of the street, before turning down an alley.

"He'll likely be running now that he's out of sight," said Laevoyt.

"We aren't supposed to chase him?"

"We don't know yet what he did, or if he did anything. The captain's been clear about that. We're not to bring anyone in until we know they've done something wrong." After a moment, the patroller added, "Wager we'll find a door with a broken lock up there, or a door someone forgot to close. Probably not much more than that, since he wasn't carrying anything."

When the two reached the warehouse entry, Beltur immediately saw that the door was ajar. Not sensing anyone nearby, he eased the door open. Snow had drifted into the small entry foyer of the narrow building, but the locked iron gate that protected the closed door at the rear of the entry hall was intact. Even in the cold air, the foyer smelled of urine and other foulness.

"Some trader's not going to be too happy." As Laevoyt stood just outside the door, he took out a folded sheet of paper and wrote the building number on it with a grease stick. "Can you do something to slide that bolt back in place from the outside?"

"Let me see." Beltur slid the bolt back and forth, then retracted it, and closed the door. Using a tiny containment pressed against the knob of the bolt, Beltur slid it into place, then checked the door. "It's in place, but the door's a little loose."

"That tramp probably shook the door long enough that it vibrated loose." Laevoyt wrote a few words on the paper and then slipped it back inside his heavy patroller's coat. "I'll add that to the report."

"I take it that the captain doesn't want to gaol men who are just trying to keep warm unless they steal or damage something."

"He also doesn't want patrollers acting as watchmen for traders."

From Laevoyt's tone, Beltur could tell that Laevoyt felt exactly the same way. That prompted him to say, "Late on oneday after noon, a pair of men in ragged clothes slammed into me in the snow. The snow was so heavy that they got far enough away too fast for me to use containments before they were out of sight. I didn't chase them, and I wondered . . ."

"I thought you always used shields."

"I did. I was thinking about something else and not paying much attention except to get home as soon as I could. They hit my shields, and realized I was a mage. Then they ran."

"Better that you didn't chase them. I wouldn't tell the captain or the Patrol Mage, though."

They hadn't walked more than another block before the workhouse crew climbed onto the two wagons they had emptied of snow, and the teamsters drove off down a side street heading east. Beltur wasn't exactly astounded to discover that the work crew had also cleared away the street around a tavern—the Oaken Barrel—although the door was closed and the shutters fastened tight.

"Did someone slip a little extra coin to get that snow cleared?"

"The Council looks the other way on things like that. They don't want those who drink too much to fall in the snow and freeze to death on the street, but they don't want to pay for clearing the snow, either."

Given what Beltur had seen of the traders, that made a kind of sense, and since there wasn't anything he could do about it, he turned his attention back to the street ahead. Past the tavern was a line of shops and a chandlery. The mercer's store was open, as was the chandlery, and so was a small café. Beltur couldn't tell whether anyone was eating there, although there was a line of whitish-gray smoke coming from the chimney.

For the next glass or so, Beltur and Laevoyt walked down River Street to the north wall and then back. Given how cold it was, and the fact that the white winter sun seemed to offer no warmth, Beltur was scarcely surprised that they encountered few on the street, and no hint of anything untoward.

"We can stop at headquarters and warm up for a fraction of a glass," Laevoyt announced as the two turned east on Patrol Street. "How are your feet? Are they numb?"

"They're cold, but not numb."

"Good. Sometimes it helps if you put soft straw in the bottom of your boots."

"I'll keep that in mind," said Beltur, although he wondered where he would be able to find straw.

When they reached the duty room at headquarters, Beltur was more than glad to get out of the cold.

"How cold is it?" asked the duty patroller, looking at Laevoyt.

"Not as cold as midwinter, but frigging cold for midfall."

"Looks like a cold winter ahead."

"Has to happen sometime," replied Laevoyt laconically.

Beltur's feet were still cold when they left headquarters, just not so cold as they had been, and the city chimes were ringing out ninth glass when the two reached the market square. Much to Beltur's surprise, over a score of vendors were gathered on the cleared section, and there were perhaps half that many shoppers looking at what was for sale, largely food items, along with some woolens. One woman was selling what looked to be an assortment of worn and shabby boots, and another, leather jackets that had seen better days.

Beltur didn't see the woman who sold acorn cakes, and he wondered if she'd sold out all she had made . . . or if she might be waiting to sell more until food became scarcer. He didn't bother with a concealment as he walked past the comparatively few carts and tables, noting that there were no spices at all in evidence. He'd made two circles of the cleared areas and looked over all the goods being hawked before Fosset arrived with his cart.

While Beltur could have used a mug of hot cider right then, he kept patrolling, trying to sense for the chaos flickers of cutpurses and lifters, but there seemed to be none anywhere near.

Another glass passed before Beltur made his way to Fosset's cart, and by then he was more than ready for a mug of hot cider to go with his small loaf.

"What do you think of the weather?" asked Beltur as he took the mug of hot cider.

"I haven't seen it this cold this early in years. If it's like this for the rest of fall . . ." Fosset shook his head.

"Do you have trouble with beggars around the inn when it gets cold?"

"They wouldn't dare."

"Oh?"

"Uncle has his ways." Fosset turned to a thin man in a heavy coat, as much as telling Beltur that he wasn't about to say more. "Large or small."

Beltur finished the loaf and the cider, put the mug on the used rack, and resumed patrolling. By the second glass of the afternoon, half the vendors were packing up, and by slightly past third glass, the square was almost deserted.

Beltur was still thinking about what Fosset had said when he and Laevoyt left the square and were walking back to Patrol headquarters. "Fosset was telling me that the Traders' Rest doesn't have problems with tramps and beggars, that they wouldn't dare hang around there."

"Not if they don't want a long cold sleep."

Beltur thought he knew what Laevoyt meant. "How do they get away with that?"

"A quick crack to the back of the head, and dragging the unhappy fellow into the corner of an alley on a cold night. He just never wakes up, and workhouse cleanup crews find another fellow who drank himself into a stupor and died of the cold. No one can prove otherwise."

"Just like that?"

"Comartyl's a mean bastard if he's crossed. Most innkeepers are. The ones who are successful, anyway."

"What about the City Patrol?"

"We know it happens, but it happens when there aren't any patrollers around. There's no way to prove what happened, except a poor, worn-out bastard who froze to death. The Council won't pay for late patrols. All we can do is pass the word that hanging around the posher inns isn't good for anyone's health, especially in fall or winter. Most of those who ignore that advice likely wouldn't live through the winter anyway."

"There aren't any places that offer shelter?"

"Only the workhouses. Except for orphans. There's an orphanage on the old northeast road. The children learn trades and work the orchards and gardens."

"But nothing for anyone else?"

"The Council doesn't like paying for people who don't contribute anything. You've seen some of them around the market. They'd rather steal than work."

But what if there isn't any work? Beltur was a black mage who could read and write and do a number of things, and it hadn't been all that easy to find work. *Except you really didn't try all that hard, and you didn't want to work the fields or as a loader.*

Beltur was definitely beginning to see why there weren't many street people in Elparta, but he didn't say more, just kept pace with Laevoyt on the way back to Patrol headquarters.

After signing the duty book, Beltur stayed in the duty room for a time, until he felt a little warmer. Then he left and headed home. While his feet had felt cold all day, they hadn't gotten numb, but if the weather got that much colder, he'd definitely need to find straw or some other way to keep his feet from freezing solid.

XIII

On fourday, Beltur shoveled more snow away from the bakery, and in front of and around the hitching rail at the side of the building, and then helped Meldryn, mostly by cleaning ovens and baking tins. On fiveday, which was slightly warmer, he walked to the smithy and spent the day working with

Jorhan to cast two delicate-looking cupridium mirrors, for which he received a single silver, just for the day's work, but not the piecework wage, which would have to wait until the mirrors sold, but he also received two golds as his share of what the Lydian trader had bought earlier in the eightday. Six-day, he helped Meldryn again, and sevenday, he patrolled with Laevoyt, and while more of the market square had been cleared by the workhouse crews, there were only a few more vendors and customers.

Eightday, he read some and then walked to Grenara's house, again bringing bread and meat pies, where he had an early dinner and had some time with Jessyla. As always, Grenara seemed less than pleased to see him, and was the first to suggest that he leave because the late afternoon was getting cold.

On oneday, since Jorhan had suggested on the previous fiveday that he didn't need Beltur until twoday, Beltur had helped unload two barrels of flour so that Meldryn didn't have to interrupt his baking. While the day was cold, it wasn't quite as chilly as eightday had been, and the green-blue sky was clear under a white sun that still did not seem to provide any warmth, even though winter was still some four eightdays away. As he went back inside, a messenger in Council blue came out of the bakery and nodded politely before hurrying on, headed east on Crossed Lane.

Beltur hurried back inside, and waited until Meldryn dealt with the three women who had lined up. Once the last one had gathered up her loaves and left, Beltur asked, "What did the Council messenger deliver?"

"I haven't had a chance to read it." Meldryn walked to the worktable where he'd set an envelope, then used his belt knife to open it. He smoothed out the single sheet and read it. Then, without speaking, he extended it.

Beltur took it and quickly read it.

> There will be a meeting of all the black mages of Elparta in the
> Council conference room at sixth glass this evening. The subject has
> not been announced, but it likely will be about the Council's
> consideration of a charter to a Black Council of Mages. I thought you
> might like to know.

The short note was signed by Veroyt. Beltur looked up at Meldryn. "The councilor's assistant is the one telling you about a meeting called by Cohndar? One that's taking place tonight?"

"Veroyt has always kept us informed. Cohndar has tended to overlook us. You or I may discover that a message to us was lost because of the snowstorm or something similar." Meldryn's voice was cool and dry, and just a touch bitter.

"Has it always been like that . . . or is it because I'm here?" Even before he finished his words, Beltur hoped he hadn't come off as negatively self-important. "I don't mean . . ."

"I understood what you meant." Meldryn smiled. "We never quite fit, even before you showed up. Athaal saw that you didn't fit, either."

"He saw a lot."

"He did. So do you, I must say."

"Not as much as I should, I think, and I'm often slow to see the obvious."

"Speed in most things is overprized. All it does in baking is ruin the results, and that's true in cabinetry and other skills and trades as well."

"It's also true in coppersmithing," Beltur agreed.

"And speed in deciding when you don't know all the facts often makes things worse. Knowing when speed is necessary and when it's not is a good part of wisdom," said Meldryn wryly. "Do you want to learn more about baking?"

"If I won't get in your way."

The older mage just smiled.

By the time Meldryn closed the bakery at fourth glass, Beltur's head was swimming with terms he'd never heard. He did understand the difference between starter-leavened bread, unleavened bread, and barm-leavened bread, and why Meldryn baked all three. He doubted he'd remember the specifics for feeding and storing the starter dough, except that it couldn't be allowed to freeze or to get too warm, and he doubted that he could mix any of the doughs.

Dinner was a fowl pie, admittedly made from meat scraps that Meldryn hadn't used in the pies he had baked for sale, but tasty and filling all the same.

As the two sat at the kitchen table, nursing the last of their mugs of ale after eating, Beltur asked, "What do you think this meeting is all about?" He had his own ideas, but he wanted to see what Meldryn thought, especially since the older mage knew more about all the mages of Elparta.

"Cohndar has wanted to be more than the unofficial senior mage here in Elparta for years. The meeting will likely reveal just how he intends to accomplish that."

"You think this is about a magely council he can head? Or maybe a special position for him with the Council, like mage assistant to Councilor Jhaldrak?"

"Your guess is as good as mine." Meldryn stood and stretched. "We should get ready."

Before long, after Beltur hurriedly cleaned up the kitchen, the two were walking south on the cleared part of Bakers Lane. They arrived at the Council building at a quint before sixth glass, just as the sun was dropping behind the trees beyond the snow-covered marshes on the west side of the river and casting a pale pinkish glow.

Once he made his way to the conference room, Beltur surveyed the mages standing there talking. The table had been moved against the wall and several lines of chairs set up, but no one was sitting. He didn't see either Cohndar or Waensyn, but he immediately recognized Lhadoraak, who was conversing with a stocky brown-haired mage Beltur had seen before at the meeting where Veroyt had briefed the blacks on their duties and assignments in defending Elparta. He also recognized Osarus, the City Patrol Mage, and Caradyn, the mage Osarus was conversing with, largely because of Caradyn's silver-streaked black hair.

Beltur turned to Meldryn. "Who is Lhadoraak talking to? I don't think I've met him."

"That's Mharkyn."

"Is this all the blacks in Elparta?" That wasn't quite what Beltur was thinking, since he'd counted all the mages present, including himself, and come up with fifteen. That didn't include Cohndar and Waensyn, who hadn't appeared, but what struck him was that out of that group, he only knew of five who had actually faced the Gallosian forces and mages. There might have been one or two others, but he doubted that there had been more than that. Felsyn, of course, had wanted to, but he'd been too old, and there was one mage besides Athaal who had been killed in battle, but Beltur had never known his name.

"I don't know of any others, except Cohndar or Waensyn."

"Why aren't they here?"

"As senior mage in Elparta, Cohndar will be the last to arrive. Presumably, as his assistant, Waensyn will accompany him."

Within moments of Meldryn's words, a side door to the conference room opened, and three men walked in—Cohndar, Waensyn, and Veroyt.

"If you all would be seated . . ." offered Veroyt pleasantly, standing in front of the table and facing the chairs.

Cohndar took a position to the right of Veroyt, while Waensyn stood at the end of the table, conveying the impression that he was just an assistant. Meldryn and Beltur took the two chairs in the second row at the left end. With Beltur on the end, Lhadoraak eased into the seat beside Meldryn, with Mharkyn beside him.

Once everyone was seated, Veroyt cleared his throat and surveyed the group before speaking. "Thank you all for coming. I asked Senior Mage Cohndar to ask all of you to be here because a recent action by the Traders' Council of Spidlar will affect you. The Traders' Council has reviewed the events surrounding the recent attempted attack on Elparta by the Prefect of Gallos. Given the contribution that the blacks have made in helping repel the invaders, the Council has decided that it would be in the interests of both the Traders' Council and the black mages of Spidlar that an official local council of mages be established in each of the major cities of Spidlar. The head of each council will report on a regular basis to the Traders' Council. Furthermore, while it is up to the black mages of each city to determine the mage-councilor from each city, until such councils are formally organized, the senior mage in each city will act as the mage-councilor." Veroyt paused and again studied the assembled mages.

While Beltur was slightly surprised, he had the sense that most of the other blacks were not and that to them the announcement was merely a formality.

Veroyt cleared his throat and continued. "Senior Mage Cohndar, to his credit, felt that it would be best if you all selected the mage who would represent you as soon as possible, and that is the purpose of this meeting. Because this is a matter for mages, and not for a representative of the Traders' Council, at this point, I am leaving, and will turn the meeting over to Senior Mage Cohndar."

Beltur had never heard the Council referred to as the "Traders' Council" so many times in such a short amount of time. *Is that Veroyt's way of suggesting that the Council wasn't about to get involved in selecting the mage representatives? Or something else?*

Cohndar turned to Veroyt. "We all thank you, Representative Veroyt, for setting up this meeting and for informing us of the Council's decision."

"It was my duty and pleasure," replied Veroyt, inclining his head to Cohndar and then walking toward the side door.

Beltur doubted that Veroyt was that pleased, although the councilor's representative had spoken evenly and warmly.

Cohndar did not speak until the door closed. Even then, he waited several moments. "We have not seen the last of the Prefect of Gallos. While the invasion failed, we all know that, without your efforts, it would have succeeded. One of the reasons it almost succeeded was that the

Council and the High Command did not use black mages in the most effective manner possible, nor did the senior officers understand how blacks can be best used. We lost three good mages as a result. If it had not been for the heroic efforts of several others, including Waensyn here, the results might have been far different. This was one of several reasons why Councilor Jhaldrak and I persuaded the Traders' Council to formalize the position and to create a structured organization of blacks in Spidlar. The last thing any of us should want is for blacks to be taken for granted either by the Council or by individual traders." The white-haired mage paused, just for a moment. "The next step is to select our councilor—"

"Cohndar should be the councilor," declared a black whom Beltur did not recognize.

"Cohndar!" insisted Caradyn.

"Cohndar . . ."

Waensyn stepped forward, smiling, motioning for quiet. "Every single known black in Elparta is gathered in this room. If a majority of you wish Cohndar to continue as our representative, then you can so decide. If not, then you can choose someone else. But . . . from what I see, it might simply be best for those of you who wish that Cohndar remain as our representative to indicate that by raising your hand."

Immediately, two-thirds of the mages raised their hands.

As Meldryn raised his hand, slightly later than the others, he murmured to Beltur, "Raise your hand. Quickly."

Beltur did so, noting that both Lhadoraak and Mharkyn had not raised their hands until Meldryn had done so.

"It appears that you all want Cohndar to continue," said Waensyn, who then inclined his head to the older mage. "You are now the Mage-Councilor of Elparta."

"Thank you," replied Cohndar, turning back to face the still-seated mages. "We face many challenges, not the least of which will likely be the hostility of the Prefect of Gallos. To meet those challenges, we need to become stronger. We need to become more disciplined, and we always need to be on our guard against those who would weaken us. I had not anticipated that any mage would have received such a unanimous selection, let alone me, but I will do my poor best to justify your choice. In the eightdays ahead, I will try to meet with each of you to learn from you your thoughts and hopes for blacks in Spidlar." He paused. "Thank you . . . again."

While Cohndar had shielded himself fully during the entire meeting, Beltur had sensed, if barely and faintly, a certain amount of chaos when

Cohndar had said he had not anticipated a unanimous choice. While Beltur hadn't immediately grasped the reasons for Meldryn's quick instructions to raise his hand, the result and Cohndar's smooth acceptance of the position of mage-councilor had been explanation enough.

Waensyn stepped forward once more. "Given the weather, it's best we don't tarry here, but thank you all for coming."

"As I said," added Cohndar, "you'll be seeing me."

After the seated mages all rose, Meldryn stepped forward to a sandy-haired black who had been sitting in front of him. "Jhosak, it's been a while."

"Meldryn . . . I didn't . . . I was so sorry to hear about Athaal."

"Thank you. Like the others who suffered or died, he was doing his best to keep the Prefect from driving us out of Spidlar."

"That he was."

"Have you met Beltur? He and Athaal were the ones who saved Lhadoraak."

"Oh, I haven't had the pleasure."

Beltur smiled pleasantly. "Jhosak, is it? I'm pleased to meet you."

"You're the other one who escaped the Prefect, right?"

"I'm afraid so. Waensyn was able to leave in a more leisurely fashion. I had to flee in a hurry. The Prefect's mages were looking for my head, as well as the rest of me."

"I didn't realize that. You're fortunate to be here." Jhosak turned back to Meldryn. "You must excuse me." With a thin smile, he nodded and turned.

"Caradyn," said Meldryn as he stepped forward and put a powerful hand on the other mage's shoulder. "I haven't seen you lately, but I'd like you to meet Beltur. You might recall that he was the one who took care of three of the Prefect's whites."

"Meldryn. It has been a while." Caradyn's shields hid any emotion he might have felt, and his smile and eyes were both warm as he looked to Beltur. "I've heard about you. Combining order and chaos, was it?"

"Only in forging cupridium. And it's always chaos bounded by order, as it was when I had to confront the Prefect's whites. Far more order, very little chaos."

"So it would seem, fortunately for all of us. I'm glad to meet you. You're a mage of many talents, it would appear." Caradyn turned back to Meldryn. "It's good to see you, and for you to introduce young Beltur. The next time I get to your part of the city, I'll have to get some of your bread and pies." With a last smile, he eased away.

Beltur realized that he and Meldryn were the last mages in the conference room.

"I'd hoped to introduce you to more blacks, but . . ." Meldryn shrugged. "They didn't seem to want to talk. We can discuss matters on the walk back home."

Beltur took that to mean that Meldryn wasn't about to say anything meaningful while in the Council building. "I appreciate your making the effort. There are so few that I've met."

"I thought it would be useful, one way or another. I suppose we should head out."

No sooner had Meldryn and Beltur left the Council building and started down the street toward Bakers Lane than Lhadoraak and Mharkyn eased up to them.

"I didn't expect that," said Lhadoraak. "I mean, I thought it likely that Cohndar would get the position, but . . . no one even seemed to think about anyone else."

"I wonder what he promised them," said Mharkyn in a low voice.

"Whatever it took," replied Lhadoraak.

"He's talked about the Council paying mages more," said Mharkyn, "but the traders won't pay more than they have to. A few extra silvers for City Patrol duty or boat inspections won't help us that much."

"He likely pointed out that the white mages in Gallos are better organized and get paid more," said Meldryn.

"When they get paid," murmured Beltur.

None of the others heard him, or if they did, chose not to reply to his words.

"I couldn't believe Caradyn," said Mharkyn. "He and Cohndar often don't agree."

"It could be that they both agree that blacks have to do something to gain more power," suggested Meldryn mildly.

"I still don't like it," replied Mharkyn.

"What do you think we can do?" asked Meldryn.

"Nothing. Not for the moment," said Lhadoraak. "That's what's so rotten about it."

"Rottenness finds its own reward," declared Meldryn, "but it spoils the pie for everyone else as well."

Lhadoraak laughed, if slightly bitterly.

None of the four said anything during the time it took to walk another block and turn on to Bakers Lane.

"Do you think things are really as bad as Cohndar says?" finally asked Mharkyn.

"As far as Gallos goes, I don't think so," said Meldryn. "The whites lost five or six strong mages and close to ten thousand troopers. I strongly doubt that the Prefect will try another invasion anytime soon."

"Then why . . . ?" Mharkyn left the question unfinished.

"Why indeed? Perhaps because fear can unite people behind the most unsuitable of leaders, especially when that fear is strong and targeted at a common enemy or those who are different, or sometimes both. When people are fearful, the last thing they want to hear is that their fears are unreasonable or unjustified."

"I'm not so sure my concerns about Cohndar are unjustified," said Beltur.

"You said 'concerns,' Beltur," replied Meldryn. "Concerns by their nature are reasoned. Fears are not."

"That's an interesting way of putting it," said Lhadoraak, "but I promised Mharkyn I'd stop by his place for a moment, and we're heading off now."

"Then we'll talk later," suggested Meldryn, "or whenever you come by the bakery."

"I can do that."

Beltur and Meldryn walked in silence, except for the occasional squeaking crunch when their boots crossed infrequent patches of snow.

"Veroyt knew this would happen," said Beltur after a time. "Our being there couldn't have changed anything."

"It changed one thing," replied the gray-bearded mage. "You saw how Waensyn and Cohndar have already gotten almost everyone to support them. Would you have felt the same way if you hadn't seen how Cohndar was immediately accepted?"

"Most likely not, but why would Veroyt want you to see that? To warn you?"

"It could be. Or he could want you to know."

"Why me?"

"You're the strongest mage in Elparta. That might have something to do with it."

"So I'm supposed to oppose Cohndar? Openly?"

"That might be best for Veroyt. It likely wouldn't be best for you."

Or for Meldryn, Beltur realized.

"What do you think Cohndar meant by blacks being better disciplined?" asked Meldryn.

"He wants everyone to think the way he does, and that sounds dangerous because we don't." For a moment, Beltur had been thinking more about himself, but had realized that, after what he'd overheard Cohndar saying about Athaal and Meldryn during the last eightday of the invasion, Meldryn was likely to be as much a target as Beltur himself.

"*Wants* them to think that way?"

"He's setting things up so that most if not all the blacks follow his lead."

Just like Wyath did in Gallos. Beltur shivered, and not from the cold. "I don't like it."

"Neither do I, but openly opposing him at the moment will only cause us more trouble."

What Meldryn wasn't saying was that most of that trouble would be centered on Beltur.

"We have a lot to think about," declared Meldryn as they neared the corner of Crossed and Bakers Lanes.

We certainly do.

XIV

On twoday, Beltur stepped out of the house at his normal time because, despite the cold, the main streets were at least half cleared. He was also glad to see Laranya, because that meant he wouldn't have cleaning to do when he returned from the smithy.

Once he left the southeast city gate, he noticed the road had been cleared for twenty yards east of the gate. At the end of the cleared section, the snow had been packed down to a hard surface no more than five or six digits deep, and there were depressions a hand-width across separated by more than a yard, with hoofprints in the middle. For a moment that puzzled him, before he realized that the snow had been packed by a horse-drawn sleigh or sledge, likely several of them. He'd heard of both, but he'd never seen either.

The packed snow made the rest of the walk to Jorhan's smithy far less difficult than it might have been, and it helped that Jorhan had cleared a path in the middle of the lane from the road to the smithy. The tracks in the snow at the bottom of the lane suggested that someone in a sleigh or sledge had visited the smith. He couldn't help but wonder who that might have been.

When he entered the smithy, Jorhan was standing at the near workbench, smoothing the interior of a mold that appeared to be for another ornate mirror.

"Good morning," offered Beltur cheerfully. "It looks like you had visitors." He unwrapped his scarf from around him and took off his coat and hung it on the wall peg.

Jorhan smiled. "I did. A merchant from Kleth came out on sevenday. Someone I'd never heard of. He bought a pair of mirrors. I let him have them for a bit less than I might have otherwise, four golds for the pair."

"That wasn't bad, was it?"

"I'd been selling them each for two golds five, but four golds in hand at the moment makes sense. He made a special trip out because he'd heard that, before long, it would be hard to get new-forged cupridium for less than four golds for even the smallest pieces." Jorhan snorted. "Some of the bargain was for what he told me."

"Trader Alizant?"

Jorhan nodded. "I'll tell you later. The first mold's ready. I don't want it to overheat."

Beltur understood that, yet couldn't help worrying as he moved to the bellows.

Whether it was the weather, or because Beltur worried so much, the day seemed to drag out, even though, by the time fourth glass arrived, the two had cast two more mirrors and a carving set of a knife and matching serving fork.

"A bit of a chance on those two, but they didn't take that much copper," Jorhan said, once Beltur had stepped away from the mold that held the fork.

"What will you charge for them?"

"I'll ask two golds and settle for something less." Jorhan grinned. "As little less as I can manage."

"That sounds good to me."

"It might not be until spring, but I didn't expect the fellow from Kleth." The smith shook his head. "Just a moment." With that, he turned and hurried out of the smithy and along the snow-packed path to the stone house.

Beltur checked the mold again, but the order/chaos net or mesh, finer than any he had done so far, held firm.

Jorhan reappeared, closing the smithy door behind him and extending coins. "Here's your pay—a gold and three for your share of the mirrors and a silver for the day's work."

"I appreciate that, especially after what you've told me, and the fact that my time as a patrol mage will end in early winter."

"Winter could be long and hard. I'm thinking about closing up here and taking a sledge to Axalt."

"Thinking about?"

"If this Trader Alizant can keep me from getting copper, I can't forge anything at all, and you can't make cupridium without copper. So neither of us would make anything."

"How does that benefit him?"

"Oh . . . after he made his point, he'd let me have the copper, on the condition I sell to him for a fraction of what the finished piece is worth. That's what he did to Tylert."

"Tylert?"

"The silversmith. None of the traders bothered with a coppersmith before. Not enough golds involved. But with cupridium . . ." Jorhan shook his head.

"What about your lands and everything?"

"One of Johlana's boys likes the place. He says he'd rather be a herder here. All the land in Axalt is rocks and trees. One of her boys would get the lands and house, anyway."

"I'd hate to see you have to leave the lands."

"They'd still be in the family, and I'd be able to smith without bending my neck to another frigging trader. That's if this Alizant does what it looks like he's going to do."

"Do you really think he will?"

"If he can find a way, he will."

"When do you want me back here?"

"Fiveday, if that's agreeable."

"I'll be here."

"Good. Likely be more small fine work." Jorhan offered a crooked smile. "We need to make the copper last."

With a nod, Beltur turned and made his way to the line of wall pegs, from which he removed his coat and scarf and put them on. Once he left the smithy, he walked as quickly as he could back to the southeast gate and from there to the Council building, where he hurried inside and toward Raymandyl's table desk.

"You're cutting it close again." The clerk shook his head as he took out the ledger.

"I know. I was working with Jorhan today."

"I thought you worked with him every day you weren't patrolling."

"Not anymore. Copper's hard to come by these days."

"Copper? That's hard to believe. There's always copper."

"Not if people don't want to sell it," rejoined Beltur.

Raymandyl frowned, almost as if he didn't want to say anything about the copper, and pushed the ledger across the table for Beltur to sign. "Do you have any tokens?"

"Not this eightday. I doubt I'll have any for quite a while." Beltur signed and returned the book, watching as the clerk sealed the entry and then retrieved two silvers.

"Here you go. One eightday's pay."

"Thank you." Beltur paused, then asked, "Can a trader just keep people from selling copper to Jorhan?" He slipped the silvers into his belt wallet.

Raymandyl sighed. "It doesn't work that way. The Council believes every trader, every person, has the right either to sell or not to sell a good or service. Likewise, a seller cannot refuse to sell a physical good to the highest bidder, but may refuse to provide services for good and valid reasons."

Beltur had to think about what the clerk said for a moment. "Then Jorhan should be able to obtain copper if he pays more."

"It doesn't always work that way. If someone offers copper for sale, they'll offer it to the traders first. Also, there are arrangements, sometimes options of first refusal. Once a trader has an amount of copper, he can refuse to sell it at all. Only if he offers it for sale does he have to sell it to the highest bidder."

Beltur was certain that there was more involved, but the gist of the matter was simple enough—Jorhan wasn't going to get copper from anyone in Elparta unless the traders permitted it, and possibly not from anyone outside Elparta if that person was known to the traders. "I see."

"I don't make the rules, Beltur. Thankfully, I don't even have to enforce them."

"But you know them."

"I just listen. I tell people what I know, but I don't advise anyone."

"I appreciate the information. Thank you."

"It's better if you don't try to cut things too close, you know? I'll see you in an eightday."

"If it doesn't snow."

"You'll be here."

Beltur smiled ruefully, knowing that was true, then left the building, thinking about Raymandyl's advice about not cutting things too close. He didn't think the apparent repetition had anything to do with his getting to the Council building in the last moments before half past fourth glass.

It had to be advice, despite Raymandyl's statement that he didn't give advice.

But what might you be cutting too close? What had he been putting off that he should already have been doing . . . or preparing to do?

XV

The next three days were uneventful, in that Beltur patrolled on three-day amid intermittent snow flurries, with no sign of lawbreakers; worked around the bakery with Meldryn on fourday, learning about how to judge the heat in the ovens and what heat was best for different types of breads; and then went back to work at the smithy with Jorhan on fiveday, where the two turned out two highly elaborate scrolled cupridium mirror castings.

"These will be the best yet," declared the smith, after having paid Beltur a silver for the day, and as he prepared to leave.

"You haven't heard anything from the traders, have you?"

"Not a thing. Like I told you, I wouldn't be expecting that for a while. Traders wait until you really need something. Then they make an offer you can't refuse." Jorhan snorted. "Unless you're thinking of dying or leaving."

"He might make an offer you can accept."

"He might. Then he might not. We'll have to see."

"Sixday?" ventured Beltur.

"That would be rushing things. There's only so much copper that Barrynt brought, remember?"

How could I forget? "Next oneday, then?"

"That would be what I was thinking."

"Until then." Beltur wound his scarf in place and headed out.

As he walked westward toward Elparta, he kept thinking over what Jorhan had said, and what he hadn't. It seemed clear enough that the smith wasn't about to stay in Elparta if Alizant wanted him and Beltur to work for almost nothing. That left Beltur in a very difficult position, because without either being a patrol mage or working for Jorhan, he'd go back to making nothing, and the golds he had stockpiled would dwindle away, slow bit by slow bit. If he followed Jorhan to Axalt, then he'd be leaving Jessyla, and there was no way, not that he could see, that he could ask her to follow him when he had no sure way of making a living. And, if he left her, then she'd be even more subject to pressure from most of the blacks and from Grenara to consort Waensyn.

You don't even know for sure that it will happen that way. Except he couldn't help but worry that events would turn out exactly that way.

A gust of wind whipped out of the north, cold, but without the sting that he'd felt on previous days, and without lifting loose snow off the expanse of white that covered the ground and fields bordering the road, an indication that there had been just enough warmth around midday to melt the loose flakes into the slight crust on top of the longer-standing snowfall.

Given all his concerns, once he passed through the southeast gate, he took the east wall road all the way to Crafters Lane and then headed west to a certain house with a green door lintel. Once there, he rapped on the door—firmly.

After several moments, the door opened, and Margrena stood there. "Beltur, what brings you here in the middle of the eightday? Oh . . . come in. There's no sense in us both being cold."

Beltur stepped inside. "Thank you." He looked around, but all he saw was Growler, sitting on the steps to the upper level, pointedly ignoring the interloper.

"Jessyla's not here. After we got back from the healing house, she went with Grenara to visit Grenara's old friend Almaya. I actually sent her. In all this cold, I worry about Grenara. They left only a quint before you arrived. I don't expect them back any time soon."

Disappointed as he was, Beltur just nodded. "I would have liked to see her, but that wasn't the reason I came by. I'd like to know if I might accompany you tomorrow, that is, if you're going to the Council Healing House."

"We are going tomorrow. I'm certain that Klarisia will be pleased. I doubt you will be."

"Are matters that bad?"

"They're likely usual for Elparta, but the early cold . . ." Margrena shook her head. "We can't do enough. The Council doesn't provide enough food for those who are hurt or violently ill, and when they can't work . . ."

"I've seen how hard they work the young men from the workhouses."

"They're more fortunate than those in the Council Healing House."

"You're not trying to discourage me, are you?"

"No. Just to warn you."

"Then I stand warned." Beltur paused. "Have you heard about what happened on oneday night?"

"About the creation of a black mages' council of Elparta, you mean?"

Beltur nodded. "And that Cohndar was unanimously selected as mage-councilor?"

"Unanimously?"

"When all but four of us immediately insisted on Cohndar, Meldryn quickly suggested we join in." It hadn't been quite that way, Beltur knew, but that was what Meldryn had meant, and describing exactly how it came about wouldn't have made sense.

"You, Meldryn, and Lhadoraak, I would guess. Who else?"

"Mharkyn."

"Most likely because he follows Lhadoraak." Margrena frowned. "I trust Meldryn's judgment, but that still worries me."

"It worries both him and me," admitted Beltur. "More than a little. Especially since Cohndar has the traders and the Council behind him."

"Is there any difference between the two?" asked Margrena dryly.

Beltur could feel himself flush, although with his face reddened by the cold, he doubted that his embarrassment was obvious. "Not really."

"Is there anything else?"

"No. Half before seventh glass tomorrow?"

"We'll see you then." Margrena moved to the door, then smiled as she opened it. "I will tell her that you came."

"Thank you." Beltur stepped back out into the late-afternoon sunlight, light that was beginning to show a slight pinkness as the white sun dropped in the western sky. At least the walk back south on Bakers Lane wouldn't be that cold.

XVI

On sixday morning, Beltur reached Grenara's house just before half past seventh glass. He didn't even have to knock, because Jessyla immediately opened the door, offering a warm smile as she did.

"I'm so sorry I missed you yesterday, but I'm glad you're here now."

"He may not be so glad as you are by the time he leaves this afternoon," cautioned Margrena.

"Mother, Beltur's already seen much worse than at the healing house."

Margrena looked as if she might reply immediately. Then she nodded and said, "Sometimes, I forget that."

"In battle, I was too busy trying to do what needed to be done that mostly I didn't have time to dwell on the injured."

"You felt every death, didn't you?" asked Jessyla.

"I did." Beltur couldn't very well lie about that, not when the cold black mist of every death had washed over him.

"Now that we've established that," said Margrena gently, "perhaps we should leave. Before the rest of the cold air outside gets into the house."

Jessyla flushed. "We should." She finished draping her scarf across her face and ears and stepped out the door.

Beltur moved with her.

The two stopped and waited for Margrena to close the door before turning west. Beltur noticed that the older healer carried a small bag in her left hand, although he couldn't determine what might be in it.

The air seemed colder to Beltur than it had been even on the walk to Grenara's, and, if anything, on a clear day with little wind it should have gotten warmer once the sun cleared the eastern city wall. He glanced to the north, but there were no clouds visible.

Three blocks later, they walked along the south side of the northwest market square, less than a quarter of which was cleared, and without any vendors, not surprisingly, given how early in the day it was. Before that long, they reached the two-story, oblong, gray stone building, its narrow blue shutters all fastened tight. Only two of the five chimneys showed smoke.

Once inside the modest foyer, Beltur was so assaulted by the amount of wound and sickness chaos that he had to steady himself on the wide white plank floor. In the main hallway just beyond, between the foyer and the door to the chamber that Senior Healer Klarisia used as her study and headquarters, sprawled two gaunt men with dirty white hair and garments more like rags than clothing, lying end-to-end on thin pallets on the left side, twitching in the chilly air as they lay in an approximation of sleep or stupor.

Beltur could sense no direct wound chaos, only very low levels of basic order and chaos, as well as tiny points of chaos spread throughout their bodies. He looked to Margrena, questioningly.

"They're starving. I told you. There's not enough food here. We all bring what we can." She held up the bag. "I'll leave this with Klarisia, but . . ."

. . . *you don't have that much to spare.* Beltur glanced farther down the hallway, only to see more pallets, one empty, and one on which a tiny older woman sat, her back propped up against the wall, looking blankly at the other side of the hall.

Margrena entered Klarisia's study, as did Jessyla. Beltur stood in the doorway.

The dark-haired senior healer looked up past Margrena for a moment before saying, "You brought help today."

"He asked to accompany us. He's at least half healer already, as well as mage."

"You're welcome here, Beltur, but I can't pay mages, you know?" Klarisia looked evenly at Beltur.

"I didn't come for pay."

"I thought not. You can hang your coat and scarf on the pegs there." Klarisia looked to Jessyla. "Make sure you take three baskets."

Beltur immediately took off his coat and scarf, as did Jessyla, after which she took a basket off the side table and handed it to Beltur, then took two more.

Klarisia went on. "I'd appreciate it if you three would go upstairs first today. There aren't any children here yet."

"Is there anything we should know?" asked Margrena.

"Nothing you don't already."

"Then we'll start." Margrena turned and nodded to Jessyla.

"No children here yet?" murmured Beltur once Margrena had stepped into the main hall.

"In the cold weather, women wait until later to bring their children to the healing house. Few have anything warm to wear, except layers of rags." Margrena led the way past the empty pallet, then stopped by the old woman half sitting, half slumped against the wall, reaching down and handing her a small chunk of bread. "Here's a little something for you."

The woman took it, almost fearfully, as if she thought Margrena might snatch it back. "May the Rational Stars bless you, Healer."

"Just eat it and rest," Margrena said gently.

At the next archway, she turned and started up the narrow staircase to the second level. Beltur let Jessyla go next and then followed her. On the second level, Margrena walked back to the last door on the east end of the corridor, which she pushed open.

Once inside, Beltur realized that he'd been in the room before, but now, there were five pallet beds where there had been four . . . and he didn't think any of the men who lay in those beds were the same as those who had been there less than three eightdays before. Since none of the previous four could have recovered in that time . . . He managed to keep a pleasant expression on his face as he stepped into the room behind the two healers.

"Good morning, Healers," began the legless man in the first bed, who started to smile before subsiding into a fit of coughing, a fit that added a bloody froth to the cloth he put to his mouth.

Margrena moved forward, letting her fingers rest on the top of the coughing man's shoulders for a moment.

Even from where he stood, Beltur could sense the points of wound or flux chaos in the man's lungs and chest, but there didn't seem to be that many. He stepped up beside Margrena.

She raised her eyebrows.

Beltur motioned for her to step back, set down his basket, then rested his fingertips on the consumptive's back just above the shoulder blades. From there he directed small amounts of free order to the points of chaos. He ignored the tiniest points, feeling that if the worst flux or wound areas healed, the body would take care of the others. *You hope.* He also knew he had to be careful with what he did, because it was going to be a long day, a very long day.

Margrena moved on to the next pallet bed.

When Beltur finished, not all that much later, he picked up his basket and stepped back.

Margrena was blotting the forehead of the man in the third pallet bed, who was fevered and flushed, but from what Beltur could sense, not saturated with flux or wound chaos.

Jessyla was cleaning a deep wound in a younger man's thigh, and he was gazing at her in rapt attention, for a moment, when he almost convulsed. Beltur immediately joined her, and realized that the bone beneath the wound was also broken.

"It's too deep," she murmured.

"The chaos around the bone, you mean?"

She nodded.

"I can do a little, I think."

"Not too much," added Margrena from beside Beltur.

"Because of the natural . . . ?" asked Beltur, not wanting to use the word chaos, feeling that would upset the man, who looked to be perhaps a few years older than Beltur.

Margrena nodded.

Once more setting down the basket whose contents he had yet to use, Beltur eased free order into the ugliest reddish-white areas around the bone ends. At least, that was what he sensed. When he finished, he looked to the man. "That should help some."

"It . . . doesn't hurt, quite so much." After a moment, the man added, "I didn't know there were men who were healers."

"Beltur is both a mage and a healer," said Margrena. "There aren't many who are both."

"You're fortunate," added Jessyla.

Beltur wouldn't have gone that far. He worried whether the free order would be enough, but he'd had the feeling that using any more than he had would have caused too much disruption of the natural chaos. *So much of this is feel . . . and you have so little experience.* As it was, he might have tried too hard without Margrena's gentle warning.

"Try to breathe easily," said Margrena, motioning Jessyla toward the fifth and last pallet bed in the chamber.

Beltur reclaimed the basket and followed.

The graybeard in the fifth bed lay on one side, half moaning, half snoring, as if every breath took a great effort. Beltur could tell that it did, and that there was little any of them could do. He stepped back and looked to Jessyla, barely shaking his head.

Margrena joined them, murmuring, "Let him sleep. If he's fortunate, he'll slip away."

When the three left the chamber, Margrena immediately turned to Beltur. "Did that take too much effort? With the consumptive?"

Beltur shook his head. "I could do it all with free order. That's not as hard."

Margrena frowned.

"You pointed that out to me a time ago. Natural order comes from us. Free order doesn't."

"You can tell the difference?"

This time Beltur was the one confused. "You can't?"

She shook her head. "Order is order." She paused. "Except to you, it's not."

"From what you said, I thought all mages and healers . . ."

"I don't know about mages, but I don't know any healers who can tell the difference between kinds of order."

"But you can tell the difference between wound chaos and flux chaos and natural chaos."

"It doesn't feel any different to me," replied Margrena. "It's where it is. Does it feel different to you?"

Beltur considered what Margrena said, and she was right, at least mostly, because natural chaos was deeper within the body and bones. He'd never thought of it that way because he'd sensed the difference in feeling a difference he felt like color.

"Beltur?" asked Margrena gently.

"I was thinking about what you said. Yes, the various kinds of order and chaos feel different to me, partly almost in colors and shades."

"I told you that—" began Jessyla.

"Later, dear. Later." Margrena shook her head. "Not here." She looked to Beltur. "Not now."

Another thought crossed Beltur's mind. "There aren't any pallets in the hall up here. Only on the first floor."

"That's because those who need them are too weak to climb the steps. The Council won't let them stay overnight, anyway. Not if there aren't beds enough. People sleeping in the hall spread the chaos and corruption."

"Do they have anywhere to go?"

"Some do. Some don't. The Council says it's not up to them to provide housing. There's no point in talking about it. That won't change anything. We need to go through the other chambers up here." Margrena walked toward the next door.

She never reached it, because Klarisia appeared at the top of the staircase, gesturing frantically. The three followed her down the steps to a chamber in the middle of the building, listening.

". . . young woman struggled in. She's been badly beaten, and she's large with child, and she's having severe contractions . . ."

"Is she bleeding?" asked Margrena.

"There's some seepage, but I don't have a good feeling about her," said Klarisia as she reached the bottom of the stairs and stepped out into the main lower corridor. "This way."

As the last one to enter the small room, even from yards away, Beltur could sense the wound chaos of the bruises around the outside of the woman's enlarged abdomen. She lay on a slightly raised pallet bed, with another, black-haired healer whom Beltur had not met standing beside her.

"The baby's in the birth canal . . ." offered the black-haired healer, mouthing, "The bleeding's increasing . . ."

Klarisia nodded.

Margrena motioned for Beltur and Jessyla to stay where they were.

Beltur still tried to sense more carefully beyond the obvious. When he did, what worried him even more than the bruises or the small trickles of visible bleeding were the streaks of chaos deeper within her body, surrounding the unborn child.

Should you do something with order? But what? What would it do to the mother or the child?

"Keep pushing . . ." said one of the healers.

"Hurts . . . Ohhh! . . . hurts . . . so much!"

Still holding the basket, Beltur could sense when the healer beside the woman offered a touch of order, but that faded quickly with another contraction and wave of pain.

Margrena did not look in Beltur's direction, but murmured something to Klarisia, and the two of them moved to the other side of the woman. Beltur edged forward, trying to get a better sense of what was happening, knowing that he knew nothing except what he'd read, and trying to reconcile those words with the reality before him.

Then . . . seemingly suddenly, the roundness of the baby's head appeared, and with it, a gush of blood . . . and more blood.

Margrena and Klarisia were there, one easing the infant from the mother, the other with cloths and order, trying to stanch the flood of blood, but there seemed no end of the blood.

In too short a time, the room was silent, and a black mist swept over Beltur.

"The child?" whispered Jessyla.

Beltur didn't have to say a word. He knew that they all sensed that the child was dead, as was her mother. But the child had been dead before birth, Beltur suspected from hindsight, since only a single black mist had chilled him, although he wasn't about to mention that unless asked.

Margrena motioned for Beltur and Jessyla to step outside. He did so and closed the door behind Jessyla, who had turned pale. He still felt stunned. *So fast . . .*

Jessyla was silent, equally stunned, he thought.

Beltur set down the basket and stood there. He was still standing there, trying to work out what he might have been able to do, when Margrena eased out of the room and shut the door.

She looked at Beltur. "You sensed something as soon as we entered the birthing room, didn't you?"

"There were chaos streaks inside her womb. I didn't know what they were, but they were from where the blood was coming, I think. Even if I'd known that she was bleeding so badly inside, I don't know what I could have done. Shields wouldn't have done any good, nor would order."

"Sometimes, there isn't anything that any of us can do." Margrena's voice was low.

"But if she hadn't been so badly beaten . . ." began Beltur.

"That was why she was beaten. Someone didn't want her to have that child, perhaps any child. There's no real way to find out. No one knows who she was. Klarisia never asked her. We don't ask. If they tell us, that's their choice."

Beltur understood that. "No. I meant that someone must know who she was."

"Someone knows, but no one here does. No one has the time to go out and ask hundreds of people if they knew a woman who was with child who was beaten and then vanished. You'd likely find more than one poor woman who vanished, but those who did it would deny even knowing her, and anyone else who did would likely be afraid to say anything."

That, too, Beltur unfortunately understood.

"We need to see to the children's room." Margrena turned.

Beltur and Jessyla picked up their baskets and followed her.

By the time the city chimes rang out the fourth glass of the afternoon, Beltur had used shields to help Margrena and Jessyla set and splint bones. He'd cleaned out wounds himself, if with Margrena watching. But the one thing that stayed with him was the woman who had hemorrhaged and died even as she gave birth to a child who had arrived stillborn.

He still had no idea what he could have done.

When the three finally left the healing house, Beltur was tired and felt he was on the verge of light-headedness. The light but chill wind helped somewhat, and after walking a ways, he looked to Margrena and said, "Earlier today, you said I was a healer and a mage."

"You are. There is little doubt of that," said Margrena. "If you work at it, you could become a great healer. Most mages turn from that path."

"Why?" asked Jessyla.

"Beltur," said Margrena, "how did you feel while that woman was dying? Honestly feel?"

"I felt I couldn't do anything, or that anything I tried would have failed or made things worse." *But how could I have made it worse? She died.*

"You were right. At that moment, it was too late to do anything at all. All too often with healing, the best we can do is not enough." She turned to Jessyla. "And, no, Daughter dear, I'm not giving up. We have to try, but we have to accept that there are times when we cannot save people."

The best we can do is not enough. Those words seemed to echo in Beltur's thoughts as the wind chilled his exposed forehead.

XVII

By early afternoon on sevenday, as Beltur patrolled the market square, his feet were again getting cold, not quite numb, even after he'd eaten his loaf and downed a mug of Fosset's hot cider. The sky was green-gray rather than green-blue because of a high haze, and the sun seemed dimmer and more distant. Uncomfortable as patrolling was becoming, Beltur worried that, from what he calculated, he only had four more eightdays of patrol duty. *Four more eightdays before steady pay disappears.*

When the chimes rang out first glass, Beltur was almost to the corner of West Street and Patrol Street to meet Laevoyt, where he could see the tall patroller standing and waiting. By now, a good half of the market square had been cleared, and the other half was piled with packed snow taller than a man. Four young men from the workhouse were still shoveling the packed snow into wagons.

As he stopped next to Laevoyt, Beltur shook his head. "They're still shoveling. And it all gets dumped in the river?" Even as he asked, Beltur realized it was a stupid question.

"Where else? Until the river freezes over. Then they dump it on the ice. What are you fretting about?"

"What everyone frets about, I suppose. Having enough coins to get through the winter." Beltur wasn't about to mention the image of the dying woman that was all too fresh in his mind, or the fact that he'd felt so helpless. In some ways, even more helpless than when Athaal had died, because, then, he'd been able to do *something,* even though it hadn't been enough.

Laevoyt smiled, but shook his head. "Sort of troubling when mages worry like patrollers."

"Not all mages. I don't think I'd worry as much if I'd been raised here. I'd be established in some way. Getting established is harder when you know so few people."

"I hadn't thought of it that way. Makes sense, though."

"It's also a problem when there isn't much copper coming to Elparta in the winter, and when there aren't many merchants and traders from other places passing through. Not many folks here want or can afford cupridium.

With all the time I spent as a mage-officer, I didn't have as much time to look for other possibilities as I'd hoped."

"I know you liked Athaal . . ." ventured Laevoyt.

"An awful lot of what he did—at least that I know about—consisted of work dealing with animals, piers, crops, and mills, and most of that doesn't happen in the late fall or winter." Beltur paused, thinking about pier inspections. *You should talk to Veroyt about that.* In fact, he should already have talked to Veroyt. *Another chance possibly missed.*

"You're so good as a patrol mage that I sometimes forget there's still a lot you don't know about Elparta. Others might think the same way."

Beltur smiled wryly. "Thank you for that."

"We'd better get back to patrolling."

Beltur nodded. "Until fourth glass." He turned and headed east on Patrol Street, since Laevoyt had headed south on West Street.

By the time the chimes rang out fourth glass, the square was almost deserted, except for one handcart that a vendor was slowly pushing away— and the two patrollers. Beltur was more than ready to sign out as he and Laevoyt walked toward headquarters.

"The acorn woman was back again," offered Beltur, just trying to make conversation. "Haven't seen her for several eightdays."

"She'll be here every so often. She's hoarding the acorns like coppers."

"For her they are."

Laevoyt laughed.

Once he signed the duty book and left headquarters and turned north on Bakers Lane, Beltur found himself walking into the teeth of a stiff and much colder wind that had come up since he'd left the market square. Or maybe the buildings around the square had blocked the wind, and the straight north-south line of the lane had channeled and strengthened the wind.

When he finally stepped into the house, he heard voices coming from the kitchen. For a moment, he wondered if Margrena or Jessyla had stopped by and were talking to Meldryn, but the second voice was male. After taking off coat, cap, scarf, and gloves, and hanging the coat on the wall peg, Beltur hurried toward the kitchen. There he found Meldryn and Lhadoraak seated at the table. Each had a mug of hot spiced cider, and there was an empty mug on the table—clearly for him.

"The kettle's still hot," said Meldryn. "After walking around all day in the cold, I figured you could use some warming up."

"Thank you. It's really cold out there." Seeing Meldryn's amused expression, Beltur added, "I know. It's not as cold as it's going to get, and the weather outside is warm compared to what's coming."

Both other mages smiled.

Beltur took the stove mitten and lifted the kettle off the iron hook over the hearth coals and filled the mug, then replaced the kettle and sat down at the table beside Lhadoraak. He took a swallow of the cider and then held the mug under his nose, enjoying the warmth and the scent of cloves and cinnamon, spices generally reserved for company, before asking, "What brings you here on this only modestly cold afternoon?"

"Taelya."

Despite the warmth of the cider, Beltur felt a momentary chill. "Is something wrong?"

"Ah . . . not . . . wrong . . . concerning."

The way Lhadoraak said the words, Beltur had a good idea what the other mage meant, but he just asked, "Concerning?"

"She's growing. She's healthy and definitely stronger. She's eating like a sailor in home port." A brief smile crossed Lhadoraak's face, then vanished. "What did you do to her?"

"I told you."

"Is that all?"

Beltur could sense the worry behind Lhadoraak's words. "That's all. Why?"

"She's showing magely abilities."

"That shouldn't be surprising. She is your daughter."

"But she's too young. Besides, I'm a black, and Tulya's enough black that she could almost be a healer."

"You're suggesting that Taelya might be a white?"

"She used chaos to light the lamps the other day. Chaos. What did you do?"

"I didn't change anything about Taelya," Beltur said. "The illness she had . . . it was hiding what she is. Or what I suspected she is. She's most likely to be a white mage." *And strong, if abilities are showing up this young.*

"Women aren't mages, and not white mages," protested Lhadoraak.

"Are you willing to tell your daughter she can't be what she is?"

"How do you know what she's going to be?"

"I don't, but her order/chaos pattern looks more like a white's than a black's, and if she can light lamps already, she's a beginning mage."

"She can be trained black."

"You can try," said Beltur. "My uncle tried to train me as a white. In the end, it didn't work."

"You're saying she has to be a white?" Lhadoraak took a deep breath. "After the invasion by the Prefect and his white mages, and the way Waensyn and Cohndar talk . . . well . . ." The fine-featured mage flushed.

"You mean how they talk badly about me, and I'm only a black raised by a white, and you're worried that if Taelya is actually a white . . . ?"

Lhadoraak nodded. "Tulya's even more worried. Especially with the way the Council's behind Cohndar."

"Has Cohndar ever paid much attention to you?" asked Meldryn.

Lhadoraak frowned. "Now that you ask . . . not really. He's only dropped by the house once in the past two years."

"Then why would he have any reason even to suspect your daughter might be a white?"

"I suppose he wouldn't . . . but he still might drop by sometime."

"He might," agreed Meldryn, "but so long as he's not close to Taelya . . ."

"I see what you mean. For a few years anyway."

"I told Lhadoraak," Meldryn said in his deep mellow voice, "that you might be able to help, since you're the only one with any real experience in dealing with chaos magery."

"That's if you're willing," added Lhadoraak. "I was wondering if there's any chance . . ."

"Become a black?" Beltur shook his head. "That would likely leave her so weak as to make her easy prey for any mage, black or white. If you and Tulya agree, and Taelya's willing, I can try to teach her how to use chaos in a way that will limit the bad effects of chaos magery and make her as strong as her talents will allow."

"But she'll be a white," protested Lhadoraak.

"I understand how you feel." Beltur took another swallow of cider, thinking about how he could make Lhadoraak understand.

"A white . . . in Spidlar," emphasized Lhadoraak.

"My uncle was a white," Beltur said slowly. "He tried to raise me as a white. I was likely the weakest white wizard in all of Gallos, if even that. It wasn't until Jessyla suggested that handling chaos with order might be better—because Athaal had said something about it—that I began to improve. Before long, it was clear that I was really a black. I only survived because I began to strengthen what I was, not what my uncle wanted me to be. Athaal once told me that going against one's nature was a certain way to destruction." Athaal hadn't put it nearly that bluntly, but that had certainly been the thrust of his words to Beltur.

"But . . . white?" The anguish in Lhadoraak's voice tore at Beltur.

"White doesn't mean evil," said Meldryn calmly. "Both Athaal and Margrena knew Beltur's uncle. They both said that he was a good man. He helped Margrena and Jessyla to leave Gallos, and he sacrificed his life standing up against the Prefect and saving Beltur. People like to give nasty names to those who are different, even a little different. Beltur likely did more than any other black to save Elparta from the Gallosians, and yet Cohndar and Waensyn are still denigrating him. Trying to make Taelya into something she is not may well destroy her."

"What can we do? You make it sound like . . ."

"Let Beltur work with her," suggested Meldryn.

Lhadoraak looked to Meldryn questioningly.

"He knows more than I do about these things, and, if she's like most children, she'll learn better from someone besides her parents. You can certainly observe. Discreetly, of course."

Lhadoraak turned to Beltur. "Could you? Would you?"

"I'd be happy to help her all I can." *Not only for your sake, and Tulya's, but for Athaal's.* "But I'll have to have your word that you'll allow Taelya to be what she must be in order to survive. From what you say, she could be a white, or she might be more gray."

"Gray?" Lhadoraak winced.

"Trying to make her what she is not will destroy her, sooner or later." Beltur felt the repetition was more than necessary.

"When . . . ?" Lhadoraak finally said.

"I could start tomorrow . . . a little after midday."

"Would you?"

"I'll be there."

Lhadoraak took a last swallow of the cider, set the mug on the table without it making a sound, and then stood, slowly and deliberately. His face was bleak. "You don't think there's any chance she might still turn out black?"

"At this point," replied Beltur carefully, as he stood, "I don't know what she is. I know what worries you. I'll know more once I work with her, and so will you."

A quick wry smile appeared on Lhadoraak's face, then vanished. "You sound like Athaal."

"I'm me, but if I have to sound like anyone, I'd choose Athaal."

"Even that sounds like him," offered Meldryn.

Beltur walked with Lhadoraak from the kitchen to the front door, then waited as the blond mage donned his coat and scarf.

Meldryn appeared a few moments later.

"Tulya and I will be interested to see what you think."

"So will I," replied Beltur cheerfully. "But now's not the time to worry. She's still young, and there's time to sort it all out."

"We'll see you tomorrow."

"I'll be there," Beltur said again.

Lhadoraak turned to Meldryn. "Thank you. Your advice has always been good." Then he opened the door and left without looking back.

After Beltur closed the door, Meldryn said, "He's more worried than he's saying."

"I know. Do you think it's just Taelya?"

"You'll have to see." Meldryn paused, then added, "You know that whites don't live nearly as long as blacks?"

"I know that, but most whites don't use order in the right way. They mingle their natural chaos with free chaos. The same sort of thing may be true of blacks. Margrena pointed out that in healing, the problem is that a healer's natural order works far better for most healing than free order, and using too much natural order can kill a healer. That suggests that there's also a danger for blacks in not keeping their natural order mostly separate from free order."

"I've never heard anyone put it that way, not even Athaal."

"You miss him."

"More than I'll ever say. Or could say."

"I'm sorry."

"Beltur . . . you have nothing to be sorry about. You did all you could, and almost died yourself trying to save him—unlike those who express no remorse, or unfelt sorrow, and on whom the guilt for his death and those of others should rest."

"I can still feel sorry for his loss and yours." Beltur managed a wistful smile. "Is there any of that hot cider left?"

Meldryn shook his head. "I appreciate the effort . . . and, yes, there is, and we both could use it."

Beltur could agree with that.

XVIII

As Beltur promised, he arrived at Lhadoraak and Tulya's door at two quints past noon on eightday.

Tulya opened the door and immediately stepped back, motioning for Beltur to enter. "Thank you so much for coming. We've been so worried."

"It's the least I could do . . . and if Jessyla and Athaal hadn't helped me to discover what I was, I wouldn't be here."

"Jessyla?"

"She told me something Athaal had told her, and that got me started. Athaal helped me the rest of the way. Now . . . let's see to Taelya."

"She's in the parlor."

Taelya was seated on a parlor bench in front of the hearth, reading, or nervously pretending to read, Beltur suspected.

Lhadoraak rose from his chair as Beltur entered. "Good afternoon, Beltur. You're punctual, I have to say." He glanced past Beltur to Tulya, who was motioning her consort to join her and leave the parlor, then turned to his daughter. "Taelya, Beltur is here, and he's going to try to help you become a better mage, like I told you. Your mother and I will be in the kitchen."

Taelya set down the book she had not been reading. "I'll be fine, Father."

Lhadoraak nodded to Beltur, saying, "Let us know when you're done."

"I will." Beltur picked up a straight-backed chair and set it at an angle to Taelya, then seated himself and studied Taelya. He could see that she was definitely taller, even seated, and her growth was noticeable only some two eightdays after Beltur had removed the order shields that had confined her natural chaos. The free chaos that swirled around her was certainly the mark of a white, but there was more than a little free order there as well. But why hadn't Lhadoraak said anything sooner? He had to have sensed and known it long before yesterday. *Because he'd hoped she'd outgrow being a white?*

"Are you going to try to make me a black?" asked Taelya calmly.

"No. I'm here to make you better at whatever you really are. If you don't learn the proper way of how to handle order and chaos, you'll end up killing yourself or dying young." *Or younger than necessary.*

"Father said you were raised as a white. You don't look that way now. You're almost as dark as Father."

"Do you see that with your eyes?"

Taelya frowned. "Not exactly. There's a mist around you."

"Good. What about the mist around you?"

Taelya paused.

"Hold out your hand. Try to look at it in the same way that you look at me."

"It doesn't look any different."

Beltur thought a moment, then managed to draw together a small point of free chaos from that which surrounded Taelya, positioning it above his outstretched hand. "What am I holding?"

"Nothing."

"Look again."

Taelya wrinkled her forehead. "There's a misty white ball. But it's really not there."

"That's free chaos. I drew it from the chaos that surrounds you. Now look around your own hand."

"Oh . . ." After a moment, she said, "Is that how I look to you?"

"The mist around you is grayish white. You've collected both free order and free chaos."

"Is that bad?"

"Right now, it's not bad or good. It's what other mages will see or sense. Or healers." He paused, then asked, "How do you feel?"

"Better than I have in a long time." Taelya smiled. "Much better."

"That's good. Very good. Your father said that you could light lamps."

"I can do it sometimes."

Beltur nodded. "Can you get a candle? We'll use it for practice."

"I can already do that."

Beltur looked at her.

"Sometimes," Taelya added.

"Go find a candle. What's important isn't just being able to do things, but how you do them. That's important in everything, but it's especially important in magery. We're going to work on that."

"You sound like Mother."

"Your mother is a sensible woman. I hope you'll be one as well."

"I'll get a candle. Can it be an old little one?"

"It can. In fact, that would be better."

Taelya bounded to her feet and for several steps, then slowed to a more decorous walk as she left the parlor headed for the kitchen.

In moments, she returned with a small squat tannish candle, with a stubby blackened wick barely protruding from the melted and remelted wax in the middle. The candle sat on a chipped ivory-colored plate barely a handspan wide.

"Put it on the side table. Then sit down on the bench facing the candle."

Taelya seated herself.

"Now . . . try to light the candle."

"I thought you were going to teach me a different way."

"I have to see what you're doing to know which way will work better for you."

Taelya looked hard at the candle, squeezing her face into an intent frown.

Beltur could sense the thin line of chaos from her to the candle as the unseen white mist around the candle strengthened into a white point. Finally, the tip of the wick glimmered and then showed a point of flame that slowly grew.

"There!" declared Taelya with satisfaction.

"Do you feel like you're reaching out to the candle wick?"

"Sort of. Should I be doing something else?"

"I'd like you to try something totally different for a moment." Beltur stood and moved his chair closer to the bench, then sat down. "Concentrate on what's above my hand." He created a small point of order there.

"There's a black point there. That's order, isn't it?"

"It is. Now, I'm going to move it halfway between us."

"I can feel that."

"Good. I want you to make a point of white chaos close to it—a very tiny point." Beltur watched as a line of chaos drifted from Taelya. "No. Don't reach out. Try just to think about that little point of chaos hanging there in the air beside the point of order. Concentrate on that point, just a tiny point of chaos there."

Suddenly, there was a point of chaos there.

"I did it!"

But the point of chaos dissolved in Taelya's enthusiasm.

"Oh . . ."

Beltur smiled warmly. "That's all right. You showed you can do it. Tell me. Why did your chaos point vanish?"

"Ah . . . I stopped concentrating?"

"That's half of it. Now . . . has your father told you what chaos is?"

"It's a kind of power all jumbled up . . ."

"That's right. Chaos doesn't like to be concentrated or confined. Or captured. It wants to escape. Chaos mages get their power from concentrating chaos, either with order or more chaos, and holding it tight, and then forcing that concentrated chaos to go somewhere else. When they stop holding it tight, the power comes from its expanding and escaping." That was a simplified explanation, but one that was basically accurate on the fundamental level.

"So when I stopped concentrating, it escaped?"

"Exactly. That's why you need to keep concentrating and follow my instructions. Make another tiny point of chaos close to my point of order." Beltur waited until Taelya had her tiny focused point of chaos, then said, "Move it toward the point of order. Keep moving it until they touch." As she did, he watched. Just before they touched, he placed a containment around them.

Whsst! A small flame flared up, then vanished.

"Oh!"

"That's what happens when pure concentrated order and chaos meet. If we'd done that right over the candlewick it would still be burning." Beltur grinned. "That is *not* the best way to light a candle. We'll get to that in a bit. Now . . . this time, I'm going to provide the chaos, and you're going to concentrate a tiny bit of order. It will likely be harder, but you need to do it."

"Why do I need to do both?"

"That's a good question. You already know the answer. You just don't know that you know it."

Taelya frowned. "I do?"

"Let's say you turn out to be a white, and you want to throw a chaos bolt. How do you get the chaos to stay together?" Beltur waited.

"Order?"

"That's right. Using order is much easier. The problem is that some whites never learn this. They just keep cramming more and more chaos together. That works, but it has a very high cost. You could do this as well, but all that free chaos around you all the time starts to unravel the order in your body. That's why strong whites who don't use enough order to channel their power all die very young . . . or make mistakes that can kill them."

"How do you know this?"

"Because my uncle trained me as a white, and I wasn't one. But it allowed me to learn to use both."

"Blacks don't have that problem, do they?"

"They have a different problem. If they don't keep free order and chaos away from their body, they have different problems." Beltur wanted to skip over that, because what he thought was only a guess. "Either way, a mage, and it's clear you're a beginning mage, needs to keep order and chaos from being too close, especially chaos. Now . . . try to sense the order and chaos swirling around you . . ." Beltur waited for several moments. "Move the darker white next to you, then put the order outside that, and the bright misty white outside the black." He just watched as Taelya struggled.

"It doesn't want to stay there."

"Just watch what I do. If it hurts, tell me immediately." Beltur didn't think it would, but he'd never tried what he was about to do with anyone besides himself. Gently, as gently as he could, he linked loosely the swirling bits of black mist into a cloud that separated the slightly darker natural chaos of Taelya's body from the larger mist of free chaos.

Taelya sat there, rigidly, as if fearing something would hurt.

"That's it," Beltur finally said. "Can you sense the differences?"

"I don't feel that different."

"I meant in the order and chaos around you."

"Oh . . . they're in a sort of pattern."

"Did you see how I linked the order?"

"I saw . . ."

"All right. I'm going to put a mist of order a yard away from you, and I want you to try to link the mist together the way I did."

Almost a glass passed before Taelya could finally repeat the linkages, and her forehead was damp.

"Good!" declared Beltur.

"You never did show me how to light a candle." Taelya's voice had a trace of resentment.

"It should be easy for you now. Just use the black order to move some white free chaos around the candlewick. It shouldn't take much. Squeeze the chaos with the order."

A flame almost five digits long flared up from the candle.

"Oh!!!"

Beltur grinned. "You see? If you do it right, it takes very little. Try again." Beltur snuffed out the candle with order.

The third time, Taelya lit the candle with just the right amount of chaos. "That is easier."

"That's why it's important to learn the right way to do things."

"Can I show Father?"

"Of course. I think we've done enough for today. You're going to feel very tired in a little while." Beltur raised his voice. "Lhadoraak, Tulya, your daughter wants to show you a few things." He used order to snuff out the candle once more.

The moment Lhadoraak walked into the parlor, his mouth dropped open. "What . . . how . . . ?"

"I showed Taelya how to keep free chaos and order from interfering with her own natural order and chaos. That way, she'll be able to use both without hurting herself."

Tulya frowned.

"She's at least part white," Beltur said. "I can't change that, but using order to handle chaos will not only make her stronger, but healthier." He turned to Taelya. "You can light the candle now."

The candle appeared to light instantly.

"Now, put it out."

Taelya did.

"You can see how little effort that took," Beltur said. "We worked on getting her to use order to control chaos."

Lhadoraak glanced at Tulya.

Tulya nodded and turned to her daughter. "You've been working hard. Would you like some bread and jam?"

"Could I?"

"Yes, but don't forget to thank Beltur."

Taelya turned to Beltur. "Thank you, ser." She inclined her head.

"You're welcome. Next time, we'll work on some new magely things."

"I'd like that." With a smile Taelya turned and accompanied her mother to the kitchen.

Beltur turned back to face Lhadoraak.

"Seeing her like that is frightening," said the blond mage. "She feels like a total white."

"I can't help what she is," Beltur replied. "I can only give her the tools to be the best at it, and I'm trying to give her the skills to be a strong white. She'll need strong shields, but that will take a while. The strongest shields are a mixture of order and chaos, and she doesn't react adversely to either."

"How did you know how to protect her that way?"

"Look at me . . . closely." Beltur waited.

Lhadoraak's eyes widened.

"My order and chaos is layered, too. The only difference is that, in Taelya's case, natural chaos is stronger. So the order separates free chaos from her natural chaos."

"I never realized . . ." Lhadoraak swallowed. "Cohndar's right to be worried about you. I don't think he can do what you can."

"My skills are mostly with forms of layers and shields," Beltur protested.

"That's like saying you're only skilled with every form of order and chaos," countered Lhadoraak wryly.

Is it really? "I never could throw a chaos bolt, and I still can't. I can use shields to redirect one."

"I'm not sure many blacks can do even that. I can't. Athaal couldn't."

Beltur wasn't going to address that. "When do you think I should come again?"

"The sooner the better."

"I'll probably be free on twoday afternoon. If I have to work with Jorhan, though, I'll still come, but it will be after fourth glass."

"Thank you. I don't know who else could help her."

Beltur didn't, either, although Athaal could have. "I'm glad I can. Until twoday." He reclaimed his coat and pulled it on, then wrapped his scarf in place before heading out.

Before that long he reached Crafters Way and turned west.

He had to knock on Grenara's door several times before Jessyla opened it.

"I didn't bring anything today," Beltur confessed, almost sheepishly.

"Good," declared Jessyla. "You don't have to bribe your way into the house, you know?" She stepped back to allow Beltur into the house before closing the door behind him.

"Not in your eyes," he murmured, glancing past her toward the kitchen, where he suspected Grenara and Margrena were. "Or your mother's." He only saw Growler, sitting on the staircase, ignoring both humans while tacitly acknowledging their lesser presences as only a feline could do.

"You've been doing something magely, haven't you?"

"How do you know that?"

"I . . . just feel it. Have you?"

"Yes. I'll need to explain it to you and your mother, though. If she's here."

"I'll get her while you take off your coat. In a moment." She put both arms around him briefly, murmuring, "*You* should have done this first." Then she released him and left him standing there blushing.

He did get his coat off and hung on one of the wall pegs and was even standing in front of the hearth in the front room when Jessyla returned with Margrena.

They sat on the bench, while Beltur took the straight-backed chair.

"What is this mysterious magery that Mother and I must both know about?" asked Jessyla, curiosity mixing with annoyance in her voice.

"It's not mysterious, but troubling. Lhadoraak was waiting at the house when I got home from patrol duty yesterday afternoon . . ." Beltur went on to tell what had happened and then gave a brief outline of what he'd discovered about Taelya and what he'd been trying to teach her.

When he finished, Margrena immediately asked, "What did Lhadoraak and Tulya say?"

"Lhadoraak's not at all happy that Taelya's clearly either white or gray. He is grateful that I'll work with her because he says there's no one else who can. Athaal could have."

"He's fortunate you can," said Jessyla.

"He's right to be worried," added Margrena. "Cohndar and Waensyn won't like the idea of a white mage in Elparta, especially a woman."

"She's only a girl," declared Jessyla.

"Beltur's only one mage among many," replied Margrena, "and they're not happy with him. They weren't fond of Athaal, and they're skeptical of Meldryn."

"Men," snorted Jessyla. "They don't like anyone except those like themselves."

"There's a certain truth in that, Jessyla dear," said Margrena, "but you'd be wise not to say that where anyone else can hear you, because those men have the ear and the support of the Council, and the Council has never been that fond of women who cross them. As your aunt can tell you."

"I know. I know. It doesn't make it right."

"Power establishes what is right," said Grenara from where she stood in the doorway to the kitchen. "Never forget that, girl."

"What those in power want, not what is right," replied Jessyla.

"For the rest of us," countered Grenara flatly, "it amounts to the same thing."

Jessyla had barely opened her mouth when Margrena said, sternly, "Jessyla, no argument. There's much we know that is not as it should be. There's little point in arguing about what should be when we can do nothing to change it."

Jessyla sighed. "I understand. I don't have to like it."

"None of us do, girl," replied Grenara, her voice much softer. "None of us."

"Even Beltur, as accomplished as he is, has to carry out the Council's will when he is serving as a patrol mage," added Margrena.

"If Beltur is staying for an early dinner, I'll need some help." Grenara looked to Margrena.

"I can do that. Beltur and Jessyla don't have that much time together these days," replied Margrena, standing and motioning to the bench from which she had risen. "Sit here. It's warmer."

"Thank you." Beltur smiled at Margrena, then nodded his head to Grenara.

As the two older healers left the front room, Beltur sat down beside Jessyla.

"They're right," she murmured, "but I hate it. You and Athaal and Meldryn are so much better than Cohndar and Waensyn and the others. Why don't they see that?"

Because they don't want to. "Most people think their way is best. They're no different from us in that fashion."

"But our way is better."

"I'm sure they'd say the same thing."

"Beltur . . . are you trying to start an argument?"

Beltur almost replied instantly, but then managed to grin, before saying, "Not if I can help it."

"Good."

Beltur hoped so.

XIX

Beltur woke early on oneday, still thinking over the pleasant eightday afternoon he had spent with Jessyla. At the same time, he couldn't help but be worried, the more he thought it over, about the problems that could arise when Cohndar and Waensyn discovered that he was essentially training a white wizard, and a young woman at that. That might be kept quiet for a time, possibly as long as a year before they discovered that Taelya was a white, simply because they wouldn't have thought of a girl as a white. Cohndar said he would visit all mages, but he might well not even notice Taelya if she were kept away.

But if you can teach her shields well enough to hide her personal order and chaos the way you can . . . Beltur almost shook his head. That was expecting far too much from a seven-year-old. In time, that was certainly possible, but not in the next year or so.

As usual, his bedchamber was cold, but it didn't seem that cold, or perhaps he was getting used to it. When he finally left the house, the light snowfall confirmed that it was warmer, since it seemed to warm up somewhat during storms . . . at least some of the time.

The snow was light enough that there was little more than a digit on the streets, and he had no difficulty in reaching the smithy.

He had just taken off his coat and scarf, when he noticed that Jorhan had a number of molds laid out on the front workbench, and that another was being heated. As he walked toward the forge, he said, "I thought we were going to space out the copper. Did I misunderstand?"

"You don't know?"

"Know what?"

"That figures." Jorhan shook his head. "I'm not blaming you. I thought you might not know, but I wasn't sure." He pointed to an envelope on the end of the bench. "Read it."

Beltur had a sinking feeling that he wasn't going to like what was in the envelope, especially when he saw the Council seal—since Jorhan had slit the envelope to avoid breaking the seal. He slipped out the single sheet and began to read. First came the elaborate letterhead of the Council, then the text.

Whereas the Traders' Council of Spidlaria has the duty and responsibility to make, maintain, and enforce standards for the conduct and safety of trade and manufactures in Spidlar, it is hereby declared that:

Effective the first oneday of Winter this year, any and all manufactured goods, devices, or materials, of which a significant aspect is the use of magery in the production thereof, shall only be sold through a trader approved by the Council. Any such approved trader must submit an affirmation to the Council that the goods, devices, or materials being sold constitute no danger and inflict no chaos upon those handling or using said goods, devices, or materials.

Failure of any individual, maker, or seller of such goods to comply with this law shall result in the forfeiture of all revenues resulting from such sale and the imposition of a penalty of twenty golds for each item so produced or sold, in addition to which shall be added a penalty of fifty golds. A second offense shall result in the same penalties and require the immediate and permanent exile of all those involved in the creation, making, or sale of such items . . .

The rest of the verbiage dealt with more technicalities, including the duty of the mage-councilor of the appropriate city, or the mage-councilor of the city closest to the point of offense, in determining that magery was indeed used in the creation of such items.

Beltur lowered the proclamation, momentarily speechless, but realizing the reason why Jorhan had heard nothing was that Alizant had been working with Cohndar to get the full Council to make the proclamation, and getting the information to and from Spidlaria had taken time. That meant that Alizant had been working on it possibly even before Beltur had finished with his duties as a mage-officer.

"They've made a law that requires us to sell to a trader so that bastard can get all the profit."

"It's a law that seems to apply to everyone," Beltur finally said, "but it only applies to us, or to anyone making black iron. Those are the only two materials that need mages."

"There might be others, but the result is the same."

"Is that why you have all the molds set out?"

"I'll be frigging damned if I'm going to give a copper to those bastards. I thought we could use all the copper in the next eightday or so. I've taken time to make repairs to my old sledge. Haven't used it in years. It'll last long enough to take me and everything we forge to Axalt. One of the boys can come back in the spring and take over the lands." Jorhan paused. "I'll have to send you your share of the golds once things sell. I can pay your daily wages, but not your share."

"That's fine. I understand." *What else can you do?* Beltur walked to the forge and stood by the bellows. "We might as well get started."

"Barrynt said there was a place for you in Axalt," Jorhan said quietly.

"That's something I'll have to think about. I have obligations . . . debts to pay . . . here in Elparta."

"Thought you might say something like that. Just keep it in mind. Always good to have options."

"What's the first mold?"

"I've got three knives set up to go first. Knives are easier to sell, and they don't take as much metal. Also, there's less tariff on knives and blades for a trader who has to go through Certis. After that, we should have time for a larger hand mirror. It's a different design."

Beltur set to work with the bellows as Jorhan moved the crucible into position.

By slightly past fourth glass, the three knives and the mirror were cast, and Beltur stood by the workbench, sensing the mirror, but the order/chaos net had definitely set.

He turned to Jorhan. "Tomorrow then?"

"Tomorrow. You're still on City Patrol duty, aren't you?"

Beltur nodded.

"We'll cast as much as we can tomorrow. I can do finish work on three-day, and we'll get back to casting on fourday." The smith handed Beltur a silver. "For now. The rest . . . I told you how that will go. I wish it didn't have to be this way, but I've always paid my debts."

"I know."

A few light snowflakes were still drifting lazily from the featureless gray clouds overhead as Beltur walked back toward Elparta along the snow-packed and ice-rutted road, his thoughts mostly on the Council proclamation. From what he could sense, almost absently, the clouds didn't hold the kind of order/chaos splitting and turmoil that signified a lot of rain or snow, for which he was grateful.

There were more people on the streets, especially on Bakers Lane near the bakery, but he didn't see anyone he knew. Then again, he really knew very few people in Elparta.

He was still mulling over what choices he had, or how few choices there really were, when he reached the house, and after taking off his coat and scarf, he walked into the kitchen.

"How did your day go?" asked Meldryn.

"The smithing went fine. Nothing else did. The Council proclaimed a new law that says any material made in part with magery must be sold through a trader and approved by the mage-councilor of the nearest city. Jorhan got a copy of the proclamation on sevenday."

Meldryn frowned. "I can't believe Cohndar would go that far."

"I don't think he had to. Trader Alizant has been telling people that he'll be the one trading in cupridium. He probably talked to Jhaldrak . . . and Cohndar. The proclamation states that the reason is to make certain goods made through magery do not include harmful chaos."

"That sounds very much like Cohndar. He's always been prating about the evils of chaos and white wizards."

"I thought as much. He was talking like that when he came to the smithy to complain that we weren't really forging cupridium."

"What is Jorhan going to do?"

"He's planning to leave Spidlar—after we forge all the cupridium we can in the next eightday or so. His sister lives in Axalt, and her consort has said he'll be welcome any time."

"He'd actually leave?" Meldryn sounded surprised. "His family has held those lands for generations."

Beltur explained about the lands and Johlana's son taking over.

"Why doesn't he just stay as a coppersmith? Or was he already having trouble?"

"He was in debt until we started forging cupridium. I think he's too much of a craftsman, and people in Elparta can't or won't pay for craft. Also, the traders here charge him too much for the copper. The last batch we got from Axalt cost less."

Meldryn nodded. "That's going to put you in a difficult position, isn't it?"

"In time. I've saved up enough silvers to get through the winter, and that includes paying you for food and lodging—"

"You don't have to do that."

"Yes, I do. Athaal isn't here to help, and you likely lost coins baking bread for the Council during the invasion. It just wouldn't be fair for me not to pay my share. I'm probably not even paying enough."

"You're paying more than enough."

Beltur was surprised to sense the absolute truth behind Meldryn's feelings, so surprised that he couldn't say anything for several moments.

"Athaal often didn't make as much as you're paying right now. So I don't want to hear any more about your not carrying your share."

"I'm sorry . . . I didn't know."

Meldryn laughed, sadly. "You wouldn't. We never told you. At first, it was because you weren't making anything to speak of, and we didn't want you to feel badly. Then, I didn't want to say anything to make Athaal feel badly . . . and . . . then . . . it didn't matter."

"I . . ." Beltur didn't know what to say. Finally, he managed, "You were both so kind. I don't know what I would have done without you both."

"You're being kind to Jessyla and to Lhadoraak and Tulya. That's what's important. We can't always control how many coins we earn. We can control how we behave toward others." Meldryn smiled. "You need an ale, and then we'll have dinner."

Beltur was more than ready for both.

XX

Beltur rose a glass earlier than normal on twoday and even then hurried to ready breakfast and call Meldryn to eat.

When the older mage hurried over from the bakery, he immediately said, "You're up early. Couldn't you sleep?"

"The worrying didn't help. That's not the reason, though. Jorhan wants a full day's work, but I promised Lhadoraak that I'd work with Taelya this afternoon. I told Lhadoraak I might be late, if I had to work, but I don't want it to be too late."

"You're trying to please everyone, aren't you?" Meldryn settled himself at the table and took a swallow of the hot cider. "I'm going to have to eat quickly."

"Go ahead. I didn't think about timing your baking. I'm not so much trying to please everyone as to get everything done while I can."

Meldryn swallowed a large bite of the breakfast hash, followed by a sip of cider, before saying, "You've always had to think ahead, haven't you?"

"Not always, and I never really had to worry about coins until I came to Elparta. Uncle worried about those, and sometimes I worried about Uncle and what I could do." *And complained silently when I had no reason to.* At least those complaints had been silent, reflected Beltur.

"Your uncle was quite a man, I think."

"More than I understood."

"What matters is that you understand now. Most young people don't understand. The problem is when they get older and still don't."

In what seemed like moments, Meldryn finished eating and hurried back to the bakery. Beltur quickly cleaned up the kitchen, washed up, finished dressing, and headed out the door. The day was clear and sunny, but the white sun seemed to provide only light and no warmth.

When Beltur entered the smithy and took off his coat and scarf, Jorhan looked up in surprise. "You're here more than a mite early, not that I mind that."

"I'm here early because I have to leave early, and I didn't want to shortchange you."

Jorhan laughed, almost harshly, shaking his head. "You'd be the last one who'd short me."

"I didn't think you'd be needing me quite so much, and I'd agreed to help someone with a problem this afternoon. I was so disconcerted by the Council proclamation that I didn't even think about that until after I left."

"Seeing you're more than a glass early, I think we'll manage."

"What are we casting today?"

"A sabre, two pair of candelabra . . . and another mirror—a small one—if we have time."

Beltur moved to the bellows. "Do you know when you're thinking about leaving?"

"That depends on how long the casting and finish work takes, and what the weather's like. I also want to look into getting another horse. I'll travel faster that way, and I can always sell a horse, especially in Axalt. Traders coming through are always looking for mounts."

"Do you have room for two horses in the barn?"

"Had four, once, years ago, when Menara and I were running sheep." Jorhan moved to the forge and picked up the crucible with his tongs.

Beltur began to work the bellows.

When he left at two quints before third glass, the two had indeed cast all Jorhan had planned, including the small hand mirror.

Beltur went down the stone lane, completely cleared of snow, at a fast walk, and he didn't slow down until he reached the north door of the Council building. There he stopped and took a deep breath, then stepped inside, where he saw a city patroller standing in front of Raymandyl's table desk. Since neither man had even looked in his direction, Beltur wrapped himself in a total concealment and eased as quietly as he could toward the clerk and the patroller, hoping he might hear something of importance.

"There you are . . . three silvers," offered the clerk.

"The bounty of the Council," said the patroller sardonically.

"It's better than the alternatives, especially with winter coming on."

"Barely enough for food, rent, and coal. Council hasn't raised pay in five years. Wasn't that good then, but it got worse when the Gallosians attacked. Everything costs more now."

"They haven't raised my pay, either," the clerk pointed out.

"Don't notice any traders suffering. They never do, but they can't pay a man a decent wage."

Beltur had the feeling that Raymandyl shrugged, but sensing under a concealment didn't reveal facial expressions or small body movements.

"Won't bother you more, Raymandyl." The patroller laughed. "Not till next eightday, anyway." He turned.

Beltur eased to the side, but the departing patroller didn't come close to him. He waited until the door closed and Raymandyl was bent over his desk before removing the concealment and stepping forward.

The clerk looked up, clearly surprised. "Beltur! I didn't hear you. You're much earlier today. Are you going to make a habit of it?"

"Most likely just today."

"Just my luck." The clerk shook his head, mock-mournfully. "Let me get the ledger. Any tokens?"

"Not today. The way things are going, there may not be any for the rest of my duty."

"There aren't many in winter." Raymandyl pushed the ledger across the desk.

Beltur took the pen, dipped it in the inkwell and signed his name, then watched as the clerk sealed the entry and then took a pair of silvers from the floor chest.

"Here you are."

"Thank you." Beltur slipped the silvers into his belt wallet, then said, "You know . . . last twoday, I mentioned the copper problem Jorhan was facing. I didn't really notice it at the time, but when I thought about it, you didn't say anything."

"Oh?"

"You always say something." Beltur smiled. "You know what I'm talking about. I think you already knew that the proclamation about goods made with magery was being worked on. Maybe the Council in Spidlaria had already sent something."

"How would I—"

"I imagine that sort of thing comes across your desk. Besides, you frowned, and you didn't say anything, and you usually do."

Raymandyl offered a rueful expression. "Can't keep much from mages, I suppose. Especially you. Laevoyt said it wasn't a good idea to try and hide things from you."

He did? "So when did Trader Alizant start talking to Jhaldrak?"

"I don't know. I really don't, and even if I did, it wouldn't be good if I said anything."

He's admitting it was Alizant without saying so. "It probably wouldn't, but it had to be a while ago if it was decided by the whole Council," Beltur pointed out. "How long does it take when Councilor Jhaldrak wants to bring something before the Council until there's a proclamation?"

"Sometimes, it doesn't happen. Not everything he wants gets approved."

"But if it does?" Beltur pressed.

"Never less than three-four eightdays." Raymandyl sighed, as if he wished the matter would disappear. "Not that I've seen, anyway."

That told Beltur enough. Whether it had been three eightdays or five, Alizant's plan had been in the works likely within days of Beltur's mentioning the value of cupridium to Zandyr. *And it never even crossed your mind that such a simple statement would come back to bite you. But how could you have known back then?*

Beltur just said, "Thank you. I'll see you in an eightday."

"If we don't get a northeaster." The clerk managed a faint smile.

"Then I'll see you later." Beltur offered a pleasant smile before making his way out.

Even hurrying as much as he could without actually running, which wouldn't have been wise since there were still patches of ice hidden in the shadows cast by the afternoon sun, Beltur didn't reach Lhadoraak's house until after half past third glass.

Tulya opened the door when he knocked.

"I'm sorry I'm later than I said," said Beltur. "I didn't know I'd have to work until late yesterday." That wasn't quite true, but he didn't feel like going into details.

"That's all right," replied Tulya. "Lhadoraak said that might happen. Come on in. Taelya's in the parlor. I'll be in the kitchen." She stepped back from the door.

Beltur entered and closed the door. "You can listen if you want, but I'd appreciate it if you'd stay out of sight."

"Thank you."

He took off his coat and scarf and hung them on a wall peg, then stepped into the parlor. "Good afternoon, Taelya."

"Good afternoon, ser."

As he seated himself in the straight-backed chair, Beltur carefully studied the girl, sensing that some of the free chaos around her was beginning to mix with her natural order barrier that separated her natural chaos from the free chaos. "Taelya . . . look at yourself. Look at where the whitish chaos is."

She immediately looked away.

Beltur waited.

After more than a few moments, she finally said, "It's work to keep them separated."

"Isn't everything work when you first begin?"

"Yes, ser."

"Reorder the levels the way I showed you."

"Is that all we're going to do . . . ser?"

"No. That's where we'll begin every time I come. Unless you've already done it before I arrive."

Beltur watched and sensed as she struggled, then said, "Use the order to separate the two kinds of chaos. Order stays together more easily."

"Moving the chaos is easier."

"Not if it doesn't stay where you want it."

"Is this really important?"

"It's more important than you have any idea," Beltur said firmly.

Not totally surprisingly to Beltur, once Taelya concentrated on order, she reestablished clear levels and separations.

"Good. Now, I'm going to see what you need to learn to develop shields. All good mages have good shields."

"I was hoping you'd show me how to do chaos bolts."

Beltur shook his head. "Shields have to come first. Shields are what you need to protect yourself if your chaos bolt comes back at you or if someone else throws a chaos bolt at you."

"Chaos bolts can come back?"

"Other mages can make them do that. Sometimes, storms can do that also." *If rarely.* "There are other important reasons for shields as well, but I can't show you why those reasons are important until you have the ability to form and hold some sort of shield."

Taelya frowned.

"I say some sort of shield because every mage I've known has shields that are different from every other mage. Sometimes, the differences aren't much. Sometimes, they're considerable." Beltur paused. "You know how to link bits of order together. You can make a shield by linking order and chaos together. I'm going to put together a simple shield right in front of you. I want you to watch closely with your eyes and senses."

What Beltur did was to create what amounted to a series of chains of free chaos, with the chains linked together by order. The shield was small, less than half a yard by half a yard.

"That won't protect anything," observed Taelya.

"No, it won't. But you have to figure out what kind of shield you can build, and it's a waste of time and effort to try to build a full shield until you know what works."

"That makes sense."

I'm so glad that it does, dear child. Beltur just nodded. "Now, you try to do what I did."

Taelya pushed together several stringy strands of chaos, with a few scattered order links, before the structure collapsed. "That's harder than it looks."

"It will likely take you at least several tries."

Beltur heard the front door open, but he also sensed a concealment and movement toward the kitchen, suggesting that Lhadoraak had returned. Taelya seemed not to notice as she tried again.

"This isn't working."

"Then don't try chains. Can you knit?" Beltur should have thought of that earlier, he realized.

"Of course."

"Then make one yarn out of order and the other out of free chaos and knit them together in a pattern you already know. That might work better for you. As I told you, each mage has to figure it out in a way that best suits them."

Beltur forced himself to observe—mostly—only occasionally giving suggestions.

After almost a glass, Taelya came up with a small shield. "I have one, and it's staying together."

"Good." Beltur could sense that. "Just hold it there. I'm going to push against it with order. Try to keep me from moving it toward you."

"I'll try." Taelya sounded doubtful.

"Holding it will be easier than making it was." Beltur offered the tiniest pressure, smiling as Taelya's shield held against it. He added a little more pressure, and pressed the small shield back. "Try a little harder."

"I'm trying."

Beltur could see perspiration on Taelya's forehead, and he released his pressure on her shield. "That was very good. You're doing well for having worked with this for so short a time. Now, the next thing you need to work on is building a shield that will surround you."

Taelya sighed, despairingly.

Beltur wanted to smile at the dramatics. "Not at this moment, but I want you to work at it once you're rested, and I want you to keep working at it."

Surprisingly, she said, "This is really important, isn't it?"

"Yes. Why do you think that?"

"You're not trying to make it fun."

"Later, when you're better with shields, we can try things that might be more enjoyable." Beltur stood, stretching a little as he realized he'd scarcely moved while working with Taelya. "Right now, you need to do something else."

"Are you done?" called Tulya.

"We're done," replied Beltur.

After several moments, both Lhadoraak and Tulya walked into the parlor.

"Father! When did you get home?"

"A little while ago. I didn't want to disturb your lesson with Beltur."

"Would you like a little something to eat?" Tulya asked her daughter.

"Could I, Mother?"

"You can indeed." Tulya smiled.

After the two left the parlor, Lhadoraak looked at Beltur. "You actually had her working on the beginnings of shields. I can't believe it."

"She'll need them." *Especially here in Elparta.*

"How did you do it?"

"I just made suggestions until we found something that worked."

"When will you come again?"

"I could come for a little while on fourday, but it would have to be close to half past four."

"We can do that." Lhadoraak paused. "I still worry about Cohndar finding out she's going to be a white."

"Lhadoraak," Beltur said gently, "she's already a white. Just try to keep her away from other mages for a while."

"You think there's a way?" Hope filled the other's face.

While Beltur did have something in mind, he shook his head. "She's a white. If we can train her early and well, she might be able to handle her talents well enough that they won't discover her too soon. She's also younger than when this much ability usually shows up. That may help." Before Lhadoraak could ask another question, he added, "They really don't believe there are whites here in Elparta."

"That's true . . ."

"I need to get back to the bakery. I'll see you—or Tulya—on fourday." Beltur moved toward the front hall.

"You have to understand," said Lhadoraak, as he walked beside Beltur. "Taelya's our only child."

Beltur not only heard, but felt, Lhadoraak's anguish. "I think I do. Remember, I'm an only child who lost everyone. I'm doing my best."

"I know you are, but . . . she's . . ."

She's all you have. "I know," said Beltur as he donned his coat and wrapped the scarf around his face and ears. "I'll be here on fourday. Remind Taelya, every so often, if you would, to use order to separate her natural order from the free chaos she attracts. She needs to make that a habit, one that happens without her even thinking about it."

"Is that . . . ?"

"That way, she'll not only live longer, but it will reinforce the patterns for her to hold shields, much earlier than most mages learn to do it." *Certainly far earlier than I learned it.*

"You've really thought this through."

"I've tried." Beltur opened the door. "Until fourday."

As he left Lhadoraak and walked through the cold air of late, late afternoon, glancing to the north where more clouds were appearing, Beltur couldn't help worrying that troubles seemed to be coming, not only at him, but at those around him—Jorhan, Jessyla, Lhadoraak and Tulya, and indirectly at Meldryn and Margrena. And besides earning as much as he could, learning more about healing, and helping Taelya to master her abilities, he didn't know what else he could do, much as he feared that he wasn't doing enough. *Not nearly enough.*

XXI

When Beltur headed out for City Patrol duty on threeday, the snow was ankle-deep and falling fast with large flakes that clung to everything, but the snow was definitely warmer and didn't crunch or squeak under his boots.

As was often the case, Laevoyt was waiting for Beltur in the duty room. Neither spoke until they left headquarters and were walking east on Patrol Street toward the market square.

"This is quite a snow," Beltur offered.

"It won't last more than a few glasses. The flakes are big and soft. That kind never lasts. By afternoon, or maybe even sooner, it'll likely be sunny and warmer than it's been in several eightdays."

"I'll take your word for it, but it doesn't seem like it'll blow over that soon." Beltur brushed more snow off his scarf and visor cap.

"You'll see. That's why we're headed to the square and not along River Street."

Beltur nodded and brushed away more snow.

When they reached the market square, the workhouse crews were shoveling off the northwest corner, seemingly barely keeping ahead of the snow, yet by a little before eighth glass, the snow had dwindled to intermittent flakes, and shortly after the chimes struck the glass, the sun appeared. There were more vendors and shoppers than Beltur had seen in some time, even one table that held rings and jewels, but Beltur had the feeling that table was there more to buy than sell, no doubt profiting off those feeling short of silvers.

By half past the glass, Beltur had unwound his scarf because he was getting too warm, and by ninth glass he walked to the corner to meet Laevoyt with his heavy coat open. The stones that had been shoveled clear were already beginning to dry under a sun that had not felt so warm in more than two eightdays.

Laevoyt, his heavy patroller's coat open, grinned at Beltur, but said not a word.

"You were right," offered Beltur. "How long will it stay this warm?"

"At least a day or two, and then it will get colder, but it usually doesn't snow for almost an eightday after one of these warm-ups." Laevoyt's voice turned more serious. "For the next glass or so, keep your eyes open. If there are any lifters at all, it'll be now."

"That makes sense. There's more than produce and woolens for sale today."

"This eightday might be the last for a while."

Keeping the patroller's advice in mind, Beltur left Laevoyt and made his way across the carts and stalls near Patrol Street to the point more than halfway across the square where snow was still piled before slipping into a concealment and moving back westward across the produce carts. He briefly sensed a flash of transitory chaos, but there was only that hint of possible trouble for the next few quints.

Just after the ten strokes of midday rang out on the chimes, Beltur felt a definite quick wash of chaos from near the table that was both selling and buying small items of jewelry. He immediately moved, still under a concealment, toward the site of the chaos. Unlike the chaos associated with lifters and cutpurses, that which he'd sensed didn't flicker, but remained around one figure standing several paces back, that of a woman, but there were two figures close together. Belatedly, Beltur realized that he was sensing a woman holding a child, and he released the concealment.

The woman seemed to be looking at a table set to one side of the jewelry vendor and did not even see him appear, although the vendor at the jewelry table offered a surprised expression.

As he moved closer, Beltur could see that the young woman was looking at the few remaining acorn cakes set on the other table. He could also sense a swirling of chaos, chaos that was something else. *More like despair.*

He turned directly toward the young woman. While he was certainly no expert on infants, he thought the child, wrapped in a small but heavy blanket that had been patched more than a few times, with only its face visible, was likely less than three seasons old. The mother wore a thin and worn cloak, and while the day was far warmer than most had been recently, Beltur doubted that the cloak provided enough warmth. Her face was thin, dark circles under slightly reddened eyes.

"Have you eaten much lately?" he asked gently.

She shuddered, as if she hadn't even noticed him approach, and her eyes widened as she took in his visor cap and medallion. "I haven't done anything, ser."

"I know that," Beltur replied. "I asked if you'd eaten lately. Please don't lie to me."

Her eyes dropped. "No, ser."

Beltur looked at the acorn cake seller. "Are the cakes still three for a copper?"

"Two coppers for five, ser."

Beltur eased two coppers from his belt wallet and handed them to the vendor. "These are for her." As the vendor wrapped the cakes in a thin paper, Beltur noticed that there were six cakes in the stack, and he murmured, "Thank you."

"Thank you, ser," replied the older woman.

Beltur handed the cakes to the young woman, who looked at him unbelievingly. "Please find some shelter and eat."

Tears seeped from the corners of her eyes as she took the package one-handed. "We . . . we've been so hungry . . ."

"I could tell."

"Thank you, ser." Then she turned and hurried off, almost as if fleeing and believing that the small stack of acorn cakes would vanish if she remained.

"She's been standing here, looking for almost a quint," the vendor said. "I thought she might faint."

"You were kind to add an extra," Beltur said.

"You could tell she wasn't a thief, couldn't you?"

Beltur nodded. "She's the kind who can't even beg." *At least not with words.* He offered a smile to the vendor and moved on, wondering about mother and child, but he never caught another glimpse of them for the rest of the time he patrolled the square.

He was still thinking about her, and the chaos of desperation that had surrounded her, even after he'd signed out and as he walked through the afternoon light along Bakers Lane, back toward the house. He hadn't told Laevoyt what he'd done, and he wasn't sure he wanted to tell anyone, because he wondered if he'd done too little, even as he considered that he couldn't keep feeding and supporting the young woman. And, if he told anyone, that wouldn't really be right, either, because, in a way, he'd be boasting. No . . . it was better to leave the strange encounter unmentioned.

Once he reached the house, he had barely stepped inside when Meldryn appeared in the archway leading to the parlor.

"The mage-councilor's here to see us," said Meldryn, adding in a much lower voice, "You mostly, I'd guess."

"Did he say why?" murmured Beltur.

Meldryn shook his head.

When Meldryn and Beltur returned to the parlor, Cohndar did not rise from the padded bench where he sat, but inclined his head in a perfunctory manner to Beltur. "As Meldryn might have told you, Beltur, I'm visiting all the blacks in Elparta. One reason for this is to tell you that the Council has passed a proclamation establishing a mage council in each of the three largest cities in Spidlar. I'm particularly pleased about this because I've been working for a long time to better the conditions for all blacks. The second reason is that the Council has issued a proclamation changing the laws affecting trade and magery."

Meldryn sat in his favorite chair, saying nothing, while Beltur took the straight-backed chair, turned it to face Cohndar, and seated himself. "Changing the laws affecting magery? I have to admit I didn't know that there were any laws, except the ones requiring mages to serve with the City Patrol."

"That was in fact the only one directly affecting only mages," replied Cohndar smoothly, "but, as you know, the attempted invasion by the Prefect of Gallos and his white wizards greatly alarmed the Council. As a result, the councilors decided that certain changes needed to be made to assure that Spidlaria, and particularly Elparta, remain free of the white influence and that chaos is kept away, chaos in all forms, not just that employed by white wizards in the field."

Beltur managed a concerned frown, not difficult because he was concerned, if not in precisely the fashion in which he hoped Cohndar would interpret the expression. "I wasn't aware that there has been any difficulty with chaos in Elparta. Is this something that has happened elsewhere in Spidlar?"

"I can't speak to that, only to the action that the Council has taken."

More like won't speak to it.

"What is this action that the Council has taken?" asked Meldryn.

"I'm glad you asked." Cohndar smiled. "The Council has issued a proclamation that requires all goods manufactured using magery to be sold to users through a trader. The trader is required to have such items inspected by a representative of the Mages' Council to make certain that no harmful chaos is in those items. The proclamation applies to all goods sold in Spidlar on or after the first day of Winter."

"Manufactured using magery?" Meldryn said musingly. "I certainly don't use magery in baking bread, pies, or pastries."

"Your baked goods wouldn't be covered by that proclamation," replied Cohndar, turning his head toward Beltur. "It's aimed more at objects made of metal, possibly wood, other more . . . tangible . . . items that could easily incorporate chaos without anyone except a mage being any the wiser."

Beltur managed a nod, before saying, "I can see the concern. I don't think anyone would like uncontained chaos floating around, and I can see the possible need for inspection by knowledgeable mages. What I don't understand is why the Council required the items to be sold to users by a trader."

"You'd have to take that up with the Council, Beltur. I'm certainly not privy as to why the councilors decide how they want something accomplished. I can only surmise that they felt that doing it that way would be more certain."

"It does make some things more certain," said Meldryn, "like sending the word that the Council has the power to restrict who can sell what to whom. That seems to me to be a disturbing precedent."

Cohndar shrugged. "As we know, the Council will do what the

Council will do. It always has. Anyway, as I said earlier, I'm just the messenger. I didn't make the new law. I just want to make certain that all the blacks in Elparta are aware of it." He smiled faintly. "Sometimes, tradesmen have a habit of not passing on what they know."

"I suppose that's possible," said Beltur flatly. "Even mages have been known not to do that."

Cohndar stiffened just slightly, then added, "You should also know that the penalty for failing to comply is ten golds per item, in addition to a fifty-gold penalty."

"That seems rather steep," observed Meldryn. "Most crafters don't have that many golds. Certainly, most mages don't."

"Then the crafter or the mage would have to be indentured until the fines are paid."

"Most would likely leave Elparta before submitting to that."

"Trying to evade a significant indenture can require execution," Cohndar said mildly. "Surely, you should be aware of that, Meldryn."

"That's never been invoked in years."

"Only because people are sensible." Cohndar rose, smiling cheerfully. "That's all I came to do, and I must be heading out to finish informing others."

"We certainly wouldn't want to keep you," said Meldryn politely, also standing. "I'll see you out."

Beltur stood, but did not accompany the two to the entry foyer. He just waited until he heard the front door close and Meldryn returned to the parlor before asking, "What do you think?"

"He didn't come up with the idea, but he certainly came up with the idea of the Mages' Council gaining control over what magery can and cannot be used for."

"He's looking more and more like the black version of Wyath," said Beltur. "Especially when he suggested that if I tried to avoid the proclamation, I'd face indentured slavery or a death sentence. Waensyn must really hate me."

"A season ago, I would have disputed that, but not now. He's also thinking about gaining more power. Did you catch his implied threat? He said my baked goods wouldn't be covered by *that* proclamation."

"Suggesting that he could get such a proclamation if you cause him trouble."

"That's the way I heard it. I knew he was slimy, but this . . ." The gray-bearded mage shook his head.

"Part of it has to be Waensyn's influence."

"That may be, but Cohndar doesn't have to take bad advice."

Beltur had to agree with that. "I don't see anyone except Lhadoraak taking exception to the proclamation."

"Oh, there will be a few others, but they won't speak up. They never do, and some like Caradyn and Osarus have been wanting a mages' group with power for years."

"I can see that mages need more power," said Beltur, "but it seems like every time someone sets up something like it, it immediately gets used for something that's not particularly good."

"That's because the people who want power the most are the ones who should be granted it the least." Meldryn snorted. "We might as well have dinner. I need to get the taste of slime out of my mouth."

Beltur nodded and accompanied Meldryn to the kitchen. *Slavery or death for wanting to sell cupridium without going through a trader?*

XXII

On fourday morning, Beltur was at the smithy well before seventh glass.

"Thought you might come early," called out Jorhan as Beltur hung his coat on the wall peg. "I'm already heating the mold for a sabre. After that, we'll move on to daggers."

Beltur walked toward the forge. "We had a visitor yesterday afternoon. Cohndar. You might recall him. He was the one who came here with Councilor Jhaldrak."

"Sleazy type, as I recall. What did he want?"

"He's now the representative of the Mages' Council, and he wanted to make clear everything in the proclamation you showed me twoday."

"Between him and that Trader Alizant, seems like they want to squeeze every copper from us."

Beltur shook his head. "Alizant wants us to forge cupridium. He'll offer a deal, more than you'd make as a coppersmith but a lot less than you're making now. Cohndar doesn't want me to make anything. He even said I'd get indentured slavery if I didn't comply."

"This have anything to do with your healer girl?"

"Just about everything." Beltur went on to explain about Waensyn.

When Beltur had finished, the smith shook his head. "World'd be a better place without some folks."

"I'm beginning to agree with you."

"Won't change anything. I've got the sledge almost ready. Hontyl's looking for a likely mount for me. Says he's going to be looking at a new lot. Want me to have him look for you?"

"Right now . . . I don't feel I can leave."

"Take her with you."

If it were only that easy. "There's her mother, and her aunt, and they're not ready for us to consort, and taking her without their permission . . ." Beltur shook his head. "When do you think you'll be leaving?"

"I'd like to leave now, but we've got another four or five days of casting, and it'll take that much time for all the fullering, hardening, polishing, and finishing . . . maybe more." Jorhan paused. "Any time you want to change your mind, you're welcome to come with me . . . and bring your healer."

"I appreciate the offer. I wish I could take you up on it." Beltur managed a smile. "We'd better get to work. I wouldn't want to be the one delaying you."

All through the day, Beltur tried to keep his mind on the work at hand. He managed that, for the most part, except when he stopped to eat his loaf or drink some of Jorhan's ale, and then his thoughts turned to Jessyla . . . and how Cohndar and Waensyn had done so much to complicate both his life and Jessyla's. Then he forced himself back to work.

At half past third glass, Beltur left the smithy, with another silver in his wallet, walking quickly. The afternoon was pleasant by comparison to the weather of the past two eightdays, although Beltur certainly wouldn't have called it that a year earlier. *So very much has changed.*

After he passed through the southeast city gate, he took the east wall street to Crossed Lane and turned west. Before that long he was knocking on Lhadoraak's door.

The mage opened it. "I thought it might be you." Lhadoraak stepped back to allow Beltur inside, then closed the door behind him.

"Did Cohndar come and visit you?" Beltur stripped off his coat and scarf.

"He did, but Tulya kept Taelya upstairs," replied Lhadoraak. "She just told her that we were talking black mage matters and that the two of them needed to stay away. So far as I could tell, there wasn't any free chaos in the parlor. Taelya's been following your advice."

"That's good." Beltur breathed a little more easily, but he still worried. "Until yesterday, I had no idea he'd be visiting all the blacks."

"Why did he bother?" Lhadoraak frowned. "None of us—"

"Except me," replied Beltur wryly. "Trader Alizant wants to get a big cut out of what Jorhan and I are forging, and that fit right in with what Cohndar and Waensyn want."

"But how?" After only a moment, Lhadoraak's mouth opened. "I can't believe . . . he'd really do that? Just to . . ."

"To keep me coinless and make Waensyn seem like a better match for Jessyla? It appears that would be one of the results of the Council's action. I can't believe he didn't know that from the beginning, since he was the one who pushed Jhaldrak into visiting Jorhan's smithy to see if we were really forging cupridium."

"He did that?"

"Before the invasion." Beltur was surprised that Lhadoraak didn't know, but, upon reflection, he realized that there was no reason the other mage would have known. "Didn't he also talk some about the need to keep chaos at bay?"

"He's always talked about that. He's been repeating that for years. That wasn't new."

"You didn't know Taelya was a white, then."

"You don't think he'd really exile her? Does he know about her, do you think?"

"No. If he did, he would have been more direct, now that he has the Council and all the traders behind him. But he did take a dig at Meldryn. He pointed out that the *present* proclamation wouldn't affect Meldryn's bakery."

"Cohndar said that?"

"Almost word for word."

Lhadoraak shook his head. "I don't like the way this is going. Not at all."

You don't like it? How do you think I feel? "I don't either, but I can't think of a way around it at the moment." *Except leaving Elparta and doing that with winter coming on isn't exactly something I'd want to try, especially if it means leaving Jessyla to Waensyn's slimy hands.* "It's even more important that I work with Taelya now."

Lhadoraak nodded, then raised his voice. "Taelya, it's time for your work with Beltur." He turned back to Beltur. "I need to talk this over with Tulya while you're working with Taelya."

"It would be good to know what she thinks." *For several reasons.*

Lhadoraak nodded, then turned and smiled as Taelya came down the narrow staircase.

Beltur studied her, then said, "Much better. You've kept the two kinds of chaos separated." Then he grinned. "Did you just do that, or have you been doing it all along?"

Taelya offered an embarrassed smile. "Ah . . . I just did. But I have been doing it at times every day."

Beltur could sense the truth of her words. "That's good. It's gotten easier, hasn't it?"

"Yes, ser."

He motioned toward the parlor, then followed her. She sat on the bench, and he took the same straight-backed chair he'd used before, positioning it to face her before sitting down. "We're going to work more on shields today."

"I've been practicing shields. I can hold a much larger one now."

"Let me see."

Taelya scrunched up her face slightly, concentrating, and presented a circular "knitted" shield almost three yards across.

"Why did you make it a circle?" asked Beltur.

"Because I could tie the loose strands of order and chaos together better that way. Mother gave me the idea. I asked her about how she did it with knitting. I thought I knew, but she helped."

"I'm going to put pressure on it again, and we'll see how strong you've made it."

"I'm ready."

Beltur created a probe, really a narrow shield containment, and first pressed it against the center of the shield, then probed various parts. While he could have broken through her shield, what was important was that the shield was equally strong everywhere, and that impressed him. "You've done a good job there. Now, I want you to try making a slightly different kind of shield."

"Isn't mine good enough?"

"It's the best one I've ever seen from someone as young as you are, and better than some of the older mages." Only one, but Taelya didn't have to know that. "But we need to look at different ways of making shields so that you learn how to make and hold the strongest shield you possibly can. Just like different yards and yarn patterns in knitting have different strengths." Beltur hoped that was so. He'd observed very little knitting.

"There are some that are stronger. Most are about the same."

"That's true of shields as well, but you're going to need the strongest shield you can hold."

"Because I'm a white?"

"Yes. Anyone who's different needs to be as good as they can be."

"Father says you're like that."

He did? "I think that's why he and your mother decided I might be able to help you."

"He said that, too."

"I want you to make a small shield, about the size of the one you did on twoday. Then I'll tell you what I want you to try."

Beltur waited until Taelya had a small circular shield, one invisible to the eye, but very present to his senses, then said, "I'd like you to try to make a special knot where the order and chaos threads cross, with chaos in the center, surrounded by order."

"That sounds hard."

"Most things that are strong take more effort and skill."

Even with Beltur's help and suggestions, it took almost two quints before Taelya could create the first knot, and by the time she did, he was wondering if he'd asked too much.

"There!"

Beltur smiled. "I'm going to probe it."

The order/chaos knot held, even against more pressure than Beltur had used before.

"I can feel that. It hurts a little."

Beltur released the pressure. "That's what it feels like when your shields aren't quite strong enough and another mage or an arrow or a sword hits them. It's very good that you can sense that, though. And your knot is much stronger than the rest of your shield. If you work on putting more of those knots in your shields, they'll be much stronger."

Beltur could see and sense that Taelya was getting tired. "You can let go now."

She released the shield and took a deep breath.

"You're doing very well," Beltur said. "I think that's enough for this afternoon. But if you keep practicing the way you have been, you'll be able to shield yourself on all sides before too long."

"How long is before too long?"

Beltur grinned. "All I'll say is that you'll have good shields at a much younger age than I did."

"Or I did," added Lhadoraak as he stepped into the parlor, adding, "I heard you say that you were through for the afternoon." He turned to his daughter. "You need to eat. Your mother has something for you in the kitchen."

Once Taelya was well away, Lhadoraak looked at Beltur. "You're either very good, or she comes by magery naturally."

"I had to learn it all the hard way," replied Beltur. "A lot of things I tried didn't work. So I have an idea of what's more likely to work. But she has strong natural abilities, and it's a good thing we're working with her. She's strong enough to burn herself out young by using too much chaos. That's why she needs to keep the free chaos separate."

"I've never heard about doing that before. Is that something you were taught in Fenard?"

"No. I wasn't taught it. I learned that from observing, and I observed a lot, because I was terrible at handling chaos in the way most whites did. That was because I was always a black and didn't know it."

"We're fortunate you were."

"So am I."

Lhadoraak moistened his lips, then finally said, "Tulya thinks we should think about moving to Suthya in the spring."

"She does? Why not Axalt? It's closer."

"It's too close, and it's even colder than Elparta. Besides, we could go by flatboat to Spidlaria, and then by ship to Armat. If Suthya doesn't work out . . . well, it's not too far to Sarronnyn. Maybe you should think about coming with us."

"I've thought about leaving, but . . ."

"There's Jessyla," said Lhadoraak.

Beltur nodded. "Whether she'll agree to consort me or not, I can't leave her here. Not with Waensyn scheming to get her. And Cohndar backing him."

"Have you asked her? Or at least talked to her?"

"I haven't had a chance. This all came up so quickly."

"I'd suggest you go from here to Grenara's and talk to both Jessyla and her mother." Lhadoraak gestured toward the front door.

"Late on sixday?" asked Beltur.

"We'll be here. So will Taelya."

Seemingly in moments, Beltur was outside and walking toward the healers' house.

Margrena was the one who opened the door when he reached Grenara's. "Beltur?"

"I have some news, and I need to talk to both you and Jessyla, preferably not with Grenara in earshot."

"Grenara's resting upstairs. Come on in. I'll get Jessyla."

By the time Beltur had his coat and scarf off, Margrena and Jessyla were in the front room, sitting on the bench. Beltur took the straight-backed chair. "Cohndar came to see Meldryn and me late yesterday afternoon. He's visiting all the blacks in Elparta personally to tell them about a new Council proclamation. Have you heard about it?"

"No." Margrena frowned.

"The Council has decreed that, in the interests of combating chaos, anything that is made through the use of magery must be sold through a trader, and that trader must obtain the approval of the Mage-Councilor of Elparta that the item contains no harmful chaos." Beltur waited.

After a moment, Jessyla spoke. "That's about cupridium, isn't it? What does that mean for you?"

"It means a lot of things. First, anything Jorhan and I forge will have to be sold through a trader . . ." Beltur went on to explain everything, including Jorhan's decision to leave Elparta and Cohndar's emphasis on indentured slavery.

"Cohndar's a sick old man," declared Jessyla. "Especially to say that." She paused. "What does this Trader Alizant have against you?"

"He doesn't have anything against me. He just sees a way to make more silvers. That means we'll make less, or we would if Jorhan stayed here, but he's had enough. The other thing is that Cohndar and probably Waensyn have decided to use this as a way to gain greater control over the blacks here in Elparta. Last night, he even said that, at present, Meldryn's bread and pastries didn't require approval of the Mages' Council."

"A veiled threat," said Margrena.

"He also talked a lot about keeping chaos at bay . . . and Lhadoraak's daughter Taelya is definitely a white. She looks as though she might be a very strong white. Lhadoraak and Tulya are very worried."

"They should be," declared Margrena.

"What about you?" asked Jessyla. "What are you going to do?"

"I've saved enough to live on for a while."

"That's not a decision," said Jessyla.

Beltur looked directly at her. "I have a problem, and you know very well what it happens to be."

"You're making me the problem?"

Beltur sighed. "No. The problem is mine. It's going to be hard to make a living here in Elparta, especially with Cohndar and Waensyn trying to make it more and more difficult. At the same time, I don't want to leave you."

Jessyla looked to her mother. "We should just get consorted and move to Axalt."

"You don't have to decide that this moment," replied Margrena. "We need to think this over." She turned to Beltur. "I know you can tell who's trustworthy, but do you know anyone in Axalt besides Jorhan and this merchant?"

"I don't, and that's part of the problem as well. I just didn't want you both surprised, because everyone will likely know about the proclamation in a few days. I probably should have told you earlier. I'd heard some rumors about what the trader was trying, but until the proclamation came out . . . there wasn't anything solid."

Margrena nodded. "Now we know, and we'll have to think about it."

"You're not to tell Auntie," said Jessyla firmly. "If you do, I'll leave."

"You're too young to consort."

"Most girls my age are already consorted. That wasn't what I meant. I could live at the Council Healing House, just like Saendya does."

"That's no life for a young woman."

"That's your choice," countered Jessyla.

"She'll find out before long, within days. Waensyn or Cohndar will tell her," pointed out Margrena.

"That's the way she should find out."

Margrena looked to Beltur. "You're not saying anything. Why not?"

"Because I don't want to be the cause of a rift between you two, or between Jessyla and me, or between you and me."

Both women looked at Beltur, the same annoyed expression on each face.

"What is that supposed to mean?" demanded Jessyla.

"I love you. That means I want the best for you. It's not the best for you if you're living in miserable conditions. It's not the best for you if you and your mother are at odds. I don't believe it's best for you if you're forced into consorting anyone before you want to, me or anyone else, but certainly not Waensyn. It's not best for your mother or you if she's at odds with her sister."

"That's just an excuse for not deciding," declared Jessyla.

"That may be," said Margrena, "but he's right. Think about it. Think about where Beltur was after his uncle was killed."

"He was with us."

"No. Before that. He couldn't go home. He had no family left to turn to. Life is hard enough. Life without friends and family is even harder." Margrena's voice softened. "Your aunt understands that. When her consort died, she had no one."

"She had you."

"I was a country away, and you'd just been born. As I've told you, I couldn't leave Fenard then."

Beltur had the definite feeling that was not a matter for him to ask about, at least not at the moment.

"You don't want us to leave her now, do you?"

"You and Beltur may have to leave, but you shouldn't rush it, especially with winter coming on."

Jessyla's expression softened. "You mean that, don't you?"

Margrena nodded.

"Can I be the one to tell Auntie, then?"

"You may. I reserve the right to add anything you leave out." Margrena turned to Beltur. "You could stay for supper."

The way the invitation was phrased, Beltur knew what his response needed to be. "Thank you. You're very kind, but I didn't tell Meldryn about the latest with Taelya and Jorhan, and I'm going to be much later than he expects as it is."

"You'll come on eightday . . . or sooner?" asked Jessyla.

"I will."

"Good." She stepped forward and hugged him tightly, murmuring in his ear, "I'm so glad now."

"So am I," he murmured back, even if he hadn't expected to get an answer from Margrena in the way they had.

All too soon, Beltur was back out in the cold, although it was warmer than most evenings had been for some time.

He did hurry, but as soon as he entered the house, Meldryn was halfway to the door even before Beltur had his coat off.

"I was a bit concerned. You're late," said Meldryn. "What happened?"

"It took a while at Lhadoraak's. I'm working on shields with Taelya. She's definitely got more ability with chaos, but I'm getting her to use order to keep free chaos from her as much as possible."

"Doesn't that restrict her?"

Beltur shook his head. "She can still use chaos, but the order makes her stronger. Also, using order and chaos that way won't make her as vulnerable to order attacks. Her shields are stronger than mine were at her age."

"That's because you're teaching her."

"Athaal could have done it."

Meldryn shook his head. "He didn't have the experience with chaos that you have."

"Jorhan's more determined than ever to leave as soon as he can. Lhadoraak's worried about Cohndar, especially about his wanting to keep chaos at bay. He's thinking they'll have to leave Spidlar, possibly for Suthya in the spring."

"He should worry. So should you."

"Then I went to talk to Jessyla and Margrena."

"You should have done that earlier."

"I know, but I told them that Cohndar had visited us last night, and I had to work today."

"That's true, if not the whole truth. We need to eat before things dry up in the hearth oven. You can tell me the rest while we eat."

"There's a lot to tell."

"You'll manage."

Beltur smiled at Meldryn's dry tone, and followed the older mage down the hall and into the kitchen.

XXIII

Fiveday dawned clear and seemingly colder than fourday—or at least Beltur thought his room was colder as he washed up, shaved, and dressed. He heard a pounding on the door as he came downstairs to fix breakfast, but by the time he'd reached the bottom of the stairs, Meldryn was opening the door to Laranya, who held a still figure in her arms.

Spots of ice dotted the front of her thin and shabby coat, and for a moment Beltur puzzled over the ice spots, until he saw Laranya's reddened eyes, and he realized that the ice spots were tears that had frozen to her coat. Meldryn had already taken Nykail from his mother and carried him toward the parlor.

"Nykail . . . he barely moves. Only you can help. Do something, please," pleaded Laranya as Meldryn eased the frail-looking figure onto the padded bench in the parlor, stretching him out on his back.

"When did this happen?" asked Meldryn.

"He has been weak for the last eightday. He has always been weak when it is cold and the snow falls. But not like this." Laranya stood on one side of the bench, her eyes darting from Meldryn to Nykail and back again.

Beltur let his senses range over the boy. *It's almost like Taelya.* That was his first thought, but the more he studied Nykail, the more he saw that, unlike order compressing chaos, in the boy's case, somehow order knots or lattices were tied together throughout Nykail's body, and those linkages were compressing both natural order and natural chaos.

Meldryn looked to Beltur, questioningly.

"I can try."

Meldryn turned to Laranya. "Beltur has been working with the healers. He is both a healer and a mage."

"Do what you can," pleaded the distraught mother.

Beltur moved the straight-backed chair next to Nykail, then looked to Meldryn. "I'll need some ale."

Meldryn nodded.

"Ale?" asked Laranya. "Ale will not help."

"The ale is for Beltur," said Meldryn. "He hasn't eaten this morning, and it will help him."

Beltur continued to trace the links and connections of the dark web, both marveling and being appalled at how deadly too much order could be within the body, while at the same time wondering what had caused the linkages to form in the first place. He was still studying the order bindings when Meldryn returned, holding a mug and a chunk of bread.

"Here you are."

Beltur ate the bread and drank about half the ale before setting the mug on the side table. Then he gently probed one of the larger knots of order. *More order isn't going to help.* After several moments, he eased the smallest bit of free chaos into the knot. Part, but not all, of the knot dissolved. He added a bit more, and the knot vanished. The problem was that there were close to a score of the large knots, and scores more of the smaller ones. Beltur really didn't like using chaos inside someone's body, and attacking the small ones would require less free chaos. *But the big order knots are the problem . . . and if you work on them . . . that isn't going to be easy on Nykail.*

But if he didn't . . .

Beltur took a long and deep breath and concentrated on the next large order knot or node.

After he'd eliminated almost half the knots, he could sense that Nykail was warmer, and he couldn't help but wonder about that. Unfortunately, the order strings linking the smaller knots to the remaining large knots still remained. That meant he had to do more or what he'd already done wouldn't be enough, because Nykail's natural chaos level was still far too low.

Even before he dissolved the last of the large order knots, the order strings linking them to the smaller knots were vanishing. His eyes were burning when he finally looked up, realizing that Nykail was warming up all too quickly.

"What did you do? He's burning up! He's burning up!"

Beltur did not answer, struggling as he was to keep the boy's natural chaos, so long repressed, from overreacting and turning into a truly killing fever.

"Sometimes a fever is good for a short time," said Meldryn. "Haven't you said that all too often Nykail was so cold you feared for his life?"

"But he's burning."

"Cold cloths will help," Beltur said abruptly. "If we can get him through the next quint, he'll be much, much better."

Meldryn hurried off, returning with damp cold cloths almost instantly.

All in all, it took more than a few applications of those cold cloths, especially on Nykail's head and wrists, over almost two quints before the boy's fever began to subside. Another quint passed before the boy stirred, and then struggled into a sitting position.

"He's going to be weak for a while," Beltur said.

"I'm . . . thirsty." Nykail looked at his mother.

Meldryn hurried off again, returning with a mug of water.

Beltur just sat there, exhausted.

The boy drained the mug.

Beltur could already sense a better balance between Nykail's order and chaos. He reached out and took the mug of ale, finishing it off in two quick swallows.

"I think Nykail should stay here with you today," said Meldryn. "Beltur needs to go to work, and there's not much else he can do." He looked at Beltur. "Is there?"

Beltur shook his head. He had the definite feeling he'd done all he should have. He just hoped he hadn't done too much.

"Go get something more to eat, and then be on your way."

"Have you eaten?" Laranya asked Meldryn.

"Ah . . ."

"Both of you go eat. I will stay here with Nykail."

Once the two men were in the kitchen, seated at the table and eating, Meldryn looked to Beltur and asked in a low voice, "Do you want to explain?"

"He was literally order-bound," said Beltur quietly. "It was a little like what happened with Taelya, but with Nykail, all the extra order was choking off his natural chaos."

"Will it happen again?"

"I don't know. I've never seen or sensed anything like it."

"I couldn't sense any of that, just that there was too much order everywhere within him. Athaal said you could sense order and chaos in the tiniest increments."

"I don't know about that. I do seem to be able to sense either in smaller bits than many mages can."

"Than most, I suspect."

"I'm sorry to leave you with all this."

"Laranya will be here anyway. She can clean it up in between watching Nykail. He'll likely sleep some, and I'd like him nearby for a while in any event."

With that reassurance, Beltur finished dressing and hurried off, under another clear sky, although, as he'd suspected, the air was colder than it had been on fourday. Surprisingly, at least to Beltur, it was only a little past the half glass when he reached the smithy and stepped inside.

"I'm sorry I'm a little late. I had to do some healing. I can work later, though." Beltur had his coat and scarf off in moments and hurried toward the forge.

Jorhan nodded. "Didn't know you were a healer."

"I got pressed into doing some healing when I was a mage-officer, and I've been working on that when I've had free time. I've been doing some healing at the Council Healing House. There was a boy. He was close . . . he was very ill. I think I was able to get him on the way to being much better."

The smith offered a sad smile. "You do too much for too many people, Beltur, and before long, none of 'em will be easy around you, especially as young as you are."

"I don't think many will ever hear about this child."

"Things always get around, sooner or later. If you're fortunate, it's later." Jorhan picked up the crucible with the tongs and nodded.

Beltur moved to the bellows. "What's first?"

"A long dagger. Then a platter."

By half past fourth glass, Jorhan insisted that Beltur had done more than enough and that he needed time to do more finishing work on some of the pieces cast earlier.

"How long before you'll be ready to leave?" asked Beltur, with some trepidation, after taking his daily silver.

"Hard to say. Hontyl's still looking for a horse for me. Looks like we'll be able to finish off the copper and the casting by next oneday, maybe twoday. I figure I'll need to be in Axalt before the first day of Winter, just to be safe. Be my luck not to make it and run afoul of Council guards outside of Axalt."

"You think they'd send guards after you?"

"They might, and they might not, but there's not much point in tempting fate or the Rational Stars. In bad weather, it could take close to an eightday to get there. I've talked to some outland traders. Two are leaving on twoday, threeday at the latest. One's from Tyrhavven and the other from Vergren. They've got guards, and they're happy to have company—and another sledge. I'm not carrying that much, except food, my tools and some clothes, and what we've forged." Jorhan shrugged.

Just listening, Beltur got a very sinking feeling in his guts. Jorhan's departure, and what that meant to him, wasn't just something that might happen. It was going to happen, in less than an eightday.

He was still thinking about that as he walked back toward the southeast gate, wondering just how long his stock of silvers would last once his patrol duty was over . . . because he didn't see much other work coming his way, unless he could persuade Klarisia to pay him as a healer, and he had real doubts about that. And then there was Nykail, and he worried about the boy more and more as he approached the house.

He opened the door gingerly, stepping inside quietly, and trying to sense who might be in the parlor as he took off his coat and scarf and hung them on the wall peg.

"Beltur?" called Meldryn from the kitchen.

"Yes?" After a moment, he asked, "How's Nykail?"

Meldryn appeared in the hallway, smiling. "He's a bit weak, still, but he's eating, and he's healthier than he's likely been in seasons. Laranya took him home around third glass."

"Was there any sign of more order building up?"

"Not that I could tell."

Beltur could feel some of the tension leaving his shoulders. "I still worry about whether that will reoccur. I don't understand why it happened."

"You need an ale, and dinner's ready." Meldryn motioned toward the kitchen. "How was the smithing . . . and Jorhan?"

"He's fine. He did say that I was doing too many things that would upset too many people once they found out, as if they haven't already." Once he was in the kitchen, Beltur took the mug from his place at the table and filled it from the small keg. He took a long swallow and, after Meldryn's gesture to seat himself, did just that.

"He's right, you know, and he doesn't even know about Taelya."

"I know. What makes things worse is that he's really leaving Elparta."

"You said he might."

"He really is. He's fixed up his sledge, and he's got someone looking for another horse. He's lined up some outland traders to travel with . . ."

"What about what he owes you?"

"He paid me for my share of everything that's been sold. He says he'll send my share of whatever he sells things for. He feels like he's telling the truth."

"It might be better if you told him to keep the silvers for you in Axalt, and you'll come there to collect them."

"Why?"

"Because if Alizant found out about it, he might demand all you made, and the Council would likely support him."

"How could he do that?"

"Has Jorhan sold any of those pieces he'll be taking to Axalt? Doesn't the proclamation state that anything made with magery and sold after the first day of Winter must be sold through Alizant and approved by Cohndar?"

Beltur didn't reply for a moment. "That means, even if we forged it before the first day of winter . . ."

"You didn't sell it before then. That's likely why Jorhan is leaving as soon as he can." Meldryn set two platters on the table, one at each place, then sat down.

"And if I want to get paid, I'll have to go to Axalt."

"It might be worse than that. If Jorhan takes the unsold cupridium to Axalt and later sells it there, no one here can prove when it was sold, but if you go to Axalt and return with silvers, or even if the silvers are sent to you, assuming that they arrive safely, that suggests that you are knowingly violating the Council proclamation because the goods were made in Elparta before the first day of Winter and sold after that date elsewhere. But the proclamation states that goods made here . . ."

"Frig!" After a moment, Beltur added, "And Cohndar would like nothing better than to declare I broke the Council's law. So . . . if I want to stay here and not get in trouble with the Council, I can't get paid for anything that Jorhan sells after he leaves Spidlar?"

Meldryn nodded. "You might be fortunate, and Cohndar and the Council might not find out, but that's a risk. Since Jorhan is the seller, if you don't get anything, they can only blame him, but if you do . . ."

"Cohndar will say it's proof I was also part of the plan to keep the most honorable Trader Alizant from obtaining his lawful extortion . . . and penalize me sixty golds I can't pay and turn me into an indentured slave."

"That's very possible."

"But . . . why? I doubt that Jorhan has made that many golds, especially compared to what traders make."

"Power. Cohndar's power, not Alizant's. Alizant will likely go along because he'll be irked that Jorhan denied him the opportunity to make a few more golds. The Council won't back you because they always back a trader."

"Will Cohndar come after you? Just because you've helped me?"

"I doubt it. I'm just a not-very-powerful black who is a good baker." Meldryn shrugged. "Everyone knows that. You, on the other hand, are a chaos-tinged renegade who, given time, might actually threaten both Waensyn and Cohndar."

"Me?"

"You," replied Meldryn, with a faint smile.

How did it all come to this? Just because you and Jorhan wanted to do better for yourselves? Beltur didn't feel all that hungry, but he still took a bite of the meat pie, and then another.

XXIV

Sixday morning was somewhat colder than fiveday, but the blue-green sky was clear when Beltur set out for the smithy, much earlier than the day before, so that he could do whatever Jorhan needed and still get to Lhadoraak's house to work with Taelya before it got too late. He couldn't help but think about the situation in which he found himself. While he had well over fifteen golds, mostly in silvers, in his hidden and protected strongbox, certainly enough to live on for over a year, as well as pay Meldryn, after what Cohndar and Alizant had done, he didn't see much chance of being able to buy a dwelling, even the smallest, or to offer much of a future to Jessyla . . . and, given Waensyn, he had no doubts that more obstacles would be placed in his path.

You could go to Axalt . . . or perhaps you should go to Suthya with Lhadoraak and Tulya in the spring. But he didn't want to leave Jessyla, and at the moment, neither Margrena nor Grenara seemed in the mood to allow him to consort Jessyla immediately, not unless matters got really bad, and that was the last thing Beltur wanted.

Beltur had choices, none of them exactly appealing, and he was still mentally wrestling with all the possibilities and their relative disadvantages when he reached the smithy.

Jorhan looked up from the polishing wheel as Beltur shut the smithy door behind himself. "You're early this morning. You plan to leave early?" His voice was terse and clipped.

"Only if we finish what you need done, because I still have patrol duty tomorrow." After shedding his coat and scarf, Beltur moved to the bellows. "What's first?"

"Another sabre. They pay well."

"How are you coming with copper?" Beltur tried not to frown, sensing that Jorhan was not pleased with something.

"Might have a stone's worth to take with me."

"Are you still planning to leave on twoday or threeday?"

"I'd leave earlier, if I could." Jorhan moved from the wheel to the workbench, where he picked up a sheet of paper. He walked to Beltur and thrust the paper at the mage. "Read this."

Beltur took the paper and began to read, his eyes scanning the words. He was shaking his head as he read.

To: Jorhan, smith of Elparta
From: Veroyt, Assistant to the Council

It has come to the attention of the Council that you, in collaboration with a mage, are engaged in the forging of cupridium items and objects. By this notice, you are hereby informed that, in accord with the earlier proclamation of the Council, with which you were served, as of the first day of Winter, all items and objects forged in part or whole of cupridium, must be sold through Trader Alizant of the House of Alizant, whether or not such items or objects were forged prior to the first day of Winter . . .

There was more, mostly about penalties for disobeying the Council edict, and offering the location to which all items should be delivered for sale.

Beltur looked up. "Alizant must really want to get his hands on what we've forged."

"Just like those bastards to come up with something like this." Jorhan snorted. "They must have got wind of all the forging we've been doing. I told you I'd need to get out of Spidlar well before the first day of Winter, didn't I?"

"You did." Beltur handed the paper back.

"They'll be after you next, if you're not real careful. You'll have to avoid that Cohndar fellow all you can. You certain you want to stay around?" Before Beltur could even form a response, the smith went on. "I know. That healer. Just be careful."

"I'm trying, but no one is making it easier on either one of us."

"You can't expect that. Now . . . the mold's almost ready." Jorhan laid the paper on the workbench and picked up the tongs.

Beltur moved to the bellows as Jorhan moved the crucible into position.

By half past third glass, two cupridium sabres lay in their molds, cooling, as did a mirror and a pair of bud vases.

"That should do it for now." Jorhan blotted his forehead, then handed Beltur a silver. "If you could come early on oneday . . ."

"Unless there's a deep snow. Then it might take longer."

"You'll manage."

Beltur pulled on his coat and made his way from the smithy and down the lane that Jorhan always kept clear of snow and then onto the road. Although it wasn't yet winter by the eightdays, the snow beyond the road covering the fields looked to be more than waist-deep in places, and even the road was covered to depth of six or seven digits with snow hard-packed by horses and sledges, and in places there were even patches of solid ice. *And it's still fall?*

Beltur glanced back toward the smithy, where a trail of smoke rose from the stone chimney, thinking that Jorhan would be pressing his luck in traveling to Axalt so late in the season. Yet, with the various blades and other cupridium pieces that the smith had finished likely able to fetch more than fifteen golds, possibly twice that, most of which would likely go to Alizant . . . or remain unsold, assuming Jorhan decided not to sell at all, Beltur could also see why the smith had decided to leave, snow or no snow.

Beltur returned his attention to the sometimes uneven hardpack and walked carefully westward. When he reached the southeast gate, he nodded to the guards, and they nodded back as he followed a messenger on horseback through the wall gate. Then he took the east wall street north and made his way to Lhadoraak's small dwelling.

The fine-featured mage was the one to respond to Beltur's knock. "I thought you might be later."

"I went to work earlier," Beltur replied as he stepped inside.

"How is that coming?" Lhadoraak frowned, closing the door. "I thought you weren't working as much because Jorhan was short of copper."

"We're finishing up with the copper he has."

"Does that have to do with that proclamation about magery? I take it he doesn't want the traders taking most of what he makes, either."

Beltur was glad he didn't have to explain. "That's about it."

"Alizant? He's the one? Cohndar didn't mention names when he told me. They say he's tighter than the bark on a red oak, and nastier than a mountain cat defending her kits. I can see why your smith doesn't want to deal with him."

"So . . ." Beltur shrugged. "I'm going to have to find more work before long."

"I'm sorry to hear that. It's slow for me now. Before long there won't be any boats on the river."

"Do you inspect anything else?"

"Wagons. That's if the gate guards get suspicious." Lhadoraak smiled faintly. "I still get a small stipend in the winter. It's enough . . . if we've been careful the rest of the year."

Beltur managed to keep his sense of embarrassment and shame hidden behind his shields. *You're worried about coins, and you've probably got more saved in two seasons than Lhadoraak and Meldryn have at all. Or Grenara or Margrena.* "Do any mages earn a good living?"

"Quite a few do. Osarus makes half a gold an eightday, I've heard. Cohndar does well, but part of that's because he works for his brother. Darcohn's a trader. Caradyn provides services to several traders. He inspects their wagons, warehouses, that sort of thing. Shalaart works with a farrier and a wheelwright. The others, I couldn't say."

"You know a lot more than I do. Is Taelya in the parlor?"

"She is. She was reading a history. A child's history. It was my aunt's."

"Don't tell her I'm here. I'm going to enter the parlor under a concealment and see if she can sense me."

"You want her to learn that now?"

Beltur definitely felt Lhadoraak's unease with that idea, but that mattered less than what was important for Taelya to know. "I do. She'll need every possible skill." *And then some.*

After concealing himself, but not shielding the order and chaos of his presence, Beltur eased into the parlor, slowly, carefully, because a concealment wouldn't block sounds, then stopped short of the bench where Taelya sat, the book in her lap, looking in the direction of the dying coals in the hearth. He was pleased that she was maintaining the order separation between her natural chaos and the free chaos that swirled around her even more strongly than before.

She did not move.

"Taelya," murmured Beltur, his voice barely audible.

The girl started, then grabbed the book to keep it from sliding off her legs, before standing and looking around.

"Don't move," Beltur murmured. "Sense where I am."

After several moments, Taelya said, "You're standing at the end of the bench."

Beltur did not reply, but moved toward the hearth.

"Now you're by the chair."

He dropped the concealment. "Good. I'm going to walk back out into the hall, under a concealment. Once I'm out there, you tell me where I am, and in which direction I'm moving."

"Yes, ser."

Beltur raised the concealment and left the parlor, moving into the hallway and toward the rear of the house.

"You're by the kitchen door . . ."

He moved back.

"You're in the middle of the hall, beside the high little table."

Beltur moved again, easing several steps up the staircase.

"You're up . . . on the steps upstairs."

After two more moves, which Taelya also determined correctly, Beltur returned to the parlor, still under a concealment, but this time, under a complete shield.

"You're gone. I can't sense you anywhere. Are you here anywhere?"

"I am," murmured Beltur.

"Where are you?"

Beltur dropped the concealment. "Here."

Taelya looked both surprised and annoyed. "I don't understand. If you can hide from being sensed, why do I need to know that?"

"There are two reasons. First, most people aren't mages, and you can sense them in the dark. Sometimes, cutpurses hide in dark lanes or alleys. Sensing them will allow you to avoid them. Second, some mages can shield themselves from being sensed, but many cannot, and even those who can often will not because it takes much more strength to use a total shield like that."

"Oh . . . that makes good sense."

"I'm glad you think so."

Taelya paled. "I'm sorry, ser."

"You need to be very polite to all mages, Taelya. It's not only good manners, but there's little point in antagonizing people, particularly when you'll likely be surrounded by blacks."

"Why don't people like whites? I'm the same as I was before I turned into a white."

"I know. There are blacks who don't like me because I was raised by my uncle, who was a white."

"That's how you know about whites, then?"

"That, and working and living with them from the time I was nine until I came to Elparta. Now . . . we need to get back to work on your shields."

"Yes, ser. Will you teach me how to shield myself like you just did?"

"That takes a lot of time and effort. You have to have very strong personal shields against order and chaos before you can even think about shielding everything. Try to put a shield completely around yourself. One tied together with order knots. You have been practicing that, haven't you?"

"Yes, ser." Her response was muted.

"But not as much as you should have been."

"No, ser."

"Go ahead and do your best." Beltur settled into the straight-backed chair.

Taelya's first attempt collapsed even before she had created a section a yard across.

"Oh . . ."

"Make the order knots smaller. Much smaller." Beltur felt that the session was going to be long and frustrating for Taelya, and her comments as they proceeded indicated just that.

"I can't do what you want . . ."

"It's too soft and squishy . . . that won't protect anything . . ."

"The yards keep unraveling . . ."

After close to three quints, Taelya finally managed a loose circular shield all the way around. She held it for possibly half a quint before she began to shake and the shield collapsed, order and chaos threads fraying and repelling each other. "I can't, can't, can't . . ."

"Taelya," Beltur said gently. "You did just fine. You've done enough for today. Please sit down on the bench."

"Yes, ser." Her tone was just short of sullen.

"You don't believe it, but you are doing very well. You've been working with order and chaos less than a handful of times, and you can do more than I could do when I was four years older than you are now." That was unfortunately true, Beltur knew. "You can't learn it all at once. But the reason why I'm pushing you to do more than you can do is because the more you try, with a mage watching so that you don't try too much, the sooner you'll get stronger. You can hold a fairly strong shield in front of yourself already. It's strong enough to stop a thief for a while, and before long, you should be able to protect yourself against those kinds of people—that's if you sense them in time to raise a shield."

"Oh . . ." sniffed Taelya, "that's why you wanted me to learn to sense."

"That's right."

"There's so much to learn."

"There is, but you're still young. Just keep practicing at what you did today. No more than you did today, but keep working on holding the shield longer. You're also doing well at keeping your order and chaos levels separate."

"I've been working at that." Taelya sniffed again, as if she'd been holding back tears, but was beginning to recover.

"It shows. I'd guess you're going to need something to eat." Beltur stood, knowing that Lhadoraak was waiting in the hall until Taelya left. "I may see you again on eightday. We'll see."

No sooner had Taelya headed for the kitchen than Lhadoraak entered the parlor and joined Beltur. "I don't mean to pry, but when you were working with Taelya on sensing . . . you . . . just . . . disappeared."

Beltur shook his head. "It's just another level of shielding."

"I couldn't sense anything. It was like you weren't even there."

"I was very much here. It takes a great deal of effort." That wasn't totally true. When Beltur had first tried multiple shields, it had tired him quickly, but practice had made carrying such order/chaos shields only slightly tiring, rather than exhausting.

"*What* are you?" Lhadoraak's voice was low, but intense.

"I'm a black who has a great deal of skill at sensing even small bits of order and chaos, and a fair amount of skill with shields, and only if those shields are fairly close to me, as you well know . . . and very limited abilities beyond that."

"I . . . hadn't thought of it that way."

"I can help Taelya with sensing and shields. Others, later, once she has strong shields, might be best to broaden her abilities."

Lhadoraak's mouth opened. "You think she could shield herself the way you did . . . so . . ."

"I can't say. It's possible, but it likely won't be for years. She'll need more purely physical strength. I'm trying to give her the tools she'll need."

"You ought to be running a school for mages."

Beltur shook his head. "I don't know enough. There's so much I don't know."

"That might be, but I couldn't have taught her what you did."

Beltur smiled. "Of course not. But that's because you're her father, and children seldom want to learn from their parents. You could probably teach other mages' children."

"You're kind, Beltur, but I know better. Can you come on eightday? Any time?"

"Early afternoon, if it doesn't snow."

"That's fine."

The two walked to the front door.

Lhadoraak was about to open it when he turned. "I can't tell you how much we appreciate this."

"I'm happy to do it." And, as Beltur donned his coat, he realized that he was.

"We're glad you are." Lhadoraak opened the door.

When Beltur stepped outside, he realized that a light snow was falling, although less than a digit covered the paving stones of the street.

He was still thinking about how few silvers most of the blacks in Elparta seemed to make, but he also recalled what either Meldryn or Athaal had said some time back—that very few men who relied on just the skills of their mind or body ever were wealthy, and that true wealth came from trade or from the use of other people's skills. At least, that was how he recalled it. *And that's what Alizant is trying to do with you and Jorhan.*

He also still felt ashamed . . . and selfish . . . about thinking that he'd been doing badly in what he earned. Compared to Lhadoraak or Margrena or many of the blacks, he'd been paid handsomely over the past season. *Very handsomely . . . even if future earnings like that are about to disappear.*

Working all day with Jorhan, and then with Taelya, had left him feeling very hungry, and he was looking forward to whatever Meldryn might have fixed. Even what the older mage called leftovers were better than some people's best dinners.

Beltur smiled and kept walking.

XXV

Beltur was up early on sevenday, because he had patrol duty and because he hadn't slept as soundly as he might have, worrying not only about whether the snow might be deep, but also about Taelya and how long before Cohndar discovered she was a white, about what he could do to make a living in Elparta once Jorhan left . . . or whether he was being foolish not to accompany the smith. *But you can't leave Jessyla . . . and even Meldryn needs the silvers you provide.*

He fixed breakfast, ate with Meldryn, cleaned up, and then finished dressing. When he stepped outside, the snow was still falling, almost lazily, and only a few digits' worth covered the stones. Meldryn had already cleared the area around the bakery, and people were walking on the streets, much the same as they had been on previous days with no snowfall.

Beltur reached City Patrol headquarters and was signing the duty book when the duty patroller said, "Ser, the Patrol Mage would like a word with you before you head out."

"Thank you." Wondering what Osarus wanted, Beltur opened the door from the duty room and made his way to Osarus's study, where the door was open. "Ser?"

"Come in, Beltur. Close the door, if you would."

That worried Beltur, but he complied.

Osarus's pale blue eyes immediately focused on Beltur. "As I recall, in the past you worked with a coppersmith to forge cupridium."

"Yes, ser. I still do."

"Then you are aware of the Council proclamation dealing with the making of objects either wholly or partly through magery?"

"I am. Mage-Councilor Cohndar made a personal visit to me and to all blacks in Elparta, I understand. He explained the provisions of the proclamation in detail."

Uncharacteristically, the Patrol Mage's hand brushed away a nonexistent strand of the black hair that was slicked back and perfectly in place before he spoke again. "You've been an excellent patrol mage. The City Patrol could not have asked for better. I understand very well that the proclamation will make your life far more difficult. I am not a trader, nor was I informed as to why the Council has chosen to do this. Unwise as the decision seems to me, it is *now* the law of Spidlar." Osarus paused and cleared his throat.

Beltur had noticed the very slight emphasis the Patrol Mage had placed on the word "now." He doubted it was accidental.

"Because the proclamation deals with trade," Osarus went on, "should any violations occur, they will be dealt with initially by Council guards. If any overt violence occurs, of course, the Council can call upon the City Patrol. The Patrol will then determine whether the Patrol should take action. I regret having to spell this out in detail, but in view of your excellent service, I thought you should know the consequences of violating either the spirit or the letter of the law as it now stands."

"I appreciate your making that clear, ser."

"I very much regret the situation. It's too bad that you can't continue forging cupridium here in Spidlar without forgoing considerable income, but that is the law as of now." Osarus paused again. "Do you have any questions?"

"No, ser. Thank you."

"Thank you for your service, Beltur. You've done well."

"By your leave, ser."

"Of course." Osarus offered a smile that could only have been described as sad, not even regretful.

Beltur hurried back to the duty room, where Laevoyt was waiting, and the two immediately stepped out onto Patrol Street and headed toward the main market square.

"Do you want to tell me what that was all about?"

Beltur didn't see any point in not doing so and gave a quick explanation of what that all meant, ending up with a paraphrase of what the Patrol Mage had said.

"Sounds like he wants to make sure you understand how serious it could be. Also sounds like he doesn't approve and can't do anything about it." Laevoyt shook his head. "Bastard traders'll do anything for a few more silvers. Frigging shame, it is. What are you going to do?"

"At the moment, I don't know."

"Thoughtful of Osarus, but it sounds strange, somehow."

Beltur thought so, also, but just said, "I appreciated that thoughtfulness."

As the two neared the square, Beltur could see that the workhouse men had already cleared the new snow off the half of the square that they had previously cleared, and that the wagons and men were working their way north on West Street. There were already several vendors set up on the stone pavement.

"Likely be the most folks we'll see here until spring," offered Laevoyt. "We'll be patrolling River Street at least half-time from now on, I'd wager." After a moment, he asked, "How much longer for you?"

"If I've figured it right, three more eightdays after tomorrow."

"You'll be seeing more of River Street." Laevoyt laughed.

After leaving Laevoyt, as Beltur patrolled the square, he kept thinking about what Osarus had said. First were Osarus's references to the law as if it were already in effect. *Was that his way of telling you that it is, at least in the minds of the Council and the traders, despite the wording that said "the first day of Winter"?* The other was the hinted suggestion that Beltur might be better off forging cupridium outside Spidlar. Or had that been the older mage's way of telling Beltur that he would never be able to do it inside Spidlar? Whichever way Osarus had meant it, it had been clear that he wasn't happy with the Council's action.

But he's not opposing it openly. Beltur smiled wryly, thinking, *You're not, either.*

By ninth glass, there were more people at the square than Beltur had seen in eightdays, possibly almost four score, between buyers and sellers, but although Beltur spent much of the time under concealment, he didn't sense any chaos. None at all.

Because most of those buying don't have that many coins and are buying necessities of one sort or another?

Roughly halfway between noon and first glass, Beltur made his way to Fosset's cart, but waited until after Fosset served two others before asking for a hot cider. When Beltur took the mug, he asked, "How are things going with you?"

"Cold. I hate standing around waiting. I suppose it's better than lugging logs at the inn, or mucking out the stables there."

"You'd have to do that?"

"I'm not the favored nephew. What do you do when you're not on mage duty?"

"I've been working with a coppersmith."

"You do? I thought mages made sure things worked, or inspected boats or piers, except Meldryn. He's the only mage I know who's a baker. But a mage as a coppersmith?"

Fosset's question surprised Beltur for a moment, but then he realized that he'd never mentioned smithing to Fosset. "More like his striker, right now, but I've been learning. Except now, the Council's saying we have to sell to a trader."

"I'm surprised they didn't do that earlier. Uncle was going to build a mill with a big hammer run by the wheel. Gave up on the idea when he found out he'd have to sell the nails he wanted to make through a trader. Council claimed they needed to maintain quality."

"Did someone else build the mill?"

"Trader named Alizant."

Beltur managed just to nod. "I can't say I'm surprised."

Fosset shook his head, then turned to his next customer.

Beltur finished off his loaf and the cider, put the empty mug on the rack, and headed back to his patrolling.

A quint or so later, he was passing along the line of produce carts when he came to the table of the woman with the acorn cakes. He was surprised to see her there, because he hadn't seen her earlier. "Did you come later today?"

"I did. A bit after noon. You noticed that. Most mages wouldn't."

"I wasn't sure, but I thought so." Beltur smiled ruefully. "I take it that acorn cakes make a good travel food?" He wasn't sure what prompted him to ask.

"That they do, ser mage. For men or mounts."

"I have a friend who may have to travel before long. I'll take two coppers' worth." Beltur handed over the coppers and took the wrapped cakes, which felt heavier than he thought they would be. He doubted that Jorhan would have acorn cakes, and if the smith didn't like them, he could feed them to the horses, but he felt he ought to make some gesture to Jorhan that showed at least some thoughtfulness.

Despite the larger number of sellers and buyers than in recent days, the square was almost empty by third glass, although the light snow had finally stopped, and the sky seemed to be clearing, and a light wind began to blow out of the north, a wind that promised a colder night to come.

After signing out at Patrol headquarters, Beltur made his way back to Bakers Lane, now totally clear, and reached the house just about two quints past fourth glass.

Since Meldryn was still in the bakery, Beltur went there after hanging up his coat and scarf. "You're working a little later today."

"I had a special order from Comartyl."

"The innkeeper at the Traders' Rest? What did he want?"

"Two pearapple cakes. Good thing I had half a barrel of pearapples left in the cellar."

"Do we have to deliver them?"

"No. His nephew picked them up just after fourth glass."

"Fosset? The one who sells cider and ale on the square?"

"The same one. I gave him a tiny pearapple tart. I made some of those for us since I had the pearapples out anyway."

"That sounds excellent." Beltur frowned. "Did Fosset tell you anything interesting?"

Meldryn shook his head.

"Something odd happened today."

"What was that?" asked Meldryn.

"Osarus called me in to his study . . ." Beltur went on to explain exactly what the Patrol Mage had said, then added, "I have the feeling that it was definitely a warning, but I couldn't tell whether he was suggesting I leave Spidlar or just that I don't do anything more with smithing."

"You don't want to leave Spidlar, for rather good and obvious reasons, but I think it would be for the best if Jorhan leaves with all that finished cupridium as soon as possible. Otherwise, it's possible that Alizant might insist that he be the one to sell it."

"I wondered about that, and I think Jorhan is concerned as well."

"He should be. Alizant isn't the most honorable of traders."

"I've wondered about that as well, but none of them seem to be what I'd call honorable."

"It's best you don't say that too loudly." Meldryn paused. "There's something else to consider. For Alizant to sell anything, it would require that Cohndar inspect whatever it might be, and he and Waensyn might find a way to say that there was too much chaos in the metal."

"I hadn't thought about that," Beltur confessed. "But how could they say that? The chaos is locked in order."

"Only Cohndar gets to make that decision," Meldryn pointed out. "Most of the other blacks won't stand against him."

"I don't like the sound of that at all."

"You shouldn't." Meldryn shook his head, then offered a cheerful smile. "We can't do much about that now, but I do have a meat pie and those tarts. If you'll carry them back to the kitchen, I'll finish here and be there in a few moments."

Beltur could do that, especially if there were pearapple tarts involved.

XXVI

Under a clear and cold green-blue sky on eightday, Beltur arrived at Lhadoraak and Tulya's house just a single quint past noon, carrying a covered basket.

Tulya opened the door, glancing at the basket.

"That's for Jessyla. I'm going there after Taelya and I are done."

"When are you two going to be consorted?" Tulya smiled as she stepped back and motioned for Beltur to enter the house.

"I can't say. That's up to Margrena, right now."

"I can see that. It takes more silvers than you think to start a household."

"And it keeps taking them, from what I've seen," replied Beltur as he closed the door. He set the basket on the side table and then took off his coat and hung it and his scarf up.

"You're right about that," said Tulya, immediately ushering him into the parlor, where Taelya, wearing light gray trousers and tunic, sat on the bench waiting.

Beltur noticed immediately both the strength of her chaos/order presence, and the clear separations in the chaos and order around her.

"Good afternoon, ser."

"Good afternoon, Taelya. You've been working, I can see." Beltur moved the straight-backed chair and then sat down. "Let's see what you can do with a shield around yourself."

Taelya immediately created her knitted shield, with tiny order points reinforcing the junctures of order and chaos yarns. "Is that better?"

"It is. I'm going to apply pressure, but I want you to hold it for as long as you can."

"I'll do that."

Beltur was pleased that she hadn't said that she'd try, but that she would. He began to apply force with an order probe, jabbing first at different places, then at the order-linked junctures. Then he stood and picked up the chair by the back and thrust it at her shield. The shield held, but Taelya slid backward on the bench. Beltur thrust again, harder, watching as she stood up, leaning forward and bracing herself. The shield still held. "That's good. You can drop the shield for a moment and sit back down. You had to work to hold it, didn't you?"

"Yes, ser."

"What happened when I thrust the chair at your shield?"

"I got pushed backwards."

"Do you think that always happens to other mages?"

"I don't know. Does it?"

Beltur smiled. "Unless they're very big and heavy, or unless they anchor their shield to something that won't break or move. Would you like to try to learn how to do that?"

The girl nodded.

"To anchor a shield, you have to link part of your shield to either the order or chaos embodied in something strong around you. Outside, it's usually the ground. Order anchors usually work better because order stays together more easily, but some whites anchor their shields with scores of tiny pieces of chaos."

"What does an anchor feel like?"

"It's different for everyone. For me, I think of it as a link in a chain that

I close around other order. I've heard others say their anchors are like hooks. I like the link idea because hooks can tear loose, but you'll have to decide what works for you." Beltur paused. "Do you want to try?"

"Yes!"

"It's not as easy as it sounds. You may have to work at it for a long time, perhaps seasons, if not longer, before you have really good anchors." Beltur paused. "One thing. Don't *ever* anchor your shields to a horse or a person or any animal. The anchors will fail, and you could kill the animal, and if you're riding a horse, that could kill you."

"I wouldn't do that."

"I didn't think you would, but I wanted you to know that. See what you can do."

Beltur observed while Taelya created her shield, but when she tried to anchor it to the floor, the small points of order holding the intertwined order and chaos yarns seemed to weaken, and the shield collapsed. Then she tried setting the anchors first and building the shield up from them, but the anchors seemed to vanish when she finished the shield.

Taelya tried a third time, and then a fourth.

Finally, she looked at Beltur. "I can't do all of it at once. I just can't."

While Beltur could hear the frustration in every word, he just asked, "Why not?"

"I can do the shield, but when I try to anchor it, the shield falls apart. When I start with the anchors, they fail by the time I get the shield right."

"Then what you need to do right now is to work on creating a strong shield that holds together without your having to think about it. That might mean trying different kinds of shields, or different order locks, or maybe using the free chaos in a different way. You also might find something that works better for you."

"What do you mean by different?"

"Try weaving the chaos in different ways, or making the yarns thicker, or thinner . . ."

Taelya tried thinner strands of chaos, more like threads. The shield immediately collapsed. Then she tried larger threads, but the shield wasn't as strong. She looked to Beltur.

"It stays together, but it's not as strong."

"That means you need to find a way to arrange the thicker chaos threads so that they are stronger." Beltur stood. "That's something you can work on yourself . . . after you rest a little."

"Couldn't we work longer?"

"It's been almost a glass," Beltur pointed out, "and you're getting tired. You need to rest before you try more ways of working with the chaos threads. That's the way you get stronger. Work until you're tired; rest; and then try again." *Time after time, until you're sick of it, always knowing that you still have to keep trying.*

"You make it sound easy. It's not."

"No, it's not," agreed Beltur. "Practicing a skill, working to make it just a little bit better each time, doing it time and time again—that's hard work. It's also the only way to become a skilled mage. Magery's like any other skill. It takes work and practice."

"Do you still practice?"

"I still practice, and I'm still trying to learn new things."

"What?"

"Right now, I'm working on knowing more about healing."

"Mages aren't healers, and healers aren't mages."

"That's what people say, but there's no reason why mages can't also be healers."

"Have you healed anyone?"

"I have. I had to try, because there weren't any healers around."

"Father says you're different from other blacks."

"All blacks differ from each other. I'm just a bit more different." *And getting to be even more different.* "Now . . . your lesson is over, and it's time for you to rest or to get something to eat."

"It is indeed," said Lhadoraak, stepping into the parlor.

"Yes, Father." Taelya's voice was resigned, but not sullen. She turned to Beltur. "Thank you. I *will* work on getting a stronger shield that won't ever fall apart."

"That's good," replied Beltur cheerfully.

After Taelya left, her father said, "She's working hard. I never thought a child of mine would be a white."

"If she keeps working, she's likely to be a strong white."

"You're not working with her on throwing chaos bolts."

"There's no point in that until she has strong shields, especially here in Spidlar."

"There is that," replied Lhadoraak ruefully. "When can you come again?"

Beltur was about to suggest twoday, but then realized that he might be tied up in finishing things with Jorhan, and threeday was a City Patrol day. "After the next few days, I may have more time. What about fourday afternoon?"

"That shouldn't be a problem. If it is, we'll send word to Meldryn." Lhadoraak smiled. "Are you headed to see Jessyla now?"

Beltur smiled back. "Where else?"

The two walked to the front door, where Beltur donned his coat and reclaimed his basket. "How are things going for you?"

"Slow. They always are at this time of year."

"Late fall and winter seem to be harder for everyone."

"Everyone who lives where it's cold enough for snow and ice." Lhadoraak followed his words with a short bitter laugh.

Beltur opened the door. "I'll see you or Tulya around midafternoon on fourday."

"Until then."

Beltur stepped out into the cold and headed north.

It was close to half past first glass when he knocked on the door of Grenara's house.

This time, Jessyla opened the door.

Beltur handed her the basket. "Bread, a meat pie, and four pearapple tarts."

"How . . . ?" Jessyla took the basket.

Beltur entered the house and closed the door. "Meldryn had a special order, and there were extra pearapples available. We had some last night. They're good."

"Everything he bakes is good."

"He'd claim that some things are just acceptable." Beltur hung up his coat, glanced around, and seeing no one but Growler, perched as he often was on the staircase, immediately threw his arms around Jessyla.

"I think you missed me," she murmured, holding him tightly with her free arm for a moment before easing from his embrace. "Mother's coming."

While Beltur had sensed Margrena moving toward the doorway from the kitchen to the front room, he'd heard nothing, and Margrena wasn't yet in sight. "You sensed her coming?"

"I can, a little. I'm getting better at it."

"I've told you before. You're more than a healer."

"You're more than a mage."

While Beltur had his doubts about being even a fully capable mage, he just replied quietly, "You're kind, but I have a lot to learn."

"I'm not kind, and I hate that word. It suggests being more generous in judging people than they merit, and I don't ever do that. If anything, I'm hard on people."

"She's being very truthful about that," added Margrena as she approached. "She tends to be direct and truthful, even when kindness might be more appropriate."

"I won't lie to Beltur. That wouldn't be right. He needs to know that."

Margrena looked at Beltur, her words gently wry. "I trust she's made that clear."

Beltur turned to Jessyla. "I appreciate the honesty. In turn, I must say that I believe you overestimate the range and strength of my abilities."

"I didn't say you were the strongest mage. I said you could do more than just a mage."

"She's right," declared Margrena. "Now that you two have cleared that up, how are matters coming with the smithing and Cohndar?"

"Jorhan is planning on leaving on twoday, but no later than threeday. He's arranged to travel with some outland merchants."

"Has Cohndar approached you again?"

"No."

"He likely will. He'll try to provoke you into doing or saying something for which he can then approach the Council to demand your exile . . . or some form of extreme penance."

Jessyla handed the basket to her mother. "He's brought gifts again."

"I don't like imposing on you without lessening the burden."

"Grenara appreciates that, and Jessyla and I are grateful." Margrena turned to her daughter. "Is that truthful enough?"

"Yes, Mother." Jessyla's reply was demure.

"But we can all enjoy an early dinner."

"Not too early," declared Jessyla.

"Sometime shortly after third glass? Would that be acceptable?"

"It would."

"Good. You two can enjoy yourselves in the front room. Within reason." With a smile, Margrena turned and carried the basket into the kitchen.

Beltur didn't need any encouragement to sit beside Jessyla on the bench.

"Cohndar and Waensyn are looking for a way to force you to leave Elparta." Her voice was calm and matter-of-fact.

Beltur didn't even sense any chaos that would have revealed conflicting feelings about what she said. "I've had that feeling for some time."

"I won't stay here if you leave." She looked at him openly, warmly.

He could sense the depth of feeling, and he wanted to hold her—and a great deal more that would not have been at all in reason. Instead, he leaned forward, intending to kiss her gently.

Except . . . her response was far more fervent, and the kiss and embrace lasted much longer than Beltur had intended or expected. Finally, he murmured in her ear. "We're not consorted. We haven't even said much about—"

She straightened. "I don't care. Don't you dare leave Elparta without me. That wouldn't be right for either of us."

As he again looked into Jessyla's green eyes, he had to agree, but it wasn't likely to be anywhere that easy. "Your mother . . ."

"She doesn't have to live my life. Besides, I can take care of myself." She offered a crooked smile and added, "Not that I'd have to with you."

"You're awfully confident in me."

She shook her head. "You've given me almost a gold in silvers, and you wouldn't have done that if you didn't have it to spare. I could sense that. Outside of a new tunic and trousers and a few shirts, you've bought almost nothing for yourself, but you've been working for the Patrol and the smith for over a season. You must have saved several golds at the least."

"I have saved a few."

"And didn't you say that you'd been offered a place of sorts in Axalt?"

"Of sorts. I'm fairly sure I'd be welcome for at least a time."

"If you'd be welcome, I'm sure that your consort, who is a healer, would also be welcome."

"Likely more welcome than an outcast black mage, because that's what I'd be."

"Then it's settled. If you leave, so do I."

"It may be settled between us—"

"I'll take care of Mother. And Auntie."

The way Jessyla said those words, Beltur had no doubts that she would. He just hoped that it wouldn't come to that, but he wasn't about to voice those thoughts. "How has it been at the healing house?"

"Does talking about leaving bother you that much?"

"It bothers me some. I worry about having already been forced from one land, and then possibly being forced from another."

"If it comes to that, we'll find the right place. You'll see."

Beltur could almost sense the black iron behind her words, but he just nodded.

Jessyla put her arms around him and drew him to her for several very long moments, before easing back slightly and whispering, "Do you see now?"

XXVII

When he woke on oneday, Beltur was still in what felt like a warm haze, despite the chill in his chamber. The two glasses or so that he'd spent with Jessyla had passed far too quickly, as had the supper, and before he'd known it, he'd been walking back along Bakers Lane in the late-afternoon cold, not that he'd really noticed it. Except that, when he rolled out of bed, the cold in his room, and the realization that he only had a day or two more of paid work from Jorhan, struck him almost with the force of a blow, leaving him standing beside the bed for several moments, immobile, the warm glow stripped away, before he finally forced himself to begin his morning routine of washing, shaving, and dressing.

Then he hurried downstairs and fixed breakfast, trying just to concentrate on what he was doing at the moment. When the egg toast was ready, and the cider hot, he called Meldryn.

"Are you all right?" asked the older mage when he stepped into the kitchen.

"I'm fine. Just a little worried. I got to thinking."

Meldryn laughed. "Unlike last night." He sat down at the table.

"Unlike last night," agreed Beltur, seating himself. "I'm worried about Jorhan's leaving. I'm worried about what Alizant and Cohndar and Waensyn might do. I'm worried about not earning anything at all in another two eightdays."

"You've got a fair bit put aside, I imagine."

"Enough for a while, but . . ."

"You're not sure how long it will last?"

"That, and what Cohndar will do to keep me from earning much in the future."

"I didn't think he was that petty, but now . . ."

"He likely wasn't . . . until Waensyn started flattering and manipulating him. Now that he's the mage-councilor, things aren't likely to get better."

"They may not. We'll have to see." Meldryn took a mouthful of the egg toast. "This is good. You've gotten to be a much better cook."

"I've had a good teacher." Beltur smiled and then took a sip of the hot cider, then ate more of the eggs. They were good, but then Meldryn's bread made anything, especially egg toast, taste better.

"The best teacher can't teach someone who won't or can't learn. Too many parents don't understand that, and that includes traders."

"You're talking about Zandyr?"

"Among others," replied Meldryn. "That's another reason why you and Jessyla might think about leaving here, come spring. From what you said last night, by spring Margrena wouldn't be that opposed."

"She wouldn't be opposed. I doubt she'd be happy."

"Unhappiness passes, if there's love. Sometimes, opposition doesn't."

Thinking of Meldryn and Athaal, and how the two had battled both opposition and the lack of familial love, Beltur just nodded.

"You'll be later tonight?"

"Most likely. Jorhan will want to finish up as much as we can. I told you that he was hoping to leave tomorrow."

"Best that he does. Clear weather won't hold for that long, and we haven't had a northeaster in a while."

After they ate, Beltur cleaned up and readied himself. He almost forgot the acorn cakes, but remembered at the last moment. The morning was again clear and cold, but not overpoweringly so, although Beltur wondered if he was just beginning to get used to the cold as he walked east to the wall street and south to the gate, nodding to the guards as he passed. He arrived at the smithy just before seventh glass, but he didn't even have a chance to take off his coat, because Jorhan was putting his on.

"I want you to take a look at the horses I got." The smith motioned in the direction of the small barn.

"Horses? I thought you were looking for one horse." Beltur handed the package of acorn cakes to the smith. "Acorn travel cakes. Good for horses or people."

"Thank you." Jorhan set the package on a stool and grinned. "Now . . . about the horses. I got a really good deal on the second. You'll understand why when you see him."

"How could you get a good deal on a horse? Even nags don't come cheap."

Jorhan opened the door, motioning for Beltur to accompany him.

More than a little curious, Beltur followed the smith. By the time he entered the stone-walled structure by the small side door, Jorhan had already lit the wall lamp. In the dim light, Beltur could see both a cart tucked away in one corner and a wagon/sledge set in front of the main double doors and partly packed with bundles and kegs. There were also three stalls.

"The one I'll be riding is the bay mare. The chestnut is my own cart and sledge horse. The other one—the one in the end stall—he's the bargain." Jorhan grinned again.

Beltur's mouth dropped open. He could only gape at the enormous brown gelding. "Slowpoke!"

"Good!" declared Jorhan. "Figured it had to be him. Hontyl let me have him. Even gave me an old cavalry saddle and a bridle. Had to do some jury-rigging on the saddle, but the girths are sound."

"Let you *have* him? But . . . how? Why?"

"The Council sold off the extra horses after the invasion was over. Most of 'em were old, or hard to deal with. Some they just didn't need. Hontyl bought a lot last eightday. Your Slowpoke was in the lot. At first, Hontyl couldn't figure why such a fine animal was still there."

"Why was he?" asked Beltur, curious in spite of himself.

"Hontyl said he was too fine to put down, too tough to eat, and too stubborn to sell. He was trying not to sell him to the renderer."

"Too stubborn?"

"Anyone could saddle him. Anyone could lead him. Anyone could mount him, but he wouldn't budge with anyone in the saddle. Wouldn't stand for harnesses, either. So he's yours."

"But I don't have anywhere to keep him, and no way to feed him. How can I—"

"Seeing as you're not coming to Axalt with me, not yet anyhow, I figured we could do a trade. You look after the place till one of the boys gets here, and you keep him here. I've already laid in fodder for Bessie, and she won't be eating it, seeing as she's going to be with me in Axalt. Be a shame to waste all that fodder. Besides, I got a feeling you just might be needing that horse. Might even be before spring." Jorhan looked at Slowpoke and shook his head. "Just didn't seem right . . ."

Beltur slowly walked over to the end stall and just looked. He winced at the scars on Slowpoke's shoulders, then reached over the stall half wall and touched the big gelding, stroking his neck, and projecting a sense of warmth and caring. Slowpoke's ears stiffened. After a moment his big head turned, and he nuzzled Beltur, making a low noise as he did.

Beltur found his eyes burning, even as he kept stroking Slowpoke's neck. *You should have looked harder for him. You should have.*

"Sure didn't forget you," offered Jorhan.

"I didn't forget him . . ." Beltur swallowed, unable to say more for a moment. "But by the time I recovered, the whole company was gone to Kleth, and I thought he'd gone with them. I didn't know . . ." He shook his head.

"Sometimes, things don't turn out. Once in a while they do."

"Would you mind if I groomed him? I'll work late."

"Go ahead. Brushes are over there on the shelf."

Slowpoke enjoyed the grooming. So did Beltur.

Two quints later, Beltur returned to the smithy, feeling both relieved, and with an additional worry. How was he going to be able to deal with having Slowpoke over any length of time? Yet how could he possibly give up the mount that had saved his life on more than one occasion? Especially after being so fortunate in being given a second chance?

"He sure looked happy to see you," observed Jorhan.

"I was happy to see him. I still can't believe it."

"There's an old saying about gift horses . . ." The smith grinned.

"I understand. What are we working on today?"

"Small things. Two ladies' knives, to start with."

As he headed toward the bellows, Beltur frowned. He'd never thought that knives would be different for women. It made sense. He just hadn't considered it, although he should have, especially recalling the precautions taken by the seamstress who had made his clothes when he'd come to Elparta . . . or the fact that both Margrena and Jessyla carried knives everywhere.

At two quints past third glass, Beltur stepped away from the mold that held yet another ornate mirror, after making certain that the order/chaos net was firmly locked into the cupridium.

"That's all I need from you right now."

"I could help with the polishing wheel."

"You could," agreed Jorhan, "if I had anything ready to polish. What I don't get done in the morning I can polish in Axalt."

"Then I'm going to walk Slowpoke before I go."

"Good thought."

Beltur donned his coat and made his way back to the stable, where he put a halter and a lead on Slowpoke and walked him out of the stable and up and down the lane for more than two quints, watching and sensing the gelding, but Slowpoke didn't seem to be bothered. After bringing him back to the stable, Beltur brushed him down quickly and made sure he had water before going back to the smithy, where Jorhan was cleaning and straightening up.

"I'll see you in the morning . . . just in case you need anything."

"That would be good. Oh . . . here's your silver."

"Are you sure? Don't I owe you for Slowpoke?" Beltur held the silver, unsure of whether he should even take it.

"He didn't cost me a thing. Hontyl likes horses. When I told him . . . I'll owe him a favor. That's all."

"Then I owe you a favor."

Jorhan shook his head. "You did me the biggest favor of all by helping forge all that cupridium. I still owe you . . . and I'll pay." After a pause, the smith added, "Wouldn't hurt if you spent a little time here at the house now and then. I'm taking everything of value that I can carry. That's anything folks could make off with easy-like. Never did put much stock in buying things that weren't useful."

Given the sparseness of the furnishings in the house that Beltur had seen when he first met Jorhan, Beltur had long assumed that. "You'd like people to get the idea that someone's here part of the time."

Jorhan nodded.

"I can do that."

"I'll see you in the morning."

"I'll be here." Beltur nodded, then turned and left the smithy. Even as he walked down the lane to the main road, his breath filtering through the scarf and leaving a slight steamy trace in the air, he was still pondering over his good fortune in recovering Slowpoke. *Except it wasn't anything you did. Jorhan was the one who made it possible.*

As soon as he reached the house, after taking off his coat, he hurried to the kitchen.

"You're back earlier than I expected."

"Earlier than I did as well. Something unexpected happened."

"Oh?"

"It appears I have a horse," Beltur managed wryly. "Slowpoke was about to be sold to a renderer because he was too stubborn for anyone else to ride."

"Slowpoke? The big horse you rode?"

"The Council sold him off as unsuitable after the invasion. Jorhan made a deal . . ." Beltur explained the trade-off Jorhan had proposed.

Meldryn nodded. "That makes sense. Who better than a mage like you to look after his place? And with your horse there, he knows you'll be there." Meldryn paused. "You'll have to use order locks out there, though, or someone will try to steal him and everything else."

"I'd thought about that. Jorhan says he's taking anything of easy value, that he really never had that much."

"He might be right about that. Still . . ."

"There's not much else I can do."

"You could stay there at times."

"Jorhan asked if I would."

Meldryn smiled. "It is a private place. About the only one you and Jessyla might find."

Beltur flushed. He had to admit to himself that the thought had occurred to him almost immediately.

The older mage's face became serious. "There's something else you should know. Lhadoraak stopped by here to get some bread for Tulya. Mharkyn told him that Cohndar is working with the traders to get small artisans and crafters to sell through traders, and that the Mages' Council of each of the cities would get some of the revenues from that, maybe even more than that."

"That wouldn't work. You couldn't sell bread through a trader."

"No. It's for hard goods." Meldryn smiled wryly. "Like cupridium, black iron, or artisans and crafters who don't have their own shops. Apparently, if you don't own or rent space just for your business, and it's not produce or food, then you'll have to sell through a trader."

Beltur frowned. "But Jorhan owns his own smithy."

"They took care of that through the magery provision, remember?"

"Doesn't that mean Cohndar and some blacks will be acting as enforcers for the Council?"

"Mharkyn didn't know about that. He just said that Waensyn was talking about it, and that some blacks would be paid. Mharkyn thought that anything that meant we got paid more was a good idea."

Beltur could definitely see the appeal of more silvers. "That would make the black council a tool of the traders. I'm not sure that's a good idea, pay or no pay."

"I have more than a few doubts, but most blacks are barely getting by. More to the point, what you and I think doesn't seem to matter these days."

"Has it ever?"

"Not that I can recall," replied the older mage in his dry fashion. "But that got me to thinking. If Cohndar really goes after you, you'll need to be ready to leave quickly. I've laid out a spare duffel in the parlor, and a heavy old blanket. You might think about what you want to take if you have to leave in a hurry. And now that you have a mount . . . that will help."

"Do you really think things will happen that fast?"

"This morning, I didn't. After what Mharkyn said, they just might. If they don't, you'll have a duffel ready when you need it without having to look for one when you don't have time."

"Thank you. I just hope it doesn't come to that."

"So do I. Sometimes, when we're prepared for the worst, it doesn't happen. I hope that's the way it goes." Meldryn shook his head. "But sometimes it doesn't. Now . . . we might as well have dinner."

Beltur had thought he was hungry, but, despite the aroma from the hot meat pie, and the taste of the smooth dark ale, he ended up almost forcing himself to eat, as his thoughts flitted from point to point—Jessyla, then Slowpoke, and Grenara's quiet opposition, all the time worrying about Cohndar, and wondering what it would be like with Jorhan gone, and how he was going to manage watching Jorhan's house and smithy . . . and Slowpoke, especially when the snows got as deep as everyone had predicted that they would.

And it's not even winter yet.

XXVIII

Needless to say, Beltur didn't sleep all that well on oneday night. He woke early in the darkness on twoday morning, and just lay there for a time. Then he got up, lit the lamp, and laid out the duffel Meldryn had insisted he take, and folded his spare clothes and put them inside, along with the heavy old blanket on top. *Nothing's going to happen today.* He smiled wryly. Most likely, it wouldn't, but the way things had been going, it wouldn't hurt to have his things ready to go.

After that, he waited until Meldryn finished washing up and headed downstairs. Then he finished getting himself ready and fixed breakfast almost a glass earlier than he usually did. He could tell, without even looking, just by his order senses, that a light snow was falling.

Once he had breakfast mostly ready, he walked down the side corridor to the bakery, where he called from the doorway, "Breakfast is ready . . . if you are."

"I'll be about a half quint."

"That's fine. I know I'm early." Beltur walked back to the front door and opened it to confirm that snow was falling, if barely, before closing the door and returning to the kitchen, warm enough with the shutters closed and a bank of hot coals in the hearth.

As soon as Meldryn appeared, Beltur dished out the egg and mutton strip hash onto the two platters and set them on the table, then poured out two mugs of steaming spiced cider.

"You were awake early. Worried, aren't you?"

"I'm sure you can sense it," replied Beltur. "Things are changing, and change hasn't been all that kind recently, for either of us."

"True enough, but we can't do much about it except accommodate it as well as we can."

"Why doesn't anyone stand up to Cohndar? Osarus and Caradyn seem like they're as strong as he is."

"For the same reason you and I don't. The Council is behind Cohndar, and we all still need to make a living. Enough of the blacks in Elparta, especially the ones doing well, are paid by the wealthier traders. If they go against the Council and Cohndar, they might lose their patrons. At least we don't have to live with that hanging over our heads."

Beltur paused, his mug not quite touching his lips, as he thought about what Meldryn had said. *That could be even worse than being a patrol mage.* "I hadn't thought of it that way."

"I don't think there's anywhere that mages aren't beholden to someone, either rulers or traders or merchants."

"After what I've seen, I'm beginning to wish that there were."

"That would be a tall order. Whites have trouble being organized, except by force, and most blacks don't have enough power to rule without armsmen to support them, and armsmen would rather not bow to mages. Wishing for that is like wishing for the return of the Rational Stars. Last time that happened was when the black angels arrived, and that was the sort of change no one wants to see again—whole lands west of the Westhorns savaged and uprooted, and the greatest empire ever shattered into ruins." Meldryn shook his head.

For a short time, both ate quietly. Then Meldryn rose. "Time to get back to work. Thank you for breakfast."

"You're more than welcome." Beltur finished the last of his cider, then began to clean up.

Less than a glass later, he was out the door and walking east through the intermittent fine flakes of snow toward the wall road. His thoughts kept going back to Slowpoke and how he'd ever be able to keep him once the fodder ran out . . . and then there was the problem of Cohndar and Waensyn.

Once he walked up the lane, covered with perhaps a digit of new-fallen snow, and stepped inside the stone-walled building, he immediately noticed that it was cold, much colder than usual, and that both workbenches were empty, with no tools in sight. Nor was Jorhan anywhere in sight. *He must be seeing to the sledge.*

His coat still on, Beltur made his way along the side lane to the stable, where, indeed, he found Jorhan strapping bundles in place on the sledge, on top of the wheels that would turn it back into a wagon come spring. "You're expecting the traders early?"

"By eighth glass. The sooner I'm out of here the better. Likely better for you, too."

"Because, if the cupridium's gone before the first day of Winter, they can't complain that I've done something wrong?"

"That'd be my thought."

"Is there anything I can do?"

The smith finished lashing a row of bundles in place and straightened. "Not a thing, except maybe watch the sledge as we go down the lane. There's not really enough snow there." Jorhan cleared his throat. "You see anyone on the way here?"

"No. Let me see what I can tell now." Beltur frowned as he concentrated on sensing at a distance. He hadn't been doing much of that since he'd been mustered out. Despite the light snow, he was sensing a mass of order headed along the Axalt road, the kind of order that could only mean a black mage. He kept working on sensing, until he could make out three riders, and two were mages. Immediately, he looked to Jorhan. "I don't sense any traders, but there are three riders heading east on the Axalt road. Two are mages, and they just might be coming here."

"We haven't done anything wrong," snapped the smith. "That frigging proclamation said the first day of winter."

Osarus had hinted at something . . . "I have the feeling that Cohndar is up to something, and it likely concerns me. Why don't you just keep getting ready?"

Jorhan shook his head. "I'm ready as I need to be. We're in this to-gether." He bent over the sledge and rummaged for a moment, pulling out a heavy hammer and thrusting it under his belt. "We'll meet them at the smithy."

Beltur saw no point in saying that the hammer was likely to be either unnecessary or useless. He just nodded and turned. The two walked back to the smithy.

Before that long, Beltur sensed the three riders, and then heard hooves on the stone of the lane, slightly muffled by the snow. He walked to the smithy door, then decided to open it and watch. There were just the three riders, two in black and one in Council blue. The one in blue was a Council guard, wearing a sword. The two in black were Cohndar and Waensyn. Both mages, Beltur observed, wore thick black wool overcoats and heavy black gloves. He would have wagered that their coats alone might have cost a gold apiece.

The guard dismounted, tied his mount to the old hitching rail anchored in two mortared stone pillars, then walked to the smithy door. His eyes did not quite meet Beltur's. "Is this the smithy of Jorhan?"

"It is," replied the smith from where he stood slightly back and to the side of Beltur.

"I'm Beltur, and I presume the two mages are Cohndar and Waensyn?"

"Mage-Councilor Cohndar and Mage Waensyn are here to inspect the smithy."

"By what right?" asked Jorhan.

"By the right established in the proclamation of the Traders' Council of Spidlar, Smith, dealing with the use of magery in the forging of metals." The guard peered past Beltur into the smithy, then stepped back and turned. "The smith and the mage are here, Mage-Councilor. The smithy appears to contain no others."

"Excellent!" declared Waensyn, immediately dismounting and tying up his horse.

Cohndar dismounted more deliberately and handed the reins of his mount to Waensyn, who tied them to the rail before turning to the Coun-cil guard.

The guard stepped back from the doorway and glanced toward Cohndar, who waited for Waensyn to join him. Finally, the guard spoke again. "Sers?"

"This is between mages, and a matter for the Mages' Council," an-nounced Waensyn, turning toward the Council guard. "You've escorted us out here and announced the will of the Council. We can handle the matter from here."

Beltur stiffened at those words, but managed to keep a pleasant expression on his face.

"Yes, sers. Thank you, sers." The guard immediately moved to the railing and untied his mount. He mounted quickly and turned his horse down the lane.

Beltur checked his shields. He had the feeling he was going to need them . . . and that he might have to shield Jorhan as well.

"Might we come in?" asked Cohndar as he neared the door.

"Might as well," replied Jorhan, "seeing as you're already here." He glanced to Beltur, who gave the slightest nod and stepped back.

"Snow isn't that much different from rain," said Waensyn conversationally. "It doesn't affect order much, but it greatly hampers chaos."

"We do appreciate your welcoming graciousness," said Cohndar sardonically. "Or perhaps you actually do recognize the authority of the Council. I did think we might find both of you here," he added, as he stepped into the smithy, followed by Waensyn, who did not bother to hide the smirk on his face.

Without speaking, Jorhan closed the door behind Waensyn.

Beltur sensed the shields of both mages, although they didn't seem especially impressive to him. But then, they might have hidden secondary shields.

"Do you sense chaos here, Waensyn?" asked Cohndar conversationally.

"I certainly do, Councilor," replied Waensyn. "There's a white residue just about everywhere."

"Only in your imagination," suggested Beltur mildly.

"That is just what I'd expect from a renegade white mage posing as a black," commented Waensyn.

Cohndar turned to Jorhan. "You must be the smith deceived by this chaos wielder. You should have known better than to try to avoid the will of the Council. You're preparing to flee. That's obvious. The smithy is cold, and you've recently bought two more horses."

"The Council proclamation isn't effective until the first day of winter," Jorhan said, an edge to his voice.

"The Council proclamation deals with both the sale of goods made with chaos and with their making," declared Waensyn. "The proclamation also provides the Mage-Councilor of Elparta with the authority to root out chaos at any time."

"I've read the proclamation," replied Jorhan. "It says 'the first day of Winter.' It won't be the first of winter for another seven days."

"That applies to the sale of such goods, not to their production." Waensyn smiled.

"So you see," said Cohndar smoothly, "we are acting within the scope of the proclamation. We are here to require you to turn over all chaos-tinged objects, to take the renegade mage into custody."

"You'll not be doing that," said Jorhan. "That's theft."

"Oh, but we will. It's what the Council wants."

"Only because you've persuaded them by promising golds to Alizant," said Beltur, checking his shields.

"Really. Do you think the senior mage would bother himself with mere golds?" asked Cohndar scornfully.

"Just if they served a purpose."

"You will drop those shields, Beltur, that is, if you don't want others to suffer."

"Then what?"

"You might get off as an indentured worker . . . if you're very, very good and obedient," suggested Cohndar.

Waensyn just smirked, an expression that suggested far worse than Cohndar's implied promise.

At that moment, Beltur slammed containments around both mages, containments with shields blocking all order and chaos. He knew he couldn't hold them for too long, but hopefully that wouldn't be required.

For long moments, both of the intruding blacks struggled against Beltur's containments. When Beltur felt Cohndar's shields yielding, he pressed that containment harder.

Abruptly, the older mage's shields failed, and Beltur lessened his containment on Cohndar, concentrating on Waensyn, who was on the verge of breaking through Beltur's containment on him.

"So . . . you've contained Waensyn and broken my shields," said Cohndar. "Now what? Murder us both? Or can't you bring yourself to do that? Or is it taking all your strength to hold Waensyn? He's stronger than you are, you know."

At that moment, Waensyn mustered more order and pushed back on the containment Beltur held. Beltur struggled to hold Waensyn, but couldn't risk moving. Then Cohndar made another effort and broke through the lighter containment, bolting toward the smithy door and seemingly forgetting that Jorhan stood there.

The heavy hammer that the smith had carried rose . . . and slammed down on Cohndar's skull.

"You're not going anywhere, black bastard!" snapped Jorhan.

Cohndar dropped like a sack of grain onto the stone floor of the smithy, and black mist flared from his form.

Waensyn hesitated, clearly stunned.

Finally able to focus all his strength on Waensyn, Beltur took that moment of hesitation to tighten the containment around the other mage so that it was skintight. Waensyn tried to force back the containment, but Beltur held firm, thinking that without all his past efforts at mastering multiple containments, he would have been the one being restrained. Moments passed, followed by more moments. Struggling vainly against the containment, Waensyn turned red, then bluish, and then another black mist chilled Beltur. He dropped the containment, and Waensyn's body pitched forward onto the stones.

Beltur shuddered, then took a deep breath. "I . . . didn't . . . want to do that."

"Good thing you did. They would have done the same to you. You'd best be coming to Axalt with me," said Jorhan.

"We'll have to catch up with you."

"We?"

"I promised her I wouldn't leave her."

"First sensible thing you've said in eightdays. What about the two of them? The traders' party is going to be here in less than a glass."

"We'll need to hide the bodies, someplace where they won't be found until spring . . . and not on your lands. After that, I'll take one of the horses with me, and leave the other in the barn until I come back here with Jessyla. Then we'll use it to carry gear."

"Is it that safe for you to go back to Elparta?"

"It's still snowing, and I can stay hidden when I need to. Besides, I promised I wouldn't leave without her."

"We'd better get moving, then. Saddle that big gelding of yours. Mine's already saddled."

In less than a quint, the two had their mounts outside the smithy, where Jorhan held the reins of both. Beltur lifted Cohndar's body up and threw it over the saddle of Jorhan's mount.

"Don't forget his wallet," said Jorhan. "No sense in leaving silvers."

Beltur found two golds, three silvers, and eight coppers in the dead councilor's wallet. When he hoisted Waensyn's still form over his own shabby saddle he found a gold and eight silvers. *So much for them looking out for other blacks.* "Where are we going?"

"Down to the road, and east to the next lane. Just a hundred yards or so on the road. Up the lane a bit is a gully. Vorgaan dumps everything there, and everyone else does and everyone knows about it. If the snow keeps up, they won't be found until spring. Maybe not even then."

Since Beltur didn't have a better idea, he walked Slowpoke down the lane, sensing through the still-falling light snow, but finding no one near. Disposing of both bodies was as simple as Jorhan had indicated. Beltur would have preferred a more remote disposal location, but given that he had to ride back and get Jessyla, tell Meldryn, and get well clear of Elparta before people started asking about Cohndar and Waensyn, the less time it took, the better.

Once back at the smithy, they stabled one of the two mounts Cohndar and Waensyn had ridden, both Council horses, Beltur suspected, which would add another crime to his rapidly growing list. Then he turned to Jorhan. "I can't see what I need to do taking less than two glasses. We'll do our best to catch up."

"I can stall them a bit."

"Not too much. You don't want to be here too long, either."

"Nasty pair like that, no one's going to hurry if they don't show up."

Beltur could only hope that was the case, but all that mattered at the moment was getting Jessyla and getting on the way to Axalt.

"Beltur . . ."

"Yes?"

"There's a way station some thirteen or fourteen kays east, maybe three kays beyond Reiks."

"Reiks? Is that a village?"

"More like a hamlet, but no one there will host folks they don't know. It's just after a long ridge on the south."

Beltur nodded. He remembered that ridge from the invasion campaign, but he didn't recall a hamlet, just a few houses set well back from the road.

"If you don't catch up to us, stop at the way station. It's got a covered well, and it's more snug than most. And don't run the horses. You don't want them to get sweaty in this weather. Better that you take a day or two more to catch up than your horse gets his coat damp down to his skin. The other winter way stations are about fifteen kays apart."

"Thank you. That's very good to know."

Beltur mounted Slowpoke and rode back down the lane, with the other horse on a lead beside him. He was about halfway to the southeast gate when he made out two sledges heading east out of Elparta. He eased off the road, raised a concealment, and waited, although he was fairly certain that the group were those Jorhan was waiting for. Once they passed, he continued on. When he neared the gate, he waited, well back, until there was no one near, then raised a concealment, and, after easing the Council mount close to Slowpoke, rode through the gate. One of the guards peered around, but said nothing. After he was inside the walls, he turned north on the wall street and headed for the Council Healing House.

As he rode, his eyes and senses alert, he couldn't help wondering whether there had been any other way to deal with Cohndar and Waensyn. *Maybe . . . if you'd toadied up to Cohndar early on . . .* He shook his head. That wouldn't have worked, either. Cohndar would have detected the deception unless Beltur had kept total shields around himself all the time when he had been near Cohndar, and that would have told the senior mage that Beltur was hiding something.

Once he reined up outside the healing house, he didn't see much alternative to tying the horses to the rail and putting a concealment around them. He hurried inside and walked straight to the chamber where Klarisia usually was. No one was there except a thin older woman in gray. "Where could I find Healer Margrena and Healer Jessyla?"

"They might be in the main admitting room, the one—"

"Thank you." Beltur smiled and left, taking long swift strides down the main corridor.

Even as Beltur stepped into the admitting room, Jessyla turned, then said to her mother, "I think it's time to go."

Margrena stepped back and said to the woman she was tending, "I'll be back in a moment."

When mother and daughter reached him, he said, "I have two mounts outside. We need to hurry. You'll have to gather up everything quickly."

"It's done," replied Jessyla. "I already have everything packed."

"You do?"

"She started packing as soon as you left on eightday," said Margrena. "What happened?"

"Let's just say that, when Cohndar and Waensyn showed up at the smithy this morning, they made it clear that my life would soon be forfeit if I remained a day longer in Elparta."

"A day longer?" asked Margrena.

"If that." Beltur gestured and turned. "This way. We need to move quickly."

Margrena frowned, but said nothing.

The three walked down the corridor. Jessyla hurried ahead and recovered her coat from Klarisia's study quickly enough that Beltur didn't even have to break stride.

Once they were outside, Beltur saw two men near the concealed horses. One started toward Beltur, a club in his hand. Beltur struck him with a small containment, hard enough to knock the club from his hand.

"Frigging mage . . ."

But both men backed off, then hurried away.

Beltur removed the concealment and stopped short of Slowpoke, turning to Margrena. "I'm sorry things happened this way. I did my best to avoid trouble, but that's what Cohndar and Waensyn insisted on. The only way I can avoid execution or permanent indenture is to leave Elparta."

"Why?"

"Cohndar insisted that I left free chaos in the cupridium, against the orders of the Council." Beltur motioned to the Council mount. "This one's yours, Jessyla."

Jessyla looked at her mother. "I'm sorry—"

"Don't be. When I was your age, I didn't have the courage to follow your father. If I had, he might have lived. You'll make your own mistakes, but I don't want you making mine. Besides, if I said no, you'd follow Beltur, and that would be far more dangerous."

Jessyla's mouth opened, and her eyes brightened.

"Just go. Every moment you spend here will make it harder, and I can tell from just looking at Beltur that you need to be away quickly."

Jessyla threw her arms around her mother. "Thank you." After a tight embrace, she mounted the horse.

Beltur mounted Slowpoke, then said, "Your aunt's house."

Jessyla nodded.

Beltur eased Slowpoke into a quick walk. "Is she home?"

"She said she was going to spend the afternoon at Almaya's, but she'll be home now."

"Then I'll wait outside with the horses."

Once they reined up outside the door of Grenara's house, Jessyla dismounted and handed her horse's reins to Beltur.

Beltur waited, uneasily, but Jessyla was back quickly, after a time that seemed to drag as Beltur kept looking around, but was likely only a fraction of a quint.

She hurried out, carrying a large cloth-covered cylindrical pack.

Grenara followed Jessyla, but stopped in the doorway. "You can't run off like this! What will I tell your mother? What will she say?"

"She already knows. She told me to go," declared Jessyla, struggling to balance the overlarge duffel over the front of the saddle before mounting.

Grenara was speechless for a moment, before turning to Beltur. "The Council won't let you get away with this. Waensyn will chase you to the end of Candar and beyond."

"If he does, it will be his undoing, and he'll deserve that and more." *Seeing as he's already gotten part of what he deserved.* Beltur turned to Jessyla. "Are you ready?"

"Go."

While they rode south on Bakers Lane, Beltur kept his eyes and senses moving, feeling that each of those they passed was looking at the two of them. And while they were, likely because very few riders were out in the snow, light as it was, none gave the mounted pair more than a passing glance.

When they neared the bakery, Beltur said, "I need you to wait here outside with the horses, while I gather my few clothes and things and say goodbye to Meldryn. I won't be long. Not at all." *You can't afford to be.* He rode Slowpoke to a point midway between the door to the house and the door to the bakery. There, he reined up, dismounted, and handed Slowpoke's reins to Jessyla.

"I'll be as quick as I can be."

"I'll be here."

Beltur hurried inside, brushing past Laranya, who had come from the parlor.

"Oh . . . you're never here in the middle of the day."

"I'm usually not. I need to get a few things. I'll be out shortly. Just get on with what you were doing."

"I wanted to tell you that Nykail is doing so much better. One of the black mages came to look at him. He had silver hair. He asked what you had done to heal Nykail. I told him I didn't know, except that you had said he had too much order deep inside. He thanked me and left."

"Did he give his name?"

"No. The one with him said he was a councilor."

Waensyn and Cohndar! But how did they know? Figuring that out would have to wait. "I see. Thank you for telling me." Beltur managed a smile before heading upstairs.

Once in his room, the first thing he did was to open the iron strongbox and take out the golds and silvers. The golds went into the inside slots in his belt, except for two, which he slipped into his pocket, and some of the silvers into his wallet. The rest stayed in the cloth bag that they'd been in, and the bag went in the duffel. *You'll have to do better than that, but not right now.*

He looked at the patrol mage medallion, then smiled wryly and put it around his neck. *Why not? They'll execute you anyway if they catch you.*

Quickly he gathered his toiletries and wrapped them in a towel. He also grabbed another towel, and packed all that in the duffel and tied it shut. Carrying the duffel, he hurried down the stairs and to the bakery, where he stood in the archway for a moment until he saw that no one was there.

"Meldryn, you were right," he said as he walked toward the gray-bearded mage. "Cohndar plans to charge me with chaos-wielding and indenture me for life, that is, if the Council doesn't decide to execute me."

"And you're still here?"

"Not for long. Jessyla is outside with the horses, and we're leaving." Beltur handed over the two golds. "This isn't even close to what I owe you in so many ways, but it's all I can afford to spare."

"You don't—"

"I do. I owe you more than I can say, but if I don't pay some of it, it will haunt me forever . . . as long as that may be." *Or at least as long as we manage to stay alive.*

"You'd better go. Your whole body says you're just quints ahead of Cohndar and Waensyn."

"Something like that." Beltur set down the duffel, then stepped forward and hugged the older man, strongly but quickly. "Thank you ever so much."

"I gained as much as you did."

Beltur doubted that.

Meldryn hurried to the middle of the bakery, picked up two meat pies and wrapped them in a cloth, then handed the package to Beltur.

Beltur decided to leave through the bakery. After picking up the duffel one-handed, he walked to the door, Meldryn beside him.

As he neared the door, Beltur took a deep breath and was almost overwhelmed by how good the bakery smelled . . . and how much he was going to miss Meldryn . . . and had missed Athaal.

He swallowed.

"Just go," said Meldryn gently, as he opened the door. "She's waiting for you, and you don't want anything to happen to her."

Beltur nodded and hurried toward Jessyla, handing her the wrapped meat pies.

In moments, or so it seemed, the two of them were riding north on Crossed Lane.

"What are we doing?"

"We're going to the smithy, where we'll load our duffels on another horse, and then we'll set out to catch up with Jorhan and the traders. If we hurry, they'll only be a glass or so ahead of us, and we should be able to catch them by the end of the day."

"If the snow doesn't get worse."

"Even if we don't we have to get away from Elparta. I'll tell you more when we get to the smithy."

"I have the feeling I know. Mother probably does also."

"But she doesn't know for a fact, and that's important."

Before long they turned south on the east wall street. Beltur questioned whether to use a concealment in approaching the southeast gate, but decided against it, especially since he'd never used one around Jessyla and since he didn't have a lead attached to her mount. "We'll just ride out through the gate. I hope I don't have to use containments on the guards, but they usually don't care who's leaving."

As they neared the gate, Beltur glanced in the direction of the Council building, wishing he dared to stop and pick up his last two silvers as a patrol mage. He shook his head. That was risking far too much for too little. Besides, what he'd taken from Cohndar and Waensyn more than outweighed two silvers. *At least you're not leaving Elparta coinless and with more than the clothes on your back.*

Beltur could feel himself getting tense when he turned Slowpoke east and rode through the gate. On the far side, one of the guards looked quizzically at Beltur, then smiled. "So you've finally got a horse, Mage?"

"I do, indeed. He's an old friend that I finally managed to get back."

"Don't be gone too long. The snow's getting heavier."

"We'll likely be staying at the smithy where I've been working. Don't expect us back tonight."

The guard nodded.

Once the two were well away from the gate, Jessyla asked, "How did he know you?"

"Just by sight. I've been walking through those gates for almost two seasons. Some of the guards recognize me by now."

"That's good. They don't see anything unusual about your leaving."

Beltur hoped not, although he seldom left the city so late in the morning, and he also hoped the guard hadn't seen him leave the first time or didn't recall it.

As the two rode closer to the smithy, Beltur kept sensing to see if any blacks or anyone else was near the smithy, but while there were low spots in the snow on the lane where the snow had lightly covered earlier tracks, most likely from Jorhan's sledge, there were no signs that anyone else had been there. Beltur rode right up to the stable, where he dismounted and tied Slowpoke. Jessyla dismounted as well, and the two entered the stable, Jessyla still carrying the meat pies.

The first thing Beltur noticed was a small sack tied to the saddle of the second Council mount, with a note attached. He read the words and smiled.

> Provisions. Figured you might not have time for them. One sack by
> the door has grain for horses. The big one has hay. It's not as heavy as
> it looks. The water bottle's old, but it doesn't leak.

Beltur realized that there was a water bottle in an older leather holder on the other side of the saddle, and an old curry brush, thrust under the leather strap. He peered inside the sack. At the top was the package of acorn cakes he'd given Jorhan. He smiled, then turned to Jessyla. "We can put the meat pies here. Jorhan was thoughtful." *More than thoughtful. Much more.*

"What happened? It happened in the other building, didn't it?"

"Cohndar and Waensyn showed up before eighth glass. They came with a Council guard, but they sent him off as soon as they discovered no one was here but Jorhan and me. They told Jorhan that he'd been deceived by a renegade white mage, and they said they were going to return me to Elparta and that I'd be fortunate to spend my life as an indentured slave. Then they told me to drop my shields. That told me I'd never make it back to stand before the Council. They would have claimed that I tried to escape and that they had to kill me. I put containments around them both. I broke Cohndar's shields, but Waensyn almost broke out of the containment I had around him. While I was dealing with him, Cohndar tried to escape. Jorhan hit him with a big smithing hammer. It killed him instantly. I tightened the containment on Waensyn and held it until he died."

"Good! They both deserved it."

"Waensyn even more than Cohndar."

"I never liked him, but he made up to Auntie. The only reason he did that was to try to get me and get at you."

"You never said anything about that."

"I thought you'd get too angry and do something foolish. Then I saw that you were wiser than I thought, and it didn't matter anymore." She paused. "I still don't see why they put you in a situation where you didn't have any choice."

"Because they thought they were much stronger than I am. That was my fault, or my doing, anyway. None of them, not even Athaal, knew what I could do. At first, I kept what I was doing to make myself stronger from everyone because I thought I was weaker than the stronger blacks, and I didn't want them to know that. Then, when I was forced into being an arms-mage, I didn't want them to know because it became obvious that Cohndar and Waensyn were plotting to put me in situations where I'd be killed. You know that. I almost was several times, and without Slowpoke, it would have been worse. So I let them think I was much weaker than I was. A lot of them can probably do more, but I don't think many of the blacks in Elparta are as strong with containments and shields, and those made the difference. I just wish they'd left us alone."

"Some people can't do that."

Unfortunately, and that makes it worse for everyone. "We need to load up the other horse and be going. It wouldn't be good to be caught here."

"In a moment." Jessyla turned and pulled him to her, her lips on his in the chill stable. When she finally released him, she said quietly, "We are consorted. It may not be formal and with a party, but it counts."

While Beltur hadn't expected the suddenness of her statement, he just said, before returning the kiss, "We are." And a flood of bittersweetness swept over him, for all those who should have been there at that moment, and who would never know, for his uncle, for Athaal, and Meldryn and Margrena . . . all because of two jealous and bitter blacks.

XXIX

A little more than a glass after Beltur and Jessyla left the smithy, the snow began to fall more heavily, although the wind did not pick up, and the air seemed slightly warmer. Remembering what Jorhan had said about the horses, he hadn't pushed them, but kept moving at a solid walk, riding with Jessyla to his right, and the Council mount that served as their packhorse on a lead to his left. The packhorse looked heavy-laden because of the sack of fodder, but the weight it carried was far less than the other two. The center of the road was packed snow, and by straining Beltur could follow the traces of the traders' sledges covered by perhaps three digits of recently fallen snow.

After two glasses passed, they stopped to stretch their legs, and to drink some of the water in the single bottle. Beltur also worried about watering the horses. He could use tiny bits of chaos to melt snow, but he didn't have anything to hold the water. *Another thing you didn't think of.*

They remounted and resumed their ride. Before that long, there was enough newer snow on the road that Jessyla announced, "We can't see the traces anymore. At least, I can't."

"We're still on the road," replied Beltur. "There's been enough travel that the snow is higher on the sides."

"I can see that. More like sense it, but it worries me, and we haven't seen anyone."

"That's probably for the best. Before long, no one will be able to tell if we came this way and how far."

"Where else could we go where we're out of Spidlar any sooner?"

Beltur laughed softly. "You're right about that."

After several long moments, she spoke again. "You never said what you did with them . . . their bodies. I mean, you're not a chaos mage."

"So I couldn't have burned them to ashes? No, I didn't do that. Jorhan knew a place. Even if someone does go looking, and we're unfortunate, it will be a few days before they're found, since they may not even be missed yet. With luck no one will ever find them, but I'm not counting on that."

"That's why you didn't tell Meldryn or Mother anything."

"They can truthfully say that they don't know anything about it. The way I phrased what I did say suggested that I was fleeing to avoid Cohndar and Waensyn. That implied that they were still alive at that time. With their mounts also missing, some people might wonder if they got lost in the snow chasing us." *Unlikely, but possible.* "Also, they're likely to find out that Jorhan bought two horses when he already had one, and that might muddy the waters more."

"They can't force Axalt to give you up, can they?"

"First, they'll have to discover that we're there. Second, Axalt has never given up anyone or anything to either Certis, Gallos, or Spidlar." Beltur brushed more snow off his coat and then off Slowpoke. "That's where Relyn went to escape the Prefect of Gallos."

"Relyn?"

"You don't know about Relyn?"

"I've heard of the Relynists. He must be the one they're named after."

"He is. According to Meldryn, Relyn built a black temple of order in Passera. The Prefect didn't like what he was telling people about order and put a price on his head. He fled through Elparta to Axalt. The Prefect had attacked Axalt before and had failed. I don't think he tried again. Anyway, Relyn was safe in Axalt. Supposedly, there are a lot of Relynists there. Some in Montgren, too, I think."

"What did he say that made the Prefect so mad?"

"I don't know. Some called him the Black Prophet."

"I never heard of a black prophet."

"I didn't either, until Athaal told me about him . . ." Beltur paused. "Come to think, it was Laevoyt who called him the Black Prophet."

"Laevoyt? The city patroller you worked with?"

"He was the one. Good man. I wish I could have said goodbye to him, too."

Another glass passed, and the road showed no recent trace or traces of mounts or sledges.

Beltur was getting the definite feeling that they were unlikely to catch up with Jorhan any time soon—not unless the smith and the traders stopped at the way station beyond Reiks. He also wondered if he'd even be able to make out the few structures that comprised the hamlet through the gloom and still-falling snow.

"How far do you think the way station might be?" Jessyla finally asked.

"I haven't seen or sensed the buildings that might be Reiks. We've only been gone for a little less than four glasses, and Jorhan said the way station was at least thirteen kays from the smithy, maybe fourteen."

"It will start to get dark in another two glasses, maybe sooner if the snow gets heavier."

Beltur was well aware of that. He was also conscious of the fact that his hands and feet were getting cold, almost numb. By the time another glass passed, he was feeling more than a little chilled, and worried. Had they somehow gotten sidetracked onto another road? All he could see was white in every direction . . . and he couldn't sense anything standing out— or could he?

He concentrated more, hard as it was through the snow, before he sensed what had to be a cot, to the north of the road and not that far ahead. *Now . . . if there's another . . .*

Before long, he sensed another, past the first, and when they were almost abreast of the first, he saw what had to be a path, if covered with new snow, heading north. He was afraid to smile, but when he sensed a third, he finally spoke. "I think we're passing through Reiks."

"That means another glass before the way station?"

"Maybe a little less."

More than three quints later, Beltur finally sensed, and then saw, the way station. It stood less than ten yards off the road, hard for Beltur to see in the dim light with the still-falling snow, essentially a timbered barn with a steeply pitched roof and two doors, one clearly for animals and the other for travelers. There were only two windows, and they were shuttered.

"I was beginning to think we'd never get here." Jessyla paused. "There's no sign anyone else has been here, not in the last glass or two, anyway."

While a way several yards wide had been packed down in the snow in the not-too-distant past, the untouched snow above it was a good ten digits deep.

Beltur rode Slowpoke right up to the door for the horses, or oxen, he supposed, but saw immediately he'd have to open that door from inside. So he rode back to the smaller door and dismounted, handing the lead to the packhorse to Jessyla. He had to pound on the door to break it free of the ice that had formed, but it gave way suddenly, so abruptly that he almost tripped and fell inside.

The inside was pitch dark, although he could sense that the travelers' side was little more than an open space with a small hearth in one corner. There was even wood in the woodbox. He turned toward the west side of the barn, looking for and finding a door, ajar, through which he hurried. Since the timbers that held the double doors shut were frozen to their iron brackets, Beltur didn't hesitate to use several bits of chaos to unfreeze them so that he could open the doors. Jessyla immediately rode inside, and Beltur stepped out, only to find Slowpoke already moving toward him.

"Good fellow!" Beltur led the gelding inside and then barred the doors. He frowned, then returned to the travelers' side, looking for and finding a bar to the smaller door, which he quickly put in place.

"Now, for some water."

"Beltur . . . it's dark, and it's hard to sense where things are. If we could get my bag down, I did bring two candles."

Beltur made his way to the packhorse and unloaded Jessyla's overlarge cylindrical duffel, but carried it to the travelers' side, where there was a very worn wooden floor, then set it near the hearth. He was surprised to see that a fire had been laid in the hearth. *Does the Council pay one of the locals to keep the way stations ready?*

He smiled wryly. He hadn't thought he'd ever again be grateful for anything the Council did. He didn't bother with a striker, but used chaos to light the kindling. By then Jessyla had appeared and had dug out a candle, and she used the fire to light it.

"Time to find out where the well is. Jorhan said there was one here somewhere." Beltur stopped. He could see and sense that Jessyla was shivering. "You sit close to the hearth until you warm up."

"I'm all right."

"You will be . . . once you warm up."

"I . . . I could stand to warm up."

"Just stay put at least until you stop shivering."

Beltur should have realized that her coat was nowhere near as warm as his was. *You should have known . . . and she never said a word.*

He did find the well, behind a door on the north side of the barn, but the water he drew up felt chaos-tinged. He swirled order into it, and promptly got very dizzy, so dizzy he had to sit on the side of the well for a time. He was still sitting there when Jessyla appeared, pale, and still shivering slightly.

"Are you all right?"

"I think so." Except when he started to stand, the well room seemed to swirl around him, and he sat down again. "I've done more than I thought. Can you get me one of those acorn cakes and the water bottle?"

"I can do that."

Beltur lowered his head. That helped a little. Had he really done all that much? Or had all the sensing through the snow worn him out? *You also haven't eaten since before fifth glass this morning, and you've done a lot of magery, especially in dealing with Cohndar and Waensyn.*

Jessyla reappeared with the package of acorn cakes and the water bottle. "I think I need some, too."

Sharing the water bottle, they both ate slowly. A good quint passed before Beltur could move without dizziness. While Jessyla was still shivering intermittently, she was no longer pale.

Beltur sensed that the water no longer held chaos, and he poured it from the chained pail into another bucket—after using a hint of chaos, tentatively, to clean the second bucket. "I need to water and feed the horses."

"Take your time."

The way he felt, Beltur wasn't about to rush anything, and he didn't, first returning to the west side of the way station, which was divided into two sections by a chest-high wooden wall, and ushering the three mounts into the north side, which seemed a shade warmer to Beltur. Then he unsaddled and watered the horses, which required several buckets to fill the trough. After that, he groomed the horses, while Jessyla unloaded the packhorse. Finally, he spread some of the fodder from the big bag into the wooden manger, adding grain in three separate places, and watching to make sure each horse got grain, before returning to the hearth, where Jessyla had dragged the sole trestle table and a bench near the fire, and had set one of the meat pies on the hearth stones to warm.

"Are you done?" she asked.

"For now. I'll have to get the horses more water later. There's really not enough fodder and grain for them for more than a few days." *If that.*

"You have enough silvers to buy some, don't you?"

"It might be possible if there's anyone close enough to the road who has horses."

"You need to sit down and eat." She motioned for him to join her on the bench. "It's getting warmer at last. I added more wood to the fire. We'll need to sleep close to the hearth."

Beltur could see the candle lying on the table, clearly snuffed out. He smiled briefly. Jessyla wasn't one to waste anything. "I brought one heavy blanket."

"So did I. Two might be enough, but we still have our coats, once they dry out."

Beltur looked at her. "I never planned for things to happen this way. I was saving silvers. I'd planned to buy us a house in a year or so."

"I know." After a moment, she added, "Sometimes, things are meant to be. You weren't meant to be a white in Fenard. We weren't meant to stay in Elparta."

Beltur had his doubts about what was meant to be or not to be, but refrained from saying so, instead soaking in the warmth from the fire.

"I know you don't believe in that," Jessyla went on. "I do. Mother does, deep inside, but she won't say anything about it."

"And your aunt?" asked Beltur.

"Auntie believes most of all in the silvers she can count. That's why I never told her about all the ones you gave me."

"But they were for you and your mother."

"We used them. We just never told her."

"That was why she wanted you to consort Waensyn." That scarcely needed to be said, Beltur knew.

"You'll do far better than he would have. You make things and do things. He just took."

"I still worry about taking you from your family."

"You didn't take me. I chose. You couldn't have taken me anywhere if I didn't want to go."

He laughed softly. "I shouldn't ever forget that."

"No. You shouldn't."

But she smiled after she spoke, Beltur could see.

"We need to eat and to get some rest."

Beltur nodded. "I am tired."

"Not too tired. I hope."

Beltur hoped that the ruddy firelight concealed the way his face flushed.

XXX

Beltur woke on threeday morning nestled close to Jessyla. His face was chill, but nothing else was. His side was also sore from lying on the hard and warped wood floor.

She turned to him, then kissed him on the cheek, wrapping her arms around him. "You were sweet. I think we need more practice."

Beltur flushed, knowing she was right, but also feeling more than willing.

"Not now, dear."

He knew she was right, but that didn't make getting the rest of his clothes on any easier . . . and he was definitely chilled by the time he had his trousers, tunic, and boots on. The last thing he put on was the City Patrol medallion.

"You took the patrol medallion. Good. You earned it."

"I thought so. I'm not sure the Council would agree." He started to turn away as she began to dress herself.

"You don't have to do that. We are consorted."

Beltur flushed again, but he took Jessyla at her word, just enjoying watching her for the very few moments it took her to get into her healer greens.

"Is it still snowing?" she asked after sitting on the bench and pulling on her boots.

"I don't think so, but I'll look." Beltur walked to the door, noticing the greater chill the farther he moved from the coals remaining in the hearth. But before opening it, he let his senses range over the area outside and the road. He sensed no one and no large animals, except for the horses in the way station itself. Only then did he unbar the smaller door and peer out.

It was earlier than he'd thought, but the sky was clear, the grayish green color it often took on just before dawn, and his breath was an icy plume in the bitter air outside. Something less than fifteen digits of snow covered the path from the way station, and Beltur didn't see any new tracks on the road, just the snow-covered depressions that remained from their mounts.

Just to be on the safe side, he re-barred the door and walked back to Jessyla, who hugged him fiercely for a moment.

"It's just before dawn, and the snow's stopped."

"Then we need to eat and get moving if we want to catch up with Jorhan and the traders."

"There are a few other things we need to do."

"You take care of the mounts. I'll see what else we can eat . . . besides acorn cakes."

"You don't like them?"

"They're food. They're also bitter, and they don't taste of much except bitterness."

Beltur hadn't thought they were that bitter, but he also hadn't thought that they'd tasted like much of anything. "We probably ought to save the other meat pie."

"I'd already thought that."

Almost a glass passed before the two left the way station, after Jessyla had found some travel bread in the provisions sack, along with a small jar of berry preserves, and a large wedge of cheese, from which she had cut several slices. The road was as of yet untraveled, but Slowpoke didn't seem to mind the ten to fifteen digits of snow above the packed base. From what Beltur could tell, the base was hard-packed snow, and while there might have been ice farther down, there didn't seem to be any ice shards that might have cut Slowpoke or the two other horses.

Riding through the new-fallen snow was a bit slower than it had been on twoday, and Beltur found himself riding with his eyes closed and using his senses much of the time because of the glare caused by the reflection of sunlight from the snow, light that brought little warmth.

Sometime after eighth glass, Beltur saw a set of tracks in the road ahead. As they neared the hoofprints and the wide runner traces of a sledge—in fact, several sledges—Beltur saw that they came down a side lane that ran due south of the Axalt road.

"Those look like they might belong to Jorhan and the traders."

"Where did they come from?" asked Jessyla.

As they drew closer, Beltur studied the traces and looked southward, where he could see several lines of smoke coming from what looked to be a stead several hundred yards from the main road. Or could it be an inn? *But an inn that far from the road? Or had one of the traders made an arrangement with the steadholder?*

He shook his head. While an inn or a hospitable stead might have been a better place to stop, there had been no way that he and Jessyla could have gone any farther the night before. "There's a stead or an inn down that lane. It must be a lane of some sort."

"We might not even have seen it in the dark."

"You might be right."

"Might?"

Behind his scarf, Beltur winced. "You're right. We were cold and tired."

"How long ago did they come this way, do you think?"

"We left the way station pretty early. I'd think that we might be able to catch up with them sometime today. Maybe by midafternoon?"

"You don't sound that certain," replied Jessyla, a hint of laughter following her words.

"That might just be because I'm not."

For the next glass, Beltur said little, studying the tracks of the party before them, hoping it happened to be the traders, especially since he knew nothing of the way ahead, only that it could take as little as four days or as long as an eightday to reach Axalt, about which he knew even less, except that it was reputed to take those not in favor in Gallos, Spidlar, or Certis, and perhaps elsewhere. He knew that they were likely more than two kays behind the others, because he could sense close to that far now that the snow had stopped and the sky remained clear.

The snow on each side of the road seemed to grow higher with each passing kay, so that his eyes, even while he was mounted, were only a yard or so above the snow, and when he dismounted to check Slowpoke's hooves to make sure ice was not building up there, he could barely peer over the white barrier on each side of the road.

Then slightly before first glass, they stopped to rest and eat some acorn cakes, along with drinking some water. Beltur could sense that the horses needed water, but what was in the water bottle wouldn't help much, and trying to find a stream under all the snow wasn't exactly practical. Nor did he have any container in which to pour the water.

At that thought, he stopped and shook his head. An open containment could handle that. If he just put a containment around some snow that looked clean, added a little chaos for heat, and then shifted the containment to allow the horses to drink . . .

In the end, however, it took some four tries to get it right, because the first time there wasn't enough snow. The second time, while there was enough snow to create a bucketful of water, in amid the snow was a sizable horse dropping. Beltur was more careful of that the third time, but the heat melted the snow on one end of the containment that he hadn't anchored, and the water ran out. The fourth time worked, and Slowpoke lapped up the warm water almost greedily. Beltur had to repeat the process for each of the other horses. He was fairly certain he hadn't overwatered them, but he wasn't sure how soon it would be before he had to repeat the process.

A quint or so after they resumed riding, he began to sense riders and mounts ahead of them, around a long sweeping turn in the road. "There are travelers ahead of us. I can't tell how many yet."

"The tracks in the road look fresh, and we just passed some horse droppings that hadn't frozen."

"I just hope it's Jorhan and the traders."

"Aren't they the most likely?"

"I'd think so, but the way the snow's been packed, there are more winter travelers than I thought." He paused, then said, "Maybe I'm being overly cautious, but I'd like to get closer to them before they see us. I'm going to put a concealment around us. After I do, tell me if you can sense where I am and where the packhorse is."

"I can do that."

Beltur raised the concealment and waited.

"I can sense everything for twenty or thirty yards. After that . . . it just gets fuzzy."

"That's good enough. So long as you can sense where Slowpoke and I are, you can stay on the road."

"I can do better than that. I can sense the sides of the road."

Beltur smiled. "That's even better. You'll improve with practice. And I did say that you are more than a healer."

"Yes, you did. I'm glad you did."

So am I. Beltur lifted the concealment. "We won't need that for another kay or so, after where the road goes around that hill ahead."

"You did something like making a shield when you watered the horses, didn't you?"

"I created a containment. It's what I had to do to restrain lightfingers and cutpurses. Except with the horses, the containment was much smaller and open on top."

"I could feel that, but . . . there were tiny black coils and fuzzy white coils, and the black ones sort of confined the fuzzy ones."

Beltur didn't sense order and chaos quite that way, but he knew most mages sensed them differently. "I sense them a bit differently, but that sounds right."

"How do you shape them into a containment or a shield?"

"I picture them in my thoughts the way I want them to be. It took me a long time to get it to work."

"You said Taelya could already do that."

"I have the feeling she'd been working at it secretly for some time."

"That doesn't seem fair."

"You mean that you've been able to sense order and chaos for much longer, but haven't been able to shape or use it?"

Jessyla nodded.

"Maybe we need to think about a different way for you to think about them."

"But they are what they are."

Beltur managed not to sigh.

"You're humoring me."

"What you're doing isn't working as well as you want it to. I'm just suggesting a change. If you don't like the change I'm suggesting, then think of a different way that feels better to you."

"I just might."

Beltur hid a wince. "It's hard to explain, because every mage, and probably every healer, senses order and chaos differently."

"You said that."

"I do repeat myself sometimes." He managed a rueful and dry tone.

"I'm sorry. It's just . . ."

"So frustrating?"

"Yes."

"I do understand that."

"I know." Jessyla sighed.

They rode a good hundred yards without speaking before Beltur said, "I'm going to have to conceal us now. When we get closer, we'll have to stop talking, because the concealment doesn't hide sounds."

"I didn't think it did."

Another half glass passed before Beltur and Jessyla neared the last sledge, the one Beltur thought might be Jorhan's. He waited until he was certain none of the riders were looking back before he lifted the concealment. He immediately could see for certain that the trailing sledge was Jorhan's, as was the mount beside the sledge horse, and presumably the bundled rider was indeed the smith.

"Jorhan!"

The smith jerked his head around. "Beltur! Where the frig did you come from?"

Beltur rode forward, closer to the rear of the sledge, before replying. "From Elparta to your smithy to the way station last night. We left early this morning, and I hoped the traces we found were yours."

"Hold up, ahead!" shouted Jorhan. "The mage is here!" As soon as Jorhan halted the sledge, he turned in the saddle to face Beltur. "I've been worrying about you two. We didn't stop at the way station. Karmult said the water there was bad."

"It was," agreed Beltur, "but we managed."

"He knew a stead where he's stopped before." Jorhan looked at Jessyla as she reined up her mount beside Slowpoke. "Pleased to meet you, Healer. I can see why he didn't want to leave you behind."

Jessyla smiled politely. "I told him he'd better not."

Jorhan laughed. "She knows her mind."

"She always has."

"Best I introduce you to the others." Jorhan motioned.

The rider escorting the second sledge eased his mount back beside Jorhan.

"Trader Karmult, this is Beltur, the black mage. He's the one who helped forge the cupridium." Jorhan looked inquiringly to Beltur.

"And this is Jessyla. She's a healer, and also my consort."

The sandy-haired and bearded man nodded. "Having a mage and a healer can't but help when we reach the foothills before Axalt. There are sometimes brigands there."

When the other rider appeared, Jorhan went on. "This is Vaenturl. He's from Vergren. He trades whatever he can. Vaenturl, this is Beltur, the one I told you about . . . and his consort Jessyla. She's a healer."

Beltur wondered about the trader, but then Vergren was the capital of Montgren and likely one of the few places where a wide-ranging trader could easily sell his goods.

The dark-bearded trader inclined his head. "Hope we don't need either of you, but it's good to have you." His eyes went to Slowpoke. "Big horse you've got."

"I rode him during the fighting, but I couldn't find him afterwards," said Beltur. "Jorhan came across him when he was looking for a mount. One of the best favors a man could do."

"He's a warhorse. You were one of the mages in the battles?"

Beltur nodded.

"And you're leaving Elparta?"

"Gratitude isn't considered a virtue by the Council," said Jessyla acidly.

"And you'd know?" asked Karmult.

"She would," answered Beltur, his voice even. "She was one of the battle healers."

"You never mentioned that," said Jorhan.

"I imagine there's much he didn't mention," replied Jessyla. "Beltur doesn't often talk about what he's done."

"It seems to me—" began Karmult.

"You're in deep enough," interjected Vaenturl, the sound of amusement permeating his voice. "Stop digging."

"I didn't mean . . ."

"Think about it. He's a mage. He's young. He's consorted to a battle healer. That mount is clearly his. He can forge cupridium, and the two of them caught up with us without any of us seeing them on an open road with no cover—"

"He was also a City Patrol mage in Elparta," added Jorhan. "That, I do know."

Karmult shook his head, then laughed. "You've made your point." He looked at Beltur. "Since I'm a Lydian and we always want all the answers . . . that doesn't answer why you're here."

"Let's just say that I'm not held in the greatest esteem by the Council at the moment. I refused to surrender Jessyla to a mage more highly favored by the Council and had to use certain magely skills to depart, against the will of the Mage-Councilor of Elparta."

The Lydian turned to Jessyla. "And you freely chose to accompany him?"

"No." Jessyla paused, then added, "I demanded it."

Jorhan grinned. "Enough answers for you, Karmult?"

"We're in good company, Karmult," said Vaenturl. "Two traders with wares from questionable sources, accompanied by a coppersmith flouting edicts of the Spidlarian Council and a mage and a healer who've done the same and likely worse. I do suggest we proceed, since none of us wish to remain in Spidlar longer than necessary."

Beltur couldn't help but like the narrow-faced trader from Montgren, who was clearly more open and honest than he described himself.

"Lead on, then." Jorhan turned to Beltur. "Best if you two stay back here. The sledges do pack the snow, and that's easier on your mounts."

"We also don't happen to know the way," added Beltur.

"That won't matter for the next few days. There's only one way to go." The smith paused, then added, "Good to see you're both here."

"We're glad to be here," replied Jessyla. "And I'm glad to meet you. Beltur's often talked of you."

"Don't believe it all. He's brought out the best in me. Better get the sledge moving or we'll be left behind."

As Jorhan eased his mount forward, Jessyla said quietly, "I like him. He's a good man."

"Better than he believes."

"Like you."

Beltur doubted that, but he wasn't about to dispute her words.

XXXI

Over the next three glasses, the travelers plodded on, seeing no one on the road, except a local steadholder who was leading a horse pulling a roller down the lane from his dwelling to the main road, packing the snow flat. Most houses appeared to be inhabited, from the thin plumes of smoke rising into the clear and windless green-blue sky, but Beltur glimpsed only a few individuals outside doing various chores.

As the sun dropped in the western sky, Jessyla looked to Beltur. "Do you know where we're staying tonight?"

"Jorhan mentioned a village named Charaam."

"That's helpful."

Beltur urged Slowpoke farther ahead. "Jorhan, I don't believe you mentioned where we'll be stopping, except that it's in Charaam."

"The Road Inn. It's the only inn there, such as it is."

"The inn or Charaam?" asked Beltur.

"Both. I hope you brought some coins. The Road Inn is costly."

"How costly?" asked Beltur warily.

"Half silver for every night. A copper for each mount, and dinner is four coppers with a single ale or lager. You can get provisions as well. They're a tad more reasonable."

Beltur glanced back at Jessyla, whose eyes had definitely widened, then back at the smith. "That seems like a lot."

"It is. But it's the only decent place to stop in thirty kays, or more. This time of year, there will be room. In summer, harvest, and early fall, it's stuffed with traders."

"Is it better than the way station?"

"It's warmer, and there's hot fare. Beds are decent. No vermin."

Beltur had his doubts about that, but order/chaos dusting could deal with that. "You've stayed there before?"

"Twice. Told you before that I've not been to Axalt that often. Barrynt told me about it. It's not like the Traders' Rest in Elparta."

"But it costs as much," called back Vaenturl.

Another half glass passed before the sledges and mounts started down a long and gentle slope into a lower area dotted with scattered steads and cots.

"There's the inn, right beside the road," called out Jorhan.

To Beltur, the Road Inn didn't look all that impressive, just a long and seemingly low brick-walled structure on the north side of the Axalt road, set apart by open ground, possibly snow-covered pastures, from the handfuls of houses and cots that apparently constituted the village of Charaam. As they rode closer, though, Beltur realized that the inn was more imposing than he'd realized, a full two stories, stretching almost thirty yards on a side, with a width of possibly twenty yards, separated by an open courtyard from a stable about the same size as the inn. The roof was steeply pitched, and probably needed to be, given the amount of snow that he'd already seen, even before winter proper had begun.

Almost another glass passed before Karmult turned the lead sledge off the road and along a snow-packed way toward the stable, where an ostler stood motioning. Beltur watched as Karmult eased the sledge to a halt outside the first of two large doors.

"The first door is for sleighs and sledges, the second for horses." The ostler looked closely at Slowpoke as Beltur rode up. "You an armsman for hire?"

"No. Just a black mage, with a healer, who's also my consort."

"Your mount looks like a warhorse." The ostler's voice was close to accusing.

"He was. I rode him against the Gallosians. The Council didn't want him after the fighting ended. I did." All of that was true, even if the implications weren't. After seeing the dubious expression on the man's face, Beltur opened his coat enough to show his black tunic and the silver patrol medallion.

The ostler stepped back. "I'm sorry, ser. We have to look out for brigands."

"I can understand that, but do you get that many in the winter?"

"There are still a few. Most stay in the hills near the border, but two eightdays ago, they ambushed a trader traveling alone some ten kays north of here."

"That's good to know. Which stalls? We have three mounts."

"Take the next door. You can double-stall the two smaller horses at the end, and the big one next to them. That will only be a copper for each stall. We charge by the stall, but feed is extra."

"How much?"

"A copper a day for each horse. Two cups of grain and hay. A stone's worth of hay a day."

Beltur nodded. He hadn't the faintest idea if that was enough, but had the feeling it might not be enough for Slowpoke.

Once they had stalled and unsaddled the horses, Jessyla watched as Beltur groomed the three. Then they waited for Jorhan and the others before they carried their duffels and the provisions sack across the courtyard to the front foyer of the inn, a red-brick-floored space far larger than any inn Beltur had visited, with age-darkened oak walls, and the faintest hint of cooked onions coming from somewhere.

There, Jessyla unwound her heavy scarf and smoothed her hair into a rough order. The man behind the counter stared. "Don't see many women traveling this time of year."

"You won't see many like this pair, Mharl," said Vaenturl, gesturing to Beltur, who had set down the duffel and provisions sack. "He's a mage, and she's a healer. And don't get ideas. They're consorted."

The stocky man shook his head. "First pretty woman in eightdays, and she's a healer consorted to a mage. Whole season's been like that."

"You expect too much of fall and winter," countered Vaenturl. "What about rooms on the south side on the west end?"

"How many?"

"Four. Three small, one large. With good shutters."

"All the shutters are sound." At Vaenturl's doubtful look, Mharl added, "Mostly." Then he looked at a large board with hooks. Under each hook was a number, and under some numbers was a line. Most of the hooks held keys.

"I can give you fourteen, fifteen, sixteen, and seventeen."

Vaenturl looked at the board. "What about eight, nine, ten, and eleven, the ones on the top level?"

"If you're only here for the night."

"We'll take them." The trader turned to Beltur. "It's seven coppers for the double."

"I'm supposed to ask for eight," complained Mharl.

"Seven will do for a mage and a healer."

"Easy enough for you to say."

"They wouldn't be here if it weren't for us, and you wouldn't have even the seven."

"You traders . . ."

"You're making it up in stalls and feed," added Beltur.

Mharl smiled wryly. "Seven."

Beltur handed over a silver and received back three coppers and the key, with the number 11 scratched into the metal. "Is there wash water in the room, or do we carry it up?"

"There's a pitcher and basin in the room. There's a pump at the end of the building on the lower level."

"Run the water for a bit before you fill the pitcher," suggested Vaenturl.

"And throw the waste water out the hall window at the end," said Mharl. "That way you don't dump it on someone."

"Meet for supper in half a glass?" Jorhan pointed to the double doors on the far side of the foyer.

Beltur looked to Jessyla, then back to Jorhan. "Three quints or so."

"We'll be in the public room," said the smith.

"Follow me," suggested Vaenturl.

Beltur and Jessyla let the trader from Montgren lead the way to a narrow staircase that creaked as they climbed to the second level.

"Upper level is a little warmer and a lot quieter," offered Vaenturl. "Even in off-times."

"Do you travel this road that often?" asked Jessyla.

"Only once a year. I've been doing that for ten-odd years. Most years, anyway. I've never been farther west than Elparta. Made it to Kleth once. Never again." Vaenturl turned right at the top of the stair and headed toward the end of the also narrow hallway.

"Why not?" Beltur had an idea, but he wondered if he was assuming too much. He had difficulty getting himself, the duffel, and the provisions bag through the opening to the hallway.

"There's nothing there you can't get in Elparta for less, and the traders there . . . they have definite ideas about their worth and the worth of whatever they trade in."

Beltur nodded. That scarcely surprised him.

"You said you left Elparta because the Council had little gratitude. That's a little vague."

Before Beltur could reply, Jessyla immediately said, "We came from Gallos, hoping Spidlar would be more hospitable. After a few seasons, it became clear that it wasn't, and that matters would get worse."

"Why was that, if I might ask?"

"Traders tend to regard mages and healers as slightly higher-paid indentured servants," replied Beltur. "And they don't like it if we discover ways to make a few more coins."

"Jorhan mentioned something like that. I wondered. Do you think it will be better anywhere else?"

"We're young enough to take that chance," said Jessyla. "From what I've seen, the older you are, the harder it is to move."

"That might be. It also might be that when you're younger, you think places are more different than they really are."

"Or that when you're older," countered Jessyla, "you fool yourself into thinking they're more alike."

Vaenturl chuckled. "I foresee interesting times for you two. You might be better off in Montgren, if I do say so."

"Why do you think that?" asked Beltur.

"We can talk about that later." Vaenturl pointed. "There's your room. It's much better than where Mharl wanted to put you."

"Thank you," replied Beltur, turning the door lever and pushing the door open. He stepped back to let Jessyla enter, then said to the trader, "At dinner, then."

"Of course," replied the trader with a smile, looking back down the hall to where Karmult was emerging from the staircase.

Beltur nodded and stepped into the room, setting the duffel and provisions sack against the wall beside the door, and then closing the door behind himself. In the dimness, he glanced around the chamber, taking in the small wash table, the line of wall pegs for clothing, the heavy brown woolen hangings over the shuttered window, and the one bed, twice the width of a pallet bed, not exactly capacious, Beltur thought, but certainly better than the wooden floor of the way station. "How are you doing?"

"A little tired. My thighs are sore." Jessyla flushed. "From riding."

"I'll fill the basin with water, and use a trace of chaos to warm it up. Then I'll get another pitcher full."

Jessyla sat on the edge of the bed, still looking at Beltur. "Vaenturl wants us to go to Montgren. Do you know why?"

"I don't know more than he's a trader out of Vergren and that Jorhan trusts him. He's not chaotic."

"I sense that as well. That's why . . ."

"You think he's trying to tell us that Axalt may not be any better for us?"

"It's possible."

"You wash up and . . . whatever. Let me go get some more water. Slide the lock plate after I leave."

"I can manage that."

After adding a touch of order to the water in the pitcher before heating it with chaos and pouring it into the basin, Beltur took his time getting the water, partly because he ducked into another vacant room and picked up a second pitcher, so that when he made his way back upstairs, he had two full pitchers.

After he unlocked the door and reentered, he saw that Jessyla was combing out her hair, not that it was that long, not even shoulder length, and peering into a tiny tin mirror nailed to the wall. He couldn't help but wish he could have afforded one of the cupridium mirrors that he and Jorhan had forged. "Do you need any more warm water?"

"Not now. You might want to empty the basin, though."

Beltur did just that, using the window at the end of the hall, and noticing a large icy lump rising from the snow below. He returned to the room and washed up. Then he shaved, not knowing when he might next get the chance. After that he changed into his better black wool tunic, since he'd been wearing his "working" tunic the whole time since twoday morning.

He also made certain that the patrol medallion was under his tunic and out of sight before turning and looking at Jessyla in her greens—and wearing the shimmersilk scarf he had given her. "You look beautiful."

"Scarcely that. Better than presentable."

"Beautiful," he said gently.

"You really mean that." Her eyes brightened. She stepped forward and held him tightly.

Beltur's arms went around her, and they stood there, locked together, for a time.

"Even after all this . . ." she murmured. "I'm so glad."

"So am I."

By the time the two left their room and made the way back down to the public room, Vaenturl and Jorhan were already seated at a round table with five straight-backed chairs. Of the close to twenty tables in the room, only seven were taken, most of them close to the hearth, where several large logs, obviously recently added to the fire, now burned.

At Beltur and Jessyla's entrance, several men turned to look, not so much at Beltur, he sensed, as at Jessyla. He strained to hear some of the comments.

". . . pretty thing with the mage . . . young . . . mage . . . good or cocky . . ."

". . . rode a warhorse . . . no wonder his consort's . . ."

Beltur repressed a smile as he looked hard at the weathered man who'd started to comment on Jessyla. The man immediately looked away.

Beltur seated Jessyla beside Jorhan, and Vaenturl switched chairs so that Beltur was seated between Jessyla and the trader.

"Karmult should be here in a bit," said Jorhan. "He's meeting with another Lydian trader who's headed to Elparta."

"With winter coming on?" asked Jessyla.

"He'll likely take a riverboat down to Spidlaria and a ship back home from there," explained Vaenturl. "Spidlaria won't freeze up until midwinter, if then."

"Did he say why he was meeting?" asked Beltur.

"I didn't ask," replied Vaenturl. "No point in it. He'd never say. Lydians are more closemouthed than Spidlarians. Traders and merchants, anyway."

"Does that go back to Heldry the Mad?" asked Beltur with a smile.

"Who was he?" asked Vaenturl.

"A duke of Lydiar."

"Never heard of him." Vaenturl shrugged.

"He wrote a book on ruling."

"Must not have been that good a duke if he had to write it all down." Vaenturl glanced toward the open doors to the public room. "Here he comes."

"How did your meeting go?" asked Jorhan as the Lydian seated himself.

"Well enough." Karmult gestured toward the serving woman as she left three younger men.

The server moved to the round table, but stood next to Jorhan, on the side where Jessyla was seated.

"What's the fare?" asked the smith.

"Mutton pie, fowl and dumplings, or coney hash and gravy."

"Fowl and dumplings, ale," said Jorhan.

"The same," added Beltur and Vaenturl, almost simultaneously.

"Do you have hot cider?" asked Jessyla.

"We do. Same as the ale."

"I'll have that with the fowl."

Karmult shook his head. "Ale and mutton pie."

"Is that all?"

"For now," said the Lydian.

"Pay when you're served. Inn's rules," announced the server, glancing around the table.

Beltur nodded, as did Jorhan and Vaenturl.

Once the server headed toward the kitchen, Karmult nodded in a satisfied manner. "Mutton pie. Can't go wrong with that."

"Not at all," said Vaenturl, "unless it's not Montgren mutton and you like lead in your belly."

"I've had the dumplings. They make mutton seem light."

"Only if you're talking about Montgren mutton," replied Vaenturl. "It makes others' lamb taste like mutton, and Montgren lamb is ambrosia."

Karmult laughed. "Some truth in that, but that much."

"More than you'll admit." Vaenturl grinned.

Karmult shook his head.

"How many more days to Axalt . . . if it doesn't snow?" asked Beltur.

"Without snow and wind, four days. Otherwise," replied Karmult, "who knows?"

"Likely won't snow for at least two days," said Jorhan. "Looks to be cold and clear tonight."

"Are there any more inns along the way?" asked Jessyla.

"There's one in Trakka," said Jorhan. "Two days. Not much to speak of, but the fare's decent."

Before all that long, the serving woman returned. When she set the platters before Jessyla and Beltur, he put down a silver. "That's for the healer and me."

The silver vanished with a quick movement of the server's hand, which left two coppers where the silver had been. Beltur left one of the coppers on the table, then took a sip of the ale, a deep amber, but not dark. It was on the bitter side, but not nearly so bitter as what his uncle had preferred.

The dumplings were heavy, Beltur had to admit, but they were tasty, and the sauce was good and necessary because the fowl seemed a little dry, not that he left anything on his platter.

"Good to have hot fare," said Jorhan. "Travel food gets old quick."

"Travel gets old quickly," added Vaenturl.

"If it gets that old, why do you keep doing it?" asked Karmult.

"Because I'm a terrible herder, and a man has to make a living." Vaenturl shook his head ruefully and gave Beltur a quick sidelong glance.

Beltur understood immediately, because he'd sensed a certain falsity in the other's quick and seemingly rueful reply. *But that means he knows you can sense that, and he's trusting you not to say anything.* But why? "Are there herders in your family?"

Vaenturl laughed, honestly, before answering. "I doubt that there's a single family in Montgren that doesn't have herders, and that includes the Duchess's family. The sheep of Montgren, especially the black sheep, are the strength and wealth of the land. No doubt your tunic is woven of the finest Montgren wool."

"I wouldn't know," admitted Beltur.

"I can tell from here."

"What else can you tell?" asked Jessyla warmly.

"That your consort is a very fortunate man."

"I'm fortunate as well. Very fortunate."

"Spoken like the newly consorted," said Karmult sardonically.

"As they should speak," replied Vaenturl. "If we don't speak that way when we're young, how can we speak well of each other after enduring the trials that life brings to everyone."

"You're speaking like a Relynist," observed Karmult.

"I'm not one, but there's wisdom in both what the Kaordists and the Relynists say, although I don't hold to either's words strictly."

"Do you hold to any words strictly?"

"Just to do what is right, as best I can. Sometimes, that's not as good as I'd wish. More than sometimes."

Again, Beltur had the feeling that what Vaenturl said was slightly off, not so much false as false self-denigration.

Two quints later, Jorhan rose. "I'm tired, and tomorrow will be early."

At that prompt, both Beltur and Jessyla also stood.

"We'll be here for a bit, yet," said Karmult.

"Then we'll see you in the morning," offered Jorhan, who turned to Beltur and Jessyla, "as I will you." Then he strode off quickly out through the doors, but once out in the foyer, not in the direction of the staircase to the upper level.

When Beltur and Jessyla stepped out of the public room, a worn-looking woman in faded brown trousers and jacket moved quickly toward Jessyla. "Healer . . . a moment . . . please?"

Beltur eased a shield around Jessyla, even though he sensed no untoward chaos.

"What is it?" asked Jessyla kindly.

"My son. He needs a healer. He got frostburn, and there is pus and stench . . ."

Jessyla did not wince, but Beltur sensed a certain discomfort.

"Where is he?"

"In our quarters, at the end of the stable. Please . . ."

"Aren't there any healers here in Charaam?" asked Beltur.

"No, ser."

Beltur sensed the truth and the despair behind the words.

"We'll do what we can," said Jessyla.

Beltur kept the shields up as they followed the woman from the inn and across the courtyard to the far end of the building holding the stables. The shields didn't do anything to protect them from the wind, and his teeth were chattering when they reached the building.

The "quarters" to which the woman led them consisted of a single room little larger than the one where Beltur and Jessyla stayed. That room was smoky, because there was no hearth or stove, just a large brazier, along with a bench, a narrow table set against the outside wall, and two pallet beds. A girl sat on the end of the bench. She was small, possibly only four or five, with wide brown eyes. At the other end of the bench sat a red-haired boy, also small, but likely ten or eleven. One hand was wrapped in a stained cloth.

Even from the doorway, Beltur could sense the wound chaos, but he said nothing, accompanying Jessyla to where the boy sat.

"Vielor, the healer needs to see your hand."

The boy held up the hand.

Jessyla unwrapped the cloth, studying the inflamed area and the greenish pus, as well as the reddish streaks radiating from the discolored distention in his palm. "He's had frostburn. You can tell from the whiteness of his skin, but the chaos isn't from that. If it were, his hands and fingers would be dark blue, even black."

"There's something in his hand, in the palm below the thumb."

"I can sense that." Jessyla turned to the mother. "I'm going to have to cut into his hand a little. It needs to be cleaned."

"Do what you must, Healer."

"Do you have a clean cloth and some water?"

The woman pointed to the table, and the pitcher on it. "I will get some cloth."

Beltur eased out his belt knife, dusting it with free order, then handed it to Jessyla, who waited until the serving woman held out a square of cloth.

"Just moisten it, and hold it for a few moments."

"You won't be able to move your hand while the healer does what she must," Beltur said, using a containment to hold the boy's hand steady.

Jessyla used the knife to cut away the dead skin, then took the cloth and began to express the pus. Beltur tried to ignore the initial smell. After a time, she looked to him. "I don't have any tweezers, and I'd rather not cut any deeper."

"Let me see what I can do." Beltur concentrated on anchoring a bit of order to the small object lodged in the boy's hand, then linked that to a small containment that he gingerly tugged free through the cut Jessyla made.

She used the cloth to grasp it. "Another clean wet cloth." She handed back Beltur's knife, which he laid on the table.

Once she had cleaned the wound as well as she could, Beltur eased in bits of free order.

"I can't stitch it up—"

"I have a needle and thread," volunteered the woman.

Beltur used a bit more order to strengthen the thread as Jessyla sutured the cut. Then he released the containment, and recovered his knife, using a scrap of cloth and order to clean it.

Finally, Jessyla turned to the mother. "You'll need to keep the wound clean and dry. He shouldn't be working in the cold until it heals."

"The stablemaster—"

"If it gets worse again, he might lose the hand," interrupted Jessyla. "He might even die. Tell the stablemaster that."

The woman swallowed.

"Tell him that both a mage and a healer told you that," added Beltur.

The woman inclined her head. "Thank you, Healer, and ser."

Jessyla looked to the boy. "Keep it dry and clean."

Once the two were outside in the courtyard and hurrying through the cold back to the inn, Beltur spoke. "How could a splinter get that deep without him noticing?" He thought he might know, but wasn't sure and wanted to hear what Jessyla had to say.

"His hands were numb from the frostburn, and he likely didn't feel it then. When his hands warmed, they hurt all over, far worse than a splinter would. He works in the stable. There was likely some corruption on the splinter, and it festered and kept getting worse. At first, his mother likely didn't notice or told him it would get better. Usually, little chaos wounds like that do. That's why I think there was some corruption on the splinter."

Beltur glanced up at the night sky momentarily, seeing the stars glittering, tiny points of light against the black velvet of the sky. He shivered as the wind gusted around them, far colder than it had been earlier, possibly because the night was so clear and the wind came out of the north. They were both shivering by the time they returned to their room in the inn, since they hadn't worn coats or gloves, not really expecting to have done some healing in the stable quarters.

Once he locked the door, he just looked at Jessyla. "We're very fortunate, compared to so many. Even if we do have to leave Spidlar."

She nodded.

He looked at her again, so beautiful.

She smiled. "Not yet, dear. We need to talk. No . . . I ate too much too quickly, and then doing healing . . ."

Beltur sensed that she was more than truthful. "Then sit down, and we'll talk. There is something that happened at dinner . . ."

"I saw. Vaenturl isn't a terrible herder at all. Or that's not why he's not a herder."

"Then there's what he said in the hallway earlier—that we'd be better suited to Montgren. He clearly felt that. We really know nothing about Axalt, except that there's one honest trader there who offered to help us."

"Help you."

"Anyone who would help a mage would certainly be more willing to help a healer."

"I suppose so."

Beltur pursed his lips. "There's something we should have talked about much earlier."

"Oh?" Jessyla offered an amused smile.

"We are young, and we don't have even a land where we belong, let alone a home or even a rented room . . ." Beltur didn't really want to blurt out what he had in mind.

"Are you trying to ask what we might do so that we don't find ourselves with a child too soon?"

Beltur swallowed. "Ah . . . well . . . yes."

"It might have been better if you'd brought this up before last night, you know?" she asked, her tone almost stern.

"I should have," he admitted.

Jessyla grinned. "I love it when you know you should have done something and are trying to make apologies without apologizing."

Beltur flushed. "I . . . don't like admitting making mistakes. I'm sorry."

"I accept your apology." She smiled gently. "It's something Mother and I talked about a long time ago, once I became an apprentice healer. She made me practice until I could do it effortlessly. It just takes concentration on order in the right place, and we won't have a child until we're both ready."

Beltur did not sigh in relief, but he might as well have done so, because he knew she could sense what he felt.

"I'm glad you did think about it, even a little late."

So was Beltur.

XXXII

As Jorhan predicted, fourday dawned bright, clear, and cold. Breakfast was egg and mutton scramble with near-tasteless, if warm, bread, and ale or cold cider. Beltur had the three mounts saddled before the sledges were ready, even though he took extra time to show Jessyla how to groom and saddle her mount. They had their gear loaded on the third horse and were waiting in the stable, which kept them out of the slight wind, when a stableboy appeared.

"You're the mage and healer? Baryla said to tell you Vielor's much better."

"Thank you," said Jessyla.

The boy looked sideways and then said to Beltur, his voice low, "Your mounts looked like they needed more. Couldn't do much with the grain. Stablemaster does that, but I put more of the sweet hay in their mangers."

Beltur kept his smile to himself and slipped the boy two coppers. "We appreciate it . . ."

"You don't have to, ser. You and the healer . . . I saw Vielor's hand yesterday. Worse'n any frostburn I ever saw. His ma says he'll keep the hand." The boy looked around. "Best be going, ser." In moments, he was nowhere to be seen.

"I'm glad to hear that," Beltur said.

"You're glad?" Jessyla shook her head. "It took two of us."

"Only because you didn't have the right tools to deal with the wound chaos."

"That was sometimes a problem at the Council Healing House. There were too many who needed help and not enough healers or even clear spirits or cloths." Jessyla peered out the door. "Vaenturl's pulling his sledge out now."

"We'd better lead the horses out and mount up." Beltur untied Slowpoke and patted his neck, then led him and the packhorse out into the clear morning, where the green-blue sky showed not a trace of haze or clouds. Once Jorhan had his sledge on the snow-packed path to the main road, Beltur and Jessyla mounted and closed up the gap.

Fourday was uneventful, if chill, with riding a glass, walking a stretch, watering the mounts, riding, walking. During the entire day, they saw one local sledge heading east that turned off before they neared it, and passed two groups of traders headed west toward Elparta.

The way station where they stayed on fourday evening was much like the one where Jessyla and Beltur had earlier spent the night, except the water wasn't tainted, and they had to share the space with a trapper who was bringing pelts to Elparta.

Fiveday was much like fourday, except there was no wind and the sky had a faint haze. The inn at Trakka had smaller rooms, harder beds, and Beltur had to dust the straw mattress with order and a little chaos to kill off the vermin, and he spent another three silvers or so for room, stalls, feed, and food . . . plus another silver for grain and some extra fodder and bread and cheese.

The end of sixday brought them to a way station within sight of the Easthorns, and at sevenday's end, they stayed in a stead that offered rooms over a stable, better accommodations than at a way station but more severe than at either inn.

Eightday dawned hazy and gray.

Once they were on the road to Axalt, still a snow-packed way, but one that curved through hills that seemed to get higher, Jorhan motioned for Beltur to ride closer to him. Once Beltur moved up, the smith said, "Often we get a northeaster after this kind of haze. Also, this part of the road is the most likely place for an attack by brigands." He pointed to Vaenturl, who now carried a bow and a full quiver.

Karmult, riding beside the lead sledge horse, also carried a bow.

For a moment, Beltur wondered what weapon the smith might have, until he saw the long staff in a bracket on the side of the sledge closest to Jorhan.

The smith gestured to the staff. "That's the best I can do. Don't see that well at a distance, and I never could get my shafts anywhere near where I wanted them."

"There don't seem to be any tracks besides those on the road, and there are few of those," Beltur said.

"After the brigands attack, even if they're not successful, they take pine branches and smooth the snow. After even a light snow, it's hard to see their tracks."

"How do they even get to the road? The snow is waist-deep out there."

"Skis."

"Skis?" Beltur had never heard of them.

"Long narrow board slats tied to their boots. They're polished and waxed on the bottom. They'll ski down close to the road and use their bows to pick off travelers. The snow makes it hard for the travelers to get to them. Most travelers aren't good enough with bows to drive the brigands off."

Beltur could see how that might work.

"Then, they take the sledges and drive them farther to where there's a hidden path off the main road. They'll dump bodies somewhere in gullies or deep snow, and wait until spring when they'll travel back roads through the high passes to Certis, and sell what they can to a fence in Rytel."

"Fence?"

"A less than honest merchant who will resell at a profit to others, usually outlanders."

"'Fence' . . . a good term for a barrier between the thieves and others who aren't averse to not looking too closely at where something came from."

"Suppose that's where the word comes from. Never thought about it. You never heard that before?"

"Trade isn't something I had to worry about. Maybe I should have."

"It doesn't hurt to know about it . . . as we've both found out. Anyway, you might do whatever you do to discover people who aren't in plain sight."

"I've been doing that, but I'll be even more on guard."

"Sometimes, they come up behind and start loosing shafts . . . and there's another group up ahead waiting."

"I'll keep that in mind as well."

"Might never see any. Then, again, we might."

"I'll keep a close watch," promised Beltur, slowing Slowpoke and the packhorse to drop back so that he was once more riding beside Jessyla. "Jorhan says we might see brigands. Even if we don't, we might end up caught in a northeaster."

"I noticed they're carrying bows. They weren't yesterday."

"They travel on skis—long wooden slats—"

"I know what skis are."

Beltur frowned. "How come you know and I don't?"

"Dear, I just might know a few things that you don't. Isn't that possible?"

Beltur winced. "It's more than possible. You know more about healing, and most likely other things that I know nothing about. But how did you know about skis? I never heard about skis in Fenard."

"I read about them. The women of Westwind use them. They have for hundreds of years."

"It's not in *The Book of Ayrlyn*."

"It's in *The Book of Saryn*."

"There is a *Book of Saryn*?"

"There is. I read part of it when I was younger. There was an older healer named Helyea. She visited Mother once. She came from Sarronnyn. I don't know where she went after she left, but I remember the part about skis because it seemed so amazing that you could glide along over the top of snow." She gestured toward the side of the road. "Seeing all this, it makes sense."

"It does."

"Let me lead the packhorse. That makes more sense, too."

Beltur almost objected, but then realized that she was right, and leaned toward her, handing her the lead. Then he slipped the lead over Slowpoke's head and reined up. "Switch the lead to your right side."

Once the packhorse was on Jessyla's right, he urged Slowpoke forward so that he was riding on her left. He couldn't have said why, but he felt that any attack, if there happened to be one, would likely come from the north side of the road.

Another glass passed before Beltur sensed the presence of people ahead. At first, he thought that they might be traveling traders on the road itself, but after riding another few hundred yards, he gained the definite impression that they were on the slope above the road around the next curve. He also could sense, not quite so clearly, at least one or two people moving swiftly down a slope behind them, but from high on the slope and at an angle that would eventually intersect the road, if just out of eyesight. He rode ahead and eased up just behind Jorhan.

"There are people on the slope of the next hill around the curve ahead, and there are some behind us on the right."

"Sounds like brigands to me. Ride ahead and tell Vaenturl."

Beltur urged Slowpoke forward, past Jorhan and up beside the bearded trader, where he repeated what he'd told Jorhan.

Vaenturl nodded, then called out, "Time to rest the horses!"

Karmult immediately turned and yelled back, "It's too early."

"Just rein up!"

The Lydian did so.

Vaenturl kept his mount and sledge moving until his sledge horse was within a yard of the rear of Karmult's sledge.

The Lydian turned in the saddle. "You're making us easy pickings."

Vaenturl shook his head. "The mage says there are people on the slope ahead, around the curve. There are some more behind us."

"They can't catch us if we keep moving."

"They're high on the slope, aren't they?" asked Vaenturl.

"Yes. They're coming downhill at an angle."

Karmult took a deep breath. "Frigging brigands."

"I wanted to rest the horses now," said Vaenturl, "because once they're on the level with us, or close to it, we can move faster than they can."

"If we're not too full of arrows," snorted Karmult.

"I can help with that," said Beltur. "I can block the arrows for a while. That's if you keep the sledges and horses close together."

"Then we should be able to outrun them," said Vaenturl. "The road's faster than deep snow. Beltur, you and the healer and your mounts should be right behind Karmult. That way you'll have the best chance of looking forward or back."

Beltur nodded, although he suspected that Vaenturl also didn't want Jessyla any more exposed than necessary.

After resting the horses for about a quint, during which time the brigands did not move closer, Karmult eased his sledge forward. "We'll move at a restful pace until they attack."

Beltur urged Slowpoke along, right behind the Lydian. Just before they came around the last part of the curve in the road, Beltur heard a rushing roar from somewhere ahead that soon died away. Even when they reached the point where the road straightened out, Beltur saw no signs of the brigands. He could sense the bodies on the slope, but all he could see were scattered pines and firs, with occasional rocky outcrops protruding from the deep snow.

Then some of the snow began to move, and he realized that the brigands were all in white, with even their scarves or head coverings white as well, and those white shapes began to move down the slope, spraying snow from their legs. Beltur couldn't make out their boots or the skis that supposedly carried them.

Then, only about a hundred yards from the road, from a point still some five yards higher than the road, the half score or so of brigands stopped and produced bows—also white. The moment the first shafts were loosed, Beltur expanded his shields.

At the same time Karmult urged the sledge horse into a faster walk.

Beltur kept sensing the brigands, discovering, to his surprise, that several of them, possibly half, were women. But then, he realized that it made perfect sense. No one was going to be able to close quickly with them through the deep snow, and anyone who tried would be a better target the closer they got.

The brigands were good archers. That Beltur could tell by the impacts on his shields.

"Beltur! Ahead!" called out Karmult.

Beltur looked forward. The brigands were just about abreast of them, if a hundred yards off the road, but ahead of the travelers was a low wall of snow across the road. A wall not all that high, possibly only slightly over a yard deep, but deep enough to block any passage by the sledges and enough to slow the horse to a crawl. *So that even if we escape, our goods are left behind?*

Beltur smiled grimly, not appreciating terribly the cleverness of the brigands.

Briefly, he wondered how they had managed it, until he glanced to the north and the steep slope, now through which ran a swath of rubbled snow that extended to the road, if in an ever-narrower path. *That was what you heard.*

Even so, he had to do something about the barrier. *What about a shield with warm chaos on the front?* Beltur glanced back. The nearest brigand was a good hundred yards away from Jorhan and the last sledge. "Come on, big fellow, we're going to see about pushing snow." He could also sense that the sledges were slowing down as they saw the low wall of snow.

"Karmult! I'm coming past you on the left! Just slow down a little. We're going to try something."

Beltur knew that snow was heavy, especially packed snow, but what if he and Slowpoke pushed away the top half yard or so? He concentrated on shaping his shield into an angled front, hoping that the shield would put a wedge in the middle of the road, and that a thin line of hot chaos would help.

When the shield hit the wall of snow, Beltur could feel the pressure, but while Slowpoke slowed he kept moving—for about three yards. Beltur let the gelding stop and studied the snow ahead. They were almost through the barrier, with less than a yard to go.

He turned Slowpoke and guided him back to before the beginning of the wall, as fast as he dared, looking back toward the closing brigands, then noticing that he'd left a good fifteen to twenty digits of snow above the level of the snowpack on the rest of the road. *Probably too much for the sledges.* He pushed that thought away and urged Slowpoke ahead once more, worrying about the time his makeshift plowing was taking. This time the gelding broke through the barrier.

Beltur immediately turned Slowpoke back and made another snow-shield run through the remaining snow before turning back to where the snow barrier had begun and gesturing to Karmult, as he edged Slowpoke to the side of the snow-packed part of the road. "Get moving. I'll keep shielding you. But move!" The snow was deeper than it had been on the road before, but Beltur knew he couldn't clear much more, not without lowering his shields, and the arrows were still coming.

Part of that urgency was because Beltur knew he was on the verge of light-headedness. Carrying wide shields while pushing snow with his shield, as well as shielding himself from the free chaos he'd drawn from somewhere, had definitely been an effort.

Karmult's sledge horse struggled with the deeper snow, slowing to almost a snail's pace, before breaking through, followed by Jessyla and the packhorse. Vaenturl's passage was easier, largely because he kept his sledge in the traces Karmult had created. Jorhan didn't slow down that much.

Beltur swung in behind the smith's sledge, struggling to keep his expanded shields in place, until the brigands stopped loosing shafts. That happened after they had covered another hundred yards beyond the snow barrier, and Beltur dropped the shield back just to cover himself. As Beltur passed Vaenturl, the trader said, "Thank you. We'd likely be dead without what you did."

"You could have gotten over the snow barrier, I think. But you would have lost the sledges."

"We still might not have made it. They're good archers. I saw where you stopped the shafts."

"They are good." Beltur smiled ruefully and moved forward beside Jessyla, expanding his shields just a bit to cover her. He'd worried about that, but he just couldn't have held the larger shields that much longer.

He kept sensing, but so far as he could tell, there were no other brigands anywhere near.

After a deep breath, he fumbled out the water bottle and took several swallows. The water, cold as it was, helped a little, but he could only hope that he didn't have to do any more magery any time soon. *Why did that take so much out of you?*

"Are you all right?" asked Jessyla.

"I'm fine. As long as I don't have to do anything more for a while. I think it's all the snow and the order and chaos tied up in it . . . and that I had to use a little chaos in clearing it away."

"I could feel that." Jessyla shuddered slightly.

"I couldn't think of anything else to do, not quickly." Not wanting to dwell on his condition, he added, "Did you know that almost half of the brigands were women?"

"I wondered about that. Some of them seemed smaller."

"They were still good archers, better than many armsmen, I think."

"You could have killed the brigands, couldn't you, one by one?" asked Jessyla.

Beltur almost froze in the saddle. "I didn't think of that."

"That's because you don't think that way."

"I killed people during the invasion."

"I'm sure you did. Did you ever go out with the idea of killing them?"

"Yes," he admitted.

"Who?"

Beltur was silent for a long moment. "The only ones I went out intending to kill were white mages. But that doesn't matter. I killed far more troopers than mages, even if I wasn't trying to kill each of them. And I knew some of them would die from what I did." *More than just some of them. Many more.*

"It does matter. Unless you're really threatened or trying to survive, deep inside you, you don't want to kill people. Defeating the Prefect's army was a matter of survival."

"I'm not so sure that's always been true. Even if it is, that may not always be good," reflected Beltur. "We escaped the brigands, but because I didn't kill them, we left them to prey on other travelers and traders."

"That was because you weren't really in charge," Jessyla said. "Vaenturl was thinking like a trader. He wanted everyone and all the goods to escape. You accepted that and acted to make it happen."

"I didn't even think of it in that way." He managed a smile. "You've given me a lot to think about . . . again." He kept sensing, but the brigands seemed not to have moved much. When he looked back, though, all he could see were trees, some few rocks, and a great amount of white snow, into which the brigands blended all too well.

"How far to Axalt?" he called back to Vaenturl.

"Another three glasses, maybe four, to the border gates. A glass beyond that to the city proper."

Beltur nodded, hoping no more brigands lay in wait.

XXXIII

Beltur looked ahead in the late-afternoon light. The slopes flanking the road were the lower parts of small mountains, with more rock and evergreens than earlier, evergreens that were largely snow-covered. He also realized that the road had been built up from the floor of a canyon cut through the land by a modest stream, but it remained a depression flattened deeply enough into the surrounding and seemingly endless snow that, even from the saddle, Beltur could barely see over the sloping sides that angled up from the layers of packed snow that covered the actual road. Beyond the right side of the road was an ice-covered stream.

He finally began to feel better after raiding the provisions sack when they finally stopped to rest after escaping the brigands. He had to admit that while acorn cakes did provide nourishment, they seemed a trace bitterer each time he ate one. He'd given part of one to Slowpoke, but the gelding had clearly enjoyed it. He also noticed that since they had escaped the bandits, their speed had slowed, perhaps because the road had a slight but definite grade that wasn't that obvious until he looked back.

"How much farther to the border gates?" Beltur called back to Vaenturl.

"Less than a glass."

Beltur was certain that he'd heard that more than a glass before, but he just nodded.

Little more than a quint later, as Beltur followed Karmult and his sledge around a tight curve, he saw a wall running from one side of the canyon to the other, a distance of a good hundred yards, if not slightly more. The road led to a gate on one side of the wall with an opening barely wide enough for a large wagon and most likely no more than three yards high. The gray stone blocks that framed the gate rose another twenty yards above the keystone of the square arch. The top of the wall was crenellated, with arrow slits on the level just below.

At the base of the wall on the side opposite the gate was a narrow water sluice from which poured the icy waters of the stream into a narrow lake, some two hundred yards in length and half that in width, bordered by the canyon wall on the south, the stone embankment on the north, on the top of which ran the road, and a spillway on the west end of the lake from which the water tumbled down into the streambed. From what Beltur could see as they approached, the sluice was constructed to keep the water in the lake in motion, presumably so that the lake would not freeze over. He wondered if that actually worked in the depth of winter. The sky to the east of the wall looked to be much darker, as if heavy clouds were rolling in, but they were too far away for Beltur to sense what form of order/chaos lay within them.

When they neared the wall, Beltur saw two guards waiting in sheltered stone niches at the side of the gates. While the heavy oak gates were recessed into slots on each side, Beltur could make out an iron portcullis suspended behind the gates. He had the feeling that there were other gates behind the obvious ones, suggesting one reason why no one had ever taken Axalt, especially combined with the narrow and twisting nature of the canyon.

Karmult slowed and then stopped the sledge just short of the guards, both of whom wore dark gray uniforms and who immediately stepped forward.

"Why are you coming to Axalt?" asked the taller of the two guards.

"I'm a trader from Lydiar. I'm passing through on my way to Rytel, then Jellico. After that, I'll go to Vergren, and then home."

"Through Weevett or Haven?"

"Why would I go through Haven? It's out of the way, and there's nothing there anymore."

"Do you have a passage letter?"

"I have one from going outbound." The trader produced a document.

The shorter guard read it and returned it. "What sort of goods do you have in the sledge?"

Karmult produced another sheet. "This is a listing of everything that's in trade."

After a few more questions the guards waved the trader on.

Beltur eased Slowpoke forward, then reined up. Jessyla followed with the packhorse.

The shorter guard looked curiously at Slowpoke and then at Beltur. "This is a warhorse and an old combat saddle. I see no weapons."

Beltur opened his coat, revealing his black tunic and showing the medallion. "I'm a black mage. I served during the invasion. The Council sold off my horse. I got him back."

"Why are you coming to Axalt?"

"My consort and I were invited by Merchant Barrynt. She's a healer."

"How do you know him?"

"I've been working with Jorhan. He's the smith with the last sledge. When the Council of Spidlar said that we couldn't sell copperwork, except through a trader—"

"You're not the first to leave Spidlar because of the Council." The guard paused. "How do I know you're a mage?"

"Try to hit me. I won't hurt you. Just try."

The guard unsheathed his blade and thrust, if cautiously, at Beltur. When the tip struck the unseen shield, he almost dropped the sword. He then sheathed the weapon and rubbed his hand. "If you aren't one, I've never seen one." Then he looked at Jessyla, taking in her green trousers and her boots. "You two can wait for the smith inside the gate."

The guard took even less time with Vaenturl, possibly because the trader from Montgren produced a document, possibly a passage letter, although Beltur couldn't hear from where he and Jessyla waited. Both guards read it, asked several questions, and passed him through.

When Jorhan moved up, the guards took quite a bit of time questioning him, but finally waved him through. With that, Karmult immediately moved out with his sledge.

Vaenturl motioned for Beltur to follow. "It's getting dark and cloudy, and we've still got another two or three kays to go. With luck, we might reach the city before the storm hits."

"The city's not near?" asked Jessyla.

"The canyon continues for another kay," explained Vaenturl. "Maybe even a bit farther. Then there are fields, and then the city."

As Beltur eased Slowpoke after Karmult, the thought struck him that they had entered Axalt on the last day of fall, just before winter began. *So, officially, we aren't even violating the Council edict.* As if that were the worst of his offenses against the Council. He shook his head and looked ahead, taking in the still narrow, stream-cut canyon and the winding road.

Jessyla and Beltur rode only a few hundred yards before a gust of wind ripped into them, so cold that it felt like Beltur's forehead was being stabbed by scores of tiny needles. After a few moments, he closed his eyes, trying to guide Slowpoke largely by his senses, although the swirling order and chaos made it hard for him to sense more than ten or fifteen yards ahead.

While the storm was coming more out of the north than the east, the walls of the canyon channeled the winds and snow so that the travelers were heading directly into maelstrom.

There was little sense in stopping, Beltur knew, because the snow and wind would last for glasses, if not days. So they plodded on, staying close behind Karmult. After what seemed like a glass, barely twenty yards away, so heavy was the snow, Beltur both sensed and saw another set of walls also crossing the entire canyon, lower than the border wall, topping out at perhaps ten yards, and seemingly in good repair, but with open and un-guarded gates. The stream just poured through a stone culvert in the walls. Beltur wondered if the second wall was older, or constructed later as a secondary defense. *Does it matter?*

Riding through the open gates was almost like riding through rapids of snow, but once past the wall, through the near-blinding snow, Beltur could discern that, east of the wall, the canyon opened into a valley. He couldn't see just how big it might be, just that there were the fields Vaenturl had mentioned, terraced on levels, through which the road continued.

They rode another kay before they reached a line of houses, as if who-ever ruled Axalt had decreed that the houses would begin at that point, and the road became a street, one recently cleared since there were only about five digits of new-fallen snow on top of the stone pavement.

Almost half a kay later, Karmult slowed his sledge to a halt at the edge of an open square, and Beltur and Jessyla reined up.

Vaenturl pulled up behind them, calling out loudly so that his voice could be heard over the howling of the wind, "We're going to the Traders' Bowl. It's on the far side of the square. We don't know where Jorhan's sister's consort lives, but he'll guide you there. We'll be here for at least a few days." After a pause, the trader added, "Just in case you two want to move on."

Moving on was the last thing on Beltur's mind, especially in the middle of a northeaster. "Thank you. We'll keep your words in mind."

"If you ever do get to Vergren, you're welcome. Ask for me at Essek's Factorage, off the main market square."

Beltur did his best to fix those names in his mind. *Essek's Factorage.* "I appreciate that."

With a nod, Vaenturl eased his mount and sledge away from Beltur and Jessyla, and their packhorse/mount, and Jorhan rode forward.

"It's not that far, less than a kay."

"We'll follow you." Beltur was more than glad to do that, especially with the driving snow, especially after two turns in the narrow streets of Axalt in less than a few hundred yards. Then they were on a slightly wider way where all the houses appeared to be at least of three stories and com-paratively narrow, given their height.

Jorhan began to slow the sledge, then turned in through a narrow opening in a stone wall surrounding a dwelling that looked to be slightly larger than those they had passed earlier. He stopped beside a covered portico leading to a small side door, dismounted, and tied his mount to a short railing. "We're here." He climbed the steps to the raised and covered side entry, where he pounded vigorously on the door.

Beltur rode closer to the steps and simply waited, glancing down the side lane toward a rear building almost as large as Jorhan's house that had to be a stable or the equivalent.

The side door opened a fraction, and then was thrown wide. Barrynt grinned as he stepped out onto the portico and into the snow. "Jorhan! I never thought you'd take up my offer . . . or you either, Mage," he added as he took in Beltur.

"Frigging Council didn't give either of us much choice," replied the smith. "Have to apologize for arriving in the middle of a northeaster."

Barrynt looked past Jorhan. "And the third member of your party?"

"Beltur's consort. She's a healer."

"A smith, a mage, and a healer! Quite a pleasant surprise. Let me get my coat, and we'll see you out to the stables to settle your horses. I'll tell Johlana you actually came. She's had a chamber waiting for you for years. Said you'd be here sooner or later."

Beltur sensed that Barrynt meant everything that he said, and that was a definite relief, although he'd been telling himself for the entire journey that the merchant had struck him as honest and direct.

In moments, Barrynt reappeared, wearing a heavy tan woolen coat and matching hat.

With him was a muscular-looking woman with silver-streaked blond hair and a wide smile, wearing a coat matching that of her consort. She threw her arms around her brother. "I'm so glad you came!" After a moment, she stepped back and said, "No more shilly-shallying. You all must be freezing. This way!" In moments, she was down the steps, leading the way toward the rear building. She had the double doors open even before Jorhan brought the sledge to a stop. "Trade goods?"

"Only a fair amount of cupridium."

"We'll need to bring that inside and put it in the strongroom. You and Barrynt take care of that. I'll deal with the horses until you finish." Johlana turned to Beltur. "You're the mage?"

"Beltur, and this is my consort, Jessyla. She's a healer."

"Axalt could use another healer, no doubt about that." Her eyes measured

Slowpoke. "He'll need a stall to himself. There are two empty at the far end. You can double-stall the two smaller horses in the larger one."

As Johlana took charge of organizing the horses, Beltur managed not to smile, but he had a definite feeling that she had to have contributed to the merchant's success.

Almost a glass passed, even with the help of Johlana and Barrynt, before the horses had been groomed and watered, and given some hay, and all the gear carried into the side hall of the house, certainly the largest personal dwelling Beltur had ever entered. Even the side foyer was large, a good three yards by five, with a whole line of wall pegs, several of which already held heavy coats. Beyond the foyer was a modest hallway leading to what appeared to be a larger center hall. The lower half of the wainscoted hall walls was a dark wood, while the upper half was a creamy white, and Beltur had the impression that the wainscoting continued throughout the main level at least.

"Cupridium's all in Barrynt's strongroom, down below," Jorhan told Beltur.

"That'll bring a few golds and then some," added Barrynt. "I still don't see why they wanted to drive you out."

"They didn't think we'd leave," said Jorhan. "They thought we'd stay and work for almost nothing."

Barrynt frowned and turned almost stone-faced for an instant. "Bastards." The single word embodied both anger and cold rage.

"Dear," said Johlana quickly, "you can't do anything to someone in Elparta."

After a moment, Barrynt shook his head and started to say something more, but stopped when Johlana gave him a sharp glance.

She then turned to Jessyla and Beltur as they shed their outer coats and hung them on the wall pegs where Jorhan had already put his. "You two are younger than I'd thought. After all you've done, Beltur . . ."

"I told you he wasn't that old," said Barrynt, following his words with a laugh.

"Well . . . he doesn't look any older than Halhana, and she's only been consorted a year. But then, she was young. If it hadn't been Eshult . . ." Johlana pursed her lips, obviously thinking. "The best chamber for you two would be the corner one on the third floor. It's an extra flight of stairs, but there's no one up there, hasn't been for years, not since Barrynt's mother passed on, but her room was on the other corner. Even an adjoining washroom. I know, that means a bit more water-carrying, but you two are young and hale."

"You're very kind," said Beltur.

"You were more than kind to Jorhan, and kind to kind is the best way for all of us. Good thing it's eightday when we always have a big family dinner. I'll have to have Asala make some changes for dinner, but that won't be a problem, and it won't take more than a glass. Besides, I want to hear everything, and after you take your things upstairs and freshen up, we can have something hot to drink in the family parlor and you can tell us, while Asala finishes readying the fare." Johlana turned to her brother. "You know where you're staying, and don't forget to wash up good."

Jorhan grinned, as much at Beltur as at his sister. "Some things don't change."

"It's a good thing they don't." Johlana looked to Beltur and Jessyla. "You two come with me." She turned and headed for the central hallway.

Jessyla and Beltur followed, as the merchant's consort led them to the main entry hallway and then up the staircase, open on both sides and wide enough for two people, with polished dark banisters. The steps to the third level were somewhat narrower and closed, but still had banisters. The center hall on the third level was more modest, but the wood floors were clean and polished, and the hallway walls were also wainscoted in the same fashion as those below.

Johlana looked at the open doorway to her right and nodded. "This is where you'll be staying."

Although the inside shutters were closed and dark brown hangings covered the two narrow windows, one of the bedside lamps had been lit so that there was a warm glow to the room. Beltur wondered when Johlana had arranged that, since she'd scarcely been out of sight since they arrived.

Johlana ushered them inside. "We'll be down in the parlor when you're ready. You will excuse me, but there are a few things I need to take care of. If there's anything you need, just let me know when you come down." She paused. "Oh . . . there is one thing. You can empty the used washbasin water down the covered standpipe in the washroom. Just the wash water, though. I'll show you where the chamber pots are emptied later." With a warm smile, she turned and was gone, closing the bedchamber door behind her and leaving Beltur and Jessyla standing there.

Jessyla just stood and looked around the bedchamber, taking in the bedside tables, each with an oil lamp; the ornately carved, high-backed wooden bench with a long brown velvet sitting cushion; the tall wardrobe; and the wide bed with its heavy quilt patterned in brown and tan interlocking circles over a cream background, actual pillows with shams matching the quilt.

Beltur opened the wardrobe doors to discover on one side hanging pegs and on the other a series of drawers.

"It's like a palace," said Jessyla quietly. "And they're so nice, and they mean it."

"We should enjoy it while we can," said Beltur.

Jessyla walked to the bed and turned back the quilt slightly. "Top and bottom sheets, and they're so smooth."

"What about washing up?"

"We certainly should."

There were already two large pitchers of water in the adjoining washroom, which also held two commodious chamber pots.

Beltur looked at the pitchers and shook his head. "They're even warm."

Jessyla's eyes went to the mirror above the wash table. "I don't even want to see how I look."

"You look wonderful."

"To you, dear. I know better."

"You can wash up first," Beltur said. "I'll unpack my duffel."

A little over two quints later, the two walked down the staircases together, with Beltur in his best blacks, cleaned as well as he could with a damp cloth, and with Jessyla wearing the green shimmersilk scarf. They made their way to the family parlor, where they found Jorhan, Barrynt, Johlana, and two young men, all seated in an assortment of comfortable chairs, except Johlana was on one settee, and another settee was vacant, clearly left for Beltur and Jessyla. Heat radiated from the iron stove set in the hearth.

Barrynt gestured. "You haven't met Ryntaar—he's the redhead and the elder—and Frankyr. You'll likely meet Halhana sometime. She stops by often."

"When she wants to tell Mother something," said Ryntaar.

"Or needs something," added Frankyr. "Or when Emlyn and Sarysta are being nasty again."

Johlana offered a sharp glance. Both young men lowered their eyes.

"There's dark lager, pale ale, or hot mulled wine," continued the merchant, "or chilled redberry juice."

"The mulled wine, please," said Jessyla.

"The pale ale, thank you," added Beltur.

"Sit down. Frankyr will get your drinks."

"Thank you," said Jessyla, seating herself.

Beltur settled beside her.

Frankyr stood and went to the sideboard, where he filled a mug and a beaker, then offered the mug, with a wisp of steam coming from it, to Jessyla, and the beaker to Beltur.

"We can't tell you how much we appreciate your kindness and hospitality," Beltur said.

"I can't tell you how much I appreciate your getting Jorhan out of Spidlar," returned Johlana. "That place has gotten worse with every year. From all I've heard, Elparta isn't the same city where I grew up."

"I have to say that I've gotten that impression from others," said Beltur, "but I didn't live there long enough to know personally if that happened to be true." In fact, he suspected that Elparta and Spidlar hadn't changed all that much, and that people felt it had changed for the worse when what the Council did impacted them personally. He took a sip of the ale and found it strong but very smooth, unsurprisingly. "This is very good ale."

"Barrynt believes that his family should have the best, not just other merchants when we entertain. Some of them can be . . . but I shouldn't talk about those who are unpleasant."

"You've made your point, Mother," said Ryntaar with a smile.

"Enough of it, anyway," Johlana replied cheerfully before turning to the smith. "How was the trip here? Outside of your encountering the north-easter?"

Jorhan laughed. "Likely as good as it could be with winter coming on. It was snowing when we left—"

"Why did you leave then?" asked Barrynt.

"Because we didn't have any choice," replied Jorhan. "The Council was trying to make me give up all the cupridium we'd made to this Trader Alizant even before the proclamation was saying we had to. It would have been even worse for Beltur if he'd stayed."

"Oh?" Barrynt frowned.

"The Mages' Council of Elparta was going to charge me with the improper use of chaos," said Beltur. "If I'd stayed, they would have turned me into an indentured servant."

"Or worse," added Jessyla. "One of the senior mages wanted to consort me, rather than letting me consort Beltur. That's why they were going to have him executed."

"And why we set out in the snow," said Jorhan. "At first, it was a light snow, and it only dropped maybe ten digits on the road. That was all until we reached the border wall when the northeaster hit." He turned to Barrynt. "Do you know why the gate guards at the border wall were so difficult? They almost didn't want to let me in. If it hadn't been for Beltur, it would have been even harder."

"I just said that I was coming with you," Beltur said, "and that we wanted to come to Axalt because the Council wanted to tariff us beyond belief. Well . . . I didn't put it that way."

"The guard said he'd let me in because black mages and healers don't lie," added Jorhan.

"Is that true?" asked Johlana. "That you don't lie."

"It's painful to tell a lie, but not impossible," said Beltur.

"In short," said Johlana, "you don't do it often or well."

"That's very true," replied Jessyla. "He even has trouble not telling me something if he thinks I should know it, and that's not even a lie."

Johlana smiled. "I suspect you're very careful in how much of the truth you tell."

Beltur smiled wryly. "I try not to get in that position. Even that makes me uncomfortable."

"So why did you decide to work with Uncle Jorhan?" asked Frankyr.

"Because I fled Gallos with the Prefect wanting to kill me, and I had no coins. Even some of the clothes on my back were gifts from Athaal."

"He was the black who took in Beltur," interjected Jorhan.

"You seem to get people unhappy with you, ser," said Ryntaar.

"It wasn't that. I was orphaned young, and my uncle took care of me. He was a white mage, but the Prefect of Gallos set six of his strongest whites after us because Uncle tried to avoid becoming an arms-mage for the Prefect. Uncle stood them off long enough for me to escape. I wanted to stay, but I wasn't a very good mage then, and he insisted that he'd sworn to my mother before she died that he'd keep me safe no matter what. I wouldn't have made it out of Gallos without the help of Athaal, Jessyla, and her mother."

"This is a story that ought to be set out as an epic poem," declared Barrynt.

"Epic poem or not," said Johlana, rising from the settee, "Beltur can tell us the rest over dinner." She made her way to the pocket doors at the end of the room from the hearth stove and opened them, revealing the dining room and a long table set for seven, although the table could easily have seated twice that number.

Johlana directed everyone to their places, except for Barrynt, who stood at the head of the table, so that she was on Barrynt's right, with Beltur beside her, while Jorhan was on Barrynt's left, with Jessyla beside the smith. The brothers sat across from each other, with Frankyr beside Jessyla, and Ryntaar beside Beltur.

No one sat as Barrynt stood behind the chair at the head of the table and bowed his head. Since the family members did as well, including Jorhan, so did Beltur and Jessyla.

"In these times of disorder," said Barrynt, "we rejoice in the order of those who are good and in the strength of an honest and caring family, always reminding ourselves to take care to embody order in all we do and think, as should always be the case for right-thinking people. May we always have the wisdom to know what strengthens order and the ability and the will to do so, following the example and words of Relyn."

Beltur managed not to show surprise. Jorhan had never mentioned that Johlana and Barrynt were Relynists. But then, there had never been any reason for him to mention it.

Barrynt cleared his throat. "Now for the fare." He glanced to his consort, and the two seated themselves, as did the others. He filled his consort's beaker with the pale ale from one pitcher, then his own oversized beaker with dark lager from the other pitcher on the table.

Immediately, a woman appeared with a large platter and a deep and broad covered dish, both of which she set before Barrynt.

"The slices on the platter are game pie," said Johlana, "red deer, rabbit, and some squirrel, thanks to Ryntaar and Frankyr."

By the time she finished speaking, the server, who Beltur suspected was the cook as well, returned with a large basket filled with small loaves of bread, and another dish.

"The second casserole is quilla, shallots, and cheese."

Beltur could sense Frankyr's almost visceral reaction to his mother's announcement.

"Frankyr . . . you need more than meat, potatoes, and pastry," announced Johlana, turning from her son to Jessyla. "That's a lovely scarf you're wearing. You don't often see one like that. It's shimmersilk, isn't it?"

"It is. It was Beltur's gift to me, his promise to me, if you will."

As Jessyla spoke, Jorhan filled her beaker with pale ale, then passed the pitcher to Beltur.

"Smart man," said Johlana.

"She should have had it earlier," said Beltur.

"Any earlier, dear, and Auntie would have thrown you out of the house." Jessyla smiled sweetly. "As you well knew."

"You may be a mage," said Barrynt, "but best you listen to her." He grinned at his consort.

"I've already learned that."

"Mostly," replied Jessyla.

"Give me time."

Once everyone had served themselves or been served, conversation dwindled for a time, as they began to eat, until somewhat later when Barrynt said, "I'd like to hear more about how you both got to Elparta." He looked to Jessyla. "I did hear it right, that you helped Beltur get out of Gallos?"

Her mouth full, Jessyla nodded, glancing at Beltur.

Beltur took a swallow of the pale ale, cleared his throat, and began. "I suppose it all began when the Prefect asked my uncle to go to Analeria . . ." While he tried to keep the story short, more than a quint had passed by the time he and Jessyla had recounted their progress from Gallos to Elparta and then to Axalt, including their encounter with the brigands.

"That's quite a story," said Barrynt. "Right up there with Relyn, I'd say."

"I think he traveled farther and longer," said Beltur. "He also did a lot more. All we've done is survive—"

"That's false modesty, dear," said Jessyla, too sweetly. "What you did in the invasion is the reason why the Prefect couldn't take Elparta, and it's also why what the Council did is so despicable."

"Ser . . ." began Ryntaar, his tone almost apologetic, "if I understand what happened, you were powerful enough to stand against white wizards that other blacks couldn't. So why did you have to leave Elparta. Surely . . ."

"It's not that simple," interjected Jorhan. "Still takes silvers to live, especially if a fellow doesn't want his consort to suffer. The Council took that away from us."

"But . . ."

"There's another aspect to that, Ryntaar," added Beltur. "My strength as a mage lies largely in two areas. I'm very strong at shielding myself and others close to me, and I can use those shields to turn the white mages' chaos back against them, but my ability to harm others through my own abilities is far more limited."

"You're sort of a magely shieldman, in a way?" asked Barrynt.

"Not entirely," replied Beltur, "but more that than anything." *So far, anyway.*

Before anyone else could speak, Johlana immediately said, "We've tariffed Beltur and Jessyla enough for this meal. I'm sure we'll hear more in the days ahead, but for now, I think we should enjoy Asala's bread pudding."

The bread pudding was good, Beltur had to admit, even if it wasn't quite as good as Meldryn's pastries and fruit pies. But then, Beltur doubted that very many sweets were as good as what Meldryn had made, which was why the older mage had been so successful, even if some of the blacks in Elparta had disapproved of his personal life.

Before all that long, he and Jessyla had climbed the two flights of stairs and were back up in the third-story bedchamber.

Jessyla surveyed the room once more before seating herself on the padded bench and looking at Beltur, as he stood by the wardrobe and looked back at her. Finally, she said, "I never expected we'd end up in a mansion when we came to Axalt—even if it is only for a little while."

"Neither did I," admitted Beltur.

"What are we going to do now?"

Beltur looked toward the bed. "Sleep?" He grinned.

"I'm certain we'll sleep . . . sooner or later. That wasn't what I meant."

Beltur's expression turned serious. "I know what you meant. I just didn't want to think about it for the moment. There's nothing we can do about that tonight."

"Do you think you and Jorhan can continue your smithing here?"

"He'd like to. So would I. I don't know if it's possible. After what happened with . . . you know who . . . anything was better than staying in Elparta."

"You couldn't stay, and you weren't leaving without me."

Beltur smiled again. "You made that very clear."

She smiled back. "We could talk about the future . . . tomorrow morning."

XXXIV

Despite the comfortable bed, both Jessyla and Beltur woke early on one-day, and Beltur's second thought was that it was the first day of winter—and that he was very glad that he and Jessyla were safe in Axalt, despite the fact that he had no idea of what the days ahead might bring. His eyes lingered on Jessyla as she began to dress.

"What are you thinking?" she asked. "Besides that?"

"Besides what?" asked Beltur mock-innocently.

She just shook her head.

"After *that* . . . well, I was thinking that we need to figure out how to earn some silvers now that we've managed to survive the Council, Waensyn, and the weather."

"I thought you said that you could keep working with Jorhan."

"Both Barrynt and Jorhan said that we could. Barrynt made his offer honestly and in goodwill. But we still have to find a place to forge, locate someone who can supply copper, and a few other things like that. I also can't believe that Jorhan could carry everything he needed on one sledge. Coming to Axalt was far better than all the other alternatives, but . . ."

"Much better for us." Jessyla paused. "I feel sorry for Mother."

"Because of what she said before we left? Or because she's left with Grenara?"

"Both. She never said much about my father, except that things don't always work out the way we expect. She just said that he couldn't stay in Fenard, and she couldn't leave her parents then."

"Was he a mage or a healer?"

"She never really answered that question. She said he could have been more than he was, but not in Gallos."

"Where did he go?"

"He was traveling to Suthya, and he died in the Westhorns on the way."

"So that was why your mother . . ."

"She never said that she could have saved him before."

"How did she know she might have saved him?"

"Mother's always had her secrets." Jessyla looked hard at Beltur. "Please don't ever keep secrets from me."

"I couldn't do that." *Especially since you'd know I was keeping secrets.*

She smiled. "I know that . . . but please don't try, either. I'm going to wash up."

Once Jessyla walked to the adjoining washroom and shut the door, Beltur straightened the disarranged sheets and then made up the bed.

When Jessyla returned, she immediately straightened up what he had done even more.

He shrugged wryly as he walked toward the washroom.

Before long the two of them walked down the stairs. The breakfast room was empty except for Johlana, but the odor of fresh-baked bread filled the air. Beltur couldn't help but notice a hint of burned crust from the baking, something he'd never smelled from Meldryn's baking.

"You two are up early." Johlana smiled happily.

"It's hard to break the habit," replied Beltur.

"Please sit down. There's hot cider in the pitcher, and it won't be long before Asala has breakfast on the table. Barrynt will be down shortly. I don't think Jorhan's awake yet."

"He probably needs the sleep."

"More than you? A journey from Elparta isn't easy any time, but especially in winter, it has to be an effort."

"We're younger," replied Beltur.

"Youth isn't everything," said Barrynt as he entered the breakfast room, followed by Jorhan. "The boys left already?"

"They said they had to bring back several cords."

"Good. I told them we'd need it with more people here." Barrynt settled into his place at the head of the table. "Good experience for Frankyr. He'll have to get used to it before Ryntaar leaves for Elparta in the spring, because he'll be doing it alone then."

Beltur poured the hot cider into Jessyla's mug and then his own before passing the pitcher to Barrynt.

The egg toast and thin fried ham strips might have been a bit better than if Beltur had fixed them, and the thick redberry syrup helped, but they weren't what they would have been if Meldryn had been the cook. *You're definitely going to miss that.* But then, there was a lot he definitely wasn't going to miss.

Barrynt didn't say anything more until he'd finished off three enormous slices of egg toast, heavily drizzled with the redberry syrup, along with the fried ham. "We'll need to talk about getting you two set up."

"Good idea," said Jorhan.

Johlana looked to Jessyla. "I think I should take you to meet Herrara. She's the head of the Healers' Guild."

"Healers have a guild here?" asked Jessyla.

"Of course. Guilds help keep the order. That is, if they work properly with the Council, but that's never ever been a problem here. The Council is very thorough and very thoughtful."

"Indeed, it is," said Barrynt heartily.

"Are you finished, dear?" asked Johlana. "Excellent. We should go. It's much easier to see Herrara early in the morning, before she leaves the healing house to see to those who can't come to it." With that, Johlana stood. "We'll see you all later."

Jessyla looked at Beltur, with the hint of a smile in her eyes.

Once Johlana and Jessyla had left the breakfast room, Jorhan looked at Barrynt. "Can you sell some of the things we forged? At a good price?"

"I'd be happy to. At this time of year, though, it's likely to be slow. Only a few traders come through in the winter, and there are only a handful of merchants who'd consider having more than a piece or two of the quality you've forged. They'd think it . . . ostentatious." Barrynt smiled. "A few might buy daggers or knives. They could claim that the way cupridium holds up is a virtue."

"I know you don't have anywhere that we could get to work . . ."

"That might be a problem right now." A slight frown crossed Barrynt's forehead, then vanished. "A place for a smithy—that would have to be in south town. We'll figure that out. You'll need coal, too. Most supplies are spoken for, but there's always someone who has some."

"The smithy can't be in Axalt?" Jorhan frowned.

"South town is part of the city. That's what we call the finger of the main valley southwest of here. Most of the time wind blows from the northeast. That keeps the worst of the smoke and dust or odors from smiths, tanneries, rendering . . . all the less . . . savory . . . crafts from settling over the city itself. All of them are there. It's only a little more than a kay from the south side of the city, and the road's kept clear year-round." Barrynt smiled cheerfully. "I can make inquiries, but there's no need to worry. Certainly, some of what you brought will sell quickly, and we're happy to have you stay here while we work everything out. I imagine, in time, Beltur, you and your consort would like a place of your own. Jorhan, that's up to you. You can stay here, or we can find some place. But there's no hurry for either of you. No hurry at all. Johlana and I appreciate the company. She hasn't had a grown woman in the house since my mother died, and she misses that."

While Barrynt meant every word that he said, Beltur still worried. "Are houses here hard to find?"

"Impossible." The merchant laughed. "There are always a few, but no one says. I'll be looking for one soon as I can. Folks talk to me. It might take time, but don't you worry. I've got a few ideas already."

"You've always been a man of your word," said Jorhan. "What about copper and tin?"

"I've kept a little in my warehouse. You have your tools?"

"Everything I need except a good solid anvil." Jorhan's voice turned wry. "I could have brought an anvil—or everything else."

That might have been an overstatement, but, as he recalled the anvil in Jorhan's smithy, Beltur suspected it wasn't much of one.

Barrynt stood. "I've got to see Pastanak first thing, but I'll be back after that. Do whatever you need to do while I'm gone."

Beltur rose. "Johlana showed us where things were in the stable last night. Is there anything else I need to know? Oh . . . and where does the stall waste go?"

"There's a bin with a hinged lid on the side of the stable. Just straw and dung there. I sell that to some of the growers come spring. Anything else goes in the refuse barrels beside the bin."

"I'll be out in a little while," said Jorhan. "I'm not in any hurry."

"I'll see you both later." With a nod, the merchant left the breakfast room.

When Beltur went out the side door a little later, he saw immediately that snow was still falling heavily. For a moment, he was surprised, until he recalled that northeasters lasted for more than a few glasses, and what had struck them the day before had definitely been just that. He was also surprised that the portico had to have been shoveled and swept not long before, since there were only a few digits of fresh-fallen snow, marked by recent bootprints.

He made his way to the stable. By the time he covered that distance, he realized that Axalt was indeed considerably colder than Elparta. But then, it was in the Easthorns and higher than Elparta.

Slowpoke was clearly glad to see Beltur, nuzzling him as he checked the manger and added some hay. Beltur went to the pump, which was inside, for reasons made obvious by the cold, working to fill a bucket with extremely cold water. He knew that cold water shouldn't hurt the gelding, but he still only allowed Slowpoke a half bucket at a time while he cleaned out the stall. He did the same for the two other horses, and then he checked all their hooves, using his senses as much as his eyes, given that the stable lantern didn't give that much light. Even though he took his time, Jorhan did not appear, although the smith had said he would be out shortly to deal with his horses. Beltur did add some hay to their mangers before he left.

After returning to the house, he was careful to brush all the snow off his boots and coat before entering the side hall, where he hung up his coat and scarf. Then, he made his way to the parlor. He'd noticed a small bookcase against the wall earlier, and he wanted to see what the volumes might be . . . if no one else was there. Since that was the case, he began to look at the volumes in the bookcase, starting with the top shelf.

None of the leather-bound tomes had an inscription on the outside, so he opened each one carefully, checking the title page of each and replacing each in the bookcase in turn. He had looked through *Codex of Candar, The Basics of Mathematics, Fables of Lydiar and Hydlen, A Guide to the Survey, Lexicon Technicum,* and a number of others before he came to *A Historie of Axalt and the Easthorns,* which he set aside while he continued to peruse the remaining books.

Before long he came to a clearly worn volume, placed at the end of the top shelf. He wasn't surprised at the bold and unornamented title *The Wisdom of Relyn.*

With a smile, he sat down in one of the wooden armchairs and began to read. Even the first words gripped him.

> I have been called an angel, but I was never that worthy. The angels came from beyond the stars in the sky. I was only a second son of Gethen Groves, a too-proud holding in the land of Lornth, later conquered by Saryn of Westwind when the lords of Lornth failed to understand the might of her black blades. Long before that, I lost my right hand to Ryba, the darkest and mightiest of all the angels, when I foolishly attacked the angels as they were building their black tower. I was saved and befriended by Nylan, a mage whose like Candar, or the world, will never see again, for he forged Westwind, as surely as he forged the blades by which the angels carved their domain from the ice and stone of the Roof of the World . . .

Certain passages interested him more than others, and he tried to fix those in his mind as he read on.

> . . . the first words of wisdom I heard from Nylan were that it was unwise to force others to make choices, because forcing a choice creates anger and resentment . . .
>
> . . . he said that because rulers can move people with words, they can come to believe that words, rather than actions, can change the world . . . and that while Ryba's visions were true, the meaning she ascribed to them was often different from the truth of the vision, for we can too often see what we wish that is not there in the truest of visions . . .
>
> . . . The greatest magery is in a man's mind . . . and a man must be in harmony with what he does. So must a woman, but from what I have observed, most men have greater difficulty being in harmony with both themselves and with the world, while women struggle more for harmony within themselves and less with the world . . .
>
> No one can teach another anything unless the listener wants to learn. A teacher can speak, but the listener cannot learn if he will not find the order within himself . . .

At that point Beltur started leafing through the book quickly, just to discover what seemed to be in it. The first part appeared to be a summary of Relyn's sayings and the second a history of at least a portion of his life. He didn't get to leaf through the third part, because he heard the front door opening and closing, followed by the sound of Johlana's voice.

"We're back! How has your morning been? Is anyone here?"

Beltur closed the book, stood and replaced it in the bookcase, and called back, "I'm here in the family parlor!"

Within moments, both Johlana and Jessyla appeared.

"You're the only one here?" asked Johlana.

"Barrynt said he had to see someone and that he'd be back soon. Jorhan is either sleeping or out in the stable."

Johlana laughed. "Sleeping, I'd wager. All he's ever done is either work or sleep."

"He might be tired. It was a long trip," said Jessyla, adding quickly, "At least, it seemed that way to me."

"I'm glad you were with him. Without you two . . . the brigands . . ." Johlana shook her head.

"That was Beltur's doing," said Jessyla.

"I imagine you were doing your share, Healer." Johlana smiled. "Just sit down. The two of you need a rest, and I've more than a few chores to tend to."

Once Johlana had left the parlor, Jessyla settled onto the settee.

Beltur took the chair closest to it. "What did the head healer have to say?"

"Herrara? She escorted me around the healing house and had me look at several injuries. Then she had me assist her, and she finally said that I was a qualified healer. She even said that I could start tomorrow." Jessyla offered a wry expression.

"You don't sound too happy."

"I think they don't have many healers who want to work there, but if I want to practice as a healer anywhere else in Axalt, I'll have to work there for a season four days out of every eightday, for a half silver an eightday. That means I have no real choice, because it's the only place I can be a healer here."

"After that, what happens?"

"If I stay at the healing house, they'll pay me a silver an eightday. I don't know how much I could make working for a merchant."

"Isn't a silver an eightday about what you made in Elparta?"

"But I won't get that for a season."

"I have enough silvers for several seasons."

"I don't like coming to you for coins."

"We're in this together," Beltur said gently. "I wouldn't be alive at all without you, and you know that."

"You would have done something."

"What? How? I didn't know enough to survive in Gallos. Until I got to Elparta and worked with Athaal, I wouldn't have been able to learn what I did, and Athaal wouldn't have agreed to let me come with him, if I hadn't learned from your suggestions and if you hadn't convinced him to help me."

Jessyla smiled faintly. "It took two of us. I had to convince Mother, and we convinced Athaal."

"You see?"

"I see that you're working very hard to persuade me."

"It's in good faith and in a good cause." Beltur grinned.

"I'll think about it. In the meantime, I think we should put on our coats and scarves and take a walk around Axalt . . . or this part of it, until we get too cold," said Jessyla. "I saw a tiny part of it this morning. You haven't seen any of it."

"That's probably a good idea."

"Probably?" Jessyla arched her eyebrows.

"It's a very good idea."

"Beltur." The single word was icier than the snow outside.

He understood immediately. The only question he had was how he could extricate himself from the verbal trap he'd created. He just shrugged helplessly.

"Well?" That word wasn't any warmer than her last.

"I'm sorry. I didn't mean to be . . . condescending."

"I know healers don't make the coins mages do. I can accept that. I can also accept I'll likely always need some help from you in that fashion. You *know* I don't like being beholden to anyone. And you should know that I hate being talked down to or condescended to . . . even in little things. I may have to accept condescension from others, but that shouldn't be the way it is between us."

"You're right . . . and I am sorry." He managed a rueful grin.

"Sorry because you shouldn't have or sorry because I got angry?"

"How about both?"

"I'll accept that, especially since you mean it. Shall we go?"

"We should. You lead the way, since I was trying to follow Jorhan last night, rather than look much at the city."

Before long, the two were walking east on the street holding Barrynt's capacious dwelling, but only to the next lane, where Jessyla turned north.

"This is the way to the healing house. I thought I'd show you that first so that you'd know how to get there from where we're staying." Jessyla paused. "I know we just got here, but how long can we stay with Barrynt and Johlana before we smell like spoiled fish?"

"I don't know. Right now, they're happy to host us. At some point, we should talk to Barrynt about how we get our own place, but doing it right now might seem like we're not grateful and trying to get away from them."

"You're *probably* right about that."

Beltur winced quietly at the slight emphasis on "probably," but only nodded and said, "All of these houses seem large." At least, they seemed large to him, since the stone three-story and multi-chimneyed mansion that they were walking past made Barrynt's dwelling seem small. "This must be where merchants and traders live."

"In another block, they start to get smaller. They're much smaller—narrower, anyway, more like where Auntie lives—near the healing house."

As they continued walking through the snow that Beltur thought was beginning to taper off, he studied each of the dwellings. He also noted a small stone structure, almost like a small house two yards on a side, with only a door, and set back from the corner of a street and a lane.

After three long blocks, his boots were squeaking with each step he took, and his feet were beginning to get cold. After five blocks, he'd seen several of the little stone houses, and he decided that, except for the snow, most of Axalt seemed largely brown and gray, the houses and buildings almost all seemingly built of oil-stained brown wood and gray stone, with the only color that of doors and shutters painted in brighter hues.

"You have that thoughtful look," said Jessyla.

"How can you tell?" he asked wryly, aware that very little of his face showed.

"You feel thoughtful."

"I am thinking."

"About what?"

"I know I don't know nearly all that you do, but could I pass what the head healer asked of you?"

"You'd work as a healer?"

"It's better than not working. Besides, I could learn more about healing while Jorhan and Barrynt do whatever's necessary to set up a smithy. I can't help much with finding a place."

"I don't know . . . Do you really want to do that?"

"More than I want to do nothing."

Jessyla shook her head, then asked, "What would I tell Healer Herrara?"

"Tell her the truth—that I'd been working with you and your mother when I could at the Council Healing House in Elparta, and that while there are likely some gaps in my knowledge, there are also things I can do that are useful, like using shields to help a healer set bones."

"I told you how little they pay, and they might not want to pay you at all. Klarisia didn't."

"You told me that she couldn't. For now, it doesn't matter. I'd rather learn than not learn."

"I think you have other ideas, as well. What are they?"

"I just wonder . . . I seem to get pulled into healing, even when I'm not trying. Maybe . . . order, fate . . . whatever . . . is trying to send me a message."

"I thought you didn't believe in the Rational Stars."

"I don't, and I don't believe in some god, like the one-god worshippers or the Kaordists do, but what if order itself . . ."

"That sounds suspiciously like you're considering order as a deity."

"No . . . just a force. I could be wrong, but, if I am, it still won't hurt for me to know more about healing, will it?"

"No. It's bound to come in useful."

"Especially if anything happens to you," he said. "One thing your mother was very clear about was that healers can't heal themselves, not if they're seriously ill or hurt."

"She was very clear about more than one thing," replied Jessyla dryly.

"Just like you," replied Beltur.

Jessyla scooped a handful of snow from the top of the low stone wall in front of a more modest dwelling and threw it at Beltur, but the snow arrived more as an additional wind-aided clump of snow than as a snowball.

They both laughed.

XXXV

By twoday morning, the snow had stopped, and the sky was a coldly brilliant green-blue, as Beltur walked with Jessyla toward the healing house of Axalt. Although the air was still, it was bitter, colder than anything Beltur had yet experienced.

"There's something else I need to do," said Jessyla.

"And what might that be?"

"Find a way to send a letter to Mother to let her know we're safe here."

"Barrynt might know about any traders traveling to Elparta. I'm sure that, for an extra silver or two, they might be willing to deliver a letter." He paused. "It might cost more than that, but we should let her know. She could also tell Meldryn."

"That's a good idea."

Because of the cold, the two walked quickly across already packed snow that crunched and squeaked with each step that took them the seven long blocks to the two-story healing house, a structure that was far more modest than the one in Elparta, some twenty yards long and ten wide, with solid gray stone walls and the same steeply pitched roof that all structures in Axalt seemed to have. The main door was single, if slightly wider than most doors, with polished but old brass hinges and fittings. Beltur opened it for Jessyla and followed her inside. Once in the small entry hall, she immediately turned to the left into a small room with wall pegs, where she hung her coat and scarf. Beltur followed her example, and the two went back to the entry, through a square arch into a corridor perhaps a yard and a half wide, their steps echoing on the gray stone floor, as they walked into the first chamber on the right.

An older woman with jet-black hair, pale brown eyes, and a narrow pinched face looked up from the table desk where she sat, her eyes taking in Jessyla. "You're here when you should be. I'll say that."

Jessyla nodded. "Healer Herrara, this is my consort, Beltur. As you can see, he's a mage."

"He looks a bit young for a mage." Herrara's expression was one of disinterest, almost as if to ask why Beltur was at the healing house.

"He was strong enough to hold off the mages of Gallos," said Jessyla.

Herrara shifted her glance to Beltur. "I presume you wish me to ask why you are here?"

"I would have told you. It's very simple. Everywhere I've been, I've been pressed into service as a healer, because I do have some healing skills. For that reason, I asked the head of the Council Healing House in Elparta to allow me to work there, as I could when I was not working or serving as a City Patrol mage, so that I would know more."

"You seem to be telling the truth, but why are you here? In Axalt, that is?"

"The newly formed Mages' Council of Elparta wished me to become an indentured slave, partly to keep me from earning silvers and partly to force Jessyla to consort with the favorite of the chief mage of the Council."

"That's not the whole truth, I think."

"No, it's not. I worked with Jorhan, a coppersmith, to make items out of cupridium, everything from blades to mirrors and candelabra. The Council issued an edict that we could only sell them through a trader. Then the Council claimed that we had violated the edict even before the date it became effective. I had to flee because both the Traders' Council and the Mages' Council were after me."

"I insisted he consort me and that I accompany him," added Jessyla.

"You are either very brave or very foolish. Perhaps both." Her eyes went back to Beltur. "You wish me to pay you while I teach you?"

"No. I would suggest that you allow me to accompany you so that you can question me, test me, and determine where I might be of assistance. If and when you decide that I might be, then you could consider whether I should be paid as other healers are."

"Begging your pardon, Mage, but what if I don't find your abilities satisfactory?"

"Then you can either instruct me or dismiss me, as you see fit."

Herrara frowned, then shook her head. "It is most irregular."

"I'm a black mage. It's painful for me to physically injure anyone. We've had to leave Spidlar because the Council's rules destroyed my ability to make a living. The last thing I'd want to do is something that would cause trouble."

"I can sense that much truth." Herrara frowned again. "Are you thinking to become a healer?"

"I've been where I've had to be too many times, where someone would have died. I've been fortunate enough to have kept that from happening in most cases. The ones where I could not were on the battlefield. Since life seems to thrust the need for healing at me, I would prefer to know more."

"Interesting. Those are the most ordered words you've spoken, although I've sensed no outright chaos." She turned back to Jessyla. "What have you seen him do?"

"He can clean wounds, both with spirits and cloth, a knife, and with order. He helped the healers in Elparta set bones in a way that was less painful and more effective than anything else . . ."

Before Jessyla could finish, Herrara gestured for her to stop. "If you, Mage, can do even that, then it seems I must accept your suggestion. Are you here for today?"

"I had hoped to be."

"Then let us see whether there is any hope for you as a healer. If you would, wait here while I take Healer Jessyla to the welcoming ward and inform her about her immediate duties." The chief healer stood and walked to what looked like a bookcase set against the wall, except that the shelves were separated into rectangles, and within most of the rectangles were what appeared to be various supplies. One held small folded cloths, another small corked bottles, another large tweezers, as well as other devices Beltur did not immediately recognize. Herrara took an oblong basket and handed it to Jessyla, then turned toward the open door.

Jessyla gave Beltur a warm smile before she followed Herrara from the small room.

He stood there, his eyes taking in the table desk on which were several books similar to ledgers, one of which was open. Without stepping toward the desk, he could only see that there were blocks of handwriting separated by small intervals of white space. He looked back to the wooden supply case, studying the contents.

He was still studying it and trying to determine what certain objects might be used for when Herrara returned.

"We will go to the upper level. There I would like you to examine several people. Do not say a word about what you think you may have learned about each until we have returned to the main corridor and closed the door."

Once on the second level, Herrara led Beltur into a room containing four narrow beds. Two were empty. Herrara walked over to the first bed. A thin-faced older man with an unkempt mostly white beard lay there, his eyes closed. He seemed to be asleep. The healer shook him by the shoulder, firmly but not roughly. Then she pinched his cheek. "He was found in the front hall of his daughter's house. He's only been here a day, but he can't swallow anything."

Following Herrara's instructions, Beltur let his senses range over the older man, noting immediately that the levels of both his natural order and chaos were low. That might have been because the man hadn't eaten for some time, something Beltur had noticed on a less pronounced scale with himself. The second thing was the dull redness inside the man's skull on the right side, not exactly wound chaos, although it might have been "brighter" earlier. He bent over the man, looking at that side of his head, but there was no sign of a wound, no bruising or cuts. Nor did he find any other signs of concentrated wound or free chaos or the kind of excessive order binding that he'd sensed in Taelya.

Finally, he stepped back and nodded to Herrara.

She moved to the second occupied bed, which held a much younger man whose eyes were open but who did not seem to see either figure. He gave several low moans as they approached, but barely moved, almost as if any motion might hurt.

"Stullak?" said Herrara. "How do you feel today?"

"My leg . . ." His face contorted. "It's like fire. Why have you brought a mage? I'm not dead yet."

"I'm glad to hear it."

Beltur could tell that wasn't the total truth, but he concentrated on Stullak, a man he realized wasn't that much older than he was. Nearly instantly, he could sense knots and patches of a different kind of wound chaos everywhere within Stullak's body—a whitish-yellow red—but especially along his left thigh, which felt like there was little but chaos there.

Overall order and chaos levels were almost as low as those in the first man, and Beltur couldn't see how the man could even speak, given the amount of chaos in his body, far more than Beltur could possibly have dealt with. He gave a slight nod to Herrara.

"We just wanted to stop in and see you for a moment. I'll be back shortly."

Stullak's face contorted in clear agony. Beltur couldn't help himself and reached out, touching the suffering man on the forehead and offering a slight balm of order.

The man's eyes opened wider for a moment. "What . . . ?"

"Just rest," replied Beltur softly, aware that Herrara's attention was totally on him. Offering Stullak a warm smile, he turned and followed Herrara out into the hall, closing the door behind him.

She looked at him. "You're not as cold as I thought. How did you do that, get him to relax?"

"It's just a little bit of free order, but if you spread it thinly, it helps, just for a little while."

"How did you learn that?"

"I don't know. It was just something I tried when troopers were badly wounded, sometimes when no one could save them. It's not the same as personal order in healing, but it does help sometimes, and it doesn't exhaust me."

Herrara pursed her lips, then moistened them. "Tell me what you could determine about the first man."

"His levels of natural order and chaos are low. He's likely dying. He's had some sort of damage in his skull on the right side. It's got the dull redness that usually comes when a wound is between healing and festering, but there's no sign of a wound. It's as if that part of his brain was bleeding. It could be that it still is. I don't know of any way to heal that."

"And Stullak?"

"His entire body is filled with a white-yellow red chaos. That's the way it feels to me. It's the worst along his left thigh. I could remove some of that, but there's far too much of it."

"Have you removed chaos from a body before?"

"Once." Beltur went on to tell the story of the boy he'd healed when he'd first come to Elparta, then added, "He didn't get over the limp, but he was still well when I left Elparta."

"I see." Herrara frowned again. "We'll see what you know and can do for the rest of the day. Come along."

As he followed Herrara, Beltur understood that those words were as much of an approval as he was likely to get.

For the next six glasses Beltur did whatever was asked of him, beginning with cleaning out the wound and burns suffered by a serving girl who had "accidentally" tripped and fallen against a hot andiron in a hearth and ground ash and coals into the wound and along her forearm. Then came helping Herrara set the broken arm of a stableboy who'd slipped on ice around an outside trough. At least that was the story, and Beltur sensed most of that was true.

By third glass, Beltur was somewhat tired, more in feelings than in body, because what he had sensed was about the same as what he'd experienced at the Council Healing House in Elparta and because he'd been also aware of Herrara's constant study of him.

Abruptly, the chief healer turned to him. "We've done all we can today. Let's go back to the study."

Beltur nodded and followed her.

This time, Herrara closed the door and sat down behind the table desk, gesturing for Beltur to take the single straight-backed chair. For several moments, she said nothing. Then she looked at Beltur, her brown eyes almost flat. "I'd be a fool to reject your help. Despite your lack of knowledge in certain areas, you can obviously do more than any healer I have ever known, and your consort is at least as good as any young healer I have encountered. Both of you have much to learn, but what you do not know can be learned. What you can do that others cannot are skills few ever possess. You are aware of that, I can tell. What I doubt that you know is that such skills are as much curse as blessing, and the greater the gifts, the more that they will weigh on you in time."

As if you haven't already begun to discover that. Beltur just nodded.

"You likely have an inkling of that, or you wouldn't be here in Axalt," Herrara went on. "I was impressed by your feelings for Stullak, but more by your understanding of what you know you cannot do."

"I've come close to killing myself more than once by trying to do too much with magery," Beltur admitted.

The faint trace of a smile crossed Herrara's lips and vanished as quickly as it had appeared. "I should have guessed that, given your comparative youth." Another pause followed.

"Despite a few shortcomings, you are a qualified healer, and you and your consort will be listed as such. Both of you will require a season serving here before you can be approved to heal without supervision elsewhere.

To avoid any questions of fairness, except in times when absolutely necessary, you and your consort will have to alternate days working here. Do you have any preference about who will be here tomorrow?"

"I'd prefer that we talk it over, and that what we decide will determine which of us shows up here in the morning."

"That's fair enough, provided that you keep to that schedule, unless one of you is ill—and that can happen, working in a healing house."

"One of us will be here," Beltur said, hoping he wasn't promising too much.

"You both get paid on oneday afternoon, or twoday if you don't work on oneday."

"We appreciate that."

"I'll see one of you tomorrow."

Taking that as a dismissal, Beltur nodded and left the study, leaving the door open behind him, since he gathered it was usually open.

He only had to wait about a fifth of a glass in the cloak or coat room before Jessyla appeared.

When she saw him, she smiled. "You're still here. That has to be good." After a hesitation, she added, "It is, isn't it?"

"I must have done something right," said Beltur. "She said that I was a qualified healer, and that we'd both be listed as such. She told me the same thing she told you, that I couldn't practice as a healer until working here for a full season."

"What else?"

"We have to work alternate days."

"I can see that. She gets another healer every day, and that avoids any suggestion of favoritism. Who gets which day?"

"We can choose. We can talk about it on the walk home, or later. One of us has to show up tomorrow morning."

"Now," said Jessyla lightly, "you have to start teaching me how to be a mage."

"I think that's a very good idea," said Beltur. *Very good, indeed.*

"You mean that, don't you?"

"I do. You can sense and feel enough that you should be able to do some magery. We just need to find out how to make it possible."

"It might take a while."

Beltur could detect a worried tone in her voice. He smiled as he lifted her coat off the peg and handed it to her. "We have time. We're likely not going anywhere soon."

XXXVI

On threeday, Jessyla went to the healing house, while Beltur accompanied Jorhan on a tour of the south town area of Axalt, just so that the two of them could become more familiar with the area. The day was slightly warmer than twoday had been, and, again, there was little wind, although the sun shining through the clear sky offered scant warmth. In midafternoon, once they had finished and noted several buildings that seemed vacant, they walked back along the stone-paved road connecting south town to the main part of Axalt in midafternoon.

"Every building there appeared to be in good repair," Beltur observed, "even the empty ones."

"That's something the Council here insists on, especially the roofs," replied Jorhan. "They'll close a shop if it needs repairs and they aren't made."

"How do they know?"

"They inspect buildings. Sometimes it's a councilor, sometimes a builder who works for the Council. Barrynt told me that yesterday. Any building that is built or empty has to be inspected before people live in it or a crafter can begin work in it."

"Even the Council in Elparta doesn't do that."

"No . . . they just tell you what you can make and who gets to sell it," said Jorhan dryly.

Beltur immediately changed the subject. "All the ways are stone-paved, and they keep them clear."

"That's because the Council levies a fee on anyone who doesn't," replied Jorhan. "The fees pay for workmen to do it."

"Is that true of the streets in front of houses, too?"

The smith shook his head. "Everyone pays a yearly fee for that. There is also a fee for each time you don't clear your sidewalks."

"What happens if you don't pay?"

"If someone is old, and there is no one in the house able-bodied enough to shovel, then the Council pays. If there is someone able-bodied, they have to do work for the Council."

"And if they refuse?"

"Then they get escorted to whichever border they choose and sent on their way. It almost never comes to that. That's what Johlana told me."

As the two neared the edge of the part of Axalt that held houses and those shops that did not require location in south town, Beltur realized something else. He'd never seen a single beggar or someone who lived in alleys, even around the small market square that he and Jessyla had visited on oneday. There hadn't been all that many in Elparta, but they had been there. *But then, you saw them on patrol duty and at the healing house, and you've only been at the healing house here one day.*

When they neared Barrynt's house, Jorhan cleared his throat. "I'm going to Barrynt's factorage. Let him know about the buildings we saw. It's better if he approaches the owners."

"Should I come?"

The smith shook his head and smiled. "He'll feel more obligated if it's just me."

Beltur laughed. "Are you sure you don't have some trader blood?"

"If I do, I never heard about it."

At the walk to the house, the two parted, and Beltur walked up the lane to the side entrance.

Once he was back inside, after hanging up his scarf and coat and then seeing that the family parlor was empty, he sat down and took *The Wisdom of Relyn* from the bookcase and began to read once more.

> . . . the angels are not gods or great forces. They are people. Some of them were foolish, and some were arrogant and reckless, and they died that first winter on the Roof of the World. Those who were wise survived. Ryba of the Swift Ships of Heaven was not only wise. She was ruthless. At times she could see what would be, and what she foretold has thus far come to pass . . .

After reading that paragraph, Beltur stopped. *The Book of Ayrlyn* had said much the same thing, but had not mentioned Relyn at all. So far, Beltur had not seen any mentions of Ayrlyn, but then, he might have skipped over such a mention, particularly if Relyn had written about Ayrlyn just in passing.

Almost two quints passed before he finally came to something about Ayrlyn.

... Ryba would tell the flame-haired healer to make a song, and the healer would. She wrote songs about the Guards of Westwind, about Nylan the mighty smith, and about the deadly blades of the guards. All those have come to pass as Ayrlyn sang that they would, long before it was so. That, too, came from the power and understanding of order ...

Belatedly, Beltur realized something else. Never had Relyn mentioned the Rational Stars. He leafed back to the beginning and reread the first few pages. *He only said that the angels came from beyond the stars in the sky. Beyond?* What did that mean?

He was still pondering that when he heard the side door open and sensed quickly a presence that could only be that of Jessyla. Closing the worn leather-bound volume, he stood and replaced it in the bookcase.

"Beltur?"

"I'm in the parlor."

Jessyla hurried in, her cheeks red from the cold. "Did you find a place for a smithy?"

"Not exactly. We just walked over to south town and walked every street and lane, I think, just so that we'd have a better idea. There looked to be several buildings that weren't being used. When we got back, Jorhan went to talk to Barrynt about them." Beltur gestured to the bookcase. "I was reading *The Wisdom of Relyn.*"

She frowned. "Why? Is it interesting?"

"It is, but I was reading it because I thought it might be useful." He hesitated. "It's been very well-read."

Jessyla's eyes widened. "Oh ..."

"It couldn't hurt, I thought. How was your day?"

"Mostly quiet. Except for Stullak and one girl."

"Stullak? He died, didn't he?"

"You're not surprised."

Beltur shook his head. "There was so much wound chaos all through his body." He took a deep breath. "What about the girl? What was the problem?"

"She wasn't the problem. Her mother was. She didn't want to believe her daughter was pregnant. So she beat her. The girl lost the child. She almost died."

"Will she be all right?"

"Herrara and I think so."

"What about the mother?"

"The city patrollers couldn't find her. They think she fled into the mountains. Herrara doubted they tried very hard."

"Why would her *mother* do that?" Beltur could unfortunately see some men he'd known doing that, but a mother?

"She wasn't consorted, and that wasn't according to order. Acts not in accord with order had to be punished. That was what the girl said her mother told her. She was telling the truth."

Beltur didn't know quite what to say. So he asked, "Did Herrara say if that sort of thing happened often?"

"She didn't say. She was upset. Really upset."

"Then it's likely something that happens often."

"Having a child without being consorted or being beaten for it? Or a mother doing the beating?" asked Jessyla almost sardonically.

"The mother . . . that seems . . ." Beltur didn't have the words for what he wanted to express.

"Women aren't always as good as you seem to think, dear."

"No, they're not," interjected Johlana as she walked into the parlor. "Sometimes, they're worse than men. Not often, but when they are . . ." She shook her head, then looked quizzically at Beltur. "Jorhan didn't come back with you?"

"He went to see Barrynt about some empty buildings in south town."

"That's good. Barrynt knows everyone, and he'll make sure Jorhan comes back with him, and doesn't stop by the inn. We've got better lager and ale here anyway. As soon as Barrynt and Jorhan and the boys arrive, we'll have something to drink before dinner. In the meantime, you two just sit down and enjoy yourselves." Then Johlana turned and headed toward the kitchen.

"I need to wash up," said Jessyla. "I'll be back in a few moments."

Then she too was gone.

Beltur looked at the bookcase, wondering if he should try to read more about Relyn.

He shook his head and sat down, waiting for whoever might first join him. He'd been waiting long enough that he regretted not having spent the time reading, and was about to get up to retrieve the book, when he sensed someone entering the room—except it was no one he knew.

He immediately stood to greet the petite young blond woman who walked into the family parlor, a puzzled look on her face.

"I was looking for . . . Jorhan."

"He'll be back before long. He's with Barrynt." For a moment, Beltur wondered who she might be, but then realized there was only one possibility. "Are you Halhana, by any chance?"

"Why, yes . . . Oh, you must be Beltur."

Beltur nodded.

"Uncle Jorhan was telling me about you earlier." She smiled.

"I'm afraid I know nothing about you, except your name and that you're consorted." *Somewhat younger than your mother would have preferred.*

"There's not much to know. I'm the oldest and the shortest and talk the most, even when I don't have much to say."

"We've all been guilty of that, I fear," replied Beltur.

"You less than many, dear," said Jessyla as she returned to the parlor.

"This is Halhana," said Beltur.

Jessyla stepped closer to the smaller blond woman. "Everyone's mentioned you. I'm glad to meet you."

Halhana looked up at Jessyla. "I've never seen a healer as tall as you . . . or as beautiful."

Seeing the two women facing each other, for some reason, Beltur was struck by what Halhana had said. He'd always known Jessyla was taller than most women and very good-looking, but he wasn't sure he'd realized just how beautiful she was. *Or has she become more beautiful?*

"Thank you."

Beltur could tell that the compliment had flustered Jessyla. At least, something had.

At that moment, Johlana entered the parlor. "Will you be staying for dinner, dear?"

"Oh, no. We're going to his parents' tonight. It's his sister's birthday. Emlyn and Sarysta made it clear that everyone should be there. She's Eshult's youngest sister."

"He does have a few," said Frankyr from the archway into the parlor.

Johlana favored her son with a knife-like look Beltur wouldn't have wanted to receive.

". . . and I'm certain they're all accomplished and charming," added Frankyr.

"A little more convincing tone would help, Frankyr," said Halhana cheerfully. "Someday, you might have daughters. Perhaps I could persuade Mage Beltur to assist in that."

"Children," said Johlana firmly. "You're not exactly showing your better sides to Beltur and Jessyla."

"Frankyr and I never do," replied Halhana in a warm bubbly tone.

"You keep this up, and this recently consorted pair may decide never to have children, and it will be all your fault," declared Johlana in a tone of mock severity, looking at Frankyr as he started to speak and adding, "Not another word. Go bring in more coal for the oven."

Frankyr grinned but immediately vanished from the archway.

"He's impossible at times," said Johlana. "It's a good thing that he's good-hearted."

"I was going to wait for Uncle Jorhan, but I need to get back home. Also, I don't want to keep Kaslaar outside in the cold any longer."

"I'll tell Jorhan you were here."

"Thank you, Mother." After an engaging smile, Halhana turned and left the parlor.

"She's very pretty," said Jessyla.

"More important, she's caring," replied Johlana. "I've known too many pretty women who cared for no one but themselves. You two settle yourselves. I'll be back in just a moment."

Neither Beltur nor Jessyla spoke for several moments. Finally, Jessyla said, "She takes after both of them."

"More her mother, I think."

"They're both strong-willed."

"Like another mother and daughter I know."

"I should have known you'd say that." Jessyla shook her head. "Speaking of Mother, I need to see Johlana about borrowing some stationery . . ."

Beltur smiled.

XXXVII

Dinner was pleasant, and Beltur particularly enjoyed the mutton burhka, spicy as it was, perhaps because the sauce added some taste to the sliced and boiled turnips that had accompanied the main dish. Neither Barrynt nor Jorhan had said anything about possibilities for a smithy, and Beltur didn't press.

After dinner, in the family parlor, Beltur turned to Barrynt. "I was wondering. Jessyla would like to let her mother know that we've arrived here safely. I know you sent missives to Jorhan . . ."

Barrynt smiled. "You'd like to know if I could arrange for a letter to go to her mother?"

"If it's possible."

The merchant nodded. "At this time of year it might be an eightday or more before someone trustworthy is headed that way. The usual fee in winter is two silvers."

"We can do that."

"Then it's settled. You don't have to pay me until the letter's sent."

"I'll have it for you in the next day," said Jessyla.

"You may well be more prompt in the writing than in its departure," Barrynt pointed out.

"That could be true," agreed Jessyla, "but the sooner I have it to you, the better the chance it will be ready for whoever is traveling west."

"Thank you," added Beltur.

"My pleasure."

For all of Barrynt's cheerful agreement, before long both he and Johlana seemed to sink into a preoccupied state, and while Beltur sensed that and wondered about the cause, Jessyla was the one to speak first.

"Thank you again for a wonderful dinner. I hope you won't mind if we excuse ourselves. Today was a very long day at the healing house."

"Of course not, dear," Johlana replied immediately. "We all have long days at times."

"We'll see you in the morning," added Barrynt cheerfully.

"I likely won't," said Jorhan. "There's not much point in me getting up when there's no work to do. I'll leave that to those who do."

Beltur sensed a certain irritation behind the pleasant tone of the smith's words.

Not until Beltur and Jessyla were back in their bedchamber, standing beside the padded bench, did either speak.

"Something's going on between Jorhan and Barrynt and Johlana," said Beltur. "Or all three of them are worried about the same thing."

"I don't think it's that. Not with Jorhan's last words."

"He doesn't like not being busy. He's a smith, and he wants to keep doing it." Beltur paused. "Do you think we're overstaying our welcome?"

"We probably are," admitted Jessyla, "but I don't get the sense that we're the problem."

"Not yet, anyway. Halhana, perhaps?"

"Not Halhana . . . not exactly, but I think it has something to do with her."

"I did notice one thing about her . . ."

"Oh?"

"You seemed at loss when she said you were beautiful."

Jessyla flushed. "It wasn't that. I didn't think you saw."

"I did. How could I not? But she's right. You are beautiful."

She turned to him. "It wasn't her. It was you. I could feel you looking at me . . . and what you felt." She put her arms around him and drew him to her for a long, lingering kiss, then slowly drew back, slightly. "I hoped . . . but somehow, standing next to someone that pretty, and feeling as though I was the only one you saw . . ."

Beltur swallowed. "How could I not? You are the only one."

"Words are one thing. Your feelings are what count, and . . . your feelings were so strong I could sense them from across the room."

As close together as they were, Beltur didn't even have to try in sensing the truth and warmth—and love—that flowed from her.

"We belong together," she added.

While he wanted to enfold her, to do far more, he also sensed that the moment was more about love than physical passion, as passionate as he felt. He kissed her far more gently than he would have liked. "We do." After a moment, he asked, "How long have you felt that way?"

"I had the first hint when we came to Elparta. We were sitting in Athaal and Meldryn's parlor, and you looked at me and said, 'Congratulations.' It meant a lot that your first words were about what I'd done. Well, almost your first words, but even your very first words were that you would have hurried if you'd known I was there."

"I would have."

"I know."

"And then?"

"When you thanked me for what I'd said in Fenard, that I'd gotten you to thinking about order. It wasn't just that. It was that Waensyn had been so awful, and you didn't dwell on that. You asked me all about healing, and you understood."

"I don't know that I really understood, but I was trying to."

"I knew that, too. That was even more important. You're always trying to understand. You always want to know more and get better. I've always known that I never wanted to be with anyone who didn't try or who . . . looked down on me. You never have."

"How could I?"

"That's another reason why I love you."

Beltur wasn't about to question that. "Are you tired?"

"Not yet."

Beltur managed not to sigh or to look longingly in the direction of the bed.

Jessyla glanced toward the bed, and back to Beltur. "Not yet, dear man."

Beltur hung on the word "yet."

"You had mentioned something about teaching me magery," Jessyla said. "We have a little time. It's not that late."

You did promise her that. Beltur unentangled himself from Jessyla.

"Please don't pout. It doesn't become you."

"I'm not pouting." *Feeling frustrated, but not pouting.*

"Good." She leaned forward and kissed his cheek momentarily.

Beltur paused, trying to clear his thoughts and wondering exactly where he could start. "If I do something in shifting and moving chaos, you can sense what I'm doing, right?"

"That's the problem. I can sense it, but I can't do what I see that you're doing."

"Watch me with your senses." Beltur eased a tiny bit of free order from the air around him and moved it toward Jessyla, letting it hang in front of her. "Did you sense that? Where's the order?"

She raised a finger, the tip of her nail almost touching the order point. "There."

"Now you try it."

Beltur focused on Jessyla, but could sense no shifting or changing of the order flow around her.

"I can't do it. I just can't. Nothing's changed."

The discouragement and disappointment in her voice tore at Beltur. Abruptly, he straightened. "Let's try something else."

"I don't see what. That won't make any difference."

"No . . . the same thing, but in a very different way."

Her forehead knit in puzzlement.

"Hold my hands."

"That's not magery."

"Just hold them."

Gingerly, she did.

"No . . . like you really meant it. Just trust me."

Her fingers tightened around his, possibly with a hint of desperation.

"Now . . . try to sense what I'm feeling, just what I'm feeling." Beltur used his senses to grasp a tiny bit of free order and then to place it on Jessyla's cheek.

"Oh . . . how . . . ?"

"Keep holding my hands. This time, try to sense both what I'm feeling and what I'm doing . . ."

Beltur again grasped a tiny bit of free order and placed it beside the first on Jessyla's cheek. "Did you sense both my feelings and my actions?"

"Yes . . ."

Beltur could sense the tentativeness of her reply. "We'll try that again. Just concentrate on both my feelings and the movement of the order." This time Beltur also focused on only those two things as well.

"Do that again," murmured Jessyla. "There's . . . something . . . I can almost . . ."

Beltur repeated the exercise, forcing his thoughts to focus on those two things, and only those two things.

"It's like I can almost touch it, but not quite."

"This time, you try to move the bit of order, and I'll just give you the feelings." Beltur concentrated on sensing what she was trying, and, as she tried to touch a bit of order, he nudged it toward what felt like her grasp . . . and the order kept moving, this time toward Beltur's cheek.

"I did it!"

Jessyla's words weren't that loud, but to Beltur, the excitement behind them was overwhelming.

"Do it again."

Beltur concentrated once more, still sensing a hint of a barrier, if less than the last time, and, again, he offered an even slighter nudge than before, but Jessyla's grasp was firmer. "Much better. Do it again."

The third time, he offered feelings, but no actual assistance. The fourth time, he offered neither, but she managed to move a small bit of order.

"Do it without holding my hands this time."

Jessyla had to try twice before she managed to move the small bit of order.

"Now . . . we're going to try something different." He stood and walked to the side table that held a traveling candle. He used a touch of free chaos to light the candle. "I want you to put enough order around the flame to snuff it out. Right now, it might take several tries."

In fact, Jessyla tried five times before she could snuff out the candle. "That was hard."

"You keep trying, day after day, and it gets easier. Now . . . I want you to try something else. I'm going to create a small ball of free chaos, surrounded by order. I want you to move it to the candlewick and see if you can light the candle."

The first time that Jessyla tried it nothing happened.

"Why didn't it light?"

"You just let go of the chaos, and it spread in all directions. This time, just move the order on one side so that all the chaos flows over the candlewick."

"How did you ever learn all this?" she asked.

"It took a long time. Almost too long. Now try it again."

The second time, the tip of the wick showed a spark, but that faded immediately.

"Again."

It took two more attempts before the candle caught, with just a tiny flame that slowly grew into a full one.

"How do you feel?" Beltur asked quietly.

"Excited . . . tired . . . How did you know that would work? Not the candle, but working with feelings."

"I didn't. I just knew that the way I learned and the way everyone else learned wasn't working. Handling order and chaos isn't just by thought. It takes physical strength and . . . a certain feel. You're strong enough, and you can definitely sense where order and chaos are—and most people can't. I just guessed that if I could get you to feel something, feel how I did it, that might open things enough for you so that you could begin to manipulate order and chaos."

"It worked." A broad smile crossed Jessyla's face. "It really did."

"I'm glad." *Especially since I'm not sure what else I could have done.*

"I'm a little tired." She looked toward the bed.

Beltur tried to take a long deep breath slowly.

"Not that tired, dear man." She took his hands. "You know . . . what you were doing at first was very . . . sensual . . ."

"I could do that again . . ."

XXXVIII

On fourday and sixday, Beltur worked at the healing house, while Jessyla did on fiveday and sevenday. When Beltur wasn't working at healing, he did his best to be helpful around Barrynt's house, scraping frost and ice off the lane and the sidewalks, grooming all the horses, cleaning the entire stable, and whatever else seemed necessary. In turn, Jessyla helped Johlana.

After four more days of cold and clear weather, when Beltur left for the healing house on eightday morning, heavy clouds shrouded the mountains, and a fine snow fell across Axalt. He walked swiftly, if carefully, given that treacherous clear ice on the stone pavement was always possible, but still arrived before seventh glass, nodding to Elisa, the young girl studying to be a healer who ran errands and carried messages.

She offered a quick smile and hurried down the corridor.

Herrara greeted him as he walked into her study. "In the middle of the night, a house burned down. It was in the hills east of south town. It happens, now and again. Except this fire was deliberate. The girl said the house was in flames when she woke. Both her parents were lying on the floor. She got her two brothers out. A neighbor brought them here well before dawn this morning. The eldest boy died right after they arrived. The girl and the other boy have bruises, burns, and frostburn on their feet. They're upstairs in the small room. I'd like you to check them and the dressings on their burns and their feet. Then let me know what you think."

Beltur could sense that Herrara was uneasy about something, but there wasn't any point in asking . . . not yet. "I'll do that immediately."

"If I'm not here, I'll be in the incoming room."

Beltur left the study and made his way to the staircase and up the steps, wondering how one child could have died when it sounded as though the other two weren't that badly injured.

The two children were in the smallest chamber on the upper level. The girl sitting on the edge of the narrow bed radiated fear as Beltur stepped inside the door, leaving it open behind him. All types of chaos swirled around her, and that didn't include wound chaos on her arms and feet, or the duller red chaos in too many places on her body. She looked to be eleven or twelve. The boy in the other bed stared at Beltur almost blankly.

"I'm Beltur. I'm both a healer and a black mage. That's why I wear black instead of green." He stopped well short of the girl. "I came to see how you two are doing."

"Toscalt died, didn't he? They took him away in the dark."

"He did."

"Pa beat him too bad." The girl looked at Beltur defiantly.

"He beat you all. I can see that." *He did more than that to you.* But Beltur wasn't ready to go into that. "Could you tell me your name?"

"Chora."

"And your brother's name?"

"I call him Bhast. Pa said he didn't deserve a name."

"I need to look at your arms and feet. That's to see if your dressings need to be changed."

"You'll hurt me, like the others."

"I'll try not to."

"That's what they said."

Beltur studied her for a moment with his senses. Her right hand was heavily bandaged, most likely with a cool compress holding a poultice of brinn and calendula. While there were tiny flecks of wound chaos everywhere, there was no sign of a large concentration. The palm of her other hand was also bound, and there was a large compress covering most of her right forearm, but the burns didn't appear that severe. Then he used his senses on her feet. There were definite chaotic signs of frostburn around her toes, but Beltur thought they would also heal, although they would bear watching. "Do your feet feel like they're hot or burning a little?"

"Not anymore."

Beltur turned his attention to her brother. He had slightly fewer bruises, and his burns were all comparatively light. His frostburn was about the same as his sister's.

Beltur looked back to Chora. "Your brother was burned less than you were."

She just looked at Beltur.

"Do you have any relatives? An aunt or an uncle?"

Chora shook her head.

He took another step toward her. "Hold out your left hand."

Warily, she did so.

Beltur barely touched her fingertips with his, but drew a slight bit of free order from around him and let it flow into Chora, then withdrew his hand. "That might help a little."

Her eyes brightened just a touch.

"Try to sleep or rest," he said. "I'll be back from time to time to check on you and Bhast."

She gave the faintest nod.

Beltur could sense that she was still fearful, but less so. He smiled gently, then eased out of the room, closing the door quietly. He had no doubts about what had happened, and he couldn't say that he blamed the girl.

He made his way back to Herrara's study. She was still sitting behind the desk, one of the ledger-like books before her, but Beltur could tell that she wasn't really looking at it.

"That didn't take long." The older healer looked squarely at Beltur.

"No. The burns and frost damage should heal before too long. I'd guess that the neighbor cooled the burns with water or compresses."

"You're not telling me everything. What else?"

Beltur moistened his lips, deciding to offer just the facts. "The girl is bruised all over. Some of the bruises are recent. There are older ones I can barely sense. That's true for the boy, if not quite so badly. I take it that the boy who died was older and was badly bruised."

Herrara's eyes widened only slightly. "He was also badly burned."

"Then he was the oldest of the children?"

"He was."

Beltur changed his view of what had happened, at least as to who had done what. "I see."

"I believe you do. I'm asking you as a healer and a mage—will they heal in the next few days?"

"They should within the eightday." *But you already know that.* "What will happen to them now that their parents are dead? Chora said they didn't have any relatives."

"They'll go to the poorhouse."

Beltur didn't know if that was a death sentence or more hope than the two had before the fire.

"They'll be all right there. We haven't had a child die there from neglect, ever. Once in a great while from illness."

"Thank you."

"I could see the question. If you would check on them every glass or so."

"I can do that."

"Please check on the rest of the upstairs rooms, now, and do whatever is necessary."

Beltur nodded and then took another basket of supplies from the shelf before leaving the study and heading for the second floor once more. He started at one end and methodically began, checking each person in each bed. After the first two rooms, he had to stop and take the discarded dressings down to the waste barrel in the outside closet that held only refuse, then wash up and gather two more baskets of supplies.

Possibly two glasses had passed when he was about to enter another room and Elisa hurried toward him. "Downstairs, ser. Healer Herrara needs you immediately in the surgery."

Beltur handed her the basket filled with soiled dressings. "Please take care of those."

She accepted the basket and nodded.

He hurried to the staircase and down to the main level. When he entered the surgery, he saw two men supporting a third seated on the corner of the surgical table. What looked to be the stub of a pole protruded from the chest of the third man, whose face was contorted in pain. As Beltur moved forward, he could see that Herrara stood behind the man, cutting away his shirt.

"Tell Healer Beltur what happened." Herrara's words were terse.

The taller man spoke, not looking at Beltur. "Poldaark was feeding the rabbits in the pen. He slipped. He fell and hit the pole on the corner of the rabbit pen. Somehow, the tip broke off and the whole pole went through his back. We sawed off the rest of the pole. We didn't know how to get it out. We brought him here."

At first Beltur didn't see how the pole could have gone through the young man, or how the young man had even lived, but closer examination showed that the pole had missed the shoulder blade. "The tip must have been awfully sharp to have cut through his coat."

"It was inside the barn. He wasn't wearing his coat."

That really didn't address Beltur's question, but determining what to do was the more urgent need. Or, more to the point, what Herrara needed him to do. He looked to the older healer. "What do you need?"

"What do you sense?"

Beltur concentrated. "There's not a lot of the dull red chaos. So he's not bleeding a huge amount inside." *Not yet.* "Not much wound chaos yet."

"Good. We'll have to remove the pole. And it's got to come out from the back. Can you use those shields of yours to stop any severe bleeding if it occurs?"

"If it's not in too many places."

"We'll have to chance that. He can't live with a pole through him. I'm starting now."

As Herrara carefully eased the pole—about a digit across—back out, Beltur immediately placed a small shield over the exit wound, slowly extending it like a tube into the space where the pole had been.

When the pole was out, Herrara said, "There's no bleeding."

"I've replaced the pole with a shield, but I can't hold it forever."

"Ease it back so that I can clean the entry wound."

Beltur did so. "Is that enough?"

"A little more. It's a bit more jagged than I'd like, and there are wood splinters." After Beltur had moved the shield back a bit, she said, "Good. Just hold that."

"OOOOH!" Poldaark shuddered.

"Just hold him tightly," ordered Herrara, using a set of iron tweezers.

"OOOH!"

Almost half a glass passed before Herrara finished cleaning and dressing the wound. By then Poldaark was limp, not moving when the two men used a stretcher to carry him to wherever Herrara was directing them.

Beltur took a deep breath, then began to clean up the surgery, first gathering everything soiled and putting it in the disposal bin, then using spirits on his hands, along with some free order, before cleaning off the surgery table.

He'd barely finished when Herrara returned, glancing around the surgery. "Good." After a moment, she said, "He's a very fortunate young man. I know you could have stopped the bleeding for a while if he'd ripped a large blood vessel, but stitching a blood vessel usually doesn't work, and only then if there's a slight cut or rip. If it's badly torn, there's no hope. We'll just have to hope—again—that wound chaos doesn't build up."

"I can reduce some of that," Beltur said.

"Then check on him often."

"I will." Beltur had no idea how fast interior wound chaos might build or when it might start. *Another thing you need to learn.*

Herrara nodded and left the surgery.

After several moments, Beltur stepped out into the corridor, immediately noticing that the two men who had brought Poldaark were standing at the far end of the corridor, presumably outside the room holding the young man. Beltur glanced around. For the moment, the corridor was empty, and neither man was looking in his direction. He raised a concealment and then moved slowly and as quietly as possible toward the pair, finally stopping several yards away.

". . . how is he?"

"It looked like he's still breathing. Moaning a lot, though. Can't you hear him?"

"The head healer thinks there's a chance he'll live."

"Impaled like that?"

"Told you we should bring him in. She and the black healer got that pole out of him, and he didn't gush blood. You ought to thank him."

"What else is he going to do? Not much call for a black mage in Axalt."

"Fortunate he's not white."

The two men laughed.

"Still say Poldaark's a lucky little bastard."

"You're the frigging fortunate one. Told you not to horse around like that."

"He deserved it. Little wiseass. How was I to know that pole was cracked?"

"Good thing none of the rabbits escaped. Then Hannon would really have had your ass."

"We'd better get back. Not much else we can do here."

Beltur just stood there as the two left the healing house, finally lowering the concealment. He shook his head and headed for the staircase. He still had to finish tending to those on the second floor.

The rest of the day was thankfully uneventful, possibly because fewer things tended to go wrong on eightday, or because people tended to stay home. *Especially in winter.*

By the time Beltur reached Barrynt's house after fourth glass, he was worn out, although not particularly tired. He'd checked Chora and her brother just before he'd left, and they were fine. Poldaark seemed slightly better, and certainly no worse, but that could easily change.

Beltur shook his head as he climbed the steps to the side entry, where he opened the door and stepped inside.

Jessyla stood in the foyer waiting. "You look tired."

"It was . . . a day."

"Tell me now. Everyone's in the family parlor, and you look like you need to tell someone."

"Let me get my coat off, and then I will." Once he'd hung his coat and scarf on a peg, and tucked his gloves into a sleeve, he cleared his throat. "It

started almost the moment I arrived . . ." Beltur gave her a quick summary
of the first three glasses. ". . . and after that, it was just checking on people."

"Do you think Herrara will say anything about the girl?"

"No. She doesn't like it, but there's no proof, and it's clear Chora was
beaten and abused."

"To a mage or a good healer."

Beltur smiled sardonically. "Anyone else would see even less."

"For her sake, I hope so."

"So do I."

Jessyla squeezed his hand for a moment, then led the way from the
foyer.

As Beltur and Jessyla entered the family parlor, Beltur saw that everyone else was already there, all with beakers or mugs in their hands.

"You two need some refreshment," insisted Johlana immediately. "You,
especially, Beltur. A mage working on an eightday. What's the world come
to?" She gestured and Frankyr moved toward the sideboard.

Once Beltur had a beaker of amber ale and Jessyla a mug of hot spiced
wine, Barrynt cleared his throat loudly. When the parlor was silent, he
announced, "I have two things to tell you two. First, I've located a Sligan
trader heading to Elparta tomorrow, assuming the weather is clear. He'll
be taking your letter. He was glad for the detailed directions."

"I thought it best to send in to the healing house," interjected Jessyla.

"And second, you know I've put out the word about a building for your
smithy, and I've talked to those who had vacant buildings . . ."

"You're saying you've found one?" asked Jorhan.

"No. There are several possibilities, but I did find something that might
interest Beltur and Jessyla. There's a fellow named Rohan. He mentioned he
had an empty cot he'd like to rent out. His mother lived there, but she died
suddenly in midfall. He's just finished cleaning it out. I think he'll be reasonable." Barrynt looked at Beltur. "Would you like to look at it tomorrow?"

"Could we do it in the late afternoon, so that both Jessyla and I could
see it together?"

"I don't see why not. Rohan's not going anywhere. Neither is the cot."
Barrynt smiled broadly.

"Thank you," said Jessyla politely.

"What do you think about the healing house, now that you're a healer
there?" asked Johlana, looking at Jessyla.

"It's a healing house. Healer Herrara is very well organized."

"She's always been that."

"Do you think we'll get another northeaster within an eightday?" asked Frankyr.

"It's not likely," replied Barrynt, "but you can never be certain. You know that."

Beltur tried to listen more than talk, through the time in the parlor and at dinner, during which time he slipped Barrynt a pair of silvers to pay for delivering Jessyla's letter. Much later, after spending time in the parlor with the others after dinner, Beltur and Jessyla repaired to their bedchamber.

"We don't even have a bed to our name," said Jessyla. "How can we rent something?"

"It can't hurt to look," pointed out Beltur. "We do have blankets."

She just shook her head. "What about the horses?"

"We'll have to see if I can work out something with Barrynt . . . or someone else." Beltur wasn't about to give up Slowpoke, especially since he knew the gelding would end up being slaughtered or going to a renderer. "Besides, we knew we'd have to find a place sometime."

"I'd hoped it wouldn't be . . . quite so soon."

"We're fortunate that we're being hosted. And, as I told you, we do have a few golds." *Even a bit more than a few.*

"I know. We are making a few silvers, and we'll make more in a season."

"By then, Jorhan should have the smithy working." *And by late spring, we might even be selling cupridium again.*

"And we're together."

XXXIX

Just before noon on oneday, Beltur finished his self-appointed chores and assorted tasks and decided to walk down to the market square, wondering what might be sold there during winter, partly because he knew that he and Jessyla had almost nothing with which to start a household. The day was, as most had been, clear and cold.

As he walked, Beltur pondered, as he had more than once, what he could have done differently, but he doubted that he had much choice besides leaving the city in some fashion or another. *If you'd killed Waensyn earlier . . .* He shook his head. Not only did that feel wrong, but it wouldn't have worked, because he was the only one with the ability to kill Waensyn who had a reason to do so. Of course, after Jorhan had killed Cohndar, there had been no choice at all. And the fact that the two of them had come to the smithy alone showed that they believed either that they were more powerful than Beltur, or that he'd accede to their demands. *Or both.* In a way, Waensyn's arrogance had resulted from Beltur's minimizing the appearance of his abilities in the battles against the Prefect's mages, out of self-preservation, just so that Cohndar wouldn't assign him to ever more dangerous duties. *So much of what you've done to try to protect yourself has led to more problems.*

Maybe that's just the way of the world.

The market square was smaller than the main square in Elparta, perhaps sixty yards on a side. The Traders' Bowl—the inn where Vaenturl and Karmult had stayed—faced the square on the east side, while a line of shops was on the north side, and the Council House on the south side, while the boulevard leading to the square from the canyon road was on the west side, flanked by several dwellings that had shops on the lower level.

To Beltur's mild surprise, there were more than a score of vendors in groups of three to six scattered almost randomly across the square. The first group he neared all seemed to be selling woolen garments, sweaters, jackets, and even gloves.

He nodded politely and moved to the next group, a larger number of sellers that all had produce for sale. He found himself peering at a dish holding what appeared to be tannish cream seeds. "What are they?"

"Pine nuts. A copper a cup."

Beltur had to struggle to understand the words that the ruddy-faced woman uttered so cheerfully, so thick was her accent. At least, her words sounded accented to him, but likely his way of speaking probably did to her as well. He wasn't certain he wanted to eat nuts that tasted like pine trees, and the cup beside the dish looked rather small.

"Try one." She pointed to the dish.

Beltur took one and popped it in his mouth, finding it surprisingly soft, and without a taste of pine resin. "Thank you. I'll have to think about it."

He could sense the smiles from adjoining vendors.

Someone murmured, "Flatlander," but the tone didn't sound derogatory.

Another vendor had lentils and dry beans, while a third had dried apple slices. Beltur didn't see any acorn cakes. The end vendor had sacks of corn, and oats. From the produce vendors he made his way to a group of three others who seemed to have an assortment of hardware—nails and spikes, a hammer, some old iron pots, one of which looked quite usable.

After he perused everything in the square, he walked toward the row of shops, spotting a small chandlery, which, after a moment, he entered, almost bumping into a rangy man wearing a stained leather apron who was stepping away from a narrow table on which sat a row of square lanterns of various sizes. "Oh . . . I'm sorry. I didn't see you."

"Quite all right." The man studied Beltur briefly, then added, "Good black wool trousers. You wouldn't be the mage-healer being guested by Merchant Barrynt, would you?"

"I fear I am. Beltur. You are?"

"Rhodos."

"This is your chandlery?"

"Such as it is, ser mage. What are you looking for?"

Beltur offered an embarrassed smile. "I don't know. I'm looking so that I know where to look for what when I do need it."

Rhodos offered a broad smile. "Look all you want. I have tools in the chests on that wall. Ropes and lines and nets and even snares over there. On the long table are some dried foods sealed for travel. Candles in the open-topped boxes next to them . . . the rest, well, you can see for yourself . . . pitch, turpentine, even some fine timbering saws." He laughed. "I get carried away when I meet someone new. A mage likely wouldn't need a timbering saw."

"I might not, but if I do, I know where to find it. What about cooking ware and the like?"

"Back in the rear corner." Rhodos paused. "You're thinking of settling here?"

There was an almost skeptical note in the chandler's voice, but Beltur replied, "We've thought of it. It seems like a well-ordered place."

"Very well-ordered, if I do say so myself. The Council's good about that. Costs a bit more in tariffs, but worth it."

"Even for people who live here?"

"Oh, no, the tariffs aren't on people, just on shops and crafts and houses."

"I just wondered. Gallos and Elparta only tariff goods coming into their lands."

"The tariffs aren't on goods. They're on buildings and dwellings. They're used to pay for the roads, the fountains and water pipes, and the public sewers."

Beltur couldn't help frowning. He didn't think there had been such tariffs in Gallos or Spidlar. Neither his uncle nor Meldryn had mentioned them. *But you never asked.* He also realized that he'd never even thought about tariffs on buildings.

"They're not that high. Some small cots pay only a half silver a year."

"If they're that low . . ."

Rhodos nodded. "Just let me know if you have any questions."

"I will." Beltur smiled.

He took his time perusing the chandlery's tables, taking in the small table that held several pairs of scissors but no needles or pins. Beltur imagined those were kept close by the chandler. The items hung on the walls included several axes and shovels, and oddly, Beltur thought, a pole saw.

When he left the chandlery, he was still thinking about the chandler's reaction to the idea that Beltur and Jessyla might remain in Axalt. *Why was he surprised?* Besides, where else could they go that would be any better?

With that thought still hanging over him, he continued his inspection of the other shops, particularly the dry goods store that displayed barrels and barrels of rolled oats, feed maize, wheat and rye flour, and white, brown, and black beans, as well as a small barrel of dried fruit.

The graystone Council House seemed almost deserted, with only a few people entering or leaving it, while there was a continual flow of people around the inn, which almost seemed to be a meeting place for many, mostly men.

Beltur finally returned to Barrynt's mansion slightly after second glass and settled into the family parlor to read more in *The Wisdom of Relyn.* This time, instead of leafing through the volume quickly, he began at the start of the short section that seemed to be historical, reading quickly through Relyn's training as a lord-holder's second son in Gethen Groves, only to discover that Relyn left out most of what happened after that, just offering a summary.

> . . . as with many second sons, I fulfilled my duties with little hope of a consort or of lands of my own, until the Lord of Lornth offered lands in the Ironwoods to any who could vanquish the interlopers and remove them from the Roof of the World. I spent all of what few golds I had to raise a band and made my way there. Seeing how few of the interlopers there were, and seeing that most were women, I pressed the attack. In what seemed moments, most of my men were dead, the few others fleeing for their lives, my right hand was gone, and a strange man smaller than many of

mine and smaller than the woman warleader of the interlopers, created flame from a metal pipe and seared the stump of my lower arm. Thus began my time and my learning among the angels. That time ended when Lord Sillek of Lornth massed his forces and attacked Westwind, for such the angels had named it, and the black tower created stone by stone by the mighty Nylan. All the angel warriors were women, save Nylan, and they slaughtered close to half of Lord Sillek's men with those short bows that looked like a child's and pierced mail and armor as if they were but thin leather. Yet Sillek's forces pressed back the angels, who seemed to break and retreat to their tower, all but Nylan and the few who surrounded him.

Just before that horde of Lornth seemed about to overwhelm the black mage, he summoned the fires of Heaven and burnt the battlefield and all upon it to ashes and dust in but an instant. I stood there, no more than a yard away. One moment, there was a mighty army charging across the trampled grass and the next there was nothing but gray ash . . . and Nylan lay still, nearly at my feet, but he was alive and breathing, and the silver-haired healer—not Ayrlyn—said he would live.

Nylan had told me that, if I wished to live, I should flee, immediately after the battle . . .

Beltur blinked. *That's all he wrote about the battle?*

He looked to see if a page had been cut from the volume, but none had. Finally, he read on, following Relyn's slow travel through Gallos, avoiding Fenard, until he reached Passera.

At that point, Barrynt walked into the parlor. "Are you still reading that book?"

"I thought I should. I don't know much about Relyn, and parts of it are very interesting." Beltur tried to mentally note where he was, then closed the book and stood, immediately replacing the volume in the bookcase. "It looks like it's been in your family for some time and been read often."

"My mother insisted we each read it. I haven't opened it since then. Johlana read some of it after we were consorted."

"Then you have brothers or sisters?"

"Not any longer. My brother Ryntaar went to sea. He was killed when pirates from Hydlen attacked his ship. His consort and son were with him."

"Oh . . . I'm sorry."

"That's all right. You didn't know, and it was a long time ago." After a pause, Barrynt went on. "That's another reason I don't read it. Ryntaar kept telling me that order would protect him. Never seemed to me that it works that way." The merchant offered a crooked smile. "Didn't work that well for you, it seems."

Beltur shrugged. "Order and chaos are part of the world. I've used order, and it certainly helped to get us here safely. Neither order nor chaos caused our problems in Elparta. Greedy people did."

Barrynt laughed. "I think we're saying the same thing."

"Most likely."

"Rohan will meet us at the cot a quint or so after fourth glass. Will your consort be here by then?"

"She should be . . . unless someone is badly hurt just before she leaves."

"That's not likely in winter. Most accidents happen in the morning or at night. There's not much theft or burgling at night in winter." Barrynt smiled. "Houses are shuttered tight against the cold."

Jessyla arrived in the side foyer just before fourth glass. Beltur and Barrynt were waiting.

"How was your day?" asked Beltur.

"Mostly quiet. The young man you and Herrara saved . . ."

"Is he all right . . . I mean, is he getting better?"

"He's not getting worse. Herrara says that tomorrow will tell."

Barrynt cleared his throat loudly.

"Oh . . . do we need to go right now?" asked Jessyla.

"The man with the cot is going to meet us there in the next quint," explained Beltur.

"It will take a little while. It's about half a kay from here," said Barrynt. "To the northeast."

After the two men had donned their coats, Barrynt opened the door and stepped outside.

Beltur gestured for Jessyla to precede him, then followed, closing the door firmly. A gust of wind whipped the end of Beltur's scarf loose, and he had to tuck the end inside his coat.

"Looks like another storm," said Barrynt. "It won't be a northeaster, though. The sky's too light for that."

"You can tell just from that?" asked Jessyla.

"After a while."

"Tell us more about this cot." Jessyla looked at the merchant.

"It's a cozy little place," said Barrynt. "The rent's not bad, either."

"What does 'not bad' mean?" asked Jessyla, even before Beltur could.

"Four coppers an eightday."

"Almost half a silver?"

"It's cheap at the price. I've seen smaller places go for more."

"How about larger places going for less?" asked Beltur cheerfully, even as he was continuing to get the impression, copper by copper, that it cost more to live in Axalt than it had in either Elparta or Fenard.

"That's possible," returned Barrynt, equally cheerfully, "if you want to live kays out of town lugging water from a spring you have to chop through the ice to get to."

Beltur decided not to offer another quip. "We do have one other problem . . ."

"Your horses?" asked Barrynt. "I'd thought about that. If you want to keep cleaning the stables the way you have been, you can keep them there. You pay for your share of the hay and feed." The merchant grinned. "I can get it cheaper than you could."

"We'd appreciate that," Beltur said.

"In return," added Barrynt, pausing and letting the silence draw out.

Beltur managed to look interested but not wince.

"We'd like to be able to call on your healing talents if we need to. Johlana's not all that fond of the healing house."

"We can do that," said Jessyla.

"Just down this side lane, now."

The lane—or the cleared part of it—was narrow, only a little more than three yards wide, but the paving stones were evenly set, Beltur noticed. A two-story dwelling stood on the corner, and a man in a gray coat stood waiting at the end of the cleared walk from the front door to the lane proper.

"There's Rohan. He lives there. The cot is next door to his house."

Beltur looked toward the small squarish dwelling, slightly more than ten yards on a side, with possibly five yards between it and the low stone walls to the north and south, walls that protruded less than half a yard above the snow that was almost a yard deep. The dark brown shutters were fastened tight, and the front door matched the shutters.

"Rohan! This is Mage Beltur and his consort Jessyla. They're both healers."

The wiry man stepped forward. "Pleasure to meet you." He paused, looking at Beltur. "A mage and a healer?"

Beltur smiled. "Both. It's a long story."

"Sometime, I'd like to hear it." Rohan began to walk toward the cot, gesturing as he did. "It's small, but it's snug, and it's neat. Comes with a couple of benches, a kitchen table and sideboard, and a bedstead."

"We have a decent mattress and some linens and towels you can have," added Barrynt. "More than we'll ever use."

Rohan walked to the door and opened it, gesturing for the others to enter.

Beltur and Barrynt stepped to the side to allow Jessyla to go first. Beltur followed her.

The door opened into a front room, essentially the parlor, perhaps five yards on a side, with a hearth set in the middle of the rear wall. An archway to the right of the stone wall that held the chimney led into the kitchen. The floor was made of wide planks that were comparatively and surprisingly level and largely without deep scratches or gouges. The only piece of furniture in the front room was a backed bench that had seen better days, but looked sturdy enough. Four stout wooden pegs were set in the wall just to the right of the door, and two modest and shuttered windows were evenly spaced in the front wall. There was only a tiny high side window, also shuttered, in the outside wall on the left side of the room. As with all the dwellings Beltur had seen, every window appeared to have outer and inner shutters, a necessity in winter, he suspected.

The kitchen was about two yards wider than the front room, and had three doors: a rear door; a door leading back to the bedroom, which was to the right of the front room, but entered from the kitchen; and a door to the washroom and jakes. The kitchen table was large and solid, and less battered than either the bench or the sideboard bench that accompanied it. The hearth, which was open on both sides—the front room and the kitchen—had two iron brackets that could be swiveled over the fire.

Rohan pointed to a small hinged door in the wall, perhaps fifteen digits square, between the shuttered rear window and the rear door. "That's for waste water. Just water. No slops of any sort. You pay the Council if you clog the standpipe. Sewer port is down the alley to the left about ten yards."

Beltur looked at the shutters, noticing that they admitted some light through small openings, possibly cracks. Jessyla inspected the sideboard, opening the hinged doors to reveal three shelves. She closed the sideboard doors.

"You won't find anything near this good for anything close to this rent," said Barrynt.

"That's because you're a black and she's a healer," added Rohan.

"It is very neat," said Jessyla politely, before heading into the bedroom.

Beltur followed her into a chamber that was also sparsely furnished, with just a side table, a stool, and a bedstead, although it was large enough for two and looked sturdy. He looked at Jessyla as she walked to the bedstead and looked it over, then checked the inside shutters on the single front window and then on the small side window.

"What do you think?" asked Barrynt.

"It's more than large enough for us," replied Jessyla. "It might be too large, since we have little enough to put in it."

Barrynt smiled. "I think we can be helping there, and you'll be helping us as well."

Beltur didn't hide his puzzlement.

"The storeroom in the stable is filled with furniture. I can barely close the door, and there are some good pieces there . . . well, let's just say that, good as they are, it would be best if you had them."

Beltur could tell that Barrynt truly meant those words. *But why would that be so?* Then he remembered what Jorhan had told him—that Barrynt had been a widower. *Those are pieces with either painful memories or links to his first consort, pieces he doesn't want to sell or destroy . . . but why wouldn't they go to his children?* Because of Johlana?

Beltur couldn't tell, but what was clear was that Barrynt was being honest.

"I can't tell you how kind that is," said Jessyla softly. "I really can't."

"Then you'll take the place?" asked Rohan.

"We will," said Jessyla before Beltur could say a word.

"That's a good choice," said Barrynt. "You won't regret it."

"I'm sure we won't," said Jessyla.

"There's a deposit of two silvers," Rohan pointed out. "And the rent's due every five eightdays, two silvers, twice a season, in advance."

"Then that's four silvers," said Beltur, "before we move in."

"That'd be right."

"If they pay now," said Barrynt, "supposing you let them have this eightday. It will take them a few days to gather everything they need."

Rohan cocked his head questioningly.

"You won't be getting any better tenants, and likely not any sooner at this time of year," said Barrynt with a smile.

"I suppose I could do that. That'd mean the rent'd be due on oneday of the seventh eightday of winter." Rohan frowned. "How about four and a half silvers for everything, and that pays the rent through winter, and the next payment's due on the first day of spring?"

Beltur had to calculate for a moment, but he thought that amounted to a savings of almost a silver over the winter, and he and Jessyla certainly didn't want to wear out their welcome with Barrynt. "That sounds fair enough." He reached for his belt wallet.

"But you fix anything that's not their fault," said Barrynt. "Roof, walls, leaks in the standpipes."

"Be a poor landlord if I didn't, and you know what the Council thinks of that," replied Rohan, with a touch of testiness in his voice.

"I know that, but they're not from Axalt, and they don't," said Barrynt cheerfully.

"Best they know," agreed Rohan.

Beltur handed over the four silvers and five coppers and received a large heavy key in return.

"Clearing the walks is your responsibility, and I'll bring over a shovel for you in a bit. It's not likely to snow in the next day."

"A pleasure dealing with you, Rohan," declared Barrynt.

"All around, it looks to fit everyone," agreed the landlord. "And seeing the cot is in good hands, I need to be off." He nodded and left the bed-chamber.

In moments, the front door opened and closed.

"He seemed to be in a hurry," said Jessyla.

"He's likely headed to the Council House to register you as his tenants."

"Register us as tenants?" asked Beltur. "Does it have to be done that quickly?"

"No," replied Barrynt, "but he's responsible for clearing the walks and making sure nothing's left in the lane in front of the cot until you're regis-tered. He's likely been paying to have the walks cleared."

"And once we're registered, he'll only have to pay half as much?"

"That would be my thought," agreed the merchant. "We should head back to the house and talk to Johlana about where we can help you. That's besides the spare furniture. She'll leave me to deal with what's in the stable storeroom."

Beltur was careful to lock both front and rear doors before they left.

Although Barrynt set a quick pace heading back, Jessyla walked a trace more slowly. For a moment, Beltur wondered if she didn't feel well, but then realized she wanted space between them and the merchant.

Finally, she said, quietly, "He really wants us to have that furniture. When I said he was being kind, there was a sadness . . ."

"I think that's because it might have been his first consort's. Jorhan told me she died in childbirth and that Barrynt was a forlorn man, and that Johlana was the only one who could cheer him up." That wasn't exactly what Jorhan had said, but it was certainly what he'd implied.

"He didn't have any children with his first consort?"

"Jorhan said he didn't."

"All of that makes sense. Poor man. Maybe our taking some of it will help with that old sadness." She frowned. "I don't see why Johlana has let him keep furniture that was his first consort's. I wouldn't have."

"Grenara is living in the house once occupied by another consort before her."

"Auntie didn't have any choice."

"Maybe, for reasons we don't know, Johlana doesn't."

"That's awful! It makes me very glad you weren't consorted before."

"I'm too young for that," said Beltur with a grin.

"Beltur . . ." She shook her head.

Beltur could tell that she wasn't even remotely close to feeling as displeased as she'd tried to sound.

When they reached the house, took off their coats and scarves, and finally entered the parlor, Johlana turned from where she had been talking with her consort, smiling happily. "Barrynt tells me that you've found a place, and that it's not too far away. That's wonderful. For us as well. There's so much furniture in the stable that's been going to waste. It should have been put to good use long ago."

Beltur could sense that Johlana was definitely not displeased.

Nor did Barrynt seem unhappy, either.

"You've already been so kind," offered Jessyla.

"Too kind," added Beltur.

"Nonsense. You've rescued my brother and brought him here safe, and that will allow Ryntaar to do what he's always wanted. It's the least we can do. And there's a good mattress in our cellar that will fit that bedstead. If it doesn't, there's a bedstead in the stable . . ."

Beltur just listened as Johlana explained to Jessyla.

XL

On twoday, Beltur woke early. *What have you done? You're committed to set-*
ting up a household in a city where you've been for less than two eightdays. You
know almost no one, and you're not making enough to pay for everything, and
the golds and silvers you have will only last so long.

But what choice did he and Jessyla have? Without Barrynt and Johlana,
things would have been far worse. Still, he couldn't help worrying.

"Are you awake?" asked Jessyla. "Are you all right?"

And you're consorted to someone who can largely sense what you're feeling.
"I woke up worrying, but other than that, I'm all right."

"You're worrying too much."

"With what little we're making?" Beltur turned toward her.

"The cot costs four silvers a season. That's a gold for an entire year.
We're each making a gold a season." She paused. "I saw how many golds
you have in the slots in your belt. We could live on those for several years,
even without making anything, if we're careful."

"I need to find a safe place—"

"Right now, as long as you keep your trousers close, that's the safest
place." She reached out and touched his cheek. "It really is."

They were the first into the breakfast room, except for, of course,
Johlana. Almost as soon as Jessyla sat down, Johlana said, "You have the
day off. So we can look over the furniture in the storeroom and see what
suits you and Beltur best. I also have some linens in the back of the linen
closet that should work . . ."

Beltur managed not to smile in amusement, although he was also very
glad that the merchant's consort wanted to be helpful. Instead, he began
to eat soon after Asala appeared with a platter of egg toast and ham
strips—but after Johlana and Jessyla served themselves.

Then Barrynt arrived, along with Ryntaar and Frankyr, and after several swallows of ale, he turned to Beltur. "I've been thinking . . ."

"Yes?" replied Beltur politely.

"I only saw a few sticks in the woodpile by the back door of your cot
and nothing in the woodbox by the hearth. We can spare some coal for
your hearth to get you started and get the place warmed up, but you'll

have to buy wood as well as coal. Most men line up their coal well before winter. You obviously couldn't do that, but there are always young fellows with strong backs who have wood for sale. Don't pay more than a silver for a cord, though, and not until it's delivered and stacked."

"That's part of the price?"

"It is, but they'll take you for an outlander. You'll need to tell them that the price has to include delivery and stacking."

Beltur couldn't help wondering just how many other unplanned expenses would crop up before they were even settled in the cot. "I appreciate the advice." He grinned wryly. "What else should I know that I don't? What about water?"

"You're not so fortunate. I paid to have a pipe run from the nearest water house to our cistern. That's what the pump brings up."

"Water house?"

"The little square houses set on corners every so often. Each one has a small cistern and a pump. Each cistern is fed by pipes from the reservoir. The pumps are designed so that when they're not used the water drains out. That's so they don't freeze up. You'll have to carry water to the cot."

Beltur imagined that carrying water to the cot could get old very quickly, but that would have been a problem anywhere that they could afford. "I didn't see any buckets."

"Rhodos at the chandlery has good buckets. Tell him I sent you. It might help. He might even have a house cistern that doesn't cost too much."

"Like a huge barrel?"

"Barrels get dirty too easily. House cisterns are made of fired and glazed clay. It might cost a silver or two to get one delivered, but if you can afford it, they're worth it. Much easier to clean, and they warm up the water to the same heat as the cot."

"Thank you." Beltur had never heard of a house cistern, but the idea made sense to him.

"I'm sure you'll have more questions, especially after our consorts go through the storeroom."

"I wouldn't wager against that."

Beltur finished the last of his egg toast and the amber ale, then rose. "Thank you, again, for such an excellent breakfast. I need to hurry off, unhappily."

"It still seems strange for a mage to be working like a healer," said Ryntaar.

"I've never heard of a mage-healer," added Frankyr.

"There are very few," said Jessyla. "My mother knew one years ago."

"What happened to him?" asked Frankyr.

"She didn't know. He left Fenard when she was very young. She didn't know why."

Beltur looked to Jessyla, trying to keep his jaw in place. "You never . . ."

"I didn't remember until Frankyr said 'mage-healer.' I couldn't have been more than five or six." She offered an embarrassed smile. "You'll be late. I'll tell you this evening."

Beltur could sense both the honesty and embarrassment. "I look forward to hearing it all." He smiled back at her, then inclined his head to Johlana. "Thank you, again."

Once he left the breakfast room, Beltur had to hurry, but he still managed to arrive at the healing house just before seventh glass.

When he stepped into Herrara's study, she looked up at him.

"You'd better look at Poldaark first."

"Wound chaos?"

She just nodded.

"Where is he?"

"In the room where Stullak was."

Beltur hid a wince, thinking of the man he hadn't been able to save. After a moment, he nodded and then took one of the oblong baskets that held cloths, spirits, and a few implements, and then headed up the stairs. The small room still had four beds, but only one was occupied.

Poldaark looked up from that bed. "It still hurts. It's getting worse."

"I know," said Beltur. "I'm going to see what I can do for you." He stood over the youth and let his senses explore the long puncture wound and the area around it. While there were quite a number of small and angry-feeling bits of wound chaos, a handful of which had a yellow-greenish tinge that he definitely didn't like, the chaos was restricted to or immediately touching the wound, unlike with poor Stullak, where it had been everywhere. But there were close to a score of those small chaos bits.

He took a deep breath and then sat down on the side of the bed closest to Poldaark. "This might take a little while."

"I don't think I'm going anywhere, ser mage."

Not if I can't get rid of most of that wound chaos inside you. Beltur just nodded and began to focus on channeling bits of free order at the largest clump of the greenish-tinged chaos, then moving his efforts to the next one. After removing five or so of the greenish clumps, he could also sense that the wound and the area around it were getting warmer, but he had the feeling that he needed to deal with all of them, if he didn't want the wound to fester.

"Are you feeling feverish?"

"Where the pole went through me feels warmer. That doesn't feel bad, though."

"Good. You may feel feverish before I'm finished."

Beltur continued, working from the larger clumps to the smaller ones, bit by bit. When he finished, he had a slight hint of a headache. He took a deep breath and looked at Poldaark. Sweat was beading on the youth's forehead. "How do you feel?"

"Hot, and it's sort of sore. Sorer than it was."

"You should cool down in a while. The soreness should pass after a while." *You hope.*

Beltur stood. "I'll stop by later."

After looking in on three others on the upper level, he went back to see Herrara.

"What do you think?"

"I took care of the wound chaos."

"So far. How long can you keep doing it?"

Beltur shrugged wearily. "For now. If I can keep it down, he'll have a chance."

"Until those other two throw him around again," replied Herrara.

"Has something like that happened with him before?"

"Not with him. I've seen others come in several times until they didn't make it. Even if he doesn't come back, in the next eightday or so, sooner or later, there will be another incident."

"It happens that often?"

"More often as winter drags on. By spring, more of the beds will be filled."

That thought disturbed Beltur, but if the chief healer said that, he didn't doubt it. "I looked at the others upstairs. There's nothing else I could do there now." He paused. "You seem to be the only healer here. How many are there in Axalt?"

"I am. The Council only pays for two. That doesn't count Elisa, since she's in training." Herrara smiled tightly. "If you must know, I am grateful that you and your consort came."

"I'm grateful for the experience."

"Now that's out of the way, you might as well come with me."

Beltur spent much of the morning preparing wound dressings, until more injuries filtered into the healing house, when he returned to dealing with an assortment of injuries.

Just after fourth glass, he left the healing house and walked back through the cold to Barrynt's, where he found that the only person there was Asala, busy working on dinner.

"Where is everyone, Asala?"

"Your consort and Mistress Johlana are at your cot. So's young Frankyr. Master Barrynt's likely at his factorage with the smith and Ryntaar."

"Thank you." Beltur turned and made his way from the merchant's small mansion, walking the half kay to the cot.

There he found Frankyr readying what had to be Barrynt's wagon to leave the cot.

"They're inside, ser mage."

"Thank you."

Beltur opened the front door and stepped into the front room of the cot . . . and just looked.

There were two oak armchairs, each with a dark green cushion, flanking a matching oak bench, with two side tables. The bench that had been in the cot had been placed against the inside wall underneath the wooden coat pegs near the front door.

"Beltur? Is that you?" called Jessyla from either the kitchen or bedroom.

"It's me." He slowly shut the door.

Jessyla burst through the archway from the kitchen, a broad smile on her face. "How do you like it?"

"I can't believe it."

"Neither can I, and Johlana insists it's really all ours." Jessyla turned and gestured to the older woman.

"It really is," affirmed Johlana. "We have no use for it, and there's plenty more for Ryntaar and Frankyr."

"We can't thank you enough," said Jessyla.

Johlana offered what Beltur could only describe as a mischievous smile. "I can't tell you how happy helping you two has made me. Now that Beltur's here, I'll ride back to the house with Frankyr. You can show Beltur everything."

Johlana was gone in moments, and Jessyla ushered Beltur into the kitchen, where there were four straight-backed chairs, which consisted of two matched pairs of different styles and slightly different heights, and a much older corner cupboard. The table that had come with the house remained, as did the bench, which had been moved underneath the small side window. There was also a stool that could seat someone at one end of the table, if necessary.

In the bedroom, the ancient bedstead had been replaced by one of golden oak, with a thick mattress, and a tall dresser and armoire that matched the bedstead.

"What did you do with the old one?" asked Beltur.

"Johlana persuaded Rohan to take it back."

Beltur frowned. "She did that?"

"She can be . . . quietly forceful."

"Sometimes not even quietly so," replied Beltur. "I wonder why. That sounds like she wanted us to have the bedstead."

"I'm sure she did. She wanted it out of sight."

"Then it had to have been . . ." He shook his head. "Barrynt couldn't have been consorted that long when . . ."

"I can't believe that he just turned to Johlana right after his first consort's death."

"I don't think he did. Jorhan said that Barrynt had been widowed for a while and was forlorn when he first met Johlana. He courted her for over two years." Beltur fingered his chin, thinking. "Still . . . Johlana seemed happy to help you. It wasn't as though she was just getting rid of reminders of a past she didn't share."

"She was very happy." Jessyla paused. "I don't think she had much say in what happened in Halhana's household or how it was set up," said Jessyla. "I don't think she cares much for Eshult's parents."

"Emlyn and Sarysta?"

Jessyla nodded. "Johlana said that they'd picked out all the furnishings in Halhana's house. That might have been why she's so pleased to be able to help us."

"Help you, I think."

"She's enjoying it, and so am I . . . except . . ."

Beltur could see the sudden brightness in Jessyla's eyes. "You wish your mother were here doing that, don't you?"

"Maybe . . . she can come to see us in the summer. I know it's a long trip . . . both ways . . . but . . ."

"We'll just have to see. There ought to be someone we can send a letter with sometime in the next few eightdays. It wouldn't be good for her to travel here in the winter anyway."

"No. You're right about that."

Beltur didn't even have to strain to sense the resigned acceptance behind her words. "We'll get word to her as soon as we can." He immediately added, "You never did tell me about the mage-healer that your mother knew."

"She said that when she was a child, she met a mage-healer, and that he was silver-haired, like the dark angel Nylan, and that he was returning home to the forest."

"The Great Forest of Naclos?"

"She never said. I didn't ask, but I'm sure I didn't even know what the Great Forest of Naclos was. I don't know why I thought about that. For some reason, when Frankyr said 'mage-healer,' I remembered what she said."

"He was probably a druid, then."

"I don't know. She never said much more than that."

"And you never asked her about him?"

Jessyla gave Beltur a look of exasperation. "How could I ask her when I didn't remember what she said until now?"

"You really didn't remember?"

"Would I have said I didn't remember if I didn't?" Jessyla's voice sharpened.

Beltur winced. "I'm sorry. It just . . . seemed strange."

"Just because it's strange doesn't mean that it didn't happen that way."

"You're right." Beltur had to admit that, but he still wondered why she hadn't recalled what had been said at some other time.

"Was that so hard?"

Beltur winced again.

"Beltur . . ."

He just offered an embarrassed expression that wasn't quite a smile.

She shook her head, but with an expression of almost rueful amusement. "We need to walk back to Johlana's. You can clean the cot up tomorrow while I'm at the healing house."

Beltur just nodded.

XLI

Threeday morning came too early so far as Beltur was concerned, but both he and Jessyla were in the breakfast room well before sixth glass, lit by two lamps in brass wall sconces.

Johlana immediately appeared. "I do so like having people who are up as early as I am." Her eyes went to Jessyla. "You're at the healing house today?"

"I am."

"Good." Johlana looked to Beltur. "No chores around here today except for the stables. You need to get that cot ready."

Beltur glanced questioningly toward Jessyla.

She smiled. "I didn't say a word."

"She didn't have to," added Johlana.

Beltur took momentary refuge in taking the pitcher and filling Jessyla's mug and then his . . . and immediately taking a long swallow.

"I've already readied a basket with rags and some soap scraps," said Johlana. "You come back here for that after you've gotten a bucket from the chandlery. Two buckets would be better. One for soap and one for rinse."

"I think you two have planned my entire day."

"Not all of it," replied Jessyla.

"You two meet me here after you finish at the healing house," Johlana went on cheerfully, looking at Jessyla. "By then, I'll have sorted through the linens and cloths, and we'll go over what might prove useful."

"We couldn't . . ." began Jessyla.

"You can, and you should," replied Johlana forcefully.

"Whatever it is," said Barrynt as he entered the breakfast room, "when she gets that insistent, it's a good idea to agree." The merchant smiled, an expression both fond and rueful.

"I'm just trying to keep a pair of very good healers here in Axalt," responded Johlana. "And my brother, who's likely to drink too much if he can't work."

"I'm working on getting a space for his smithy."

"Good. Now, you all should eat. I've said enough for now."

Beltur was more than happy to dig into the scrambled ham and eggs, along with the warm bread. Once they finished breakfast and Jessyla had left the house, Beltur cleaned the stables. When he finished, he washed up again and then made his way to the chandlery under a gray sky from which scattered snowflakes intermittently fell. He didn't even have to ask for Rhodos, because the chandler appeared before Beltur had taken three steps inside.

"What can I do for you, ser mage?" asked the chandler.

"Barrynt mentioned that you might have house cisterns."

Rhodos frowned, cocking his head slightly. "I don't have any large ones."

"What do you have?" Beltur was willing to look at anything that might make life easier.

"Come take a look. I have kitchen cistern in the storeroom." Rhodos turned.

Beltur followed the chandler to the storeroom in the rear of the building, where Rhodos pointed to the object in the corner.

"There. That's what I've got."

Beltur studied the cistern that looked more like a stoneware barrel—standing on a sturdy wooden platform that only raised its base less than ten digits from the floor. Even on the platform the top of the circular cistern only came to Beltur's chin. The circular top looked to be perhaps a yard and a third across. There was a square wooden lid set in the top near the rear. At the base in front was a spigot tap, much like the tap on a cask of ale.

"Why the platform?"

"The Council requires it. That way you can tell if it's leaking before it damages the floor. Also, you can clean under it."

"How much does this one cost?"

"I could let you have it for four silvers. That includes the base."

Four silvers? That was almost as much as Jessyla made in half a season. "How many buckets does it take to fill it?"

"I've never counted," admitted the chandler. "According to Halstaff—he makes the stoneware—it takes fifty regular buckets filled to the top, but you wouldn't want to carry buckets that full. It's also not a good idea to fill it that full. Two-thirds is probably about right. And put it on a solid floor. The base supports will go right through a weak one."

Beltur could see that. Water was *heavy.* And carrying those buckets of water would take a lot of effort. "What about delivering it?"

"I can arrange that. You'll have to pay for it. That will likely be five coppers."

Four and a half silvers total. "Would you buy one of these if you didn't have water piped to your house?" Beltur looked to the chandler.

"I had one for years. I never regretted it." Rhodos offered a rueful expression. "Having water piped to the house is better, but you can't do that in winter anyway, and you don't want to do it if you don't own the house."

Beltur could see that as well. "I also need two buckets. Good ones."

"Buckets I have." Rhodos headed to the other side of the storeroom.

In the end, Beltur spent five silvers and three coppers for the cistern—including the fee for delivery, which Rhodos promised by second glass—and for two new and sturdy buckets, which he then carried back to Barrynt's. There he picked up the basket with cleaning supplies—and a length of line—and made his way to the cot.

While the cot had looked neat and relatively clean, once Beltur got to looking at it closely, there was dust everywhere, and dirt in too many corners. That meant more than a few trips to the water house almost a block away and then back with a bucket of water. The really dirty water had to go to the sewer standpipe behind Rohan's house.

Every single time that Beltur put the single scrubbing brush on the well-worn wooden floor, it came away dark with dust and dirt. By ninth glass he was glad he'd worn his worst trousers and that the cot wasn't any larger. By the time he finished scrubbing everything at around second glass, he began to wonder if the place was too big.

He'd barely finished rinsing out and cleaning the brush and dusting and wiping down all the furniture when the teamster and his assistant arrived with the cistern. Once they left, Beltur lugged another bucket of water back to the cot and poured it into the cistern, set in the corner of the kitchen. When he tried the tap, the water came out cloudy.

"Frig!" *Now you'll have to clean out the cistern.* That would have to wait, at least until he went back to Barrynt's to meet with Johlana and Jessyla. He left the rags and cloths to dry on the line Johlana had included, which he tied to two brackets set in the walls on opposite sides of the kitchen, which he hadn't appreciated until he'd been left with an assortment of damp cloths.

When he reached the house, the only one there was Asala.

"The mistress is visiting Halhana. She said she'd be back by fourth glass."

After deciding that there was no point in standing around waiting, Beltur went into the family parlor and extracted *The Wisdom of Relyn* from the bookcase once more. He settled into a chair and began to read, this time about the matter-of-fact chronology of Relyn's travels through small towns in Gallos as he avoided Fenard and made his way to Passera. Another passage stood out.

> . . . in those days, Passera was almost a land unto itself. The Prefect of Gallos was worried more about the dark angels of Westwind, and in time, his son assembled a massive army and invaded the Westhorns, to no avail, for Ryba of the Swift Ships of Heaven and Saryn of the black blades brought down a mountain upon that multitude and buried it under hundreds of cubits of rock and earth . . .

That's not in The Book of Ayrlyn. More than ever, Beltur wondered if there might be more about that battle in *The Book of Saryn,* which Jessyla had had mentioned. *Did she even read that part?* He'd have to ask her if she remembered anything about a battle. He resumed reading, continuing until he reached another intriguing section.

> . . . I saw the strength of the black tower. In witness to that, and to Nylan and what he taught me, I built a temple of dark stone. I talked with each person who asked me why. My answer was always the same—to show the quiet dark strength of order and harmony . . .

Beltur nodded. He was about to resume reading, when Johlana appeared.

"I see that you're here. I'm glad Jessyla isn't here yet. I didn't finish with sorting out the linens. I'll be in the linen closet off the washroom."

"Can I help?"

She shook her head. "It's women's work. You've been working hard, I can tell. Just send Jessyla to me when she arrives."

"Are you sure?"

"You'll have plenty to load and unload once we're finished." Johlana smiled and hurried out of the parlor.

Plenty to load and unload? After several moments, Beltur returned to reading.

> . . . after several years, I had thought that my presence in Passera had gone unremarked by the new Prefect, but that was not to be . . .
>
> . . . after Amosaph the vintner brought me the news that two score armsmen were riding toward Passera, and a score had crossed the river to block the road to Certis . . . gathered all that I could and went to embark upon a flatboat down the river to Elparta. Armsmen attacked me, but I was fortunate enough to prevail, and to reach Elparta. There I found more bounty-seekers pursuing, for the Prefect had placed a price of fifty golds on my head . . .

Fifty golds? Beltur kept reading.

> . . . with the help of a shepherd boy and his widowed mother, whom I rewarded as best I could, I dealt with my pursuers and made my way safely to Axalt . . .

Beltur frowned. *Shepherd boy? Rewarded as best he could?* Abruptly, he recalled Jorhan's story about his ancestor, the one who had helped a mercenary captain. *It has to have been Relyn. Who else could it possibly have been?*

He was still thinking about that when Jessyla hurried in.

"I'm sorry I'm late. There was a little girl with a broken arm . . ."

"That's all right. Johlana was late, too. She was at her daughter's, I think. She said for you to join her in the linen closet in the washroom. She was very specific. You, and only you. I'm to fetch and carry when you two have worked out whatever she has in mind."

"Are you certain? Or would you rather read?"

"I asked her if I could help as soon as she arrived. She was most definite."

"I have the feeling that she usually is." Jessyla smiled for a moment. "Go back to your book." She paused. "Is it that interesting?"

"It's far, far more interesting than I would have guessed. I'll tell you why later."

She frowned.

"It's not terrible. You'll understand."

"You're making me very curious."

"Good."

Jessyla screwed up her face into an absurd grimace, then smiled again, and left the parlor.

Beltur resumed reading. Several pages later, another passage caught his attention.

> . . . always learns from failure, if one is fortunate enough to survive that failure. My failure in Passera was in trying to embody order within a building, for people believe that the power is the building . . . Power lies within each of us, not within stone or brick or finely polished marble . . . not even within a bow or a blade, or a hammer. The force of Nylan's hammer lay in his understanding and his concentration. Saryn's terrible black blades would have been nothing without the power inside her. Ayrlyn's songs were far less when sung by another . . .
>
> For that reason I never built another temple to order, for the lasting temples are in the mind . . .

Beltur was still pondering that when Jessyla reappeared.

"Can you saddle up Slowpoke and carry several bundles of linens over to the cot? They're too heavy to carry that far on foot, and too few to harness up a cart horse."

"I can do that." Beltur stood and replaced *The Wisdom of Relyn* in the bookcase.

"We'll have them in the side hall shortly." With that, Jessyla vanished.

Beltur made his way to the side hall, donned his coat, and headed out to the stable, where he entered Slowpoke's stall. The big gelding seemed to look inquiringly at him.

"Yes, we're going to take a ride. And no, it won't be that long, but I should be better about riding you."

After saddling Slowpoke, Beltur led him to the side portico, tying him to the railing, and climbed the steps and went inside, where he looked at the three large bundles sitting on the floor, then at a smiling Jessyla. "Just these three?"

"There will be one more . . . I think."

"Then I'll take two this time, and two on a second trip."

"I thought so." She handed him a short length of rope. "You could tie them together . . ."

"Thank you."

"We should have the other one ready by the time you get back. Just put them on the kitchen table."

Beltur tied the two bundles together and then carried them out to Slowpoke, where he slung them over the front of the saddle.

At that moment, a black coach trimmed in silver pulled up to the end of the lane. Halhana stepped out and began to walk up the lane, stopping after several steps and calling out, "Beltur! Is Mother home?"

"She's inside with Jessyla," Beltur replied.

"Good!" Halhana turned and said, "I'll only be a few moments." Then she hurried up the lane and then up the steps. Even before she reached the side entry, the door opened and Johlana stepped out.

Halhana immediately leaned close to her mother and murmured something.

Johlana stiffened for just an instant, then nodded.

Halhana stepped back, saying something else.

Beltur *thought* that Johlana said, "I understand, dear." But whether she understood or not, beneath the forgiving smile, she wasn't that cheerful, Beltur felt.

Then the daughter turned and hurried down the steps.

"Halhana!" called Johlana. "Why don't you introduce Beltur to Eshult and his parents?"

Halhana hesitated for a moment.

"If we don't introduce Beltur and Jessyla to the right people, who will?"

From the momentary swirl of chaos around Halhana, Beltur could sense that introducing Beltur to the others was about the last thing on Halhana's mind, but the young woman immediately turned to Beltur as she neared him. "You really should meet Eshult."

"I'd be happy to meet him." That much was true, but while Beltur likely needed to meet Emlyn and Sarysta, especially from what he'd heard, he was wary of meeting them and resolved to be extremely polite. He also didn't want the introductions to take long, given Halhana's discomfiture.

The two walked swiftly to the coach, where Halhana opened the door, and offered a smile to the three inside. The older couple, seated facing forward, had to be Emlyn and Sarysta. Sarysta was slender, wearing a long coat of silver fur, trimmed in dark gray, while Emlyn wore a dark silver-gray woolen coat with matching silver-gray leather gloves. The top of the coat was unfastened enough that Beltur could glimpse a white shimmersilk shirt that alone doubtless cost more than every bit of clothing Beltur owned, and a shimmersilk blue cravat. Eshult also wore a dark gray coat, plain, but also of obvious quality.

"Beltur, I'd like you to meet my consort, Eshult, and his parents, Emlyn and Sarysta. Emlyn is the preeminent trader in Axalt, and Sarysta's family is equally distinguished." Halhana looked from Beltur more to Eshult, if not obviously, rather than directly looking at his parents, and went on, "Beltur is the accomplished black mage who's helped my uncle so much. He and his consort—she's a healer—have been staying with Mother and Father while they ready their own place."

"That's your uncle . . . the smith?" asked Sarysta, with scarcely veiled condescension.

"I've heard he was the best coppersmith in Elparta," said Eshult quickly. "That's why he and Beltur came to Axalt."

"Johlana is so good at taking people in," said Sarysta, her voice dripping false sweetness. "So very good. She's always so thoughtful."

Beltur could also sense a complete coldness behind Sarysta's words, despite the apparently pleasant smile.

"There's something to be said for that," added Emlyn evenly, but more politely than warmly, adding, "It's good to meet you, Beltur. A trading city like Axalt can always use another good mage and healer."

"I've heard that it's renowned for order and fairness, ser, and that's very appealing. I've heard of all of you, and it's very good to be able to put faces to names. Since it's cold, at least for me, and since you're all attired for some occasion, I would be the last to want to keep you." He smiled, inclined his head, and was about to offer Halhana a hand into the coach when Eshult did so.

The young man smiled, more warmly than his parents, and said to Beltur, "I look forward to seeing you when we have more time."

"As do I," said Beltur, closing the coach door carefully and stepping back.

The driver immediately flicked the leads, and the coach eased away from the lane.

As Beltur walked back toward Slowpoke, he had to wonder why Halhana had even stopped at the house, since she'd only spent a moment talking to her mother. He glanced toward the steps, but the door was closed, and Johlana was nowhere to be seen.

After several moments thinking over the quick meeting with Eshult and his parents, Beltur untied Slowpoke and mounted. As he started down the lane, he had to admit that riding to the cot was much faster and far easier than lugging the bundles would have been. Slowpoke almost pranced for the first several hundred yards, a reminder that Beltur did need to make time to give him exercise.

Once he reached the cot and dismounted, he tied Slowpoke to the old iron post with a solid ring frozen or rusted in place and then carried the two bundles to the door, unlocked it, and took them to the kitchen, where he untied them.

When Beltur came out of the cot, he found Rohan walking toward him.

"Good afternoon, Mage. Is that your horse?"

"He is."

"He looks like a warhorse."

"He was. He was mine."

"I thought you were a black mage."

"I am. My task in the fight against the Gallosians was to provide shields against arrows and blades . . . and against the firebolts of their white mages."

"You must have been good at it. You're still alive."

"Good enough."

"You're not keeping the horse here, are you?"

"Stars, no. I'm paying Barrynt with services so that he can stay in Barrynt's stable."

"Good to know. The Council takes a dim view of horses not in proper care."

Is there anything the Council doesn't take an interest in? "It was just easier to carry some of our belongings here with Slowpoke, and he needs to be ridden anyway."

Rohan nodded. "Is everything as it should be in the cot?"

"So far as we can tell. It will be a few days yet before we'll have everything ready."

"I noticed a kitchen cistern earlier today."

"Barrynt thought it would be a good idea."

"They are. Rather costly, though."

Beltur understood Rohan's unspoken point. "I did have some silvers saved. Enough to set up a household. At least, I hope so. The cistern was just about the only thing we've purchased so far, except for two buckets. That's because healing doesn't pay so well as merchanting, and we do have to be careful."

"Don't we all? A pleasant evening to you."

"The same to you."

As Rohan walked back toward his house, Beltur wondered if everyone in Axalt watched everyone else. He shook his head and remounted Slowpoke.

Jessyla and Johlana were both waiting in the side hall when Beltur returned to Barrynt's. So were two large bundles and a small one.

"Johlana's been so generous," declared Jessyla. "There are bed linens, and a blanket and a quilt, and lots of towels—"

"And not a one of them matching any other one," interjected Johlana. "Except one pair. Save those for when your mother visits."

We'll be using mismatched towels for a very long time. Beltur wasn't about to say that, especially since he'd never had matched towels . . . and times when his sole towel had been little more than an oversized rag. He gathered the bundles and then tied them together. "I shouldn't be long." He paused. "Since I'll have to ride back here, why don't I saddle one of the other horses, and we can ride over and back together. We really need to give the horses some exercise."

"I need to help Johlana straighten—"

"Nonsense! You can help me while he saddles the other horse. It won't take all that long. Beltur, you just go saddle up that mount."

Beltur decided not to argue.

He didn't hurry in saddling one of the Council horses—*except that they've turned out to be ours, after a fashion*—but he wasn't deliberately slow, either, and Jessyla was waiting at the side portico when he led the mount there.

"We expect you for dinner!" declared Johlana from the door.

"We won't be too long," replied Jessyla as she mounted.

Beltur mounted Slowpoke and then led the way out onto the street.

"This is much better than walking," said Jessyla from where she rode beside Beltur. "There aren't even any wagons on the road."

"I haven't seen many going this way. Most of them stay on the main road—except for the one that delivered the kitchen cistern. I didn't have time to rinse it out thoroughly, though. It came less than a glass before I had to meet you, and by the time we had it in place . . . Well. I did put a bucket of water in it, but it came out cloudy. Not really filthy, but dirty enough that I'll need to rinse it and wipe it out."

"So we won't have to lug water all the time?"

"Not after the first times," he replied wryly.

"Couldn't we use the horses?"

"That would only work if we work together. Trying to pump water and then mount holding a bucket of water . . ." He shook his head.

"Then we'll have to do it in the late afternoon."

Beltur wasn't about to argue about that, although he knew he'd be the one carrying the buckets. Still . . . he wouldn't be walking carrying them, and they couldn't be that full.

Before long, Beltur, Jessyla, and the two horses arrived at the cot. Although Beltur didn't actually see Rohan, he had the sense that the landlord was watching as he dismounted, tied up the horses, and then carried the bundles inside the cot. Once he set the bundles next to the others on the side kitchen table, the one that had come with the cot, and not the better one that Barrynt and Johlana had provided, Beltur looked to Jessyla.

She was clearly studying everything in the kitchen, and then, without looking back at him, she went into the bedchamber and then the washroom before returning. "You really did scrub everything. It's all so clean."

"That's what was needed. There was a lot of dirt in the corners, and dust everywhere."

She shook her head. "Who would believe it?" Then she stepped forward and hugged him tightly. "Thank you. You're so much more than most people see."

Just because I know how to clean? It wasn't as though Beltur hadn't had lots of experience, first with his uncle and then doing what he could for Athaal and Meldryn. Besides, he hated dirt. *Is that because you're a black?* Somehow, he didn't think so. He hadn't liked being dirty or around dirt when he'd thought he was a white. "Are you going to show me what's in the bundles?"

"Not right now. We need to get back for dinner, and we'll need to un-saddle and groom the horses."

Beltur nodded.

Jessyla was right, of course, because everyone else was in the family parlor by the time he and Jessyla finished with the horses and washed up.

As soon as they walked into the parlor, Johlana said, "I'd thought that Halhana and Eshult would be here for dinner so that you two could spend some time with them, but they had to go somewhere with Emlyn and Sarysta."

Beltur managed not to frown. Johlana had been at Halhana's earlier. Was that why Halhana had stopped, and why Johlana had been upset and trying not to show it?

Especially after thinking about that, Beltur was more than ready for a beaker of pale ale and was sitting on one of the straight-backed chairs enjoying his second or third swallow when his eyes drifted to the book-case. He set his mug on the side table, then rose and walked across the parlor, where he extracted the worn volume from the bookcase. "Jorhan . . . I read something interesting in *The Wisdom of Relyn.*"

"I can't believe there's anything interesting in that," murmured Frankyr, who dropped his eyes as Johlana shot him a sharp glare.

Beltur quickly turned the pages until he found the words. "Here!" He started to hand the book to the smith.

"You can read it," said Jorhan. "You'll do it better than I would."

"We don't need a homily before eating, do we?" asked Barrynt.

Beltur almost missed the twinkle in the merchant's eye before he re-plied, "No. It might not hurt, but this is about something that happened to Relyn."

"He was supposed to have had an adventurous life before he came to Axalt," said Ryntaar almost cautiously.

"One of his adventures reminded me of something you said," Beltur told Jorhan.

"Something I said? Couldn't be," replied the smith. "I'm not that good a person. I'm not learned and witty, either."

"You don't do badly," replied Johlana, "no matter what you say. Beltur, go ahead and read it."

Beltur studied the words for a moment, debating where to begin, then said, "This is in the part where he tells about leaving Passera and coming to Axalt." He cleared his throat.

"Before the Prefect could send yet more armsmen after me, I gathered all that I could and went to embark upon a flatboat down the river to Elparta. Armsmen attacked me, but I was fortunate enough to prevail, and to reach Elparta. There I found more bounty-seekers pursuing, for the Prefect had placed a price of fifty golds on my head, but with the help of a shepherd boy and his widowed mother, whom I rewarded as best I could, I dealt with my pursuers and made my way safely to Axalt . . ."

Beltur stopped and looked at Jorhan. "Does that sound familiar?"

Johlana wrinkled her brow. "I've never read that part of the book."

Jorhan swallowed, then said, "It's just a coincidence."

"How many shepherd boys with a widowed mother are likely to have helped a man with a price on his head and been rewarded, especially back then?"

Johlana's mouth opened. "That's an old family story, about the stranger who never gave his name, but who left six golds in repayment and discovered the family's coal when he was looking for a place to bury the assassins." She looked at her youngest son. "He was named Frankyr, too."

"It seems to me to be too much of a coincidence," said Beltur.

"That was hundreds of years ago," said Jorhan.

"Who else would have left six golds?" asked Johlana. "Only a man with a price of fifty golds on his head would have been that grateful."

"Are you saying that one of our ancestors helped Relyn to come to Axalt?" asked Frankyr. "And he was called Frankyr?"

"I doubt it's something that you could prove," said Barrynt, "but it sounds possible. Besides, it's a good family story. You can tell it to your children."

Beltur noted the slight emphasis on the word "family."

"Now there's one other thing," added Barrynt, with a smile. "It appears that one of those buildings you two looked at earlier is open to be rented as a smithy." He turned to Beltur. "I know you work tomorrow at the healing house so I arranged for us to look over the place on fiveday morning."

"You mean we can get to work?" asked Jorhan.

"First we have to make certain that the building is suitable. After that, it will still take a bit to assemble everything. But it's a start."

"About time," declared the smith.

"You've always been impatient," said Johlana. "That's one thing that's never changed." She smiled and rose. "I think it's time for dinner."

Beltur replaced the book on the shelf, and he and Jessyla followed the others into the dining room.

After a hearty meal of what Beltur thought was a cross between a stew and burhka, and twice as spicy, which required him to alternate mouthfuls of bread and stew in order to keep the considerable sense of burning in his mouth to a tolerable level, and after some pleasant conversation in the parlor after eating, he and Jessyla repaired to the room that they likely would be leaving before long.

Once the door was shut, she looked at him. "There's something about all of this that bothers me."

"What's that?"

"About you, me, Jorhan, and now Relyn . . ."

"Don't you think we deserve a little good fortune after being chased out of two different lands?"

"I know. It's not as though you didn't save Elparta and then get chased out, or that you didn't help Jorhan when he was deep in debt . . . but it's still . . . strange."

"It's about time that something strange turned in our favor. And we're not exactly minting golds working at the healing house. Oh . . . Herrara told me the other day that the Council only pays for two healers. That's one reason why we're alternating."

"I know. She told me." Jessyla shook her head. "It's still strange."

Beltur couldn't help but think the entire year had been strange . . . and that was just life.

But that reminded him of what he hadn't had a chance to tell Jessyla. "There was something else strange this afternoon . . ." He recounted his meeting with Eshult, Emlyn, and Sarysta, then looked to Jessyla.

"Sarysta actually said it like that?"

"No. It was more subtle, but it was there. And I think that Halhana had agreed to come to dinner, because Johlana was at her house earlier today. When she stopped this afternoon, it was to say that they couldn't. I thought you should know."

"Poor Johlana." Jessyla shook her head.

After several moments, Beltur said, "We really ought to work on some mage exercises, or you won't get better."

"I'm tired, but you're right."

"Working at it when you're tired makes you stronger . . . if you don't overdo it." Beltur paused. "Why don't you start by lighting the traveling candle?"

"That's easy."

"And after that, I want you to put a shield around it."

"Oh . . ."

"Go on." Beltur grinned.

"You can be mean, sometimes." But she smiled back.

XLII

Fourday at the healing house was largely uneventful for Beltur, although he did have to spend time dealing with Poldaark's wound chaos, albeit a smaller amount than on twoday. As soon as he finished, he hurried to Barrynt's, where he saddled Slowpoke and then rode to the cot, carrying a load of wood, where Jessyla was organizing and arranging furniture and linens. After setting and lighting a hearth fire, over the next glass and a half the two pumped buckets of water that Beltur and Slowpoke carried back to the cot and used first to clean out the kitchen cistern, and then to fill it possibly a third of the way before closing up the cot and returning to Barrynt's.

Early on fiveday, Beltur carried more wood to the cot, and made arrangements through Rhodos to have two cords of wood delivered, before he and Jorhan rode to meet Barrynt at his factorage. From there, the three took the narrow road to south town. Beltur noticed that the snow piled alongside the paved way was now almost chest-high.

"How high will the snow be here by late winter?"

"Not more than another yard, usually," replied Barrynt. "That's as high as they can pile it. After that, they have to cart it to the river."

Before long they rode down the main street of south town, where the smoke from chimneys hung low over the various buildings. The air had a bite beyond mere chill, and Beltur had the feeling that in warmer times, that bite would be more pronounced and redolent of even more unsavory odors. He glanced at the other two, but neither seemed to notice, or they were better at ignoring the bitter tang that he was breathing.

"It's not far," announced Barrynt. "Another block on the right."

"You said this building was the one that had been a smithy," said Jorhan.

"Years ago. It's been empty for a while. Widow Santhela decided no one in her family wanted it, but she didn't wish to sell it. I persuaded her son to get her to allow it to be rented."

"For how much?" asked Jorhan.

"Truly a pittance. A bond of two silvers, and three coppers an eightday, but any improvements you make, you pay for, and they remain."

"There's nothing inside, then," groused Jorhan. "I'll need to make workbenches and who knows what else."

"Why so little?" asked Beltur.

"She'll save two coppers an eightday. That's what the Council's charging her to clear the walks and curbs."

"It's the reddish-brown building there."

The building was modest, a one-story rectangular stone structure, scarcely four yards back from the battered stone curb. Two narrow windows, with sagging shutters, flanked the door facing the street. The roof was less steeply pitched than most of those in Axalt, but the short walk had been cleared, and there was a stone-paved area with a hitching rail adjoining the walk. Barrynt guided his mount up to the hitching rail and dismounted.

Beltur and Jorhan did the same, and Beltur tied Slowpoke and Jorhan's horse to the railing.

"That might be Theltar. He's the youngest son."

As Beltur turned, he immediately wondered why the youngest son was the one dealing with the widow's property. The approaching rider wore a coat with cross-barred gray-and-black patterns, something that Beltur had never seen, and his cap was made of the same fabric.

"That has to be Theltar," said Barrynt. "Recognize that gray-and-black plaid anywhere."

Plaid? Was that what that sort of fabric pattern was called? "I've never seen a coat like that before."

"Comes from Sligo. They weave those patterns there, all sorts of them." Barrynt raised a hand as the rider reined up, dismounted, and tied his mount. "We just got here, Theltar. The thinner one is Beltur, and the brawny one is Jorhan. He's the smith."

The angular-faced man, possibly five years older than Beltur, nodded. "I'm pleased to meet you. Shall we go inside?" Without waiting for an acknowledgment, he turned and walked to the door, quickly unlocking it and opening it. He beckoned for the others to enter.

Once inside, in the dim light coming through the cracks in the shutters, Beltur saw that the main room was totally empty, and that there were two smaller rooms in the rear.

"The chamber on the right was just for storing things. The one on the left was a woodshop."

Jorhan moved to the west wall of the front room, where a knee-high rectangle of stones stood. "Looks like this was once a forge. Have to rebuild it, though . . ."

"I doubt that Widow Santhela would have a problem with that, so long as you did it proper," replied Barrynt, turning to Theltar. "Would she?"

"A deposit of an additional two eightdays' rent if you make changes. That's what Ma said."

The slight hesitation and a certain swirling of some small fragments of chaos around Theltar suggested to Beltur that the young man hadn't talked that over with his mother, but before he could say anything, Barrynt did.

"A small deposit. That sounds reasonable enough . . ."

Beltur glanced around, noting the footprints that they had left in the dust, footprints suggesting that no one had been inside the building for some time, then walked to the storeroom, which had wall-to-wall shelves on one side—very dusty shelves. Then he walked into the woodshop, where he saw a solid-looking workbench. After that, he eased back toward the door and waited while Barrynt and Jorhan worked out the payment details with Theltar—essentially a silver deposit, with the rest to be paid before Jorhan and Beltur moved anything into the space.

Less than a glass had passed from the time Theltar had arrived until the other three left the building and began their ride back from south town to the main part of Axalt.

"Now that you have found a place that you can turn into a smithy," said Barrynt, "you have to make a proposal before the Council."

"Why the frig do we have to do that?" asked Jorhan.

Beltur was more than happy that the smith had asked, because he'd had the same question.

"So that the Council is aware of what is happening. Smithies are permitted, but the Council has to keep track of what is located where."

"You said that the building had been used as a smithy before." Jorhan frowned. "Why do they have to approve it again?"

"It was a smithy," replied Barrynt patiently. "That was why I suggested that building, but the Council still must grant permission. I doubt that it will be more than a formality."

"How long will that take?" Jorhan's voice contained both resignation and impatience.

"They meet every sixday evening at fifth glass. You can present your proposal tomorrow. I already made sure that you are on the Council agenda."

What Barrynt said meant, at least to Beltur, that he and Jorhan had little choice in which building they could rent for the smithy. At the same time, it appeared that the merchant was doing what he could to speed up matters.

"Will they decide then?" asked Jorhan.

"Stars, no," replied Barrynt. "It could take until the next meeting. Sometimes, it takes two meetings."

"But if it's just a formality?" said Beltur.

"It's a formality if everything's done properly. If it's not, then the Council will say what else needs to be done."

"Needs to be done?" Jorhan's voice sharpened.

"If the roof leaks or if there are other problems, she can't rent it until they're fixed. That way, you aren't stuck with repairs you didn't count on. That wouldn't be fair. She'd be deceiving you. Not that I don't trust her and Theltar, but you can see how that might be a problem. Much better to nip that sort of thing in the bud. That's why the Council's inspector will go over the building before the Council will approve the smithy."

Much as Beltur could see the reasoning, it still bothered him.

"Do they have to approve every frigging thing we do?" asked Jorhan.

"Not after the Council approves the smithy. Not unless you dump waste in the sewers or break the law."

"Do we have to write up some sort of document?" Jorhan glared into nothingness.

"Nothing like that. You just tell the Council that you intend to build and operate a coppersmithing forge in the Widow Santhela's building in south town, and you pay a silver."

"*Another* silver?" Jorhan sounded incredulous.

"Every crafter pays a silver a year to the Council."

"Tell me about the Council," said Beltur quickly, trying not to sound dubious, despite his experiences with the Traders' Council of Spidlar.

"We've always had a council, at least since the time of Relyn," Barrynt said. "There are eleven members. That's so that there's always a decision. I suppose there could be thirteen or nine or seven, but thirteen gets unwieldy. Seven's really too few because the Council has to have landholders, merchants, and at least two crafters. That had to be Relyn's doing. He was always looking for balance, and balance is one of the things that holds Axalt together."

"Seems to me that with everyone in these two valleys," said Jorhan with a snort, "it'd be hard to go very far."

"Axalt isn't just these two valleys. There are at least a score of vales, not to mention the forests, to the east of the city. The city's the only part that's fortified, though. The winters would kill any invaders. So would some northeasters."

"You mentioned Relyn," said Beltur. "I know he didn't want a temple here. He said so in the book. But did he leave any other writings or a house where he lived?"

"I don't know of anything."

"Did he have any children?"

"Oh . . . his daughter and granddaughter were the only ones left in the end, and they just rode off one summer night. They left thirty golds to build the Council House. They rode east. That's what everyone says, anyway."

"They just let them ride away?"

"She was a mage, just like you." Barrynt laughed heartily. "I don't see that anyone was able to stop you."

"Does anyone know why?"

"The daughter left a note. All it said was that it was better that way, that what Relyn wanted was for his teachings to be followed, not his heirs."

"And no one knows what became of them?"

"Oh . . . there are stories. Some say that the granddaughter consorted the Duke of Vergren. Others say she ended up in Westwind. Still others claim she returned to the Stars of Heaven."

Stars of Heaven? Beltur hadn't heard that phrase before, but it made sense, and that made him wonder why he hadn't heard it before.

Neither Jorhan nor Barrynt said much more on the ride back. Beltur thought that was likely for the best.

XLIII

Just as Beltur was putting on his coat, ready to leave for the healing house on sixday morning, Jessyla stepped closer to him.

"Beltur . . ."

He could tell she was concerned about something. "What is it?"

"I hate to ask . . . you know how I hate to ask for anything . . ."

He smiled. "I know. What do you need?"

"Four silvers . . . I know we have to be careful, and you've spent so much already . . ."

"What don't we have?"

"Things for the kitchen. We'll need flour and butter and salt, pepper, other herbs, cheese, potatoes. I was thinking I could start getting those kinds of things at the chandlery and at the market square . . . I still have two silvers, but they won't be enough. None of what we need costs a lot . . . but we really need so much."

Beltur managed to keep an impassive expression. "I can't give you four silvers."

Jessyla swallowed. "Are things that bad?"

He smiled, fumbling for his wallet, and extracting a coin. "I can only give you this. See if Johlana can give you silvers for it."

"A gold? Can we spare it?"

"For now. I know you'll make it last as long as possible." He grinned. "We aren't that badly off."

"You! You know how I hate to ask for anything!"

Beltur could see her flushing, and he quickly said, "I know. I wasn't thinking about all the little things that go into setting up a cot or a house. And I likely wouldn't have. Sometimes, you will have to ask. Sometimes, I'll have to ask you."

"For a moment, you made me feel so guilty for asking. I feel guilty enough about everything that Johlana has given us." She paused. "You really don't have enough silvers?"

"After buying buckets and the kitchen cistern? I only have two silvers and a few coppers, besides the golds, that is." He shook his head. "I probably should have given Rhodos a gold for the cistern and buckets, but I didn't."

"You don't want people to know what we have, do you?"

"I don't want them to get the wrong idea."

"I'll see if Johlana has enough silvers."

"If she doesn't, Barrynt should—at his factorage."

"I'll work it out. Just be careful at the healing house."

"I will." *You don't dare to be any other way.*

Once Beltur was outside, he immediately looked to the north and east, but the sky was clear and cold, and the white sun shed very little warmth as he walked toward the healing house, thinking about his conversation with Jessyla. *Are you being too cautious about silvers?*

He might be. Yet he'd seen just how quickly life could change, and how little choice he'd had when he'd had no coins to speak of.

Once he reached the healing house and doffed his coat, scarf, and gloves, since no one was waiting with an injury, he made his way up the steps to the room that held Poldaark and three other empty beds. The young man was staring at the wall and didn't seem to notice Beltur.

"How are you feeling this morning?"

Poldaark started. "Ser?"

"I asked how you were feeling."

"About the same. My shoulder hurts. Sometimes I get hot. Sometimes, I'm shivering."

"Let me see." Beltur's fingertips touched Poldaark's forehead. "You're not feverish." All the same, he did sense some slight traces of the yellowish-red wound chaos in places along the wound, but using free order to remove them took only a fraction of a quint. Then he checked the dressings. The upper wound in front was healing well, but there were still fluids draining from the lower wound in the young man's back.

"How long do I have to stay here, ser?"

"Until there's no more wound chaos inside you. It might be another eightday."

"Hannon won't be happy."

"He'd be a lot less happy if you came back too early and died."

"It doesn't hurt that much."

"It would if I weren't dealing with the chaos in you every other day."

Poldaark frowned. "You're not like the other healers."

"I'm not. For one thing, I'm a man."

"I didn't mean that way. They don't talk much about chaos."

"That's because I'm both a mage and a healer."

"Can women be mages?"

"They can. There just haven't been many who were."

"Do you know any women mages?"

"I know two, and there are histories that mention three others." Beltur didn't think he was stretching things too much. Taelya was equivalent to a beginning white mage, and Jessyla had magely skills and was making progress.

"Have there been any in Axalt?"

"Relyn's daughter was said to be a mage."

"No one ever told me that."

Beltur shrugged. "I didn't know that until recently." He offered a smile. "I'll be by later. You should be walking around the room, you know?"

"Healer Herrara told me that. So did Healer Jessyla."

"If you won't listen to me, listen to them."

Poldaark gave a puzzled look. "You're all saying the same thing."

"That should tell you something," said Beltur as he left the chamber.

He had just come down the stairs when he saw Herrara walking out of her study with a man he didn't recognize, not that there were many in Axalt that he would. The healer immediately gestured for Beltur to join her.

When he reached the pair, she turned to the man and said, "Councilor Taegyn, this is Beltur. He's the healer and black mage I told you about."

"I'm pleased to meet you," replied Taegyn, inclining his head, but also frowning, as if trying to recall if he'd seen Beltur before.

Beltur smiled politely. "I'm pleased to meet you, Councilor."

"The councilor is making an inspection of the healing house."

"We take turns," said Taegyn. "One of us each eightday. I'm happy that Herrara has such a capable healer here."

"I'm happy to be here."

Taegyn smiled pleasantly before glancing to Herrara. "We should continue."

Beltur stepped aside and watched as Taegyn and Herrara proceeded, apparently either entering or looking into each chamber. *Just what is he inspecting for?*

Beltur kept wondering about that, but he didn't have a chance to ask Herrara, because just after that a woman brought in her son with a broken arm, and since it was a simple break, Herrara left the setting and splinting to him while she continued with the councilor.

Some time later, Beltur managed to find Herrara in her study.

She looked up. "You want to know about the inspection, I take it?"

"I had wondered."

"The healer who was in charge before allowed those who were without housing to remain here so long as there were beds. The Council decided that encouraged people not to find work. They also declared that the healing house was for healing, not another poorhouse."

"There is a poorhouse?"

"Two of them. They're both in south town, thankfully at the north end."

"What happened to the healer?"

"She left Axalt. The Council began inspecting to discourage any return of that practice, but if we don't heal, especially the poor, no one else will."

"Those well-off have arrangements with other healers?"

Herrara nodded. "If you choose, after a season here, you can do the same."

Beltur could easily read her unspoken words—that he and Jessyla would be better off, but that many of the poor wouldn't be. "Thank you for explaining that."

"You would have learned that before long. Was there anything unusual about that boy's arm?"

"No. The mother said he'd tripped and hit it on a porch railing. She was telling the truth. He didn't have any bruises or any signs of older injuries."

Herrara smiled. "I didn't ask that, you know?"

"Not in words," replied Beltur with a smile of his own.

"Go check some of the dressings that haven't been changed." Despite her words, Herrara was still smiling.

The remainder of the day was routine—changing dressings, treating a bad burn, and stitching up several slashes caused by various accidents, as well as the drudge-like tasks, such as cleaning bottles before refilling them with spirits. Beltur was just thankful that healers didn't have to empty chamber pots.

He left the healing house at fourth glass, and once he reached Barrynt's, he cleaned the stables, then saddled his and Jessyla's mounts, partly because the horses did need exercise, and partly because Beltur was tired of walking. Jorhan saddled his own horse, and the three left Barrynt's house at a quint before fifth glass to ride to the Council House, where Barrynt had promised to meet them. They rode around the empty market square to the two-story graystone structure. They had just dismounted and tied their horses, when Barrynt rode up.

"It's good that you're early. The Council appreciates that." Barrynt glanced quizzically at Jessyla.

She said, "I thought I could learn more about the Council."

Beltur had a good idea of what she wasn't saying, something along the lines of wishing she'd known more about the Traders' Council of Spidlar.

"I don't know as there's much to learn," replied Barrynt with an amused smile. "The Council's pretty straightforward. We should go in."

The three followed the merchant through the double doors set in the middle of the lower level. Immediately inside was a foyer with another set of doors, most likely to serve as a windbreak, and beyond the foyer was a corridor some three yards wide. Barrynt walked to the first door on the left—which was open—and gestured for them to enter. "Take the first bench in front of the dais on the right and leave space for me on the side next to the aisle."

Beltur and Jessyla led the way.

There were three rows of low-backed wooden benches on each side of the center aisle, and a space of three yards between the front row and the dais, which was raised about a third of a yard above the light gray stone floor. Beltur saw three others seated in the chamber, all on the left side, with one younger man sitting in the front row on that side. The eleven chairs behind the long table on the dais were empty.

Once all four were seated, with Jorhan farthest from the aisle and Barrynt the nearest, Beltur asked the merchant, "What happens now?"

"The councilors come in and ask if anyone has proposals. You and Jorhan are second, after Shaeltyn." Barrynt nodded toward the man in brown seated alone at the other front bench. "They ask questions. Jorhan answers them. Then they tell you what happens next. Either they want more information, or they'll say that they'll verify what you've said, and if it's correct, they'll make a decision, most likely at the meeting next eightday."

"Sounds like a lot of dithering," muttered Jorhan.

"I wouldn't say that to the Council," replied Barrynt cheerfully. "There are rules, and the Council is bound by them as much as you are."

Beltur wasn't certain he agreed with all of that, especially after his brief encounter with Councilor Taegyn, but he was glad he asked, if only so that Jorhan knew what to expect.

Two more men entered and sat in the back benches. Then two women and a man. Beltur sensed a certain amount of blackness around one of the women, more than enough for her to be a healer, but he didn't see healer green trousers beneath the thick coat.

Then a side door at the end of the dais opened, and the councilors filed in and took their chairs. The moment Beltur saw the blacks of the third councilor, he immediately shielded himself fully, so that not even a strong black would have been able to sense that he was a mage. He couldn't have said why he did it. He just did, perhaps because he was wary of blacks on councils. All of the councilors were men, and all seemed at least as old as Barrynt. Beltur picked out Taegyn, who sat one seat in from the left side of the table.

Taegyn's eyes passed over Beltur without pausing, most likely because Beltur still wore his heavy outer coat, and Taegyn couldn't have seen his blacks. Nor could the mage-councilor, who was graying and much older.

After a long pause, the dark-bearded man in the center of the councilors cleared his throat, and then declared, "Shaeltyn, please step forth and state your proposal."

The clean-shaven man in brown stood. "Councilors, I have a small house on the far northeast side of the city. It is located at the end of the Old Pinyon Road. It is the house farthest from the square. You have the information I provided to you two sixdays ago with my proposal to be able to tan the hides from animals that I have hunted and killed. No one else would be tanning there. I am requesting that you grant me the Council's permission." He inclined his head and stood waiting.

The head councilor, if that was what being in the middle meant, did not speak for several moments. Finally, he said, "The laws of Axalt are most clear, Shaeltyn. Any activity that creates noxious odors or wastes that could foul our waters must be conducted either in south town or in dry mountain valleys that do not drain into any stream. Even then, one must obtain Council approval. For this reason, the Council must reject your proposal."

"I am but a poor hunter, Councilors. I have no golds to purchase such land. I have no silvers to rent a place. My cot is more than a hundred yards from any other cot."

The councilor smiled gently before replying. "We all understand that. Should we approve your request, then what can we say to a renderer who wishes to locate his rendering also a hundred yards from other dwellings . . . or the tinsmith with his lead and tin? Perhaps you can reach an agreement with one of the renderers in south town."

Beltur could sense the councilor's sympathy . . . and that nothing was going to change.

Shaeltyn's shoulders sagged. "That is a long, long walk, and the renderers charge more than I would make from the leathers." He just stood there.

"The proposal is rejected. You may go."

After the hunter trudged from the chamber, the councilor spoke. "Jorhan, smith and recent arrival in Axalt, please step forward."

Jorhan stood and took a step forward.

"The Council has received a proposal for the use of a property owned by the Widow Santhela for coppersmithing. Do you affirm that such is the proposed use of the property?"

"It is, Councilor."

"How many people will work there?"

"Just two, sir."

The councilor nodded, then said, "Seeing as the property has been used as a smithy previously, there is no objection to the proposed use. Two members of the Council must make an inspection of the premises to assure that the building remains in good repair. They will also meet with the owner to make certain that she has entered into the agreement to rent in good faith and without coercion. A fee of one silver must be paid before the Council makes that inspection. Do you intend to make that payment today?"

"I do," Jorhan said.

"Then step forward with your coin."

The smith placed a silver on the polished wood. "For the Council."

"Thank you. The Council will approve or deny your proposal at its next meeting." The councilor surveyed the room. "Does anyone else have a proposal to offer?"

There was no response.

"Then the Council meeting is over."

The councilors rose and filed out.

Once the side door closed, Jorhan looked to Barrynt. "Seems to me that they don't need an eightday to decide."

"They may not, but it may take several days for two of the councilors to talk to the widow, and follow up if they need to."

"Still seems like a waste of time."

"Are there that few proposals all the time?" asked Beltur, not wanting to get into what the Council should or shouldn't do.

Barrynt shook his head. "From spring to midfall, the Council meetings last at least a glass. Folks don't do a lot of building or change things much in winter."

"Aren't there other things they decide?"

"Everything in Axalt is decided by the Council, and by law. Everyone knows the laws."

"What happens when people don't obey the laws?" asked Jessyla.

"The patrollers lock them up—unless they flee Axalt first. Then the Council reviews what happened and makes a decision based on the law."

"Does that happen often?" pressed Jessyla.

Barrynt shook his head.

"You didn't mention that there was a mage on the Council."

"Oh, that's Naerkaal. He never says much . . . unless he thinks someone is lying."

That definitely made sense to Beltur.

"We need to head back for dinner. Johlana won't be happy if I'm the one to make us late. Besides, it's a fowl pie, and Asala makes a very good fowl pie."

Beltur doubted that the pie would be as good as one of Meldryn's, but he certainly wouldn't say so, especially with all that Barrynt and Johlana had done for him and Jessyla.

XLIV

All in all, it took until fourday evening of the next eightday before Jessyla and Beltur had the small cot ready to occupy, and as the sun vanished behind the snow-covered heights to the west, Beltur and Jessyla stood in the kitchen, looking at each other.

"Do we have everything we need?" asked Beltur.

"Most likely not," replied Jessyla. "It will be eightdays before we find out everything we're missing. We have enough to get by."

Beltur's eyes went to the lower shelf of the open cupboard that held, among other items, a blackened iron skillet, a battered but watertight brass kettle, large and small cookpots, along with a miscellaneous assortment of unmatched plates, platters, and bowls that Johlana had dug out of the cluttered storeroom in the merchant's stable. Beltur had bought the two cookpots, which had taken far more than he and Jessyla had earned from their previous eightday's work at the healing house.

The upper shelves of the cupboard held various provisions, as did what might have been a narrow bookcase that stood beside the cupboard. The kitchen cistern in the corner was two-thirds full, which meant that they didn't have to go out for water all the time, and the narrow kitchen table gleamed, the result of a bit of linseed oil and a great deal of effort by Jessyla while Beltur had been at the healing house.

"I can't believe it," Jessyla finally said. "We have a place of our own."

Beltur nodded. "We certainly do." *But it wouldn't have been much without everything from Barrynt and Johlana.*

"What can we do for them?"

"Be ready to help them however we can. They have everything else that they need." Beltur glanced through the door to the bedchamber, with the newer bedstead from Barrynt and Johlana, the older one having been returned to Rohan, a side table, a linen chest, a chest of drawers, a back-less wooden bench, and a very old and doorless armoire. Not a single piece matched any other piece except that all were close to the same darkish brown shade.

The linen chest against the bedchamber wall held three sets of unmatched sheets, two spare blankets—which were the ones they had brought—and quite a number of unmatched towels, as well as a thick but worn spare cover-let for the bed.

"We could sit down in front of the hearth," suggested Jessyla, "while the burhka that Johlana sent heats up. That was kind of her."

"She knew you wouldn't have time to cook today or tomorrow," replied Beltur.

"That means you'll be the first one to cook a meal here," replied Jessyla, with a smile, "since I know you can cook breakfasts." She paused. "I've never eaten anything you've cooked."

With a start, Beltur realized that was true. He'd fixed breakfasts and some dinners for Meldryn, but never for Jessyla. "It's likely a good thing the first meal will be breakfast—except there won't be any bread, not until we get a hearth oven. I can do skillet biscuits, though. Meldryn improved my breakfast cooking more than my dinners."

Jessyla moved from the kitchen into the front room and settled onto the bench in front of the hearth.

After a moment, Beltur sat beside her. "We're already low on wood. The woodcutters are supposed to deliver two cords tomorrow, but I'll need to buy an ax from Rhodos in order to split some of it. I'll see if he has a hearth oven as well."

"Do we need the oven?"

"If we want to make decent meat pies or bread. Perhaps I should say that if I want to, because that's how I learned from Meldryn. In Fenard, we just bought bread."

"You'd better buy the oven, if you can. Mother could make skillet bread. I usually burned it."

Beltur couldn't help frowning.

"You have to watch it all the time. I was always thinking about some-thing else."

"But you're a good healer."

"People are much more interesting than bread."

"Good food is always interesting."

"To eat, but not to cook. Not for me, anyway."

That reminded Beltur about the burhka, and he extended his senses to the cookpot hanging over the fire on the kitchen side of the hearth. "It won't be long before the burhka's ready."

He was getting the feeling that he'd be doing most of the cooking, but he smiled and asked, "Are you ready for a few more order exercises?"

XLV

On sixday, Beltur was up early fixing breakfast, an effort that went far better the second time around, largely because he'd spent several glasses on fiveday at the chandlery and the market square, buying various items that he'd overlooked in initially stocking the cot, such as lard, a few more eggs, and a small keg of pale ale. He hadn't relished drinking water at breakfast on fiveday. He'd saddled Slowpoke and ridden him, not only to make carrying goods back easier, but also to give the gelding a little exercise. At the chandlery, he'd found an old but serviceable hearth oven. All in all, the supposedly "small" supplements to their provisions and kitchen utensils had cost him almost five silvers, and he knew that there were still other items they were missing. The bread he had baked on fiveday afternoon had turned out acceptably, especially as a basis for egg toast on sixday, with the mixed-berry syrup that had cost three coppers just by itself.

By the time Beltur left to clean the stables on sixday morning, and then, after washing up there, for the healing house, a fine snow drifted down, but there wasn't that much of an order/chaos conflict in those clouds, which suggested that the snow wouldn't be all that heavy. What was also clear to Beltur was that because Axalt was considerably colder than Elparta, what snow did fall didn't melt, and small snowfall after small snowfall added up to an ever-increasing amount of snow piling up everywhere, except where the Council mandated it be cleared.

When he reached the healing house, he immediately went into Herrara's study. "Is there anything I should know or that you need me to do?"

"Look at Poldaark first. I thought I sensed some chaos in that wound, but you're better at finding chaos deeper inside. After that, look at the man in with him. I don't think there's much we can do but make him comfortable, but if there is . . ."

Beltur nodded. "I'll see."

"Then come back here. It's quiet now, but you can never tell."

Beltur picked up one of the oblong baskets and made his way up to the second level and the middle room. Poldaark sat on the edge of the bed. An older man lay in the bed closest to the door, and Beltur could sense instantly from the chaos in his chest that he would not be there long. That didn't even count the frostburn on the man's hands, forearms, and feet.

"The patrollers brought him in last night," said Poldaark. "They found him in the middle of the main street. No one knows who he is. He's been like that ever since."

Beltur took another look at the man, who lay on his back with a blanket up to his chin, his eyes closed. His weathered and ravaged face and tangled beard, as well as all the chaos in his body, had given Beltur the initial impression that he was older than he was. The man was likely not even fifteen years older than Beltur himself . . . and possibly even younger, but he'd clearly had a hard life. And Herrara had been right. There wasn't a thing that Beltur could do. He turned his attention to Poldaark. "How do you feel?"

"My shoulder still hurts, but not as bad as it has been. That's why I'm sitting up. Lying back on it hurts a lot after a while. Even with the blanket folded up for support so it doesn't touch anything, it still hurts."

"Let me see." Beltur let his senses range over Poldaark. Herrara had been right. There was a small bit of yellowish-red wound chaos deep in the shoulder, but it only took a few moments to ease free order into place to destroy the chaos. "That should do it. Did you feel anything?"

"Like a quick burn with a hot needle, but it's gone."

"Can you raise your hand and lower arm?"

Poldaark did so.

"Try to lift your whole arm, just a little."

"Oooooh . . . that still hurts."

"It might be some time before the muscles in your shoulder heal fully." *If they ever do.*

"How is it, ser? I mean . . ."

"Do you mean whether you'll live? So far, it looks like you're healing well. By next eightday, you just might be out of here."

"I won't be able to do much with that arm."

"You'll have to do more with your left arm for a while."

Poldaark looked at Beltur glumly. "Hannon won't like that, either."

"You're fortunate to be alive," Beltur pointed out.

"If you say so, ser."

"Poldaark, you're alive. You're getting fed. You've gotten to look at an attractive healer every other day."

"She's your consort, isn't she?"

"She is. You can look, but not touch," Beltur said lightly, hoping to cheer the young man.

Poldaark smiled faintly, if only for a moment.

Beltur had barely gotten downstairs when Elisa appeared.

"Healer Herrara would like you in the surgery. Immediately."

"I'll be right there." Beltur didn't run, but he did walk quickly.

When he stepped into the surgery, he saw a woman sitting on the edge of the surgery table, blood-soaked rags bound around her thigh. He could sense that her natural order level was low, and from all the blood he saw, that had to be the reason.

Herrara gestured. "I need you to use your shields to stop the bleeding. There's the tip of a knife buried in the bone, and every movement she makes causes more injury."

What the head healer wasn't saying was that the woman, perhaps a few years younger than the healer, didn't have that much blood left to spare.

Beltur began extending his senses as he moved toward the woman, placing himself on the side of her good leg and feeling the dark coldness of the sliver of iron whose tip was embedded in the bone. He extended a shield around the metal, except where it touched the bone, extending it slightly to press muscle away from the metal. "The shield's in place."

"Good. Can you also immobilize her upper leg, except around the wound?"

"Mostly." Beltur couldn't get another shield totally in place around the first shield.

"That will have to do." Herrara used a set of pincers to grasp the large end of the metal, then wiggled it slightly, then seemed to ease the fragment out of the bone.

That wasn't nearly as easy as it looked, because Beltur could sense the strength it took to control the pincers and remove the iron without causing more damage. Nor was it painless, because he could feel the woman stiffen and shudder, although only a low moan escaped her lips.

"Now . . . hold open the flesh above that blood vessel."

Beltur did so, watching as the healer stitched closed the slash in the vessel, amazed at the deftness in Herrara's fingers.

"Now . . . need to clean this up and close it . . . you'll have to let go of those shields."

Beltur released them, ready to replace them if Herrara so directed. "Good."

Suturing and closing the wound took far more time than removing the metal shard had required, especially since Herrara and Beltur then had to bind the upper leg on each side of the sutures.

Then Herrara looked to Beltur again. "Take care of the chaos there, if you would."

Beltur could sense tiny points of chaos where the metal had impacted the bone, as well as elsewhere, and it took him half a quint to deal with them all. His forehead was damp when he finished, despite the coolness of the surgery.

"It's gone for now," he replied, blotting his forehead with his sleeve.

Elisa appeared with the wheeled chair, and Beltur and Herrara eased the injured woman into the chair.

"Thank you . . . healers," murmured the woman. "I don't know . . ."

"You'll be fine," said Herrara warmly.

Beltur could sense that Herrara had her doubts.

"How long must I stay?"

"We'll have to see," replied the chief healer. "There's a blood vessel in your upper leg that has to heal."

"But . . . what will I do?"

"You'll get well. That's better than dying." Herrara gestured to Elisa. "The empty room near the west end."

Once Elisa and the woman were out of the surgery, Beltur asked, "How did that happen?"

"She's a serving woman at the Traders' Bowl. One of the traders from Certis took a fashion to her. She wasn't interested. He'd had too much to drink. He stabbed her. She fled. She didn't realize how badly she was hurt or that the knife had splintered. One of the ostlers found her. I think he borrowed a horse to bring her here. He didn't dare stay because the horse . . . wasn't his."

"A trader from Certis, at this time of year? And he got away with it?"

"It's his word against hers. He'd claim she was trying to seduce him and then rob him. The Council doesn't like to upset traders. If he was from Certis, I'd guess that he's likely one of those who comes regularly for silver . . ."

"Silver's mined near here?"

"Not all that near, but the mountain folk bring it here to sell. A trader

named Emlyn handles it. Knowing Johlana, you may have heard of him."
Herrara's mouth twisted slightly.

"I know the name and relationship, but I've only met the man briefly.
Why do the mountain folk trade with him?"

"They trust us more than either the Elpartans or the Certans, and you
have to have golds to trade in silver." Her mouth twisted. "The Certans are
the worst."

"Worse than the Gallosians?"

"There's no comparison."

Beltur had his doubts about that, given his own experiences, but then,
he'd already gotten the feeling that there was nothing some people
wouldn't stoop to in order to get what they wanted. *Or to stay alive and hold
on to the woman they love.* He managed just to nod.

"After we clean up here, you'd better look in on Maelyn. She's the serving woman. Then finish up looking in on the others." Herrara paused.
"How's Poldaark?"

"You were right. There was a tiny bit of chaos deep in the wound. I
took care of it. It's looking like he'll make it."

"That's your doing. I hope he's thankful, but he won't be. He's too
young. He might realize it later."

Another quint or so passed before Beltur made it to the chamber where
Maelyn lay, her head and upper body propped up. She watched him warily
as he entered the chamber, but said nothing. "I just came by to see how
you're doing."

"I'm here, ser." After a pause, she said, "You're a mage, aren't you?"

"I am, and you'd like to know what I'm doing here, wouldn't you?"

Her eyes didn't meet his.

"I'm also a healer, but I still have some things to learn. So I'm working
here for a time. Now . . . I need to see some things."

Maelyn immediately stiffened.

"I just need to touch your forehead." Beltur brushed her brow with his
fingertips, but she wasn't any warmer than she'd been earlier. Then he concentrated on her thigh. *So far, no more chaos.* If there had been, so soon, he
would have been really worried. "Just try not to move that leg more than a
little at a time, at least for now."

"It really hurts."

Beltur managed not to sigh. "I'm going to try something. It won't make
things worse, but it might help." He leaned over and lightly touched her

skin just above the leg bindings, allowing a bit of free order to flow through the sutures and down to the bone.

Maelyn's face relaxed slightly. "That's . . . better."

"It will help for a little while." Before she could ask anything, he said, "I'll look in on you later." Then he turned and left.

Beltur had almost finished seeing the other patients on the second level when Elisa again appeared, a concerned expression on her face.

"She needs me in the surgery?"

The healer-to-be nodded.

Beltur headed downstairs once more.

He almost froze for an instant when he walked into the surgery when he saw a man lying on the table, two other men beside him, with Herrara cutting away fabric to reveal a bloody smashed mess below the knee. Herrara didn't look toward Beltur, but continued cutting away fabric as she spoke. "This is Wurfael. He's a timberman. He slipped on an icy patch, and his leg went under a moving sledge. The bones below the knee look like they're shattered. I'll need to take off the lower leg." Herrara's voice was calm. "Otherwise he'll die."

She looked to Beltur. "It will be easier if you can immobilize the leg." Then she turned to the two men who had carried their comrade in. "You two will have to hold him down."

Beltur moved closer, to where he could see without getting in Herrara's way.

He had to admire the older healer's speed and skill in not only sawing through bone, but especially in sewing shut the blood vessels. He tried not to wince when the healer used a rasp to smooth the end of the bones.

Almost before Beltur realized it, she finished off by sewing the skin so that only a small area was left open to drain.

"You'll need to take out as much chaos as you can," she said to Beltur.

Beltur was definitely light-headed when he finished.

"Go get something to eat," Herrara said. "There's some bread and cheese in the study."

Beltur didn't question her. He just left the surgery. Behind him he caught a few words.

". . . healer and a mage . . . getting the chaos out is hard . . ."

Once in the study, Beltur found the cheese and bread, and slowly began to eat. A good quint passed before he felt better, and it wasn't long after that before Herrara appeared.

"I'm sorry, but there was a lot of chaos there."

"He just might live because of what you did. It took them two glasses to get him here."

"You've done that more than a few times," Beltur observed.

"Enough," she replied dryly. "Between sledges, wagons, and timbering, I do a score or so a year. This one was easier because you kept his leg absolutely still. If you can keep the chaos out of it, he should recover, and the damage was low enough that he'll be able to walk with a peg leg."

The rest of the day was comparatively uneventful, for which Beltur was most thankful.

At a quint past fourth glass, after walking back to the cot through the scattered snow flurries that had barely dropped a digit of snow, Beltur stepped inside, still marveling at the fact that he was consorted and had a place for the two of them as he took off his coat and hung it on one of the wall pegs.

Jessyla hurried out from the kitchen and hugged him. "It's good to see you. You look a little worn."

"I could use some of that ale."

"Just sit down. I'll bring you a mug."

"I can get it."

"Beltur . . . I can tell you've had a hard day. Sit down."

He didn't argue. He just accepted the mug of ale gratefully when Jessyla returned with it, and took a long swallow.

"What happened?"

"It started with the serving woman who was stabbed by a trader from Certis . . ." Beltur summarized the day's events, ending with, "You've never mentioned things like that, but I can't believe they haven't happened to you."

"I haven't had to watch Herrara take off a leg, but we've had broken bones, bad burns, some deep, deep cuts."

"She's very good. I could never do what I watched her do with that man's leg. My fingers aren't that deft."

"You're good with other things. She might not have done it so well without your help."

Beltur took another healthy swallow of the ale. "This does help."

"I'm glad." She paused. "You don't mind if I don't come to the Council House with you this evening, do you?"

"So long as you don't mind if I go."

"I don't mind. I think it's better that you're there. Also, I can have dinner ready when you come back."

"Can I ask—"

"No, you can't. It's a surprise." Her smile was wry. "Not too much of a surprise, I hope. Just sit here and talk to me for a few moments. If you're going to take Slowpoke, you can't stay long."

Jessyla was right about that, and less than a quint later he was at Barrynt's stabling Slowpoke. Jorhan had already saddled his mount and one for Barrynt. Then the three rode to the Council House. This time, Beltur raised full shields before entering the chamber. Again, they sat in the front row.

Beltur turned to Barrynt. "Is the councilor in the middle the head councilor?"

"Karanstyl is for this season. They change every season. Except the mage-councilor never heads the Council in the public meetings."

Others began to drift into the chamber, close to a score by the time the councilors filed in. Once again Beltur sensed the woman with the strength of blackness to be a healer, but unlike at the previous Council meeting, when she had been alone, this time she had come with another woman, since the two exchanged a few words every so often. Neither Taegyn nor Naerkaal seemed to recognize Beltur, and that was for the best, Beltur thought.

Karanstyl addressed the chamber. "The first matter is that of the proposal of Jorhan the smith. Jorhan, please stand."

The smith stood and waited.

"Jorhan, the Council has approved the use of the Widow Santhela's building for your use as a coppersmithy. You are limited to yourself and no more than two other assistants or smiths at any one time. No more than two barrels of wastes may be stored on the premises. All wastes must be carried to the dump at the southwest corner of south town and placed in the area for slag and metal wastes. Since you will be rebuilding the forge in the building, the Council will inspect that forge at some point after it is completed. Repairs may be required if the Council finds the forge unsafe. You owe the Council two silvers, one silver for a season's worth of dumping wastes, the other for snow clearing of the street in front of the premises. You will owe another silver for dumping in the first eightday of each season." Karanstyl paused. "Is that clear?"

"Yes, Councilor. Can I pay you now?"

"You can indeed."

Jorhan handed over two silvers.

"You may go, Jorhan. The Council has several other proposals to consider."

Barrynt rose and nodded to the Council. Beltur followed his example, and the three walked from the chamber.

Once they were outside, Jorhan looked at Barrynt. "Every time I come here, I have to pay more silvers."

"You don't owe anything more until the first eightday of spring," said Barrynt.

"Except what it will cost me for stone or bricks and mortar . . . and a good solid anvil. That chandler of yours promised he'd have one for me by the end of the eightday."

"If he said he would, he will."

"He did have a few things I liked enough to buy," admitted Jorhan.

Beltur hid a grin in his scarf.

After the ride back to Barrynt's, he quickly groomed Slowpoke, then walked back to the cot, where he was greeted with the warm odor of cooking, with a hint of something burned. He almost made it to the kitchen before Jessyla spoke.

"The burned stuff you smell isn't for dinner. We're having fowl in a sort of pearapple sauce. Just sit down at the table. No . . . pour us each a mug of ale, and then sit down."

Beltur did just that and then asked, "Where did you get a fowl?"

"Johlana brought the fowl for us. We talked for a glass. She's really very nice. I think she misses Halhana."

"But Halhana lives right here in Axalt."

"I think Johlana would like to spend more time with her. I get the feeling that Eshult's parents look down on Barrynt and Johlana, especially Johlana."

"That was obvious when I met them, and I told you what they were wearing, and how much it likely cost. I learned a little more today. Herrara mentioned Emlyn. He's as wealthy and powerful as the large traders in Elparta. He's the one who handles the mountain silver trade."

Jessyla set a platter in front of Beltur, with half a fowl breast and a leg, along with quilla strips, and boiled potatoes. "I know it looks odd, but it tastes all right."

He looked at her platter, which had the wing with half a breast.

"The other half of the fowl is for tomorrow night."

"I suppose Johlana told you only to give us half tonight," said Beltur, mock-mournfully.

Jessyla laughed as she seated herself. "She did."

Beltur cut a morsel, making sure it had some sauce, and ate it. "That's rather good."

"I'll take 'rather good,' only because you've been spoiled by Meldryn's cooking."

"I said it was good," Beltur protested.

"'Rather good,' I believe." Jessyla spoiled the severity of her words with a grin. "For that, you owe me another lesson in magery. After dinner."

"I can do that. And this is good."

Smiling, Jessyla shook her head.

Beltur laughed sheepishly.

XLVI

On sevenday, Beltur cleaned up the kitchen and the rest of the cot, cleared the night's snowfall snow from the walks, and walked to Barrynt's, where he cleaned the stables—after he spent some time with Slowpoke, talking to him as he groomed him and checked his hooves. After that, Beltur walked to the side door, where he knocked.

Asala opened the door. "The mistress says that you and Healer Jessyla don't have to knock. You're family. You do have to clean your boots."

Beltur grinned and cleaned his boots before taking off his coat and making his way to the parlor, where he actually found Johlana, seated in an armchair, apparently sewing.

"Good morning, Beltur. What can I do for you?"

"I didn't have anything in mind. What are you sewing?"

"I'm not properly sewing at all. This is lace. I used to do it for Barrynt, but I made him promise not to tell anyone that I'd done it. This will be for Halhana."

Beltur looked more carefully, taking in the design. "That's beautiful."

"My mother taught me. It's better than anything Barrynt found anywhere, and it helped him back then, but . . ." She smiled. "Merchant's consorts aren't lacemakers, and if anyone found out, especially Sarysta, it wouldn't have been good."

"He wants the best for you."

"He always has, and I'd rather not see him unhappy . . . or angry. He can be terrible. Not at family, but at those who belittle or hurt those he cares for. He's very protective of his family and his close friends."

Beltur recalled Jorhan saying something of the sort. "I don't want to pry, but . . . you worry about Halhana? Eshult's parents, perhaps?"

Johlana lowered the small frame she held. "You see more than most men, Beltur. Or you listen to your consort," she added. "That's almost as good."

"Some of both," admitted Beltur.

"In the family, it's no secret. Sarysta wasn't all that keen on her boy consorting Halhana, but they're so much in love, and he wouldn't have anyone else. Not that there was a girl in Axalt to compare to her."

"Is he the oldest son?"

"The oldest of two. He's much older than Escaylt, and compared to Eshult, Escaylt's gray ash, not even a clinker. Despite pretty faces and figures, their daughters aren't much better. Thankfully, Ryntaar and Frankyr have already seen that."

"Sarysta wanted Eshult to consort for more golds?"

"That was part of it. The rest . . . it was turned to ashes a long time ago."

"I'm sorry."

"I appreciate your kindness. You don't have to be sorry. You and Jessyla have already been through more than I ever had to weather, and you're still young." She smiled. "I am grateful that you brought Jorhan here."

"It's more like he brought me."

"He couldn't have come without what you did."

"We work well together."

She nodded. "He'll be happier once he's back to work. He's never liked being idle."

"I'll be riding to south town to see how things are coming with the smithy."

"No matter how much he complains, that's what he'd rather be doing. You know that."

"That . . . and that he wants everything he does to be the best." Beltur looked at the lace. "As do you, I suspect."

A smile flashed across Johlana's face. "I can't imagine that."

"I'd better be going."

"If Jorhan complains about your not being there earlier, tell him I kept you."

Beltur just smiled before he turned.

After leaving the house, he saddled Slowpoke, then led the gelding out into the cold, where he mounted, and the two set out for south town. As he rode, he thought over what Johlana had said. For some reason, the trouble between Eshult's parents and Halhana's parents dealt with Johlana and also had something to do with Barrynt's first consort. He also couldn't help but wonder about Barrynt being terrible when he felt those he cared for were threatened. But then, a few times, he'd seen a momentary bit of anger, and he had the feeling that Barrynt kept that anger walled away— and that was dangerous when the wall broke.

Maybe he should watch Barrynt more closely, especially when Halhana's name came up.

Once he reached the smithy and dismounted, he made sure that Slowpoke was securely tied to the hitching rail before entering the building. In one corner were laid out Jorhan's tools and everything relating to smithing, including some copper and tin ingots.

Jorhan was mortaring bricks into place to build up the forge.

"Wondered when you'd show up." The smith did not look up.

"I work even-numbered days at the healing house, remember."

"You're wasted there."

"I'm not wasted. I can help you forge things here and earn more coins. But you don't need me every day, and I need to get better at healing so I don't get into real trouble. I might as well get paid for learning as doing it for nothing."

"Something to be said for that. Would you fetch me bricks from the pile by the door?"

"I'd be happy to." Beltur walked back toward the door. He carried an armload back and stacked them neatly. He did the same once more, and repeated those efforts until there were enough bricks where Jorhan could reach them fairly easily.

"Appreciate that."

"I'm glad to help. How are you coming with finding coal and copper?"

"Coal's more of a problem than copper. Hard coal, anyway. It's like Barrynt says. Nobody wants to mine when it's cold. I don't see why. It's not that cold inside a mine, especially if you've got doors on the shaft, like you ought to anyway. They insist on keeping the roads clear." Jorhan shook his head. "Took me almost an eightday, but a fellow will be delivering some tomorrow. By then, I should have the forge finished. Not to be used. Take a few days for the mortar to set the way I want. Could have started earlier, except I couldn't get enough mortar. Had to pay extra silvers."

"You seem to be doing well."

"The way things are going, it's going to be close to an eightday before I can even think about forging. The only thing I can get for molds right now is clay. You can help with that on oneday. Good thing I brought a good amount of wax. Would help if I had plaster as well . . ."

Beltur just listened for a time. When Jorhan seemed finished, he said, "Just let me know if there's anything I can do."

"You'll know. I'd really like to get started."

Beltur frowned. "You didn't think we'd be doing that much in winter. Do you have something in mind? A new buyer?"

"Not a buyer. I asked Johlana what I could do for them. She said that she'd like a larger mirror on a stand for Halhana . . . if we could. That would be something special." The smith barked a rueful laugh. "Something that would even impress her consort's parents."

"Emlyn and Sarysta?" *Again?* "I met them the other day. They're very, very well-off, most likely because he handles the silver trade for the mountain people. For some reason," said Beltur sardonically, "they don't trust the Gallosians or the Certans . . . and apparently not the traders of Spidlar."

"Those mountain people know a thing or two . . . but if Emlyn's the best . . ." Jorhan didn't finish the statement.

As far as Beltur was concerned, the smith didn't have to. "I've got Slowpoke outside. He needs to be ridden a bit more. Is there anything I can get for you?"

"Not today. I want to get the brickwork done here." Jorhan snorted. "I'll need to be careful, what with the frigging Council poking around. Last thing I want is to have to redo it."

"What about moving that workbench from the back room?"

"We'll do that later. It'll just get in the way right now. Do whatever you have to. You might stop by on oneday."

"I'll be here." Beltur nodded and turned, deciding that he'd ride Slowpoke around south town for a bit, just to get a better feel for the place.

XLVII

Eightday and oneday passed uneventfully, but by twoday morning the snow was coming down in sheets so thick that Beltur could only see a few yards as he struggled first through the whiteness to Barrynt's stables and then, after tending to stables and horses, to the healing house. He was glad that he'd ridden all three horses on oneday, and that he'd been able to help Jorhan wrestle his "new" anvil into place. He and Slowpoke had also carried two heavy bags of clay for molds to the smithy from a potterage at the north end of south town.

When he reached the healing house, Herrara immediately dispatched him to look in on Wurfael, whom he found in a chamber near the west end of the main level.

The burly man was propped up in a sitting position on the bed. His eyes went to Beltur and then dropped.

"Good morning. I need to take a look at that leg."

"What's left of it."

"There's a lot left." Beltur studied the man's stump with his senses, finding some small patches of chaos, but very few compared to the amount that he'd had to deal with in Poldaark's case. That made sense, given Herrara's skill. After taking care of the chaos, he said, "That looks like it will heal cleanly."

"Suppose that's for the best."

"Suppose?" Beltur raised his eyebrows. "If Healer Herrara hadn't taken off your lower leg, the chaos would have killed you."

"Ser mage . . . there's not much use for a one-legged timberman . . ."

"Healer Herrara says you'll be able to use a peg leg to walk."

"Still won't be able to do timber, not in most places. That's what I'm good at. Was good at. Ground's too rugged."

"Seems to me you could be a teamster."

"I could if I had the golds for a horse, wagon, or tack . . ."

"What about working for someone else?"

"Not many'd hire a former timberman." Wurfael turned his head.

Beltur didn't know what to say that wouldn't be condescending or a simplistic platitude. He managed a pleasant smile, then said, "You'll feel better before long." *The most acceptable of simplistic platitudes.*

Wurfael didn't even nod as Beltur left the chamber and then headed upstairs to see how Poldaark was coming. Herrara joined him just after he entered the chamber where Poldaark sat dejectedly on the side of the bed. Beltur noticed that the other beds were again empty.

"How are you feeling?" asked Beltur as he stopped short of the young man and began to sense whether there was more wound chaos.

"Better. It doesn't hurt as much. Except when I forget and lean back too hard."

Herrara looked to Beltur.

"There's still some dull red of healing, but none of the points of nasty wound chaos."

"Good." Herrara turned to Poldaark. "It looks like you'll be able to go home in the next day or so."

"Do I have to?" asked Poldaark almost plaintively, looking not at Herrara, but at Beltur and offering a pleading expression.

"You can't stay here when you're well enough to take care of yourself," replied the head healer.

"I don't have anywhere to go. Hannon sent Sorvyn. He doesn't need me any longer."

"Don't you have any family?" asked Herrara.

"My folks died in a flash flood two years ago. Hannon's first consort, Aellana, was my cousin. She sort of took me in. She died last spring. Most of my folk's people live in the north part of the Easthorns west of Quend. Hannon never really liked me, and Sorvyn and Handyl were always doing things to make me look bad."

Herrara looked to Beltur, who nodded. The head healer pursed her lips. "We've got empty beds . . . for now. You can stay here until the end of the eightday. If there's still no chaos in your wound tomorrow, and when this snowfall stops you'll have to go out and see if you can find a place somewhere. That will give you a few days."

"Thank you, Healer."

"That's all I can promise."

When the two healers were out in the corridor and well away from Poldaark, Beltur said, "When will the next Council inspection be?"

Herrara smiled amusedly. "Shansyl was here yesterday. Poldaark's wound is one where it would be hard to argue about a few days. Beyond that, though, especially by next eightday . . ."

"So you knew what happened with Hannon."

"I didn't *know,* but it seemed likely when I saw someone come in, talk to Poldaark, and then leave in a hurry."

"You wanted to get him looking rather than just insisting that he leave immediately once he was well enough to cope."

"He won't be well enough to cope before he has to leave." Herrara's voice was bleak. "Too many of them aren't."

"The Council doesn't leave you much choice."

"No. We all have to make the best of the choices we've made."

Beltur was about to say that, unlike Herrara, his choices had largely affected him and those closest to him. Except . . . *they really hadn't.*

"You see?"

Beltur nodded.

The rest of the day consisted of changing dressings, dealing with minor wound chaos, and other chores.

As soon as Beltur stepped out of the healing house at fourth glass, he knew that the walk back to the cot would be even worse, since the snow was still falling just as heavily and the walks and streets had not yet been cleared. The snow in most places was at least knee-deep. But when he neared the cot, he saw that only a few digits of snow covered the walks around it. He was careful to knock as much snow as he could off of his boots before stepping inside.

Jessyla hurried out of the kitchen. "I'm glad you're home. This has to be a northeaster."

"I'm sure it is. You shoveled the snow, didn't you?" asked Beltur as he took off his coat.

"Of course. You shovel when I'm working."

Beltur couldn't argue with that. "Thank you."

"You're welcome."

"I've been thinking . . ."

"About what?"

"That we're going to work on shields before dinner." Beltur paused. "What are we having tonight?"

"Fowl soup with fried noodles and biscuits. I told you that this morning. I wasn't about to waste what was left of the fowl."

Beltur didn't recall there being anything left of the fowl Johlana had brought.

"You'll like it," she promised. "Don't look so doubtful."

"We need to work on your shields."

"Do you think I'll need them any time soon?"

"I certainly hope not. It takes a long time to develop good shields. That's why—"

"You're insisting on it now."

"You did tell me you wanted to learn magery." Beltur grinned.

"Where do I start?"

"By moving next to the hearth so that I can get warm."

Once they were between the bench and the hearth, Beltur stepped back. "Raise a shield, the same size as you did last time, but make it a circle."

"I'll try. Circles are harder."

Beltur waited, then studied the web of interlocking order. "Put a tiny bit of chaos surrounded by order at five places around the rim."

Jessyla managed three such nodes before the shield collapsed. She blotted her forehead and looked at Beltur.

"This time, try it around the innermost ring. That way, they'll be closer together."

"I know you say that chaos makes it stronger, but why is that?"

"Chaos is more . . . flexible . . . Once you can pattern chaos within a shield, the shield can hold against greater forces. It's like your body. Without natural chaos—"

"That makes sense." Jessyla squared her shoulders.

Beltur just hoped that the chicken soup with the fried noodles was good.

XLVIII

By sevenday morning the northeaster had passed, and the sky was a crystal clear green-blue, and the air even colder. When he set out on foot for south town and Jorhan's new smithy, some of the walks were clear, but many were not, and only the main road through Axalt itself was cleared. While the road to south town wasn't clear, Beltur followed some sledge traces. Even so, it took him three quints before he stepped inside the smithy, shivering slightly. After knocking the snow off his boots and trousers, he walked toward the forge.

"I wasn't sure I'd see you today," offered Jorhan, who was feeding coal to the forge fire.

"I had to shovel and clean the stable. Then I had to walk. It's too cold to leave Slowpoke tied outside."

"He'd do better than you."

"Not being tied up. Parts weren't too bad. How do they move that much snow so soon?"

"Same as in Elparta. They use men from the workhouses. Some of the women, too. They're the teamsters. Each day they clear snow counts for two days of their time, and they get a copper a day."

That was slightly more generous than in Elparta, Beltur thought. "The Council seems to want the roads clear."

"That's because open roads are worth golds. Axalt's the only way through the Easthorns from late fall through early spring."

"What about the roads in Certis? Or Spidlar?"

"You can travel by sledge where it's flat, not through the Easthorns." Jorhan shrugged. "Maybe they don't get as much snow in Certis. Barrynt just told me that they get trade because the roads are clear year-round. Also because they don't have to worry about brigands in Axalt."

"No . . . just west of the border wall." Beltur looked at the molds on the workbench. "Are those for the big mirror?"

"The supports. We'll have to cast it in four sections—base, supports, and mirror. The mirror comes last."

"I can work the fire if you want to do something else."

"Be much obliged."

Beltur took the small metal shovel from Jorhan.

By the time Jorhan had the molds the way he wanted them, and had them heated, it was after first glass, and another glass passed before he'd poured the bronze into them, and Beltur fixed the order/chaos patterns in the hot metal.

Then he had to hold them for longer, and holding two patterns was more than twice the effort and work, besides which was the problem that it had been eightdays since he'd last done it. Despite the chill in the smithy, he was sweating by the time he finally stepped away from the molds.

"There's nothing else for you to do," said Jorhan.

"I need to cool down and dry off some. Do you plan to cast the base on oneday?"

"I'd thought to."

"Then I'll be here."

Beltur didn't ask about getting paid, not when the mirror was for Halhana, especially given how much Barrynt and Johlana had provided. "Has anyone else asked about forging anything?"

"Not so far."

"The Council hasn't inspected the forge yet, have they?"

"They'll be here on oneday or two, most likely. That's what Barrynt says, anyway. Might have been here today, hadn't been for the snow."

"They inspect the healing house once an eightday, a different councilor each time."

"Seems like they'd have better things to do. Healers do the best they can. You and your consort do. People either get better or not. Councilors prowling around won't change that."

"They don't want poor people staying there after they're well enough to leave."

"Who'd want to stay? I'd think that even the poorhouse'd be better than being surrounded by folks that ill or injured."

"I'd thought so, too, but . . ." Beltur shook his head. "Axalt's different. Better than Elparta, so far."

"The Council's almost as greedy, but at least there aren't traders around trying to grab every last silver from a working man."

Beltur nodded, although he wondered, after what little he'd heard about Emlyn and his consort.

Abruptly, Jorhan looked toward the door. "No sense in your staying around here. You've got someone to head home to. Best you do it."

Beltur grinned at the smith. "That's a very good idea."

XLIX

Eightday at the healing house was largely uneventful for Beltur. That was to say that he only had to deal with two simple broken arms, a dislocated shoulder, and the city patrollers bringing in a white-haired woman who had almost frozen to death—yet without any sign of frostburn—all of which Herrara left largely to him. After finishing his healing duties, Beltur walked home, washed up, thankful for the kitchen cistern, and he and Jessyla walked to Barrynt and Johlana's for dinner, as well as for refreshments before and afterward.

Oneday found Beltur at the smithy, where he and Jorhan cast the base of the mirror for Halhana. He left early because Jorhan didn't need him, and he wanted to give Slowpoke a little exercise before he returned to the cot and prepared a decent dinner, one that wasn't soup, although the fried noodle and fowl soup had been tasty. That, he had to admit.

His dinner amounted to a mutton shank stew with onions, potatoes, and chunks of quilla. He wasn't that fond of quilla, but it was more than palatable in stew. He had enough shanks so that the stew would last several days, longer if he put it in the cold box off the kitchen. When he served it, Jessyla liked it at least well enough to eat it, possibly because his bread turned out well.

Twoday was again clear and cold when Beltur left the cot for the stable, although it seemed a touch warmer when he finished there and walked to the healing house. He began by visiting all those on the lower level. The last room he entered was that of Wurfael. "Good morning, Wurfael."

"The sun says it's morning."

"Let's see how that leg is coming."

"What's left of it, you mean."

"You've still got enough that you'll be able to get around."

"Much good that'll do."

Before Beltur could think of an appropriate reply, Herrara looked into the small chamber. "I need you in the surgery."

Even without Herrara's tone, Beltur knew that, when she wanted him, it wasn't going to be simple, and he said, "I'll be back later."

When he reached the surgery, a man, barely more than a youth, sat on the edge of the surgery table. He wore faded brown trousers, and a patched shirt of the same color. A brown jacket lay beside him. His face was white, and he cradled his left arm. Elisa stood beside him, as if uncertain as to what she could do.

Beltur could instantly sense that whatever had happened to the arm was more than a simple break. As he approached, he could sense multiple breaks in the lower part of the arm, and in one place, part of the bone had broken the skin.

"The lower arm . . ." said Herrara.

Beltur nodded. "There are several breaks."

The young man blanched, then winced. "Don't take my arm, Healer."

"You might die if we try to save it."

"A one-armed poor man is dead already."

Herrara turned to Beltur. "I'll need some careful help with those shields." She motioned for Elisa to step back. Then she looked to the young man. "You never told me your name."

"Yuareff."

"Tell us again exactly how you did this to yourself, Yuareff."

"Like I told you, I didn't do it. Naarstyn did it. Frigging piss-poor excuse for a teamster. We'd just finished loading road snow, and he started the sledge. He didn't even look to see if we'd secured the tailboard. Just headed out. Snow moved. Tailboard came down right across my arm. Frigging Naarstyn . . . dumb bastard . . ."

"We'll need to cut away your shirt first," said Herrara firmly.

"You can cut away anything but my arm."

"We'll do what we can. I'm going to support the broken arm. You let go." After Herrara held Yuareff's arm, she looked to Beltur. "Immobilize his upper arm so that he doesn't jerk."

Beltur eased a containment around the man's upper arm and another around his torso.

Although tears ran from Yuareff's eyes, the young man uttered not a sound as Herrara straightened the lower arm.

"Extend the shield farther down the arm and support it so I can cut his shirt away."

Beltur held Yuareff's arm steady while Herrara removed the fabric and then began to manipulate bones into position.

Beltur followed Herrara's directions as she continued to manipulate the arm.

"Now . . . hold the entire arm steady while I get the splint ready."

"No cast?"

"Not until tomorrow. There will be swelling, and I'd like it to subside before I immobilize the arm in a cast."

"You're not taking my arm?"

"Not now. Maybe not ever . . . if you're careful for the next few eight-days."

"Thank you, Healers. Thank you."

"Don't thank us yet," said Herrara as she eased the splint into position. Yuareff's face clouded.

Herrara finished binding the splint in place. "You're staying here for the next day or so. After that, we'll see." She turned to Elisa. "Find an empty chamber for him."

"They said I'm supposed to come back to the workhouse."

"You're not ready to do that. They won't come for you. They might come to make sure you're here. They can't make you leave until I say so."

Yuareff's face relaxed slightly.

"This way," said Elisa gently.

After the two had left, Herrara turned to Beltur. "Some of the workhouse supervisors will have him doing chores as soon as we release him. We need to see how the healing on his arm begins."

"You're worried about chaos around where the bone broke the skin?"

"There's always chaos when that happens. It's your task to deal with it."

Beltur wondered if his own ability to remove some chaos was one of the reasons she'd agreed to set Yuareff's arm rather than amputate it. "So far there's no sign of any."

"So far." She paused. "How is Wurfael doing?"

"I was about to see when you came in. I'll let you know after I see him and Poldaark."

Wurfael was still sitting on the side of the bed when Beltur returned. "When Healer Herrara asks for you, it means someone's hurt bad, doesn't it?"

"That, or it's something I haven't seen and should know about."

"Mostly hurt bad, I think," said the timberman.

Beltur nodded and took his time sensing the area around the stump of the leg. Again, he found small bits of the nasty yellowish-red wound chaos, but they were small enough that dealing with them took neither much time nor much effort. "There. Another eightday or so . . ."

"And then what?"

"Then you might be able to be measured for a peg leg." Beltur had no idea who might be able to do that, but he was fairly certain that Herrara would.

"So I can walk around looking useless?"

"That's likely better than not being able to walk around."

"Not much," groused the timberman.

When Beltur entered the upstairs chamber, Poldaark was pulling on his patched jacket.

"You're going out to look for a place?" Beltur didn't know what else to say.

"What else? I can't work much yet. The poorhouse doesn't take young men, and I can only stay here until the end of the eightday."

"You might be able to find something. Did you ask Rhodos the chandler? He knows people." Beltur quickly sensed the youth's chest and shoulder area. There were still areas that held the dull red tinge of healing flesh, but he found no sign of what he considered active wound chaos or muscles that had no natural order, which would have indicated that they were dying or about to die. "You're doing better."

"Leastwise, that's one thing that's going well." Poldaark shook his head mournfully.

As Beltur headed back down the stairs to meet with Herrara, he couldn't help wondering what would happen to the three men.

L

On threeday, a light and feathery snow began to drift down on Axalt as Beltur left Barrynt's stable on the walk to the smithy. The snow reminded Beltur that it was already midwinter, and he wondered how that much time had passed so quickly. *Because you're both busy?*

He kept walking and reached the smithy at two quints past seventh glass, the time that he and Jorhan had agreed upon. "I tried to get here a bit earlier, but cleaning the stable took longer."

"You're spoiling young Frankyr by doing that." Jorhan's voice was gruff, but not unfriendly as he shoveled some coal into the forge.

"It's the only way I can pay for stabling the horses."

"I know that, and so does Barrynt. You do a better job than Frankyr did." Jorhan laughed. "Now Frankyr has to do more at the factorage. Probably better for him that he's not getting away with so much."

"He may not think so."

"Most young fellows want the most coin for the least work."

"Not just young fellows."

"True enough. How long are you going to work at the healing house?"

"You don't need me here all the time now. When you do, I'll have put in enough time and know enough that I won't have to work there." Beltur wasn't certain he'd give it up. "Have you had any buyers approach you?"

"One or two of Barrynt's merchant friends might be interested closer to spring. You ready to do the bellows?"

Beltur nodded and moved into position.

"We're going to have to do the mirror in three pieces," said Jorhan.

"The mirror itself has to be thin. Trying to cast a thin center with a thick frame in one piece won't work. Making the frame in two parts will make fitting it all together much easier."

"Which part do you want to do first?"

"The center. That's going to be the hardest part. Even getting the mold heated properly could be a problem. I made two just in case."

Beltur began pumping the bellows to get the coal ready.

Half a glass later, Jorhan began to pour the bronze melt.

A sharp crack was followed by a hissing sound.

"Frig! Frig! Frig!" Jorhan righted the crucible to keep the rest of the melt from spilling through the break in the mold, and Beltur used the shovel, as well as his shields, to save what of the bronze he could from damaging the cooling grid.

While the second mold heated, Jorhan worked on forming a third.

The pour on the second mold went well enough, but, glasses later, it was clear that Beltur had implanted the order/chaos mesh with the nodes too close together, so close that the cupridium was effectively unworkable— and that meant Jorhan couldn't polish it to the finish necessary for a mirror.

The third mold was heating when Beltur heard a series of sharp knocks on the door. "Do you want me to get it?"

"Better you than me."

Beltur stepped back from the forge, then made his way to the door, which he opened. The man standing there looked vaguely familiar, but Beltur couldn't place him.

"Are you Jorhan, the smith?" asked the heavyset and red-bearded man.

"No, I'm Beltur, his assistant."

"I'm Councilor Zulkyn. I'm here to inspect the forge."

"Do come in, Councilor." Beltur stepped back and opened the door wider. "Jorhan is at the forge." He gestured, then shut the door behind the entering functionary and followed him, stopping several paces back.

"Councilor Zulkyn, Smith. This is the new forge?" The councilor's words were brusque, almost clipped.

Jorhan used the tongs to set the crucible with the melt components in it on the top of the forge wall closest to him. "The base was already here, Councilor. We added the upper lines of brick and leveled it off. We also added the coal box at the back."

Zulkyn peered at the forge, then appeared to study every line of bricks on each side. His hands went up and down the sides of the forge, as if to determine if there were gaps in the brickwork emitting hot air or gases. Then he studied the chimney above the forge.

After a good quint, he turned to Jorhan. "The forge is simple, but adequate. I will report on that to the Council. Occasionally, members of the Council will return to inspect the premises." He nodded and then turned, walking toward the door.

Beltur hurried to open it, nodding politely as Zulkyn departed. The councilor did not nod in return. Beltur closed the door and walked back to the forge.

"Not that friendly," observed Jorhan.

"He seemed fair enough. He didn't hint for coins, and he was quick and thorough."

"First quick thing with the Council since we got here," muttered the smith. "Time to get the mold ready."

By slightly after third glass, the thin casting was cooling, and Beltur had a better feeling about it—that it would be almost as hard as black iron but workable to the extent of being able to be polished to the necessary sheen.

Since there was nothing else for him to do, he hurried off through the intermittent fine snow that was still falling. With the growing chill in the air, and the hint of clearing sky to the north, the night was going to be very cold, possibly one of the coldest nights since he and Jessyla had come to Axalt.

He stopped by the stable, saddled Slowpoke, and rode the gelding down to the market square, where he found someone with a fowl for sale. Then he took Slowpoke around the square twice and back to the stable, where he quickly unsaddled and groomed him before setting out for the cot. He'd no more than set foot inside than Jessyla turned from the hearth, where she had laid a fire and flames were slowly rising over the wood.

"Where have you been?"

Beltur didn't have to strain to hear the edge to her voice. "We had trouble pouring the mirror sheet. Then the councilor came to inspect the forge. After that we finally cast the third sheet. I hurried off to the stables and gave Slowpoke a short ride—not a fast one because I didn't want him overheated. But I picked up some fowl at the square. After dealing with Slowpoke, I hurried home."

"You could have come home first, and we both could have ridden."

"We have three horses," replied Beltur. "Two have scarcely been ridden. I thought we could ride them after we eat."

"That will be a while. You haven't started anything, and I'm too tired to think about it."

"I can cut the chicken into strips, season it, and fry it, then make a gravy to put over it and the leftover potato slices." He paused. "You had a hard day, it sounds like."

"The City Patrol brought in three children with bad frostburn. Their father had beaten the mother so badly she might die and then left all four of them. The oldest is four. Then one of the women from the women's workhouse got in the way of a wagon, and it rolled over her foot. She said she didn't even feel it because her foot was already numb. After that—"

"Why don't we go into the kitchen. You can sit in front of the hearth there and have a little ale while I get supper ready, and you can tell me the rest of what happened while I do."

"An ale sounds good."

Beltur thought so, too, even as he wondered what he might face at the healing house on fourday.

LI

Fourday was another long day at the healing house for Beltur, and while he did have to deal with some wound chaos in Yuareff's arm, solidly encased in a plaster cast, the bones looked to be healing as well as a simple break would, possibly because Yuareff wasn't that far from being a youth, and young bones healed faster.

Fiveday was another day at the smithy, where the only casting was two small pieces for the mirror, and Beltur got back to the cot in time to ride Slowpoke as well as make several trips from the water house to partly refill the kitchen cistern. Sixday saw snow and only a few minor injuries appearing at the healing house.

On sevenday, Jorhan set Beltur to work on the foot treadle that powered the polishing wheel. Beltur worked the wheel, with breaks, for nearly four glasses straight, polishing and smoothing the mirror destined for Halhana.

Beltur watched as Jorhan finally slid the polished surface into the frame. Each corner of the frame featured a delicate rosebud, or rather half of one as seen from the side, as if the cupridium flower had been captured half in and half out of the silvery metal, with the yellowish sheen between gold and silver. A spray of rosebuds in relief decorated each end of the base from which the mirror supports curved upward.

Simple elegance. That was how Beltur saw the mirror, even before Jorhan was finished.

"When will you give it to Halhana?"

"I'll give it to Johlana at dinner on eightday. It's up to her to present it to Halhana."

"That's the best piece you've done—that I've seen, anyway."

"Most likely is," agreed the smith. "Had enough sense not to mess it up with too much in relief the way some silversmiths do, except unornamented metal in gold or silver is an invitation to scratches. They're too soft. Near impossible to scratch cupridium except with black iron. The reflected image is clear, too, and the mirror's better than anything a glasswright can produce. More durable. Won't shatter if it's dropped, either." Jorhan smiled happily. "Wouldn't have been able to do it without you."

"It took us both." After a moment, Beltur looked at the mirror again. All Jorhan had to do, it appeared, was to mount the mirror in the supports, using the two pin pieces they had cast on fiveday. "Maybe . . . if someone sees this . . . we might get an order."

"I don't think that's likely," replied Jorhan. "Only people to see it will be family."

"What about Eshult's family?"

"Not likely. They're all into silver, remember?"

"I think this makes silver look tawdry."

Jorhan grinned. "So do I. So does Johlana. Think that's why she wants it for Halhana. Wants to give her something that's special. So she can have a fine piece that's not from his family." Jorhan looked to the door. "You might as well go now. Nothing else you can do here."

"Then I'll see you on oneday."

"Tomorrow night," corrected Jorhan. "Johlana said you were coming to dinner."

Beltur hid a frown. Johlana had said nothing to him, and neither had Jessyla. "Then . . . tomorrow night and on oneday."

"Off with you. Don't want your consort saying I kept you when I didn't."

With a smile at Jorhan's mock-gruff tone, Beltur turned and headed toward the door.

He reached the cot by third glass, and that gave him time to start a fire and then shovel away the snow that had fallen on the walks intermittently throughout the day before he began to make a much milder form of burhka than favored by most Gallosians, but one more suited to his taste and, he hoped, to Jessyla's.

When she arrived, the burhka was cooking in the covered pot suspended over the kitchen side of the hearth fire, but Beltur met Jessyla in the front room.

"You got home earlier today."

"Jorhan didn't need me any later. All he has left is the finish work on the mirror. He said he hoped to present it to Johlana tomorrow." Beltur kept his face in a pleasant expression.

"Good! I'd like to see her expression."

"Are we going to be there? I wasn't aware—"

"Beltur! I told you last night."

"You did?"

"Your mind . . . and your hands were occupied elsewhere."

Beltur flushed. "I . . . didn't remember."

She laughed. "I don't think you heard a word."

"That's appearing very likely," he admitted sheepishly. "What else did I miss?"

"Only that I found a satchel filled with scores of golds in the snow yesterday afternoon."

"You didn't."

"No . . . I didn't, but I don't think you would have heard that, either."

She's probably right. "Let me get you a mug of ale, and after you have some, while we sit here in the front room, we'll have time to work on your shields. Supper won't be ready for a while."

"What are we having? It smells familiar, but not quite."

"It's a surprise."

"Mutton?"

"That's one ingredient."

"Anything hot would be good." She settled onto the bench facing the hearth.

Beltur returned shortly with two mugs of ale, handed her one, and sat down beside her. "How was your day?"

Jessyla didn't answer immediately, instead taking a swallow of the pale ale. Finally, she said, "We had a woman from the poorhouse. She came in bleeding. We couldn't save her."

"Just bleeding?"

"The warder said she had a miscarriage. Herrara didn't think so. There were bruises . . . and a lot more . . . cuts." Jessyla shuddered. "It was awful. I managed a small shield to stop the worst of the bleeding, but that wasn't enough, and there was chaos everywhere. The warder woman wasn't at all concerned."

"Bad blood between the two."

"Or worse." Jessyla shuddered again. "I'd never want to be in the poorhouse or a workhouse. Never!" She took another swallow.

"I think that's one reason why Herrara tried to save Yuareff's arm, even though the bones broke through the skin."

"She wouldn't have done it that way if she hadn't known you could remove wound chaos. She told me that."

"How is he doing?"

"There's some fuzziness, beginning chaos, between the bones and the skin. You'll have to get rid of that. I can sense it, but I can't focus free order and move it where it needs to be the way you can."

"You probably could."

"I don't want to try it the first time without you there." She paused. "I know you did, with that boy in Elparta, but he would have died if you hadn't. Yuareff's chaos is barely there. I would have tried if you weren't around."

What Jessyla said made sense, but it also worried Beltur. Was she being too cautious? Or had he been too rash? *Probably not then . . . but . . .* Then again, for whatever reason, so much of what he'd tried had been when there hadn't been good choices.

After a time, he said, "It's time to work on your shields some more. You still need more tiny bits of chaos at the nodes in your shield."

Jessyla winced. "Chaos feels . . . ugly."

"It's just chaos. It's disorderly, but not ugly."

"Disorderly *is* ugly."

"Try to think of it as disorderly," said Beltur.

"Why?"

"Because, if you think of it as ugly, you'll be repelled, and you won't use it as effectively. Think of it as disorderly, and that you're making it more orderly by surrounding it with order. Which you are."

"Sometimes . . ." Jessyla shook her head.

"Please try it that way."

Jessyla set her mug on the floor.

Lines in her forehead told Beltur that she was concentrating, and he immediately sensed the web-like pattern. He nodded. "That's it! Can you sense how much stronger it is that way?"

"Not really."

"It is. Take my word for it."

"Don't I always?" A mischievous smile appeared.

"Mostly." Beltur picked up a billet of wood from the hearth firebox. "I'm going to pound on your shield. Hold it for as long as you can."

"That might not be long."

His first blow was moderate. The shield held. His second blow was harder, and the third was hard enough that the shock through the wood forced him to drop the wood. "Very good."

"Now what?"

"Keep holding it. As long as you can. In time, you'll need to carry shields all the time."

"Like you? I don't know . . ."

"You can carry them close to your skin most of the time. Besides, carrying shields all the time makes you a stronger mage."

"Am I a mage yet?"

"You can't do everything a full mage can do, but that will come. I started you with shieldwork because without protection none of the rest matters." *Especially for a woman.* "That's particularly important because you're consorted to me."

"You're sounding like every mage in Candar is after you."

"Not every mage. Just all those in Gallos and Elparta, except for Meldryn and Lhadoraak."

"But we're in Axalt."

"I still think it's necessary. If I'm wrong, your having strong shields can't possibly hurt. Now I'm going to probe your shield with order." He focused an order probe and jabbed.

"That hurts more than the wood did."

"Both order and chaos will."

The two continued the exercises for almost a quint before Beltur said, noticing the sheen of perspiration on Jessyla's face, "That's enough. I think we're both ready for supper."

As he headed for the kitchen, mug in hand, he just hoped the burhka was ready for them.

Before long he had dished out two portions into the mismatched earthenware bowls, and they sat down with their mugs at the kitchen table. Beltur watched as Jessyla took a mouthful.

"This is almost like burhka, except it's not as spicy hot."

"It *is* burhka. I didn't see why it couldn't be spicy without burning out the inside of my mouth and throat."

Jessyla took another mouthful. "It's good. I'm not sure I'd call it burhka."

"You mean it's not burhka unless it's so spicy hot that you can't taste anything but the peppers?"

"*I* wouldn't say that . . ."

"But some people would. Like your aunt. Is that what you're saying?"

"She might. I don't care. I like it either way. You can fix it this way any time."

And you'll fix it your way. Beltur smiled ruefully. At least she liked it.

LII

As often occurred in Axalt after a light snowfall, eightday dawned bright, clear, and bitterly cold.

"I'm really glad I don't have to go out," said Jessyla, as Beltur prepared to leave to deal with the horses and stable.

"You could always come to the stable . . ." Beltur grinned. "You will have to refill the woodbox."

Jessyla shuddered. "Thank you for filling the cistern. I still don't see how you managed by yourself."

"I told you. I put a containment over the top of the buckets. I should have thought about that earlier. That way I didn't have to worry about spilling the water."

"You're still learning. You're not that old for a mage, and you can do things others can't. That means you can't learn from them."

"It also means I can't learn from their mistakes, only from my own." He paused, thinking. "Maybe that's why some of the great mages made great mistakes."

"That may be, but you'd better get going, or you'll be late."

"And Herrara will give me a long-suffering expression."

Jessyla just looked pointedly at the door.

"I'm going. I'm going." He finished pulling on his coat and wrapped his face and ears in the heavy scarf, then opened the door, wincing at the blast of frigid air that swept into the cot, before plunging forward.

Cleaning the stables and feeding the horses went quickly, and he even had a little time with Slowpoke, just talking to the big gelding, before heading off to the healing house.

Once Beltur was there, even before telling Herrara he had arrived, he went to find Yuareff, who was sitting on his bed, staring at nothing.

"You're here early, ser mage."

"Not early. You're just the first person I'm seeing. I need to look at that arm."

"You can't see much . . . Oh, you mean in the way only you mages can see?"

Beltur nodded.

"It feels fine. Well . . . not fine. It hurts, but a little less each day."

Beltur concentrated on Yuareff's forearm, nodding as he sensed the three small points of wound chaos—small, but ugly yellowish red. It took several long moments to remove all three.

Yuareff winced. "What did you do? It felt like three hot needles inside my arm."

"There was some wound chaos there. I took care of it."

"I never heard of that, except with you."

"Not many mages can heal, and even fewer healers can learn magery. Also, healing pays much less than magery, not that magery pays all that well for most of us."

"You could work every day."

"I do. I work as a smith's assistant on the days I'm not here."

Yuareff frowned. "You work every day of the eightday? As a smith's striker? And you are a powerful mage? I cannot say I understand. A mage should earn more than a crafter."

"A wise man once told me that people who only have their skills to sell are never wealthy. It is only those who control the work of others and the sale of many goods who have great piles of golds." That wasn't quite what Meldryn had said, but it was close, Beltur thought. "We're not starving, and we have a small cot in which to live, and we're young."

"Then you will be wealthy someday."

"I have my doubts about that." Beltur laughed softly. "Your arm is doing better. If I can keep the chaos at bay for an eightday, it should heal without problems." He paused. "It won't be healed by then. It just should heal normally after that. It will take at least several eightdays more once the chaos is gone." *At least that long*. He nodded. "I need to see to the others."

From Yuareff's room he went to Herrara's study.

The healer looked up at him. "Elisa said you've already been to see Yuareff."

"I worried about wound chaos. Jessyla thought she sensed the beginning of more yesterday. It was definitely there today."

"He's a very fortunate young man."

"He had a good healer set his bones," said Beltur. "I couldn't have done it nearly as well. Jessyla might have come closer."

"But neither of us could remove that wound chaos from within him."

"I have skills you don't. You have skills I don't."

Herrara smiled, even as she shook her head. "You can learn what I know. Few mages can do what you can."

"I'm sure there must be others."

"Oh . . . do you know of any? Have you even heard of any?"

"No, but I'm young and have not been many places."

Herrara offered a sad smile. "I'm older, and much of the world passes through Axalt, and I've never heard of a mage like you. You may live in Axalt for years, even for the rest of your life, but you do not belong here. You and your consort are bigger than Axalt. Axalt is a small land. It could not remain as it is without the mountains and the winter. They protect it. As does the fact that we have neither gold nor silver or anything of value except the skills of our people."

"Axalt is prosperous and well-ordered. Why would we wish to leave?"

"You may not. That is your choice."

"But?" asked Beltur. "There's something you're not saying."

"Well-ordered is also confining." Her smile vanished. "You'd best look over the others, especially Wurfael."

Beltur could tell that Herrara wasn't about to say more. "I'll take care of that right now."

He was still thinking about Axalt being too small when he walked into Poldaark's chamber. Wurfael could wait, if only for a bit. "Good morning. You look like you feel better."

"I do. A little. The shoulder still hurts when I move it." Poldaark smiled. "I have somewhere to go. It's not much, but it's a warm place to sleep and two meals a day. Healer Herrara found it for me. I have to do all the chores for an old widow who has trouble getting around. I'll only get a copper a day, but she says that she'd rather pay me than the Council."

Beltur hadn't thought about that, but he recalled that there was a fee charged for not clearing snow and probably for other things as well. "That sounds better than where you were."

Poldaark nodded. "I start tomorrow."

"I'm very glad for you." Poldaark wasn't the brightest of young men, but he was good-hearted—that Beltur could tell—and he was willing to work, and helping a widow seemed far better than where he'd been.

"If it hadn't been for all you healers, I don't know what I'd have done."

"We did what we could." *Especially Herrara.*

After leaving Poldaark, Beltur went downstairs to check on Wurfael. The young timberman had a long face. Beltur ignored the sad expression. "Good morning."

"What's good about it?"

"You're awake and alive. There's no more chaos in your leg. Is the hurting less?"

"Unless something hits it."

"It's likely to be sensitive for a time."

"For the rest of my life, short as it's going to be."

"You don't know that. More than a few men have lost a limb and gone on to live long lives. It happens every time there's a war or an invasion."

"Not in Axalt. We don't have wars or the like."

"Timbering is a form of war. You're cutting down trees for your advantage. In war, the victor cuts down the troopers of the loser to gain an advantage."

"How would you know that, Mage?"

"Because I've been a battle mage."

Wurfael's mouth opened. "But you're a healer."

"I've healed men. I've killed many more than that." *And that's an understatement.*

"Begging your pardon . . . but . . . ?"

"I was with the Elpartan forces that defeated the Gallosians." Beltur looked coolly at Wurfael. "I've seen men who've lost much more than you. The man who saved my life died when I couldn't do enough to save him."

"You must be older . . ."

"Than I look?" Beltur shook his head. "Things started happening when I was young. They didn't stop. Now . . . start thinking about what you can do, not what you can't." He managed what he hoped was an encouraging smile before he turned.

Once out in the corridor, Beltur wasn't quite certain why he'd said as much as he had to Wurfael, except somehow . . . Wurfael seemed to be obsessed with what he couldn't do. *But then, how would you feel if you lost the ability to be a mage? What else could you do?*

He felt like shaking his head. Had he been too hard on the former timberman? Wurfael didn't have much choice except to deal with what he faced. *Really . . . is it different for any of us?* Yet another disturbing thought followed. *But you have advantages and abilities he doesn't.*

The remainder of the day was like any other day—a beggar woman with frostburned fingers; a serving maid with bruises and a dislocated shoulder, something Beltur hadn't seen before, which was why he watched Herrara intently as she relocated the shoulder; another youth with a broken arm. For all that, Beltur still worried about what he'd said to Wurfael.

Beltur left the healing house right at fourth glass and hurried home, where he washed up and changed into his better blacks, thinking that he really needed to wash his others. *That will have to wait until tomorrow.* He'd put that off because the only place where he could hang them was in the kitchen and it took more than a day for them to dry. At least he had several shirts.

At two quints past four, they set out for Barrynt's.

"What did you do today?" he asked Jessyla as they walked westward.

"I went to the market square. They had some eggs, and even some dried beef, and a scrawny fowl. I made dumplings so that we could have fowl and dumplings for the next few days and you wouldn't have to fix as much."

When they reached the merchant's house, Frankyr greeted them at the side door. "Everyone's in the family parlor. Except Halhana. She never comes on eightday anymore."

"How have you found working in the factorage?" asked Beltur as he took off his coat and hung it on a wall peg.

"Different, ser. I've had to learn more, but it's not as physical as dealing with the horses."

"The factorage is where your future is," said Beltur, "not the stables."

"Father's made that clear. So has Ryntaar." Frankyr laughed softly and humorously.

The first thing Beltur noticed as he stepped into the parlor was the cupridium mirror, standing on the larger side table.

"Isn't it just gorgeous?" asked Johlana, looking to Jessyla. "You've already seen it," she added to Beltur before turning back to Jessyla. "It will make a stunning addition to her house."

"When will you give it to her?" asked Jessyla.

"In a few days."

"It will be good for her to have some craftsmanship in something other than silver," said Barrynt. "And in a metal even more valuable."

"Uncle Jorhan's crafting is better than that silver stuff she has," said Ryntaar. "Old Emlyn thinks things are good if they're made of silver or gold, no matter what they look like."

"You may be right, Ryntaar," said Johlana, "but that's an opinion best kept to yourself. Those words could only cause trouble for Halhana. I don't think you'd want that."

"None of us do, but it's true."

"Enough said," declared Johlana. "Please see to whatever Beltur and Jessyla want."

Ryntaar nodded.

"The hot spiced wine, please," said Jessyla.

"Pale ale, thank you," added Beltur, settling on the vacant settee beside Jessyla.

Whatever was cooking in the kitchen smelled wonderful, and Beltur felt it might be a pork roast. His mouth watered at the thought as he took the beaker from Ryntaar, just glad to be in a warm parlor and not having to worry about fixing dinner, especially since the food was bound to be better than his efforts.

Even so, his thoughts drifted back to Wurfael.

LIII

When Beltur reached the smithy on oneday, he found Jorhan busy at his workbench, working on a small mold, and there was only a modest fire in the forge, more to warm the smithy than anything, Beltur suspected.

"What's that?"

"Something new," replied the smith. "After you two left the house yesterday, I talked some with Barrynt. He thought we should try casting a few smaller pieces."

"That would take less bronze, but what pieces did he think might sell? We've already made belt knives and daggers, even small platters and mirrors."

"Smaller than that. What he called bud vases, with some ornate relief work. He also suggested I meet with artists who paint miniature portraits and see if they'd be interested in cupridium stands or frames."

"Would they pay enough?"

Jorhan shrugged. "No one's buying now. Making a bud vase or stand for a miniature won't take that much copper and tin. We'd need an example of each to see who's interested. I thought we'd start with the little vase. Likely take as much work on the mold as something three times as big. I've been at it since sixth glass."

"Can I do anything?"

"Think about what might go on a miniature frame besides rosebuds . . . and shovel more coal in the forge. It's cold in here."

Shoveling the coal was easier than coming up with a design, since Beltur had never been that good at drawing and his penmanship was barely readable, hard as he had tried. His uncle had told him that it was a good thing he was a mage, because he never would have succeeded as a scrivener. All that brought Beltur's thoughts back to Wurfael. He couldn't help feeling that he'd been too hard on the timberman. *You'd be in a very hard place if you weren't a mage.*

He was still thinking about that when Jorhan cleared his throat.

"What thoughts do you have for the frame?"

"Grapevines . . . ivy." Beltur knew he wasn't being that creative.

"Don't know about vines. Some folks might not take that well. The ivy'd be easier."

"What about just a pattern, interlocking diamonds or something?"

"That might be better. Meantime, we need to work on the melt. It won't take that long to heat the mold."

Beltur moved to the bellows and began to pump.

Later, after Jorhan poured the melt, and Beltur set the order/chaos pattern, the smith turned. "Not much else for you to do." Jorhan gestured. "No sense in you wasting time here."

Beltur nodded, donned his coat, then walked back to the stable, where he saddled one of the other mounts and rode her, then came back and rode Slowpoke. Even after riding and grooming them, he was back at the cot before third glass, where he began to prepare supper, a sort of fowl and root vegetable pie. After he put the pie in the oven, he turned to his neglected laundry.

Jessyla arrived at a quint past fourth glass. "Whatever you're cooking smells good."

"It's a sort of fowl pie. It's going to be a while."

"I need to wash up."

"Be careful in the kitchen. I've got laundry hanging there and a set of greens I did also."

"Thank you. I could have done that."

"There may be a time when I'll need my blacks done."

Beltur got a smile before Jessyla headed to the washroom. He went back into the kitchen, where he checked on the pie and how his bread dough was rising. Then he returned to the front room, where he tried to visualize possible patterns for a miniature frame.

"What are you thinking?" asked Jessyla when she rejoined him.

"Patterns to put around the end of a cupridium miniature frame."

"A miniature frame?"

"One that would hold a miniature painting. The kind artists paint for merchants."

Before Jessyla could say more, there was a series of raps on the door.

"I can't think who that might be," said Beltur.

"Rohan . . . or Frankyr or Ryntaar bringing something from Johlana," suggested Jessyla.

Beltur frowned as he turned and walked toward the door. Was he sensing the blackness of order outside? Almost instinctively, he strengthened his shields before easing the door open. His mouth opened as he saw Lhadoraak standing there.

"What . . . how . . . ?"

"It's a very long story . . ."

Behind Lhadoraak stood Tulya . . . and Taelya.

"Is this the place?" shouted the teamster of the wagon in the street.

Beltur still didn't know what to say. He did know that the three being there didn't signify anything particularly good. Finally, he managed to say, "I take it that you left Elparta in a hurry. You'd better come in with whatever you have. We'll sort it all out as we can." He turned to Jessyla. "We have company."

"Lhadoraak! Tulya! Don't stand out there in the cold. Beltur, help them with their things."

In a fraction of a quint, the three travelers were standing in the front room, three large bags stacked under the bench beside the door and their coats hanging on the wall pegs, piled partly on top of each other.

"We didn't know where else to go . . ." began Lhadoraak.

"We couldn't go anyplace else," added Tulya tersely. "The river's frozen over, and we had only an eightday before we had to leave."

"The Council exiled you all?"

"No," snapped Tulya. "They exiled Taelya. What else were we supposed to do? After you and Jessyla left, and then Cohndar and Waensyn vanished, Caradyn took over as senior mage, and the Council decided that, after their experience with you, no whites were to be permitted in Elparta. Somehow, they found out about Taelya . . ."

"And here we are," concluded Lhadoraak.

All that raised questions Beltur wasn't certain he even wanted to entertain, but knew he would have to face sooner or later. "How did you get here? How did you know where we live?"

"We came with a trader from Hydlen. He wanted a mage who could shield him from brigands," said Lhadoraak.

"We still had to pay him," added Tulya. "Besides Lhadoraak's stopping the brigands."

Lhadoraak smiled. "I just asked at the chandlery. The chandler knew who you were and where to find you. You've been there a great deal, I understand."

"It takes a lot to set up even a small place like this," Beltur said, still stunned at the appearance of the three. His eyes and senses went to Taelya. He almost nodded. The white aura was all too evident, and he had the feeling she hadn't been practicing shielding herself, especially keeping her natural order and chaos separate.

Taelya did not meet his eyes.

"You can stay with us," declared Jessyla. "We don't have much space, but we'll work it out. We'll have to share a bit with supper tonight, and it likely won't be ready for another glass. We didn't plan on company, but we do have plenty of ale." She looked directly at Beltur.

He immediately headed to the kitchen, where he poured two mugs of ale and carried them back to Lhadoraak and Tulya, seated with Taelya on the bench facing the hearth. "We don't have much else right now . . . except water."

"Taelya can have a third of a mug." Tulya looked to her daughter. "That's all. If you're really thirsty you can also have water."

"We do have plenty of water," said Jessyla. "Beltur bought a kitchen cistern."

Beltur slipped off to the kitchen and then returned with a third of a mug of ale, which he handed to Taelya. "Here you are."

"Thank you, ser." The girl took it, her eyes dropping quickly from Beltur.

Jessyla added more wood to the hearth, then said, "You three just sit here and warm up while Beltur and I make some additions to supper."

"Can't I help?" asked Tulya.

"Not right now," replied Jessyla.

"Just get warm," added Beltur.

Once he and Jessyla were in the kitchen, she murmured, "It must have been awful for them. They left with almost nothing."

Beltur decided not to point out that neither he nor Jessyla had been able to bring much. *Except you had someone who invited you, and you had golds.*

"It's hard to believe that Caradyn and the Council could be so cruel. Taelya's no danger to anyone."

"Neither were you . . . until they forced you to act in self-defense. Enough of that now. What else can we fix?"

"Skillet bread is easy and doesn't take that long. There are some fowl thighs and wings that I can turn into a sort of hash with the two potatoes we have left."

While the three travelers rested and warmed themselves in the front room, Beltur threw together the skillet bread and the makeshift chicken hash, then fried them both up, while Jessyla removed the drying laundry to the bedchamber before setting up the small table for five, and then returning to the front room to check on their company.

Before all that long, all five were seated in the kitchen, eating.

"This is so thoughtful of you," declared Tulya.

"It's what friends do for friends," declared Jessyla. "You can stay here until we can find a place where you can settle in, unless you just want to rest until you head for someplace else." She paused. "I wrote Mother. Do you know if she got my letter?"

"Meldryn said she'd gotten a letter from you and that you were safe and working as a healer. That's all he told us."

Beltur could sense Jessyla's relief. "That's good. Very good." He looked at his consort. "You don't have to worry about her not knowing."

"I still worry." Jessyla looked to Lhadoraak. "I'm sorry. I interrupted you. I just wanted to know about Mother. You didn't say what you were going to do."

"We really don't know," admitted Lhadoraak. "We had to leave so quickly. They only gave us an eightday."

"That's all?" asked Jessyla, her voice rising.

"That was all," replied Lhadoraak. "There was a Council decree."

"What about your house, all your things . . . ?" asked Beltur.

"We were only renting the house. We never had enough golds . . ."

"To buy one," finished Tulya.

"I liked that house," murmured Taelya.

"All our furnishings are either with Meldryn or in a storeroom owned by a relative of Mharkyn," added the blond mage. "We told Meldryn to sell what's in the storeroom as he can, when he can."

"How is he doing?" asked Beltur.

"He says the bakery is doing as well as it ever has in winter, and, so far, he hasn't had to deal any more with the Council or the Mages' Council."

"That sounds like he's worried."

"This bread is crumbly," said Taelya.

"Just eat the crumbs," said Tulya quietly.

"Anyone who's not in solidly with Caradyn should worry," said Lhadoraak. "Caradyn's claiming that you killed Cohndar and Waensyn."

"If he did," injected Jessyla, "it's only what they deserved. Cohndar was trying to get the Council to kill Beltur so Waensyn could consort me. As if I'd ever have consorted that sleazy, greasy, slimy, little excuse for a mage."

"He is that," said Tulya dryly. "Or was."

"Did you have anything to do with it?" asked Lhadoraak.

Beltur saw no point in dissembling. Both Lhadoraak and Tulya would be able to tell unless he totally shielded himself, and that would convey the same message in a different and even less favorable way. "They sent away the Council guard and attacked me in Jorhan's smithy. Jorhan killed Cohndar, and I took care of Waensyn."

"How could Jorhan . . . ?"

"I stripped Cohndar's shields, but I couldn't do more while I was struggling with Waensyn. Cohndar forgot about Jorhan, and Jorhan took a smithing hammer to Cohndar's skull. Once Cohndar was out of the way, I put a total confinement around Waensyn."

Lhadoraak winced.

"What else could he have done?" asked Tulya.

Taelya's eyes widened.

"You're not to talk of this except to anyone here," said Tulya. "Ever. Is that clear? Very clear?"

"Yes, Mother."

"How did all of them get that way?" Lhadoraak shook his head.

"They were always that way," declared Tulya. "You just didn't want to see it. Beltur not only saved you, he saved Elparta. Yet they immediately tried to destroy his smithing with Jorhan, and then him."

"And take away the woman who loves him," added Jessyla.

"Beltur was never a threat to them," protested Lhadoraak. "It doesn't make sense."

"Ambition and hunger for power can make men very stupid," said Beltur. "I saw that in Gallos. Uncle wasn't a danger to the Prefect or anyone, but the Prefect had him killed, and that sent me to Elparta."

"And sending you to Elparta doomed his invasion," finished Jessyla.

"Well . . . I don't think the blacks of Elparta or the Council will attack Axalt over me," said Beltur. "What would be the point? The blacks wanted me gone, and I'm gone. Waensyn wanted Jessyla, and he's gone. Caradyn wanted power and control, and he's got it."

"Except for one thing," said Lhadoraak slowly. "Caradyn knows you're more powerful than he is, and you're in Axalt, and Axalt's not that far from Elparta."

"How does he even know where I am?"

"We knew. There's also that letter from Jessyla. Sooner or later, he'll find out."

"He won't go to war over Beltur," said Jessyla.

"Most likely not," agreed Lhadoraak. "But he'll try to find some way to force you from Axalt so that you're even farther away."

"I don't doubt his motives, but how could he do that? Axalt isn't about to throw me out because the traders or some black mages in Spidlar demand it."

"That's true enough," replied Lhadoraak, "but he'll find a way if he can."

"Enough of that," said Tulya. "That's something we can't do anything about. This fowl pie is good."

"Not as good as Meldryn's, but far better than what I cooked before I learned from him."

"I like the mashed-up fowl," added Taelya.

"Good," replied Tulya. "Eat as much as you like."

"Did you have any trouble with the guards at the border wall?" asked Beltur.

"Some. They wanted to know why a black mage and his family were coming to Axalt in the dead of winter. I told them my family's lives were in danger because the Council thought we were associated with a black mage who'd fled Elparta." Lhadoraak shook his head. "I didn't know what else to say, and I didn't want to mention Taelya or lie outright, because I didn't know how Axalt and the Relynists feel about whites."

"That was probably for the best," said Beltur. "I don't know, either. It hasn't come up. For now, I wouldn't mention it."

"It was for the best," added Tulya. "One of the guards remembered you. He said it was sad when blacks chased their own out and that it reminded him of the stories about Relyn."

Beltur couldn't help but think about Jorhan's forebear, and an amused smile crossed his face. "There's a mention of Jorhan's ancestor in *The Wisdom of Relyn*—that's a book about Relyn . . ." Beltur went on to briefly tell the story, ending with, "And it appears that no one in Axalt even knew about it, but that's because Johlana didn't even know."

"Johlana?"

Beltur realized that neither he nor Jessyla had even mentioned the couple that had done so much for them. "Johlana is Jorhan's sister. She's consorted to Barrynt, and he's the one who said we were welcome in Axalt. They actually gave us all of the furnishings."

"You've managed so well in such a short time," declared Tulya.

"That's all due to them. The furniture came from their storeroom," said Jessyla. "And all of the crockery and linens. It doesn't all match, but it's good, and we'd have almost nothing without them. Barrynt even found this cot. We're renting it, but things will get better in the spring. Beltur and I are both working at the healing house, and we'll get paid more then."

"Beltur, too?" asked Tulya. "I thought he was working with a smith."

"He's doing both," replied Jessyla. "He's always had some healing abilities. He was examined by the head healer. She found that he was qualified as a healer."

Lhadoraak and Tulya exchanged glances.

"You really are a healer, too?" asked Taelya.

"Yes, he is," replied Jessyla. "After we finish eating, we'll work out things for you to sleep in the front room. We do have some extra blankets, and there's the bench pad . . ."

"We do have some blankets," Tulya said. "Are you sure . . . ?"

"You're not going out in the cold," declared Jessyla.

And you're going to need every silver you have. Beltur wasn't about to say that, although he doubted that the couple had all that many.

"There's no way we can thank you," said Lhadoraak.

"You don't have to," replied Beltur.

Later, after everyone was settled, and Beltur and Jessyla lay side by side in their bed, she turned to him, her voice low. "How could the Council have been so cruel? How could they? Taelya's barely seven."

"But that may be part of it. She's incredibly strong for a mage that young, and the blacks in Spidlar have this unreasoning fear of whites."

"But she's Spidlarian, and her parents are, too. I don't understand people sometimes."

"Neither do I." Except that wasn't quite true. Beltur could see exactly what people did and how they justified it; he just didn't understand how they could deceive themselves so much.

But haven't you done the same?

He stiffened slightly at that thought.

LIV

The only ingredients Beltur and Jessyla had sufficient to feed five people for breakfast turned out to be an oat porridge and a few pieces of egg toast with a drizzling of not quite bitter berry syrup.

Before Beltur left for the stable and the healing house, he slipped Jessyla four silvers, with the words, "Get what you can at the market square and the chandlery . . . or anywhere else."

"I'll do what I can," she mouthed back.

Beltur could also see that they'd need more ale before all that long if Lhadoraak and Tulya remained with them.

As he walked toward Barrynt's stable, he couldn't help wondering how long he and Jessyla could help Lhadoraak. *You have enough to support two families for almost a year . . . if you're very, very, careful.* But that was if nothing went wrong. *And things always go wrong at the worst times.*

Once at the stable, he found himself murmuring to Slowpoke as he curried the big gelding. ". . . how did we get into this . . . never really wanted to leave Fenard . . . just tried to do the best I could . . ." Abruptly, he shook his head. What he was saying was what his uncle would have called self-pity. He smiled sardonically, recalling just what Kaerylt had said more than once.

"You want to have a pity party, boy, you'll be the only one there. Nobody cares. There's no sense wasting words on self-pity. No sense at all."

For some reason, remembering those words made him feel better, and he stroked the gelding's neck. "We'll work it out."

Slowpoke whuffed. Beltur would have liked to have thought the gelding agreed, but he just might have wanted more hay, which Beltur gave him.

When Beltur reached the healing house, Herrara hurried him into the welcoming room, where he immediately had to deal with a boy with bruises and a broken arm. He just nodded at the woman's story, knowing that it was largely a fabrication to cover up abuse. At least, that was Beltur's suspicion, since the woman was also bruised, although her injuries weren't visible, but they were recent enough that Beltur could sense the residual chaos.

Yuareff's arm had almost no residual wound chaos, and he was comparatively cheerful, but Beltur was still worrying when he entered Wurfael's ground-floor chamber.

"Good morning."

Wurfael looked up from where he was propped up in the bed, but did not speak.

"I'd like to look at your leg."

"What's left of it. I'm not stopping you, Mage."

Beltur managed not to sigh. He'd been afraid of Wurfael's reaction. Rather than respond, he let his senses range over the leg and the stump. Finally, he said, "Your leg's healing well."

"Good for it."

"Does it hurt?"

"Some. Not as much."

Beltur noticed the wooden crutches in the corner. "How are you coming with those?"

"I can get around here. They'll be useless outside."

"Not on cleared walks and streets, I wouldn't think. Besides, they're only for a while. Once you get a peg leg, you ought to be able to get around with a cane."

"So everyone can look at the cripple?"

"You're still a strong man, Wurfael, and you've got good hands. You could be good at a lot of things. You know woods. What about working with them?"

"I don't know them like that." The young man's voice was sullen.

"You likely know them better than you think." Beltur paused, then added, "It can't hurt to think about who you know and what you know that could prove useful." He reached out and touched Wurfael's shoulder, offering the slightest bit of free order with a little warmth behind it.

The young timberman looked up, surprised.

"I think you can do it," said Beltur with a smile, before turning and leaving the room.

The rest of the day at the healing house was more routine, changing dressings, making up dressings, and dealing with small wounds and ailments, usually of poorer folk who lacked basic supplies.

Beltur left a quint early, with Herrara's permission, and hurried back to the cot. From there, he and Lhadoraak walked swiftly to Barrynt's factorage.

As they neared the factorage, a two-story structure some fifteen yards wide, and more than twenty deep, Beltur realized that he'd never actually been inside. Every time he'd come, he'd met Barrynt at the doorway or just outside. In fact, he'd never actually read the signboard, which proclaimed MOUNTAIN FACTORAGE. Beltur thought that slightly odd, because most signboards had the name of the town or city or the owner, or, in the case of inns or public houses, a greater indication of what goods or services were available.

Ryntaar appeared as they stepped inside. "Mage . . ." He frowned slightly as he took in Lhadoraak's black coat and trousers. "Or mages?"

"Lhadoraak's also a black mage from Elparta. Is your father available?"

"He's in back, ser."

"Thank you."

Beltur did indeed find Barrynt standing beside a tall open cabinet containing bolts of cloth, each in its own separate section. Several bolts were of black wool.

The merchant looked preoccupied as he studied the cabinet, and a faint haze of chaos swirled around him. Abruptly, he looked up, startled. "Beltur . . . what can I do for you?"

"You've done more than enough for me. This is Lhadoraak. He's another black mage from Elparta. He and his consort and their daughter arrived late yesterday. They're staying with us until they can find a place . . . and until Lhadoraak can find some sort of work."

"I see. I think I do, anyway." Barrynt frowned, then addressed Lhadoraak. "Welcome to Axalt, although I'm not quite sure I understand why you'd leave Elparta in winter and come to a place where you know almost no one." Barrynt's voice was mild, slightly concerned.

"The Council insisted that we leave, because they decided that I was not the kind of mage they wanted in Elparta. They insisted that my family accompany me."

"That doesn't tell me why."

"The Council seems to believe that anyone close to Beltur and Jorhan may be tainted. Beltur saved my life and that of my daughter. The Council believes those acts tainted us both."

Beltur could sense Lhadoraak's overtly concealed unease, but also admired his friend's ability to present the truth in a fashion only slightly deceptive.

Barrynt turned to Beltur. "I don't understand this. Can you make it clearer?"

For a moment, Beltur hesitated, but he could only see that any evasion was just going to make Lhadoraak's position worse. "I can. I didn't wish to upset you unduly, but Jorhan's and my escape from Elparta wasn't without cost. Two mages tried to kill us as we were leaving the smithy. In the struggle, Jorhan killed one with a hammer, and I killed the other with magery. We hid their bodies and left as quickly as we could. They were trying to kill us for the reasons I told you earlier. I suspect that, because I'd spent quite a bit of time in the eightdays before we left in healing Taelya—that's Lhadoraak's daughter—when the Mages' Council could not find the missing mages, they believed Lhadoraak had something to do with that. He knew nothing of that, but suspicion clearly fell on him."

Barrynt frowned, if but slightly, then addressed Lhadoraak. "Did you know of this?"

"No, ser. That is, not until Beltur told me last night. Meldryn had only told me that Beltur had left Elparta one step ahead of Cohndar and Waensyn. Those were the two mages who tried to kill him and Jorhan." Lhadoraak paused. "I did know that both Cohndar and Waensyn had schemed to stop Jorhan and Beltur from forging cupridium."

"When mages get involved in trading . . ." Barrynt shook his head. "A mage and a smith find a way to make something and profit from it, and everyone wants to take advantage of it." He smiled sadly. "I know Beltur can make a living here. He's already doing it. What did you do in Elparta?"

"I inspected boats and wagons to make certain goods were not hidden from the tariff inspectors."

"Were you good at it?"

"I'd like to think so. I found things the inspectors could never have discovered."

"Hmmm. I don't know that our council has considered that. We only have a few mages here in Axalt. I might be able to talk to Naerkaal about that. You might be able to help the border guards. What else can you do?"

"My grandsire was a cabinetmaker. I'm still skilled enough to assist in such a shop. I can tell if there are faults in the wood before it's cut."

Beltur hadn't known that. *But you never asked.*

"Do you have any tools?"

Lhadoraak shook his head. "The tools all went to my uncle."

"Tools can be replaced. Skills have to be learned." The merchant pursed his lips. "You do know, Beltur—"

"Ser . . . you have been incredibly welcoming and generous to us. All I'm asking is for any suggestions you may have as to whom Lhadoraak might talk to and how best to approach them. I've not been here long enough to know many people except for you and your family, those at the healing house, and a few others."

Barrynt smiled, if faintly. "That's more than fair. So is your hosting of your friend and his family. I'd like a day or so to think over who might be best for you, Lhadoraak, to contact."

"I greatly appreciate that, ser." Lhadoraak inclined his head. "I also appreciate your taking the time to hear me out."

"If a man doesn't hear things out, he's likely to make mistakes he'll regret. I've already too many regrets to add to them."

While that statement surprised Beltur, he wasn't about to ask. "I do thank you. We won't take any more of your time. You and Johlana have been·more than helpful in so many ways."

"You were helpful to her and to Jorhan. Fair's fair."

Beltur inclined his head, then stepped back.

"Hear good things about you at the healing house, Beltur. Word gets around." Barrynt returned his attention to the wool.

Both mages slipped away.

Once they were outside, Lhadoraak said quietly, "Something's bothering him. I don't think it was us, either."

"I got that impression. But he will think about where you might be useful. He's always been a man of his word."

"He strikes me that way, although I don't think I'd want to get on his bad side."

"He has a temper. I've only seen it once, but I don't think I'd want him in a rage," replied Beltur as they turned eastward toward the cot.

LV

Threeday's breakfast was far better than that of twoday, with enough egg toast for everyone and ham strips, if thin, to accompany the toast, as well as more berry syrup, all as a result of what Jessyla had been able to purchase on twoday. At the same time, Beltur worried about how long he'd need to support Lhadoraak and his family.

Even as he thought that, he felt ashamed, especially after thinking about how long Athaal and Meldryn had supported him.

Yet why are you so worried about everything? He smiled wryly as he thought about the answer to his own question. A single mage, even a pair of mages, couldn't stand against a united group, either the council of a city or a land, or a group of traders or merchants with thousands of golds who could hire or pay both armsmen and other mages. While Beltur himself was stronger than most mages he'd met, there were doubtless others stronger and more experienced . . . and Jessyla was just beginning to learn what she could do. *So . . . you have to do what you must to get along while you and Jessyla learn and, hopefully, earn.*

He nodded to himself as he prepared to leave.

Both Beltur and Jessyla left at the same time, Beltur for Barrynt's stable and Jessyla to the healing house. After he finished with the horses and the stables, Beltur hurried to the smithy, once more under a cold and clear green-blue sky, his breath trailing him like white smoke.

When Beltur entered the smithy and began to take off his coat and scarf, Jorhan looked up from the workbench. "Understand we've got another black mage here."

"Lhadoraak. The Council exiled him and his family. They're staying with us until they can get settled somewhere."

"Seems like it might be a trace crowded in your cot."

"We hadn't planned on anything like that." Beltur walked to the forge. "It's a good thing there are only three of them."

After a moment, Jorhan said, "Barrynt's worried about how we left Elparta. He asked if there had been any other way. I told him I hadn't seen any."

"I was afraid of that, but I didn't want to lie. Lhadoraak's arrival made any further evasion impossible without outright lying."

Jorhan offered a wry smile. "You're still a black in that regard."

"I'm afraid that's not going to change."

"We might as well get working on the melt for the bud vases."

Beltur moved to the bellows.

By two quints after third glass, two cupridium bud vases and an oval frame for a miniature were ready for Jorhan to begin the final polish and finishing work.

"When you finish polishing them," asked Beltur, "then what?"

"Barrynt's going to put them on display in his factorage. Over time, he thinks people will be interested."

Beltur hoped Barrynt was right. *But then, he's the trader, and he hasn't done badly.* That brought up another question. "Do you know why it's called Mountain Factorage?"

"Because it's in the mountains, I guess. Why?"

"Most factorages bear the name of a town, a river, or the owner. I just wondered."

"Barrynt's never said. Johlana hasn't, either. I never thought about that." The smith's brow furrowed. "What made you think of that?"

"I was thinking about Vaenturl, the trader we accompanied. He said that if we ever got to Vergren to ask for him at Essek's Factorage. Then I thought about Barrynt's place, and I realized that it was the only factorage I'd seen with a name like that, not that I've seen that many."

"Never thought of it that way." Jorhan shrugged. "You might as well head back. I'll see you on fiveday, unless I see you in the stable."

"Until fiveday."

On the walk back, Beltur found he was still worrying about what he'd said to Barrynt. *But if you hadn't said what you and Jorhan had done, then what Lhadoraak said wouldn't have made sense . . . unless he'd admitted that Taelya was a white.* And Beltur felt that definitely wasn't a good idea, although he couldn't have said why.

When Beltur stepped inside the cot and took off his coat and scarf, he saw that there was a fire in the hearth, and the smell of something good cooking. He also noticed that the woodbox had been refilled and a stack of kindling and split wood set to one side.

Lhadoraak greeted him with a smile. "I split more logs and set the split ones on the side of the woodpile."

"Thank you. I do appreciate it."

"Tulya's cooking up a hearty ham and bean soup, and some maize bread."

"Both Jessyla and I will appreciate that." Beltur walked over and stood before the fire.

"I also carried some water to the cistern and used order to remove the little chaos that there was."

"You've been busy."

"All that didn't take that long. I walked around Axalt some and talked to one cabinetmaker. His shop is just off the main square. He'll pay me to look at woods, and he did give me half a silver for going through his stock." The blond mage smiled crookedly. "Every copper helps."

Beltur nodded at that. "How are Taelya and Tulya doing?"

"Tulya's worried and happy. She's happy to be out of Elparta, but worried about the future." Lhadoraak smiled. "Right now, Taelya's in the kitchen, helping her mother, but she's been working hard on keeping her two kinds of chaos separate and practicing her shields. It dawned on her this morning that you'll be here all the time." He shook his head. "Children."

"That's because you're her father, and I'm not. I didn't pay as much attention to my uncle as I should have. Athaal was the one who really taught me."

"That may be, but you know more than I do."

"Athaal likely knew more than both of us."

Lhadoraak frowned. "You're being generous. He knew a great deal, but you've done things he never thought possible."

"No. I just carried them further than he thought possible." Beltur laughed ruefully.

They both turned as the front door opened and Jessyla stepped inside.

Beltur immediately walked toward her, wrapping his arms around her even before she could escape the confines of her coat. "How was your day?"

"Not much happened for once." Jessyla smiled as she slipped out of the coat and left Beltur holding it. "I even talked a little with Herrara. I do like her. She works hard."

"She does. How is Wurfael?"

"He doesn't seem quite as gloomy as before. I talked to him a little. He wanted to know if you had any idea about hard times. So I told him a little about your life. He was surprised."

"You mean he thought I'd never had hard times?" Beltur thought he'd at least suggested that.

"He thought you'd had hard times, but that you'd come from a well-off family."

At that moment, Tulya walked out from the kitchen, followed by Taelya. "Jessyla! You're home."

"You must be the one cooking. Whatever it is, it smells wonderful," declared Jessyla.

"It's just a hearty ham and bean soup, more beans than ham," said Tulya. "I made enough for two nights. It'll keep."

"Thank you so much."

"It will be ready as soon as you are."

"Just let me wash up."

Less than a quint later, all five were seated around the kitchen table. The bean soup was every bit as good as it smelled, and Beltur had to admit that Tulya was a better cook than either he or Jessyla was.

Once dinner was over, and the kitchen cleaned up, Beltur announced, "It's time for lessons. Magery lessons, here in the kitchen. Taelya?"

"Yes, ser."

Beltur just nodded at Jessyla.

Lhadoraak and Tulya slipped back into the front room.

Beltur studied Taelya for several moments, then said, "Taelya . . . your separation of natural chaos and free chaos is good."

"You didn't have me do that," murmured Jessyla.

"You're black, through and through. You tend to keep free chaos at a distance, by instinct. So that wasn't as important for you as learning to use order to handle chaos. Taelya needs to use order to separate natural chaos from free chaos."

"Why is that, ser?" asked Taelya.

"If you mix natural chaos with free chaos, over time it will hurt you very much. That's why you need to always separate free chaos from natural chaos. Because she's a black, Jessyla naturally tries to keep free chaos away from her. So she has to learn how to use order to gather and handle free chaos." Beltur looked hard at Taelya. "Now . . . let's see your shields."

The girl formed a circular shield. The order nodes holding the chaos threads were barely present.

"Taelya . . . your shields aren't any stronger than when you were in Elparta. Did you practice much?"

"I sort of forgot while we were traveling. It was cold. I was hungry, too."

"I can understand that. Are you hungry now? Is it cold in here?" asked Beltur gently.

"No, ser."

"You need to make the order knots stronger. Otherwise, your shield will fall apart at the slightest touch."

The girl immediately began to concentrate.

"Just watch her with your senses," Beltur told Jessyla.

Taelya's second effort was clearly stronger than her first, with slightly larger order nodes.

"Taelya, that's better, but it's not as large as you were doing in Elparta. Rest and watch Jessyla with your senses." He turned to his consort. "Try a complete shield around yourself."

Jessyla did just that.

"All right. I'm going to jab at it with order. Hold it as long as you can."

Beltur's first thrust was moderate and didn't even dent the shield. Her shield held as well against a second, much harder thrust. "Good." His eyes went to Taelya. "Now you try a shield all the way around yourself."

The girl's first attempt collapsed before she could link the order and chaos threads. Beltur said nothing. The second attempt held, although Beltur knew it would have collapsed under even modest pressure.

"Keep holding that, just like it is." Beltur looked to Jessyla. "Now . . . I want you to create a shield that blocks everything, all sight, all order and chaos. You've seen me do that. It's your turn to try it."

Jessyla nodded and rebuilt her shield, then added another layer. With that, she was invisible, both to sight and to order/chaos senses.

"Both of you, keep holding those shields."

Taelya's shield collapsed after about half a quint. Beltur let Jessyla hold hers for a while beyond that before he said, "Jessyla, you can drop your full shield, but keep the one that protects you from physical damage."

Jessyla reappeared, standing next to the kitchen table.

"Taelya, you need to practice holding that shield until you can hold it a full quint. Do you understand?"

"Yes, ser."

"I'd like to have you both try something else. I want you each to see how many points of free chaos you can call up. Each one has to be surrounded by a shell of free order."

Taelya frowned.

"I know," Beltur said. "There's not much use for that skill. By itself, that is. But once you can create lots of points of chaos shielded by order, you'll be able to do other things." *Like multiple containments.*

Taelya could do one point, easily, but every time she tried to create a second point, the first point disintegrated.

Jessyla managed two points, but trying to create a third point resulted in her losing the second point after a few moments, although after she'd tried for almost a quint, the third point held for several moments.

Both Taelya and Jessyla looked relieved when Beltur finally said, "I think that's enough." Beltur smiled at the girl. "You worked hard, Taelya. You need to work that hard when I'm not around . . . but just on what I've showed you."

"I can do that."

"Good night, Taelya."

"Good night, ser."

As Taelya left the kitchen, Lhadoraak appeared, glancing at his daughter as she passed him and then to Jessyla. "I didn't see it before. You're not just a healer. You're a mage, too."

"A beginning mage."

"If you can do full shields, you're more than that."

"I can't hold them that long."

"But they're strong. I could sense them from the other room." He looked to Beltur. "How . . . ? First Taelya, and now Jessyla."

"They both have the ability. I just had to find ways to get them to be able to use it."

"Did Cohndar know you could teach magery?"

"I doubt it. I never tried until I started working with Taelya. I just followed what I'd learned from Uncle and especially from Athaal."

Lhadoraak shook his head. "I worked a little with Athaal. You do things I never saw from him."

"He wasn't working with a true white," Beltur pointed out.

Lhadoraak smiled. "Tell me. Did your uncle teach you what you've done with Taelya?"

Beltur had to think, then said, ruefully, "As best I can recall, he didn't do anything with me that I've done with Taelya . . . or with Jessyla." After a moment, he added, "But what he did worked, at least partly. What everyone else did wasn't working with Taelya or Jessyla."

"That's why you're a better teacher. You try to find new ways to do things when the old ways don't work."

"And some of what I've tried hasn't worked for me, either."

"From what I've seen, quite a bit does."

"He's right about that, dear," added Jessyla.

"How did you know Jessyla could be a mage?" asked Lhadoraak.

"Because she could sense so much about order and chaos. It didn't seem right that she couldn't be. So I just worked until I found a way."

"That just might be the story of your life," replied Lhadoraak.

At least, until I run out of ways. Not wanting to voice that, Beltur merely said, "Possibly. We'll have to see."

"Well," replied Lhadoraak, "we need to get Taelya to bed. Good night."

"Good night," replied Beltur and Jessyla, almost simultaneously.

They didn't say anything more until they were in their bedchamber with the door closed.

"I think Lhadoraak respects you a lot, but he's also just a bit scared," said Jessyla.

"Of me?"

"Of you. You saved him when no one else could have. You killed four powerful white mages during the invasion, and two of the most powerful mages in Spidlar when they tried to kill you, and you healed Taelya when no one else could."

What Jessyla said was undeniable, but . . . "I don't like it that a friend is scared of me."

"Power always frightens people," Jessyla said. "You just have to show that only those who want to harm you or those you love need to fear you. You'll find a way. You always have."

"So have you."

"That's a compliment I don't deserve, but I'll take it." She leaned forward and brushed his cheek with her lips.

LVI

By the time Beltur left Barrynt's stable on fourday morning, the sky held a greenish haze, and the air was noticeably warmer, with a light wind coming from the northeast, suggesting to Beltur that a northeaster just might be on the way. He'd barely hung up his coat and scarf in the healing house when Elisa appeared.

"Healer Herrara requests you in the surgery, ser."

"Thank you." Beltur followed the healer-in-training. Even before he stepped through the door into the surgery, he could sense the wound chaos. He could also hear the moaning.

A man was stretched out on the table, talking, with moans in between phrases. ". . . didn't do anything . . . didn't . . . plaques just turned up right . . ."

Herrara looked up for a moment. "He was beaten and left by the back door of the Traders' Bowl. He's got frostburn in places, but except for his hands, he's not that badly hurt." Beltur looked at the man's hands, but one was a swollen mass, and the other wasn't much better. As he moved closer, he could see that the end of one little finger seemed barely connected.

"I'm going to have to splint his hands—the fingers that I can try to save."

"Don't take any fingers . . ."

"We'll do the best we can." Herrara looked to Beltur. "I need you to immobilize his hand while I splint the individual fingers. Then we'll wrap the hand with a support . . ."

Beltur listened intently, then followed Herrara's instructions, beginning with the more badly injured right hand, and then the slightly less injured left hand. Despite Herrara's deftness and skill, more than a glass passed before both hands were splinted.

Although the man had stopped moaning, Beltur could sense his pain, as well as the wound chaos dotted throughout his hands.

"You're going to be here for a while," declared Herrara as she stepped back. "Your hands will likely throb all the time. Healer Beltur is going to do his best to remove the worst of the wound chaos. In time, that might help."

"Bastards . . . crippled me."

"That's what happens when you play plaques for high stakes with strangers."

"The City Patrol—"

"I've already told them. The men you said you played with left Axalt before dawn."

"Bastards . . . all of them . . ."

Until that moment, Beltur hadn't realized fully what had happened to the man . . . and most likely why. He repressed a shudder.

"That may be," said Herrara, "but it doesn't say much for your choice in selecting those you played with." She nodded to Beltur.

"I'm going to reduce some of the chaos." *The worst of it, anyway.* There were so many spots that removing them all would have created too much heat in the man's battered hands.

The man frowned. "Remove chaos? Haven't been around any white mages."

"Wound chaos," said Beltur.

"If he doesn't," added Herrara, "you could lose your hands entirely."

The man shuddered, then winced.

Herrara turned to Elisa. "Once the mage-healer is done, take him to a vacant room."

"Mage-healer?"

"There aren't many. You're fortunate." Herrara's voice was coolly pleasant.

Beltur could tell that she wasn't especially pleased, but he just stepped forward. "Don't move your hands."

"If I could do anything with 'em . . ."

Beltur concentrated on removing the ugliest of the yellowish-red spots. None were that large, but there were enough that removing close to a score took a good quint, largely because Beltur paused after each one. When he finished, he said, "I never heard your name."

"Klaznyt."

Beltur smiled pleasantly, but not warmly as he looked directly at the bleary-eyed man. "Can you tell me honestly that you didn't cheat at plaques, Klaznyt?"

"No more . . . OOOHH . . . than Grassyr did . . . less than . . . weasel Choraan . . ."

Beltur turned to Elisa. "I'm done. You can take him to a room." Then he looked back to Klaznyt. "You won't be able to do anything with those hands for quite a while. I'd be very pleasant to Elisa and everyone else." He smiled politely again, then left the surgery. Playing plaques for silvers was dangerous enough, Beltur suspected, but to try to cheat at it could clearly be deadly.

But then, what you did in leaving Elparta had also been dangerous. Except you didn't have many choices. But had Klaznyt? Beltur doubted if he'd ever know.

Beltur walked back to Herrara's study, where he looked at the older healer. "You weren't too happy with Klaznyt."

"Were you?"

"No."

"It's one thing when someone gets hurt loading, or sliding under a wagon . . . or if it's an innocent child . . . but cheating at plaques, playing with those who do . . ." Herrara shook her head.

"Does that happen often?"

"No. Most of the time, people like him disappear or end up being found somewhere when the winter snows melt."

"Is there anything else you'd like me to do first?"

"Just check on everyone and see that there's no hidden wound chaos. You can catch that sooner than I can. Sooner than any healer I've known." Herrara paused. "You've been working with your consort, haven't you? She feels more like a mage than a healer."

"She is a mage. She always felt that she was. She just didn't know how to use order."

"What made you able to show her?"

"All the mistakes I made, and those who helped me recover from them."

"That's not the whole truth."

"It's close enough."

Herrara smiled wryly. "That feels close enough. Go look in on Wurfael and the others."

Beltur nodded, then left the study and made his way to Wurfael's chamber.

The former timberman was sitting on the side of the bed, his crutches up against the bed beside him. He looked at Beltur, then swallowed. "Ser mage . . . I'm sorry . . . I had no idea . . ."

"That's all right, Wurfael. I've likely been a bit hard on you. It's just . . . well . . . I think you can do more than you think you can."

"I'll try, ser."

"I know you will. Now . . . let's look at that leg."

Beltur could find no sign of new wound chaos, and he smiled at Wurfael. "It's definitely healing well. I'll see you later."

"Yes, ser."

Beltur left and began his visits to the rest of those injured, but the remainder of the day was much quieter than the beginning.

He was still thinking about Klaznyt and Wurfael—and even Poldaark—when he walked into the cot a little after fourth glass and hung his coat and scarf above the bench by the door.

"The women are in the kitchen," said Lhadoraak, rising from the bench in front of the hearth. "They said it was too crowded with me in there. How was your day?"

"For a day at the healing house, it went well enough. What about you?"

"I visited Rhodos and got the names of the cabinetmakers he knew in Axalt. There were three others. I saw all three. I might get some work in the spring. There's a fellow in south town who would like me to help when he starts building a mill there in the spring. I stopped by the Council building. I'm supposed to meet with a Councilor Naerkaal on sixday at fourth glass."

"He's the mage on the Axalt Council."

"That's what the Council clerk told me when I asked who was in charge of mages."

"I didn't do that," Beltur admitted. "It might have been because I had a position with both Jorhan and the healing house." After a moment, he added, "Then it might be that I haven't had the best fortune in dealing with mages and councils."

"I don't have your skills, Beltur."

"You also don't have my history. I'm sure you'll get along fine with Naerkaal." Beltur hoped so, even though he wished Lhadoraak hadn't presented himself to the Council.

"Axalt seems like a very ordered place."

"From what I've experienced and seen so far, it very much is."

"You sound doubtful."

"I'm just wary . . . or cautious. Elparta seemed very ordered to me, at least until Waensyn got to Cohndar."

"There aren't very many blacks in Axalt, the clerk said—only a handful. Not many healers, either."

"Herrara said that there were only about ten she knew of. With what they pay, I can see why there aren't many."

"Do you think you'll stay here?" asked Lhadoraak.

"We haven't even thought about it," Beltur replied. "Jorhan's just got the smithy working, and we should be able to make a decent living here come spring and summer. I've already had to leave two lands, and I'm not all that interested in moving again."

"You've got a nice place here." Lhadoraak glanced around.

"Better than we'd hoped for." *Much better . . . but that was Johlana's doing.*

"I'd like to think we could do that." The blond mage shrugged. "We'll just have to see. We're certainly not going anywhere until the snows let up."

"Things will get better in spring." Beltur smiled as Jessyla walked out from the kitchen.

LVII

The northeaster that Beltur had anticipated arrived before dawn on five-day, and Jorhan sent Frankyr to tell Beltur that he wasn't about to struggle through the driving snow to get to the smithy. No such message arrived from Herrara for Jessyla, but Beltur still headed out, right after she left, to deal with Barrynt's stable and the horses.

He did saddle Slowpoke and ride him around the square and the center of Axalt, if very carefully, after which he used Slowpoke to carry water to the cot to refill the cistern, where Lhadoraak helped and used order to remove any traces of chaos. After riding back to the stable, Beltur groomed Slowpoke and rubbed him down, a process that the big gelding enjoyed—as much for the attention as anything.

After walking back to the cot, Beltur gave Taelya another lesson, including different exercises in magery, while Lhadoraak went outside and shoveled the snow off the walks.

Lhadoraak finished shoveling, and Beltur had just completed his instructionals with Taelya when there was a rap on the door.

"Who could that be?" Beltur frowned as he neared the door and opened it to find Rohan standing outside.

The older man immediately spoke. "I've been patient . . . I leased the cot to you and your consort. Everyone has friends who visit, but visiting and moving in are two different matters."

Patient? Beltur barely managed not to snap that word back at Rohan. Instead, he stepped outside into the snow, closing the door behind himself. "Lhadoraak and his consort and child only arrived on oneday afternoon—"

"Do they intend to live here forever? Were you deceiving me when you said it would only be you and your consort?"

"We didn't know that the Traders' Council of Spidlar was exiling every mage that the head mage doesn't like. Lhadoraak lost almost everything. He's looking for a position, and he has several prospects."

"In the middle of winter? That's a likely story."

"It happens to be true," Beltur pointed out. "Why else would a black mage leave everything behind in winter?"

"I can't say as I see that Axalt needs that many more black mages."

Beltur had the definite feeling that Rohan wasn't listening . . . or that he had something else in mind.

"I didn't expect to have two families in my cot."

"Neither did we. Neither did Lhadoraak. None of us can plan on the unexpected."

"Do you just expect me to stand here and take it?"

Beltur repressed both anger and a sigh. Instead, he eased two silvers from his belt wallet and extended them to the landlord. "This is extra rent for the rest of the season, if it takes that long, for them to find a place of their own."

"Just until then. Not a day longer. I'll bring it before the Council. I will." With that, Rohan turned and walked back through the heavy snow to his own house.

Beltur shook his head, then opened the door and stepped into the cot, shaking off the snow that had coated his shoulders.

"What was that all about?" asked Lhadoraak from where he stood by the padded bench.

"My paying him the last of the rent until spring," replied Beltur, not wanting to say more. Lhadoraak had more than enough to worry about.

"Is there a problem?"

"Not now." *Not until spring, anyway.*

Jessyla didn't arrive back at the cot until two quints past fourth glass.

"I must have brushed off a bushel of snow on the front stoop," she said as she hung her coat on the last available coat peg.

"How was your day?" asked Beltur as he crossed the front room to join her.

"Quiet." She turned and headed toward the kitchen. "I need to get these boots off. Somehow, I got a lot of snow in them."

Beltur could sense a certain concern, but said nothing as he followed her into the kitchen and then into the bedchamber, closing the door behind them.

Jessyla sat on the edge of the bed and pulled off her boots. Some snow flew from her boots and trousers, but not that much. She looked at Beltur. "One of the councilors came to see Herrara today. One visits the healing house once a week. Herrara told me that they alternate."

"That had to be Naerkaal." said Beltur.

"Whatever he said, she didn't look happy. She didn't say anything to me about why, though. She just told me to be careful going home. She's thoughtful that way. I still worry."

Beltur frowned. "I don't think we've done anything to upset anyone. Maybe it didn't have anything to do with us." Trying to change the subject, he asked, "How is Klaznyt—the man with the smashed hands?"

"He was very polite. Not happy, but polite. I managed to remove a little of the wound chaos." Jessyla offered a pleased smile.

"You did? That's wonderful!" Beltur couldn't help but smile broadly. "Did Herrara notice?"

"She did. She was surprised. Then she said she probably shouldn't be, that we kept surprising her. I had the feeling that there was more, but I couldn't actually sense it. The bits were likely too tiny. You might have to remove them tomorrow."

"I knew you'd be able to do it. Before long you'll sense the smaller bits as well."

"Not as well as you can."

"You're just starting."

She looked into his eyes. "Beltur . . . I've always been able to sense. How well I do hasn't changed. What I can do with what I sense has improved. It will continue to get better. How well I sense will not."

The complete honesty in her response stopped Beltur cold for a long moment.

She added softly, "That's not your fault. We are what we are. You've already given me what was first denied."

"You gave me everything I've become," he returned. "Everything."

She stepped back. "I just told you the obvious."

"Except it wasn't obvious to me or to Uncle." He smiled, but that faded as he remembered Rohan. "We may have another problem." He went on to tell her.

"We have a little time to think about that. Does he really want to anger three mages?"

"It's not about three mages," Beltur replied, acknowledging that Jessyla was indeed a black mage. "It's about what the Council of Axalt might say . . . or decide. We've already seen how strict the Council is. That's good for some things, but I worry about how they might deal with Lhadoraak if they discover Taelya's a white."

"She's seven. Why under the Stars would they want to make life harder for a girl that young?"

"Why did Wyath want to kill Uncle? Why did Cohndar and Waensyn want me dead? Why did the Council decide to exile Lhadoraak?"

Jessyla sighed. "People are so stupid."

"No. They just want things the way they want them. They don't much care about what happens to other people, and that makes it hard on everyone else."

"Do you really think the Council of Axalt would be that cruel?"

"I hope not. But it could happen. That's why I cautioned Lhadoraak and Tulya not to say anything about Taelya. The longer we're here, and the more people trust us, the less likely the Council is to get upset about what they discover. Don't you think Herrara wants us to stay?"

"I'm sure she does . . . but she looked worried."

"I'll see if she says anything tomorrow."

Jessyla stood. "We ought to join the others, don't you think?"

"In a moment." He wrapped his arms around her.

LVIII

The snow was still falling heavily on sixday morning when Beltur left for Barrynt's stable, and was still coming down when he made his way through the knee-deep whiteness to the healing house. After stamping the snow off his boots and brushing it from his coat and trousers at the door, Beltur stepped inside, where he hung his coat and scarf. Then he walked along the chilly hall to Herrara's study.

She turned from the supply shelves. "Good morning. We'll not likely see anyone new today, not with the snow so deep. Tomorrow will be different."

Beltur nodded. There were always injuries after a winter northeaster. Absently, he wondered if it would be the same in spring or summer, when what fell was a deluge of water. "Then I'll just look at Klaznyt and Wurfael and the others. How long do you think it will be before Wurfael can be fitted for a peg leg?"

"He's healing well, but it will likely be at least another eightday, probably two. See what you can do with Klaznyt. He makes Wurfael seem cheerful."

"You don't care much for him, do you?"

"Gamblers always come to a bad end, either murdered or dying alone without even a copper for lager. I could care less about what they do to themselves, but they hurt everyone, most of all those who love them or those who try to help them."

"It sounds like a few have passed through the healing house."

"More often, it's the ones they've hurt, one way or another." Herrara paused, then added, "Not all gambling deals with plaques or silvers, Beltur."

Beltur nodded. "I've understood that for a long time. Sometimes, life only offers you a choice of risks." He picked up one of the baskets of supplies before leaving the room, heading down the corridor.

Klaznyt barely looked up as Beltur entered his chamber. Each of the crippled plaque player's splinted hands rested on a small pillow.

Beltur walked to his bedside and let his senses range over the injured hands. As Jessyla had suspected, there were more than a few spots of yellowish-red wound chaos growing around the broken bones. He concentrated on the largest patch of wound chaos.

"That burns," said Klaznyt. "Why do you bother?"

"So that you'll get better."

"I'll be fortunate to be able to hold a staff or a broom. That's no kind of life."

"What kind of life is it where people try to pound your hands to a pulp?"

"It's the only way I know to make a decent living."

"Decent? Gambling with plaques looks dangerous to me."

"Living is dangerous, Mage. I'm surprised you don't know that."

"I should have said 'unnecessarily dangerous.'" Beltur continued to gather and focus free order to remove the largest and ugliest points of chaos.

"You folks around here walk around like you've got a staff up your backside. So frigging straight and upright."

"It sounds like you're not from Axalt. Where's home for you?"

"It's not like I've ever had a home. Not in years. Grew up in Worrak."

That didn't surprise Beltur, not with the little he'd heard about the port city, supposedly controlled, if indirectly, by pirates. "Is Worrak as bad as some say?"

"It's like any other city. You have to know who has the real power."

"Why did you leave?"

"I didn't learn the difference between silvers and power quick enough."

"From what I've seen," answered Beltur, "silvers are just another kind of power, like weapons or magery."

"Power and magery are direct. Silvers aren't." Klaznyt laughed, a harsh and sardonic sound. "They're also a shield for those who don't want their power known."

As are councils and councilors, Beltur thought as he stepped back. "Your hands will be warmer for a little while. They should cool in a quint. They might not hurt quite so much then."

"You've more power than most, Mage. Why don't you use it to better yourself?"

Beltur was glad he'd already considered that question. "Because I don't have enough silvers or enough support from other mages to hold off those that the use of power would anger." *Yet.*

Klaznyt offered another short burst of laughter. "Thinking that way, you'll never have enough power or silvers. You have to know when to gamble and when not to." He grimaced. "Sometimes—like now—I've not judged well. That doesn't mean I'm wrong. It just means I judged unwisely."

"Sometimes we don't have a choice."

"We *always* have choices. Sometimes, all of them are bad. And, some-times, not very often, none of them are bad." Klaznyt forced a smile. "You've done all you can for me right now, Mage. Go tend to the others."

"I'll be back later." Beltur inclined his head, then made his way to Wurfael's room.

The timberman actually smiled as Beltur entered. "Good morning, ser."

"How are you doing today?"

"Better, ser. An old tinsmith came to see me yesterday. He thinks I might be able to help him."

"That's very good. How do you know him?"

The young timberman grinned. "I don't. The head healer told him about me. I think she must know a lot of folks."

"I haven't been working here that long, but I've gotten that feeling." Beltur used his senses to study Wurfael's leg, but could find no new wound chaos, and less of the dull, almost grayish red that signified something nearly healed. "You're doing much better."

After leaving Wurfael, Beltur made his way through the rest of the rooms, dealing with small bits of wound chaos where it would help. It was close to noon when he returned to the supply room. There he began to check the shelves, making certain that chaos hadn't infiltrated the dress-ings stored there. He'd been working at that for little more than a quint when Lhadoraak appeared in the doorway. Beltur immediately sensed the almost chaotic flow of order around the blond mage. "What are you doing here?"

"Looking for you."

Turning from the shelves, Beltur frowned, worrying about what could have gone wrong, since he couldn't think of any other reason for Lhadoraak to come looking for him. "Has something happened to Jessyla . . . or Taelya or Tulya?"

"No, they're all fine."

"Then . . . why . . . ?"

"I just got a message from Naerkaal. You're supposed to accompany me to meet with him at fourth glass." Lhadoraak extended a single sheet of note paper.

From the traces of brown wax, Beltur could see that the paper had been not only folded, but sealed, at least until Lhadoraak had broken the seal. He unfolded the sheet and read.

Mage Lhadoraak—

You are requested to bring Mage-Healer Beltur with you so that both of you may meet with Mage-Councilor Naerkaal at fourth glass this afternoon.

For the Council.

There was no signature, only a seal.

Beltur looked to Lhadoraak. "Did the messenger say anything at all about the message?"

"I asked. He didn't know what the note said."

"I can't say that I like this."

"Neither do I," replied Lhadoraak. "Do you have any idea what it's about?"

"Not really. The Axalt Council already has to know that I'm a fugitive from Elparta. I told the border guards. I've told Herrara and Barrynt. Axalt's been a refuge for many over the years. You told them why you and your family came. Why would two black mages be a problem? I've been doing good work here. That's what Herrara's told me, and she wasn't lying."

"What about Cohndar and Waensyn?"

"They're likely still missing. It's been snowing for eightdays since they disappeared. If it were spring . . ."

Lhadoraak nodded slowly. "I still worry."

"So do I. I'll meet you outside the Council building just before fourth glass."

"Will that be a problem?"

"It shouldn't be. It's a summons from the Council, and I'll only be leaving two quints before I'd normally get off."

"You're sure . . . ?"

"I'm sure."

After Lhadoraak left, Beltur finished his inspection, then walked to Herrara's study.

She looked up. "The other mage was here. What was that about?"

"He and I have been summoned to meet with Councilor Naerkaal at fourth glass. The message from the Council didn't say why."

The healer frowned. "Naerkaal was here yesterday. He was asking about you. He'd heard that one of my healers was also a mage. He wanted to know how good a healer you were. I told him the truth, that you were one of the best younger healers I've ever seen, and that you'd likely become one of the very best if you continued as a healer."

"Did he ask about Jessyla?"

"Not a word. Did you do something to concern Naerkaal?"

"I told you why we had to leave Elparta. I've done nothing but help the smith Jorhan and help you here since we came to Axalt."

"I told Naerkaal what you told me. He said that there was more, but that most of it didn't concern you or your consort."

Beltur frowned. "I can't believe that Lhadoraak could possibly have done anything."

Herrara offered an amused smile. "That's another of your absolutely ordered statements. It suggests that if anyone should be of concern to the Council, it's not your friend."

"I don't think either of us should be of concern to Axalt."

"Could you say that of Elparta?"

"No . . . but that's why we're here and not there."

Herrara shook her head, then said, "Don't argue with Naerkaal. He won't listen. Most of them won't."

"How do you deal with them, then?"

"I try to anticipate and bring up things before they have a chance to make up their minds. That way, they don't have to change them. Most times, they won't."

"And you don't ask permission if you think it's within your responsibility."

"Why should I? That's what responsibility means."

"Is there anything else I should know?"

"Don't be late, and don't offer any statement to Naerkaal that isn't absolutely true."

"I'll leave at two quints before the glass, then."

"Make it a little earlier."

"Thank you."

"How are Klaznyt's hands?"

The question told Beltur that Herrara had said all she would about the Council. "I need to go back and remove more of the wound chaos this afternoon. It's still manageable."

"Good." Herrara stood. "I'm going to meet Elisa in the welcoming room."

"Do you need me?"

"Not unless someone arrives and needs surgery."

Beltur nodded, then eased his way out of the study, making his way to Klaznyt's room.

Following Herrara's suggestion, Beltur left at two quints past third glass. Even so, he only made it to the front door of the Council building at about half a quint before fourth glass.

Lhadoraak stopped his pacing and looked up.

"Where are we supposed to go?" asked Beltur.

"The main Council room, I think."

Beltur nodded toward the door, suggesting Lhadoraak lead the way, then followed the older mage inside.

A guard stood before the closed door to the Council chamber. He studied the two. "You're the mages?"

"We are," replied Beltur.

"Just a moment, sers." The guard opened the door and stepped inside the chamber, quickly closing it behind himself.

"A guard, yet?" said Lhadoraak.

"That might be just to keep people from intruding." Beltur certainly hoped that was the case, but, then again, one guard certainly couldn't restrain or hold two black mages.

Close to half a quint passed before the guard returned, again closing the door quickly. He looked first to Beltur, then Lhadoraak.

"You may enter, sers. Just walk up to the dais and wait for the councilor to address you."

Beltur decided against full cloaking shields, because that would definitely send the wrong message to Naerkaal, but as soon as he entered the Council chamber, he almost froze. All eleven councilors already sat in place behind the long table, but this time Naerkaal sat in the middle position, as the head councilor. *Whatever it is, it doesn't look good.*

When they reached the foot of the dais, Beltur stepped up beside Lhadoraak on his left.

Naerkaal said nothing.

Neither did either Beltur or Lhadoraak.

Beltur could feel Naerkaal's sensing of both of them.

Finally, the mage-councilor spoke. "Axalt has always served as a refuge for those who have fled the excesses of other lands, particularly for mages and others of an orderly persuasion. Both of you sought that refuge, and you did not conceal that you were fugitives. There is some question as to whether you concealed other matters." He looked directly at Beltur. "You, Beltur, are not only a black mage, but a healer of considerable skill. Is that not so?"

"I am a black mage, and I have some talent in healing. The degree of that talent is better assessed by Healer Herrara, although I do have some abilities that other healers do not." Beltur felt that he had answered that question fairly and honestly.

Several other councilors looked to Naerkaal.

"His response is truthful and without qualification or evasion," said the acting head councilor who looked to Lhadoraak. "You, Lhadoraak, are a black mage of moderate ability. Is that so?"

"It is."

"The Council recently received a dispatch from the Traders' Council of Spidlar. We seldom receive such communication. The last time was over a year ago. This dispatch claimed that you, Beltur, attacked and dispatched two black mages, kidnapped a healer, and fled to Axalt to escape punishment. Is this true?"

"I fled to Axalt to escape the efforts of the Council to either kill or permanently indenture me. That is true. I did not kidnap the healer. She insisted that she accompany me and become my consort. An older black mage was forcing his attentions on her. Those attentions were unwelcome."

"So far, everything Beltur has said is in perfect order." Naerkaal cleared his throat. "Did you attack two black mages?"

"No. They attacked me and Jorhan, the smith with whom I had been working. Their intent was not to restrain me, but to kill me. The two mages were the head of the mage council of Elparta and his chief assistant. That assistant was the mage who tried to press his attentions on my consort."

"Before she was your consort?"

"Yes, but we were promised to each other."

Again, the other councilors looked to Naerkaal, who nodded and said, "The mage has not uttered any untruths." Then he asked, "What happened to the two mages?"

"I tried to hold them both in containments."

"Both of them? At once?"

"I did. I learned to use multiple containments as a City Patrol mage in Elparta."

"What happened?"

"I held the containments too long."

"They died?"

"They did."

A momentary frown crossed Naerkaal's face, but he immediately said, "The Traders' Council only wrote that the two mages were missing and presumably killed."

"I hid the bodies where they will not be found until spring. I needed the time to rescue my healer and leave Elparta before others discovered what had happened."

Naerkaal nodded, adding, again, "He has spoken the truth. Are there any questions for Mage Beltur?"

"How did you feel about your acts, Mage?"

Beltur didn't know the man who asked the question, but he answered as if Naerkaal had asked. "I'm angry that I was forced into a position where the only thing I could do to save myself and keep my consort from being abused by Waensyn was to try to stop them, and that my efforts to restrain them resulted in their deaths."

"You don't regret their deaths?" asked Naerkaal.

"No. I regret that I was forced into that position. I regret that they were so consumed with getting what they wanted that they didn't even consider the effects of their actions."

"What do you mean by that?" Naerkaal seemed honestly curious.

"If I had not done what I did, I would be dead, and Jessyla would be the slave and consort of one of them. I did what I did, and they're dead, and we had to flee. Either way, the outcome could not have been good. It is likely that the Prefect will again try to attack Elparta. The city now has three fewer strong black mages because one of them wanted to force a woman who did not want him and thought that killing the mage whom she loves would gain him what he wanted."

"Killing is still killing," said one of the councilors.

"It is," replied Beltur, "but even Relyn found it necessary to reach the safety of Axalt."

A flicker of a smile crossed Naerkaal's face before he said, "The mage Beltur has been truthful. He has not concealed anything. Shall we move on? Does anyone object?" Seeing no objections, he looked to Lhadoraak.

"Lhadoraak, the dispatch from the Traders' Council stated that you were not exiled, but that you chose to leave, rather than submit to an order of the Council. Is this true?"

"It is true. It is also misleading to the point of being false."

"Please explain that for us."

"My consort and I were not exiled. That is true. The Council exiled my young daughter. She's barely seven. She is hardly old enough to make her own way in the world, especially in the middle of winter."

"For what reason was she exiled?"

"The Council declared that she is a white mage."

Beltur could see that the declaration about Taelya came as no surprise to any of the Council, indicating that the dispatch from the Traders' Council had revealed that. Given that, he had to wonder why Naerkaal had asked the questions he had.

"Were you aware that the laws of Axalt do not permit a known white mage to remain permanently in Axalt?"

"I was not. I had not heard that until this moment."

"Did you even consider that possibility?"

"We had no choice. She was given an eightday to leave Elparta, and no more than two eightdays to leave Spidlar. The river was frozen over, and we could not have reached Spidlaria in that time in winter. Going to Gallos would have meant my death, and we could not have reached any other place within the time required. I had hoped that Axalt would be more merciful than Spidlar."

"The mage has answered those questions with complete honesty," said Naerkaal. "Are there any questions?"

"Why would the Traders' Council exile a child?"

"I think my daughter was an excuse. I believe the Council wished to punish us because we were friendly with Beltur. Our daughter is barely seven. She will likely become a white mage but certainly is not one now. A seven-year-old poses no threat to anyone."

"Did you have anything to do with Beltur's dealings with the missing mages?"

"No. I did know that they were trying to find a way to keep him from earning silvers and to keep him from consorting Jessyla. He did not tell me anything about what happened until after we arrived here. I didn't even know when they left Elparta until a day or so later."

"Do you have reason to believe anyone else was involved or knew?"

"No. I did know that Beltur and Jessyla left Elparta with Jorhan the smith."

Naerkaal looked to one side of the table and then to the other. No one else spoke. Finally, Naerkaal said, "The Council will consider these matters." Then he addressed Lhadoraak. "In accord with the laws of Axalt, as mage-councilor I will be visiting where you are staying in order to meet your daughter and consort. That will be tomorrow. Please be there. After that meeting, I will report to the other councilors, and the Council will meet an eightday from today at fourth glass to set forth the decisions of the Council. Is that clear?"

"Yes, Councilor," replied Beltur.

Lhadoraak just nodded.

"Then this meeting of the Council is concluded. You may go."

Beltur led the way out of the meeting.

Neither spoke until they were outside and walking away from the Council building.

"What do you think they'll do?" asked Lhadoraak.

"I don't know. There were questions Naerkaal could have asked that would have been much worse. I have the feeling he's trying to help without breaking the laws of Axalt."

"Some of the councilors didn't look all that friendly."

"I didn't notice," Beltur admitted. "I was concentrating on Naerkaal and trying to think of totally honest ways to answer his questions."

"You did that well. You didn't mention Jorhan."

"I'm glad they didn't ask about him. He was just trying to keep me alive."

"What should we do now?"

Beltur shrugged. "There's not much point in doing anything different until the Council decides on what they're going to do."

"Do you trust them?"

Beltur barked a laugh. "More than the Traders' Council, but that's not saying much. They could have been much tougher."

"Maybe they've already made up their minds."

"We'll find that out soon enough."

By the time the two reached the cot, the white sun had long since dropped behind the mountains to the west, and Axalt was totally in shadow. Despite the coat and scarf, Beltur felt colder than usual. *Because of the meeting or because you haven't eaten?* He shook his head and opened the door.

Lhadoraak followed him and closed the door.

"What happened at the meeting?" demanded Jessyla even before Beltur had removed his coat. Tulya stood right behind her.

"The Traders' Council of Spidlar sent a nasty dispatch to the Axalt Council suggesting I murdered Cohndar and Waensyn and that Lhadoraak and Tulya really didn't have to leave Spidlar."

"That we didn't really have to leave?" Tulya's voice rose in anger. "How could they have had the nerve!"

"According to their decree, they're correct," said Lhadoraak. "I pointed out that since Taelya is barely seven the Traders' Council's claim was both accurate and completely misleading."

"What did they say then?" demanded Tulya.

"Maybe we should sit down around the hearth," suggested Jessyla, "and let Beltur and Lhadoraak tell us what happened from the beginning."

"With some ale," added Beltur.

"We can do that." Jessyla motioned to Tulya.

Beltur had the feeling that it was going to be some time before anyone ate.

LIX

Dinner was late, and by the time the kitchen was clean, and Beltur and Jessyla were in their bedchamber, with the door securely closed, it was close to eighth glass. Beltur was definitely tired, Jessyla less so as she sat on the bench and looked intently at her consort.

From where he sat on the side of the bed, Beltur asked, "What are you thinking?"

"That the Traders' Council had something more in mind than informing Axalt that you were a dangerous black mage. Or that a seven-year-old girl was a deadly white." Jessyla's last words were delivered sardonically.

"That's obvious. What do you think they're after? Besides what you said earlier?"

At dinner, Jessyla had only suggested that the Council had a grudge against both Beltur and Lhadoraak, and Beltur had refused to speculate then, partly because Taelya had been there and partly because he'd wanted some time to think.

"They don't want us to stay in Axalt."

"That's also obvious . . . but why? All I wanted to do was to consort you and work with Jorhan so that we'd have enough golds to buy a house and be comfortable. Either in Elparta or Axalt, why would that be a problem?"

Jessyla raised her eyebrows. "That would have lasted a year or two. Then what? What would happen when it became obvious to everyone and not just a few, that you were the most powerful mage in Elparta or possibly in Spidlar?"

"Jessyla . . . there's so much I can't do."

"I didn't say you were the most accomplished. I said you would likely be the most powerful. Even if you aren't, exactly, there's no other mage who can break your shields. Would Caradyn want to defer to you? What about the Traders' Council?"

"But we're in Axalt, not Elparta. A single mage can't invade an entire land."

"No, but you could ride unseen and unsensed to Elparta and do whatever you liked."

"I wouldn't do that. What would be the point of that?"

"*You* wouldn't, but if they had your abilities, they'd certainly think about it. They're uneasy about you being in Axalt."

"So they want to push us farther away. We've been pushed far enough. I'd just like to stay here and make them uneasy. They more than deserve it."

"They do," Jessyla agreed. "Is that what you want from life? To make people uneasy?"

"Of course not. I want to make a life for us, one where we're not relying on other people, and where you don't have to worry about where every copper or silver comes from. I just don't have a problem if it makes Caradyn and the other blacks uneasy."

Jessyla nodded. "I'm glad of that. Then what?"

"Then what what?"

"You made more golds in a season than most crafters make in a year."

More than that, most likely. But Beltur didn't really want to admit that.

When Beltur just waited, Jessyla gave a little headshake and went on. "If we're allowed to stay here, you'll have more than enough golds for us within a year or two. I can see that. What comes after that?"

"I still want to learn more about healing."

"You should, and I want to learn to be a much better mage."

"You're saying that we won't be happy here for very long."

"We might be. I worry about that. I also worry that Caradyn might send a mage under a concealment into Axalt."

"He won't do that soon. He'll wait to learn what the Axalt Council decides." Beltur could see what she wasn't saying—that his shields were strong enough, but hers might not be, and certainly Lhadoraak's and Taelya's weren't, and Tulya barely had any shields.

"You know what I mean."

Beltur sighed. "I do. But we don't have to decide this very moment, perhaps not for even a season, or a year. And, if it's all the same to you, I do owe something to Jorhan. Without him, I'd have nothing."

"I understand, but he's done well by you also, and he has family that can help him."

"That's true." Beltur paused. "We'll just have to see. In any event, I don't think it would be wise to just leave this moment, not with another three eightdays of winter left—if not more. And not after all that Johlana and Barrynt have given us."

"The Council may not give us much choice . . . or they may let us stay and give Lhadoraak and Tulya little choice."

Beltur winced at the last possibility. "That would be cruel."

"Councils often are," Jessyla reminded him.

As are prefects, power-mad mages, viscounts, and dukes . . . "We'll just have to see," he said quietly.

She nodded. "We need to get some sleep. Tomorrow might be a long day, for both of us."

Beltur could hardly disagree.

LX

When Beltur woke on sevenday, a thin icy fog stretched across Axalt. The inside of the cot was even colder than usual. While Tulya was making breakfast, Beltur hurried over to Barrynt's, hoping to catch Jorhan before he left for the smithy.

The smith was just coming from the stables as Beltur turned up the cleared drive beside the small mansion. "Beltur, you're here early."

"I just came to see you for a moment. Something's come up. The Council summoned Lhadoraak and me to question us yesterday at fourth glass. I didn't find out until around noon yesterday. It wasn't a regular Council meeting. The Traders' Council of Spidlar sent a dispatch stating that I'd fled and had likely killed two mages, and that they hadn't exiled Lhadoraak."

"That they *hadn't*?" Jorhan frowned.

"They didn't exile Lhadoraak or Tulya; they exiled his seven-year-old daughter because they claimed she's a white mage."

"A seven-year-old? What sort of man would do that? Makes me glad we left."

"That's why I can't come to the smithy today. Naerkaal wants to see Lhadoraak and his daughter, and I don't know when he's coming."

"What did you tell the Council, and what did they say?"

"I said that I'd put containments around both of the mages, and that they'd died. I also said that the two were trying to kill me. Naerkaal told the others I was telling the truth. They'll let us know what they decide next sixday. I think Naerkaal wants to meet Taelya to find out if she's really a mage."

"Is she?"

"She can do some things, but she's certainly nowhere close to being a full mage."

Jorhan frowned. "You didn't tell the whole story."

"No, but everything I said was true. Naerkaal knew that I'd left out something, but he didn't press me."

"That sounds like he's not happy about what the Council's doing."

"I can't imagine any honest mage would be, but he's only one of eleven councilors." Naerkaal wasn't the most powerful of black mages, but there was no way to tell how much that had affected his questioning, if it had at all. Not wanting to say more about what had happened with the Council, he asked, "How are Barrynt and Johlana?"

Jorhan frowned.

"Are they all right?"

"They're fine. Eshult's parents are causing some problems. I haven't seen much of Halhana. When I said something about it, Johlana told me she'd tell me later."

"Did Halhana get the mirror?"

"Only a couple of days ago. Johlana said that there was a right time to present it and a wrong time."

"I'm glad she got it. I hope she likes it."

"Johlana said she was pleased. She said it was the most elegant piece in her house."

Beltur grinned. "It should be. It was one of the best you've ever done."

At that moment, the side door to the house opened, and Johlana called out, "Is that Beltur, Jorhan?"

"It is."

"Could both of you come in for a moment?"

"We'll be right there." Jorhan turned to Beltur. "I think you'd best tell her about what happened, before she says anything or anyone else tells her." He led the way up the side steps and into the side hallway.

Even as he was closing the door, Beltur addressed Johlana. "I need to tell you what's happened and why I came here so much earlier than I usually do." He did so as quickly as he could.

After he'd finished, Johlana shook her head. "You're not the favored son of the Rational Stars, that's clear. Never seen someone who's tried so hard to do right have so many folks against you." She offered a crooked smile. "That might be because too many people aren't that interested in what's right."

"I've been saying that for years," said Jorhan.

"You've been wasting your breath, Brother. People like that don't listen. People who aren't that way already know." She turned back to Beltur. "I was going to invite you and Jessyla for eightday dinner, but now I think I should include your friends, especially with what the Council is doing. Fussing and worrying about a seven-year-old girl? That's disgraceful." A hint of a smile crossed her face. "I'd like to meet the child who's so upset our beloved Council . . . and her parents. Besides, we haven't had much company in a while, and it would be good to have a child in the house again. Stars knows, we won't be seeing one here in years."

Beltur thought he could almost hear the words "if we ever do." "You're very kind, as always."

"I like to hear about what goes on beyond merchanting, and it's good to share a good meal with people who enjoy conversation." She glanced at her brother.

"Never been much for that," declared Jorhan.

"You have other strengths." She turned back to Beltur. "Half past fourth glass?"

"We'll be there."

"Good. I won't keep you."

Beltur took the hint, nodded, and made his way outside. From there he hurried back to the cot, where everyone else was already gathered around the table.

"What took you so long?" asked Jessyla.

"When I told Jorhan I wouldn't be at the smithy today, he thought I should tell Johlana why. When I did, she invited all of us to dinner on eight-day evening, especially Taelya."

At Tulya's quizzical look, Beltur added, "She said she wanted to meet her and her parents. We've told you how warm and welcoming she is."

"That sounds just like her," said Jessyla. "She's also said that it's nice to occasionally have another woman around, especially now that her daughter's consorted and out of the house."

Beltur sat down and immediately began to eat the oat porridge, mixing mouthfuls with bites of bread and morsels of a single crunchy ham strip.

After a few moments, Jessyla asked, "Did Johlana say anything about Halhana and whether she liked the mirror?"

"She didn't mention it. Jorhan told me that she only gave it to Halhana a day or so ago . . . something about it being the right time."

"It's beautiful enough that any time should be the right time," replied Jessyla. "Halhana seems sweet enough, but to me it sounds like her consort's parents rule her life."

Beltur couldn't imagine either his mother or father ever doing that, even if they had lived longer. *But then, one way or another, you likely never would have met Jessyla.*

Before that long, Jessyla left the table and hurried off to the healing house.

After that, Beltur donned his coat then looked to Lhadoraak. "I'll be back as soon as I can be with Slowpoke. That way I can spend some of the morning hauling water to refill the cistern. Send for me if he comes."

While Beltur had the feeling that Councilor Naerkaal wouldn't show up first thing in the morning, he also didn't think that Naerkaal would put off his visit until late in the day.

In fact, by ninth glass, Beltur had cleaned the stable, refilled the cistern, returned Slowpoke to the stable, groomed the gelding, and walked back to the cot.

At just past the first glass of the afternoon, there was a knock on the cot door.

"You should get it," said Lhadoraak with a grin. "It is your cot. Besides, you have stronger shields."

Beltur grinned back. "Excuses yet." Then he walked to the door and opened it.

The gray-haired Naerkaal stood on the stoop alone. "Might I come in?"

"You certainly may." Beltur stepped back, then closed the door once the mage-councilor entered. "There's an empty coat peg there."

"I thought you might be here," said Naerkaal as he took off his black coat and scarf.

"Considering that Lhadoraak and his family were forced out of Spidlar at least partly because we were friends, I thought it only fair." Beltur gestured toward the bench and chairs.

"As would I, were I in your boots." The mage studied the front room. "You've only been in Axalt a little more than half a season. You look remarkably well-settled for a couple who arrived with three horses and little more than the clothes on your backs."

The mention of three horses told Beltur that Naerkaal had definitely done some looking around, but he replied, "Most of the furnishings came from Barrynt. They had been languishing in his storeroom for many years. A few items came with the cot."

"That seems most generous."

"His consort is Jorhan's sister. She was glad that he left Elparta and came to Axalt."

"So I have heard. Is it true that your ability to help him forge cupridium enabled him to pay off his debts in Spidlar?"

"He did tell me that after we had sold a number of pieces that he'd been able to pay off the factors he owed for copper and tin. We never talked more about it."

"You're very careful about what you say."

"I've discovered that's the wisest course, ser."

"You also have the strongest shields I've ever sensed. Yet you are a fugitive from two lands."

"I didn't have those shields when the Prefect's men and white mages were after me, and they weren't as strong as they are now until I'd worked with Athaal, a mage in Elparta."

"Could he not have interceded for you?"

"He was killed in the invasion by the Prefect's white mages, as were several others."

"Without Beltur, the Spidlarian forces might well have lost," interjected Lhadoraak. "He also saved me and others."

"Yet you fled Spidlar?"

"You've heard what I said before."

Naerkaal offered a sardonic smile. "Yes, I have." He turned to Lhadoraak, who stood beside the chair closest to the door. "Your daughter and consort are here?"

"They're in the kitchen."

"Before I talk with them, I have a few questions for you." Naerkaal walked to the chair on the far side of the bench and seated himself.

Lhadoraak sat on the bench, and Beltur took the other chair.

"I take it that your daughter has some tendencies toward the white, since even the traders of Spidlar would likely not go so far as to commit a total fabrication. Do you agree?"

"Not totally," replied Lhadoraak. "They would fabricate anything that served their ends. Taelya does have tendencies toward the white, but she is far from being anything close to a mage."

"Why do you think they exiled her, and not you? I'd like a complete answer, not the partial one you offered the Council."

"I'll do the best I can, ser. I don't think I know all the reasons the Council may have had. When Beltur and Jessyla left Elparta, none of the mages knew anything about Taelya. Oh, they knew I had a daughter. I doubt any even knew her name. But when Cohndar and Waensyn disappeared, none of the mages wanted to select a successor until they knew that the two were really gone."

"Did you know they were dead?"

"No, not until Beltur told me after we arrived in Axalt."

Naerkaal nodded. "Then what?"

"After an eightday or so, Caradyn acted as head of the Mages' Council in Elparta. It took several eightdays after that before the mages agreed on him and for the Traders' Council to approve him. Once he was confirmed by the Council, he began to visit every black in Elparta, asking each of us about Beltur and Jessyla, and whether we'd known anything about the disappearance of Cohndar and Waensyn."

"No one did that earlier?"

"There were questions, and certainly suspicions that Beltur had something to do with their disappearance. But there was the troubling problem that the guard accompanying Cohndar and Waensyn to Jorhan's smithy was dismissed and told that the two mages had the situation well in hand."

Naerkaal turned his eyes on Beltur. "Is that true?"

"Yes. That was when I realized that they wanted to kill me."

"Did they say anything to that effect?"

"That I'd be fortunate to survive as an indentured slave, or words to that effect."

"What did you do then?"

"As I told you. I put containments around them both and held them."

Naerkaal nodded again and looked back to Lhadoraak. "And you knew nothing of anything about this except what the guard said? Until you came to Axalt, that is?"

"I heard from Meldryn—he's the baker with whom Beltur lived—that Beltur had stopped by the bakery with Jessyla and said that they were leaving because Cohndar planned to charge him with chaos-wielding and would either indenture him for life or have the Council execute him."

"Interesting choice of words," mused Naerkaal, turning back to Beltur. "That suggests you'd already killed them."

"They were dead within a quint of the time they dismissed the Council guard."

"Lhadoraak, how soon did this . . . Caradyn . . . visit your house?"

"Within a day of the time his appointment was confirmed by the Council."

"Hmmm. What did he ask you?"

"Some of the same questions you did. If I knew where Beltur was, if I knew what happened to Cohndar."

"What did you tell him?"

"That Beltur was likely in Axalt with Jessyla, because that was what Meldryn had told me, and that I had no knowledge of what happened to Cohndar and Waensyn, but that it was certainly possible that Beltur had done something to them—but that he never would have attacked them unless they attacked first."

"Do you know that for a fact?"

"Yes."

Once more Naerkaal nodded. "Your presence in Elparta might have proved embarrassing, then?"

A look of surprise appeared on Lhadoraak's face. "Embarrassing?"

"You're clearly a very honest man. You're not a strong enough black to be able to shield a lie. The fact that you know that Beltur is the kind that never attacks first would sully the reputation of Cohndar, and by extension, that of the Mages' Council. Yet . . . exiling you would call attention to you directly. I think it's time for me to meet your daughter and consort."

"Tulya, Taelya! Please join us," called Lhadoraak, rising from the bench.

"Is anyone else in the house?" asked Naerkaal.

"No, today is one of Jessyla's days to work at the healing house."

"I'd almost forgotten that you're a skilled healer as well. That lends a certain credence to your friend's point that you tend to react rather than attack." Naerkaal stood.

Seeing as he was the only one seated, so did Beltur.

As Tulya and Taelya entered the front room, Lhadoraak gestured to the bench. "The three of us can share."

Beltur felt Naerkaal's gentle and quick sensing of Taelya, but waited to see what the mage-councilor would do.

Surprisingly, Naerkaal turned to Beltur. "You'd throw one of those confinements around me if I tried anything against her, wouldn't you?"

"I hadn't thought about it, but, yes, most likely I would."

The councilor offered a soft laugh, then turned to Taelya. "Young woman, do you know why I'm here?"

"Yes, ser. You want to see me. You want to know if I'm a mage. I'm not. Not yet."

"Fairly said. Can you light a fire?"

"No, ser. I can light a candle."

"Would you show me?"

"I'll have to get her one from the kitchen," said Tulya, rising.

"Please do."

In moments, Tulya returned with a short traveling candle and set it on the hearth before Taelya.

"Try to light it," said Naerkaal.

Taelya concentrated, using a point of free chaos confined by order. The candle flared into flame.

Beltur could sense Naerkaal's surprise.

"Can you do anything else, like throw chaos bolts?"

"Oh, no, ser. Beltur won't let me try that. He says I have to have shields before I work with lots of chaos."

Naerkaal turned to Beltur. "You've been teaching her?"

"I asked him to," interjected Lhadoraak. "He was the only one who knew anything about chaos. He was raised by his uncle who was a white mage."

"But you're clearly a black."

Beltur could see he was going to have to explain. "I grew up in Gallos.

My parents died when I was quite young . . ." He went on to give a summary of how he had ended up in Elparta.

"I see," said Naerkaal, "but how did you end up teaching Taelya?"

"She was ill. She was almost dying," interjected Lhadoraak. "Beltur was
the only one who realized she was order-bound."

"Order-bound?"

"Her natural chaos was so constrained by bands of order that she
couldn't grow, and she was slowly dying."

"I've heard of that, but never seen it. Have you run across this before?"

"Just one other time."

"What did you do?"

"Loosened some of the bands and removed some, just enough that she
was in balance."

"You can . . . Of course, you're a healer as well." After a moment,
Naerkaal addressed Taelya again. "What else can you do?"

"I still have to work to keep my own chaos separate from the free
chaos."

Again, Naerkaal turned to Beltur, inquiringly.

"The reason, I believe, that whites die so much younger than blacks is
that they mix free chaos with their body's natural chaos and that they don't
handle free chaos with order. The free chaos corrupts their system after
time. Taelya already had problems, and I didn't want her to compound them
with bad technique."

"I see." The councilor returned his attention to Taelya. "What else can
you do?"

"I'm working on getting better shields."

"Can you put up a shield for me?"

Taelya looked to Beltur, who nodded, and then concentrated. After
several moments, she had a shield around herself, not a strong one, but one
that might have stopped a single sharp blow from a blade or a staff.

Naerkaal order-probed the shield gently, but it held.

Perspiration began to appear on Taelya's forehead as she continued to
hold the shield.

"Oh, you can lower it now. Can you do anything else?"

"No, ser. Beltur says I have to work on getting stronger shields."

The councilor was silent for several moments, finally saying, "Taelya, I
need a few moments with your father."

Tulya rose and took her daughter's hand. "We'll get you something to eat."

Once Tulya and Taelya were in the kitchen, Naerkaal studied Beltur for several moments. "She's very, very strong for her age. You've also been very careful with her. I would expect no less from a mage-healer, but so often expectations are not met."

"Do you have any other questions?" asked Lhadoraak.

Naerkaal shook his head. "You all have been more forthcoming than I could have expected."

"Do you have any idea about what the Council will do?" pressed Lhadoraak.

"I'm not at liberty to discuss what the Council might or might not do. That would be premature and unwise."

"Even to discuss what the possibilities are?" asked Tulya, from where she stood at the door to the kitchen.

"Even that," replied Naerkaal, rising from the chair. "This . . . situation . . . is without precedent. With no precedent, it would be most unwise for me to offer anything beyond saying that the Council will consider everything carefully."

"Might I ask what makes it unprecedented?" asked Beltur, also standing.

"You may ask," replied Naerkaal, "but what makes it unprecedented bears on what the Council must decide, and I cannot and should not infringe on the responsibilities of the Council."

A diplomatic way of saying you aren't about to tell us. Beltur managed a polite smile, then moved toward the door. "We do appreciate your thoroughness in considering the matter."

As he donned his black wool coat and black leather gloves, Naerkaal said, "The Council would have it no other way. We've observed the results of hasty decisions elsewhere. Seldom are the results good for anyone."

"I've seen that also. That's why I appreciate thoroughness." Beltur opened the door.

"You appear to be most thorough, Beltur, and that is unusual at your age." Naerkaal nodded. "We will see the four of you at fourth glass next sixday when the Council decides the matter. Good day." He smiled pleasantly, then stepped out through the open door, not looking back as he walked toward the street.

Immediately after the door closed, Tulya asked, "What do you think?"

"I think he doesn't want to make us suffer, but there's something in the laws that's a problem." Lhadoraak looked to Beltur. "Do you know what that might be?"

"The only thing that I've heard is that white mages aren't permitted to stay in Axalt. Taelya's certainly not a mage."

"Yet," replied Lhadoraak.

"He *seemed* sympathetic," ventured Tulya.

"If he is, he'll have to persuade the Council without seeming sympathetic," replied Beltur. "That's hard."

"What do we do now?" asked Lhadoraak.

"Wait," replied Beltur. None of them knew any of the councilors, or anyone of power in Axalt, and contacting anyone now would only make matters worse. Herrara had done what she could, either out of self-interest or kindness, if not both, and while Barrynt was a prosperous merchant, from what Beltur had observed, he wasn't one of the more powerful merchants or traders, unlike Emlyn and Sarysta, who clearly looked down on Barrynt, or at least Johlana.

Rather than just sit and wait, Beltur decided he should head back to the stable and take out the other two horses. Neither had gotten as much exercise as they should have, and he could ride one and lead the other. Besides, that would keep his mind off the councilors and what they might do.

LXI

On eightday morning another fine snow was drifting down across Axalt, but less than a digit had accumulated when Beltur left to tend the stable, and the snow was not that much deeper when he left the stable for the healing house. Once he arrived there, he took off his coat and scarf and immediately made his way to Herrara's study.

She looked up from the ledger in which she was entering numbers and returned the pen to its stand before asking, "Do you want to tell me what happened at your meeting with the Council?"

Beltur told her quickly, with a slight emphasis on Taelya, then looked at the head healer. "Did Naerkaal share any of that with you?"

"He only said that you were likely more talented and more dangerous than you seemed. I told him I'd already gleaned that. I told him I didn't think you were the type to attack anyone, unless you or those you care for were threatened. I also told him that Axalt would lose a great deal if you and your consort were forced to leave."

"Did he respond to that?"

"He said that he respected my judgment more than many members of the Council might. He also wanted to know just how good a healer you and your consort were. I told him the truth—that you both had things to learn, but that you were better than many healers and that you could do healing I'd never seen done before." Herrara paused, then asked, "Do you know what the Council plans?"

"They'll talk it over this eightday, and let us know on sixday, at fourth glass. So I'll have to leave a little early then."

"We'll hope for the best." After the slightest of hesitations, she said, "You'd best start with the gambler. He's been complaining about his hands . . . among other things. Elisa says he's been difficult."

"Difficult" could mean quite a number of things, none of them good. "Oh?"

"He'd have roving hands, if not worse, except that he can't use them, and his language is more than flirtatious."

"One of those." Beltur shook his head, then picked up a basket of supplies before heading up the stairs to the chamber that held Klaznyt, announcing, "Good morning," as he walked in.

"I see that the healer sent for you," said Klaznyt sourly from where he was propped up in the bed with his splinted hands resting on his abdomen.

"She told me to look in on you, and that your hands hurt more."

"How could they be otherwise?"

"They couldn't be, not after what happened." Beltur walked over to the bed and began to use his senses to search for wound chaos. Despite what Klaznyt said, while there were still some small areas of chaos, one of which was definitely yellowish red, some of the others had either shrunk or not grown. Beltur set to work, and this time was able to remove all of the wound chaos, at least all that he could sense.

"That makes my hands and fingers hot."

"They'll cool in a bit."

"They hurt more."

"That pain should fade before long."

"You have answers for everything, don't you, Mage?"

"Hardly," replied Beltur. "Just about some things in magery and healing."

"You don't like me very much, do you?"

"I don't know you well enough to like you or dislike you," lied Beltur.

"I've heard that you've been difficult with the healer-in-training. That's something I don't like."

"I was only teasing, maybe flirting a little. What's a man to do when he can't do much?"

"She didn't take it as teasing. Neither did the head healer. If they don't, neither do I."

"You've still got that staff up your backside."

"And you've got a lot of broken fingers," said Beltur pleasantly. "We could just send you off, if you're not comfortable here."

"Don't make threats you can't carry out, Mage."

"I could," replied Beltur. "Or I could do worse, but you're not worth the bother. I was just suggesting you might think over things a bit more."

"Have you done worse?"

Beltur just smiled pleasantly. "I wouldn't worry about that. You need to worry about letting your fingers heal and what you'll do after that." He turned, glad that he hadn't answered the question, because one answer would have been a lie, and the other taken as a boast.

His next stop was Wurfael's room, where he was surprised to find the young timberman sitting on the side of the bed with what had to be a peg leg and the padding and leather harness to strap it in place. "It looks as though you're coming along."

"It's going to take some getting used to. It hurts like demon fire after even a little while. Healer Herrara said I should only wear it for a little while at a time, right now. She said once everything heals, in a season or so, I should be able to get one with a boot attached."

"She'd know about that." Beltur wondered how Herrara had arranged for the peg leg, and if that was part of what the healing house did.

Before he could say more, Elisa appeared. "She needs you in the surgery."

"I'll be back later," Beltur said before turning to the young healer-in-training. "I'm on my way." He hurried out of the room and down the stairs. The first thing he saw when he entered the surgery was a woman in dark gray standing by the surgery table, and a younger woman, barely more than a girl, sitting there.

Herrara was examining the girl's right arm. She looked up. "Her father is a weaver. Somehow, the loom tipped and the side upright smashed her arm."

Beltur could barely detect the sardonic tinge to Herrara's words.

"That is how it happened," declared the mother, red-eyed, but not crying. "Ragnar said it was like that."

As Beltur let his senses study the girl's arm, he sensed far more bruises than had yet appeared or than would have been caused by a single impact. He glanced at Herrara.

"How it happened doesn't matter now," replied Herrara. "Both bones are broken below her elbow. They haven't broken through the skin, and I need you to make sure they don't as we set them."

"Can you make it so her arm will heal straight?" asked the mother.

"She'll need to stay here for several days, until the swelling goes down and we can put a cast on her arm."

"I cannot stay."

"She'll be fine here."

Safer than at home, suspected Beltur.

At Herrara's direction, Beltur used a combination of tiny shields to make sure that the broken bones did no more damage as the healer set and splinted them. She did not put the arm in a cast, and likely would not for a day or so, given possible swelling . . . and the bruises that everyone except Herrara and Beltur seemed to be ignoring. Once the girl's arm was splinted and she was led to a room and settled there, Beltur followed Herrara back to her study.

"You're not asking me how often this happens," she said.

"I'm guessing that it happens every so often, and that there's very little you can do about it unless the girl's or boy's injuries are severe and obvious."

"That's a good guess. Sometimes, not very often, if there's more there, and the girl is old enough, I can find a place for her elsewhere."

Beltur knew very well what she meant by "more there," and he just nodded.

"Do you still want to be a healer?"

"I need to know more about healing. When I do, then we'll see."

"What you're seeing won't change."

Beltur offered a half-humorous smile. "But I might."

Herrara's laugh was sardonic. "You just might make a healer."

The rest of Beltur's day at the healing house was uneventful, and he left right at fourth glass. The fine snow had continued throughout the day, but slowly enough that the streets and walks were clear as he walked swiftly back to the cot, where he washed up and quickly changed into his better black tunic and trousers, before the five of them left to walk to Barrynt's dwelling.

Beltur led the way up the drive to the side door, where he knocked.

In moments, Johlana opened the door. "Come in, come in. Don't stay out in the cold."

Once the five were in the side hall, Johlana smiled. "And you must be Taelya?"

"I am, Lady." Taelya inclined her head solemnly.

Johlana smiled broadly. "It's good to see you . . . and the rest of you as well. Hang up your coats and follow me."

Barrynt, Jorhan, Ryntaar, and Frankyr were already in the parlor, and all stood as Johlana led the newcomers in, immediately saying, "This is Tulya, and her daughter Taelya, and Lhadoraak, and, of course, Jessyla and Beltur."

"Beltur's said a lot about you," said Jorhan immediately.

"We've never had two mages in the house before," said Barrynt, adding with a broad smile, "Until we met Beltur, we'd never had one."

Beltur was slightly surprised that Naerkaal had not visited, since he was a councilor, but said nothing.

"We have pale and dark ale, dark lager, mulled wine, and redberry juice," offered Johlana. "Just tell Frankyr—he's the dark-haired one—what you'd like."

Taelya looked to her mother.

"Yes, you may ask for the redberry juice."

"Might I have the redberry juice, please?"

Frankyr smiled warmly. "I have a special glass for you."

When everyone was seated, some in chairs brought in from other rooms, Beltur could tell, Johlana stood. "Enjoy your drinks. When the time comes, we'll be having my special cassoulet, and there's plenty of it. Barrynt won't let me make it unless we have company because he says he'll eat too much of it."

"Much better than burhka," murmured Frankyr.

Beltur thought he was the only one who heard that, just because Frankyr was sitting just to his left.

After a long moment of silence, Ryntaar spoke up, addressing Lhadoraak. "You've been here since, when, last oneday?"

"That's right," replied Lhadoraak. "We surprised Beltur and Jessyla late that afternoon."

"The more I hear about what's going on in Spidlar, the gladder I am I left when I did," said Jorhan. "Idiots'll drive out all the good people."

"How did your meeting with the Council go?" asked Barrynt.

"They asked us both a number of questions, and then yesterday Councilor Naerkaal came to the cot to meet Taelya and asked a few more," said Beltur.

"I don't know as I understand this," began Barrynt. "They think that this young woman might be a white mage? She's far too young for that."

"The Spidlarian Council just wants to make trouble," said Jorhan. "They're angry that Beltur and I didn't put up with their sow—their garbage, and because Jessyla had enough sense to reject that sleazy mage from Gallos. They're after Lhadoraak because he and his family are close to Beltur and Jessyla. That's all there is to it."

"But exiling a girl?" pressed Barrynt.

"For some reason," said Beltur, "even the Axalt Council has concerns."

"That seems to be a concern to both Axalt and Spidlar," replied Lhadoraak, "even if she's just turned seven."

"Well, then," said Johlana, "I for one am glad you're here, and I do have a special honeycake." She looked to Taelya. "Would you like that for dessert?"

"Yes, please."

"You shall have it." Johlana smiled again. "It's so good to have a child in the house again."

Barrynt stiffened at her words, if only for a moment.

What was that all about? wondered Beltur.

"Was the trip long?" asked Frankyr. "Did you have problems with brigands, the way Beltur and Uncle Jorhan did?"

"We were followed for a while, but they didn't attack us. We came with some merchants who had quite a few guards. One came close, but I put a shield around him for a moment, and he yelled something about mages, and they decided to leave us alone."

"How are you liking Axalt, Taelya?" asked Ryntaar.

"It's cold, but it's nice. I get more lessons from Beltur. That's good."

"Doesn't your mother give you lessons?" asked Barrynt.

"Those are lessons in reading and writing and numbers. Beltur's teaching me so I'll be a mage when I'm older."

"That's likely to be a while," said Lhadoraak with a soft laugh.

Beltur could sense his friend's unease at Taelya's words, true as they were.

"This is excellent lager," offered Lhadoraak.

"I'm glad you like it," replied Barrynt. "It's my favorite."

"Everything's your favorite," said Johlana warmly.

"That's because we don't serve anything we don't like."

As the interwoven conversations went on in a halting fashion, Beltur largely listened, as did Jessyla. He knew the cassoulet and the honeycake would be excellent and that nothing more would be said about the Council and the upcoming meeting . . . or, for that matter, about anything unpleasant, including the fact that no one was talking about Halhana.

LXII

The snow had dwindled off on eightday night, and oneday was bright and bone-chillingly cold, a cold increased by a sharp wind out of the northwest. Ice crystals sifted out of a clear sky that was almost pure green, instead of the usual greenish blue. As Beltur walked to the stable, he was definitely glad he'd exercised all the horses on sevenday, because he wouldn't have wanted them out in the bitter chill.

Once he cleaned the stable and dealt with the horses, he made the long walk to south town and the smithy, wondering what Jorhan might have in mind. Even though he was well-wrapped in his coat, scarf, and gloves, his hands and feet were numb by the time he reached the smithy, and he walked straight to the forge, which was filled with more coal than usual, far more, an indication that Jorhan had also needed to warm up.

"Bitter cold out there," offered the smith.

"It's as cold as I've ever felt." That was not even the slightest exaggeration on Beltur's part, and if the rest of winter were that cold . . . He shook his head.

"Same here." After several moments, Jorhan said, "Once you're thawed out, thought we might start casting some larger hand mirrors. Larger than the ones we did before, but not as big as the one we did for Halhana. Since you couldn't come on sevenday, I got to thinking, decided we should try one or two. Made the molds, and one of them's heating up now."

Beltur didn't ask if anyone had heard from Barrynt and Johlana's daughter, because they hadn't heard the night before, and Halhana seldom visited in the morning.

"I'm thinking the larger mirrors should have a longer and more decorated handle. They'd look better, and they'd be easier to hold." Jorhan smiled wryly. "Another thing. We're not going to be getting more copper and tin for a while, except for the little Barrynt's got, and I've got lots of time."

Despite the lingering chill in the smithy, the two castings went well enough that Beltur left the smithy by third glass.

Twoday at the healing house was very quiet, most likely because the bitter cold still swathed Axalt, and few were outside or engaged in anything likely to cause accidents. Beltur did help Herrara put a plaster cast on the arm of Noirya, the weaver's daughter, although Herrara really didn't need his help. Later, she did caution Beltur that, after long periods of cold, injuries from quarrels or brawls fueled by overindulgence in ale or lager would most likely rise.

Threeday at the smithy, Beltur and Jorhan worked on a small decorated cupridium jewelry box that didn't turn out quite so well as Jorhan had hoped, but the subsequent effort on fiveday turned out far more to Jorhan's satisfaction.

Even so, by sixday morning, Beltur's thoughts were far from smithing, and he was not only tired of the continuing bitter cold, but even more worried about what the Council might decide. The fact that Naerkaal had given the faintest hint of wanting to help, but also had offered not the slightest real encouragement, didn't lessen Beltur's concerns.

As Beltur stood by the front door, putting on his coat and scarf, Jessyla announced, "I'll meet you at the Council building just before fourth glass."

"They didn't—" began Lhadoraak.

Beltur had thought about saying Jessyla didn't have to be there, but as strongly as he felt her determination, he immediately decided that was a bad idea, as was the impulse to smile at Lhadoraak's reaction.

"I'm just as much affected as anyone, and I should be there." Her eyes fixed on Lhadoraak. "Shouldn't I?"

"I . . . I didn't mean that."

"Naerkaal did ask about Jessyla," Beltur said quietly, "and she's right. Her presence can only help, since it would remind the Council that they'd lose not one but two healers."

"She is right, dear," added Tulya, who didn't even try to conceal her smile.

Lhadoraak shrugged helplessly. "I really didn't mean it that way." Then he offered an embarrassed smile. "You're right. You should be there."

"I will be."

Beltur then left for the stable. From there, once he finished his chores, he made his way to the healing house, where Elisa informed him that Herrara wouldn't arrive until around ninth glass.

"Did she say why?"

"No, ser. She just sent a message saying that she was confident you could handle anything in her absence."

"Let's hope nothing comes up that tests that confidence," replied Beltur dryly. He knew he could deal with quite a few things, but he also knew he didn't have anywhere close to Herrara's surgical skills, especially in matters that might require amputation or the like.

Since no one was waiting in the welcoming room, Beltur took a basket of supplies and began visiting all those in the center, beginning with Klaznyt, simply because he preferred to deal with the gambler first, in order to get the potential unpleasantness out of the way.

Even before Beltur was more than a step inside the door, Klaznyt glared at him and asked, "When will I get these torture devices off my hands?"

"When the bones have knit enough that you won't break them again."

"When will that be?"

"Whenever Healer Herrara says so, but it's usually around four to five eightdays." That was what she'd told Beltur.

"What am I supposed to do until then?"

"Heal . . . and don't make too much of a fuss. You're getting fed, and you're not losing silvers."

"You're so cheerful, Mage."

"Things could always be worse."

"Are you speaking from vast personal experience . . . or is that just a platitude from what you've heard?"

"I've complained," *if only to yourself,* "and things have gotten worse, enough times to learn that it's not a good idea."

"You're rather young for that, I think."

"Then you're not thinking," replied Beltur calmly, as he sensed Klaznyt's hands and then began to remove the yellowish-red bits of chaos that still kept appearing, no doubt because of the brutality of the beating the gambler had taken.

"You haven't exactly gotten rid of that rod up your backside."

Beltur smiled pleasantly. "Your hands are better, but, as before, they'll be warm for a glass or so."

"Is that all you have to say?"

"For now, it's all that's necessary. I'll check on you later."

As he left the chamber, Beltur wondered why he was being so stubborn. It would have been much easier to point out that he'd lost his family and the man who'd saved him, been forced to leave two lands, fought against the Gallosians, and demon-near died twice. But that didn't feel right. *Was it because comparing what you've been through to what he's suffered is wrong? Or because doing that is somehow "winning" when no one wins if both have suffered? Or that while you've had problems, you've been fortunate, and to mention those problems would claim more than you've really suffered?* Beltur didn't know which of those might be the most valid, if even if any were, but he trusted his feelings.

By the time Herrara returned, at a quint past ninth glass, Beltur had finished his first set of rounds and was replacing supplies in his basket from those on the shelves in Herrara's study.

"How was the morning?" she asked.

"Quiet. No one needing surgery," he said with a wry grin, "because they'd have had to wait or take a huge risk."

"You'd have managed."

"There's a difference between managing and doing it well. I sense chaos and remove it better than you, but you're far, far better with surgery than I'll ever be."

Herrara just nodded.

"I see that Noirya is gone. Home?"

"Yes, unhappily. I couldn't find a place for her anywhere that would have been better."

"You've done well with Poldaark and Wurfael."

"It's always harder with girls and women."

Beltur could see that.

"That's part of your problem, you know?" Herrara continued. "Or it will be."

"Oh?" Beltur had an idea what she meant, but he didn't want to guess.

"I'll be charitable, and say you're being cautious, rather than stupid. You know very well what I mean. You're training Jessyla to be a mage, and she'll be good at it. Once that becomes obvious, people here, maybe anywhere, will be wary of you two. About the only things men are comfortable with women doing—besides spreading their legs, having children, and running a household—are being servers, cooks, and healers." She smiled. "Watching this happen could be very interesting." After a pause, she said, "No, I haven't told Naerkaal that. He might not mind, but he'd have to tell the rest of the Council, and most of them would."

"You're wary of the Council, aren't you?"

"They're mostly good men, doing the best they can, but they're very traditional, and they have trouble with anything that might disrupt the way things are and have been."

"I've gotten that impression."

"You should have. You're a mage who works with a smith and who is a good healer. You've obviously been successful, at least to some extent, as a war mage. You've also been forced out of two different lands. Those facts alone would concern most of the Council."

"That's no different from Relyn."

Herrara laughed. "Relyn would have made them just as uncomfortable. Except he's safely dead. You're not."

"You're saying that they'll push us out of Axalt?"

Herrara frowned. "Only the Council knows what they'll do. They like being a sanctuary, especially for people wrongly accused of something. The fact that you're both healers is also in your favor. So is the fact that the Traders' Council exiled a seven-year-old girl. I wouldn't want to guess. I'd prefer you and Jessyla stay. That's selfish on my part. You've made my life easier. You've also saved some that I don't think would have lived otherwise. In time, you may wish to leave. Axalt, as I've said, is traditional. *Very* traditional."

"Well . . ." said Beltur slowly and deliberately, "we'll see what the Council has to say."

"We will indeed. How are Klaznyt's hands?"

"There are still bits of yellow-red wound chaos popping up. They're getting fewer."

"That's not surprising with the beating he took. Without you, I might not have been able to save what I did. Have you told him that he lost the end of one little finger?"

"No. I didn't mention it."

"He'll begin to notice it in the next few days when the swelling and pain are less."

"He's fortunate to keep what he did."

"His kind won't think so. His hands will be stiff and likely hurt some of the time for the rest of his days."

The rest of the day at the healing house was without event, and Beltur left at two quints past third glass, not wanting to have to hurry the way he had the previous sixday. This time, he was the first to arrive at the Council building, and Jessyla was the second, followed closely by Lhadoraak, Tulya, and Taelya.

Beltur almost wanted to ask if everyone was ready to deal with the Council. Instead, he just said, "Shall we go in?"

Lhadoraak nodded and led the way. Beltur and Jessyla followed the other three inside.

The guard outside the door, once more, made them wait for close to half a quint, until the chimes outside struck fourth glass. Then he slipped into the chamber, returning almost immediately and gesturing for them to enter.

As the five walked toward the front of the Council chamber, Beltur noticed immediately that Naerkaal remained in the center of the councilors seated at the long table.

Once the five stood before the Council, Naerkaal's eyes scanned the group, lingering a moment on Jessyla, who stood at the end beside Beltur. "I see that all of you are here. That's good." After several long moments, he continued. "As I have told you, and as the Council has reaffirmed, the situation that the presence of you five in Axalt presents is unusual. In fact, it is so unusual that it is unprecedented." He paused and said again, "Unprecedented."

Beltur and the others waited.

"You, Mage Beltur, are not only one of the most powerful mages to arrive in Axalt during the tenure of any of the members of this Council, but you are also a healer, able to do feats that only a few healers can do, despite your comparative youth. Yet you also can work with a smith to forge cupridium. Despite all these skills, you were forced to flee Spidlar." Naerkaal's lips almost formed a quick smile. "That may well have been because of the skill and beauty of your consort, who is also a talented healer." He moistened his lip, then went on. "Mage Lhadoraak, your situation is even more puzzling. You are a strong, but not overpowering black mage. Your consort is neither mage nor healer. Yet you have a daughter who most definitely bears the traits and abilities that will doubtless lead to her being a white mage. At the age of seven, she stands condemned and exiled for what she might become. Do any of you dispute what I have set forth?"

"No, ser," replied Beltur and Jessyla, while Lhadoraak shook his head, as did Taelya. Tulya continued to look straight ahead, at no one.

"The Traders' Council of Spidlar has declared that, in effect, two of you have used chaos in a fashion contrary to the laws of that land. After due consideration, the Council of Axalt has rejected that finding, with certain observations and conditions . . ."

Beltur did not quite hold his breath, waiting to see exactly what those observations and conditions might be.

"Before I state those conditions," declared Naerkaal, "I must state, so that you understand fully, the law of Axalt with regard to chaos and its use. As the great Relyn said, one must accept chaos in its natural form, for chaos in that form is found in all nature. What Axalt cannot accept is the use of chaos to coerce, destroy, or otherwise cause harm to any person, any livestock or domestic animal, or to any structure or crop. Such a use defines a white mage, and no mage so defined can remain in Axalt for more than an eightday, or, in winter, until the roads are clear and safe enough for that mage to depart." He paused again. "Is that clear to each of you? All of you, except Taelya, please answer individually." Naerkaal nodded to Lhadoraak.

"It is clear, Councilor."

"Yes, Councilor," said Tulya, followed by Beltur and then Jessyla.

Naerkaal leaned forward and looked at Taelya, speaking firmly, but gently, "Taelya . . . you are not to use your abilities as a handler of chaos to threaten or harm anyone or anything. Will you promise that you will not harm anyone or anything?"

"Yes, ser. I wouldn't do that."

"Thank you."

Naerkaal straightened and cleared his throat. "It is the finding that the five of you are allowed to remain within Axalt so long as you abide by its laws and the conditions governing the use of chaos."

Beltur found that he was still releasing, if slowly, the breath he thought he had not held, but he still managed to say, "Honored councilors, we thank you for the thoughtful and thorough consideration you have given to our unusual situation, and we deeply appreciate your efforts."

"My daughter and I thank you also," added Lhadoraak.

"This meeting of the Council is hereby closed." Naerkaal actually smiled, if briefly. "You all may go."

Jessyla led the way outside.

Once the five stood facing the market square, now completely deserted, Lhadoraak shook his head. "I don't believe it. They were actually fair." He looked to Beltur. "Did you think it would come out this way?"

"I didn't know. I knew they were worried about it, but . . . I'm just glad it turned out the way it did."

"Can we stay here, then?" asked Taelya.

"Yes, we can, dear," answered Tulya.

"So long as we're good," Beltur said.

"So long as we're good," agreed Lhadoraak cheerfully.

"I think we should go home and have dinner," suggested Tulya.

Beltur nodded, as did Jessyla.

The five set out, into a light but chill wind more out of the east than the north, which left Beltur wondering if it was a forewarning of a northeaster, except usually the wind warmed, comparatively, before a northeaster.

Some moments later, as they walked away from the square, Beltur looked to Jessyla. "On the way back to the cot, I should stop briefly and let Jorhan and Johlana know what the Council decided. I'm sure they're concerned." *If for different reasons.* "I won't be long."

"That would be a good idea," replied Jessyla. "It will take us a little time to get dinner ready, anyway."

As they neared Barrynt's mansion, Beltur walked ahead and then strode up the side drive and the steps. When he knocked at the door, Ryntaar was the one to open it.

"Is Jorhan or your father here? I thought I should tell them about what happened at the Council meeting."

"Ah . . . Father's not seeing anyone right now, but Uncle Jorhan's around somewhere. If you'd come in and wait here in the hall . . ."

"That would be fine. I won't be long, but I thought everyone should know." Beltur stepped into the side hall.

"I'll get Uncle." Ryntaar immediately hurried away.

Beltur frowned. The young man seemed preoccupied. *He didn't even ask what the Council decided.* That seemed odd.

Several moments later, Jorhan appeared, also looking concerned.

Beltur could sense from the swirled mix of chaos and order around the smith that he also was perturbed or concerned. "Are you all right?"

"Oh, I'm fine. Barrynt's in one of his moods. He won't say why. He never does." Jorhan snorted. "Even I can tell that it has something to do with Sarysta and Halhana. Now, how did things go with the Council?"

"They decided we all could stay in Axalt," replied Beltur, adding dryly, "so long as we don't use chaos to coerce or harm anyone or anything."

"That's wonderful! I was worried . . ."

"So were we, but I have to say that, this time, it appears that all the Council's insistence on thoroughness and following procedures worked for us."

"About time that it did. About time."

Beltur thought he heard, or more likely sensed, muffled words from the parlor, loud enough that Beltur could hear some of them, if barely . . .

". . . that bitch Sarysta . . ."

"Beltur . . . we can talk more about this tomorrow. You'll be there?"

"I will."

"Good." Jorhan opened the side door. "Until then."

Beltur felt he had no choice but to leave, but, as he hurried down the steps and lengthened his stride, he wondered just what Sarysta had done to set Barrynt off. From what he'd seen, Barrynt didn't anger easily. But then he recalled Sarysta's snide comments about Johlana, the single time he'd met her, and the cruel coldness behind them.

He shook his head. *There are so many things you don't know about people.* He smiled ruefully. *You really didn't understand how much Uncle cared until he was gone.*

He blinked away the tearing in his eyes and kept walking.

LXIII

As he walked to the smithy on sevenday, a day slightly warmer than those previous, but still far colder than anything he'd experienced before coming to Axalt, Beltur couldn't help but think over the preoccupation and concern shown by both Jorhan and Ryntaar the day before. Clearly, something had upset the merchant, and upset him enough to concern Jorhan, and Beltur had never seen Jorhan that disconcerted. *Angry, yes, but not disconcerted.*

Once he'd reached the smithy and taken off his coat, Beltur made his way to the workbench near the forge where Jorhan was working on a mold.

"It's another decorative box."

"Both you and Ryntaar seemed very disconcerted last night," Beltur offered, not wanting to ask bluntly what had happened, but hoping that Jorhan would explain.

"Barrynt was in one of his moods. Worse than usual. Really angry. I told you I wouldn't want to get on his bad side."

"It doesn't seem like he's the type to hurt people," said Beltur.

"Johlana says he's never hurt anyone in the family. He's very protective of his family. Once he threw a fellow in the river for being rude to her."

"Was this something that Eshult did?"

"Demon stars, no. That boy might have despicable parents, but he does his best for Halhana. Trouble is that he's trying not to displease them. No . . . from what I heard, Halhana had said that she and Eshult were coming for dinner on eightday. Then, she said that they couldn't come because something had come up with Eshult's parents. This was the third or fourth time it happened, and Johlana was upset." Jorhan shook his head. "Barrynt usually gets stone-faced. This time, he was yelling about how manipulative Sarysta was, how hurtful she was. He was shouting about how Emlyn indulged Sarysta's every whim."

"Sarysta sounds spoiled."

"They're all snobs. Emlyn might as well be a trader in Elparta. Same selfish pride. Doesn't help that Sarysta's brother is just as wealthy, and he's on the Council."

Beltur couldn't help but wonder if that had helped or hurt as far as he and Lhadoraak were concerned—or if they were considered so insignificant that the brother hadn't even known about any connection.

"How was Barrynt this morning?"

"Pleasant enough. Quiet, though."

Beltur decided not to pursue that matter. "How is this mold different?"

"Longer and narrower. Thought I'd try ferns, rather than rosebuds."

Beltur nodded, then looked at the forge. There was already enough coal there that he didn't need to add any more.

"I'll be ready to start the melt in just a bit. Wouldn't hurt if you brought in more coal for the firebox."

"I'll take care of that."

By a quint after second glass, there was nothing else for Beltur to do, and he left the smithy. There was little point in his staying because he wasn't getting paid for his time, and whatever he earned from his share depended on what might be sold in the eightdays after spring-turn. Selling a piece or two before then, from those displayed in Barrynt's factorage, was possible, but hardly likely.

Because he was finished early and Jessyla was at the healing house, Beltur decided to walk by the square just to see if there might be anything he could buy there . . . and possibly also stop by the chandlery.

He was almost to the square when he saw a coach drawn up beside the shop next to the chandlery, with the driver standing beside the horses. He looked more closely at the black coach with silver trim that looked somehow familiar. *Black and silver?* Beltur eased into the shadows of the next building and drew a concealment around himself. That way anyone looking would have thought he just walked the other way.

Then he moved swiftly as he dared toward the coach, hoping to get there before whoever was shopping finished. He wasn't certain what he might discover, but after what Jorhan had said, Beltur couldn't help being curious. As he neared the coach and the driver, he could sense that there was one person in the coach, likely a man. *Emlyn? Eshult?*

The man's order/chaos levels suggested someone older, and that most likely was Emlyn, possibly waiting for Sarysta. Beltur slipped up beside the coach, its side door slightly ajar, taking a position far enough back that Sarysta, or whoever Emlyn was waiting for, could enter without bumping into Beltur in his concealment.

Almost half a quint passed before a woman left the shop and walked swiftly to the coach, carrying a package of some sort.

Emlyn leaned forward and pushed the door open. "That took a while."

"Don't provoke me, Emlyn. I'm still furious. That business with the mirror. I can't have that sheepherder's brat Johlana interfering with Eshult's happiness. She's already created too much misery." Sarysta leaned into the coach and set the package on the rear-facing seat.

"It's only a mirror. Who'll see it?"

"I know it's there. It simply doesn't go with the décor." Sarysta eased herself into the coach. "Besides, it's the principle."

"You mean that Johlana commissioned something of taste—"

"It's an awful silver copper color, and before long she'll be changing everything that I spent so long doing for Eshult. You wouldn't want that, would you?"

Beltur winced, not only at the falsely sweet tone, but at the veiled and menacing hints behind the words, hints he was certain he was not imagining.

"He loves her. Why are you making—"

"He only thinks he loves her, dear. I'm sure he'll see. I'm only thinking about Eshult . . ."

The rest of Sarysta's words were lost to Beltur as she shut the coach door firmly. He stepped back, half stunned by Sarysta's words.

He was still standing several moments later. Finally, he turned and began to make his way back toward the cot. He did stop at the next alleyway to duck into the shadows and lift the concealment before continuing, his thoughts still on the brief interchange he'd overheard.

Johlana creating misery? Somehow, he couldn't see that.

Beltur was still mulling it all over when he returned to the cot just after third glass, where he found Tulya giving Taelya lessons in reading and spelling at the kitchen table.

Taelya looked up immediately from the small chalkboard in front of her.

Tulya turned. "Lhadoraak's out talking to the owner of a sawmill. He was hoping there might be work there come spring. We're just about finished with today's lesson."

"Do we have to do more, Mother?"

Tulya smiled. "Well . . . you could do mage lessons with Beltur."

"If you're not too tired," added Beltur.

"I'm not too tired. Can we start now?"

"In the front room," said Tulya. "That way, I can start dinner."

Taelya almost bounced out of her chair on her way into the living room.

"Best of fortune," offered Tulya in a low voice. "She still gets restive when she has to correct her mistakes."

"That's like most of us. We just don't say anything. Children more often do."

Beltur walked back to the front room, where Tulya sat on the bench, and settled into the chair farthest from the door. "I thought we might work on your shields first. Then, we'll see about whether you can use chaos to light some kindling. That's harder than lighting a candle." It was also another step toward teaching Taelya how to handle larger amounts of chaos on the way to her learning how to create and use chaos bolts . . . but a step that Beltur intended would teach Taelya how to do that in a way that kept free chaos well controlled by order and, if necessary, natural chaos.

That control was going to be absolutely necessary, given what the Council had declared . . . and especially what Naerkaal had not said.

Beltur smiled. "First, raise the best shield that you can."

LXIV

Beltur wasn't about to discuss what he'd overheard until he and Jessyla were alone, and it was well after eighth glass before he closed the door to their bedroom.

"What is it, dear?" Jessyla immediately asked. "You've been very quiet. Something's bothering you. Is it something with Jorhan? Or the Council?"

"Neither. We finished early at the smithy, and I thought I'd walk to the square before heading home . . ." When Beltur finished telling her what he'd heard, he asked, "What do you think?"

"She said it just like that?"

"It was even worse. I can't even imitate the false-sweet tone. And I've never sensed anyone so cold . . . well, except maybe Waensyn."

"She's that bad?"

"If you could have heard her."

"I believe you." Jessyla frowned. "But how could Johlana have created this misery that Sarysta was talking about?"

"I've been thinking about that. More than a little. Do you think that Sarysta was related to Barrynt's first consort? That wouldn't be something anyone would talk about."

"No," mused Jessyla. "They wouldn't. That might explain the furniture, but Johlana had nothing to do with his first consort. She didn't even know Barrynt then. And if it happened that way, why wouldn't Sarysta be angry at Barrynt, not Johlana?"

"Maybe because Sarysta wanted Barrynt to be miserable for the rest of his life, and Johlana made him happy," suggested Beltur.

"From what everyone's said, Barrynt was miserable for several years. That should have been enough."

"For someone like Sarysta . . ."

Jessyla shook her head. "I don't think that makes sense. It shouldn't, anyway."

"So what do I do? From what I've seen, if I mention it to Barrynt, he'll get really angry again, the way he was the other day. And I really don't want to tell Johlana, because she'll either get upset or tell Barrynt . . ."

"If not both," said Jessyla.

"And I don't want to put Barrynt in one of his moods again. Not right after he's been so angry."

"Why don't you just wait a day or two, then," suggested Jessyla. "Let him calm down before you tell him something that will upset him."

"I don't want to wait too long. I didn't like the way Sarysta was talking about the mirror and Johlana."

"You could stop by there tomorrow after the healing house. That will at least give Barrynt another day to calm down. Come home and the two of us could go over there together."

Beltur nodded. "It might be better if you were with me."

"Then we'll plan on that."

Beltur took a deep breath.

"Do you feel better about it?"

"Better. I still worry." But the last thing Beltur wanted to do was to send Barrynt into a rage, and a day, really, even less than a day, to let things settle was probably a good idea. Beltur hoped so, anyway.

LXV

Eightday morning was slightly warmer than it had been on sevenday, but it was still clear and cold, not warm enough, nor cloudy enough to presage a northeaster. When Beltur entered the stable, he was surprised to see Frankyr there, saddling one of his father's horses.

"Good morning, Frankyr. Are you going riding?"

"Just to give Starshine a little exercise. The horses need it, even if it is cold."

Beltur nodded, then asked, "How are you doing at the factorage?"

"I'm learning. There's more to know than I thought." A rueful expression crossed the young man's face.

"There always is . . . in everything."

Frankyr gave a gentle laugh of agreement.

"How's your father doing?"

"Well enough, ser."

Frankyr's almost too calm and flat statement told Beltur that Barrynt still wasn't a happy man. "Well . . . give him my best. I hope he'll be feeling better soon."

"Thank you." Frankyr smiled, partly out of relief that Beltur hadn't pursued the inquiry, most likely, and added, "I'll tell him . . . after I get back."

Frankyr's words confirmed Beltur's feelings that it probably had been a good idea to wait until that afternoon to talk to Barrynt. Even so, as he picked up the pitchfork and started for the end of the stable, he still worried somewhat about Barrynt, given that he'd heard earlier that Barrynt's "moods" usually passed quickly . . . and the present "mood" definitely seemed not to be passing. *But what else can you do, especially when it's a family matter that Barrynt and Johlana aren't sharing with you?*

Beltur tried to put aside his worries as he dealt with the stable. Before long, Frankyr finished saddling Starshine and rode off.

The young man still hadn't returned before Beltur finished his stable chores and headed off to the healing house, still pondering over everything. After his two encounters with Sarysta, he was beginning to see why Barrynt was so upset. *On the other hand, it isn't as though people are trying to kill him or his family, or even drive them out of Axalt.* But then, he could recall the young Undercaptain Zandyr during the invasion, a man still really a youth, but one so involved with position and who consorted whom, and who wasn't considered to have position—like Beltur—and who was.

Given that, he could understand Barrynt's being upset at the clear social jabs being leveled at Johlana. What he had trouble understanding was why people like Sarysta needed to be nasty to those they thought beneath them. *Maybe they don't even see themselves as nasty, but just as holding to their "traditional" standards.* After all, Trader Alizant likely hadn't even considered the hardship created for Jorhan and Beltur by his desire to control the trade of cupridium, and if he had, he certainly would have dismissed Beltur and Jorhan as undeserving inferiors. Even in Axalt, the Council had had difficulty with the "unprecedented" situation with which Beltur and Taelya had presented them.

Beltur was still shaking his head when he walked into the healing house and took off his coat and scarf. Then he walked to Herrara's study.

"You're looking thoughtful this morning," said Herrara.

"Just thinking."

"Jessyla told me what the Council said. They didn't change their minds, did they?"

"Oh, no. I was thinking more about how they decided and how close it likely was because we represented something new and unprecedented and how people don't like change."

"Most people don't. Do you?"

Beltur laughed, then shook his head. "For the last year my life has been nothing but one change after another. Well . . . most of the last year. It's not as though I ever had a choice."

"You didn't answer the question." Herrara's tone was dry.

"Some of the changes were terrible, and I didn't like those. Some were for the best, and I knew that, and some weren't for the best, but I learned from them."

"That's likely the way most of us feel, but most people dread change when it looks to affect the way they've always lived. The Council's no different."

"They seem to be fairer than the Traders' Council of Spidlar."

"From what you and Jessyla have said and from what I've heard, that wouldn't be hard." Herrara paused, then said, "There's another man found in the snow near the Traders' Bowl last night. He's upstairs in the room across from the stairs. I'd like you to take a look at him first."

"Anything else?"

"No, but come back here before you look at Klaznyt or the others."

Beltur nodded and took a basket of supplies from the shelf, just in case, then left the study and made his way up the stairs. Just when he was about to cross the hall and enter the room, Elisa stepped out of the adjoining room. Beltur stopped.

"I'm glad the Council decided that you and Jessyla could stay in Axalt."

"Thank you. So are we."

"You're both such good healers, different, but good."

"How would you say we're different?" Beltur could immediately sense that his question had flustered the young healer-in-training and offered a warm smile.

"Ah . . . you both care. She shows it more. You don't . . . but . . . you both work so hard to heal people." After a moment, she said, "You're a powerful mage. I can sense that. You don't say much, but you work so hard as a healer . . ."

"And you want to know why?"

Elisa nodded.

Beltur smiled ruefully. "I'm not sure I know . . . except it's important, somehow." He shrugged. "That's not much of an answer, but it's all I can say." And it was.

After another hesitation, Elisa said, "You're looking in at the old man there?" She looked toward the half-open door.

"I am."

"We couldn't get much water or even ale into him. I don't think . . . it's not my place to say . . ."

"Wait here, if you would," said Beltur.

"Yes, ser."

"I won't be long." Beltur crossed the hall and entered the room. He immediately understood what Elisa had meant. The man lying under the blanket drawn up to his neck was breathing, as evidenced by a labored wheezing, but otherwise unmoving. His salt-and-pepper beard was so tangled that a rat's nest was doubtless better looking, and there were patches of frostburn on the exposed skin of his face, as well as elsewhere, from the reddish wound chaos Beltur could sense. Most telling was the very low level of both natural order and natural chaos, as low and possibly lower than Beltur had seen before, even in those who were dying or had died soon after he'd sensed such levels. There were also scores of patches of reddish wound chaos spread within his skull, dull chaos, but so many that Beltur could have spent days trying to remove them.

Yet as Beltur looked more closely, he could see that the man was likely not any older than Athaal had been, possibly even younger. He could also sense that both natural order and chaos were slowly seeping away . . . and that there was little or nothing that he could do. Neither free order nor chaos would help, and might actually hurt, so fragile was the man's condition, and using Beltur's own natural forces would only prolong the dying.

He took a deep breath, then touched the man's forehead, and offered just the slightest bit of order and warmth before stepping back and leaving the room.

Elisa stood outside in the hallway, waiting, her eyes on him.

"You're right. He won't last long, and there's nothing I can do. I don't think anyone could." He paused. "That bothers you, doesn't it?"

She nodded, then said, "It bothers you, too."

"Yes. It bothers Herrara, too. I don't think you ever get used to it."

As he headed back downstairs, another thought struck him. *And you shouldn't ever get used to it.*

Herrara looked up from the ledger as Beltur entered the study. "What do you think?"

"He's dying. There's nothing I can do to stop it. Elisa said you couldn't even get him to drink."

"Not when they're that far gone. That could have happened to Klaznyt, if they hadn't found him as soon as they did."

"How often does this happen?"

"Several times every winter. Three years ago, there were more than a half score, but that was the coldest winter than I can remember."

Beltur tried not to wince. The winter so far had certainly seemed bitter to him.

"You might as well get to the others now. I just wanted your opinion."

Beltur nodded. He understood why.

Taking his basket, he headed for Wurfael's room. The young timberman would certainly be more cheerful than Klaznyt.

Wurfael was indeed cheerful, possibly because he was getting used to the peg leg, and had learned that he could sleep in the tin shop once Herrara said he could leave. Klaznyt didn't want to talk, and that was fine with Beltur, who found only a few new spots of wound chaos.

More than a glass later, he had just finished putting a new dressing on the arm of a young girl in the welcoming room when Elisa appeared.

"She needs you in the surgery."

Beltur hurried down the corridor and through the half-open door.

A dark-haired and stocky man sat on one side of the surgery table. From his ruddy complexion and weathered face, Beltur would have guessed that he was perhaps ten years older than Beltur himself and that he was someone who worked outside.

A woman stood beside him, talking to Herrara. ". . . not right, I say, not at all."

"I'm fine . . . just short of breath," declared the man.

"It might be more than that," said Herrara, glancing toward Beltur. "Does your chest hurt?"

As Beltur drew nearer, he saw that the man was sweating profusely, and that his face was pale beneath the ruddiness of his weathered skin.

The man shook his head, then said, "Maybe a little."

Herrara took the man's wrist, holding it for a time, before releasing it and asking, "Have you been working hard today?"

"On eightday? No. Only day I don't work."

"Have you been hurt recently?"

"Not really."

"Not really?" The woman glared at him and turned to Herrara. "The log pile at the mill shifted on him, logs rolled over his legs, bruised him all over them."

"That was the pile of the smaller logs, not the big ones."

"When did that happen?"

"An eightday back from sixday," answered the woman. "He was so sore he could hardly walk for two, three days. He still walks like he's sore."

"Just bruises . . ." The man's eyes fluttered, and then he slumped forward.

Beltur managed to catch him, and he and Herrara stretched him out on the table.

Beltur immediately tried to sense what might be the problem.

"What is it?" demanded the woman.

"We're trying to find out," said Herrara tersely as she leaned down and listened to the man's chest. "His heart's still beating fast. Too fast."

The man shuddered slightly, and his eyes opened for a moment. He tried to speak, but all that happened was that a slight foam, tinged with blood, issued from his mouth.

"Has he had any signs of consumption?" asked Herrara.

"Bartrand? Never. Never even got the sniffles."

"What sort of chaos do you detect?" Herrara asked Beltur.

"There's nothing around the heart, but there's a lot around his right lung, and, of course, in his legs and thighs, especially on the right side."

Abruptly, Bartrand stiffened. Beltur could sense that his heart had stopped beating. In moments, the black and chill mist of death that Beltur had felt too often drifted across him.

"What happened? What did you do?"

Beltur swallowed, then looked at the woman. "We didn't do anything. He . . . he just . . . died."

"What did you do? Why couldn't you do something? You're healers!"

"There wasn't anything we could do," Herrara replied. "The chaos from his legs, from all that bruising, rose through his body and got into his lungs and heart."

"He said they were only bruises. He only had a few scrapes and cuts."

"Sometimes, when chaos is inside someone, they don't even know it," Herrara said gently.

"But he was so strong. He was good. Why did it have to happen to him?"

"That kind of chaos," said Herrara, her tone still gentle, "doesn't care whether someone is good. It's a hidden kind of wound chaos. I'm so sorry . . ."

Tears seeped from the corners of the woman's eyes. "Why Bartrand? He was so young. I told him yesterday . . . told him he needed to see a healer . . ."

Beltur stood there unmoving. He'd seen more than enough death, but he'd always seen an obvious cause—a sword, an arrow, a chaos bolt, one of his own order confinements, or even a massive growth of wound chaos too great and too widespread to stop—but this . . . ? A little chest pain, a small froth of blood, and bruising in the legs and thighs, and points of chaos in the lungs and chest? And a strong man was suddenly dead.

"Sometimes . . . there's nothing we can do," said Herrara.

Beltur could sense both sadness and fatalism from the older healer . . . and the swirling of order and chaos from the bereaved woman.

"You can go, Beltur," said Herrara. "There's nothing you can do."

Nothing at all.

Beltur still felt numb as he walked from the surgery, and he wondered why. He hadn't known the man. He'd only seen his last moments. *But it was so sudden . . . and so seemingly without cause.*

Because he really didn't want to see or talk to anyone for a time, he walked back to Herrara's office and sat down on the straight-backed chair in the corner.

After a time, Beltur wasn't certain how long, Herrara walked into the study, closing the door before making her way to the desk and sitting down behind it. She looked evenly at him.

"You've had quite a day, Beltur."

"So have you."

"I'm a little more used to it."

"I've probably seen more death than you have," he replied, "but not . . . like this."

"Why is it different?"

Beltur thought she honestly sounded interested.

"In battle, you know people will die. You hope you're not one of them. Except you really don't think about it. You can't afford to. Then . . . when it's over, you're relieved that it's not you. Later, sometimes a lot later, you feel guilty about others, at least I did, about the ones you might have saved, and the ones . . . the ones you tried to save and couldn't. But there were reasons, likely senseless reasons, but people did things based on those reasons. Here . . . is there any real reason why one man will survive with clumsy hands and another will die, and there's nothing we can do about it? Or that another man dies, somehow, of a wound he never knew he had, and that we can't do a thing about?"

"That's what healing's all about. We often don't know who will live and who won't. Or why. We can only do our best . . . and hope." She smiled sadly. "Isn't that what life's about?"

Beltur nodded.

After a long silence, she said, "It's time to make another round. Spend a few moments with Wurfael. It will do you both good."

As he stood Beltur couldn't but help smiling briefly at her no-nonsense tone.

The rest of the day was, thankfully, far less eventful, and Beltur left, slightly before fourth glass, at Herrara's behest.

As he walked back to the cot, still thinking over everything that had happened during the day, he realized that the wind had indeed shifted to the northeast, and that he could see dark clouds just lurking at the end of the narrow canyon that led eastward to Certis. *Definitely looks like a north-easter.* At least it wouldn't start snowing until well after dinner, and he and Jessyla could go see Barrynt before the snow started. He wasn't looking forward to that, either.

When he opened the door to the cot, Jessyla immediately was there to meet him by the time he'd taken off his coat. She started to speak, then paused for a moment before finally saying, "You look like it was a hard day."

Beltur nodded. "A man came in having trouble breathing and in less than half a quint he was dead . . ." He explained quickly, then said, "I'm sure you've seen things like that."

"Not since we've been here. It happened more often in Elparta."

"Somehow the chaos from those bruises in his legs got to his lungs and heart."

"I've never seen that before."

"I don't think Herrara had either."

THRAPP!!! THRAP!! THRAP!! The insistent pounding at the door sounded almost frantic.

Beltur looked at Jessyla.

"I have no idea."

He turned and opened the door. As the frigid air blasted past Beltur, he gaped at Frankyr, who stood there with his chest heaving. "Beltur! You have to come quick! Father's going to do something awful! Maybe he already has."

"Where? What is it?"

"Ryntaar's saddling your horse and another. They'll be ready by the time we get to the house. I'll tell you on the way."

Beltur grabbed his coat, gloves, and scarf and followed Frankyr, not quite at a run, asking, "What's he going to do?"

"Something terrible . . . Sarysta returned the cupridium mirror you and Uncle Jorhan made to Johlana."

The mirror! Was that what she meant? "And?"

"Sarysta said that the color didn't match the décor of Eshult and Hal-hana's house. That it had too much of a gold tint to it and that didn't go with the silver and black . . ." Frankyr slowed somewhat and went on. "Father'd been out riding. He said that the horses needed the exercise before the northeaster hit. When he came in and heard what had happened, he didn't say a word. He just walked out to the stable. Mother thought he had just gone out to the stable to calm down. He does that, you know. But when he rode down the lane, she sent me to get you. He has to have gone to Emlyn's house."

Beltur had a very bad feeling about that, especially after what he'd heard on sevenday. "You're worried about what he might say?"

"You don't understand, ser. Father's in a rage. It doesn't happen often, but when it does, nothing at all will stop him. Mother says this is the worst she's ever seen."

"He's that upset?" Beltur was afraid that Barrynt just might be.

"That mirror was better than anything Halhana and Eshult have, and likely worth more. Halhana loved it. Sarysta either took it without Halhana knowing it, or Emlyn and Sarysta threatened to break the consorting . . . something like that."

"They can do that?"

"Sarysta's brother's a councilor. Emlyn's the wealthiest trader in Axalt. They can do anything they want."

That almost stopped Beltur dead. He could see that happening in Elparta . . . but the Axalt Council hadn't struck him as that bad.

Ryntaar and Johlana were leading Slowpoke and another mount from the stable as Beltur and Frankyr hurried up the drive.

"Please get to him," pleaded Johlana. "I know you can stop him without hurting him or anyone else. Jorhan's told me about how you've done that when you were a patrol mage. Ryntaar will show you the way. Please hurry."

"I'll do what I can. How far is Emlyn's house?" asked Beltur as he mounted.

"More like a grand mansion," muttered Frankyr.

"Less than half a quint's ride at a walk," said Ryntaar.

Beltur almost suggested that Slowpoke could do better than that, but realized that, although the streets were cleared, there were more than a few patches of ice, and that a riding accident wouldn't be helpful. "We can do a fast walk, maybe a trot." He really didn't like the idea of galloping over icy stone streets.

Ryntaar immediately headed down the drive, but Slowpoke kept pace as they turned toward the market square. They stayed on that street only until the next corner, where they turned north. The street widened after some two hundred yards into what Beltur would have called a boulevard, flanked by dwellings that made Barrynt's house look modest by comparison. The boulevard curved gradually westward, climbing slightly as it did.

"The gray stone house with the dark green shutters and trim," called out Ryntaar. "That's Emlyn's."

Beltur could see that Emlyn's mansion, a good four levels high and still more than a hundred yards away, was surrounded by a stone wall not quite two yards high, but the gates were open, and there was no guardhouse. He followed Ryntaar through the gates. The drive made a circle around what was likely a garden in warmer seasons, but was merely a large snow pile at present. On the far side of the circular drive was the covered entry to the mansion.

"That's father's horse tied there!"

When Beltur reined up short of the hitching rail to the side of the entry, he saw that the front door was ajar, and seemed to be at a slight angle. He dismounted quickly and thrust Slowpoke's reins at Ryntaar. "You stay here with the horses!"

Then he checked his shields and hurried through the damaged door and into a large square entry hall. A door to the left opened into a parlor, which appeared empty. Beltur glanced into the room on the right, which appeared to be a study of some sort, where at least one chair lay on its side.

Beltur immediately hurried into the study, only to see two bodies—with a woman in the corner and a tall man in dark green livery, a blade still in his hand, turning toward the door . . . and Beltur.

The swordsman slashed at Beltur, his blade rebounding from Beltur's shields.

Beltur clapped a containment around the swordsman, quickly taking in the two bodies, one flat on his back in front of the ornate hearth and the other on the thick carpet beside a dark wooden desk. For a moment, Beltur did not recognize the man who lay on his back, his head at an angle that suggested his neck was broken. The blood pooled on the cream tiles below the hearth suggested that the back of his skull had been crushed. The well-tailored jacket, shimmersilk shirt, and tooled and polished boots, as well as the silver in his still well-groomed hair and beard, only confirmed that the dead man was Emlyn.

Barrynt lay on his side, his face still contorted, either in rage or anguish. There was a single slash across his neck, and the darkness of blood on his jacket and the carpet.

Beltur reached out with his senses, but he was already too late. Both men were dead.

"Stop him, Mhorgaan!" snapped a woman—Sarysta—standing in the corner of the study, one side of her face reddened.

"I cannot, Lady. The mage has me trapped."

"I'm not here to attack anyone. I was trying to get here in time to stop Barrynt from hurting someone."

"Likely story!" snapped the swordsman.

"What are you doing here?" demanded Sarysta imperiously.

"Trying to stop Barrynt, like I told you, Sarysta."

"Lady Sarysta to you."

"Ser, to you," retorted Beltur. "You're the cause of this mess."

"I did nothing, except exercise good taste."

For a moment, Beltur was stunned. While Barrynt had obviously attacked her as well as Emlyn, why was she talking about good taste? Except she'd been prating about that and décor to Emlyn the day before. *Good taste?*

"And your presence is most distasteful. Nonetheless, as party to this . . . atrocity, you will remain until the city patrollers and the Council guards can be summoned."

Beltur repressed a sigh. There was no help for that. The last thing he needed was to flee a mess like the one he'd stepped into. He addressed the swordsman. "If I release you, will you set down that blade and do what's necessary to summon the city patrollers, and, as Sarysta sees fit, the Council guards?"

"I'll sheathe the blade. It hasn't done much good against you."

"No . . . lay it across the desk. Since you used it to kill Merchant Barrynt, it should remain."

"I'll be unarmed."

"Just do as he says, Mhorgaan. He's being sensible, if not terribly respectful."

At that moment, Ryntaar appeared in the doorway.

Beltur released the containment, ready to reimpose it instantly. "Ryntaar, step inside and stand back from him."

Ryntaar did as Beltur directed, and Mhorgaan moved to the door before looking to Sarysta. "Who shall I send to assist you, Lady?"

"Escaylt. He's in the library. Dispatch Albard to summon the guards. Then return here."

Mhorgaan inclined his head and then hurried off.

"You actually seem to be a mage," said Sarysta. "I still can't imagine what you had to do with that insufferable fellow Barrynt, except I suppose mages are useful for certain things."

Useful? "He did me several favors," Beltur replied, finding himself both repelled by Sarysta's coldness, and the cold-ordered chaos of her very being, and wanting to strike her down.

"They must have been great favors for you to invade this house."

"I didn't invade it. The doors were open, and I was trying to get here before Barrynt did something terrible."

"You must have known him well. Very well."

Beltur understood what she was trying to do.

"Not that well, or I might have been able to do something much earlier. I met him only about a season ago."

"Still . . ." Sarysta drew the word out as she eased into the side chair closest to her.

"You know," Beltur said conversationally, "I'm always surprised when I run into people who use every word and every action to manipulate people, often into taking unwise actions that are designed to benefit the manipulator."

"She's always done that," said Ryntaar quietly. "Even before the time when Eshult and Halhana were consorted, she was doing that." Tears streamed down his cheeks.

"Better that consorting never happened. After this, it will be as if it never had. Even a mage can't change that."

"I suppose that's also a matter of taste?" asked Beltur sardonically.

"All life with any meaning is a matter of taste. That's something that . . . some people never understand."

Beltur glanced from Sarysta to where Emlyn still lay, wondering just how the woman could be so cold, then back to Sarysta, just in time to see her looking at Barrynt, with the hint of a satisfied smile, a smile that vanished as she looked away.

At that moment, a young man, more properly a youth, burst into the room. "Mother!"

His eyes went from Sarysta to Beltur and then to his father. He paled, standing there, almost swaying.

"Gather yourself together, Escaylt. Going to pieces won't change anything. The mage and I . . . and that other person . . . are waiting for the city patrollers." Sarysta motioned for her son to join her.

The youth stepped around Barrynt's body and avoided looking at that of his father.

Beltur didn't feel like saying more, especially knowing that Sarysta would likely twist anything he said. So he stood and waited, shifting his weight from one leg to the other, trying to sense what might be happening beyond the study, but nothing appeared to be occurring anywhere near.

Sarysta murmured a few words to her son, but did not address Beltur or Ryntaar. That was fine with Beltur.

More than a quint passed before Beltur heard the clatter of hooves, and then the sound of men entering the mansion.

"This way, sers, this way, in the study."

Beltur didn't recognize the voice, although he thought it might be that of Mhorgaan, which suggested that Emlyn's bodyguard had needed to go to the city patrollers himself. Beltur did recognize the first man to step inside the study. "Councilor Naerkaal . . . I'm glad you're here."

"Am I going to be happy you're here?"

As Naerkaal spoke, another man appeared. While Beltur didn't know his name, he recognized him as a councilor. Behind them stood several guards.

"Were you a part of this?" pressed Naerkaal.

"No. I arrived after whatever happened. Both were dead before I even entered the house."

Naerkaal looked to Sarysta. "The mage says that he arrived after the deeds were done. Is that correct?"

"He arrived later. Very soon after Mhorgaan killed the intruder who had broken into the house."

"Have either of you touched anything?"

"No."

Naerkaal turned back to Beltur. "How was it that you just happened to arrive so coincidentally? Please explain."

"It wasn't coincidental. Barrynt's family summoned me. I'd just returned to our cot from working at the healing house when young Frankyr appeared and pounded on the door . . ." Beltur went on to relate absolutely factually everything that had happened until Naerkaal had appeared. He did not relate his conversations with Sarysta.

Naerkaal turned to Sarysta. "What do you know of what happened here?"

Sarysta straightened in the chair, but did not stand. "I was in my study. The door was ajar. I heard some sort of noise at the door. Then several moments later I heard an angry voice. Emlyn answered the angry man calmly. Then he called out for me to stay out. But there was another crash, and I called for Mhorgaan. Then I ran from my study into the hall and in here. Emlyn was lying right where he is now. Barrynt turned to me and struck me so hard that I fell into the desk and then to the floor. Barrynt stood over me. He uttered despicable language. Then Mhorgaan arrived and immediately slashed Barrynt across the neck. I had just struggled to my feet when the mage rushed in. I thought he might kill me and Mhorgaan. Mhorgaan thrust at him, but his blade did not strike him. Then the mage said something about being too late to stop Barrynt, and he restrained Mhorgaan with magery."

The only part of what Sarysta said that didn't ring quite true to Beltur were the words about despicable language. For the moment, he said nothing.

"Then what happened?" asked Naerkaal.

"I said the City Patrol and the Council should be summoned. The mage agreed and released Mhorgaan. Mhorgaan left. Escaylt joined me. The . . . other person there joined the mage. We waited. You finally arrived."

Naerkaal turned to Beltur. "Do Lady Sarysta's words agree with what you saw?"

"I cannot say about what happened before I arrived. Everything she said about what happened after I entered the study is exactly as I saw it. I would be interested to know what sort of despicable words Barrynt uttered. I was told that when he was extremely angry he seldom spoke."

"Did you ever see him angry?" asked Naerkaal.

"I never saw him angry enough to do something like this. There was one time when I went to see him and his family said he was in one of his moods and that I should talk to him later." They hadn't quite said it, but that had been the unspoken message.

"Why did you need to see him at that time?"

"When I came to Axalt, he helped us find and furnish the cot, and helped Jorhan the smith and me find the building for Jorhan's smithy. I took care of his stable in return for being able to stable our horses there."

Naerkaal nodded and turned back to Sarysta. "I would also be interested to know if you heard anything that your consort and Barrynt said to each other, or what Barrynt said to you or you to him."

The other councilor stiffened slightly.

Sarysta looked levelly at Naerkaal. "I only heard the few words Barrynt said before he killed Emlyn. He said, 'You and your bitch consort won't destroy my daughter's happiness with your backbiting foolishness.' I was just in the doorway when he picked up Emlyn as if he were nothing and threw him into the hearth. I ran toward Barrynt. I think I screamed. He turned and hit me. I fell, and he stood over me. He said that I was a bitch worse than any in Westwind and that I'd destroyed a good man . . ." Sarysta swallowed.

"Go on."

". . . that I deserved even worse than what happened to Emlyn."

"And?"

"Mhorgaan rushed in and killed him."

"There's only one wound on Barrynt," observed Naerkaal.

"Mhorgaan is very good. That's why he's been with Emlyn for years. We . . . never . . . expected someone to force their way into the house . . ."

Naerkaal turned to the other man. "Councilor Sarstaan . . . they've both told the truth. They both agree on what happened. Considering their positions, it would appear that matters are exactly as the bodies and what they have said would indicate. Do you have any questions for either?"

Sarstaan immediately asked Beltur, "Did you have any idea that Barrynt meant to harm Emlyn or Sarysta?"

"No. I knew that he felt that they were trying to interfere with his daughter's life, but he never said anything that suggested he meant to do anything violent to them."

Sarstaan looked to Naerkaal, who nodded. Then he looked to Sarysta, "Did Emlyn ever say anything about fearing or worrying about Barrynt?"

"No. Never. He said he was a bit of a buffoon, and that he was a tool of his consort."

Naerkaal motioned to the guards, who stepped forward. "The mage and the young man may remove the body of Merchant Barrynt. Nothing more." Then he turned to Sarysta. "Your brother and I will be using your study for a short time. The guards will assist you in moving your consort's body."

"Thank you." Sarysta's voice was even. "Escaylt and I will wait for a moment until the . . . other body is gone." She glanced at Ryntaar, and Beltur could not only see anger and scorn, as well as condescension, but also feel it, as well as almost . . . *vindictive joy?*

Still, he did not move until Naerkaal and Sarstaan were in the hallway and well away from the study. Then he stepped toward Barrynt's body. "It's time we took your father home."

Without even looking at Sarysta, he sent out his senses and withdrew a large amount of natural chaos from Sarysta, a very large amount that he let bleed into the air.

So much for satisfaction and vindictive joy.

Then he and Ryntaar lifted Barrynt's limp form from the carpet.

"The Council will deal with the likes of all of you," declared Sarysta as Beltur and Ryntaar carried Barrynt out into the hall. "We will see to that."

Beltur did not reply, nor did Ryntaar. They carried the merchant out of the mansion and out to where the horses were tied at the hitching rail. Two Council guards watched as they neared, but said nothing.

"We'll put his body over his mount. I'll lead his horse, and we'll follow you. I didn't pay much attention on the way."

Ryntaar only nodded.

Once Beltur was convinced that Barrynt was securely in place, he took the other horse's reins and mounted Slowpoke. Then he gestured for Ryntaar to head out.

As he rode, so many thoughts crossed his mind. *Why had Barrynt attacked Emlyn when Sarysta was the problem? Or was he looking for Sarysta? What if you'd ridden at a gallop? How could you have known that Barrynt would kill Emlyn? Should you have realized how angry Barrynt was about the way Sarysta treated Halhana? What would have happened if you'd told Barrynt earlier? At least, you would have been there. But would he have waited the way he did with Johlana?* Belatedly, another thought popped up. *If Emlyn was so upstanding, why did he need a bodyguard close every time he left his mansion?* The last thought was simpler. *Let's just hope that Naerkaal doesn't understand what's about to happen to Sarysta.* But then, he doubted that there was any way to prove what he'd done. If he'd figured it correctly, Sarysta would be dead before he and Ryntaar reached Barrynt's house.

She'll have died of grief . . . and that's better than what she deserved.

But . . . was that the right thing to do?

How could he not do something, especially since Sarysta would have found a way to destroy Johlana with Barrynt dead, and when Sarysta was talking about destroying Halhana's and Eshult's love for each other?

He kept riding, thoughts churning through his mind.

LXVI

Even before Ryntaar and Beltur headed up the side drive in the growing darkness of the winter evening, Johlana rushed down from the porch, her face drawn and pale.

Jessyla followed her, but kept well back. Beltur wasn't surprised. In fact, he realized he would have been surprised had Jessyla not been there. Frankyr remained at the top of the side steps, just looking at Barrynt's body, as did Jorhan.

"We didn't get there soon enough," Beltur said as he reined up. "He'd already picked up Emlyn and thrown him into the hearth. He did it so hard that it crushed Emlyn's skull and broke his neck. Emlyn's bodyguard had killed Barrynt before we reached the house."

For a long moment, Johlana said nothing. Finally, she said, "Sarysta?"

Much as Beltur wanted to say something about what he had done, he dared not even a hint. "The guard got to Barrynt before he could do anything to Sarysta except knock her down."

"She's the guiltiest of all. Emlyn . . . everyone was her tool."

"I could see that in just a few moments."

"Beltur did everything he could," added Ryntaar, softly. "We rode as fast as we could on the ice."

"I'm so sorry," said Beltur. *What else can you say? And how can you possibly admit that if you'd told Barrynt last night . . . ?* Or would he have waited, just the way he did with Johlana?

Johlana shook her head. "I've always . . . always worried . . . that someday . . ."

"Where . . . ?" Beltur really didn't want to ask, but he also didn't wish to assume or do something horribly wrong.

"In the formal parlor," replied Johlana.

"Could I help you?" asked Jessyla.

"If you would."

Jessyla nodded to Beltur, who immediately dismounted.

Frankyr came down the steps. "I can take care of the horses."

"Thank you," said Beltur, who fully intended to relieve the young man once he and Ryntaar had carried Barrynt into the house.

In moments, Beltur and Ryntaar had Barrynt's body off his horse and carried it up the side stairs and into the house. Jessyla and Johlana followed them.

All told, it took more than a quint to get a table in position and to set up the formal parlor in a suitable fashion. After that, Beltur and Ryntaar slipped away, leaving the parlor and the rest of the arrangements to the two women, but by the time they reached the stable Frankyr had just about finished grooming the horses.

When he stepped out of the stall where he'd been grooming the last horse, the one Ryntaar had ridden, Frankyr turned to Beltur. "Tell me what happened. All of it."

"I'll tell you what I know. Ryntaar may want to add some things. We rode at a fast walk to Emlyn's mansion. The streets were clear of snow but icy, and we didn't want the horses to slip because that would have taken even more time . . ." Beltur gave a quick summary, then turned to Ryntaar. "Have I missed anything?"

"Sarysta would have killed us both with a look if she could," said

Ryntaar. "Her guard tried to cut Beltur down, but his shields stopped his blade. Young Escaylt came in after a while. He was trying not to cry. She just told him not to go to pieces. She didn't shed a single tear, and she was the cause of it all. She doesn't even see what she did. She was talking about good taste, with her consort and Father lying dead on the study floor."

"She'll get away with it. They always do," said Frankyr.

"Maybe not," replied Ryntaar. "Eshult's of age. That makes him the heir, not Sarysta."

"Eshult wouldn't do anything against his mother."

"No . . . but he loves Halhana, and he won't have to do everything his mother says any longer."

"We'll see." Frankyr's tone was dubious.

"We can hope," said Beltur, as the three left the stable and walked toward the house through the deepening chill of the evening.

He stopped in the side hall, not wanting to intrude into the formal parlor or the family parlor, which was where Frankyr and Ryntaar had apparently gone. As he stood there, he wondered whether anyone had gone to tell Halhana what had happened to her father and was trying to think about how to bring that up when Jessyla appeared.

"What are you doing here?"

"Waiting for you and trying not to intrude."

"Everyone's asking where you went. They want to hear more from you."

Beltur wasn't sure he wanted to say more, but he could understand people wanting to know. "I'll be there, in a moment. Do you know if anyone sent word to Halhana?"

"Johlana sent Asala."

Asala? Then Beltur remembered she was the cook. "That's good. I didn't want to ask."

"That made sense," added Jessyla. "If one of the family went . . ."

"It would force Halhana to make a choice between her father and her consort and his father."

"Johlana just told Asala to say that the two had a quarrel and both were dead, and that the family was at home mourning their father, and that everyone was thinking of Halhana. Now . . . we need to join the others."

Beltur followed Jessyla into the family parlor.

Johlana looked to Beltur. "We've heard what you said earlier, and Ryntaar has added some . . ."

"You'd like to hear it in a less hurried fashion."

Johlana nodded.

"I'll try to tell what happened as clearly as I can, starting when we rode through the gates at Emlyn's house. The gates were open, and there was no guard there. We rode around a circular drive to the covered entrance. Ryntaar immediately noticed his father's mount tied to the hitching rail. I could see that the front door was ajar, and it looked a little bent on its hinges . . ."

More than a glass passed before the family had heard enough and Beltur had answered all the questions that they had.

The night was cold and clear, almost heartlessly cold, Beltur felt, as he and Jessyla walked back to their cot.

"You were kind to tell everything, or almost everything," said Jessyla.

"Everything about the deaths and the councilors was what happened," Beltur said. "There is a little bit more, but that will have to wait." And it would, because the one thing he hadn't mentioned was his use of order to remove the natural chaos from Sarysta. He'd have to tell Jessyla later, but if she knew now and were questioned by Naerkaal . . .

"You've always kept your word not to hide anything from me."

"I will on this, too. Just not at this moment. You can judge if I was right when I do tell you."

Jessyla was silent for a long moment, then said, "I do have a question . . . two, really."

"Go ahead."

"Why did Barrynt attack Emlyn and not Sarysta?"

"I've thought about that. I think he was trying to get to Sarysta. Emlyn was likely trying to stop him. Sarysta said that Emlyn's last words were for her to stay out of the study."

"That makes more sense. Why does Sarysta hate Johlana so much?"

"I don't know, and no one's ever said. Did Johlana say anything when you were . . . laying out Barrynt?"

"She just talked about how warm and loving he'd always been, how he'd always taken care of her and the children."

"She said she'd always worried, but she didn't finish saying what she worried about."

"She didn't tell me, either."

Beltur wondered if Barrynt had been so protective because Johlana had never been fully accepted by the wealthier traders in Axalt, but that certainly wasn't something he could ask about. *Not right now.*

They'd also have to tell Lhadoraak and Tulya about Barrynt's murder of Emlyn and then Mhorgaan's killing of Barrynt. Beltur just hoped that what happened wouldn't lead to more trouble that might change the Council's mind.

But you weren't anywhere near when Barrynt attacked Emlyn.

Beltur couldn't help but worry that the Council might not see it that way. *If the councilors don't, you'll find out soon enough, even with the methodical way they approach everything.* "If I'd only told Barrynt earlier . . ."

"Do you think that would have changed anything?" asked Jessyla quietly. "Frankyr told me how Barrynt waited and then left without telling anyone. He might well have done that with you."

"He might . . . but he might not have." *How will you ever know?*

"Dear . . . how could you have possibly known he was that angry with Sarysta? Angry enough to try to kill her?"

"I should have known. I saw how evil she was. Even with two men lying dead at her feet, she was glad that Barrynt was dead."

"How do you know that?"

"I felt it . . . but she looked down at Barrynt, and for an instant, she smiled."

Jessyla shuddered.

LXVII

On oneday, Beltur didn't feel like going to the smithy, but what else was he going to do? Stay around the cot and get in everyone's way? He certainly didn't want to intrude on Johlana and her family, but he did take care of the stable, trying to do so as quietly as possible. Then he walked out to the smithy through a dusting of snow that fell from thin gray clouds.

Jorhan was working on a mold when Beltur joined him by the workbench.

"Morning, Beltur."

"Morning," replied Beltur. "How are you doing this morning?" He flushed. "That's a stupid question. Yesterday was terrible."

"We've all seen better," replied the smith.

"We have. What about Johlana?" Beltur imagined that she was bearing up, but with Barrynt's death occurring so suddenly, she might not be. "And what about Halhana?"

"I couldn't say for sure about either. Asala said they were both in the study with the door closed. Still there when I left. Figured they might be a while, and there wasn't much I could do." Jorhan paused. "Ryntaar told me that they'd have the farewell on threeday night. They want you and Jessyla there."

That said a great deal. Most farewells were just for family, with family members taking turns tending the pyre throughout the night. "We'll be there."

"Good." Jorhan pointed to the mold. "Working on a pearapple hanging from a branch. Wasn't sure we should do anything."

Beltur understood that, given that the last piece they had forged had led, if indirectly, to three deaths. "But?"

"Johlana wanted something herself. Said she wanted a happier reminder."

"That makes sense."

"Barrynt always liked pearapples."

"That's a good idea."

"Would have done a bust of him if my talents ran that way. They don't. This'll have to do."

"It's more personal and private that way," Beltur pointed out. "Johlana will know what it means, and it's for her."

"Hadn't thought of that." Jorhan nodded. "Be a while before we're ready to cast."

"I'll bring in more coal."

"That'd be good."

Beltur had just finished filling the coal box near the forge when there was a knock on the smithy door, almost preemptory, and two men walked in. One wore mage blacks—Naerkaal. The other was Sarstaan. Beltur stepped forward, inclining his head. "Councilors."

Sarstaan gestured to the corner of the smithy farthest from the forge, then moved toward it. Beltur and Naerkaal followed.

Beltur stopped when the councilors did. He waited without speaking.

Sarstaan nodded to Naerkaal.

Naerkaal's voice was low, but firm. "We came to see you about . . . what happened yesterday."

"I truly wish I'd gotten there faster," Beltur said. "I didn't know what Barrynt had in mind, and I didn't want to take my horse at a run with ice on the stone."

"That's more than understandable. It's also clear that you had nothing at all to do with either the death of Emlyn or Barrynt."

"No. I can't imagine how angry Barrynt was, to have picked up Emlyn and thrown him like that. Emlyn may be . . . may have been a little smaller than Barrynt, but he wasn't a small man."

"You haven't heard?" asked Naerkaal.

"Heard what?" Beltur frowned. Had something happened to Sarysta so soon? He didn't have to work to offer an expression of puzzlement.

"About Sarysta."

"What about her? I know she was angry and very contemptuous of me, Ryntaar, and Barrynt, but Ryntaar and I had nothing to do with it. I thought she understood that, no matter how much she was upset."

"She was upset enough to go to bed and not wake up."

"What?" That did surprise Beltur, if mildly. He'd thought she might either collapse shortly after he and Ryntaar left, or die a more lingering death . . . or possibly not die at all, but just be weak for eightdays, possibly even a season.

"You *are* surprised. Possibly not as much as you might be, but given your ties to Barrynt and Johlana and your treatment by Sarysta, that's understandable."

"Sarysta had a right to be harsh," said Sarstaan coldly. "The merchant murdered her consort in cold blood."

"But I had nothing to do with that. I was trying to get there as fast as I dared once his family told me he was in a rage."

"I'm curious," said Sarstaan coldly. "How long did it take the family to get in touch with you?"

"I don't know. It was soon. I do know that young Frankyr ran much of the way to our cot, while his brother was saddling the horses, and we trotted and ran back to Barrynt's. Ryntaar had the horses waiting, and we left immediately."

"How did you know he ran?"

"He was flushed and so winded he could hardly speak. He kept saying we had to hurry. I was still fastening my coat when we were on the way back."

Sarstaan looked to Naerkaal, who nodded. Then Sarysta's brother said, "I can't believe she just died."

"I can't either," said Beltur, although his reasons certainly weren't the same as Sarstaan's.

Again, Naerkaal nodded, then said, "There was no sign of poison or any other form of excess chaos."

"You may be telling the truth, Mage, but I don't trust you," said Sarstaan.

"Councilor, I understand. You don't know much about me. At the same time, I don't know that much about the Council. I came to Axalt in good faith, and I feel I've been judged and weighed on everything I've done. I've worked as a healer, and I do believe I've saved lives. Jorhan and I have been working to forge fine cupridium, and that's an honest trade. I truly tried to get to Barrynt to stop him, even when I didn't know what he had in mind—"

"Why?" snapped Sarstaan.

"Because I liked him. Because his family was afraid he'd do something that would only hurt himself and his family."

"That's a very honest answer, Sarstaan," said Naerkaal.

"I still don't know . . ."

"What else would you like to know, ser?" asked Beltur politely. "I've told you everything that happened."

"How did you come to know Barrynt?" asked Sarstaan.

"I was working with Jorhan in Elparta, helping him cast and forge cupridium. He told me his sister was consorted to a merchant in Axalt. I only met Barrynt twice, but when he learned that we would have to give up forging cupridium in Spidlar unless all the profit we made went to a trader, he said we should come to Axalt. As I've told the Council, that was what we had to do."

"Why was he so good to you?"

"I suspect it was because Jorhan could not have made cupridium without me, and he wanted to help the brother of his consort. He never said that, but that is what I believe."

The questions went on for another quint before the two councilors exchanged glances.

Then Naerkaal straightened and said, "We appreciate your time and forthrightness, Mage. It does appear that your role in this unpleasant matter has been exactly as it appears and as everyone has said. If the Council needs to know more, we will let you know."

Beltur nodded in reply. Then he escorted them to the smithy door, leaving it slightly ajar as the councilors walked back toward their mounts.

Sarstaan's murmured words drifted back to Beltur. ". . . what comes when a trader consorts below himself . . ."

Beltur did not fully close the door until the two had ridden away. Then he slowly walked back to the workbench.

"What did those two councilors want with you? One of them was the mage-councilor, isn't he?"

"He is. That's Naerkaal. The other one is Sarysta's brother."

"What did they want?" Jorhan repeated impatiently.

"Sarysta died in her sleep last night. They wanted to know if I knew. I didn't. Then they went back over all the questions they asked me yesterday . . . and a few others."

"Sarysta's dead? That bitch actually died?"

"That's what they said. I can't believe two councilors would lie about that."

"No, they likely wouldn't. Do you think Barrynt hit her hard enough that something happened? Later?"

"I never thought about that." Beltur hadn't, either. He really hadn't sensed Sarysta, except superficially, during the whole time he'd been in the study. Not that it made much difference, except if Barrynt's blow had done something to her head, that might have been why what Beltur had done had affected Sarysta in the way it had . . . and as soon as it had.

"Doesn't matter. Bitch deserved to die."

"It might matter very much," Beltur said slowly. "The Council wasn't that happy with Lhadoraak, Taelya, and me before. Now . . . with this . . . and Sarysta's brother being a councilor, I have to say that I'm worried." *And without Barrynt, it could be very much worse.*

"You did the best you could," said Jorhan. "We'll just have to see. Won't be long before I've got this ready."

In fact, it was well past first glass before Jorhan was ready to heat the melt, and close to fourth glass before Beltur released his hold on the order/ chaos mesh that turned soft bronze into cupridium.

The walk home wasn't too cold, not for Axalt, although scattered snowflakes continued to fall from the gray clouds, but he didn't reach the cot until almost two quints past fourth glass.

Jessyla was waiting for him just inside the door. As he took off his coat and scarf, she said quietly, "Two councilors came to the healing house to talk to Herrara today. One of them wore blacks."

"That had to be Naerkaal. He's the only black on the Council. The other one was likely Sarstaan. He's Sarysta's brother. They came to see me this morning. The first thing they asked me was if I knew about Sarysta's death.

She died in her sleep last night. I certainly didn't expect that, and I told them I was surprised because I was."

Jessyla frowned. "Were they telling the truth about her death?"

"They seemed to be. Later, after they left, and I talked to Jorhan, he wondered if Barrynt had hit her hard enough to have caused her death. I hadn't thought about his hitting her causing that much damage, but . . . he was in enough of a rage that he picked up Emlyn like a child's toy."

"How was Sarysta's brother?"

"Quietly angry, I'd say. He and Naerkaal spent almost two quints asking me question after question. Before they left, Naerkaal said that everything seemed to be the way I'd reported it, and Sarstaan said that, while I might have told the truth, he still didn't trust me. I said I understood because I'd done everything according to the way the Council had required, and it seemed as though the Council didn't trust Jorhan and me. I didn't say it quite that way, but that was what I meant." Beltur paused. "In a few moments, before dinner, I think you and Taelya should have some instruction in magery."

"You're worried, aren't you?"

"Yes. I want you both to learn as much as you can as fast as you safely can."

"That makes sense. Four mages stand a better chance in anything than do two."

Beltur turned and called, "Taelya! It's time for lessons."

Both Taelya and Tulya emerged from the kitchen.

"I told her you might be giving her a lesson this afternoon."

"She did," affirmed Taelya. "Can I call you Uncle Beltur?"

Beltur looked to Tulya, quizzically.

"She asked."

"I still have to do what you say," said Taelya.

"My uncle was the one who first taught me magery, and he was stricter than other mages. If you want me to be your uncle, you have to know that I'll expect more from you, not less." Beltur looked directly into Taelya's green eyes.

"That's all right."

Beltur laughed softly. "Then we'd better begin."

After almost a glass spent largely working on shields, Tulya announced that dinner was ready. Beltur had to admit that they were eating better with Tulya doing the cooking, cramped as the cot sometimes felt.

Much later, once he and Jessyla were alone in their bedchamber, she turned to him. "Why do all these things keep happening to us and around us?"

"Because in one way or another, we've thwarted the desires of people with great power, and they're anything but happy about being thwarted. The Prefect wanted Uncle to support him and use his magery for conquest. He also wanted Uncle to give him an excuse to attack Westwind or the Analerian nomads, if not both. Uncle didn't do either, and neither did I. You know what Cohndar and Waensyn wanted, and what Trader Alizant wanted. Caradyn and the mages used Taelya as an excuse to strike back at Lhadoraak for supporting us . . . and to send a message to other mages not to stand up against either the head mage or the Traders' Council. Emlyn and Sarysta wanted to lord it over Halhana, and when Jorhan and I, mostly Jorhan, came up with a piece that put theirs to shame, they struck back through Halhana, and that led to Barrynt's rage . . ."

"They were trying to make the point that they were in control, and that Halhana's parents, especially Johlana, didn't matter." Jessyla paused. "I don't understand why Sarysta had to reject the mirror. One ornamental mirror shouldn't matter. It would have remained in Halhana's bedchamber. Almost no one would have seen it."

"She likely has a dressing chamber," replied Beltur dryly. "There's another possibility. Emlyn controlled most of the trade in silver. Cupridium is just as valuable, if for other reasons. If wealthy women want more of what Jorhan produces . . ."

"It wouldn't reduce what Emlyn makes by that much."

"But Barrynt is the trader whose factorage displays it. He'll make more. I mean, he would have. We'd have paid him some for what he sold, and that would also have drawn more people."

"Power and position . . . again."

"Isn't it always?" Beltur yawned.

"You're tired. So am I." She smiled, then used order to snuff out the single lamp in the bedchamber.

LXVIII

When Beltur went to the stable on twoday, he didn't see anyone. Jorhan had already left for the smithy, and there were no signs of visitors, such as coaches or horses, at the house. He pondered that as he walked to the healing house, but decided it only confirmed what he already knew—that Barrynt had no living siblings, and since Johlana's only sibling was Jorhan, there weren't any other family members to come stay or visit, and most likely, few merchants or their consorts would dare until matters settled out.

When he stepped into Herrara's study, after reaching the healing house, she immediately addressed him. "You had quite an eightday, I hear."

"And a oneday," replied Beltur. "Councilor Naerkaal and Councilor Sarstaan came to the smithy and asked me more questions."

"They came here as well." Herrara looked evenly at Beltur. "For someone who's a black mage and a healer, troubles seem to cling to you like snow to a northeaster. I have to ask you why you think that keeps happening."

"Because people want things to stay the way they've always been, and, if I let things stay that way, I'd be dead."

Herrara frowned. "That's . . . rather . . . self-centered."

"Jorhan and I found a way to make a very good living in Elparta. Our work paid off our debts, and before long we would have been very comfortable. That meant we didn't owe everything to the traders, and that I could afford to consort Jessyla. Neither the traders nor the senior mages liked that. We were starting to do that here, and the excellence of a piece we produced for Barrynt's daughter as a gift caused resentment and jealousy on the part of Sarysta and Emlyn. They took it out on Halhana. That enraged Barrynt. We weren't trying to harm anyone. We were just trying to better ourselves."

"You're suggesting that, in three separate lands, you've done nothing wrong."

"Have we? Besides upsetting people with power and golds?"

"Upsetting those in power is often the greatest of evils, at least for those in power, and it's often fatal." Herrara smiled sardonically. "Failure to defer and show obvious subservience to those in power can be almost as deadly. You and Jessyla are well-mannered and polite. You're definitely not subservient. I happen to like that, especially in healers. Most people in power don't. And those with wealth and less power like it even less."

"Believing all that, how have you managed to do so well with the Council for the healing house?"

"I don't do well. The healing house barely survives on what the Council provides. They provide it because it makes them look good, and there are fewer deaths in the poorhouse and the workhouses. I also train healers. Most of them go on to work for wealthy traders and merchants. Those who don't fit leave Axalt, sooner or later. I can also seem subservient when necessary. I doubt that either you or Jessyla will ever be able to do that."

"Why? You're an outstanding healer."

"Who else is there? Someone less apparently subservient would destroy the healing house, as would someone truly subservient. Who else would the workers and the poor have?"

Beltur nodded. He already knew the answer to her questions.

"Beltur . . . Axalt is far from perfect, but it's also far better than most lands. There is no perfect land. Destroying a good but imperfect land doesn't make the world better. It makes it poorer. The only meaningful choices in life are either to maintain something good or to build something better. Did the Prefect's invasion of Spidlar do either?"

"No. You know that."

"Did Barrynt's death—or Emlyn's—make Axalt better?"

"Most likely not. Sarysta's death though . . ."

"It's very hard to stop killing once it starts. Each death enrages more people . . ."

Unless it's seen as natural or accidental. Beltur didn't know from where that thought came, but he hung on to it as something to remember . . . just in case.

". . . That's one reason why wars seldom end until one land is ravaged or destroyed—or both are destitute."

"You should be a councilor."

Herrara shook her head. "I see enough of bad decisions. Here, I can do something to help." She smiled. "I've kept you enough. Go do your rounds . . . and try to smile now and again."

Beltur smiled in return.

As he picked up a basket and then stepped out into the corridor, he thought over what Herrara had said . . . and what she hadn't . . . and that her words suggested that he and Jessyla were not all that suited to a long stay in Axalt.

LXIX

Just before Jessyla headed out the door on threeday, she turned to Beltur. "Remember, the farewell is at noon, and I can only be there for a glass or so before I have to go back to the healing house. I'll be back as soon as I can be around fourth glass."

"I'm going to the smithy. Jorhan could use some help with what he's doing for Johlana."

"That was a good idea after what happened with the mirror. She needs something different and more about Barrynt."

"I told you. It was Johlana's idea. She wanted something that reminded her of other times."

"You did tell me. I've been . . ."

"Are you all right?"

"I'm fine . . . that way . . . physically."

Beltur could sense the truth of that. "Did I do something to upset you?"

A soft smile appeared. "No. It isn't you. All of this with Barrynt and the Council . . . I've been thinking a lot."

"Matters aren't turning out the way either of us planned."

"No. I don't want to be late. We'll have time to talk later." She leaned forward and kissed him, holding tightly, for several moments before letting go and easing out of his arms, smiling. "Later."

Beltur was smiling also as he watched her leave, because whatever was worrying her didn't have to do with him. *You hope.* Although he hadn't sensed that, he still worried.

Then he hurried off to the stable, where he finished quickly. When he started for the smithy, he saw that the base of the pyre was already in place, although he didn't see either Frankyr or Ryntaar.

Jorhan was already polishing the memorial pearapple branch when Beltur got to the smithy and took over the foot treadle so that Jorhan could concentrate completely on the finish work.

More than a glass later, Jorhan motioned Beltur off the treadle. "That's as good as it's going to be."

"It's beautiful."

"That it is, if I do say so myself." Jorhan paused. "Some say cupridium's been cursed since the fall of Cyador. Others say that it was cursed by the black angels and that caused the fall of Cyador and will blight the lives of all who forge it or use it."

"I never heard that."

"Barrynt told me that, right after we got here. Said that it was balderdash, an excuse for what men did. Said that curses were what men used to explain away their faults." Jorhan looked at the glistening silver-gold sheen of the leaved branch that held two cupridium pearapples side by side. "Don't see how anything this good should be cursed." He sighed. "Thing is, more bad than good's come from what we've forged."

"You could say the same about gold, silver . . . gems," replied Beltur. "Maybe even black iron. Anything that's worth a lot makes men greedy. Look what Cohndar's greed or the greed of Trader Alizant led to. The cupridium didn't reach out and possess them. Sometimes, men claim that beautiful women are evil, just because they're attractive to men. The evil isn't that they're beautiful. The evil comes from what men will do to possess such beauty."

Jorhan laughed. "You'd know. You've seen what those supposed upstanding black mages did to try to possess your beauty." After a moment, he said, "Sad to think that beauty drives people to evil."

"Beauty doesn't. Wanting to possess it at any cost does."

"You ought to be a philosopher, Beltur."

Beltur shook his head, for some reason thinking about Heldry the Mad, who hadn't seemed mad at all in what he wrote . . . or Relyn, whose words seemed more reasonable than those who said they followed his teachings. "I'm just a mage and a healer, and an outstanding smith's sometime striker."

"You're going to have to be more than that to survive in this world."

"Why do you say that?"

"You're proud. You try to hide it, but you can't always. You're more powerful than many, but you bow to those who aren't half the man you are. Thing is, you're only being polite, and they know it. You want to do right, even when it offends those in power. Your consort is beautiful."

Beltur wasn't sure he liked the image that Jorhan had presented. "Am I really that bad?"

"Wouldn't say you're bad at all. You're trying to hide what you are."

"I had to."

"That's right. You had to. Do you now? Doesn't mean you need to be like Emlyn, or those blacks who drove you out of Elparta." Jorhan smiled ruefully. "I'm a good smith. Likely better than just good. That's what I am. Not a trader. Not a councilor. You need to work out who you are, what you want to do besides survive. I figure any decent mage can survive. So can any decent smith." After another pause, Jorhan shook his head. "Said enough. More than I should have, likely. You need to head out and get ready for the farewell. So do I. I'll be along shortly."

Beltur was still thinking over what Jorhan said when he left the smithy and walked back along the south town road toward the city proper. Jorhan was right. He'd been so busy reacting to what everyone else was trying to do to him and Jessyla that he'd really not thought about what he wanted to be. But that wasn't all Jorhan had said. *What you want to do besides survive.*

He knew he wanted to be a good healer and better than a good mage, but . . . being wasn't doing. Herrara wasn't just a great healer; she was healing people whom no one else would heal. She was making the lives of others better.

So what do you want to do?

When the question was put that bluntly, Beltur didn't have an answer for himself.

Once he returned to the cot, Beltur washed and changed into his good blacks, and even wore the silver medallion of a patrol mage, the one he'd kept, and shouldn't have, when he'd fled Elparta. *You more than earned it.*

"We won't be here for dinner," Beltur told Tulya, unnecessarily, he knew, but he had to say something as he passed through the kitchen on his way out.

He was nervous as he walked from the cot to Barrynt's small mansion—a dwelling he still thought of as Barrynt's, although it now belonged to Ryntaar—because he'd never really been to a farewell, not that he fully recalled. Beltur had heard about farewells most of his life, but the only one he'd ever actually attended had been for his father, and he remembered little of that. Athaal had been turned to ashes by chaos fire, as had his uncle, and, while there had been a farewell for Athaal, without a pyre, Beltur had been too injured to attend. Obviously, a farewell for his uncle had been impossible, and no one else close to him had died.

Beltur arrived possibly half a quint before midday, making his way up the side steps by himself, where Frankyr opened the door.

"It's good to see you, ser."

"I'm glad to see you, Frankyr. How are you doing?"

"Better than on eightday, ser." The young man's eyes fixed on the silver patrol medallion as Beltur removed his coat. "I haven't seen that."

"It's a City Patrol medallion from Elparta."

"It's quite impressive."

"It's meant to be, but it never impressed most lawbreakers."

"Everyone's gathering first in the family parlor. I think the only one who isn't here is your consort."

"She's at the healing house. She said she'd be here by noon."

"Then I'll wait here."

"I could do that."

"No, ser. Mother said I was to be the one to greet everyone. She was quite firm. Please go into the parlor."

Beltur could certainly believe that. "If that's the way your mother wants it, that's what I'll do." He smiled, then made his way from the side hall into the family parlor. Everyone present was dressed in their best, which didn't surprise him. What did was the presence of Eshult, standing beside the chair where Halhana was seated. Beltur hoped he'd concealed his surprise.

"Pale ale, ser?" asked Ryntaar.

"Yes, please."

"Where's your consort?" asked Jorhan.

"On her way from the healing house." *I hope.*

"You're both healers, I've heard," said Eshult pleasantly. "Isn't that unusual for a mage?"

"I suspect a number of blacks have the talent, but don't choose to develop it. I made the mistake of trying to save people, especially during the invasion, and then realized I might harm someone if I didn't learn more. That's one reason why I've been working at the healing house."

Ryntaar handed Beltur a beaker of pale ale. "Here you are."

"Thank you." Beltur sensed a certain blackness and turned to see Jessyla step into the parlor, wearing her best greens and the green shimmersilk scarf. "I see you managed to escape the healing house."

"I did. I was afraid I'd have to go back for part of the afternoon, but Herrara told me not to."

"Good for her," said Jorhan.

Frankyr appeared behind Jessyla.

"I need to get you both a drink for the toasts," said Ryntaar, looking to Jessyla.

"Do you have the mulled wine?"

"We do . . . and you want lager, Frankyr?"

The younger son nodded.

After Ryntaar served the two their drinks, he walked to the center of the parlor. "Now that everyone's here, we should move to the formal parlor. Mother . . . if you would?"

As Johlana led the group from one parlor to the other, Beltur and Jessyla let the others precede them.

Farewells were simple, at least from what Beltur had heard. First was a toast, followed by the sharing of memories, followed by a second toast, after which the departed was borne to the pyre, where the pyre was lit, and farewell verses were offered, and family members and close friends tended the fire until all was ashes. The memory sharing began with a memory from the person closest to the one being sent off, followed by a single memory from each other person, and a second and final memory from the one who offered the first memory. The last part of the sharing was a second toast.

Barrynt, wearing a brown tunic trimmed with a gold fabric, lay on a simple wooden bier, positioned on an oblong table against the back wall of the parlor. The farewellers formed an arc facing the bier. In the center of the arc were Johlana and Ryntaar.

Ryntaar raised his beaker. "To Father, for whom family meant everything, to the very end, and for whom he always did his honest best, honoring us, and those around him."

"To Father," came the reply, and all lifted their beakers or glasses.

"The first time I saw your father," began Johlana, "he was standing in Jorhan's smithy outside Elparta telling Jorhan that he'd never make a living as a coppersmith because what he made was too fine to be sold at the price it would bear. Jorhan told him that there had to be people in the world who would buy fine copperware, and that he should take some of what Jorhan had forged and see if it weren't so." Johlana smiled softly. "Barrynt turned to me and asked me what I thought. I told him he sounded too sour for a man so young and handsome. He said I hadn't answered his question. I told him that he shouldn't take Jorhan's work if he felt that way because he wouldn't do it justice, and he said that we were both impossible, but he did smile. He didn't take any of it. Not then, but he came back three days later and bought two pieces and promised me that he wouldn't be sour when he showed them to others. He must not have been, because he came back in the fall and bought even more."

Beltur saw a trace of a smile on Halhana's face as her mother finished.

Ryntaar cleared his throat, then said, "What I remember most isn't one single memory, but how often he insisted on my doing my best, and how he smiled when he knew I'd done it . . . and he could definitely tell when

I hadn't. I can remember that, too, like the time when I only unrolled a bolt of wool halfway . . . and the inside wasn't the same quality . . ."

Beltur listened intently as each offered a memory of the merchant, all touching, some amusing, some inspiring, trying to think what he'd say when his turn came.

The one before Beltur was Eshult, who looked slightly uneasy when Halhana looked to him and who took several moments to speak. "I think . . . the memory . . . that I recall . . . I felt a little like I do now . . . It was when I came into this very parlor to ask Barrynt for Halhana's hand. I knew I was too young to ask, and that Halhana was too young to accept. I also knew that, if I waited, my mother would throw obstacles in our way, and that we would lose our chance at happiness together. So . . . I came here. He was sitting in his chair, and there were just the two of us in the room. I swallowed. I had trouble speaking. He smiled. It was a warm smile, and he had the warmest smile. He asked me, 'Don't you think you two are a bit too young to consort?' I told him that we were, but that sometimes it was better to dare than to wait and lose the best life had to offer. He laughed. It wasn't a big laugh. It was cheerful. He said that he'd felt the same way when he asked for Johlana's hand. It wasn't that he was too young. He just hadn't known her long enough or well enough, but he knew that he also might lose the joy of his life. Then he said Halhana and I could consort . . . and that Halhana's joy was in my hands." Eshult swallowed. "That's all."

Beltur could see the tears oozing from the corners of Eshult's eyes. *Honest tears.*

For a long moment, no one said anything, except that was because, Beltur realized, he was supposed to speak next.

"Jessyla and I are here, safe in Axalt, because of Barrynt's kindness to a mage he did not know struggling to make his way in a strange land. When it became clear that the traders of Elparta were going to make it impossible for Jorhan and me to forge cupridium, Barrynt suggested to Jorhan, and he'd done that previously, I understand, that Jorhan would be happier in Axalt, and that Johlana certainly would be happy to have her brother close. Without hesitation, he turned to me and said that I would be welcome, too. As a mage, I can tell when someone says something out of politeness. Barrynt wasn't being kind or polite. He meant it from the first and from the heart. And when Jessyla and I arrived—he knew nothing of her at all—he and Johlana put us up, and then found us a cot . . . and provided most of the furnishings. He was pleased that we were safe . . . and happy. To me . . . there are many people who say good things, and do little. He was one of a handful who did not dwell on words, but on making good his word." Beltur didn't know what else to say. So he turned to Jessyla.

"I never met Barrynt until the day we arrived in his drive. We'd traveled an eightday in winter. We'd been attacked by brigands. We were near frozen from a northeaster. Beltur had told me of Barrynt's offer. He didn't mention that Barrynt didn't even know I existed. But the moment we arrived, he smiled. It was the smile of a man who loved life and people. I knew at that moment that we were more than welcome. He and Johlana took us in, fed us, and then made sure we had a place here . . . and in Axalt." Jessyla looked to Johlana.

"There's one last memory I'd like to share." Johlana paused. "It's not a great or grand memory. It was when Barrynt and I first rode up to this house. He turned and looked to me, and he said, 'You're home now.' I was, but what made it home was Barrynt." Unshed tears glistened in her eyes.

After another silence, Ryntaar raised his beaker. "To Father. In farewell."

The others raised their glasses or beakers, then said quietly, "In farewell," and drank.

Then, within moments, after setting aside their beakers, Ryntaar, Frankyr, Jorhan, and, surprisingly to Beltur, Eshult lifted the bier on which Barrynt rested, and carried it from the formal parlor out to the pyre that had been built on the drive between the house and the stable.

When the bier had been placed in the center of the pyre, and everyone was gathered there, Ryntaar stepped forward with the torch and lit the dishes of oil placed at the north, south, east, and west sides, then returned to stand beside his mother.

Johlana began with the first line of the farewell, and Ryntaar spoke the second, Halhana, the third, and Frankyr the fourth, the family alternating, until they came to the last two lines, which they all spoke together.

> "Farewell to this house, and the shelter of each wall,
> Farewell to this hearth, and the warmth you shared,
> Farewell to the blooms of spring, and leaves of fall,
> And to the seasons and the hearts for whom you cared.

> "Farewell to the sorrows that weighed upon you,
> And to the joys that carried you the seasons through.
> Farewell to the cares you bore through each and every day
> To purposes both large and small, to words you could not say.

Farewell to dawns and sunsets, rains and snows,
To days so still the wind of time never blows.

"In chaos and in order, we say this last farewell and bid you go
To the skies and to the stars that in life we never know."

For several moments, they all stood, just watching, as the flames rose.

Then Halhana turned, putting her arms around Eshult, sobbing silently, but almost uncontrollably.

Even from a few yards away, Beltur could sense the grief consuming the young woman. He could also sense something similar from Eshult.

"I was surprised to see him here," murmured Jessyla.

"Me, too. He's upset as well."

"He doesn't want to lose her."

That seemed so to Beltur, but he wondered why Eshult felt that way . . . possibly because he'd lost both parents so suddenly? Or was there more?

He was still mulling that over when Johlana eased over to him and Jessyla.

"I'm glad that you came and spoke. We all, Eshult especially, needed to hear what you remembered." Johlana paused. "I wanted to tell you that. I need to go inside for a little."

Left unsaid was a request not to leave, not yet, anyway.

Then Johlana turned and walked toward the steps. Ryntaar joined her, and the two climbed the steps together.

"I don't know how she did it," said Jessyla. "If anything happened to you . . ."

"You'd manage . . . just as she has." *You're both stronger than you know.* Beltur was beginning to wonder if he could have been that strong.

Again, for a time, they stood there, until Beltur realized that he was shivering. He was about to head up the steps to reclaim their coats, when Ryntaar reappeared, along with Frankyr, each carrying armloads of coats and scarves, for which Beltur was definitely glad.

He helped Jessyla into her coat, then donned his own. They both moved a bit closer to the fire, and Beltur wondered when he should offer to add more wood.

"Ser?"

As Ryntaar returned, Beltur almost jumped, preoccupied as he'd been with his own thoughts.

"Yes? I'm sorry. I was thinking."

"Most of us are, likely," replied Ryntaar. "I just wanted to thank you. If we'd only been a little sooner . . ."

Beltur shook his head. "You and Frankyr hurried as fast as you could. We couldn't have gotten there that much sooner. That's not something that you could have done anything about. It really isn't." *Perhaps I could have, if I'd told Barrynt what I heard, but you couldn't.*

"You're kind—"

"I'm not kind. Your father had been dead for a considerable fraction of a quint when we arrived. Remember, I'm a healer, and that's something I can tell."

Ryntaar said nothing for a moment. "I hadn't . . . thought about that."

"It's true. You can't blame yourself for something you couldn't have changed." That was certainly true, Beltur knew. But the danger was in knowing what could have been changed and what could not. *What if you had told Barrynt? What if you and Jorhan hadn't forged the mirror?* Could that have been changed? *But that would have meant refusing Johlana's request.* Beltur wanted to shake his head, even as he realized that, at times, events combined into results that couldn't be foreseen until it was too late to change. *And that means trying to think about the consequences well before acting.* And that was anything but easy.

"Thank you, ser."

After Ryntaar went to stand by his brother, Jessyla said, "That was kind."

"It was also mostly true."

"That helps."

Jessyla looked at Beltur. "I'm going inside."

"To see to Johlana?"

"To see if I need to, at least."

Beltur nodded, then watched as she walked toward the house, followed by Halhana.

A while later, how long Beltur wasn't certain, Eshult approached Beltur. "Might I have a word with you, ser?"

While he wondered at the young man's formality, Beltur immediately replied, "Of course."

"You were really the only one there when my father died, except Mother, and I didn't get to talk to her before she died. Halhana said I should talk to you."

"Mhorgaan and Ryntaar were there," Beltur pointed out.

"They're both good people, but . . . you're likely to be more impartial. Halhana pointed that out."

Beltur smiled sadly. "No one is truly impartial, Eshult. Both Barrynt and Johlana helped Jessyla and me a great deal when we arrived in Axalt. Barrynt was the one who offered the possibility of our finding our way in Axalt even before we left Elparta."

"I think you've just proved that you're more impartial . . . or less partial, if you will."

"What do you want to know?"

"Why Barrynt killed Father. Why he truly did . . . what drove him to that."

"I can't tell you that. I can only tell you what I saw and what I heard. That might help you draw your own conclusions. It also might make matters more confusing."

"Then tell me what you have reason to believe that might give me a better understanding."

"While I am no connoisseur of sculpture or art, the mirror that Jorhan forged was a very good mirror and piece of art. It was also made with love and great affection, and it was gifted to Halhana with love by her mother." Beltur looked to Eshult. "Do you wish me to continue?"

"Please do."

"It was returned to Johlana, as I understand it, by your mother as not being in accord with the décor in your dwelling. Shortly after that, again, as I understand matters, Halhana told her mother that the two of you could not come to eightday dinner because of arrangements made by your mother. Had this not occurred several times previously?"

"Twice, I believe." Eshult's words were clipped.

"I am not judging, Eshult. I am telling you what I know."

"This is difficult."

Especially since you're not sure whether you really want to know what you've asked. "Barrynt was upset by the return of the mirror. I saw indirect evidence of that. Now . . . consider that the mirror was forged by Johlana's brother. Consider that he is not just a smith, but a craftsman whose work has been bought by traders from throughout the east of Candar. Then, when Halhana stated, again, that you two could not have dinner with her family, consider how that might have affected Johlana."

"She would be upset."

"Do you love Halhana? Deeply? Deeply enough that it would torment you if someone did things that continued to hurt her?"

"Why do you . . . you're saying that Barrynt was so angry because of how Johlana was hurt . . ."

"I can think of no other reason. Can you? Your father and Barrynt were not on unfriendly terms as merchants, were they?"

"No, ser."

"Your father did not express hatred of Barrynt, did he?"

"No."

"Also, I never heard Barrynt say hateful things about your father." *Slightly unkind, but not hateful.* What Barrynt had said or implied about Sarysta had been far more than slightly unkind. "Your mother did not like Johlana, it seemed to me. Am I mistaken?"

"No, ser."

"Do you know why that might be?"

Eshult was silent.

Beltur waited.

The young man took a deep breath. "It makes little difference now. They're all dead except Johlana." His laugh was short and bitter. "My late aunt, my mother's sister, thought she would be Barrynt's consort. Whether there was any formal arrangement I do not know. When Barrynt consorted Johlana . . . Then my aunt died shortly thereafter . . ."

"Your mother was displeased?"

"That would be too mild, I fear. What does this have to do—?"

"I do not believe Barrynt ever intended to hurt your father. Your mother said that your father told her to stay out of the study. Then Barrynt hurled him away. I don't think a man who is trying to murder another man would throw him away. I believe, and it is only my belief, that your father was trying to protect your mother, and Barrynt was so enraged that he didn't know how much force he'd used. Barrynt's last words, according to your mother, and she was telling the truth, was that your mother was a bitch worse than any in Westwind and that she'd destroyed a good man. I don't say that to hurt you, but to show you what Barrynt felt at that moment."

"Oh . . ." Eshult stood there, trembling. "No wonder she died that very night. Father died trying to protect her . . . from something she'd caused . . ."

"I'm sorry," said Beltur gently.

"You have nothing to be sorry about, ser. Like all of us here today, you were caught in a net not of your making." Eshult smiled sadly. "I need to talk to Halhana. If you will excuse me . . ."

As Eshult walked away, Beltur felt the taste of ashes in his mouth . . . and not from the pyre, even though he'd allowed Eshult a better last view of his mother than she deserved. *But isn't that better for him and Halhana?*

His mouth still tasted of ashes.

LXX

As he walked from the stable to the healing house on fourday morning, Beltur couldn't help but worry how the Axalt Council might react to the deaths of Barrynt, Emlyn, and Sarysta . . . and not only what they might do to Beltur and Jessyla, but whether there might be more trouble for Johlana and Ryntaar.

When he stepped into Herrara's study, the ledger on her desk was closed, and beside it was a thick square of folded black cloth. She asked immediately, "Have you heard anything else from the Council?"

"Nothing new. No one's approached me since oneday. If I hear anything else, I'd think it would be after the Council meets on sixday."

"That's most likely. Before you start today, we need to take care of one thing."

Beltur felt both worry and puzzlement immediately.

"It's not anything to concern yourself with," added Herrara, "but it will make matters much simpler for both of us." She pointed to the folded black cloth on the side of the desk. "You need to wear this when you're here. You can certainly wear it elsewhere if you wish, but you need to wear it here."

Frowning, Beltur stepped forward and picked up the heavy but fine woolen cloth to discover that he held a black tunic with two wide green bands at the end of each sleeve.

"That seems appropriate for a mage-healer, don't you think?"

Beltur couldn't argue that, but . . . "You didn't pay for this, did you?"

She shook her head. "I do have a budget for supplies. Elisa's tunics are paid out of that budget. Later, I should be able to obtain another set of greens for Jessyla, but since you only need a tunic, I thought I'd start with you. Also, because I can't pay you what you're worth, you can call this a different form of pay. At the least, your wearing this will limit questions. It also might allow your other black tunics to last longer."

"Thank you." Beltur was grateful, given that his blacks were indeed limited. "Are the green bands something you've seen or read about?"

"Something I recalled from when I was a child. Even if I hadn't, the idea makes sense." She smiled. "Try it on."

Beltur did so, and found himself smiling. "It fits well."

"I'm a good judge of that, usually."

"Is there anyone new that I should know anything about?"

"There's another casualty from the Traders' Bowl upstairs, next to Klaznyt's room. Far too much ale or lager, and a broken arm. If the swelling's gone down, we'll cast the arm this afternoon and send him off. It wouldn't hurt for you to look in on him. He was still dozing it off when Elisa saw him before she left this morning."

Beltur nodded.

Herrara opened the ledger, and Beltur left the study, first taking his old solid black tunic and hanging it up under his coat before heading upstairs to check on Klaznyt and the others.

As soon as he walked in, Klaznyt said, "You're wearing a different tunic."

"The head healer decided that I should have one that showed I was both mage and healer. It seems right to me, and I wasn't about to argue." Not that Beltur had even thought about that.

"You're a mage, and you don't mind deferring to her?"

Beltur smiled. "I need to know more about healing in some areas." More than a few, but he didn't think admitting that was the best thing to say. "She's teaching me that. She's also paying me. Why would I mind deferring?"

"But . . . you were an arms-mage, a strong one."

Beltur wondered where Klaznyt had heard that, because he'd taken pains never to mention that to the gambler. "I don't recall saying anything about that."

"The other healer did—the redheaded one. She said that you'd saved Elparta. Healers don't lie." Klaznyt grinned. "You don't, either, but she might have been mistaken. So . . . I'll ask you. Was she right?"

Beltur smiled in return, not quite sardonically. "The black mages of Elparta were conscripted into the fighting. I was assigned to a reconnaissance company at first, and then later to assist a senior officer—"

"You were a conscript as a mage?"

"No, they conscripted mages as officers. I was an undercaptain. I did what was necessary, as did the other mages. If we hadn't done what we did, the Prefect would have taken Elparta. So . . . yes, I was part of the small group of mages that helped save Elparta."

Klaznyt laughed. "I think I believe her version more. Why don't you want to talk more about yourself?"

"I just did," replied Beltur with a smile. "Except for what I learned about healing during the fighting, what I did as an arms-mage doesn't have much to do with what I do here."

"You're a strange one, Mage."

Beltur shrugged and concentrated on sensing Klaznyt's hands. "Your fingers are beginning to heal now."

"They itch and hurt. They'll never be the same. You know that."

"But you'll be able to use them."

"For what? Holding a spade? Loading wagons?"

"That's better than dying or not being able to use them."

"We'll see, won't we?" Klaznyt turned his head away.

Beltur eased out of the room, walked down the hall, and stepped into the small chamber where two men lay in adjoining beds.

The one who was awake was an older man found freezing in the square, according to Jessyla. He looked at Beltur. "You must be the mage-healer. Your magery won't help me."

"Why do you think that?" From his quick sensing, Beltur suspected that already, but was curious as to why the man had spoken so.

"I'm old and tired. I have no place to go, but there's nothing wrong with me except being old and not having enough to eat for too many eightdays."

"How did that happen?"

"How does it ever happen?" The gray-faced and white-haired figure shrugged. "One son went to Vergren. The other went hunting last fall. He never came back. His consort died trying to have a child. I was a loader, got too old to keep doing it. Never able to save much. Finally the coppers ran out. It didn't help that I drank a shade too much." He glanced to the somnolent figure in the other bed. "Not stupid enough to drink that much. It doesn't seem to matter in the end. Neither you nor the other healer will be able to keep me here that long. Then what?"

Beltur didn't have anything to say that wouldn't have sounded like false comfort. The best he could do was: "You can likely stay for a few days, if not longer. It's not that long before winter's over."

"You're an optimist, but I appreciate the thought."

Beltur nodded and turned his attention to the second man, the one whom Herrara had mentioned. In addition to the chaos around the broken bone in the arm, he could sense tiny bits of dull red chaos on the man's skin everywhere, suggesting that the man had suffered frostburn on more than a few occasions recently. He removed the worst of the chaos around the break, and then left the room.

He had the feeling that the rest of the day would be about the same.

LXXI

Another light snow dusted Axalt on fiveday, although it mostly stopped before Beltur left the smithy to return home. Jorhan called it a day after casting just one small decorative vase, not only because they were running low on copper, but because obtaining more was likely to be difficult as a result of Barrynt's death, especially because they had already used most of the small stock that had been in Barrynt's warehouse. Since he left early, Beltur went to the stable, saddled Slowpoke, and took him for a modest ride, then rode one of the other horses for a time.

Sixday passed without incident at the healing house, although Beltur half expected Naerkaal to appear, and late in the day, Jorhan stopped by the cot to tell Beltur that he didn't see much point in forging much more until he could locate and purchase more copper and tin. So Beltur tended to the stable and spent time working with Taelya late on sevenday morning.

At a quint past second glass, there was a knock on the door, and Beltur immediately sensed a black presence, far stronger than that of Lhadoraak, who was doing some work for a cabinetmaker. As he walked to the door, he had few doubts about who it had to be. When he opened the door, he saw the man he expected—Naerkaal.

"Please come in, Councilor." Beltur motioned toward the front room, since Tulya and Taelya were in the kitchen.

"Thank you. I rode out to the smithy, but found no one there."

"We're not doing much smithing right now. Copper and tin appear to be in short supply, at least for us at present." Beltur gestured toward the wooden armchair.

Naerkaal seated himself and asked, "Do you find that surprising in late winter?"

Beltur took the bench and turned to face the councilor. "I don't find it surprising, but I doubt that it has much to do with the season."

Naerkaal merely nodded, then said, "The Council had a closed meeting yesterday."

"I've heard from no one until you showed up."

"There was no need to summon you, or anyone else. I just came for a visit."

"I doubt that you visit without a purpose."

"There are purposes and purposes." Naerkaal offered a pleasant smile.

"I assume that the Council met to discuss the death of Barrynt and that of Emlyn."

"Assumptions can be dangerous, but, yes, you are correct in that. Also, the death of Sarysta."

"Of course, since she is the sister of a councilor," suggested Beltur.

"And the consort of a most noted merchant of Axalt."

"There is that." Beltur paused. "Does Councilor Sarstaan have an accomplished healer as part of his various affairs?"

"He does. She attends all public meetings of the Council, but not the private ones. That may be why he asked so many questions . . ."

Beltur managed not to swallow. *The woman who felt like a healer was one!* And she went to the meetings so that she could tell Sarstaan if either councilors or witnesses were less than truthful, which was why Naerkaal had likely been so careful in his questioning.

"That does not change the facts. As I told the Council, there was absolutely no sign of poison, or the symptoms of violence or even of excessive order when I was summoned after Sarysta's body was found by her youngest son. She clearly died quietly in her sleep."

Beltur could sense that Naerkaal was telling the truth and making no attempt to conceal what he felt. That, in itself, was disturbing. "You and Sarstaan mentioned that she died in her sleep, but not that you had been summoned to examine her."

"There is one cause of death that is impossible to determine unless one is present when death occurs. As a healer and a mage, I'm quite certain that you know what it is."

Beltur shrugged, even as he felt a certain chill at Naerkaal's words. "I see it occasionally at the healing house, usually in older men, when their natural chaos levels drop too low to sustain them. I imagine it's far less common in people who are younger, but I have seen it in those of Sarysta's age, occasionally younger." *If only once.*

"I thought you might have. Others might, as well, over time."

Particularly if a certain mage-councilor pointed out that possibility and that a mage-healer was present late in the afternoon before Sarysta died. "I doubt many people know that."

"At present, most likely only the two of us."

Beltur didn't miss the slight emphasis on the words "at present." "Do you think it should remain that way . . . or merely at present?"

"That's a very interesting question. I'd like to address that in a bit." Naerkaal paused, looking at the hearth. "You know, I've watched Barrynt for years. He was extremely unhappy, wretched really, after his first consort died so unexpectedly. Many feared for his life. Unlike some, when I saw how happy Johlana made him, I thought that was a consorting that benefited both, and indeed benefited Axalt. The two raised three solid children, and young Ryntaar and Frankyr, I think, will prove to be credits to their parents. Halhana will also provide a more gentle guiding spirit for Eshult." Naerkaal turned his eyes on Beltur. "What do you think?"

"I haven't known them as long as you have, but I've been impressed with the children."

"So have I, as I've said. I think it would be a great tragedy if any shadow persisted over them. You did mention that Jorhan was having difficulty obtaining copper and tin, I believe?"

"That is what he told me, and he was telling the truth."

"I, too, am certain that he was." Naerkaal fingered his chin. "There is also another complication, and that is the fact that you're training a white mage. In time, some might even refer to her as a white witch. People's perceptions change to match what they wish to believe, and, again, in time, they might connect that shadow I mentioned to her, as well."

Beltur had known, almost from the time Naerkaal had seated himself, that their "conversation" would likely head in the direction it had, but what he hadn't anticipated was Naerkaal's feelings, feelings that seemed to be of sadness and regret. "And what would raise this shadow?"

"I would guess, and it is only a guess, that, in this instance, the shadow would become darker with the passage of time. Certainly not within eight-days, possibly not even within seasons." The mage-councilor shrugged. "Who can say? It might only remain a vague and slightly troubling miasma, that is, if those possibly connected to it were seldom seen."

And that is most unlikely for two mages consorted to each other. "Your thoughts on this are most interesting," replied Beltur. "You know, it's been a bitter winter. At least, it seems bitter to those of us raised in warmer climes."

"Most winters are like this. Some are worse. That's one reason why no one really expects anyone to travel from Axalt, especially to the east, until winter wanes and the roads are clear."

"Certis isn't the most friendly of places these days," Beltur pointed out.

"The north of Certis is much different from Jellico, and I've heard from those I trust that Montgren is most receptive to those with certain talents, such as healers. One can travel from Rytel to Montgren or Sligo without coming near Jellico."

"I doubt that even a most perceptive ruler would take a mere healer's word . . ." Beltur raised his eyebrows.

"They might not take a Council's word, either, but the Council might regard lifting shadows favorably . . ."

"In some form of document?" Beltur offered a laugh that conveyed amused disbelief.

"One never knows. Axalt values being as fair as possible. Sometimes, though . . . tradition is valued more than fairness. Under such circumstances," this time Naerkaal shrugged, ". . . accommodations may be possible. Assuming those shadows remain a mere miasma, that is."

"What if there are those on the Council who may not see it that way?"

"It is now to their advantage not to see it any other way. In time, though . . ."

"I am new to Axalt, so I must defer to your far greater understanding of the situation, and this will bear considerable thought."

Naerkaal nodded. "I would be surprised if it were otherwise. Some thought is called for, and given that it is still winter, there is time for thought." He rose from the chair. "Those were the thoughts I wished to share with you." He smiled almost sadly. "What we hope for cannot always be, I trust you understand."

Beltur stood and accompanied Naerkaal to the door. He definitely understood much of what Naerkaal had conveyed. He did wonder at what he might have missed, but he also understood that the conversation needed to be indirect, especially since Sarstaan would have an accomplished healer present when he talked with Naerkaal about his conversation with Beltur.

After Beltur opened the door, Naerkaal stepped out and inclined his head. "I will assist you as I can, given my position."

"We do appreciate that." Beltur nodded in return, then watched as Naerkaal walked to his horse and then mounted. Several moments later, he closed the door.

Tulya walked from the kitchen, with Taelya behind her. "What did the councilor want?"

"To convey a message."

"He seemed sad," said Taelya.

Tulya looked surprised. "You never saw him."

"I could feel him. Was he sad, Uncle Beltur?"

"He was. He didn't want to convey the message." Beltur addressed Tulya. "I need to think about things. Once both Lhadoraak and Jessyla are back, we all need to talk over what he said." *And what he didn't.*

"Lhadoraak shouldn't be that long."

"He'll be here before Jessyla, I'm sure."

That, in fact, was the case. Lhadoraak returned to the cot around third glass, but Jessyla did not arrive until almost two quints past fourth glass.

Beltur waited until she had her coat off and was standing in front of the hearth warming herself before he said, "I've already told Lhadoraak and Tulya. Naerkaal came by today, and the rest of you need to hear what he had to say."

"If he came here, it's not good." Jessyla glanced at Lhadoraak and Tulya, who appeared in the doorway from the kitchen. "Especially with everyone gathering around."

"It's not . . . but it could be worse. Let me tell you exactly what he had to say, at least as well as I can remember the very words he used."

"Taelya . . ." began Tulya.

"She should stay," said Beltur gently. "It affects her, too."

"You can listen," added Tulya. "Not a word, no questions until after Uncle Beltur finishes."

Beltur forced himself to sit down in one of the wooden armchairs. He waited until everyone was seated before he began. "Naerkaal was calm and pleasant. He was directly indirect, and began by saying that the Council had a closed meeting yesterday. He avoided saying directly what the councilors discussed. Instead, he discussed, in very general terms, the deaths of Barrynt, Emlyn, and, especially of Sarysta. He pointed out that Sarysta's death was of interest for several reasons . . ." Actually, Beltur had pointed out the first reason, but the way he had started he needed to segue into the actual conversation.

When he finished, he just waited.

"He's suggesting that you had something to do with Sarysta's death," asked Lhadoraak, "and because of that . . . ?"

"He suggested that because of the unknown nature of Sarysta's death, as time goes by there will be more and more rumors about a mage-healer who was present and close to Barrynt, and who owed a great deal to Barrynt," replied Beltur, "and that Councilor Sarstaan will eventually take action against me and Jessyla."

"That's not fair," declared Taelya.

"Dear," said Tulya firmly.

"It's still not fair," murmured the girl almost under her breath.

"It is what it is," Beltur pointed out. "There are also the hints about Taelya, but if Jessyla and I leave Axalt, it will be some years . . ."

Tulya shook her head. "The three of you are much stronger together."

"We don't have to decide this today," Lhadoraak said. "According to you, Naerkaal as much as said that no one was going to do much, if they do anything, until well after winter. I think the Council is being unduly harsh, Naerkaal especially. He, of all people, should understand."

"Naerkaal understands," replied Beltur.

"He was sad," affirmed Taelya.

Lhadoraak glanced at his daughter in surprise.

"He was, Father."

"Naerkaal's only one councilor out of eleven," added Beltur, "and there are few mages in Axalt. There might not be another. I've never heard another one being mentioned. There's also one other thing Naerkaal said. I kept wondering why he's been so careful in what he asked. I knew that Lhadoraak, Jessyla, or I could have sensed another mage around, and we haven't, but because of the questions Sarstaan raised and the way Naerkaal phrased what he said, I had the thought that a strong healer, like Herrara, could sense truths and falsehoods on the Council. So I asked Naerkaal. He told me that Sarstaan has a strong healer who attends all the public Council meetings."

Jessyla's mouth opened for a moment. "That's why . . . She can likely tell if anyone's lying or if Naerkaal fully shields himself."

Tulya frowned.

"That means that Naerkaal has to be very careful," Jessyla added. "It also means that Sarstaan has far greater power than just one councilor out of eleven."

"None of this is right," protested Lhadoraak.

"Councils have a way of doing what they wish," Beltur said.

"Dear," interjected Tulya firmly, "we never planned to come to Axalt in the first place. From what you said a long time back and from what the councilor said, Montgren might be a much nicer place. It can't be any colder. Beltur and Jessyla have much more to lose than we do."

Lhadoraak paused for several moments before saying, "You're right.

I hadn't thought about that." He offered a wry expression. "I just don't like being told what to do. Even quietly and indirectly."

"None of us do," said Jessyla. "But it's better than having white mages chasing us with chaos bolts or blacks trying to kill Beltur and turn me over to Waensyn. Or your being forced out of Spidlar in less than an eightday."

Tulya nodded.

Beltur could tell that she wasn't totally displeased with the idea of leaving Axalt, but then, she'd never wanted to come in the first place.

"We might as well get dinner ready," said Tulya. "We do have time to think it over."

Beltur managed to stifle a wry smile. Tulya had already decided.

At dinner, both Beltur and Jessyla avoided any more talk about Naerkaal and the Council, and Jessyla talked about what had happened at the healing house, while Lhadoraak briefly described what he'd been doing for the cabinetmaker.

Once Beltur and Jessyla were alone in their bedchamber, getting ready for bed, Beltur turned to her. "You know . . . all of this is my doing."

"You've always tried to do what's right."

"I don't know about that. Sometimes, it was what I had to do to stay alive."

"Dear . . . if you don't stay alive, you're not around to do what's right. There are at least five people who are alive who'd be dead without your skills as a healer. Taelya would be dying, if she weren't already dead. What else could you have done in Elparta?"

"Not much, not without losing you."

"Am I worth it?"

"Absolutely!" Beltur's smile faded. "About what's happened here, what do you really think?"

"I felt that the way things happened when we came to Axalt was almost too good to be true," said Jessyla quietly. "It was."

"If I hadn't—"

Jessyla put her index finger across his lips. "Not a word. I know. You don't have to say it. If Sarysta hadn't died, she would have destroyed both Johlana and Halhana . . . and Ryntaar and Frankyr, if she could have. Eshult's not as strong as his mother, and with her gone, he'll listen more to Halhana. Frankyr will definitely need Eshult, because Ryntaar doesn't want to stay in Axalt, and Eshult will find he needs Frankyr. In the end, life will be better for both families."

"Do you *know* this?"

Jessyla smiled, not quite mischievously. "It's best not to ask a woman how she knows what she knows."

Not wanting to dispute that, Beltur said, "Then I won't."

"Good." Her arms went around his neck.

LXXII

When Beltur reached the healing house on eightday morning, he took off his coat and scarf and walked into Herrara's study. She wasn't there. He picked up a basket, debating whether to wait for her, or head for the welcoming room to see if she needed any help.

At that moment, she walked in and said, "Good morning."

"Good morning. I was hoping you'd be here."

"Where else would I be?" Herrara offered an amused smile.

"I thought you'd like to know. Yesterday Councilor Naerkaal stopped by the house."

Herrara merely nodded.

"He suggested, very indirectly, that my contacts with Barrynt and his family, as well as my proximity to Sarysta on the afternoon before her death, would slowly change from a misty miasma into shadowy murmurs, and eventually worse, unless Jessyla and I removed the source of such rumors from Axalt." Beltur paused, waiting.

"I can't say I'm surprised."

"Naerkaal believes he's right. Is he?"

"If Naerkaal even hinted that, he's correct."

"You suspected something like this, didn't you?"

Herrara nodded. "You're both young and very able, and your presence has already had an effect. Some of that will last long after your departure. That's if you choose to leave."

"But should we?"

"That's your decision, not mine. You both make my life much easier. You've saved lives and limbs I likely couldn't have. You both could work here for the rest of your lives. Or you could work with Jorhan and become comfortable. Physically and financially, anyway."

Beltur understood what she wasn't saying. "Like Johlana, you mean?"

"More so. She's a woman who consorted a prosperous merchant. She's very capable, but not powerful, and her consort was thought to keep her in her place. You can't and won't do that for Jessyla, and she wouldn't for you. You're both anything but traditional. All people, but especially those in Axalt, resent young people who are capable and powerful."

"If we're so powerful, why are we being pushed out of lands?"

"From what I understand from Jessyla, you weren't at all powerful when you fled Gallos. You were more powerful when you left Spidlar, but I doubt you knew just how powerful you were. You're strong enough to stay here, but once Lhadoraak's daughter is known as a white witch, it may take all the power and capability you have. There will be greater and greater opposition. It could turn into open conflict. You're the most powerful mage in all Axalt, but do you want to force your presence onto a city whose ways and traditions are not yours? It will take force, you know? Axalt is very resistant to change. That's both its strength and its weakness."

"I'm getting the feeling that who and what Jessyla and I are won't likely fit easily into any land. Can you honestly tell me that's not so?"

"No, I can't. Neither of you fit in Gallos or Spidlar. You don't fit here, and likely never will. I do believe there's a place for everyone, if you can find or make it."

Beltur raised his eyebrows. "That doesn't happen often."

"Relyn made his place here. The dark angels made their place in Westwind. Saryn made her place in Sarronnyn. The druids made their place in the Great Forest."

"We're scarcely that powerful," demurred Beltur.

"Neither were they when they started." Herrara shrugged. "Much as Naerkaal can suggest, the Council can't force you out. Not now, especially. It's your decision, not theirs."

"We'll need to think about it."

"I'm glad for both of you that you phrased it that way." After a quick smile, she added, "You won't have to check on Wurfael. He left yesterday."

"What about the two old men?"

"The one with the broken arm is gone. Once his arm was set, he went to his daughter's cot. The other one . . . I'll be able to keep him for another few days."

"Klaznyt's still complaining?"

"He's been behaving himself."

"That might be because he's realized he needs as much time here as he can get."

"It also might be because he's finally realized who and what you are."

"I'd like to think it reflects his better nature," said Beltur wryly.

Herrara just smiled and said, "You might check on him."

Beltur left the study and headed up the stairs.

The rest of the eightday at the healing house was quiet, and Beltur left almost exactly at fourth glass, heading for Johlana's house. He'd told Jessyla not to expect him until around fifth glass because he felt he needed to talk to both Jorhan and Johlana as soon as possible.

When he reached the house and knocked, Frankyr opened the door. "Good afternoon, ser."

"The same to you, Frankyr. I'd like to talk to Jorhan. Is he here?"

"He's in the parlor with Mother, ser. You can go right in."

"I wouldn't want to interrupt them."

"I'm sure they'd want to see you," insisted Frankyr.

Beltur wasn't certain of that, although he doubted either Jorhan or Johlana would say anything or turn him away. "I'll try not to be long."

"You never overstay, ser."

Beltur appreciated the words, even if they were a form of flattery. He hung his coat and scarf on one of the pegs.

"That's a different tunic, isn't it?"

"Oh, that's because Healer Herrara thought I should have a tunic that showed I was both a mage and a healer."

"That was a good idea."

Beltur nodded and then made his way to the parlor. "I hope I'm not intruding . . ."

"You never intrude, Beltur," said Johlana warmly.

"Hardly ever, anyway," added Jorhan, with the hint of a smile. "I see you're wearing that new tunic."

"You seem to know about it."

"Herrara asked me about how wide the sleeve bands should be. That was several eightdays ago."

"Then you knew about it long before I did."

"She usually does," said Jorhan.

"I wouldn't be here, except something else has come up. Councilor Naerkaal paid me a visit late yesterday."

"Now what?" asked Jorhan, his voice turning gruff.

Johlana frowned.

"Some members of the Council have hinted that I had a close relationship with Barrynt . . . and that Barrynt's and Emlyn's deaths came rather soon after Jessyla and I arrived in Axalt." Beltur was elaborating on what

Naerkaal had hinted, but he really didn't want to get into some of the other hints. "Sarstaan is also concerned that I was one of the last people to see Sarysta alive."

"What does all that mean?" asked Jorhan.

"He's suggesting that it might be best that Jessyla and I leave Axalt sometime after winter lifts. Otherwise, the gossip and rumors could get very ugly. He didn't quite say that, but the implication was there."

"I'm sure it was," replied Johlana. "Sarstaan is a councilor, and he's influential. Barrynt worried about him."

"What about the smithing?" asked Jorhan.

"Naerkaal made it very clear that, if I stayed, over time you'd have trouble getting copper and tin."

"This Council doesn't sound much better than the bastards in Spidlar."

"They're not trying to kill us," Beltur said dryly. "It might be that I can suggest to Naerkaal that, as part of Jessyla and my agreeing to leave, you get copper and tin now. That way we could forge quite a few pieces in the next eightdays."

"If it weren't for Johlana, I'd think about coming with you." Jorhan paused. "Where are you thinking about going?"

"We won't want to stay in Certis, and we'll need to avoid Jellico. We'll likely try Montgren. If that doesn't work out, I really don't know. We'll find a way to send word where we end up."

"You're going to let them push you out?" asked Johlana.

"I had a talk with Herrara about it," Beltur said. "She pointed out that no one could force us to leave, but that it would get uglier as time passed. Then there's the problem of Taelya. She will be a white mage. That won't set well over time, either, and Lhadoraak and Tulya never really wanted to come here. Axalt was the only place they could safely reach in time." He turned directly to Johlana. "Somehow . . . I feel as though our presence has disrupted your entire life."

Johlana shook her head. "Barrynt and I were having problems with Emlyn and Sarysta long before you and Jorhan arrived. Both of you didn't have any choice, and Barrynt and I invited you." A sad smile crossed her face. "Sometimes, things just have to be what they are. Halhana and Eshult will be much happier this way. Likely, so will Ryntaar and Frankyr. In the late spring, Ryntaar wants to go back and take over Jorhan's lands. He'll do well there. He and Frankyr have planned to build a warehouse there so that they'll be able to handle more trade."

"What about you?" asked Beltur.

"I'm here," declared Jorhan.

"Emlyn and Sarysta weren't without enemies," added Johlana. "Things will settle down. Tradition is good for smoothing things over." Her face brightened. "Halhana and Eshult are coming to dinner in a while. She said that you made things easier with what you told Eshult."

"I just told him what happened."

"No one else did, especially not Sarstaan."

"He wasn't there," Beltur pointed out.

"He wouldn't have wanted to say anything that reflected badly on Sarysta. He wouldn't want to admit she was the cause of everything."

Beltur just nodded. He hadn't said that, although he'd suspected it. He'd only pointed out certain facts and how Barrynt might have felt. After several moments, he said, "I didn't have anything else to tell you, but I felt you both ought to know how Naerkaal and the Council feel about what happened."

"Think about it for a while," said Jorhan.

"We've thought about it, and we'll keep thinking about it. But if it doesn't look like matters will change . . ."

Johlana nodded slowly.

Beltur stood. "I hope you have a good dinner with Eshult and Halhana."

"I'm sure we will," declared Jorhan.

Beltur managed a pleasant smile as he left the family parlor. *Are you rushing into something you'll regret? Or will waiting too long just make matters worse?*

As he walked back toward the cot, he felt slightly numb, and not from the cold, or the light snow that had begun to filter out of the gray clouds that hung over Axalt. What Herrara had said made sense, unhappily, and if he could persuade Naerkaal to allow Jorhan to purchase more copper, he and the smith could at least forge a few more blades and other items to make Jorhan more comfortable for a while.

Even with that thought, Beltur still felt that somehow, he hadn't handled matters as well as he could have . . . and likely still wasn't.

LXXIII

After finishing his stable chores on oneday, Beltur headed for the Council building, hoping to find Naerkaal there or, if not, someone who could tell him where the mage-councilor might be. All he could find was a single bored-looking guard sitting on a stool outside the Council chamber.

"I'm looking for Mage-Councilor Naerkaal."

"None of the councilors are here on oneday."

"I can see that. Would you happen to know where Councilor Naerkaal might be."

"In his shop, I'd guess."

"Where is his shop?"

"It's a block north and east of the square."

"What kind of shop is it?"

"He's a scrivener. I know that. A bookshop? Whatever scriveners sell, I guess."

With that information, Beltur went looking. More than a quint later, he discovered the small shop south and west of the square. The sign on the outside just proclaimed SCRIVENER without any elaboration.

He opened the door and stepped inside, looking at the rows of books set neatly in shelves on the side wall away from the door.

Naerkaal looked up from where he sat behind the wide copy desk. "I thought I might see you one of these days."

"I hadn't thought of you as a scrivener."

"Why not? As you've already discovered, magery doesn't bring in many silvers, and I don't have your ability as a healer. Most mages don't. Besides, I happen to like books." Naerkaal gestured to the chair beside the desk.

Beltur seated himself. "We've talked over the question of the shadows. How real are those shadows?"

"How real? You'd know that better than I would. Certain people, beginning with Sarstaan, think they're very real. He will try to make them more real for reasons I'm certain you understand."

"If . . . *if* Jessyla and I decide to leave Axalt, that leaves Jorhan in a very bad position, and he's done absolutely nothing to deserve that."

"Sometimes that happens."

"There is a way to mitigate that."

"Oh . . . ?"

"You had mentioned that it wouldn't be necessary for us to leave until after the end of winter and until the roads were largely clear."

"I don't believe I said necessary. I said something about the shadows not getting much worse over that time because of the common sense of people in Axalt."

"I didn't mean to put words in your mouth. What you did suggest was that it would not be that amiss if we waited until traveling was not so dangerous and that most people would understand. If Jorhan were able to purchase copper and tin at a reasonable price over that period, we could work together for a time to increase his stock of cupridium goods to sell. That certainly wouldn't hurt anyone in Axalt and would allow him to assist his sister more . . . and to establish him in Axalt."

"I see your point. I'm not certain others would."

"Jorhan doesn't need everyone to see that point, just those who deal in copper and tin."

"Why would they wish to see that?"

"Well . . . I owe a certain amount to Jorhan. I don't like the idea of his being forced to choose between helping his sister and leaving here in order to continue smithing. If that were to be his choice, it just might be that Jessyla and I might have to stay longer and deal, as necessary, with what comes from those shadows."

Naerkaal smiled sardonically. "I wondered if you'd get to that point. I could suggest that leaving as early as possible in spring would be to your advantage."

"It might well be, but I'd find it difficult to leave Jorhan without adequate goods to sell for a time, and there are those, from what you've hinted, who would prefer our leaving to be sooner than later."

"I do know some factors and merchants who might prove . . . helpful." Naerkaal paused. "I would take it very much amiss if Jorhan receives such materials and you delay your departure. At present, you have always been truthful, if at times not fully revealing what you might."

Beltur realized that, at that moment, he had to decide. "I understand, but not until the snows stop and the roads are clear."

"That is reasonable, especially if it is obvious that you and your consort plan to leave." Another pause followed. "What do you know about the other black mage and his plans?"

"They will do what they feel best . . . after they know what we have decided."

"It will become more and more difficult for their daughter as she grows older."

"They are aware of that."

"I thought they might be." Naerkaal nodded. "Is there anything else?"

"I read some of *The Wisdom of Relyn*. Why did he stay in Axalt? Do you know?"

"He had no choice. Both the Viscount of Certis and the Prefect of Gallos wanted his head, and the traders of Spidlar were so weak that Gallos held the lands immediately to the west of Axalt. In turn, Axalt had no choice but to rely on him. You are fortunate that the Viscount has no idea that you even exist. That could change, of course."

Another not-so-veiled threat. "That might not be to Axalt's advantage."

"I would agree. For others, hatred and anger override common sense."

While Beltur already suspected he knew the answer, he asked, "Does Sarstaan's healer attend all the Council meetings?"

"She does, but she does not wear greens when she does."

"I assume the other councilors know this."

"So do I, but no one ever speaks of it." Naerkaal smiled. "Everyone is most honest in the public meetings."

Beltur rose from the chair. "Thank you for taking the time."

"It's always better when matters can be resolved quietly and as fairly as possible. Too often those matters resolved in public are less fair, no matter what anyone says, because power always makes itself felt."

"I'd think it might be the opposite at times," suggested Beltur.

Naerkaal shook his head. "In public, if those in power concede anything, they're thought weak. The thought of weakness leads to greater use of power, and that's even less fair."

"I hadn't thought of it that way." *But it makes a sort of sense.*

"Sooner or later, you would have."

Beltur nodded, but he wasn't so sure. After an envious look at all the books, he turned and left the shop.

From there he walked quickly to the smithy, but he was nearly a glass later than he usually arrived. Once there, he took off his coat and scarf and hurried toward the workbench, where Jorhan was working on a mold.

"Are you all right?" asked the smith.

"I'm fine." *Or as well as I can be, given how things are going.*

"Wasn't sure if I'd be seeing you today."

"I went to see Naerkaal. I got to thinking about you and all you've done for me. I told you yesterday that I'd see if I could persuade him to influence people to sell you copper and tin. I suggested we might have to stay longer if you couldn't get materials fairly soon. He said that he'd do what he could. I think it's likely you might just find some factors willing to part with those materials at a reasonable cost." Beltur offered a crooked smile. "It was worth a try."

"If it weren't for Johlana . . ."

"I know. But she needs you, especially now. And I think Ryntaar and Frankyr could use a little of your knowledge and support, at least for a time."

"Well . . ." Jorhan drew out the word. "We still have some copper and tin. You want to work on another sabre?"

"That sounds like a very good idea."

Jorhan smiled broadly.

Beltur stayed at the smithy until almost a quint past fourth glass, when he was able to release his hold on the order/chaos net embedded in the bronze that had become cupridium. Then he walked home through the late afternoon that had almost become twilight in the valley between the peaks of the Easthorns.

Jessyla was already at the cot when Beltur arrived and met him as he was hanging up his coat on the wall peg.

"You're later today."

"I went to see Naerkaal this morning . . ." Beltur quickly explained his conversation with the mage-councilor and then that he and Jorhan had been casting a sabre.

"Do you think we're doing the right thing?"

"What do you think?"

"I asked you."

"It's a huge gamble, but if we stay here, things will get harder, not easier. What if we'd left Elparta earlier?"

"We couldn't," Jessyla pointed out.

"That's true. Here we have the choice."

"You're going to have to teach me more magery . . . and soon."

Beltur nodded. "There is one other thing. You need to write a letter to your mother tonight. I'll take it to Ryntaar tomorrow and have him work out a way to get it to her. She needs to know where you are."

"Where we're not, you mean."

"That also." He frowned momentarily. "We'll need to think about getting more horses. I don't like the thought of relying on others for getting places."

Jessyla nodded, then said, "You know that Lhadoraak and Tulya don't have much in the way of silvers."

"I know, but we have enough, and we'll be much safer—"

"If we travel together," murmured Jessyla, glancing toward the kitchen, and adding in an even quieter voice, "Tulya can't wait to leave Axalt. That's good."

"What about you?"

"I'm more of a gambler than I thought." She smiled. "Except wagering on you isn't that much of a gamble."

Beltur didn't voice his considerable doubts about that.

LXXIV

The first thing Beltur did upon leaving the cot on twoday was to see Ryntaar before the young merchant left for the factorage. He found Ryntaar in the side hall and gave him Jessyla's letter to her mother.

"I'd appreciate it if you could arrange for this to be sent to Jessyla's mother in Elparta. She's addressed it to her at the Council Healing House there."

"It may take a while. Not many traders travel to Elparta in winter."

"That's why you're getting it now. She wants her mother to know. Otherwise Margrena might decide to visit, and we wouldn't want her to make that trip and find us gone."

"You're really planning on leaving, aren't you?"

"The Council hasn't given us much choice, except in when we choose to leave."

"That's scarcely fair."

"What happened hasn't been fair to you and your family, either, especially your mother. Your parents put us up, fed us, and then let us have all that furniture. That has to come back to you. It wouldn't be right any other way."

Ryntaar nodded. "That might not be too much of a problem. Frankyr and Mother have already agreed that I can take anything you leave to Elparta. Uncle Jorhan . . . well . . . he's never been much for furnishings. His place is pretty bare, from what he's said. I'll be honest. I'll have a better chance of attracting the kind of a consort I'm looking for that way."

"You're not interested in anyone here in Axalt?"

"After what Mother and Halhana have been through?" Ryntaar shook his head. "I need to head to the factorage. I need to spend a lot more time there with Frankyr."

After leaving Ryntaar, Beltur took care of the stable, then headed out. A quint later, as he neared the healing house, he saw an unattended wagon tied up to a post outside, not even a hitching post, and he thought he saw splotches of blood on the snow. He immediately hurried inside, shed his coat and scarf, dropping them on the hanging pegs, and headed toward the surgery, glancing into Herrara's empty study as he passed.

A figure was stretched on the surgery table, where Herrara was doing something to the man's shoulder. A youth stood in the corner of the surgery, his face pale.

"You're here. Good!" snapped Herrara. "I need you to use your skills while I deal with the puncture in his shoulder. He'll lose too much blood if I release the pressure. Can you sense where I'm holding it?"

"Yes. You want me to block that?"

Herrara nodded.

Beltur moved in beside Herrara and eased a containment into place beneath her hand. "I've got it."

Immediately, Herrara cut away the cloth around the wound, then studied the torn flesh under the transparent containment. "There's a small bleeder there." She gestured with the tip of the scalpel. "Can you block that a little lower, leave the torn part exposed?"

"Tell me when."

From that point on Beltur just followed Herrara's orders, first as she dealt with the deep shoulder wound, then as she went on to the score of cuts and lacerations on the man's arm. Looking at the slashes in the man's arm, Beltur couldn't understand how a woodworker could have done that to himself, or how the youth could have, not that he believed the pale and shivering figure in the corner had done anything deliberate.

When Herrara finally stepped back for a moment, Beltur could see bloody splinters or pieces of wood in the small basket that held surgical wastes. "Do you know how . . . ?"

"Boissaen was using a lathe. His son was using a foot treadle. The chisel blade caught in whatever was being turned. It snapped out of its handle and went through his chest, and fragments of wood splinters sliced up his arm. His son wrapped the arm and shoulder and borrowed a wagon to drive him here. Boissaen managed to keep pressure on the deep wound until they got here."

"Had the lathe running too fast. Bad wood . . ." mumbled the woodworker.

"You're going to be here for a few days, until we're sure there's no chaos in that wound."

"What . . . my arm?"

"You'll have plenty of scars. It will be a while before you'll get full use back. We'll have to watch for wound chaos in the shoulder for some time as well." Herrara looked to Beltur. "You might look now."

"There are a few tiny points." Beltur concentrated. "They're gone. There'll be more tomorrow and the next day."

"If you got rid of them," demanded the boy, "why will there be more tomorrow?"

"I can't sense the smallest ones," said Beltur. "Wound chaos grows from tiny points. When they get bigger, I can remove them." *If there aren't too many.* "That's why we have to watch for a time."

"Your father is fortunate. Not many healers can do what Beltur can do." Herrara gestured to Elisa, who had slipped into the surgery without Beltur noticing her. "Elisa will finish cleaning your arm, and she'll take you to a bed where you rest."

"I have to get back to my shop."

"You need to rest right now, and we'll need to check you in a glass or so," said Herrara. "Then we can talk about when it would be best for you to return to your shop."

"Now," insisted the woodworker.

Beltur stepped forward. "You're wounded. As badly as if you took a spear thrust or a crossbow quarrel in the shoulder. You just can't go back to work, just like you couldn't go back to fight—not unless you wanted to get killed."

"What do you know about fighting?"

"I was an undercaptain and a Spidlarian arms-mage during the invasion. I fought with a recon company. I also healed a few men and saw far more buried. You can leave . . . if you want your son to bury you." That was an exaggeration, but not much of one.

The woodworker slumped slightly. "Didn't seem that bad."

"It will later today, and tomorrow." Herrara gestured to Elisa, who moved forward, carrying a bottle of spirits and clean dressings.

The two older healers left the surgery and walked back to Herrara's study. There Herrara turned to Beltur. "You're spoiling me, you know? With you, I can do things better, or faster, than I can with anyone else.

We've done some healing I wouldn't even have tried without you because it would have killed the patient."

"You're talking as if we're leaving tomorrow."

"I need to get used to the idea. Most of Axalt won't know what they've lost, but I do."

"They have you, and you're more than the Council deserves."

"That may be, but what about the people who don't have their own healers? Or those in the poorhouse or the workhouses?"

Beltur definitely didn't have an answer for her questions. "That's why you're here."

"Can you think of a better reason?"

"No," he said with a rueful smile.

"Wherever you go . . ." she began, then shook her head. "I don't have to tell you anything like that. You've already seen how power ignores poverty."

"They don't ignore it," said Beltur. "They don't even see it. They think everyone is like them, except without silvers, and that they're poor because they're lazy or have to work hard because they make bad decisions."

"As if those in power don't make bad decisions," said Herrara gently.

"Silvers and golds can make up for a lot of bad decisions," replied Beltur.

"We both know that. Knowing that won't change anything. You might as well look in on those still here. There's an older serving maid upstairs. She says she fell and broke her leg. The older man without any family died last night. He never would tell anyone his name. I wonder if he actually had family and didn't want to be a burden on them."

Beltur had wondered that himself. He turned toward the shelves and picked up a basket and a bottle of spirits, then left the study and headed toward the stairs.

LXXV

Threeday brought another light snow, and Beltur trudged through it along the south town road to the smithy, walking past two workhouse wagons whose crews were busy shoveling the road clear. When he reached the smithy and took off his coat and scarf, he could see that Jorhan was busy at the workbench, and that several molds were laid out, and one was heating on the forge.

Jorhan didn't said anything until Beltur walked over to the workbench. "Don't know what you said to that councilor mage, but late yesterday, this metals factor came by. Fellow named Stahlyn. Said he had ten stones' worth of good copper and a stone of tin. Wasn't cheap, but I've paid more, sometimes a lot more. He even had it on his wagon, like he knew I'd buy it. Had to have him drive me back to the house to get the silvers, but he didn't seem to mind."

Beltur nodded. The copper was another message. "So you've got molds going here."

"Might as well. Be better for both of us." Jorhan paused. "You'll still get your share. Might be a while, but we'll find a way to get it to you, wherever you two end up."

"It's likely going to be five of us. Lhadoraak and Tulya are less than impressed with Axalt, and it's awfully cold for Tulya."

"I can't say I blame them, the way the Council questioned them about their daughter. Seven years old and the Council worrying about whether she'll be some sort of white witch."

"She'll be a white, but a mage, not a witch." After a momentary hesitation, Beltur asked, "Are we back to working on blades?"

"A dagger and a sabre first, then a pair of candelabra. The melt's ready to heat."

Beltur nodded and walked over to the bellows.

When he left the forge at fourth glass, he was vaguely surprised that he wasn't particularly tired, but then he'd been using magery at the healing center, and he'd also been doing more than a little walking and riding.

Jessyla and Tulya were in the kitchen when he arrived, and Lhadoraak was outside splitting wood. Taelya was sitting on the padded bench looking at the hearth. So Beltur smiled and said, "Time for a magery lesson, Taelya."

"Right now, Uncle Beltur?"

"Why not? I'll wager you've not been practicing with your shields as much as you should be."

"I have too."

"Then you should be able to show me." Beltur sat down in the wooden armchair. "Raise a full shield. This time, make the order binding around the chaos knots stronger than before."

"That's hard."

"It is. That's why only very good mages can do it and hold shields like that all the time."

"Am I a good mage?"

"You're a very good mage for your age. But that doesn't count if you run into a nasty mage who's older and stronger. That's why we're working on making you a better mage."

Beltur watched as she built the shield, noting that her order knots were slightly larger, and certainly her shield was far better than his had been when he'd been close to twice her age. "That's good. Now . . . I'm going to hit at it with an order probe. You hold it as long as you can."

"Yes, Uncle Beltur."

Beltur's first probe was light, and made no impression on Taelya. The second was harder, but Taelya's shield still held. Rather than increase the force of the probe, Beltur just kept hitting with the same force, so that she'd get a sense of what a continual attack was like. He watched her and tried to sense just how much strength she had left.

Abruptly, her shield collapsed.

"I just couldn't hold it any longer."

"You did just fine. Take two deep breaths. Now, put your shield back together."

"Right now?"

"Now. Whatever shield you can put together, but get a shield around yourself."

The shield wasn't quite as strong as the first, but it was complete.

"Now . . . just hold it. I won't bang on it. I just want you to keep holding it. This kind of practice makes you stronger."

Surprisingly, Taelya held the shield for almost a quint before it collapsed. Her face was sweaty, and she was breathing heavily.

"That was excellent. We're done for today. Go tell your mother that you get a treat."

"I was good, wasn't I?"

"You were," Beltur admitted.

As Taelya left the room, Jessyla came in from the kitchen and sat down on the bench. "I was doing what you had her do, except you weren't beating on my shield. That's still hard."

"It has to be hard, or you don't get better."

"For her age . . ."

"She's very talented. That's why she'll need the strongest shields she can develop."

"Because she's still a girl?"

Beltur nodded. "You'll need stronger shields, also."

"I know."

"I found out something interesting today." Beltur offered a rueful smile.

"Interesting in a way I won't like, I think, from your expression."

"You know how Jorhan's been having trouble getting copper?"

"Don't tell me that he's not."

"A factor named Stahlyn showed up yesterday afternoon and offered him ten stones' worth of copper and one of tin, at a decent price. He had the metals in his wagon."

"It sounds like Naerkaal and the Council want us out of Axalt."

"It does look that way. So we cast a dagger, a sabre, and a pair of candelabra today. Jorhan will work on finishing them tomorrow."

"Does that mean more silvers?"

"Not until they're sold."

"But we won't be here."

"Jorhan insists I'll get my share, whatever it takes. He's been more than fair. He's given more than he promised all along."

"But . . . how will he manage that?"

"Through Ryntaar, or Frankyr, probably, since Ryntaar might be in Elparta by then. The merchants have arrangements with other merchants. He'll likely send a bill of disbursement to a merchant wherever we end up, and a copy to me, and then I'll collect it from that merchant."

"Anywhere in Candar?"

"Well . . . I don't know about the Great Forest . . ." Beltur grinned.

Jessyla shook her head.

Beltur just enjoyed looking at her.

LXXVI

The light snow ended well before dawn on fourday morning, and the workhouse crews had the main streets largely clear by the time that Beltur walked from the stables to the healing house, where Elisa informed him that Herrara wouldn't be returning until early afternoon.

Hoping that he wouldn't be faced with some injury that required immediate surgery, Beltur went to work checking on patients.

As he had anticipated, more wound chaos had developed in Boissaen's shoulder and in places in his arms, but not so much that Beltur couldn't deal with it. The older serving maid had developed additional yellowish-red chaos around the broken bone in her leg, and Beltur spent almost two quints dealing with that. On the other hand, Klaznyt's hands were healing better and faster than Beltur could have hoped for.

The only person who showed up in the welcoming room was a mother with an eight-year-old boy who had an ugly sore filled with pus and chaos. Beltur cleaned the sore and removed the chaos and applied a clean dressing.

Herrara didn't return until first glass in the afternoon, but the remainder of the day was relatively quiet, with only two more people showing up, one a young man from a workhouse shoveling crew with two broken fingers, whose supervisor hadn't believed they were broken, the other an older woman with an ulcerated leg.

On fiveday, Beltur worked on more blades and another pair of candelabra, while nothing of note occurred at the healing house on sixday. Before Beltur knew it, he was leaving the healing house at fourth glass on eight-day, heading back to the cot before going to Johlana's for dinner with Jessyla, an invitation that also included Lhadoraak, Tulya, and Taelya.

The five arrived at the side door of the house at half past the glass, where Frankyr met them and ushered them inside and then into the family parlor, where Jorhan and Johlana were talking with Eshult and Halhana.

Ryntaar stood by the sidebar, smiling. "A pale ale for you, Beltur, and mulled wine?" he asked as he looked to Jessyla.

"Please."

In what seemed moments, everyone was seated with a beverage in hand, including Taelya, who had a small tumbler of pearapple cider.

"Hard to believe that we've only got another eightday of winter," said Jorhan.

"Not that all the snow's going to melt overnight nine days from now," said Eshult, with a smile. "We'll still have snows, just not nearly as often."

"How long is it usually before the roads are clear enough for safe travel?" asked Lhadoraak.

"Travel now is safe," replied Eshult. "It's just cold and takes longer." He hesitated, then added, "It's safe within Axalt, and there aren't many brigands in Certis at any time. The Viscount's men patrol the main roads. If they catch brigands, I understand most of them are killed trying to escape."

"Even if they haven't tried to escape," added Ryntaar.

"They usually leave traders and merchants alone. That's why it's a good idea for most travelers to accompany traders."

"Do you know of any traders who might be leaving in early spring?" asked Lhadoraak.

Eshult and Ryntaar exchanged questioning glances.

Finally, Eshult said, "Not right at the moment. It's likely some will start talking about their plans in the next eightday."

"We'd be interested," said Beltur.

"So soon?" asked Johlana.

"It's better that way," replied Beltur. "That is, given how things stand with the Council."

"We could use a new Council," murmured Frankyr.

"It wouldn't change things much," said Eshult, "not if my uncle stays on it."

"If he doesn't," said Beltur, "it could be worse."

Almost everyone in the parlor looked at Beltur as if he'd lost his mind.

"All of you know that I don't care much for Sarstaan," Beltur finally said. "But there's something most of you don't know. He has his personal healer attend every Council meeting."

"Is he that ill?" asked Halhana.

"No. She's a fairly strong black healer. That means she can tell when councilors aren't telling the truth. The entire Council knows this."

Eshult's mouth dropped.

"Think about it," said Beltur. "He knows if anyone lies in the public meetings. I imagine he's very good at asking questions in public that would show if a councilor lied in a closed meeting. I also imagine she's placed where she can overhear what others say to him in his factorage."

"You're saying the Council is less deceptive than it might otherwise be?" asked Eshult.

"That's only my surmise. But it might work the other way as well. If Sarstaan went too far, someone might bring up the matter, and the others might suggest to other traders that he has an unfair advantage in trading." The more Beltur thought about it, the more confused he got, because he could see so many ways of using that situation, on both sides.

"He never mentioned that, so far as I know," mused Eshult.

"Not all healers can tell that," said Jessyla.

"Only the very good ones, I'd guess," added Beltur.

Eshult offered an amused smile. "I'm seeing another reason why the Council is not so favorably disposed to your remaining in Axalt."

"Why is that?" asked Halhana. "Because more and more that they want hidden might be revealed?"

"That's one reason. I'm sure I could think of others if I tried."

"We've heard enough of all that . . . and about the Council," said Johlana, turning toward Beltur. "Do you all know where you're going?"

"Our plan is to go to Montgren, Vergren at first. A number of people suggested it's more favorable to mages and healers, and there is one trader who said to get in touch with him if we do go there."

"That fellow Vaenturl, right?" asked Jorhan. "He seemed pretty solid. Did wonder what he was trading, though. Seemed like he had one of every-thing."

Beltur hadn't noticed that, but then, he'd had a few other matters on his mind at the time. "He even told us how to find him."

"That's good," said Eshult. "Vergren's not a large city, not like Elparta or Fenard or Jellico, but it's not small, either."

"He was honest," added Jessyla.

"You could do worse than honest." Jorhan looked to Lhadoraak. "You haven't said much. What do you think?"

"We'll do better together. I hope we can find someplace that suits us . . ." The blond mage grinned. "And isn't too cold."

"Herrara will be sad to see both of you go," said Johlana. "She came by and told me so."

"She'll be sad to see you go?" groused Jorhan. "Not so much as I will."

"Don't complain too much," said Johlana, "or I'll send you after them."

Beltur wasn't sure, but he thought he sensed a little something more than good-natured joking behind Johlana's words, but he couldn't tell what that might have been.

Jorhan mock-glared at his sister. "The only way you'll get me out of Axalt is to drag me all the way."

"Don't tempt me," replied Johlana with mock sweetness.

"Women . . ." said Lhadoraak, breaking off his words as Tulya looked at him.

"Sometimes . . . we really should listen to women," said Eshult, adding quickly, "The right women, that is."

"I am glad you said those last words," said Halhana.

"I'm learning," replied Eshult. "Growing up, I didn't have the advan-tage of a sister close to my age."

"Advantage?" asked Frankyr.

"It is, Brother dear," rejoined Halhana. "By the way, I heard that Lyseana has visited the factorage several times in the last eightday." A knowing smile followed her words.

"Lyseana?" asked Ryntaar. "Trader Lyandyr's daughter?"

"She just came to offer her condolences," replied Frankyr.

"Three times?" Halhana raised her eyebrows.

Frankyr flushed.

Chuckles and smiles filled the parlor.

"On that happy note," said Johlana, "it's time for dinner." She rose from her chair.

As Beltur stood, he had the feeling that both the dinner and the conversation would be enjoyable.

They were.

LXXVII

The first thing Beltur noticed when he left the stable on his walk to south town on oneday morning was that not only was the sky a deep clear green-blue, but he could feel actual warmth radiating from the white sun. *A sign of spring approaching or just a momentary burst of warmth?*

When he reached the smithy, he loaded more coal into the forge and worked with the bellows for a time to get the fire ready for the melt. Once Jorhan had poured the bronze into the mold for another sabre, and Beltur had eased the order/chaos mesh-like net into the hot metal, he turned to Jorhan.

"We're going to need two more horses, possibly three, and if we're to leave Axalt by early spring, I need to find them. After we finish here today, I was thinking I'd stop by the factorage and ask Ryntaar if he has any ideas about who might have some mounts for sale."

"I can help with one of those. I'd be happy to let you have my second horse, the mare I bought to come to Axalt. It's no favor to her to have her mostly in the stable, and I'm not going to need more than one horse. Barrynt was paying for her feed, and that will be a bit less for the family to handle. She's gentle enough for anyone, even little Taelya."

"Are you sure? You paid good silvers for her."

"Tell you what. I'll deduct what she cost me from what I owe you. Fair's fair. Besides, you need another horse, and I don't."

Beltur couldn't argue with what Jorhan said. "Thank you."

"Once you've got that sabre set," said Jorhan, "I thought we'd do a pair of candelabra. After they're done, you can go talk to Ryntaar. He'll know someone."

The sabre seemed to take longer than Beltur had anticipated, but that had to have been in his imagination, because he finished setting the order/chaos net in each candelabrum only a quint or so after third glass. After that, he left the smithy.

The sun was still shining out of a clear sky, and Beltur could see traces of moisture at the foot of the snow piled back from the stone edges of the road. *Maybe spring will actually come.*

As he neared the factorage, Beltur looked up, taking in the signboard. He still wondered about the reason for the name, but realized he'd never actually asked Barrynt. Once inside, since he didn't see Ryntaar immediately, he walked toward the back of the building.

Ryntaar looked slightly surprised as Beltur walked toward him. "Ser . . . is anything wrong?"

"I hope not." Beltur smiled. "I just wanted your thoughts on something. We're going to have to be leaving in a few eightdays, and we'll need some more horses, for Lhadoraak and his family. Jorhan's selling me one of his horses, the mare. He says that one horse is enough for him . . . and that way you'll have to buy less grain and fodder."

"Uncle Jorhan worries about being a burden." Ryntaar shook his head. "I can see that he might not want to worry about another horse, but the fodder wouldn't have been a problem."

"I know that," replied Beltur, "but it does make matters a little easier for us. I was wondering if you know anyone who deals in horses who's trustworthy or who might have another two or three mounts for sale."

"I can certainly ask around and let you know."

"I'd appreciate that. There's one other thing. We're planning on heading out to Corumtal, then going through Rytel on the way to Vergren. Would you know any factors or merchants in those places who might also be trustworthy?"

"Let me think about that. I can also check the bills of disbursement to see the houses with whom Father dealt most often."

"I don't know that we'd even call on them, but it can't hurt to know names."

"I can see that, ser." Ryntaar paused. "I could also give you a letter of disbursement for a small amount . . . in case of unforeseen circumstances. That might help, even if you don't need to use it."

"You're very kind. Let me think about that."

"I'll let you know what I find out about the horses."

"Thank you."

When Beltur reached the cot, because it was still before fourth glass, Jessyla hadn't yet arrived, but Lhadoraak and Taelya were in the front room, where Lhadoraak was working with Taelya on her letters, using a small slate and a piece of chalk.

The blond mage looked up. "Do you have a moment after I finish this bit with Taelya?"

"I do." Beltur suspected he knew what Lhadoraak had in mind, since they had not talked about their departure from Axalt after returning from Johlana's the night before.

"I'll fix some bread and cheese for Taelya in the kitchen," added Tulya, from the doorway to the kitchen.

"Is there anything else, Mother?" asked Taelya, not quite plaintively.

"Not until dinner. You don't have to have bread and cheese, but that's all there is."

"Then I'd like the bread and cheese, please."

Once Taelya was settled in the kitchen, the three adults settled around the hearth, heaped with coals on the kitchen side for the stew that Tulya was fixing for supper.

"You had something in mind," prompted Beltur, smiling easily.

"You know very well," replied Lhadoraak, with a smile far more rueful than that of Beltur. "Just how are we going to manage this travel?"

"We'll accompany suitable merchants, or go by ourselves, if necessary, as soon as it's practicable."

"We're not equipped, not really . . . I mean Tulya, Taelya, and I . . ."

"I know that. Jorhan's selling me one of his horses, the mare. She's gentle enough for Taelya. He only bought her to come to Axalt. Ryntaar's looking for three more horses for us. That's a mount apiece, plus a second packhorse, or a spare mount. Taelya's light enough that the mare can carry extra, most likely fodder and grain for the time it takes to get to Corumtal."

"Beltur . . . we can't afford horses."

"Lhadoraak . . . I know that. I can, and you need them, and I need you three with us."

"I can't let you do that," protested Lhadoraak.

"You and Tulya and Taelya need horses. We all are traveling together, and we can travel faster and not be dependent on merchants if we all have mounts. It's to our advantage as well. Two full mages, and a healer, and two beginning mages are far more likely to avoid trouble than if we split up."

"You've been planning this, haven't you?" asked Lhadoraak wryly.

"Not until the Council started giving us trouble." Beltur paused, then added, "But I did consider it some even before that. Herrara told me eight-days ago that we really didn't belong here, and that got me to thinking." He looked to Tulya. "I understand that anywhere in Montgren is warmer than Axalt."

She shook her head. "Did Jessyla tell you to say that?"

"No. She said you felt that way, and I stole the words from her. She doesn't mind that when she's right, especially if I admit something is her idea."

"What if it's wrong?" asked Lhadoraak.

"That doesn't happen often, but then," said Beltur with wry humor, "I say it was my idea." *Most of the time, anyway.*

Tulya laughed softly. "Even without us adding to your problems, you two wouldn't have lasted much longer here."

"Probably not."

"I need to check on Taelya and the stew." Tulya rose and headed for the kitchen.

Lhadoraak looked at Beltur. "I doubt we can ever repay you."

"Friends don't balance ledgers," Beltur said gently, "and people who count every silver can't count on anyone. We're in this together." He stood. "We need to bring in some wood."

LXXVIII

By sevenday, despite a light snow on fiveday, the air and sun were warm enough that when Beltur walked to the smithy he could see that the snow piles alongside the roads were shrinking some, although that morning, clear ice had formed at the base of the piles.

By the time Beltur reached the smithy and had his coat and tunic off, Jorhan had the mold for an ornate platter heated and ready for the melt. Beltur immediately went to work with the bellows, but he hadn't been working it that long when there was a rap on the door and a man entered—Eshult—so great a surprise that, for a moment, Beltur just stopped pumping.

"Don't let me interrupt you," Eshult said immediately.

"We won't," replied Jorhan, nodding for Beltur to continue with the bellows.

Later, when the platter had been cast and Beltur stood beside the cooling mold, infusing the metal with the necessary order and chaos, and then holding it in place while the bronze that would become cupridium continued to cool, Eshult cleared his throat and said, "If you wouldn't mind, I'd like you to make something for me . . ."

"What did you have in mind?" asked Jorhan.

"I'd like a shaving mirror in a stand, along the lines of the one you did for Halhana, except . . . well . . . for a man, you understand . . ." Eshult offered a smile that was part embarrassment, part rue, Beltur thought. "You put rosebuds on hers, I think. I don't know about thorns . . . but . . . I'd likely deserve them."

"How about oak leaves and acorns?" suggested Jorhan. "Oaks mean power."

"What about crossing that with a pine or spruce branch?"

Jorhan frowned for a moment, then said, "Suppose I could do that. A bit extra."

"Whatever it takes."

Beltur understood that Eshult meant every word he spoke.

"It won't be inexpensive."

"Would ten golds cover the cost?"

Jorhan smiled. "Not that expensive. Be five or six, depending on how difficult the oak and pine branch design is."

"Do I pay you now?"

Jorhan shook his head. "When you're satisfied. It's likely to be a good eightday."

"Would you mind if I spent a moment with Beltur?" Eshult asked, looking at Jorhan.

"No. I need to get some things from the other room for the next mold."

Once Jorhan left, Eshult moved closer to Beltur. "You're still working, aren't you?"

"Yes. It takes a certain effort to hold the order/chaos net in place."

"For how long?"

"For this, around a quint. It varies a little with each casting."

The trader fingered his chin. "I have been thinking about what you said. I can foresee . . . certain difficulties . . . with Uncle Sarstaan. Have you any suggestions that might help?"

"Be very polite," replied Beltur. "That's not what you meant, though. You might try cultivating Herrara, the healer who runs the healing house. Pay her to accompany you to any meetings where Sarstaan has his healer . . . or she may be able to recommend another healer you can trust." Beltur paused. "Remember . . . if you can't sense truth or falsehood, you need to trust the person who can. Absolutely. You don't have to like them, just trust them."

"It's too bad you won't be here."

Watching Sarstaan was the last thing Beltur would have wanted to do, but he just nodded and said, "Sometimes, things don't work out the way we think they will."

Eshult nodded. "The last eightdays have shown that." He hesitated, then said, "Healer Herrara . . . her discretion . . . ?"

"I've found her to be very discreet, and very honest. Don't expect flattery. Be honest with her, and she'll be very helpful. Try to deceive her or mislead her, and she'll likely be very polite and very deferential, and of minimal assistance." After a moment, Beltur added, "She probably won't want to do what you need. That's because she relies on the Council to pay to keep the healing house going. I do think she could likely find someone who could, though."

"You don't like misleading people, either, do you?"

"No. Usually the result is worse than not misleading them. It just takes longer for the damage to occur. That's what I've seen, anyway."

Eshult stepped back and inclined his head. "I thank you. I'll be sorry to see you go, but it's likely for the best. Axalt's too small for you and Jessyla."

And too "traditional." "As I said, sometimes things don't quite work out."

Eshult nodded once more, then turned and left the smithy.

In moments, Jorhan returned. "What did he want?"

"Advice. I did the best I could."

"Better'n he got from his parents, I'd wager." The smith frowned. "About that mirror he wants?"

"How else can he show Halhana that he values the one his mother tried to remove?" Beltur thought for a moment. "It's also a statement in cupridium that he values her and her judgment."

"Best we do a very good job, then."

"Very good," agreed Beltur. *For more than a few reasons.*

When Beltur left the smithy, heading back along the south town road, the clear ice had melted again in most places, and the puddles were larger.

He was still thinking about the mirror and Eshult when he reached the Mountain Factorage and stepped inside, only to see, near the rear of the front room, Eshult and Ryntaar talking. Both immediately turned, and Ryntaar gestured for Beltur to join them.

Wondering exactly what the two had been discussing, Beltur offered a pleasant smile and made his way to where they stood.

"We've been talking about horses," Ryntaar said. "And other things."

"I've got two I'd like to see have a good owner," offered Eshult. "I didn't expect to end up with Father's horses in addition to my own. Even his stable isn't big enough for them all. They're both eight-year-old geldings, good riding horses, and strong. They'd be a gold each, and four silvers for saddles and gear for both. We might be able . . ."

"That's a generous price," Beltur said, "and, if you're offering, I'm accepting."

Eshult smiled. "I'm offering."

"And I've located a pack mule that's a little less stubborn than most," added Ryntaar. "He's six silvers, but sturdy. Mortaak says he's good on rough ground, too."

"Why's he selling?"

"Same sort of reason Eshult is. His older brother died last fall. Green flux. He's got too many mules for now, and he needs silvers."

"I'll keep the geldings until you're ready for them," said Eshult. "I know Ryntaar's stable would be cramped."

"I appreciate that." Beltur turned to Ryntaar. "You'd mentioned some traders . . ."

"I won't know about when they plan to leave until twoday, maybe three-day. It might change if there's a storm. Sometimes, we get one right after the first warm spell."

"Most times," said Eshult.

Working out the details of when to pay what took another half quint, and it was almost a quint before fifth glass when Beltur walked in the front door of the cot.

The others were seated around the hearth, but Jessyla immediately stood and walked toward him, asking, not quite tartly, "Where have you been?"

"Working on a commission that will pay me before we leave Axalt and buying two more horses and a pack mule, as well as saddles. We're one saddle short, right now."

"You have been busy." The edge to her voice vanished.

"I have been, and I can tell you had a very long day."

"The warm weather loosened the snow, and a logging party got caught in an avalanche. Broken arms, broken legs . . ." Jessyla shook her head.

"I'm sorry."

"Herrara will definitely need you tomorrow."

"It sounds that way."

"It also sounds like you two need something to eat . . . and soon," offered Tulya, rising and heading for the kitchen. "Especially you, Jessyla."

"She's right, you know," said Beltur.

"I hate it when you're right, you know?" Jessyla offered the hint of a smile, then turned and followed Tulya before Beltur could reply.

And it's likely better you didn't, he told himself.

"Can I offer something toward the horses?" asked Lhadoraak quietly, once the two women were in the kitchen.

"Just save your silvers. I'm certain we'll need them later. I don't know for what, but traveling anywhere takes silvers and more silvers."

"You're sure?"

"I'm very sure. The horses cost much less than I'd thought they might. Eshult found himself suddenly with far too many horses, and not enough stable space, and he's likely trying to make amends in a number of ways."

"I could see that."

"I'm afraid I'm not too proud to let him, since his uncle is one of the reasons we need to leave." Beltur smiled wryly.

"Whatever you did, it was for the best."

"That remains to be seen. It's done, for better or worse." *In some ways, all because Jorhan and I made the best mirror we could for Halhana, out of the best intentions, and who could have foreseen what that led to?* After a pause, Beltur said, "Whatever Tulya fixed smells wonderful, and I am hungry." He headed toward the kitchen.

LXXIX

Despite the comparative warmth on sevenday, eightday dawned cloudy, and by the time Beltur reached the healing house a heavy wet snow was falling, one that was close to being slushy underfoot, and that combined the worst features of rain and snow, being both cold and wet enough to soak through almost anything.

After getting the slushy snow off his trousers and boots, he made his way to Herrara's study. "I need to let you know something."

"When are you leaving?"

"I don't know when, but that's not what I wanted to let you know."

"Is it better or worse?" asked Herrara sardonically.

"That's up to you. I've had several conversations with Eshult lately—"

"Even after everything?"

"He claims I've been honest and that I've helped him. He believes what he says. I can't explain it." Beltur wasn't about to offer a guess as to why.

"He's listening to Halhana at last, then. Go on."

"I'd mentioned that his uncle was likely using a healer to attend all public meetings of the Council—"

"He is?"

"I already knew that a woman with a strong black presence was at the public meetings I attended, but when I asked Naerkaal later about why Sarstaan had asked so many questions about Sarysta's death, he revealed that Sarstaan had a healer who worked for him . . ." Beltur went on to explain his suspicions and what else Naerkaal had said, then said, "After all that, yesterday Eshult came to the smithy to commission a piece. When he finished with that, he drew me aside and asked my advice on dealing with his uncle." Beltur paused. "I told him that if he couldn't tell whether Sarstaan was telling the truth he might be able to find a healer who could, and that he should talk to you."

Herrara nodded. "I'd wondered why Sarstaan hired Khaerlyna. He and his consort are still in good health, as are their children."

"I don't know if he'll take my advice, but I didn't want you to be surprised if he does show up and ask to talk to you."

"I appreciate your letting me know." She paused. "That might cost me yet another healer."

"Elisa?"

"I can't pay her what Eshult could, not anywhere close."

"Can she sense honesty and deception as well as you can?"

"Not quite as well, but she has the ability, and young Eshult is going to need someone like that for quite a while if he's going to avoid getting too deeply entangled with his uncle in ways that will not benefit him."

"I didn't anticipate that. I suppose I should have thought about the possibility."

"You happen to be both a healer and a mage, Beltur, but you think more like a mage."

"I still should have thought about that. It's not been easy for me to find ways to make silvers, and I know how hard it's been for Jessyla, but I wasn't thinking that Eshult or Sarstaan would pay that much more . . ."

"You're still naïve in some ways. People will pay to obtain skills they need, sometimes a great deal if it will make them more golds."

Beltur nodded. *You should have seen that just from dealing with Jorhan.* Except Jorhan was paying for what Beltur considered the honest use of his skills, and Beltur had the feeling that Sarstaan was using what he learned from his healer for less honest ends. *Then again, you should have remembered that some traders will do anything to gain an advantage.* "I'm still sometimes surprised at the depths to which people will stoop for silvers."

"At times, even now, I am, too," replied Herrara.

"I hope that you don't lose Elisa because of me."

"I can't hope that. Not for Elisa's sake. If she can do better for herself working for Eshult, then she should. She has no family left, and few men, besides mages, will consort a woman who is a healer." Herrara smiled sadly.

"You've raised her, haven't you?"

The healer shook her head. "She came here two years ago when her mother was dying. I could sense she had the ability. So I offered to teach her and gave her a small room and food. It's only in the last year that I could pay her. That was after Khaerlyna left."

Beltur winced, realizing that Herrara would be hard-pressed with Beltur, Jessyla, and possibly Elisa leaving in the next half season or season. "I'm so sorry. I should have realized . . ."

"No," replied Herrara. "If it comes to that, I'll be happy for Elisa. She's not had an easy life, and I want the best for her." She paused. "I can't say that I haven't also appreciated all that you and Jessyla have done. I also doubted you'd be able to stay. Now . . . if you wouldn't mind checking on patients. Start with the men who were hurt in the avalanche, and then Boissaen . . ."

Beltur nodded and walked to the shelves for a basket.

As he left the study, he couldn't help but think about how trying to help one person was likely going to harm another . . . and all the poor and working folk who needed the healing house. *Does it have to be like that?*

Beltur was still mulling things over when he left the healing house just before fourth glass. As he neared the cot, he saw Rohan step out of his house and walk swiftly toward him.

"Those folks are still there, and tomorrow's the first day of spring."

"You're right." Beltur reached for his belt wallet and extracted two silvers, handing them to the landlord. "That's the rent for the next five eightdays. All of us will be leaving sometime in the next two or three eightdays. You get to keep the two silvers of the deposit as well."

"You said they'd be gone."

"They will be. So will we."

"I said I'd take it to the Council . . ."

Beltur looked coldly at Rohan. "You're getting paid extra. You can take it to the Council if you want, but the Council already knows all of us are leaving, and I doubt the Council will do anything since you're being paid well for the inconvenience."

Rohan opened his mouth and then shut it, then finally said, "No more than three eightdays."

"Agreed." *Unless we get buried in northeaster after northeaster.* But Beltur would deal with that if and when it happened. He smiled pleasantly. "Enjoy the rest of your eightday."

Then he turned and walked to the cot.

LXXX

On oneday at the smithy, also the first day of spring by the calendar, if not by the weather, Beltur and Jorhan worked on Eshult's mirror, casting the base, as well as two of the supports, and Jorhan pronounced himself pleased with how the raised oak leaves and acorns turned out, because the smith had decided that adding a pine branch would have made the embellishments too cluttered.

Even by the end of twoday at the healing house, Eshult had not appeared or contacted Herrara, and Beltur began to wonder what had happened, or if the young merchant was merely so busy in dealing with his factorage and everything else that he hadn't had time to think about whether he needed a healer.

When Beltur set out for the smithy on threeday, the day was the warmest yet since he'd come to Axalt, if still barely above freezing, although most of the slushy snow that had fallen on oneday had melted. The workhouse crews had shoveled trenches in the snow piles beside the road so that the meltwater could flow away from the stone pavement, rather than gather in puddles that would have frozen solid at night.

Certain aspects of Axalt seemed to be well thought out, Beltur reflected. *Unless you're poor and without silvers and skills.* But wasn't that true everywhere? Was it even possible to have a land where the poor and unskilled had a chance to improve themselves without working themselves to death? He was still thinking about that when he reached the smithy.

Even from the door he could see that Jorhan had molds laid out on the workbench and was working on another. He hung up his coat and tunic and walked to where Jorhan waited. "What are we casting today?"

"The mirror frame. Maybe the mirror, depending . . ."

Beltur understood—depending on how long it took to cast and set the order and chaos in the frame sections. "The oak leaves and acorns turned out well on the base."

"They aren't raised as much on the frame. Otherwise, they'd overshadow the mirror and the base. Leastwise, that's the way I see it. We'll find out if the way they turn out matches what I had in mind."

"It usually does," Beltur pointed out.

"Best hope this is usual." The smith paused, then said, "Before I forget, you need to see Ryntaar this afternoon. He thinks he knows of some traders who'll be heading for Rytel late next eightday. They might even pay you a little to keep off brigands." The smith added, "I'll be happier when this mirror's done."

Beltur just nodded.

In the end, Jorhan decided against trying to cast the mirror sheet that afternoon, and Beltur walked into the Mountain Factorage just before fourth glass, then waited in a corner, behind a concealment, while Ryntaar dealt with an older man, likely another merchant.

Once the other left, Beltur dropped the concealment and approached Ryntaar.

"Oh . . . Beltur. I didn't hear you come in."

"I just stayed out of sight while you were busy. Jorhan said that you knew of some traders who could use some mages . . . and might pay. Who are they?"

"I don't know all of them, but Jhotyl's the one putting the group together. He works for a fellow in Jellico who's the furrier to the Viscount of Certis. Or something like that. That's why they'd be happier with a few mages with them."

Beltur didn't even pretend to understand. "Why does a fur trader need guards?"

"Ever heard of ermine? That's the winter fur of a stoat. Pure white, except for the tip of the tail. Takes well over a hundred to make a full-length coat, and that coat might cost a hundred golds, except the only ones who can wear ermine in Certis are the Viscount and his family. Jho-tyl's the one who buys the ermine pelts from the mountain folk. He's likely got five hundred pelts in his wagons, and it's better to transport them while it's still cold. That's also when there are likely to be more brigands in the hills east of Axalt before you get to the flatter lands. The Certans don't patrol the hill roads much in winter. They lost too many men that way. That's why most traders don't venture traveling until spring and the roads are clear."

Beltur wasn't so sure he wanted to deal with brigands again, but the thought of traveling with others, as well as possibly getting paid, had a certain appeal. "Is there anyone else planning to leave any time soon?"

Ryntaar shook his head. "I'd say it'd be at least another eightday or two. Now there could be someone coming from Elparta on the way to Rytel and down the river to Tyrhavven."

Traders or merchants coming from Elparta sounded even less appealing. "It wouldn't hurt to talk to them. Where do I find Jhotyl?"

"Right now, he's in the public room at the Traders' Bowl. I'll take you over there and introduce you." Ryntaar turned. "Frankyr, I'm taking Beltur to meet Jhotyl. Watch the door."

"I can do that," called back the younger brother.

In moments, Ryntaar had his coat on, but didn't bother to fasten it as he walked out of the factorage with Beltur.

"How long have you known Jhotyl?" asked Beltur.

"I wouldn't say that I know him all that well. Father did business with him for a good ten years. Said he was always fair. He's not that easy to get along with, not if you're younger than he is, anyway."

"A bit prickly, it sounds like."

"He likely has to be, dealing with mountain trappers."

Beltur nodded, thinking that someone tough and prickly might not be so bad if brigands happened to show up. *But then, they want mages so that they don't have to use weapons. Or risk all those pelts.*

Before long, the two were walking into the public room in the Traders' Bowl, which looked somewhat similar to the Traders' Rest in Elparta, with heavy square timbers, reddish brick walls with traces of soot, and small leaded windowpanes. Unlike the Traders' Rest, the Bowl had simple straight-backed chairs at all the tables, and, except for two longer oblong tables, all the tables were round, although some were small, with only two chairs, and others could seat four easily, six if crowded. The fire in the hearth was mostly reddish coals.

Ryntaar led the way to a larger round table, at which sat five men. The oldest-looking man immediately stood. He had a weathered face, a square-cut black beard that still needed trimming, and longish black hair. "Ryntaar, good as your word."

Ryntaar nodded. "This is Mage Beltur, Jhotyl."

"I'm pleased to meet you," offered Beltur, inclining his head slightly.

"You're youngish for a mage." Before Beltur could reply, the fur trader went on, "Ryntaar says that you can protect traders on the road and that you'd go as far as Rytel. That right?"

"We'd go to Montgren if you're headed that way."

"Just to Rytel, then upriver on the river road to Jellico. Don't need mages from Rytel south. Ryntaar says you've got womenfolk you want to bring."

"My consort and the consort of the other mage, and their young daughter. My consort is a healer and a partial mage."

"Partial?"

"She can handle shields and a few other things."

"Never heard of a woman mage."

"There aren't many."

"How do I know you're what you say? Anyone can put on blacks and claim they're a mage." Jhotyl looked to Ryntaar. "Not that I don't trust you, but trust doesn't stop blades or brigands."

"Can you use that blade?" asked Beltur, glancing at Jhotyl's scabbard.

"Is that a question or an insult?"

"It's a question, but treat it like an insult."

Jhotyl frowned.

"Go ahead. Just try to touch me with it. If you can." Beltur offered almost a sneer.

The trader shook his head and turned to the shorter but more massive man still seated at the table. "Mheltyn, we'll see what the mage can do. Not in here. The innkeeper might not see it the way we do." Jhotyl gestured toward the door.

Beltur and Ryntaar followed the two back outside, onto the stone pavement.

"What do you have in mind, Mage?"

"Just have him try to hit me with his blade. Or anything else."

"You heard him, Mheltyn." Jhotyl stepped back, as did Ryntaar, who moved even farther back, if quietly.

Beltur just stood there.

"You aren't going to do anything?" Mheltyn thrust at Beltur. His blade slid to the side. He tried again, with the same result. The third time he delivered an angled cut with a fair amount of force. The blade stopped, and Mheltyn dropped it, shaking his hand.

"I've seen better," declared Jhotyl.

Beltur dropped tight containments around both men, giving them barely enough room to move. "I doubt it."

"What do you—" The trader's face paled as he realized he couldn't move. "Mheltyn, hit him with that blade."

The guard actually grinned as he replied, "If I could move, I would, but I'd likely break the blade. You'd have to pay for it."

"Do you want more of a demonstration?" asked Beltur.

"I . . . I think that will do." After Beltur released the containments, the trader turned to Ryntaar. "Have you seen him in action?"

"Just once, when he was attacked without warning and disarmed a bravo. He was a Spidlarian arms-mage and a City Patrol mage in Elparta."

"Is that true?"

"It is." Beltur nodded.

"Why in the name of the black angels are you offering to guard a trading group?"

"Because the Axalt Council really doesn't want me to remain in Axalt, and we need to get to Vergren. I'd prefer to make some coins while going there, since the Council frowns on my staying here and doing that."

"He's been working with a smith to forge cupridium," added Ryntaar.

Jhotyl shook his head. "Sometimes . . ." He looked to Beltur. "What about the other mage?"

"Lhadoraak was also an arms-mage during the invasion. He was exiled from Spidlar for a number of reasons, but mostly because he was my friend."

"Is there anything else I should know?"

"Beside the fact that his consort and daughter will be coming? No. Both have their own mounts, and the mother will take care of the daughter."

"What about the healer, your consort?"

"She has strong enough shields to protect herself. She's been working at the healing house here. She can set bones, do most anything a healer should do."

"Young like you."

Beltur nodded.

"She ever deal with battle wounds?"

"She was one of the healers dealing with the wounded in the invasion."

"I can't pay all that much," Jhotyl said. "A few golds at most."

Beltur could sense the truth of that. "We'll have six mounts and a pack mule. What about fodder for them?"

"Two golds and food and fodder for all of you."

"That's fair."

"You're no trader."

"You were telling the truth," Beltur countered. "I could have forced another few silvers out of you, but that wouldn't have served either of us well."

Abruptly, Jhotyl laughed.

So did Mheltyn.

"You can tell that all the time?" asked Jhotyl.

"Unless it's a powerful white or black mage who's fully shielded."

The fur trader nodded, almost as if Beltur's words explained something. Then he said, "We're waiting for one last set of pelts. We plan to leave at sixth glass on twoday morning. That's unless it snows, or we get a spring northeaster that ices everything."

"Where should we meet you?"

"Right here. If things change, I'll let Ryntaar know."

After a few more questions and answers, Beltur and Ryntaar headed back to the factorage.

"That didn't take long," said Frankyr as the two walked inside.

"Beltur has a way of getting to the heart of matters, quickly." Ryntaar smiled. "I've not dealt with Jhotyl that often, but this afternoon was the first time I've ever seen him surprised."

Beltur smiled. "Thank you for setting it up."

"I'd say it was my pleasure, except everyone in the family will be sorry to see you go. Even Eshult, I think."

"He seems to be almost happier, in a sad sort of way."

"Happier in a sad sort of way," repeated Ryntaar, musingly. "I wouldn't have thought of it that way, but it fits."

"It fits," declared Frankyr.

"Thank you, again," said Beltur. "I need to get home and let Jessyla know what's happening."

As he walked from the factorage toward the cot, Beltur just hoped that nothing would go wrong with the forging of Eshult's mirror, because, if it did, he and Jorhan would be working very late in order to finish before Beltur and Jessyla left.

Somehow . . . it seems almost unreal. You have a cot and a home, and, most likely, in an eightday, you'll have neither, and you'll be headed for a place you've never seen, just in hopes that you can find a place that won't force you out.

When Beltur opened the cot door and stepped inside, Jessyla was waiting.

"You've obviously been doing something. What, might I ask?"

"Arranging with a group of traders to accompany them to Rytel, for which we'll get paid two golds, and extra if we have to deal with brigands. They'll also supply food and fodder, not that I don't think we shouldn't bring some of our own supplies. They're planning to leave next twoday morning."

"That soon?"

"It will be the second eightday of spring," Beltur pointed out.

"That's not much time. We'll need some oilcloth," said Jessyla. "The ground will be wet, and more blankets than we had on the way here . . ."

Beltur nodded and continued to listen.

LXXXI

Fourday morning Beltur was at the healing house half a quint early, and Herrara was in her study, as if waiting for him.

"I need to tell you something," began Beltur, "if you haven't already heard."

"I've heard. Johlana told me last night. Next twoday?"

"If we don't get snow. We'll be traveling with a fur trader named Jhotyl. He's headed back to Jellico. We'll just go as far as Rytel with him, and then keep heading east to Vergren."

"I haven't heard anything about Jhotyl. What do you know about him?"

"Barrynt traded with him for at least ten years. Ryntaar says that his father had no problems with Jhotyl."

"He's likely halfway honest, then. Did he ask you much?"

Beltur smiled wryly. "He wanted a demonstration of my skills as a mage."

"He didn't ask if you'd actually killed anyone, did he?"

"No. I didn't volunteer anything like that."

There was a silence before Herrara asked, "How many men have you killed?"

"I don't know. At least hundreds. It could be more."

There was another silence before she said, "I suspect it's much more, but how can a black . . . ?"

"I'm very limited, unless a white mage throws a chaos bolt at me. I can often catch chaos bolts with order and throw them back with greater force. The Prefect had at least six or seven powerful whites. Someone's troopers were going to die, and someone's mages. I thought it was better that those who died were the invaders."

"You could have just blocked the chaos."

Beltur shook his head. "We were outnumbered. Doing that would have assured that those who died were Spidlarians."

"You could be wealthy as an arms-mage."

"I'd also die younger than I'd prefer."

"With your abilities?"

"Anyone can be killed, and the greater a threat a mage is thought to be, the more likely it is that someone will try. I've already seen that too many times in my life."

"For a mage so young and talented, you're very old and cynical in some ways."

"And very young and inexperienced in others," added Beltur wryly.

"Just keep that in mind. True old age and treachery often triumph over youth and great ability."

"I've seen some of that everywhere I've lived."

"Just don't ever forget it." She paused, then shook her head. "Better you than me." After another pause, she went on. "I'd like you to look at one of the loggers caught in the avalanche. His foot was so mangled that we had to take it off."

"I looked at him on eightday and twoday. Errakyn, isn't it? There was a bit of wound chaos there both days, less on twoday. He seemed to be healing well."

"He was in a lot of pain, but he kept saying that the pain was coming from his foot."

"The one you took off, you mean?"

Herrara nodded. "I thought that might be better suited to your kind of healing."

"I can look at him . . . but I'm not sure how to stop pain from a foot he doesn't have."

"That's happened once or twice before. I couldn't do anything then, or last night. Maybe you'll have more success. Then I'd like your thoughts on Klaznyt's hands. They seem to be healed enough to take off the splints, unless you can sense anything different. You don't need to come back down here until you look in on everyone."

"I can do that." Beltur moved to the shelves and picked up two baskets, then made his way out of the study and down the hallway to the large room that held the three remaining injured loggers, two of whom would likely be leaving the healing house before long, since their broken bones had been set in casts on threeday, according to Jessyla, somewhat later than usual because the swelling had not subsided as much as Herrara thought it should have for putting on casts earlier.

The three loggers had moved their beds so that one was being used as a table for some sort of game of plaques.

"Here comes the mage-healer," said Saebasyn.

Errakyn looked up. "About time. My foot's killing me."

Voortaan, the third logger, with one leg in a long cast from nearly knee to toe, shifted his weight on his bed awkwardly, but said nothing.

Beltur checked Voortaan and Saebasyn first, removing some small bits of wound chaos, before he moved to Errakyn. "Where exactly is the pain?"

"In my foot."

"The one you don't have anymore?"

"It still hurts."

"Does the pain go up into your leg at all?"

"Maybe a little. Hurts so much that it's hard to tell."

"Let's see if I can sense anything." Beltur concentrated. He found several small points of wound chaos, which he removed. "How does your leg feel now?"

"My leg feels fine," replied Errakyn. "The foot hurts a little less. I know my foot's not there, but it still hurts."

Beltur tried to see if he could sense something like an order binding in the stump of the lower leg. He didn't find that, but he did sense what he could only describe as a small knot that didn't feel as though it should have been there. At least, he'd never sensed a knot like that before. Rather than remove the knot, he just eased a small bit of free order into the knot.

"OOO!!!" Errakyn paled, and swayed as he sat on the bed. "Stop whatever you're doing!"

Beltur stopped and waited several moments before asking, "Has the pain stopped or gone back to where it was?"

"Hasn't stopped. It's maybe a little worse than it was."

"In a moment, I'm going to try something else." This time, Beltur eased a tiny bit of free chaos into the knot. From what he could tell the knot seemed to relax, but it didn't get any smaller. "How's that?"

"It's better. It just aches now."

"Good. We'll just have to see whether it improves or whether you'll need another treatment."

"You won't do that first thing again?"

"No," promised Beltur. "I tried the one I thought would hurt less first. I was wrong. There's no way to tell unless you try." *For me, anyway.*

"It is better," said the logger.

"We'll have to see how it goes. I can't do any more right now." Beltur just hoped that what he'd done had actually removed some of the pain and not that the pain that Errakyn had just seemed less after the use of order had triggered more severe pain. "I'll check back later."

The loggers were back at their plaques almost before he was out of the room, and that was a good sign, although he wondered where they'd gotten the deck of plaques. He climbed the steps and made his way to Klaznyt's room.

The gambler was looking morosely at the wall. After a moment, he turned to Beltur. "Are you ever taking off all these splints?"

"You'll get them off when the bones are mostly healed. That's what I'm here to check on. Even when you get the splints off, you'll have to be very careful for almost half a season, or you could break them again."

"I didn't break them the first time," groused Klaznyt.

"You could be the one to break them the second time."

Beltur let his senses range over Klaznyt's hands, first the left and then the right. He thought he could sense why Herrara was concerned. He straightened.

"Well . . . ? When am I getting them off?"

"That's up to Healer Herrara. I can say you're getting closer."

"Is that all you can say?"

"She has much more experience with multiple breaks than I do."

"But you're a mage."

"She's a very experienced healer. I've only been a healer for a year or so." *And that's an exaggeration.* "That came long after I became a mage."

"I hope you two don't keep me here forever."

"We wouldn't think of it," replied Beltur cheerfully.

Almost two glasses passed before Beltur finished all he had to do and returned to Herrara's study, where she was talking to Elisa.

Instead of entering he waited in the hall until the young healer left.

"What did you find out?"

Beltur relayed what he'd discovered about Errakyn's pain and what he'd done.

Herrara frowned. "I wish I could sense the way you can."

"I don't know if what I'm doing will work. I'll have to check him later today."

"What about Klaznyt?"

"I looked at Klaznyt's hands. You've got much more experience than I do with broken bones. This is the only time I've been anywhere that I could even see how bones healed."

"From the way you say that, you're worrying about something."

"Have you thought about splinting his middle finger and index fingers on each hand together for another eightday or so? I don't know . . ." Beltur shrugged.

Herrara smiled. "You've got good instincts. That's what I planned, but I wanted to see what you thought. What did you tell him?"

"Just that it was getting close to the time that some of the splints might be able to come off. I did say that when they came off, his fingers wouldn't be fully healed and that he'd need to be careful. I'm not sure that he will be, though."

"That's his problem. We can let him go once he's got some use of his hands . . . and Elisa will be very happy about that."

"Have you heard anything . . . from Eshult?"

"He sent a note, saying that he'd like to meet with me, but that it would have to wait an eightday or so."

"That suggests he really wants to, but that he has to be careful for some reason."

"That was my thought. We'll just have to see."

Beltur nodded. He had the feeling that there were a great many things about which he was just going to have to see, especially about where he and Jessyla, and Lhadoraak, Tulya, and Taelya, might end up.

At the same time, he did have the feeling that the rest of the day at the healing house was going to be uneventful, and that would be just fine with him.

LXXXII

Worried as he was about being able to finish Eshult's mirror before he had to leave Axalt, Beltur was at the smithy earlier on fiveday, early enough that he was the one building the forge fire while Jorhan made some adjustments to the mold for the mirror sheet of cupridium.

Then he stood by watching as Jorhan heated the mold.

"Warmer again this morning," offered the smith. "Either it's spring or we've got a northeaster coming in tomorrow. Don't envy you traveling this early in spring."

"I'm not looking forward to that," admitted Beltur, "and I don't like leaving you and Johlana. It just seems that there's some force out there, maybe it's chaos, that doesn't want us working together."

"Had that feeling myself. Thought about going with you, but not with what happened to Barrynt. Johlana, it wouldn't be right to leave her. Maybe later, if she's settled, and maybe not."

Beltur could see that. Even though he'd never thought himself that close to his uncle, there was still an emptiness there. *And there might always be.*

"Time to get the forge ready for the melt."

Beltur moved to the bellows.

Almost a glass passed before Jorhan was satisfied with both the mold and the melt, and the liquid bronze flowed into the mold. Then Beltur began setting the order/chaos mesh in place, trying to feel so that it was perfectly aligned and balanced. In a way he couldn't describe, he could sense that the mesh was too low, yet when he eased it upward, it felt somehow . . . off.

More than two quints later, he knew he'd been right, and he turned to Jorhan as he surveyed the mold. "I think we're going to have problems with the mirror sheet. Now that I'm sensing it, I have the feeling it's going to split if you try to work it at all." Beltur knew what the problem was—that with the thinness of the bronze both the structure of the order/chaos mesh net and its placement had to be perfect.

"You're sure?" asked Jorhan.

"Fairly sure. I haven't been working with that thin a casting in a while, and . . . well, it doesn't feel right, and I didn't sense that it wasn't right until the bronze was too cool to move it."

"Sometimes, things just don't go right. First time around, with Halhana's mirror, I couldn't get the mold right."

"This time, it wasn't the mold."

Beltur spent another half quint, still studying the cooling metal, until he had a better feel.

By the time Jorhan had adjusted and trimmed the second mold and they had the melt ready it was well into afternoon. All in all, Beltur didn't finish setting the order/chaos mesh in the second pouring until close to fifth glass, but he could sense that it was solid when he stepped away from the mold.

"That's much better," Beltur said to the smith.

"That means the hardest part is over, and I can get on with the finishing tomorrow."

"What else do we need to cast?"

"Just a set of pins. I won't be able to mold them until I have the mirror polished and set in the frame sections. They won't take long. We can do those on sevenday."

"I'll see you then." Beltur nodded and made his way toward the door.

"Johlana told me to remind you that all five of you are coming to dinner on eightday."

"Thank you. I'm reminded." Beltur doubted that he would have been able to forget, since Jessyla had already told him twice.

The late afternoon was warm enough that he didn't have to fasten his coat or wrap his scarf around his ears for the walk back to the cot. A sheen of water covered the paving stones at the end of the road, and he could hear the gurgling of meltwater in places.

As soon as he opened the cot door, Taelya turned from where she sat on the padded bench. "Uncle Beltur's home!"

Jessyla hurried out from the kitchen. "You didn't stop by the factorage, did you?"

Beltur shook his head as he finished hanging up his coat and scarf. "Was I supposed to? Is something wrong?"

"I hope not, but you're later than usual."

"That's because we had trouble pouring and casting the mirror sheet for Eshult's mirror, and we're getting short on time. It took two pourings to get it right. And since Eshult's paying when it's finished . . ."

Jessyla nodded. "That's a few more silvers."

"Quite a few," Beltur said.

"We've talked about this before, but it doesn't seem like . . . that something . . . doesn't want you to be a smith." She shook her head. "That's just silly, I know, but I feel that way."

"Whatever that something is, it doesn't seem to want us to stay long in any one place."

"Maybe that's because we're not in the right place yet."

"If that's so, I hope we don't have to travel through all of Candar to find the right place . . . if there even is such a place."

"There is a place. We just have to find it."

And just how will we know what place is the right place, even if we do get there? With a rueful smile, Beltur pushed away the question and walked toward the kitchen with Jessyla.

LXXXIII

For Beltur, sixday and sevenday seemed to go by in almost a blur, although sixday was much colder and several digits' worth of snow fell, most of which had melted by afternoon on sevenday. And when Beltur left the smithy on sevenday afternoon, Eshult's mirror was complete, and Jorhan was doing some final polishing.

Eightday felt slightly cooler when Beltur walked to the healing house for what was his last day working there, barring a northeaster or some event totally unforeseen. In some ways, it felt as though he'd been working as a healer far longer than just a season, but then, he'd learned a great deal from Herrara, although it had also become clear that there was always more to learn and the variety of ways in which people could injure themselves or others was clearly endless.

After he'd reached the healing house and stepped into Herrara's study, she motioned for him to sit down across the table desk from her. "This looks to be your last day here." She put two silvers on the desk and slid them toward Beltur. "Since you've always been paid an eightday in arrears, and you won't be here on either twoday or the next day, those are your pay for the last two eightdays."

"I should have been paying you for all that I've learned," replied Beltur.

"You didn't ask to be paid. I offered. I've learned a few things from you as well."

Beltur thought that Herrara was being too generous, but merely said, "I appreciate both the knowledge and the pay. I feel I should offer to reimburse you for the mage-healer tunic."

"If I'd paid for it, I'd accept your offer," replied Herrara. "I didn't. The Council did, and they can well afford to pay for it after the way things have turned out."

Sensing the truth of her words, Beltur smiled wryly. "They can indeed."

"Do you have any idea what you're doing, besides leaving Axalt and heading to Montgren? Or what you'll do when you get there?"

"That's not really a question, is it?"

Herrara smiled. "Not really. And that's not an answer."

Beltur chuckled. "No, it's not. I can only say that I don't intend to try to settle down anywhere that we can't live the way we want to—all of us, and that includes Taelya. With three mages, two healers, and a budding white, we have enough behind us to treat for what we need. At least, I hope so."

"Forget about hoping. Just be straightforward from the beginning. I've heard that the Duchess is rather direct. I don't know as it's true, but a woman in power in Candar usually has to be very strong and straightforward or incredibly devious and cruel. I think we'd know were she that cruel. Then again, the most devious people can appear straightforward. Some people who are very straightforward seem scheming to those who are devious because the deceivers cannot believe that such directness is anything but a ploy or a stratagem."

"In short, people may be what they seem, but they just might not be."

"You're direct, Beltur, but that directness serves a deeper goal. I'm not sure you even know what it is, but for your sake and all those who follow you, and who will follow you, I'm asking you to make sure that it's a worthy goal, one that's beyond mere survival. Any mage with your abilities can survive, no matter what you think."

"You've offered a good example of a goal beyond survival," Beltur said quietly.

"I've tried. Time judges more accurately than we do." She offered a quirky smile. "That's far too long a homily. You need to see to the patients, especially Klaznyt and Errakyn."

She nodded toward the door.

Beltur nodded in return, then took the silvers, stood, and walked to the shelves for a basket before leaving the study, his thoughts swirling around what Herrara had said.

He slowly made his way up the steps to the room that held Klaznyt, deciding to deal with the gambler first. *Except he just might be a former gambler, but only for a while, unless he learns from his experiences.* Beltur smiled wryly. *And that was one of the things that Herrara was trying to get across to you, if politely, that you can't keep running from things. You have to decide what you're going to do and where you'll do it . . . and make it stick.*

He was well aware that trying to make things work out didn't always turn out well. They hadn't for his uncle . . . or for Athaal . . . or Barrynt. *But doesn't that make it more important that you succeed?*

Even when he was barely inside the door of the room, Klaznyt began to talk. "Mage, when can I really use my fingers? Any of them? Even the fingers that aren't bound up are stiff, and they hurt to move, and they don't move that far." Seeing the expression on Beltur's face, the gambler quickly added, "I know. I've got most of my hands back, except for one little finger, and that was on my left hand, and without the two of you, I might not have any fingers at all. But a man has to have a way to live, that's what I meant."

"You want to know when they'll be flexible enough to hold a plaque deck so that you can get them all broken again . . . or get yourself killed?" Beltur's voice was mild.

"You don't understand. You have the talent for magery. My only real talent is plaques . . . or it was. After . . . this . . . my hands likely won't be strong enough for anything heavy. What do you expect?"

"I expect that you'll do the best you can. Isn't that what all of us try to do?" Beltur paused, then decided against saying more along those lines. "Let me check your hands and fingers. Hold up your left hand first." Beltur let his senses range over the still-injured hand, removing a few small points of wound chaos. "Now your right hand."

When he finished, he said, "They're both healing nicely. Just keep moving the ones that aren't splinted. Don't force the movement. Moving them might hurt some, but increase how far you move them gradually." Beltur stepped back.

"Why don't you like me, Mage?"

"I don't dislike you," Beltur replied. "I worry about you. Your hands were broken because the others thought you cheated. What's to stop that from happening again if you go back to gambling?"

"You think I cheated?"

"You said you didn't cheat as much as others. That suggests that the best cheaters win. If you don't win, there's little point to gaming, and, even if you win without cheating, people will think you cheat. Sooner or later, someone will break your hands again . . . or do worse."

"Everything in life is a gamble of some sort."

Beltur nodded. "You're right."

"Then why are you against my gambling?"

"From what you've said, you can't win. It seems to me that there are gambles worth taking and those not worth taking. You're telling me that gambling at plaques will always have you ending up losing, one way or another. Is that a gamble worth taking?"

"You're twisting my words."

"I just repeated what you told me. If I misstated them, I apologize. The question stays the same. Is going back to gambling at plaques worth it? That's your decision, not mine."

"Have you ever gambled for anything really worth it, Mage?"

More than you know, Klaznyt. More than you know. "That's something I've had to decide, just as you'll have to."

"That's not an answer."

"It's enough of one," replied Beltur, smiling pleasantly as he headed for the door.

"You don't understand . . ."

Beltur resisted the temptation to reply and kept walking.

When Beltur entered Errakyn's room, the logger was alone, the two other loggers having left on oneday, according to Jessyla, and he sat morosely on one side of his bed dealing out plaques in a form of solitaire that Beltur didn't recognize.

"How are your leg and foot coming?"

"The stump's sore, but the pain's the same as before."

"The same as before what I did on eightday . . . or afterwards?"

"The same as after."

"Then we'll try another round. Just the second type," Beltur added quickly as he saw the logger's face tighten. "I couldn't tell which would work better without trying both."

"You sure about that, Mage?"

"It feels better now, doesn't it?"

"It still hurts."

Beltur checked the lower leg, finding a few points of wound chaos, which he removed, and then began to ease a tiny bit of free chaos into the knot he'd discovered earlier, a knot that he thought had shrunk just a bit. Finally, he straightened and looked at Errakyn. "Is that a little better?"

"There's some pain, but not so much."

"Good. I'll be back later, close to fourth glass, and I'll see what else I can do."

"You can't do more now?"

Beltur shook his head. "Your leg would get too hot." He didn't know that for certain, but from what he'd learned while at the healing house, using too much order or chaos, especially free order or chaos, caused too much heat in the flesh. "It needs to cool down and recover for a while." He definitely wanted to remove the pain, or at least get it down lower, before he left Axalt.

After stepping out of the room, he couldn't help thinking, *No matter what you do, or how long you stay, there will be something more you could have done if you stayed longer.*

Basket in hand, he started for the adjoining room.

The remainder of eightday was quiet, and just before he left the healing house, he returned to see Errakyn.

"Is the pain still less?"

"Yes, ser. It's not bad at all."

"Let's see if we can lessen it more." Beltur concentrated once more on the knot, definitely smaller than it had been earlier, easing a touch more free chaos into it. Then he stood back and looked to the logger, inquiringly.

"It's better. A bit of a twinge, still."

"That's good. This is most likely the last time I'll see you."

Errakyn frowned. "You can't do more?"

"That's not the question. The Axalt Council prefers that Healer Jessyla and I leave Axalt. So, unless a northeaster hits in the next day or so, we'll be leaving on twoday."

"But you're healers."

"So is Healer Herrara, and she's very good. You'll be in good hands." Beltur managed a warm smile, then quickly turned and left the room.

What else could you say without creating more problems?

After that, he made his way to Herrara's study.

"You're getting ready to leave?"

Beltur nodded. "I gave Errakyn a last treatment with another small bit of free chaos. He says that pain is down to a twinge."

"I can't even sense that knot that you talk about."

"It's not very big."

Herrara shook her head. "We'll miss you. I'll certainly miss you."

"I'll miss you. I've learned a lot here, and not all of it was about healing."

She offered a mock-serious expression. "I would hope not."

Beltur couldn't help grinning, even knowing that Herrara had provoked his reaction. "Be careful, I might come back with an army."

"You don't need an army," she said lightly. "Just gather a few more mages and healers, and no one will dare cross you."

"That might be harder than it sounds."

"You'll manage."

"Do you have the kind of foresight that Ryba did?"

"Me? Hardly. I've just watched you and Jessyla." After the briefest hesitation, she added, "You need to be on your way, or you'll be late to dinner at Johlana's."

"How did you—"

"It wasn't magery. Now go." The smile belied the firmness of her last words.

Beltur inclined his head and left.

As Herrara had implied, everyone was waiting and ready to leave for Johlana's when Beltur arrived at the cot. So he washed up quickly, trying not to keep the others waiting, then hurried to rejoin them.

Once they were outside and walking westward, Jessyla said, "Tulya and I have most things packed. Most of what we can take is packed into a bundle for the pack mule. Two, really. One's for food. Our clothes will still fit in the duffels we used before."

When he remembered the duffel Jessyla had brought to Axalt, Beltur looked at his consort. "As I recall—"

"Don't say a word. I put a few of my things in your duffel. I also made up bedrolls with the oilcloth I got last fourday."

Beltur decided that the less he said, the better. He also thought he could sense Lhadoraak's amusement.

When the five reached Johlana's, Halhana was the one who answered the side door. "You're all here. Good! Come on in, and I'll tell Asala so she knows she doesn't have to delay dinner."

By the time Beltur had his coat and scarf off and hung on one of the hall wall pegs, Halhana had returned and escorted them to the family parlor. When Beltur and Jessyla entered the room, the first thing that Beltur noticed was the mirror for Eshult, its silvered-bronze cupridium shimmering in the light cast by the oil lamps in their wall sconces.

"Now you can say something about the mirror, Eshult," said Johlana from where she sat in her customary armchair.

"You don't have to say anything," rumbled Jorhan. "Man commissions a mirror and likes it, that's good enough for me."

"It's magnificent," said Eshult, "as I said earlier."

"But Beltur needed to hear that," said Johlana.

"Jorhan did most of the work, and the artistry is all his. I just made sure than the cupridium was good."

Tulya looked at the mirror without moving for several moments, then eased close to where it rested on a side table. "It's gorgeous." She looked to Beltur, then to Jorhan. "I didn't know . . ."

For an instant, Beltur wondered what she meant, then realized that neither Tulya nor Lhadoraak had ever seen any of the work that he and Jorhan had produced. Even Lhadoraak looked surprised as he studied the mirror.

"The councilors are idiots to stop Uncle Jorhan and Beltur from working together," declared Frankyr.

"They didn't say we couldn't work together," replied Beltur. "They said that I shouldn't stay in Axalt."

"That's the same thing," returned Frankyr.

"Halhana and Eshult have the two best pieces we've ever done," said Jorhan. "Can't think of a better place for them."

Beltur couldn't, either, although he doubted his reasons were quite the same as Jorhan's, since he hoped that the blood and loss caused by the first mirror might be healed in some fashion by the second—or by the fact that Eshult had asked for the second mirror.

"I do think, if I do say so myself," Jorhan said, a slight twinkle in his eye, "that oak leaves and acorns match better with rosebuds than thistles or thorns would."

Halhana turned to her consort. "You *asked* for thorns?"

From her tone, and what he sensed, Beltur could tell she was teasing Eshult.

"You have noted that I come from prickly stock," Eshult bantered back.

Halhana turned to her uncle. "Thank you for the oak leaves and acorns. I like what that foretells much better."

"So do I," said Eshult.

At that moment, Ryntaar handed a mug of mulled wine to Jessyla and a beaker of pale ale to Beltur, while Frankyr provided Taelya with a tumbler of pearapple juice. Ryntaar then went back to the sideboard and returned with lager and mulled wine for Lhadoraak and Tulya.

"And now, a toast for good traveling," offered Ryntaar, raising his own beaker, "and fair weather."

"Good traveling and fair weather," came the response.

Johlana raised her mug of mulled wine. "Tonight will be my farewell. The last thing you all need is someone hanging around when you're trying to deal with horses and packs. So . . . a fond farewell to friends who are like family, and to the hope we will indeed meet again . . . before too long."

"A fond farewell."

Beltur definitely had the feeling that he was going to enjoy the evening, and that was good, because he was clearly going to be very, very busy on oneday.

LXXXIV

Even before Jessyla left for the healing house on oneday, Beltur was at Johlana's stable—he thought of everything as hers, even though, by law, everything except Johlana's personal property and jewelry belonged to Ryntaar, unless Ryntaar gifted it to Frankyr at some point. Ryntaar had already left to pick up the two additional mounts from Eshult and the pack mule, along with the necessary tack, and Beltur immediately went to work on giving each of the horses a thorough grooming, as well as checking them over once again. He'd almost finished with the first four, including the mare from Jorhan, when Ryntaar arrived with the others.

Beltur helped the young merchant lead the three animals into the stable.

"It's going to be crowded for a while," observed Ryntaar after the three were secured, "but the weather looks good. The roads are dry at least until you reach the east wall. That's what the post riders say."

That meant the first two days would be uneventful. At least, they should be, because there hadn't been any brigands in years along the stone roads that ran from the east wall through Axalt and the city proper to the west wall. Outside those walls, however, was another question, and the reason why he and Lhadoraak would be paid for accompanying the merchants.

"So we'll run into wet snow or rain once we're out of Axalt?" asked Beltur humorously.

"Well . . . you will be in Certis, and with the Viscount you just never know."

"I was afraid you might say something like that."

"Is there anything else I can help with?" asked Ryntaar.

"No, you've done more than enough. Thank you for bringing the horses."

"It's little enough."

"It's more than that, and we appreciate everything you and your parents have done for us."

"Then I'll see you later."

After Ryntaar left the stable, Beltur went back to work, beginning by grooming the mule, who, true to the nature of mules, tried to shy away from Beltur. Beltur, as he once had with Slowpoke, simply used containments to keep the mule in position.

More than a glass later, as Beltur was putting away gear and tack, the stable door opened, and a figure in black entered. For a moment, Beltur thought it might be Lhadoraak, but then realized the black was none other than Councilor Naerkaal.

"I've been looking for you. Lhadoraak told me you'd be here, getting the horses ready for your departure tomorrow."

"Making sure we depart?"

"As we both know, whether you wish to acknowledge it or not, there is no way I could force you to depart . . . or do anything you do not wish."

Beltur was struck by Naerkaal's gentle honesty, and not only struck, but also surprised, despite what Herrara had said days earlier. "Perhaps not directly, but as I learned in Elparta, by restricting someone's ability to earn a living or by other indirect means, you can usually accomplish what can't be achieved by force."

"That is true, but that was not my doing, and not to my liking. I'm also subject to indirect pressures, and I'm far less powerful than you are." The councilor smiled warmly. "That wasn't why I sought you. I wanted to give you this." Naerkaal extended a book bound in black leather.

Not even trying to conceal a puzzled expression, Beltur took the book, a volume that felt old.

"Since I suspect you haven't had the chance to finish it," the older man went on, "and even if you have, I thought you'd like to have your own copy. This is an older version, and that seemed appropriate. It's still in very good condition. It's good for thought . . . and you'll find, I think, as I have, some of it will work for you, and some won't. You and he have a great deal in common, I think."

With what Naerkaal had said, Beltur had a good idea of what the book might be, but he opened it to the title page, which read *The Wisdom of Relyn*. He nodded, closed the book, and looked to Naerkaal. "Thank you. You were right. I didn't have a chance to read more than a bit of Barrynt's copy." He paused. "I'm not certain that I have that much in common with Relyn, other than being forced out of several lands."

"There is that. You're also a more powerful mage than Relyn was. It's hard to tell from reading his book, but I wonder if he was really a mage at all. Yet he accomplished a great deal. You could do more, if you put your mind to it."

Me? A mage forced out of three lands? Part healer, part mage, with my only real strengths being shields and sensing tiny bits of order and chaos? "You seem to have more confidence in me than I do."

"You'll learn. I hope it won't be too painful for you and those around you. I wish you well in your travels." Naerkaal inclined his head.

"Thank you . . . again."

"It was my pleasure." The councilor turned and slipped out of the stable.

Beltur set aside the book, carefully, and went back to work.

By midday, Beltur had done all that he could with the horses, and he walked back through a day that had become increasingly hazy, almost foggy, and he had to wonder if that had something to do with the melting snow. He was surprised to find Jessyla in the front room at the cot, where she and Tulya were cleaning.

"You're already here?"

"Herrara paid me at noon and told me to leave."

"And you're cleaning?"

"We're not going to leave the place a mess," declared Jessyla. "Not when poor Frankyr has to move things out after we leave."

"It'll be as neat and clean as we can make it," added Tulya. "Lhadoraak's out back, splitting more wood, leaving it for that grouch Rohan."

"He doesn't deserve it," added Taelya, who even had a cleaning rag in her hand.

"Councilor Naerkaal came by the stable."

"He was here earlier," said Tulya. "Lhadoraak talked to him."

"What did he want?" asked Jessyla. "Your promise that we'd really leave Axalt?"

"No. He handed me a gift."

"What? A map to get out of town?"

"A book. A copy of *The Wisdom of Relyn*. He said I might find it useful, since Relyn and I were similar in some ways."

"You and Relyn?"

"Well . . . we were both forced out of three separate lands." Beltur paused. "Actually, I think he was forced out of four."

"Don't try for that similarity . . . please," said Jessyla.

"I'm not trying for any similarity. Naerkaal was the one who said that. He also said that he wasn't the one who wanted us to leave." Beltur could hear the door open and sensed Lhadoraak entering the cot. The door closed.

"But he's the only mage on the Council."

"He might well be the only mage in Axalt except for those of us here, and he's not that powerful a mage. That was what he said, or close to it."

"That might be another reason why they want us gone," said Lhadoraak. "They can overrule him and pressure him. They'd have more trouble with us."

"Don't even think about trying to stay here," said Tulya. "I hate it here. Besides, we'd have no friends except for Johlana's family. Everyone else would be like Rohan."

Will it be different anywhere else? Beltur felt a wry smile, one that he did not show. *It will be unless we take steps to make sure it isn't.* The only problem was that he had no real idea what those steps should be, except that upsetting those in power wasn't a very good idea.

"Wherever we end up," suggested Beltur, "we need to make it clear that we are what we are, and that we stand together." *That would be a start, anyway.*

"Now that you've decided that, dear," said Jessyla, "would you mind dumping out the waste water and getting a bucket of clean water?"

"I can do that." Beltur smiled as he walked toward the bucket to which she had pointed, setting the black-covered book on the side table as he passed.

LXXXV

Beltur was up well before dawn, as was everyone else in the cot, and he and Lhadoraak hurried over to the stable, where Beltur started to ready the horses, but stopped when he saw Lhadoraak just looking at the tack.

"Beltur . . . I can ride some, but I've never saddled a horse."

That was something Beltur hadn't even considered, but he should have. Lhadoraak had been a city mage, just the way Beltur had been until his uncle had taken him on the mission to Analeria. "Then you're about to learn. Watch what I do. Watch closely."

Saddling the five mounts took time, especially since Beltur had Lhadoraak saddle one while he watched. Even Beltur had a little trouble figuring out the pack straps for the mule. The spare mount took a saddle. After dealing with that, he was glad that he'd bought a fair amount of rope at the chandlery earlier, because the pack straps for the mule wouldn't have been enough to hold the mule's load securely in place, let alone whatever the spare mount would be carrying.

The time wasn't the problem, because Beltur had counted on that, but he realized that he really didn't want Lhadoraak leading more than a single mount back to the cot, and that would have required Beltur to ride Slowpoke and lead three mounts and the mule.

He was considering that problem when Frankyr appeared, followed by Jorhan.

"Ryntaar said you might need help getting all the horses over to the cot," offered Frankyr.

"We'd really appreciate that," admitted Beltur.

Jorhan motioned to Beltur, drawing him aside. "You never asked about pay, but I figured you could use your share of what Eshult paid for the mirror." He handed Beltur a small bag. "There's two golds and nine silvers."

"I thought you charged Eshult six. With the cost of the copper and tin . . ."

"He paid seven, and was happy to do it."

"Thank you."

"Now . . . you be sure to let Ryntaar or Frankyr know where you end up so I can send you your share of what we did that hasn't sold yet."

"I'll do that."

Jorhan reached out and put a hand on Beltur's shoulder. "It'll all work out. You'll make it work out, just like you made the cupridium work out." Jorhan stepped back. "Like Johlana, I'm not much for long farewells." He turned and slipped away into the darkness outside the stable.

Beltur took a moment to slide the golds into the slots hidden in his belt and the silvers into his belt wallet.

Even with Frankyr's assistance, it was close to fifth glass by the time the three had the mounts tied up outside the cot, and they began to load their gear in place. Another three quints passed, and the sky over the mountains to the east was lightening when Beltur said, "We need to mount up. Now." Then he turned to Frankyr. "Here's the key to the cot. Thank you for everything."

"I'm glad I could help, ser."

Beltur and the others slowly rode away from the cot, heading toward the square and the Traders' Bowl. As they rode past Johlana's, Beltur saw someone standing on the side porch watching, but he wasn't certain who it might have been.

"How big is this group of traders?" asked Jessyla. "Do you know?"

"It can't be that big. Two or three traders and their wagons, I'd guess."

As they neared the square and the inn, Beltur could sense several men, horses, and what seemed to be three high-wheeled wagons outside the inn. As he neared the group, he rode forward, looking for Jhotyl. He found the fur trader inspecting the second high-wheeled wagon. While Beltur waited for Jhotyl to finish the inspection, he noticed a long board with one end curved upward fastened to the side of the wagon. *To turn the wagon into a sledge of sorts in case of snow?* In that case, there had to be another of the boards fastened to the other side.

Beltur tried to sense the far side of the wagon and thought he could make out something similar, but stopped trying when Jhotyl looked up.

"You all here?"

"We're here and ready to ride. Where do you want us? Front, back, or middle?"

"One of you mages up front with me, the other in the rear with Mheltyn. The rest of your party one place or the other. Up to you."

"We'll start out with me and Jessyla up front and Lhadoraak in the rear. We'll switch positions on and off." *Depending on how Lhadoraak and his family ride and what you sense.* "The three wagons and how many other riders?"

"Just me. Paastar'll be driving his own wagon, and me and Mheltyn. Mheltyn, he'll switch driving the wagons or walk. Thought Camoros was going to join us, but he's waiting for something from Kleth, and the black angels only know when that'll show up. Like to get close to Corumtal before the spring rains start."

"How long will that take?"

"Two days to the east wall, another four, maybe five from there to Corumtal. That's if we don't get heavy snow or rain."

"And from Corumtal to Rytel?"

"Depends on the river, and who's got a flatboat handy. If we have to take the road, rather than the river, it's more than an eightday." Jhotyl frowned. "You don't seem like you've done much traveling."

"Not going east. I've traveled from Fenard to Elparta, from Elparta to Axalt. Going west, I've traveled from Fenard into Analeria as far as a place called Kasiera. That's where the nomad raiders are, and we fought off several attacks there and then on the way to Paalsyra. We also ran into brigands on the way from Elparta to Axalt."

"How close is Kasiera to the Westhorns?"

"You could see them from there, but Kasiera is farther west, much farther west than Fenard. The Westhorns curve west south of Fenard."

"What were you doing there?"

"Carrying out the Prefect's orders. That was before he and his whites killed my uncle and tried to kill me. Also, we never got paid for doing what he wanted, either."

"Very few people have much good to say about the Prefect. If what happened to you is usual, I can see why."

"What is the Viscount like?"

"I'll tell you later. We'll have plenty of time for that. Right now, we need to head out."

Beltur nodded. "I'll get Lhadoraak in position. Ten yards back of the rear wagon?"

"No closer than five and no more than fifteen."

"We'll keep that in mind." Beltur turned Slowpoke and rode back toward where the others waited.

LXXXVI

The ride from Axalt to the midpoint way station on threeday was moderately long and colder than Beltur had anticipated. Taelya did well but Tulya, Beltur could tell, was miserable for most of the ride. Beltur himself was tired by the time he dismounted, because he'd been sensing both what was in front of the traders and what was behind, although most of what he sensed beyond the road happened to be red deer, and an occasional mountain cat that seemed to be stalking and, in one instance, killing the deer.

The way station was better than any of those in Spidlar, with solid stone walls and a slate roof. The floors of both the wayfarers' space and the stable were stone, and there was an ample supply of wood, as well as a pipe from a spring whose water was like liquid ice. The space for travelers consisted of nooks against the wall, all open to the central fireplace and chimneyed hearth. The food supplied by Jhotyl was cold sliced mutton, bread, and cheese, along with slices of pickled pearapples.

Beltur ended up sleeping with most of his blankets and bedroll under him, given that the raised "beds" in the nooks were solid stone, but he was so tired he didn't mind it much.

While Beltur and Jessyla were a little stiff on fourday morning, both Lhadoraak and Tulya were so stiff they had trouble moving. Taelya was fine. Breakfast was bread and cheese.

Jhotyl explained that by saying, "We'll get hot food tonight at the inn at the east wall. Might not be all that tasty, but it will be hot."

Beltur nodded, rather than admit that he hadn't known there was an inn there.

Once again Beltur not only saddled Slowpoke and Jessyla's horse, as well as reloaded the mule and spare mount, but also watched, and offered pointers, as Lhadoraak saddled the mounts that he and his family were riding.

The group was on the road again shortly after sixth glass, moving eastward and gradually upward through a canyon that seemingly narrowed with each kay. After a glass or so, although the sky above was a bright green-blue, shadows still cloaked the road, and the air was cold enough that the ice in the stone gutters alongside the road remained largely unmelted.

Beltur glanced ahead at the empty road, then to the right at the stream-bed that had dwindled almost into nothingness, before saying quietly to Jessyla, riding beside him, "I can see why no one worries about brigands on this part of the ride. They can't approach except by the road, and there's nowhere to go except to Axalt or the east wall."

"Couldn't they block the road in both directions?"

"They could, but where would they go? Also, they'd lose the advantage of numbers." What Beltur didn't point out was that Axalt could easily block the road and hold off invaders with a comparatively small force— possibly another reason why it had never been conquered.

As Beltur and Jessyla rode another three kays up a comparatively gentle incline, the canyon walls seemed to get shorter and shorter, except that was an illusion, because the rocky walls remained the same height as the road rose to meet them. After another several kays of riding, Beltur could see that the road leveled out where it passed through a rocky swale between two tall peaks.

"We're nearing the top of the pass," called Jhotyl from behind them. "We'll stop where it's flat to rest the horses before we start down. This is the coldest part of the journey. Even the eastern wall is warmer than Axalt."

"Is that because it's lower?"

"It is somewhat lower, but the farther the wind blows over the mountains, the colder it becomes, and most of the winds come from the northeast, not from the west or northwest."

With each step that Slowpoke carried Beltur toward the flatter area be-tween the peaks, the wind strengthened. By the time Jhotyl called a halt, a brisk wind was scouring the heat out of the travelers. Beltur dismounted and tied Slowpoke to the lead wagon, then walked back to the rear where he found Lhadoraak standing beside his mount, stretching his legs.

"How are you doing?"

"I'm wondering how you survived all the riding you've done."

"You'll get used to it. My legs were raw the first time I rode a lot. How's Taelya?"

"Better than either of us." Lhadoraak's words were wry. "How is Jessyla doing?"

"She's a bit sore." So was Beltur, but he clearly wasn't suffering as much as Lhadoraak and Tulya were. "Jhotyl says that the first part of the trip is the hardest."

"That's some small consolation."

"If we survive it," added Tulya.

"It's also warmer east of the pass."

"So it will take us twice as long to freeze?" asked Tulya sardonically.

"Something like that. I just wanted to let you both know that."

"Thank you," said Lhadoraak.

Beltur turned and walked back to where Jessyla stood beside her mount, stretching her arms and alternating lifting her knees.

"How is Tulya?"

"Cold, unhappy, and sore, I'd say. She wasn't even cheered much by the idea that it will be warmer as we get closer to the eastern wall."

"She's never liked the cold. That's one reason why she was more than happy to do the cooking. She could stay close to the hearth and still be useful."

"The good thing might be that anywhere we go likely won't be as cold as Axalt."

"There's Westwind," pointed out Jessyla with a smile.

"You know we're not going there. They'd never let two black mages who are male remain there anyway." Beltur smiled. She'd said that just to tease him, knowing he'd feel it necessary to explain.

The ride down from the top of the pass was slower than the climb had been, and colder, because the road on the eastern side wound back and forth across an exposed field of boulders for a good six kays before it finally descended into another canyon, one more valley-like than the canyon on the west side of the pass. Once they were out of the wind and riding along a stretch flanked by pines and spruces that had lost their snow cover, Beltur definitely felt less chilled.

It was close to fifth glass when he rode around a wide sweeping curve in the road and saw the east wall, a structure as high as the western wall, but almost half again as long. As with the western wall, there was but a single well-fortified gate, but there were several structures of considerable size set against the wall and constructed of the same gray stone. Smoke rose from a number of chimneys into a sky that had become covered with thin and high gray clouds.

"The stable is the building on the right side of the gate," said Jhotyl from where he rode directly behind but between Beltur and Jessyla. "The first building on the left is for the tariff inspectors, and the inn is the next one north of the inspectors' building. The guard quarters are the last building on the left. We must stop and inform the tariff inspectors before we can use either the stable or the inn."

"Must you pay them before using the stable or inn?"

"No. We must report what we have, but we do not pay until just before we go through the gates. An inspector from Axalt and one from Certis will both go over what we report. We make one payment. What goes to which land depends on the goods."

"How highly do they tariff ermine pelts?"

"I have the Viscount's marque. Certis will not tariff the pelts. Axalt makes traders pay five silvers even if nothing is subject to tariff."

"How do they know . . ." Beltur broke off the question and asked instead, "Do they inspect everything everyone carries?"

"Usually, they do not, just wagons and large packs. But they can if they wish."

Beltur nodded.

Another two quints passed before Beltur and the others reined up outside the small graystone building of the tariff inspectors.

"Just wait here." Jhotyl dismounted and then tied his mount to the lead wagon, before walking toward the building carrying what looked to be several sheets of paper in a roll.

Several moments later, Paastar followed Jhotyl into the building. He also carried a rolled sheet of paper.

A good half quint, if not longer, passed before Jhotyl and Paastar emerged from the smaller stone building, accompanied by two men, one wearing the dark gray uniform of Axalt and another wearing a differently cut green coat and brown trousers, suggesting that he represented the Viscount of Certis.

The Certan inspector looked to Jhotyl. "We still need to inspect the wagons."

"You've seen the Viscount's marque."

"It is only for pelts, trader."

"That's all that's in the wagons, except for personal things, food, and fodder."

"We must look."

"Look all you want, but if you damage the pelts, His Mightiness won't be pleased."

"We will be most careful."

Jhotyl did not snort until the inspector was inside the first wagon.

Over the next quint, the inspectors looked through all three wagons, referring again and again to the sheet of paper each carried.

In the end, they returned to the lead wagon, where the Certan inspector asked Jhotyl, "What about the pack mule?"

"That belongs to the mages." Jhotyl gestured toward Beltur.

In turn, the Certan looked up to Beltur, still mounted. "What's in the bundles on the mule, Mage?"

"Personal goods, inspector. Blankets, clothing, a few cooking pieces, some bedding . . ."

"That seems . . . strange."

"We're leaving Axalt. It's far too cold for the health of the other mage and his daughter, and Axalt has little need of us."

The inspector looked at Beltur for a long moment, then at Jessyla. "Is what the mage says true?"

"It is, inspector."

The Certan turned his eyes back to Jhotyl. "Then that takes care of everything but payment when you pass through the gates."

In moments, the two inspectors were gone.

Jhotyl gestured toward the stable, then untied and walked his mount toward the entrance, saying to Beltur as he did, "We pay separately for the stable and the inn."

As soon as Jhotyl approached the stable doors, they opened and two stableboys hurried out, followed by a graying ostler. In the end, the stable was much like the one at the way station, except that the stone-walled stalls had wooden doors, and mangers for fodder, as well as stableboys and ostlers. Hay was provided for the cost of the stall, two coppers a night, but grain was extra.

Once the horses were settled, Beltur and his party followed Jhotyl to the inn, lugging their gear—except for the packs on the mule and spare mount, which were kept, for an extra copper, in a locked storage room in the stable.

"What do rooms cost?" asked Beltur as they neared the door to the inn.

"They're small but more comfortable than most. Five coppers a room for each night for the smallest rooms."

Beltur winced. In his experience, rooms had cost around three coppers a night. "Is fare that much more costly also?"

"Not for the fare, but for ale or lager."

A clerk stood waiting behind a counter just beyond the entry foyer of the inn.

"I'll need a large and a small room. Just for tonight," said Jhotyl. "Next to each other."

"That will be a silver and a copper, ser."

When Jhotyl finished paying, and Mheltyn and the other two teamsters joined him, the four headed down the corridor away from the entry.

"How many rooms, ser?"

"Two. A small will suffice for two, will it not?"

"Yes, ser. That will be a silver."

Beltur handed over a single silver, and received two keys, each with a different image, one with a pinecone, and the other with a mountain columbine.

"The image on the key and the room are the same. Both rooms are on the next level. The stairs are past the public room. When you return the key, you get a token to give the ostler."

Meaning you don't get your horses without relinquishing the key. "Thank you."

Beltur handed the pinecone key to Lhadoraak.

"You shouldn't—"

"We'll talk about it at dinner," said Beltur quietly, turning and heading down the hallway.

Some ten yards farther along, they passed the public room, less than a third filled, but a space that could seat possibly four score easily, and walked another fifteen yards before they came to the wide wooden steps and started up. The room with the pinecone carved into the door was the second from the top of the steps on the next level.

Lhadoraak stopped and turned to Beltur.

Before he could speak, Beltur said, "We'll meet you in the public room in about a quint."

"In the public room, then," agreed the older mage.

The columbine room was four doors farther along. Beltur unlocked the door with the large and heavy key, then motioned for Jessyla to enter.

She did and, once inside, set down the heavy duffel with relief.

Beltur closed the door, walked several steps past Jessyla before lowering his own duffel to the worn but clean wide plank floor, and looked around the room. The small window was double-shuttered, with wall pegs for clothing and a side table with one straight-backed chair. On the table were a washbasin and a pitcher. Beltur looked into the pitcher, which was empty. "We'll have to carry up water."

"We have a quint. You told Lhadoraak that."

Beltur glanced to the far corner of the room, which held a chamber pot, then to the bed, large enough for two without crowding. He leaned over and pressed down on the mattress, then tried to sense if it held vermin. He didn't sense any.

"The mattress is hay and horsehair with lots of marigold leaves and petals. Marigolds kill most vermin," said Jessyla, who had obviously felt his sensing. "It's not a bad mattress."

"That's good," said Beltur with a smile.

"I need something to eat, and so do you," replied Jessyla. "But first, we need to wash up. And you did promise Lhadoraak we'd meet them in the public room."

Beltur managed not to sigh as he picked up the pitcher and headed for the door.

LXXXVII

By the time the traders' party rode through the gates of the eastern wall early on fiveday morning, Beltur had laid out almost half a gold for lodging, food, drink, and stabling, while telling Lhadoraak several times just to hang on to his silvers, because the way things were going, his turn would come.

Possibly much sooner than you thought, Beltur told himself as the eastern wall slowly receded behind them. He glanced up at the sky, covered with high thin clouds just heavy enough to take any warmth out of the early spring sun.

"We likely won't see any sign of brigands for close to a day," said Jhotyl. "Then again, if they have an informer in the stable at the eastern wall, it could be within a few glasses. It likely won't be any sooner because an attack close to the wall would make both the Axalt Council and the Prefect angry . . . and very suspicious of the tariff inspectors."

Even with those words, Beltur continued to sense as far out as he could, beyond the evergreens that rose away from the road. A half kay or so along the road and downhill from the wall, a small stream flowed out from a ravine on the left. Beyond the stream, the ground was steep and rocky, but dotted with occasional spruces. To the right was a gradual slope toward a ridge a kay away, beyond which were much higher hills.

At that moment, Beltur realized, truly realized, that they had left Axalt. That meant he had to take care of something. He eased Slowpoke over so that he was riding close to Jessyla.

She looked at him. "What is it?"

"Now that we're out of Axalt," said Beltur, "I'll tell you the last bit of the story about Sarysta. She didn't die of a broken heart. I let Eshult think that because it was kinder, but that was a lie, and it bothers me. I removed some of her natural chaos."

"I already guessed that. That was all it could have been. Evil people like Sarysta don't die of broken hearts. You were trying to protect me, weren't you?"

He shook his head. "I'm not that good. It would have protected you, but I did it to protect me."

"That protected us both." She smiled gently. "I'm glad you told me."

"I said that I would."

"That's one of the things I love about you."

Beltur was glad he remembered before she recalled that he hadn't told her.

Less than a glass after leaving the wall, he began to sense men ahead, although at first, he could barely make them out, and he wasn't certain whether they were travelers in front of them or possible brigands waiting for the traders.

As he rode, he studied the terrain on each side of the road, especially on the left side. Although the snow wasn't nearly as deep as it was higher in the Easthorns and around Axalt, it was certainly at least knee-deep.

Then, after riding another quint, Beltur could sense that the men hadn't moved, and he turned in the saddle and said to Jhotyl, "There are men ahead, near the north side of the road about a kay ahead, around the curve in the road that starts at that rocky outcrop on the right. I can't tell exactly how many yet, but there are more than just two or three."

"Are they mounted?"

"There are some horses there, but no one is mounted now."

"What do you plan?" asked Jhotyl.

"Let them attack. There's no way two mages can deal with as many as half a score brigands if they scatter, and we'd have to leave you unprotected. We'll shield you and the horses, and take them out as we can. You just keep moving."

"You just can't kill them with chaos bolts?"

Beltur managed not to gape. "We're blacks. We defend. We can use defenses to kill, if necessary, but the brigands have to be close. You hired us to protect you. That's what we'll do."

"How many have you held off . . . before?"

"Over a hundred, but I'd prefer not to do that again." That was more than true, but was misleading without explanations that Beltur didn't want to get into, especially before dealing with possible brigands.

"Then do as you must. What do you suggest?"

"Ride as close to the lead wagon as you can. I'll let you know if I need something else. Now, I need to tell Lhadoraak. He can't sense quite as far as I can." Beltur turned to Jessyla. "I'll be back in a bit. I'm going to send Tulya and Taelya up to ride with you."

Then Beltur eased Slowpoke around, then patted him on the shoulder, saying quietly, "This might remind you of times better not remembered, fellow." He rode back along the side of the road and pulled in beside Lhadoraak.

"You look like there's trouble," observed the older mage.

"There are men and horses up ahead around that curve. About a kay. They're on the left right now. Can you keep a shield around Paastar and the horses when they attack?"

"For a while, if I'm riding close to him, but what about Tulya and Taelya?"

"They're going to ride beside Jessyla. She'll be on the far side of the first wagon when the attack begins."

"I worry . . ."

"You need to concentrate on your shields and Paastar and his wagon. Jessyla and I will worry about Tulya and Taelya."

Lhadoraak looked as though he might object, then nodded. "I'll do that."

"Good." Beltur nodded, then turned in the saddle toward Tulya. "Let me have the lead rope for the mule. You and Taelya follow me."

Before that long, Beltur had eased the mule forward and past the three wagons, if with the help of a few containments that limited where the mule could go, and was riding behind Jessyla and the spare mount.

"Tulya and Taelya are behind me. I've got the mule, but I can't deal with him and the brigands. So it's up to you and Tulya. I thought that if you three stayed on the stream side of the wagon, your shields should be strong enough to deal with any shafts that might go over the wagon and my shields."

"We'll work it out. You deal with the brigands. I think two of them have moved closer."

"You can sense them?"

"Just barely."

Beltur handed the mule's lead rope to Jessyla then moved ahead and to the north side of the road, riding slightly forward of Jhotyl. He could sense that Jessyla had been right in that two figures waited closer than the other brigands to the oncoming trading party.

Halfway around the wide and sweeping curve, Beltur noticed that where the curve ended and the road straightened, the incline also steepened, and there was a whitish sheen to the road itself, unlike the dark gray of the nearer stones, and the sheen appeared roughly even with where the first of the brigands hid in the trees to the left of the road.

Why would the road shine—Ice!

Beltur turned to Jhotyl. "I think that part of the road where the brigands are waiting is covered in a layer of ice."

"Those swill-sucking bastards . . ."

"I take it that we'll have to cross the ice slowly."

"If we don't, we'll end up in the snow on the left or in the stream on the right."

"What if we just stop short of the ice?" asked Beltur.

"They'd like that, I'm certain."

"How sure-footed are horses on ice?"

"They could break a leg if the rider isn't careful."

Beltur took a moment to sense just how many brigands there seemed to be. So far as he could tell, there were just eleven.

"Then it just might be better to stop short of the ice and let them come to us."

Jhotyl frowned. "Why would that be better?"

"Two of them are in the trees just about where the ice begins. The others are some fifty yards farther along. We can deal with the first two, and the others will have to come to us."

"What if they don't?"

"Then Lhadoraak will stay here, and I'll go down to them, very carefully. They'll either attack, or retreat. If they attack, then I'll deal with them. If they withdraw, then you can bring the wagons down slowly while I make sure they don't change their minds."

"Seeing as you're taking all the risks . . ."

"Do you have a better idea?" asked Beltur. "If you do, I'd like it."

Jhotyl shook his head.

"Then I'll tell Lhadoraak and Jessyla the new plan." Beltur once more turned Slowpoke and headed back to brief Lhadoraak.

Less than half a quint later, he was back at the front of the group, and riding slowly toward the clump of trees that jutted out from the sparse forest to the north of the road, a clump that concealed two men, some three hundred yards ahead. From what Beltur could tell, the icy section of the road began about twenty yards beyond the waiting brigands.

He kept close watch on the two groups of brigands, but neither moved as the trading party continued eastward. Once the distance narrowed to less than two hundred yards Beltur extended his shields. He could sense, but not see, that the first two brigands were crouched behind what appeared to be a large snowdrift between two trees, but that there were no tracks visible in the snow, suggesting that they'd approached from the forest and used a pine branch or something like it to smooth away traces of their presence.

"It's too quiet," said Jhotyl.

"None of them have moved yet."

"Where do you want us to stop?"

"See that clump of trees there. Stop about thirty yards short of that, maybe a little farther."

For Beltur, the moments seemed to drag as he and Slowpoke rode toward the trees, yet he was still surprised when Jhotyl called out, "Wagons! Halt!"

Beltur looked toward the trees, but neither man moved.

After a time, he called out, "You two, between the trees! Show yourselves."

Still, neither man moved.

Beltur took a deep breath, then placed a containment around each man, holding it tightly, enough that neither could likely breathe easily, until he thought each might be close to being unable to breathe at all. Then he released both containments. One man turned, scrambling northward and away from the road. He had covered possibly ten yards of the twenty-five or so between the clump and the first trunks of the forest when he staggered, then fell with an arrow in his back.

The second man stood and, bow in hand, began to loose shafts at Beltur. The arrows hit Beltur's shield and fell into the snow at the edge of the road. Then another group of brigands emerged from behind false snowdrifts some fifty yards east of Beltur and began to move up the slope, trying to stay close to the road. All carried bows, and wore blades in shoulder scabbards, which made sense to Beltur for anyone having to struggle through knee-deep or deeper snow.

None of them loosed shafts until they were about thirty yards away.

Those shafts also dropped short.

"You really don't want to do this!" called out Beltur.

"We can wait all eightday!" called back a broad-shouldered man in what looked to be a coat and trousers made out of whitish leather.

Beltur dropped a containment around him, then let man and containment pitch forward into the snow.

"He can't do that to all of us!" shouted another, drawing a blade and running toward Beltur.

Beltur formed another containment, well aware that he couldn't hold ten containments at once, and let the second man drop into the snow as well. He forced himself to wait until the seven remaining brigands scrambled onto the dry stretch of road north of where the wagons had stopped. All of them drew blades and charged.

Beltur waited as long as he dared, then urged Slowpoke forward, creating a small shield in front of him, but one wide enough to strike all the attackers.

All of them went down, but Beltur barely managed to slow Slowpoke short of the ice. He turned, to see that four of the attackers were getting up, blades still in hand.

Abruptly, Beltur realized something else, although he had no idea from where he'd gotten the idea. *Small containments don't take as much effort.* With that thought, he clamped vise-like containments around the throats of the four men trying to advance on Jessyla and the wagons.

In moments, if long moments, the four were grasping vainly at their throats. Then they began to fall.

Beltur forced himself to hold the containments until the four who had tried to continue the attack were dead. By that time, so were the men in the two full containments. Two of the men who had been flattened by Slowpoke and the shield were not moving, and eight black mists of death, likely unseen and unfelt by anyone except possibly Jessyla and Lhadoraak, had penetrated to the depths of Beltur's bones.

The one brigand on the road who had survived scrambled away, leaving his blade on the paving stones, and plunged northward through the snow toward the trees. He was followed by the surviving man from the clump of trees.

Beltur found himself shaking in the saddle as he sat there looking down at the six bodies on the road. He didn't look at the two in the snow.

"I thought you said you couldn't kill." There was an appalled tone to Jhotyl's words.

"I didn't say that. I said what blacks do is better suited to defense. I don't like killing. And the way I have to do it is terrible."

"What they wanted to do to us was terrible," said Rhamtyl, the teamster of the lead wagon, who stood beside the wagon horse.

Beltur could sense the shock coming from Tulya, and what seemed to be sadness from Jessyla.

Taelya looked both puzzled and worried.

"The one with the arrow in his back is still alive," said Jessyla.

"Just leave him," said Rhamtyl, the usually silent teamster.

Beltur shook his head. "We might find out something from him." *Besides, for whatever reason, he never tried to attack us.* "If Mheltyn can carry him back, I'll go with him to make sure nothing happens."

Bringing back the wounded man took more effort than Beltur would have liked, since he wasn't about to ride Slowpoke over snow-covered ground that could conceal anything, but a quint later the wounded man, a youth, really, lay on his stomach on the rear tailboard of the lead wagon. The youth was so scrawny his ribs almost showed.

In the meantime, Jhotyl and his men had stripped the valuables, weapons, and coins from the dead brigands and then dragged the bodies into the woods.

The youth winced, but was otherwise silent as Jessyla used Beltur's knife to ease out the arrow, and then sewed up the wound. After that, Beltur did his best to remove what wound chaos there was, although he knew there would be more by sixday, and for some time thereafter.

"He's lost a lot of blood, but he's young," said Jessyla.

Once the young man was sitting up on the tailboard, Beltur looked at him and said, "The wound wasn't that bad. Why didn't you move?"

The youth looked at Beltur. "You're a mage, aren't you?"

"Yes. So is Jessyla, as well as a healer. So is Lhadoraak. Now . . . why didn't you move?"

"Vhister would have shot me again. If he thought I was dead, he might have just left me."

"Vhister was the leader?"

"Yes, ser."

"How did you know we were coming?"

"Vhister got word last night."

"Who told him?"

"I don't know. He goes up to the wall some nights. Most of the time, when he does, he either says we stay away from the road or that we might have good pickings."

"How does he know when to go up to the wall?"

"I don't know, ser."

Beltur could tell that was a partial truth. "You have a good idea, though, don't you?"

The youth sighed. "It's just an idea. Once I started to ask him. He beat me so bad I couldn't walk the next day."

"Why didn't you leave?"

"Where would I go? Vhister was my uncle. Only relative I had. What would I tell folks about what I'd been doing? You know what they do to brigands." After a pause, the youth asked. "You killed him, didn't you?"

"If he was the one in the white leathers with broad shoulders. Now . . . how do you think he knew?"

"He seemed to look at the wall. Maybe it was the banners. It might have been something else."

"What else did Vhister and his men do?"

"We all worked as timbermen when we could. There was never enough work. The trees are better in Axalt."

Beltur looked to Jhotyl, who had said nothing, just listened. "Do you know anything about that?"

"He's right. You'll see when we get into the lower hills. Everything there is scrub pine or scrub oak. Up here, it's too far to cart timber down to Corumtal and too hard and too costly to lug it up to Axalt. Only a few hamlets and villages. Not much need for a lot of timber."

Beltur had more than a few other questions, but those had nothing to do with brigands, and he could tell Jhotyl wanted to get moving. He looked to the youth. "What should we do with you?"

"Ser . . . please take me to Corumtal, or anyplace else. Tie me up and stick me in a wagon. They'll kill me if the cold doesn't."

Beltur looked to Jhotyl. "He never fired a single shaft at us."

"It's your choice, Mage."

"Tie his hands in front of him."

Jhotyl frowned.

"If they're tied behind him, the wound won't heal. Don't worry. He won't get free."

"Magery?"

Beltur nodded. He watched as Jhotyl tied the youth's hands. Then he eased free order into the ropes, linking the very strands together, in a way that even the sharpest knife would likely slip off the bonds.

"Into the wagon, boy," said Jhotyl. "You've got a long rough ride."

"Thank you, ser."

"Don't thank any of us yet," said Beltur. "What's your name?"

"Faeltur, ser."

"You do anything remotely brigandish, and you're in the snow with your hands still bound. Do you understand?"

Faeltur shuddered, then, using both hands, struggled into the back of the wagon.

Beltur turned and walked back to where Slowpoke was tied, drinking from a bucket that Beltur suspected Mheltyn had placed here. He looked to the relief teamster. "Thank you. I was a little tied up."

"I could see that, ser." Mheltyn paused, then asked, "You were an arms-mage once, I hear?"

"I was."

"An officer?"

"Just an undercaptain."

"It shows. The way you dealt with the brigands. I don't think most mages would do it that way."

Beltur smiled wryly. "I wouldn't know. I didn't work that much with other mages, except at the very end. I spent most of my time with a recon company."

"Doesn't surprise me, ser. Thank you." The teamster watched as Beltur waited for Slowpoke to finish drinking before he untied the gelding and led him forward to where Jhotyl waited.

"Ready, Mage?"

"I'm ready." Beltur mounted quickly. "You want us to take it slow and steady on the ice, I take it?"

"A very slow walk is best."

Almost a quint passed before all the wagons were clear of the ice that had been created by the brigands. Only then did Beltur speak again. "Whoever was the informer, it wasn't likely to be one of the two inspectors, especially the Certan inspector."

Jhotyl nodded. "Because he asked about the pack mule, and I said it belonged to the mages." The trader smiled wryly and added, "Unless he had a reason for getting rid of the brigands or wanted to teach them a lesson."

"Or to make the point that he deserved more of a cut of their booty," called out Mheltyn from the seat of the lead wagon.

"What's the likelihood of more brigands?" asked Beltur. "You said earlier that there wouldn't be many, if any, when we near Corumtal."

"If we do run into any more, it will be likely in the low hills before we reach the Viscount's wagon road."

That didn't exactly surprise Beltur, and he nodded, wondering what in the name of the Rational Stars he was going to do with Faeltur.

LXXXVIII

By sevenday evening, Beltur was tired, as well as slightly discouraged, largely because he hadn't realized just how wide the Easthorns were. After six days of solid riding they were still in the high hills on the eastern side of the mountains, spending the night in a shabby way station, one with cracks in the wooden planks that made up the upper half of the walls, and with no wood for the hearth. That had required foraging, which, in turn, had reinforced what Faeltur and Jhotyl had said about the lack of real trees in the hills, because the comparatively small branches and dead wood that they had been able to find burned quickly and without much lasting heat.

Beltur and his party—and Faeltur, whose hands were still bound—had finished their rations of salted mutton and hard bread and cheese and were huddled against the old and uneven stone wall that only rose a yard and a half from the packed clay floor before giving way to the uneven planks comprising the upper part of the wall.

"I need to check your shoulder," Beltur told the youth.

"You check it every night and morning, ser."

"If he didn't," said Jessyla sharply, not quite snapping, "your shoulder would be filled with wound chaos. You'd be moaning, or trying not to, and on the way to dying. There was likely something smeared on that arrowhead."

"Just bear fat, the grubby fat that doesn't render well. The good stuff's for cooking."

Beltur doubted that the chaos that kept cropping up around Faeltur's wound came from the fat, but rather came from something that had clung to the fat. "Hold still."

"Yes, ser."

Beltur slowly sensed the area around the wound, finding more of the small but reddish-yellow wound-chaos bits, then used free order to destroy them. There were more than he would have liked, and that meant more heat in Faeltur's shoulder.

"Oooo . . . that's hot."

"You'd be much hotter if I didn't do this."

"I never knew there were mage-healers."

"You said that before." Jessyla's voice was terse.

"I'm sorry. I've never been with mages. It's . . . different. Are there many mage-healers?"

"No," replied Jessyla. "Mage-healers or healer-mages are few. You were fortunate. Otherwise, you might be dying."

Faeltur was silent.

Beltur turned to Taelya, who was cuddled next to her mother. "I need you to create a shield."

"Now, Uncle Beltur?"

"Now. You have to practice all the time or you won't get better. It helps if you practice when you're tired."

"I'll try."

Beltur could sense that the small shield took effort, but it was solid enough to stop perhaps one or two arrows. After a time, he said, "That's enough. You can let go now." Then, smiling, he added, "Faeltur isn't sure you could be a mage. Do you think you could create a little chaos flame right in front of him?"

"I can too be a mage." Setting her jaw, Taelya concentrated. A flame the size of her small fist appeared less than a yard in front of Faeltur, with enough heat that Beltur could feel it.

So could Faeltur, who jerked back, then winced at the pain in his shoulder.

"That's very good, Taelya. Let it go, now."

The flame vanished.

"See? I did it."

"You did it very well," said Beltur. "Now . . . for a little practice sensing. I'll put a concealment around me, and you point to where I am." He stood, then placed a concealment around himself, easing to the left.

"You're there!" Taelya pointed directly at Beltur.

Beltur moved again, and Taelya again pointed to where he was.

"The next thing is that I'm going to put a concealment around you. It will be darker than night, but you can still sense where I am. Just point to where I am."

Taelya was silent for several moments. "You can't see me. How do you know where I'm pointing?"

"The same way you can sense where I am," replied Beltur, moving as quietly as he could.

"You're there!"

After several more movements, Beltur dropped both concealments and returned to settle beside Jessyla. "That's all for tonight."

"That's good." Taelya yawned.

Several moments later, in the dim light cast by the dying coals of the fire in the crude way-station hearth, Faeltur looked to Beltur and said quietly, "The little girl . . . she is already a white mage?"

Beltur shook his head. "She can do enough to protect herself if she's warned, and she can light lamps and candles, as you saw. She still has much to learn, and she has to grow and get stronger to be able to do more."

"The fur trader said that when you were an arms-mage, you killed hundreds. Are all mages that powerful?"

"Some are likely more powerful than I am. Some aren't. Part of how good a mage becomes is how well they are trained. I was fortunate to learn from someone who could help me." *And in the end, I couldn't save him, hard as I tried.* That memory would always bring pain, Beltur knew.

Abruptly, Faeltur looked down and away.

Later, when Faeltur, Taelya, and even Lhadoraak and Tulya had drifted into what had to be uneasy slumber, Jessyla said quietly, her lips at Beltur's right ear, "Did you see Tulya's expression when Taelya made that flame?"

"No. I was watching her and shielding Faeltur, just in case Taelya put the flame too close. She was surprised?"

"A little afraid, too."

Beltur frowned. "Maybe I should talk to Lhadoraak. He should be doing more of the disciplining of Taelya."

"Just in case she lashes out?"

"Yes, I've already been worrying. That's why I've had her working on shields and delicate control of chaos. I didn't think she'd be this strong this young."

"That's because no one's thought to teach someone with the ability the way you have," said Jessyla.

"That's part of it, but she just has a great amount of ability."

"She doesn't even have to try to keep her natural chaos separated from free chaos anymore. It's habit. You made sure it was habit. That might be part of it."

"You're doing well with that, too. I can sense that."

"It's still not as much of a habit as it should be."

"Just keep working at it, and it will be."

"How did you get able to hold so many containments at once? I know Athaal taught you about them at first."

"I practiced on holding them around birds, as many as I could at a time. That was while I was walking to and from Jorhan's smithy."

"Sometimes . . ."

"Sometimes, what?" asked Beltur softly.

"How you push yourself scares me, just a little. Why is that? That you do that, I mean?"

"There have been times when I couldn't save people. I suppose it might be that I never want to be in that position again."

Jessyla leaned even closer and kissed his cheek. "We need to get some sleep."

Beltur knew that . . . but still he worried about what might lie ahead.

LXXXIX

By noon on oneday, the hills through which the travelers rode were much lower, and there were only scattered patches of snow on the south-facing slopes. While chilly, the air was definitely warmer than it had been even on eightday, and with each kay that passed, the road continued to slope downward. Also on eightday, the stone-paved road had given way to a rutted track that had once been graveled, but remained that way only about half the time. Jhotyl had no explanation for why either Axalt had paved the road into the lands of Certis or Certis had paved the section closest to Axalt.

Beltur wondered how old the stone paving was, but the fur trader had no idea. Parts of it looked ancient, but others seemed newer. *Does the paved part date back to the time of Relyn?*

Earlier that morning, Beltur had noticed that the road had kept to an easterly direction, while the stream that had bordered it turned south into a narrow and winding gorge. He couldn't help thinking he didn't like being that far from water, especially given how much Slowpoke drank.

While Tulya was clearly more cheerful with the warmer air, even smiling at times, Beltur was beginning to worry again. He wasn't certain, but he had the feeling that a number of riders lay somewhere ahead. Whether they were armsmen serving the Viscount or more brigands he had no way of knowing, but he doubted that they served the Viscount.

He became more concerned when he sensed a single rider behind an outcropping half a kay ahead, and even more so when that rider slipped away, riding to the east without returning to the road until he was well out of sight of the traders.

"Someone's scouting us," Beltur reported to Jhotyl. "The scout's riding east. I have the feeling there are more riders there, but it's too far to say."

"Let me know when you can tell."

By the time another glass had passed, Beltur turned to Jhotyl. "There are close to a score of riders behind a ridge in the vale ahead."

"How far is the ridge from the road?"

"It's about half a kay to the north. The riders are about in the middle of the ridge."

"There's no other passable way to Corumtal from here. Not at this time of year. And if we turn back, they'll likely just follow us. Twenty sounds like more than you'd want to handle."

"We might be able to avoid them, or at least surprise them," Beltur suggested. "If you don't mind traveling like blind men."

"What do you mean?"

"I can put a concealment around all of us, the way I did the other night in the way station when I was teaching Taelya."

"Mage . . . I was sleeping."

"A concealment hides people, like this." Beltur dropped a concealment around Slowpoke and himself.

"Where are you? Are you still there?"

"I am." Beltur released the concealment. "Unhappily, there are problems with using a concealment as you'll see when I put one around you." Beltur cloaked the fur trader and his mount in a concealment.

"You've blinded me. I can't see."

Beltur turned in the saddle. "Rhamtyl! Can you see Trader Jhotyl?"

"Where did he go?"

Beltur released the concealment, and Jhotyl seemed to appear from nowhere.

"What good is that if we can't see where we're going?"

"You can't. Lhadoraak, Jessyla, and I can. We can sense where we are. Now . . . if each teamster walks and leads his horse with one hand, and holds to the wagon before him, and the lead teamster has a rope tied to Slowpoke's saddle, we might be able to get across most of the vale ahead before the brigands realize we're there."

"If they can't see us, how would they know?"

"A concealment doesn't stop sound, and if we raise dust, it will hang in the air behind us once the concealment passes that dust."

"If they come after us, how will that help?"

"Because they'll be bunched together on the road." *If we get far enough along.* "It's much easier to deal with them if they're in a bunch. If they attack us from the side—"

"They can strike many more places. I understand that." Jhotyl frowned.

"Also," added Beltur, "at the end of the vale, the land on each side of the road rises steeply, and it appears to be uneven. If we can get close to the east end of the vale before they discover us, that will force them closer together."

"And you can do something like you did in the mountains?"

Let's hope so. "That's the idea."

"Don't you ever attack first?" asked Jhotyl.

"Not often."

"Have you *ever* attacked first?"

Beltur had to think about that for a moment. "I've taken the attack to someone once they started something, but I can't recall ever attacking first. Letting others make mistakes first seems to work better for me."

"Seems to me that you're letting others set things up to their advantage."

"That might be because I've never had the advantage of numbers or position," replied Beltur.

"You should think about that," suggested Jhotyl.

At times, the trader's words seemed . . . untrader-like. "You sound like you know something about arms and tactics."

The trader smiled. "Very little. For a time, I was close to those who did. I listened." He shrugged. "Listening is useful. More useful than talking, most times."

Beltur could sense that Jhotyl wasn't telling the entire truth.

"When will you put us under this concealment?"

"When we get to where we can almost see the ridge in the vale. If we can't see where they are, they'll not likely see us."

"I'll call a halt now, and you can tell everyone the plan."

More than a quint later, the travelers resumed their measured pace through the end of the wider valley and then between the hills leading into the smaller vale—a far better place for an ambush. Just before the space be-tween the hills widened, Beltur lowered the concealment over the group. Beltur was more than glad that he'd shown Taelya about concealments and that she had enough ability with sensing to know what was around her, although her abilities only extended thirty or forty yards, less if she hap-pened to be hungry or tired.

Beltur led the party, with Jhotyl on the right of the lead wagon horse, led by Rhamtyl.

Jessyla rode between the first and second wagon, with Tulya beside her and Taelya farthest to the right, the mule and spare mount following, while Lhadoraak led the third wagon.

As the group moved into the vale, Beltur kept sensing the riders hid-den among the bush-like pines near the base of the ridge, but none of the riders moved out of hiding, even as Beltur reached a point on the road almost even with them. From what he could tell, there weren't any riders posted farther ahead, at least not for several kays.

He kept sensing, having the feeling that there was . . . something . . . something not quite right. Then he swallowed. A swirl of chaos! *Frig! They've got a white wizard . . . maybe only a scrub mage . . . but it won't be long before he senses something.*

While Beltur could have used full screens over the entire party, total screens over that distance while riding two kays would have exhausted him, and the last thing he wanted was to have no shields or weak shields when the attack came, and it was indeed likely to come. He turned in the saddle in the direction of Jhotyl. "The raiders have a scrub mage. He hasn't sensed us yet, but it likely won't be long. Where the hills come together is still about half a kay away, and they're about half a kay to the north of us. Can the wagons take a fast trot for a half kay?"

"Not unless the teamsters can see where they're going."

Beltur thought. Traveling under a concealment meant the attackers couldn't see exactly where the travelers were, but neither could anyone but mages know where the attackers were, and Beltur could shield against just arrows until the brigands got close. That was as far as his thoughts got, because he sensed the raiders throwing themselves into saddles.

Beltur dropped the concealment. "Keep moving as fast as you can safely! Lhadoraak and I will hold them off." He moved Slowpoke to the north side of the road.

"Teamsters! Fast trot! Now!" yelled Jhotyl.

"Lhadoraak! Join me!" shouted Beltur. Then he glanced eastward. The distance to the narrowing of the open ground was still close to a thousand yards, and the riders bursting out from cover were likely to reach the travelers before they reached that point.

"What do we do now?" asked Lhadoraak as he reined up beside Beltur.

"We follow the wagons. I'll shield for arrows and when they get close we'll try a few tricks of sorts." Beltur turned Slowpoke and urged him into a trot. He hadn't covered more than two hundred yards before the brigands loosed their first shafts, but those dropped out of the sky when they hit Beltur's outermost shield.

That didn't seem to slow the riders at all as they angled toward the road and the travelers.

Beltur took a moment to again sense to the north, but the only large bodies he sensed were those of his party. He glanced to the side. The leading attackers were perhaps three hundred yards back and perhaps two hundred yards from the road, but they all seemed to be converging on the road. *Because they think they can ride faster there? That just might make things easier for us.*

Beltur turned to Lhadoraak, who was holding onto his saddle to stay on his mount. "When we stop and rein up, I need you to throw a concealment across the road behind us, maybe a hundred yards deep. Can you do it?"

"If . . . If I'm not trying to stay on the horse. Why do you want to conceal them?"

"I don't. I want them to be unable to see."

"Oh . . ."

"Then I'll have a little surprise for them."

After covering another hundred yards, Beltur glanced back. *If you wait any longer, you won't have time . . .*

"Lhadoraak! Rein up! Now! Turn and cover the road with a concealment!" Beltur reined up Slowpoke and turned to face the oncoming raiders, most of whom seemed to be wearing worn uniforms of brown and dark green.

Lhadoraak seemed to have trouble slowing his mount and turning, but he finally managed, although the leading riders were less than two hundred yards away.

Beltur felt his shields blocking more arrows, and he waited, hoping that Lhadoraak could create the concealment, knowing he was going to need all the help he could get.

Abruptly, the brigands vanished from sight.

In moments, though, a command rang out. "Keep going!" shouted one of the brigands. "The road's clear except for two riders. Just ride on! The mage will take care of them!"

Even as the brigand spoke, Beltur sensed the modest chaos bolt that arched from a rider well back near the rear of the brigands, angling straight toward Lhadoraak. Just as he had had to do so many times during the invasion, almost without thinking, Beltur used his shields to catch and fling the chaos bolt into the first rank of their pursuers. Two riders and their mounts went down in a charred heap. A second and stronger chaos bolt followed, this one aimed at Beltur, and Beltur used that to take out three more riders.

The only problem was that the riders were going to reach Beltur and Lhadoraak before the white mage had flung enough chaos for Beltur to eliminate even a sizable fraction of the score or so of brigands.

The mage didn't give up, this time flinging an even stronger bolt at Beltur. This time Beltur turned the bolt, added a black order, and drove it back through the shields of the scrub mage. Order and chaos combined into a flare that took out several more riders, but by now the oncoming riders were less than a hundred yards away, and about to reach the end of Lhadoraak's concealment.

Beltur steeled himself, then formed a half shield a little more than a yard high just outside the concealment, doing his best to anchor it to the stone beneath the road.

When the first riders burst out of the concealment and struck Beltur's shield, horses screamed, but few of the raiders yelled. Beltur felt as though several of the horses had run over him, and his vision blurred for several moments, but when he could see, there were men and mounts seemingly lying everywhere. He'd felt several black mists, but Beltur sensed that most of the fallen seemed to be alive, but largely injured to some extent. Possibly five riders were still mounted, and they had pulled back, as if uncertain as to what to do. Beltur immediately dropped his shields back down to just around himself and Lhadoraak.

"If you want more of that, just keep coming!" Beltur shouted.

None of them moved toward Beltur and Lhadoraak.

"It's time to start moving again," said Beltur.

"Most of them are down," said Lhadoraak.

"If I have to do that again," replied Beltur, his voice suddenly shaky, "I'll be down with them. If the five who are left attack, we can likely take them out, but some of those on the ground might just recover if we go looking for spoils."

"Not many of them," said Lhadoraak.

"We'll leave them . . . unless they come after us." Slowly, still looking over his shoulder, Beltur turned Slowpoke, then urged him into a trot. Belatedly, Lhadoraak did the same.

Beltur kept sensing and looking back, but the would-be brigands showed no inclination to follow them.

After a time, Lhadoraak said, "Where did you come up with that idea of using a concealment on them?"

"It was something I figured out when I was with Second Recon during the invasion."

"You really are an arms-mage, no matter what you say."

Beltur got out a water bottle, and took a long swallow of the bitter watered lager. He hoped it would help the throbbing in his skull. He'd forgotten what battle magery could do to him.

Almost a quint passed before Beltur and Lhadoraak caught up with the wagons, stopped a good two kays farther along the road.

Jessyla and Jhotyl were waiting, mounted at the rear of the wagons.

"What happened?" asked Jhotyl as Beltur and Lhadoraak reined up.

"Beltur turned the scrub mage's chaos against some of the brigands," said Lhadoraak, "then against him. I threw a concealment over them so that they charged into an order barrier Beltur created. That brought down all but five of the survivors. They decided not to follow us."

"How many are left?"

"Only five that weren't dead or injured," said Beltur. "There was one thing I did see that I didn't care for. Most of them were wearing worn uniforms of brown and green."

"Most likely deserters," suggested Jhotyl.

"An entire squad's worth, with a mage?" asked Beltur.

The fur trader shrugged. "It happens. The life of a Certan ranker isn't the best, and they can't return to anywhere decent. Their lives are forfeit if they're caught."

"And the mage?"

"Most mages in Certis have to serve the Viscount."

Beltur nodded slowly. The idea of going to Montgren was definitely looking better, assuming that they could get there. "How far is Corumtal from here?"

"Another day and a half. Two days if the road is muddy."

"I thought you said we'd be reaching the Viscount's wagon road soon."

"We're *on* the Viscount's wagon road. You should see the roads that he hasn't had his men work on."

Beltur was certain he didn't want to see such roads . . . and that he probably would, sooner than he wished. Still . . . he had to ask. "What happens when we reach Corumtal? Do we follow a river road to Rytel, or can we take flatboats downstream?"

Jhotyl shrugged. "We'll find out. Often, this early in the spring, the river is low, and there are no flatboats. Then we follow the river road. If we're fortunate, we'll take flatboats to Rytel. Either way, once we near Corumtal, there will likely be no more brigands." He shook his head. "Most years there are only a few. This year . . . eleven outside Axalt, and a score in the low hills . . . last year's harvests must have been poor indeed."

"Or the Viscount raised tariffs on them," suggested Beltur. "Or cut the pay for his rankers."

Jhotyl frowned, but he neither agreed nor disagreed.

"Lhadoraak and I need something to eat before we start again."

Jhotyl glanced from Beltur to Lhadoraak and then to Jessyla, then smiled slowly. "I'm beginning to see why the Council preferred you leave Axalt. Will bread, cheese, and lager suffice?"

Beltur returned the smile. "That will be just fine."

XC

A little before second glass on threeday, as Beltur, Jessyla, and Jhotyl reached the top of a low rise of the road beside the Corum River, Jhotyl gestured to the town ahead, the outskirts of which appeared to begin less than a kay away, where plots of land gave way to scattered cots alongside the road, which had improved to a graded and graveled way that suggested it was indeed one of the Viscount's wagon roads.

"Corumtal, such as she is, Mage. Looking at the river, I fear we will be taking the road to Rytel. I can see mudbanks where there should be water."

"How long will that take?"

"Not as long as getting here from Axalt, possibly five days. Six if it rains."

As Beltur and Jessyla rode closer to the cots, she said quietly, "Those poor people. Those are worse than those near the renderers in Fenard."

Two scrawny children, wearing little more than shapeless, grayish-brown rags, stood in front of the second cot that Beltur and Jessyla neared. Their eyes were vacant.

"Pay them no mind," said Jhotyl from behind them. "You give a single copper and a score will appear, beleaguering you and begging as though they were all dying."

Jessyla glanced to Beltur, her lips forming the words, "They look like they're dying."

Beltur could sense that was not true, but the pair were so thin that he could not see whether either was boy or girl. He forced himself to look ahead, knowing he could spend every silver he had and that it would make little difference in another eightday. *And that is deplorable.*

Ahead of them, past the first scattering of cots, set on the right side of the road, but back from both road and river, stood several buildings constructed of reddish sandstone, with weathered reddish roof tiles, surrounded in turn by a stone wall.

"That's a post for the Viscount's guards," explained Jhotyl.

"It looks almost deserted," observed Beltur.

"Once there was a company posted here. Now . . . there might be perhaps two squads."

"Why might that be? Is that why the brigands are more prevalent?" Beltur turned in the saddle to look at the fur trader.

Jhotyl shrugged, then said, "The Viscount has troubles in the south, it is said."

"With Gallos?" Beltur recalled his uncle mentioning something about that.

"Not only with Gallos but with Lydiar, it is said. Even with Hydlen."

"But not with Montgren?"

"The Duchess prefers to remain on good terms with all."

"What sort of troubles?"

"Who knows? I am but a fur trader." Jhotyl smiled pleasantly.

"How long will we be staying here?" asked Jessyla, slightly impatiently, as if she were tiring of the trader's partial answers.

"Today and tomorrow. All of us, and the horses, need rest. We also need provisions and fodder, especially for that beast of yours, Mage. Not that he hasn't earned every bushel's worth." After the briefest hesitation, Jhotyl went on. "We will stay at the River Inn. It is the only place worth staying at. With the water so low, it will not be crowded."

Beltur wondered just how many River Inns there might be across Candar.

The River Inn, as its name indicated, was located on the north side of the main square with its north side on the river road and the south side facing the square. A warehouse flanked the lodging on the east, and the stable on the west. The two-story lodging building was constructed of sandstone blocks, much like the guard post, with the same faded reddish tile roof, while the warehouse and stable were of mud-red brick. Narrow covered porches graced both the front and rear of the inn proper.

After stabling the horses, and, at Jhotyl's suggestion, putting the mule's and spare mount's packs in the second wagon, Beltur and Jessyla followed Jhotyl to the square side of the inn, carrying their personal gear. Lhadoraak and his family trailed behind.

A narrow-faced but not-quite-rotund man with a bald pate stood behind a desk counter, but turned as he heard Beltur and the others approach. His eyes narrowed as he looked at Jhotyl. Then he offered a resigned smile. "Master Trader Jhotyl. Welcome to the River Inn."

"Thank you, Innkeeper Granois."

"How long will you and your party be staying, Master Trader?" asked the innkeeper.

"Tonight and tomorrow night. We'll need five rooms. Two for the mages and three for me and the others in the party."

"You haven't brought mages before."

"I haven't needed them before. The brigands are worse this year. Worse than any time I recall."

"In case you haven't noticed, Master Trader, everything is worse. There is little water in the river. Late rains and early frosts spoiled much of the harvest. There are fewer guards at the post, and they have fewer coppers to spend."

"I think I've heard that before," replied Jhotyl.

"That is because times have been hard before." Granois turned to a board on which hung keys, a board from which Beltur saw that only a few keys were missing, removed five keys and turned back to the group. "These two keys are for the mages." The innkeeper looked at Beltur, then at Jessyla, quizzically.

"These two are both mages and healers—"

"Women mages are rare." The innkeeper inclined his head slightly, then looked at Beltur. "Even rarer than men healers." Then he returned his eyes to Jhotyl. "Truly, you have surprised me . . . again."

Beltur took both keys and passed one to Jessyla. "For Lhadoraak."

She in turn handed it to the blond mage.

Granois handed the remaining keys to Jhotyl, then said, "If you will excuse me, Master Trader, I need to tell the cooks to prepare more for supper." He slipped from behind the counter, gracefully for a man of his bulk, and began to walk across the foyer to the archway leading into an empty public room, though that was scarcely surprising in early midafternoon.

"The stairs are beyond the public room," said Jhotyl. "The water pump is behind the door opposite the stairs."

"Thank you," said Beltur.

"I will meet you mages for dinner here at fifth glass. Now, I need to see to the wagons." The trader turned and made his way from the inn.

Beltur and Jessyla carried their gear up to the second level and found their room, graced by simply the number eight, on both key and door. Beltur unlocked it, opened the door, and motioned for Jessyla to enter. He followed her and closed the door, then said, "Did you notice that the innkeeper did not ask for payment?"

"I did. He was also overly deferential to Jhotyl. Jhotyl must come here often."

"Or he's more than just a fur trader."

"If not both."

Beltur walked to the window, which only had inside shutters, rather than the double shutters so common in Axalt, and looked out over the river. The nearest pier was opposite the inn's warehouse, but there were no boats tied up there, doubtless because there was mud showing under the first ten yards from the river's edge. He turned and studied the room, not overly large, but certainly larger than the one at the eastern wall inn. There were two straight-backed chairs and two pitchers and washbasins on a wash table. The pitchers were empty.

"I'll go down and fill the pitchers," he volunteered.

"I'll make the second trip," replied Jessyla.

Beltur smiled. "I can do that as well. You'll need more to wash your hair, even as short as you keep it."

"Thank you."

It took more than a few trips, both for fresh water and to empty the basins, since there was no waste pipe in the room, and since they both had a great deal of dust and grime to wash away.

Later, while Jessyla was struggling with her hair, Beltur took out the copy of *The Wisdom of Relyn*, deciding to start at the beginning and to read the volume all the way through. While he'd read the first few pages before, he opened to the very first page once more, wondering what else he might discover.

He found himself reading beyond the page where he had stopped before.

> . . . was saved and befriended by Nylan, a mage whose like Candar, or the world, will never see again, for he forged Westwind, as surely as he forged the blades by which the angels carved their domain from the ice and stone of the Roof of the World.
>
> Never has there existed a mage like Nylan, for when he wielded the fires of Heaven and swept the land before the Black Tower clean of all the attackers from Lornth, the deaths of those attackers nearly claimed him as well, though none ever came within a sword's length of him. He was not a man of great stature, and at first glance, seemed more like a stripling youth, for all that he was the oldest of all the angels. Yet his silver hair was not that of age, but truly bright and young, as if it belonged to a child. A man of wisdom, with the strength of a giant, but the appearance of a youth. Yet I could not have bent iron to my will as did he, nor could any other of the angels.
>
> For all that fierceness, he would sing to his infant children lullabies so moving that they would sleep through the tempests that buffeted the Roof of the World, and he crafted a cradle for his eldest, the daughter Dyliess who will come to rule Westwind after Ryba, her mother . . .

Beltur lowered the book for a moment and looked to Jessyla. "I'd like to read something from Relyn's book to you."

"Go ahead. I'm listening."

Beltur read the part about Nylan, ending with the words about Nylan's daughter.

"Daughter? He had a daughter with Ryba?"

"That's what Relyn wrote. *The Book of Ayrlyn* mentions a son—"

"It does?"

"It does, but it doesn't mention a daughter who went on to rule Westwind."

"It makes sense, though," mused Jessyla. "Nylan was powerful, and so was Ryba. Their daughter likely was as well." She paused. "She must have been. Westwind still rules the Westhorns."

"And the part about him singing to his children . . . Somehow that doesn't fit with a man who destroyed armies."

"Why do you say that? Maybe that's why he could, because he loved them so much that he'd do anything to make them safe."

"Or maybe," said Beltur, "because he really wasn't a cruel man, he did what he did so that he wouldn't ever have to do it again."

"That sounds more like you, dear."

"Except I seem to have to keep doing it for us to survive."

"That will change."

"You think so."

Jessyla just offered a smile that Beltur could only have described as enigmatic.

Somehow, before Beltur even realized so much time had passed, the two were hurrying down to the public room, Beltur wearing his mage-healer tunic because the other two were hanging up drying from a semi-cleaning with wet cloths.

Jhotyl was already in the public room, seated at the head of an oblong table, with Lhadoraak, Taelya, and Tulya on one side. There were only two other occupied tables. One held two young men with beakers of something on the table, and around the other were the teamsters and Trader Paastar, and Faeltur, whose wrists Beltur had freed late on twoday.

Jessyla took the chair farthest from Jhotyl, making sure that Beltur would be seated next to the trader.

"I've never seen a mage wear a tunic like yours."

"It's a mage-healer's tunic. It's what I wore when I was working in the healing house."

"You . . . a mage . . . you actually served in a healing house? With . . . healers?" Jhotyl's voice contained traces of both surprise and almost a sense of being scandalized.

"He did," said Lhadoraak, clearly amused at Jhotyl's apparent consternation.

Beltur wondered about the trader's reaction, but only said, "How else could I have learned what I needed to know about healing?"

Jhotyl did not pursue the question, instead looking up for a serving woman. "Dinner is my pleasure. I would not have any pelts, and possibly not even my life, except for all of you. I cannot pay much more than I promised, but Granois—he is the innkeeper, and he owes me many meals and much lodging. So you may choose from whatever there is." A lopsided grin followed his words.

"Thank you. We appreciate it." Beltur did not ask why Granois owed so many meals—and lodging—to Jhotyl. The fur trader would explain if and when he wanted to, if ever.

A very young-looking serving girl hurried toward the table, looking immediately to Jhotyl. "Ser . . . Master Trader, tonight we have valden-schnitz or mutton chops with cream gravy. There is red wine, white wine, golden ale, and dark lager."

"I'll have the valdenschnitz and dark lager," declared Jhotyl.

"Can you tell me about the valdenschnitz?" asked Beltur, never having heard of the dish.

"It's valdenschnitz, ser," said the serving girl, almost helplessly, as if anyone should know what valdenschnitz was.

Beltur looked to Lhadoraak, who shrugged helplessly.

After a moment of silence, Jhotyl said, "It's pork pounded thin and dredged in frothed eggs and then coated with crushed floured nuts and local spices and then fried and covered with a chili-lemon-cream sauce. Spicy hot but very good. You'll need bread with it. Ale or lager won't cool your mouth."

"Is it hotter than burhka?"

"About the same, but the taste is very different."

"I'll try it," decided Beltur, hoping that wasn't a mistake, "with the golden ale."

"I'll have the mutton chops," said Jessyla firmly, "with golden ale."

Lhadoraak, Tulya, and Taelya followed Jessyla's example, except Taelya got watered ale, since there was no juice.

After the serving girl left, Jhotyl said, "Mutton here is good, more like lamb. A bit bland for my taste, but good."

In only a few moments, the beakers of ale and lager arrived, along with a large basket containing three warm loaves of a darkish bread, not really brown bread, but not rye, either.

Beltur took a cautious sip of the ale, but it was full-bodied without any hint of sourness or bitterness.

Tulya immediately broke off a chunk of bread and handed it to Taelya, leaning over and whispering something in Taelya's ear.

"Thank you, Mother. Thank you, Trader Jhotyl."

"You're most welcome, young . . . woman."

After several modest swallows from his beaker, Beltur asked, "Are we likely to run into more brigands on the road to Rytel?"

"When we've had to take the road before, we haven't seen any. Now . . .

with last year's poor harvests, there might be a greater chance. If there are any, they won't come in the numbers of that last bunch."

Another silence followed.

Then Taelya spoke. "Ser, how many coats will all those hides make?"

Jhotyl smiled. "When they have fur on them, they're called pelts, Tae-lya. It depends on how long the coat is. A really long coat might take two hundred pelts. That's why it takes most of winter to gather enough of them."

"Do you have a coat like that?"

"No, I don't. Those coats are for important people, like the Viscount or his consort. I'm not that important."

At that moment, the young server returned, accompanied by a much older woman, both quickly setting platters, as well as battered cutlery, in front of the dinners, and then returning to the kitchen.

Beltur looked down at his platter, which held the valdenschnitz, definitely covered with a heavy cream sauce and accompanied by fried lace potatoes, and three long thin slices of what looked to be pickled quilla.

Beltur broke off a large chunk of bread and set it on the edge of his platter, then cut a thin piece of the valdenschnitz, trying not to seem too ginger in his movements as he conveyed the morsel to his mouth. He chewed, but the pork was tender, or had been pounded enough to make it tender, and the initial taste was smooth and slightly tart lemon cream.

The second taste was like liquid fire filling his mouth and flaring up through his nostrils. He grabbed the bread, and quickly bit off a piece. The fire subsided, and the aftertaste was almost mellow. He took a small swallow of ale.

"What do you think?" asked Jhotyl, who had eaten a far larger bite than had Beltur, and seemed not at all discomfited.

"It's hotter than any burhka I've ever tasted, but with the bread, it's actually quite good."

"Your forehead's sweating," said Lhadoraak blandly.

"I said it was hot, but I still like it."

"Better you two than me." Lhadoraak laughed softly.

"I like this," declared Taelya. "Thank you, Trader Jhotyl."

"You're welcome."

"What can you tell us about Certis and the Viscount that we should know?" asked Beltur. "All I really know is that the Viscount rules and that he and the Prefect of Gallos appear to have . . . different views."

"Different views," replied Jhotyl with a laugh. "That's a polite way of saying they don't much like each other."

"I don't know even that," Beltur said.

"They don't much care for each other. I don't have the faintest idea why the Prefect does what he does, but he seems to want everyone in Candar to pay tariffs to him and feels that he shouldn't have to pay tariffs to anyone. That's why more and more traders in Jellico are shipping goods down the River Jellicor, all the way to Tyrhavven in Sligo, and then having coasters carry them either to Spidlaria or Lydiar."

"Does the Viscount insist on high tariffs as well?"

"He is far more reasonable. The tariffs are modest for any goods except those from Gallos, and that is only because of the Prefect's actions and arrogance. Lower tariffs are much better for all lands. That's the way it should be."

"Have you ever met the Viscount?" asked Jessyla. "Do you know what he's like?"

"I couldn't say, lady mage. I've provided furs, and my workshop has made coats for some of his family. They have all been most courteous. The Viscount is said to be forbearing and reasonable unless his patience is greatly tried. That is what I have heard. I have no experience in such matters." Jhotyl shrugged.

Beltur could see that the trader was not likely to say more. "What is the city like?"

"Jellico? It is a magnificent city, with tall and well-kept walls a good twenty yards in height at the lowest. The streets are paved and smooth, and there are four market squares, each serving a different quarter of the city . . ."

Beltur smiled pleasantly, listening carefully as Jhotyl went on to describe a city he obviously knew very well.

XCI

Beltur hadn't realized just how tired he was until he woke on fourday . . . and found it was well after seventh glass, but part of that might have been that they stayed up later than usual as well. Beltur smiled, recalling that that time had been well-spent, as he looked at Jessyla, still asleep. She slept for another quint before waking.

They did manage to get down to the public room for breakfast, well after anyone else had left, but the serving girl did not complain, but provided egg toast, a bitter berry syrup, and thin ham strips and bread. Again, they were not asked to pay, which, in a way, bothered Beltur. At the same time, it did mean that his silvers would go further.

After eating and washing up, they decided to walk around Corumtal to see what they could see and learn what they could. The white sun was warm enough that neither wore their heavy coats, a fact that amused Beltur, because a year earlier, he wouldn't have thought the day that warm.

As they left the River Inn and walked across the river road to the pier opposite the inn's warehouse, Beltur began, "Something about dinner bothered me . . ."

"Besides the spiciness of the valdenschnitz?" replied Jessyla with a smile. "I liked that, hot as it was."

"I could tell that . . . even before last night . . ."

Beltur flushed and quickly said, "No . . . it was the way Jhotyl explained what valdenschnitz was. He didn't sound like a fur trader. It was as though he'd been in charge of the kitchen at a great house or even a palace. He also didn't answer the question about the Viscount and his family."

"I did like his description of Jellico," said Jessyla, "but it wasn't what I expected from a fur trader. He also admitted that his workshop made the coats. Do you think he's related to the Viscount?"

"If he is, he can't be a close relative. He really does trade furs, and he doesn't travel with any guards . . . although Mheltyn certainly is familiar with a blade and likely other weapons."

"Rhamtyl carries a blade, and so does the other teamster."

Beltur stopped before he reached the shore end of the pier. While the timbers were weathered and looked mostly solid, the thin layer of dried dirt and mud made it clear that the pier had not been used recently. He and Jessyla turned and continued eastward on the side of the river road, which had no walks, unlike the streets in Axalt.

The first shop that they came to was a chandlery.

"Should we go in?" asked Beltur.

"Do we need anything?"

"I'm sure we do," he replied lightly.

"Enough to put out coppers for it?"

"Most likely not."

Down the road, across the road from some rotted posts sticking up from the river mud, a sign on a shop caught Beltur's eye. There was just one word—Pots—and a line drawing in black of three pots of the same shape and different sizes. "We could look in."

"We can't carry pots."

"That's why we won't be tempted. I'd just like to see what sort of pots there might be."

Jessyla offered an amused shrug. "Why not?"

Beltur had only taken two steps into the small shop when he spied a black vase, simple, but somehow appealing, perhaps because its curved body was neither too rounded nor too straight, and the neck was narrow, only wide enough for the stems of a few flowers, and given that small a neck, it had to be for flowers.

"You're not from around here," said the white-haired woman seated behind a plain table. "A healer and . . . a mage? I've never seen a mage's tunic with green cuffs."

"That's because he's a mage and a healer," replied Jessyla.

"I'm surprised that the Viscount hasn't sent for you both."

"We're not from Certis," explained Beltur.

"I don't know as that would make much difference to him."

"It might to us," said Jessyla.

"I wouldn't worry if you're passing through. The guards posted here aren't about to insist on confronting a full mage."

"What about in Rytel?" asked Beltur.

"I wouldn't know, and asking that sort of thing these days isn't useful."

"The black vase there . . . it's striking," said Beltur.

"One of my better pieces. I did it for me. Most folks just want simple pitchers, bowls, and platters. It gets boring doing them, but they make me enough to get by. They might not if the guards from the post didn't break so much crockery. Then, they wouldn't be posted here if they were really good. They'd be in Jellico. Where did you two come from?"

"Axalt," answered Jessyla.

"Most folks want to get to Axalt, not to leave it."

"We're not most folks." Jessyla smiled pleasantly.

"That's obvious."

"Is there anything someone passing through should see?"

"No. I can't think of a thing, but it's been pleasant talking to you."

Beltur glanced around the shop, looking at the shelves, but as the potter had said, there were simple, but well-made, platters, bowls, and pitchers. "Thank you."

The potter nodded.

Jessyla didn't say anything until they were back outside. "She was . . . different."

"She's a good potter. Should we head back to the Inn?"

"Not yet."

After spending little more than two quints walking through the streets that held shops and crafters, none of which looked particularly appealing, Beltur and Jessyla finally headed back toward the River Inn.

"We ought to walk through the market square at least," Beltur suggested.

"If it's like the rest of Corumtal . . ."

"Sometimes, you can learn things," Beltur said.

Another quint later, they stood at the edge of the square, which held a scattering of vendors and those looking. From what Beltur saw and sensed, few of those selling offered foodstuffs, outside of a few root vegetables, and one woman with dried fish of some sort. There were three or four basket sellers, and the baskets were either of grass or withies.

"What are you learning?" asked Jessyla.

"The town is even poorer than I thought, and I have my doubts that things will get better any time soon. I think it's time for us to give Slowpoke and the other horses a thorough grooming and check their water."

"You just miss Slowpoke."

"Of course." Beltur grinned.

The two walked from the square toward the stable.

XCII

When Beltur and Jessyla rode out of the stables at the River Inn on five-day, the early morning was hazy, cool enough that Beltur wore his coat and gloves, but not his scarf, and he had left the coat open.

He couldn't say he was unhappy to leave Corumtal, but all he said to Jhotyl as they rode past the shops was, "The town seems like it's seen better days."

"Every time I come here, it's a little more run-down."

"Do you come here every year?"

"No . . . more like every other year." Jhotyl frowned and leaned forward in the saddle. "There are guards up ahead. They'll likely stop us."

"Why? What are they looking for?"

"Whatever they can find that traders aren't supposed to have, or don't have the papers for."

"What goods do you need papers for?"

"Weapons, mostly. Camma bark, though camma trees don't grow here. It's too cold. Also, gold and silver bars."

Beltur had never heard of camma bark, and he had no idea why gold and silver bars required documents. "Not pelts?" he asked humorously.

"They're not required, but I did take the precaution of having the Certan tariff inspectors seal a paper saying that the pelts came from Axalt."

"And not from Gallos?" asked Jessyla.

"With the troubles between Certis and Gallos, I thought that wise."

Beltur looked ahead, where, just beyond the last cot, several guards in brown-and-green uniforms stood on the side of the road away from the river. In front of them was a single uniformed guard with a single slashed stripe on each shoulder of his tunic. Since Beltur didn't see collar insignia, and since there were less than a half score of guards, he thought the mounted man had to be a squad leader.

When Beltur reached a point less than ten yards from the squad leader, the man called out, "Halt the wagons!"

Beltur, Jhotyl, and Jessyla reined up.

"You!" snapped the squad leader at Beltur. "Are you in charge?"

"No, Squad Leader. Trader Jhotyl is." Beltur shifted his weight in the saddle as he inclined his head toward the trader, as well as letting his coat open more to show his blacks.

"Mage," the squad leader's voice became more pleasant, "might I ask what you are doing here, rather than being in Jellico?"

"I'm accompanying Trader Jhotyl," replied Beltur pleasantly.

With a puzzled look, the squad leader turned to Jhotyl. "Is that correct?"

"It is, Squad Leader."

"What do you have in those wagons?"

"Ermine pelts." Jhotyl took a leather case from his saddlebags, then eased his mount slowly forward, just enough that he could hand the case to the squad leader. "The Viscount's marque, and the necessary papers."

The squad leader took some time to read the papers, most likely because his reading skills left something to be desired, Beltur suspected. Finally, the squad leader replaced the papers in the case and addressed Jhotyl. "Where are you headed?"

"To Jellico. We would have taken a flatboat to Rytel, but the river's too low."

"The pelts . . . whose are those?"

"They are for coats for the Viscount and his family."

The squad leader nodded. He looked back at Beltur, then studied Slowpoke. "That's a big gelding, more like a warhorse. Just where did you get him, Mage?"

"He is a warhorse," replied Beltur. "He's been with me ever since I was an undercaptain. That was before I came to accompany the trader."

"You're an arms-mage?"

"When necessary. As a black, I'd prefer not to be."

"Might I ask . . . ah, where?"

"Against the Gallosians."

"I see."

The squad leader doubtless did, but what he saw was what Beltur implied, not the entire truth. His eyes went to Jessyla, belatedly seeing the healer greens. After a long moment, he extended the leather case and handed it back to Jhotyl. "Thank you, Mage, Trader, Healer. I wish you safe travels. I doubt you will have trouble."

"And we wish you success in your patrols," returned Jhotyl.

The squad leader guided his mount off the road, watching as the riders and wagons passed. Beltur could sense the squad leader's puzzlement for some distance.

Once they were a good kay farther east on the river road, Jhotyl looked to Beltur. "Your presence made that encounter . . . less difficult than it might have been."

"I understand that mages not under the . . . auspices . . . of the Viscount would likely be regarded with some suspicion."

Jhotyl laughed. "That squad leader is still suspicious, but he'll never dare to ask. He'll just report and hope a superior officer will explain."

Beltur nodded. "Something like that was my hope."

"Mage . . . I thought . . . blacks had . . . some difficulty in . . . avoiding the truth."

"They do," replied Beltur. "That's why everything I told the squad leader was true."

The trader shook his head. "I foresee interesting times for you."

So did Beltur. He just hoped they wouldn't be too interesting.

XCIII

The next five days were long, tiring, and uneventful, except for a hailstorm that swept over the party on sevenday afternoon, which, as the hail melted, left the road ahead muddy, but not impassable, for almost four kays, just about to the point where the Corum River met the River Estal, and since the Estal was larger, that was the name of the river that led the rest of the way to Rytel.

While mornings were chilly, by midday Beltur shed his coat, but kept wearing his gloves. When there seemed to be no other travelers near, Beltur took time with both Taelya and Jessyla, giving them exercises, starting Jessyla on containments as her shields strengthened.

Just before noon on threeday, as the travelers rode past small steads set back from the river, much higher with the greater flow from the Estal, Jhotyl gestured ahead. "Once we're around that curve past that orchard, you'll be able to see Rytel."

"How big is Rytel?" asked Jessyla.

"Larger than Axalt and smaller than Elparta. Considerably smaller than Jellico."

When they rode past the orchard, Beltur saw that the trees showed a hint of green, as if the leaves were just starting to break from their buds.

They looked like apple trees, but he hadn't seen an apple tree not in full leaf before. "Are there many apple orchards here?"

"Some, I think. I'm not much on trees." Jhotyl gestured ahead.

All Beltur saw ahead was a welter of cots, many little more than huts, crowding the right side of the river road. Half a kay farther along was a low pier that extended possibly ten yards into the river. Beyond the ramshackle pier, an earthen wall began, and after another hundred yards the road merged with the top of the river wall. The cots from there on were several yards lower than the river wall. A narrow lane ran along the land side of the base of the wall.

"Does the Estal flood often?" asked Beltur.

"It never floods," replied Jhotyl. "The Jellicor floods often. When it does, some of the floodwaters back up into the Estal."

Looking ahead, Beltur squinted. It seemed as though the road ahead was higher. He looked back over his shoulder, then forward again. After they had ridden for another quint, Beltur looked back once more. They were higher, but the road and river wall seemed level, and the ground to the right of the road was higher as well, so that the road was only about a yard higher than the accompanying lane. The cots had given way to wooden houses, and farther to the south, Beltur saw low forested hills.

"The Estal meets the River Jellicor another kay to the northeast," declared Jhotyl. "We won't be riding nearly that far. We'll take the South Market Boulevard east to the factorage."

"Factorage?"

"I have an arrangement with a factor—Greshym. I stay with him in Rytel, and he stays with me when he travels to Jellico. Neither of us travels that much, and it suits us both."

"Since we're not accompanying you to Jellico, where would you suggest we stay in Rytel?" asked Beltur.

"If you don't mind cramped quarters, you can stay in the stable rooms at Greshym's."

"Ah . . . what will he say about that?"

"Nothing. You're part of my party until we go our separate ways." Jhotyl offered an amused smile. "Greshym used to trade in horses. Now he trades more in wagons and whatever may happen to be in them. He changed some of the stable into lodgings and locked spaces for other traders and factors who visit Rytel. Those he does not know well pay a modest sum for the safety of their wagons. Others trade accommodations and security with him."

"You're one of the others?"

"Of course. A secure haven in Jellico is costly otherwise, and that I can provide."

Beltur nodded, as much to himself as to Jhotyl, who, it was becoming most clear, was far more than a mere fur trader. But what exactly was another question.

Off to the right, less than half a kay away, a yellow brick wall some three yards high surrounded other buildings, and squat square towers on each side of a gate suggested a much larger post for the Viscount's Guard.

"Another guard post?" asked Beltur.

"Indeed. Two companies of the Viscount's guards are posted here, but a company is always patrolling the River Jellicor road. That's why there are seldom brigands there."

"What about the road to Montgren?"

"There are some brigands near the hills that separate Montgren and Certis, but they prey on those who cannot defend themselves. The pickings are too slim to support large numbers of brigands. I would doubt you will have that sort of trouble, not from what I have seen." Jhotyl pointed beyond the post. "After the Guards' Bowl public room is the South Market Boulevard. It's not far from there."

Even after what Jhotyl had said, Beltur was surprised when they reined up inside a compound the size of a small square surrounded by a red brick wall two and a half yards high, and with solid iron-bound gates. At the rear was a house roughly the size of Johlana's, except it was wider and only had two stories, but a large covered entry. Unlike the three other long buildings, one of which was clearly the stable, all of which were constructed of the same red brick as the wall, the dwelling was built of what looked to be limestone blocks and had large glazed windows.

More than a glass passed before Beltur and Jessyla had taken care of the horses, the mule, and carried their personal gear from the stable to the long barracks building, where they stood with Lhadoraak, Tulya, Taelya, and Jhotyl.

"These two rooms are yours," said Jhotyl, handing two keys to Beltur. "There's a washroom for clothes three doors down, and a pump there for wash water for your rooms."

His eyes went to Beltur. "Greshym has invited you and your consort to dine with us." Jhotyl looked to Lhadoraak. "You and your family are welcome to eat in the small public room with Paastar and the others." The fur trader grinned. "You won't find anything that good elsewhere . . . and it's far cheaper."

Lhadoraak raised his eyebrows, then said, with a smile, "When a trader says I won't find anything better and less dear . . ."

Jhotyl laughed. "Greshym charges everyone the same. One copper for a meal, and that includes one ale or lager. Every ale after the first costs four coppers. He found that tariffing teamsters and factors less for ale . . . caused certain . . . damage."

Beltur could definitely see that. He didn't like excluding Lhadoraak, not that he had a choice. At the same time, he also didn't want to offend Greshym, who was providing safe lodging without requiring payment.

"Go and enjoy yourselves," murmured Lhadoraak.

Tulya nodded as well.

"That's most gracious," said Beltur.

"As much self-interest as grace, I think," said the trader. "He expects us at fifth glass."

"Thank you . . . and Greshym."

"At fifth glass, then," said Jhotyl, turning and striding across the brick-paved courtyard toward the large house.

When Beltur and Jessyla entered their room, he could see that it was not large, but neither was it small, four yards square. It held a bed for two, a bench at the foot of the bed, a wash table with a pitcher and two basins, wall pegs for clothes, a side table, a stool, and a chamber pot. There was one window with inside shutters. The bed had a brown quilt, with the only design being a large "G" in a lighter rust brown, over a blanket.

"Can we afford the price of this free lodging?" asked Jessyla wryly.

"We'll find out at dinner," replied Beltur.

"We need to make ourselves presentable . . . and you do need to shave. You only look shabby, not dashing, with that stubble."

"I know. I know."

"And wear the mage-healer tunic. It's the cleanest, anyway."

"You think so?"

"You look more distinguished."

Beltur doubted anyone his age looked distinguished, but he nodded anyway.

"Should I show the patrol medallion?" Beltur had worn it under his outer tunic since leaving Axalt.

Jessyla shook her head. "Not here, I think."

More than a glass and several quints later, when Beltur and Jessyla reached the entry of the large house, where a tall doorman in dark green livery stood, Jhotyl stepped out to meet them, wearing a fine gray tunic that Beltur hadn't seen before. Beltur was glad to have taken Jessyla's advice about wearing his mage-healer tunic.

"I thought it best to meet you here and escort you in."

In moments, the trader guided them across the polished white limestone floor of the entry hallway into a small parlor, whose limestone tiles were largely covered by a green and rust carpet. The wall hangings flanking the windows were dark green trimmed in a light brown. The mantel and fireplace were of limestone, and a low fire burned there.

The man who rose from the armchair wore a cream dress tunic under a dark brown jacket that matched his trousers and even his polished boots. Greshym was almost a head shorter than Jhotyl, with jet black hair, and black eyes that seemed to bore into Beltur. "Mage Beltur, Healer Jessyla, thank you for accepting my invitation. After the few words that Jhotyl has spoken about you, I did so wish to make your acquaintance." He gestured to the settee and the armchairs, arranged in a semicircle facing the fireplace. "I thought we might enjoy a drink before dinner." His eyes went to Beltur. "I understand you prefer pale ale." Then he looked to Jessyla. "Your preferences vary more, I hear."

"If you have a smooth dark lager, I'd like that."

"My preference as well." Greshym nodded to the young man in dark green livery, who had stood silently in the corner, and who immediately left the parlor.

After the four had seated themselves, Beltur and Jessyla on the settee, with Beltur nearest to Greshym, their host went on, "Jhotyl has told me of your prowess in vanquishing brigands."

"I'm sure he was too kind," demurred Beltur.

"He's never kind that way. His judgment is excellent, I've found. It's too bad that you can't stay in Certis, but that wouldn't be for the best. Not for anyone." Greshym smiled, almost regretfully. "I understand you are headed to Montgren."

"We are," replied Beltur. "We've heard it might be amenable to black and white mages."

"Montgren is amenable to most anyone who follows the laws and doesn't mind a plethora of sheep. The Duchess, I understand, values productivity and honesty over any form of blind belief. That is both a virtue and a weakness, I fear."

"Why do you say that?" asked Jessyla pleasantly.

"I may be mistaken, but those who believe blindly usually try to press their beliefs on others. Of course, they insist that what they believe is only the truth, and who could possibly object to supporting the truth, with force, if necessary. Those who do not value such 'truth' as highly are inclined to dismiss those who do until they are facing lances, blades, or chaos fire. By then, they are usually at a disadvantage. But . . . I really am being far too pedantic." He smiled again as the server returned with a tray, presenting a beaker of dark lager to Jessyla first, then one of a faintly golden ale to Beltur, and more dark lager to both Jhotyl and Greshym.

Jessyla sipped the lager, then said, "While I've not tasted that many lagers, this is the best I've ever had."

"I'd be surprised if it weren't at least among the best," added Jhotyl.

"The pale ale is also excellent." Beltur paused, then took the bit in his teeth. *Better now than later.* "You've been incredibly kind and welcoming—"

"And you're wondering why, and what I would like in return." Greshym nodded. "I do prefer polite directness. It's much easier and more refreshing. I would like several things, all dealing with what you know. Knowledge, I've found, is far more valuable and enduring than most other objects people value." He chuckled humorously. "It also makes the acquisition of objects, as well as golds and silvers, far less costly in the long run."

"What would you like to know that you think I can provide?" Beltur took another swallow of ale, savoring it.

"What do you think of the traders of Spidlar and their Council, and why do you think that?"

Beltur thought for a moment. "They think too much in terms of how many golds or silvers they can obtain at the lowest possible cost."

"Doesn't every merchant or trader?"

"That's true, but . . . well . . . when you want to control things to the point of driving people who are producing things . . . I can't talk around it. I worked with a smith to produce cupridium. We did moderately well, enough that I could pay off debts I owed to those who hosted me when I had to flee Gallos. Then the Council passed a proclamation declaring that we could not sell what we produced ourselves, and that what we produced had to be sold through a trader, at whatever price he would pay. We left Spidlar."

"I see what you mean." Greshym looked to Jhotyl, then back to Beltur. "Why did you leave Axalt?"

"The Axalt Council decided that our producing cupridium in Axalt was . . . I guess I'd say . . . too disruptive for Axalt to handle. The smith has family there. I didn't. He stayed. We left. Also, Jessyla is a healer, and they pay healers less in Axalt than in Spidlar."

"Jhotyl tells me you're a healer as well. Isn't that what the green bands mean?"

"That's correct. I'm not as far along in healing as in magery, though."

"In some things," corrected Jessyla. "In others, he can do more than most healers. He can find tiny bits of wound chaos before others can."

"I'm curious about another matter. You were an arms-mage when the Prefect attacked Elparta, I understand."

"I was."

"The Prefect has many white mages, and Spidlar none, but Spidlar prevailed. How did that happen?"

"It wasn't just arms-mages. I was with a recon company, and it looked to me that the armsmen in Spidlar were better trained. They were also fighting to survive. The black mages in Spidlar had solid shields against chaos fire, and when the chaos bolts weren't effective because of those shields, it looked to me that the Gallosians lost heart when they took casualties."

"Interesting. I would have thought it would work the other way."

Beltur shook his head. "A weak chaos mage will likely always best a weak ordermage. But a truly strong black can withstand several strong whites, that is, if he's careful. The blacks of Spidlar were careful."

"That is very interesting." Greshym turned to Jhotyl. "Don't you think so?"

"I do."

"Do you think either Certis or Spidlar or Gallos could conquer Axalt?"

"Why would they want to?" asked Beltur. "The border walls are the highest and thickest and strongest I've ever seen. The winters are brutal, and there's nothing of value there except the skills of the people. Any conquest would destroy those. The fact that Axalt doesn't belong to any of the other three lands is what makes it useful." He looked at Greshym. "But you likely know that already."

Greshym laughed. "Of course, but I wanted to know if you did." He looked to Jessyla. "You're young, attractive, and clearly skilled as a healer. Why did you consort Beltur, rather than an older, more powerful mage? Besides for love, that is?"

"Besides love?" Jessyla smiled. "Because he cared for me, because he valued me. And because he was able to protect me . . . and teach me."

"Those are good answers. Very good answers." Greshym stood. "I do believe it's time to dine. At table, in return, I will tell you what you may not know about Certis."

The dining room was not excessively large, with a dark wooden table that could have seated twelve comfortably. The wood of the chairs, as well as the sideboards, matched that of the table. The green tapers of a single branched silver candelabrum in the middle of the table provided the only illumination besides the fading light of twilight coming through the high windows on the east side of the room.

As Greshym seated himself at the head of the table, gesturing for Beltur to sit at his left, Jhotyl his right, and Jessyla beside Beltur, he said, "I would have made preparations for a less modest meal, had I known I was to have company. Would anyone prefer a change of beverage from your customary? I can offer good white or red wine as well as ale or lager. Dinner will be what I call beef Viscount. I prefer red wine with beef."

"As do I," said Jhotyl.

"I'll try the red wine," offered Jessyla.

"I'll stick with the excellent pale ale," declared Beltur.

"That would have been my second choice, I admit." Greshym waited until the server had filled the three goblets and one beaker, then lifted his goblet. "To friendship, despite the perils we all face."

"To friendship."

"Why do you call what we will be served beef Viscount?" asked Jessyla.

"Because it's not quite what it seems, like the Viscount, although I wouldn't tell him that. But then, he has a sense of humor and would appreciate any good dish named after him, unlike a ruler such as the Prefect of Gallos, who, I understand, has no sense of humor at all. His idea of a jest is more like an execution."

"I've thought most rulers don't like jests at their expense," said Beltur. "Or am I mistaken?"

"It depends on who bears the expense," replied Jhotyl dryly. "That's why the Prefect of Gallos found it amusing that Saryn of the black blades conquered the rather boorish lords of Lornth, but a great deal less humorous when she and Ryba destroyed his entire army."

"And what of the Viscount?" asked Jessyla, a glint in her eye.

"From what I know," replied Greshym, "he laughs at small pranks played on him by his family, smiles at wordplay that does not always flatter him, and accepts certain playful behaviors by those of wealth and power.

He still punishes those whose acts or pranks seek to undermine his authority."

"At times," added Jhotyl, "he even has forgiven a first offense."

At that moment, the server, the same man who had brought drinks both in the parlor and earlier in the dining room, began to present each diner with a platter on which was a circular golden brown pastry, from the corners of which seeped a brown sauce. Each diner also received a small loaf of soft dark bread. The platters, however, were of a cream-colored porcelain, with a dark green rim, as were the smaller plates that held each loaf of bread.

Once the server retired to the corner of the dining room, Greshym said, "Beef Viscount isn't as elegant a dish as one might find in Jellico, but I have a weakness for it. I find I prefer taste to elegance, especially in what I eat. See what you think." With that, he cut into his pastry.

Beltur followed his host's example, cutting through the browned pastry crust, and then took a small sampling of what lay beneath—a brown sauce covering thin strips of beef, along with chunks of potato, and two other vegetables he did not recognize, one slightly slippery, if buttery, and the other with almost no taste, except a tinge of bitterness that somehow just offset the richness of the sauce enough that the result was pleasantly piquant. He took another mouthful . . . and another.

The brown bread was slightly sweet. *Molasses bread.* And the molasses had come from somewhere else. Northern Certis was too cold.

"I see you like the beef Viscount," said Greshym.

"I do," said Beltur. "I didn't recognize the vegetables."

"Most people don't, for different reasons. The ones that taste buttery are mushrooms—"

Beltur stiffened. Had he been wrong to trust Greshym? "Mushrooms? Aren't they poisonous?"

"Some are. Most aren't." Greshym smiled. "I have a small cellar where I raise the safe kind."

Beltur could sense the truth of that, but he still couldn't help worrying. "And the other vegetable?"

"Oh, that's quilla, cut into chunks. The cooks soak it in watered wine for a time. That takes out the bitterness, all but a touch. Now . . . I did promise to tell you about Certis while we finish dinner. If you were to travel the river road south to Jellico with Jhotyl, you would see that in most places the river walls are high. Those walls were built by the grandsire of the Viscount . . ."

Near the end of dinner, after Beltur and Jessyla had each lingered over an almond honeycake, Greshym said, casually, "You should stay another day before you start your trek to Vergren."

"That wouldn't be a problem?" asked Beltur.

"Stars, no. You did a favor to all of us by dealing with those brigands. We're not crowded, and you need a day of rest. So do your horses. The grazing on the way will be slender. Please feel free to pack as much hay as you can carry."

"Thank you." Beltur didn't like being indebted, even for information, but he wasn't about to turn down such an offer. He also knew that they couldn't carry that much hay, perhaps enough for two days, if that. "Are there places to buy hay and grain?"

"At this time of year, those who have it will be glad to sell," said Greshym.

Beltur had almost forgotten that he wanted to bring up one other matter. "About the brigands . . . most of those in the second attack were wearing old uniform tunics that looked like uniforms of the Viscount's guards."

"I heard. Jhotyl provided me with one."

Beltur looked askance at the purported fur trader.

"Mheltyn ran back and stripped one off one of the dead."

"It might prove useful to all of us," added Greshym. "Now . . . I do have some fine brandy. And let me tell you what I know about the road to Vergren . . ."

Beltur understood that what remained of the evening would deal with their coming travel and pleasantries.

XCIV

Both Beltur and Jessyla were glad to be able to sleep later on eightday, later being seventh glass, and they spent the morning washing clothes, grooming horses, and cleaning tack. After that, Beltur spent more than a glass working with both Taelya and Jessyla on magery, and in the case of Jessyla, with learning and holding containments, in addition to her shields. The later afternoon was spent in more pleasurable activities.

They did not receive another invitation to dinner, not that Beltur expected such, but the meals in the small public room were better than in most of the inns they had visited . . . and far less costly, as Jhotyl had pointed out. They also did not see Jhotyl, although they encountered all the others of the traders' party on and off, and late on eightday, another two wagons rolled in, accompanied by two riders.

Oneday morning, Beltur gathered the others together, making sure that the bundles of hay were securely fastened to the mule, and especially behind Taelya, since she was so much lighter than the other riders.

Beltur finished that and turned to go find Jhotyl. He'd been reluctant to press for his golds on sevenday night, and no one had known where Jhotyl was on eightday.

He needn't have worried, because the trader was standing outside the stable, as if he'd been waiting for Beltur. He immediately handed Beltur a small leather bag. "I would that I could pay you more, but I am not as wealthy as those who could. I trust you will find this sufficient. It is a little more than I promised."

"I'm curious," said Beltur. "You've gone out of your way to be more than fair. Might I ask why?"

"You might. It's because I'm looking out for myself. I do not know where you will end up. I daresay you don't either. But the odds are that you will do well and will find a position of power. In that position, you may be able to help me, at least in areas where our interests coincide. You have also gained me a young man who might become a good and loyal teamster."

Beltur noted the slight emphasis on the word "loyal." "He seems like he's appreciative of an opportunity not to continue in past endeavors."

"He also saw what you could do." Jhotyl offered a rueful look. "Also, if I may be honest, for similar reasons, I do not ever wish to be considered your enemy, even if your future interests and mine do not align themselves."

"I would not wish that, either."

"Good. Then, we are agreed. I wish you the fortune of the black angels and the guidance of the Rational Stars."

"The same to you, and may your journey to Jellico be most uneventful. I do have one last question."

"Oh?"

"The other night you mentioned there was a ferry to the other side of the river. What is the best way to get there?"

"That's something I can answer. Take the South Market Boulevard to the next wide avenue. It's not marked, but it's the one with a public house on the corner—the Green Pitcher. Turn left, and take it until it reaches the river. Then turn right. The ferry is no more than half a kay east."

"Thank you."

"You're more than welcome." Jhotyl offered a parting smile before turning and walking toward the warehouse where Faeltur was watching and listening closely as Mheltyn loaded one of the trader's wagons.

"*Who* is he?" asked Jessyla, as she edged out from the stable.

"Someone who is much more than he seems, and who has created friends and allies everywhere. Beyond that . . . in time, we may find out." *And I really don't want to be on the other side. It could be far too costly.* Beltur smiled ruefully. That was what Jhotyl had as much as said as well.

Because the bag felt heavier than it likely should, unless some of the golds were in the form of silvers, Beltur untied the leather thong holding the bag closed and gingerly poured out the coins, his mouth opening. Then he counted them and looked at Jessyla. "Four golds and ten silvers."

She nodded as if unsurprised. "It's only fair."

"I'm still surprised when someone I don't know that well treats me fairly."

"That should tell you something."

"I think it says more about Jhotyl than me." Beltur put the silvers in his belt wallet, and two golds in the notches in his belt, holding on to the other two. "I need to pay Lhadoraak his share."

Jessyla nodded and followed Beltur back into the stable to where Lhadoraak stood waiting by his mount.

"What did he want?"

"To pay us." Beltur extended the two golds. "Here's your share."

The blond mage's eyes widened. "That's what he promised for all of us."

"He decided we were worth more after we got rid of the second group of brigands."

"You didn't have to . . ."

"He gave us five."

"Then two is too much. You've paid—"

"Two is fair. Just make sure Tulya knows." Beltur grinned. "Are you all ready to leave? We need to head out."

He walked back to where he'd tied Slowpoke and stroked the big horse, getting a nuzzle in return. "You ready for more riding?" Then he led Slowpoke out to the courtyard, where he mounted and adjusted the visor cap to best shield his eyes.

Jhotyl's directions were easy to follow, and two quints later, Beltur led his party toward the ferry slip, following the gestures of a man standing at the end of the slip where the ferry would dock. He reined up in front of a wooden gate on the left side of a stout wooden fence.

The ferryman stood on the other side. "You're fortunate today. There won't be much of a wait. It's a copper a horse. You pay as you pass, once we've offloaded. Keep your mounts behind the fence railing there. When the ferry comes in, they'll be offloading steers, and you don't want to get in the way."

"Offloading steers?" said Tulya.

The ferryman grinned. "Where do you think the beef comes from?"

While that response didn't exactly answer the question, the ferryman turned to watch the river and the large capstan from which a heavy cable ran.

Beltur looked to the far side, where, after a time, a large green banner rose to the top of a pole.

"Boat's ready!" called the ferryman.

Beltur looked down to see that two oxen were yoked to capstan bars on the lower level, and they began to move, turning the capstan. Slowly the rectangular ferry moved through the water toward the west shore. As it drew nearer, Beltur made out the forms of ten black steers, behind the solid hull planks of the ferry.

When the ferry reached the slip, the entire pier and slip shuddered. Then the two ferry hands threw lines around bollards, and seemingly in moments, two drovers guided the steers into a chute that led to a sturdy-looking corral, presumably a holding pen.

Shortly the ferryman opened the gate. Beltur handed over seven coppers.

"No more than two mounts side by side!" The deckhand looked at Beltur and added, "Ser, move him forward to the bar."

"Healer, a little more outboard. That way."

Again, before long, the ferry was moving across the river, swaying in a motion that was part up and down and seemingly side to side.

The deckhand closest to Beltur kept looking at him, then finally said, "Mage, not wanting to pry, ser, but where might you be headed?"

"East," Beltur replied. "There's something we need to do there." That wasn't exactly true, but Beltur didn't want the deckhands spreading exactly where they were headed, although he couldn't have said precisely why, just that if somehow the Viscount's Guard did inquire, he didn't want them to find out more than anyone could have seen.

The ferry soon docked on the eastern shore, again with the thudding shudder.

As they led their mounts off the ferry, Beltur glanced around. Outside of several largely dilapidated piers, two buildings that looked like warehouses, and a row of shops—and almost a score of corrals, some with sheep, but most with steers—all he could see were small cots, and a few larger houses, none of which looked to be more than half a kay from the ferry slip.

Ahead of them was a road leading eastward roughly through the middle of the village.

Although the road was graveled and smoothed, Beltur couldn't help but worry how far they could travel before it turned into a rutted track.

He urged Slowpoke forward.

XCV

Five days later, as the sun burned off the late-morning spring mist, Beltur and his party were still in Certis, but riding across rolling plains toward hills that seemed to recede with each step that Slowpoke took. They'd passed a handful of traders heading west, most with two or three wagons, presumably with enough men to discourage small groups of brigands, but had not overtaken anyone heading east, except near hamlets.

There had been grass that had sprouted in sheltered places, allowing some grazing, and they'd been able to buy some hay along the way, but Beltur worried that the horses weren't getting enough to eat, and he'd insisted on more stops wherever he saw grass that looked good. Slowpoke seemed perfectly willing to feed on most grasses, and that also bothered Beltur, because he doubted he knew which were best, but the fact that there were grasses the gelding didn't like reassured him a little.

By the time the sun had neared its zenith, the hills had stopped retreating and were beginning to grow larger. Then Beltur saw a keystone, half buried in the withered grass of the past year, with the barely discernible inscription BORTAAN 5K.

"According to the people in the hamlet we left this morning, that's the last town in Certis, isn't it?" said Jessyla. "They weren't as friendly as they might have been. But everyone seems wary of mages and the Viscount's guards."

"Except we haven't seen any, except for dispatch riders. The last one circled around us, as if we carried the green flux." That also bothered Beltur, because the longer they'd been in Certis, the clearer it was that mages were kept under very tight control by the Viscount. That suggested that, like the Prefect of Gallos, the Viscount had a group of very strong mages at his command. While it was unlikely that any would show up on the road from Rytel to Bortaan, it still concerned him. "I think the people are more uncertain about us, because we're not supposed to be here, and they don't know what that means. I'm more worried about the border post ahead."

"No one mentioned a border post."

"This is a trade road. It's not a busy one, but it does go to Montgren. I can't imagine that there isn't a post with tariff inspectors there, at least on the Certan side. If there's not, I'll be relieved, but I wouldn't wager on it."

"Neither would I," said Lhadoraak from where he rode behind them. "What do you have in mind if they give us some difficulty?"

"First, we need to see if they have any mages here and how many arms-men or guards. After that, we'll decide."

Almost a glass passed before the group came over the top of a gentle rise and saw a small town set on a flat that extended almost to the bases of two rugged hills that showed frequent rocky outcrops, and occasional steep but short cliffs. Beltur reined up and gestured for the others to join him as he studied Bortaan. The road ran straight to the town, bisecting it almost evenly, and there was a wall on the far side of all the buildings that extended almost a kay on each side of the road, seeming to turn right into the steep inclines and ending there. A larger brick building stood between the wall and the other buildings in the town, and Beltur thought he could make out a gap in the wall where the road seemed to go through it.

As the others moved their mounts closer to Beltur and reined up, he said, "Take a look and tell me what you think."

After several moments, Tulya said, "That wall is like the walls on each side of Axalt, except smaller."

"There's a fort there," added Lhadoraak. "That means armsmen and tariff inspectors."

"Couldn't people just walk around the wall?" asked Taelya.

"I was just thinking that, dear," said Tulya.

"They could," said Beltur, "but people aren't the reason for the wall. Those hills look pretty rugged. People and horses could get around the wall, but I don't think wagons could. Even for people, it doesn't look easy. The wall's to make sure it's hard for traders to avoid paying tariffs. I'm not sure they care that much about travelers who aren't armsmen or traders."

"They might care about mages," said Jessyla dryly.

Beltur looked over his party. "Any other thoughts?"

"What do *you* think?" asked Lhadoraak.

"I'd like to get out of Certis as soon as possible. When we get into the town, we should stop at the square or wherever we can to water the horses and give them a little rest. While we're doing that, I should be able to tell if there are any mages there. If there aren't, I think we should just ride up to the gate as if we were what we are, travelers on our way to Montgren."

"What if they try to stop us?" asked Tulya.

"I don't think it will come to that, but if it looks like trouble, we just agree to turn around, and we ride away and then use a concealment and make our way around Bortaan." For Beltur, that was very much the last resort. He *really* didn't want to blunder through rocky hills in a land he didn't know. On the other hand, he also really didn't want to have to use magery against the Viscount's Guard, not unless he had to. It somehow seemed wrong to use order/chaos force against the lawful authority of a land that hadn't done anything against him or those in his party. *Unless they try to detain us simply because we're mages.*

Beltur waited for any of the others to speak. When no one did, he smiled. "We might as well find a fountain or somewhere to water the horses." Then he patted Slowpoke on the shoulder and urged the gelding forward.

There was what passed for a market square, close to the middle of Bortaan, and on the main road, which was scarcely surprising. It had a fountain, and only a handful of vendors were present, including only one gray-haired woman apparently looking at a bushel of some root vegetables.

Even before dismounting, Beltur used his senses to check to see if there was chaos in the water, but there wasn't any in the water itself, although there were traces in the basin beneath. "We'll use the bucket to water the horses," he said as he dismounted.

None of those in the square gave more than half a glance to the travelers until Beltur had finished watering Slowpoke, Jessyla's mount, and the mule and spare mount and turned the bucket over to Lhadoraak. Then a woman at a nearby cart looked up. Beltur could tell that she was studying him, then Jessyla, and finally Lhadoraak. After several moments, the woman walked to the older man at the next cart and spoke several words to him.

Beltur watched as word passed among the vendors, and he could sense an increase in the natural chaos surrounding the vendors, although none of them moved from the square. That prompted him to use his senses to search for any concentration of order or chaos that might indicate a white or black mage nearby, but the only concentrations were those around him.

When Lhadoraak returned with the bucket, Beltur said, "I can't sense any whites or blacks, but the people here in the square are uncomfortable with our presence."

"I had that feeling," interjected Jessyla.

Lhadoraak nodded, then asked, "Do you still want to continue on?"

"More than ever. If the people here are uncomfortable, there's a reason for it, and I'd just as soon be out of Certis, without having to force our way out, before that reason shows up."

"You're in command," said the blond mage.

Beltur managed not to wince. That was as close as Lhadoraak would come to saying he was uncomfortable. But then, Lhadoraak had never been happy about conflict, at best being reluctantly resigned to it when absolutely necessary. That observation brought home to Beltur that he was becoming far less resigned to using magery. *Is that really a good attitude?* All he said was, "We'll just mount up and ride to the wall gate. It's less than a kay."

Lhadoraak nodded once more and walked back to where Tulya held their horses. "We need to mount up. Beltur thinks he can get us out of Certis without forcing our way."

That was Beltur's hope. He'd have to see how well he would do at it. He mounted Slowpoke, then eased the big gelding across the square, politely inclining his head to the one vendor whom he passed only a few yards away.

Her eyes widened.

Beltur studied the buildings on the main street that the road had become as Slowpoke carried him toward the wall, a direction that was more south-east than due east. He passed a chandlery that seemed tiny, little more than five yards wide, and then a potter's shop across from what looked to be a weaver's, beyond which was a larger structure that clearly held a blacksmith.

In what seemed moments, but what was actually more than a quint, Beltur found himself riding past the reddish-brown brick wall that surrounded the guard post and then across a space of about fifty yards to where the road passed through the wall.

Two of the Viscount's Guard stood before the open gate in the wall, a space wide enough for two wagons. The wall itself was of a brownish brick and little more than two yards high, just high enough and thick enough to block wagons and carts and anyone in a hurry. The shorter guard stepped forward, while the taller one took one look at Beltur and Lhadoraak and headed for the small building to the right.

Going for a squad leader or undercaptain, no doubt. Beltur glanced at the gate, still open. In fact, it didn't appear to have been closed in years, but that could easily be deceiving.

Still . . . he could throw a shield around his party and just have everyone ride through, blocking the gate with a containment, if necessary. He hoped it wouldn't be.

"Ser mage . . . if you would wait but a moment . . ." The guard's voice was strained.

Beltur didn't blame the young man. "Of course."

It took more than a few moments before the taller guard returned, followed by an older man with single silver bars on his collar, which would have meant an undercaptain in Spidlar. The undercaptain's face was narrow and lined, and Beltur suspected the officer was a good fifteen years older than Beltur, and likely had come up through the ranks.

The officer frowned as his eyes focused on Beltur's visor cap, with its Elpartan City Patrol insignia above the brim, as if he struggled to make sense of the apparently unfamiliar device. "Ser, we received no word that mages would be coming this way." His eyes went to Jessyla and her greens. "And not about healers, either." He paused and added, looking particularly to Taelya, "Or others."

"What you have heard or not heard," Beltur said firmly, keeping his voice level and pleasant, "is not my concern, Undercaptain. We have been sent to Vergren. Why is not your concern, just as what you have heard or not heard is not mine."

Beltur could sense the consternation his words raised in the older officer.

"This . . . it is not according to the standing orders of the Viscount, ah . . . ser. We should have been told . . ."

"That is, as I said, scarcely my concern." Beltur smiled coolly as he eased the large silver patrol medallion from under his tunic and let it and its solid silver links rest on his chest. "This should mean something to you, Undercaptain." He doubted that the officer had ever seen anything like it. He waited for a long moment. "Of course, if necessary . . ." Beltur let the words hang there.

The officer swallowed, finally saying, "No, ser. That . . . I mean, I would not wish to intrude upon your mission. Might I enter your name for my records?"

"Beltur. Captain. Black mage. Out of Jellico."

"Thank you, ser." The undercaptain stepped back.

Beltur inclined his head, urging Slowpoke forward, but also casting a narrow shield around his entire party, as he led the way through the gate, just in case one of the Guard decided on something rash. No one did.

Your time as an undercaptain came in very useful. Beltur did not smile and held the shield in place until they had ridden almost half a kay along the road between the gray rock outcroppings that began about a hundred yards from the wall.

Since Beltur didn't quite know what to say, he said nothing, not until they passed through the narrowest point between the rocky hills and he saw two brick posts flanking the road ahead, and behind the one on the left, a small brick building. Behind the posts the space between the hills widened somewhat, and Beltur thought he saw roofs farther eastward through the bare limbs of trees that showed some green but that had not fully leafed out. "I think I see the official entrance to Montgren ahead."

As he rode closer he saw a man standing behind the road post on the left, just in front of the small building. He also sensed what seemed like a shield, the kind he was working on with Taelya, but the shield wasn't anywhere near the posts.

The man wore a blue tunic and trousers with a blue visor cap that showed a brass insignia above the visor, and smiled as Beltur approached and then reined up. "Welcome to Montgren."

An expression of mild surprise followed as he looked from Beltur to Jessyla and then Lhadoraak.

"Two mages and a healer coming from Certis? That is a surprise."

Although Beltur knew very well why the border patroller was surprised, he said, "We came from Elparta by way of Axalt and then through Certis. It occasionally took a little persuasion. Are you a tariff inspector?"

"Hardly. The Duchess doesn't hold for border tariffs. We're just here to make sure the Viscount's men don't come into Montgren chasing after folks who want to leave Certis."

Beltur couldn't help wondering just how a few men could stop even a squad of the Viscount's Guard. "Just you?"

"Oh, not me. I just keep count of who and what comes and goes. Might I ask whatever names you choose to go by?"

Beltur smiled and said, "Beltur, black mage and healer; Jessyla, healer and apprentice mage; Lhadoraak, black mage, and his consort Tulya, and their daughter Taelya."

"Where might you be headed?"

"To Vergren."

"Not Lavah?"

"No." Beltur had no idea even where Lavah was. He was slightly disconcerted, because he sensed that the mage who held the shield was approaching, even before the mage stepped out of the small brick building and walked toward the first border keeper and the five riders.

The approaching mage wore a blue uniform tunic identical to that of the first patroller, with the exception of wide white bands at the end of his sleeves. His hair was blond, shot with silver, although he looked to be close to the same age as Lhadoraak. He studied the group without speaking for several moments. Then he inclined his head to Beltur and asked, "Did you get through the Certan border guards by concealment or force?"

"Neither. Subterfuge and the merest suggestion of force."

The white mage offered a smile Beltur could tell was forced. "Subterfuge? That seldom works."

"We rode up. We were challenged. I said we were on a mission to Montgren, and displayed this medallion. The undercaptain said he had no orders or notice. I told him that was no concern of mine. He reconsidered. Here we are."

"He was a very wise man. I hope he is wise enough not to report your passage." After a moment, the mage continued. "I've never sensed shields as strong as yours. The shields and your mount . . . and your bearing . . . suggest a certain . . . past."

"I was an arms-mage in Spidlar when the Prefect invaded. So was Lhadoraak."

"Are you looking for a similar position here?"

Beltur shook his head. "We did what was necessary. We're traveling to meet a friend in Vergren who suggested he might have prospects for us." Saying Vaenturl was a friend was a slight exaggeration, but the offer had been real enough.

"Oh?"

"He's a trader who often travels to Elparta. We traveled with him from Elparta to Axalt."

The mage nodded. "I wish you all well."

"Are there lodgings near? We've been on the road an eightday."

"There are two inns another three kays east. That's where the springs are. They both have rooms this time of year. I'd suggest the West End."

"Thank you."

The mage looked at Lhadoraak, Tulya, then Taelya.

Beltur could see him stiffen, and said, "Yes, she is . . . or will be once she learns more."

"She's very young, but . . . I've never . . ."

"I've been working with her."

"You're a black."

"I was raised as a white by a white. It's caused certain problems for me, but it made it easy for me to help her."

The mage shook his head. "I don't think I need to know. Just be aware that the Duchess doesn't much care for magery as a weapon except in self-defense."

"None of us has ever behaved otherwise." *Except in a war we didn't begin.*

The mage looked to the other border patroller.

"They gave names."

The mage gestured for them to continue.

Beltur urged Slowpoke forward, but he was ready to throw shields around everyone if the white mage showed the slightest hint of raising chaos. After another half kay, he began to relax.

"They were more friendly," said Jessyla. "I don't think they care much for the Certans."

"I'm not sure about that. They don't care much for the Viscount, but the mage is certainly aware that the Viscount's guards are following orders and even showed some sympathy for that undercaptain."

"I hope the West End is a good and comfortable inn."

So did Beltur.

XCVI

Sevenday morning, Beltur woke up in the darkness to what sounded like small hammers thudding against the walls of the West End inn. He bolted upright from the most comfortable bed he'd slept in since they'd left Rytel, then realized that the sound was that of rain, and the intensity meant that it had to be a northeaster.

"What's that?" asked Jessyla, lifting her head and looking toward Beltur, her voice heavy with sleep.

"Rain."

She turned to him. "It sounds like a northeaster. Did you sense that yesterday? Was that why you wanted to get out of Certis?"

Beltur leaned back, settling next to her, yawned, then shook his head. "I'd like to say I did. You know my magery doesn't run to that. I just felt that it would be better. I don't have a good feeling about Certis." He paused, then said, "That's not right. I don't have a good feeling about the Viscount."

"You scared Tulya yesterday," said Jessyla softly.

"I wasn't going to let anything happen to her or Taelya. She should know that. How many glasses have I spent, day after day, working with Taelya?"

"That wasn't what scared her."

"Oh?"

"What scared her was the person you became when you talked to that poor undercaptain. You frightened him to death. He was almost shivering with the fear that you were going to destroy him on the spot."

"If he could have, he would have kept us locked up until the Viscount's mages arrived to cart us off to serve the Viscount, using Tulya and Taelya as hostages for our 'cooperation.' What we saw in the short time we were in Certis—"

"It wasn't that short. It seemed like half a season."

"What we saw," repeated Beltur, "was just like what the Prefect is doing in Gallos."

"You don't know that. Not for certain."

Beltur sighed. "You're right. I don't know it for certain. But when almost a score of former guards turn into brigands, when villagers look at mages warily, when mages are under the thumb of the Viscount—"

"The Viscount's tariff inspectors let us into Certis without a word."

"Of course they did. Why wouldn't they? There was also the possibility that we might already be working for the Viscount. Especially since Jhotyl was under the Viscount's marque. Didn't you see how that squad leader in Corumtal reacted?"

"It might not be that bad."

"You're right. It might not be. But I'd just as soon not find out by staying in Certis. And I wouldn't want to find out by anything happening to you."

Jessyla did not reply, but just looked at Beltur through the gloom.

"Well . . . would you want anything like that to happen?"

"I love you when you get so serious and protective."

"You!!!"

Jessyla started to giggle.

Beltur offered an overly broad smile. "You know . . . with this rain, we're not going anywhere at all today."

"I know." Her arms went around his neck.

XCVII

The northeaster lasted well into evening on eightday, and Beltur had no desire to wade through muddy roads on oneday, especially since oneday dawned clear and bright, and a day of sunlight would dry the road and make it far more passable on twoday.

He even worked in a little more reading in *The Wisdom of Relyn,* coming across a passage that disturbed him for more than a few reasons, enough that he was still mulling it over on oneday evening when he finally dropped off to sleep.

> Once in my misguided youth I tried to gain a holding by killing the angels. What happened made me avoid all killing after that. I avoided it so much that it drew others after me, who thought I was weak, and they almost killed innocents. I could only stop that by killing those who followed me. What that revealed was that, sometimes, when you try to avoid something too much, you end up drawing it to you.

Beltur was still thinking that over on twoday morning when, after another hearty breakfast at the West End, and quite a few more silvers spent on lodging, food, and fodder, but with far more rested travelers and mounts, he led Slowpoke out of the inn's stable into a crisp and clear early morning, then mounted and guided the others southeast on the road to Vergren.

For the first ten kays or so the road wound through the rocky but heavily forested hills, then opened out onto a vista of rolling hills that seemed half covered in hardwoods that were not quite finished leafing out and regular sections of meadows and pastures. As the party continued riding through the late morning, it became apparent to Beltur that about one in four of the meadows held sheep, and there was always a sturdy cot or even a small house near the flocks, with a large walled garden. It also seemed to Beltur that either a not-quite-full-grown boy or girl tended the black-faced sheep, usually accompanied by one or two good-sized dogs that never barked or paid any attention to the riders even when Slowpoke was within ten or fifteen yards.

By midday, Beltur discovered something else—that the air, even though still moderately cool, was damp, and that he was sweating because of that dampness.

By the time they had ridden another three days through what seemed to be the same rolling hills, meadows, and forests, the land no longer seemed quite so idyllic to Beltur, for all the seemingly cheerful people they passed, often walking beside a cart, and by noon on fiveday, Beltur was getting worried. *Is all Montgren like this?* He had heard, more than once, that Montgren was all sheep, meadows, and forests, but no one had mentioned the continual dampness—cool dampness, warm dampness, and hot dampness. By comparison, Spidlar was dry, and much of Gallos a pleasant desert—and Beltur had never thought he would be remembering anything about Gallos favorably.

So when, shortly after first glass on fiveday, the road carried them around yet another hill and the land opened up into a wide valley with few trees, except a few woodlots, Beltur let out a deep sigh of relief.

"I've never heard so much sighing from you," said Jessyla. "It's been a pleasant ride, and the people here are much friendlier."

It's all the same, and it's warm and sticky, and we're only in early spring. Except, Beltur realized, that it was far closer to midspring, and he really didn't want to count the kays they'd traveled. He was also worrying about Slowpoke's shoes, which he'd reinforced with a little order, but before long the gelding, as well as most of the other horses, would need to be reshod.

Perhaps in Vergren.

XCVIII

After reaching the more open valley on fiveday, Beltur had hoped that Vergren would not be that far, but the valley was far longer than he had anticipated, with more wooded areas than he'd initially expected, and that night they ended up staying at an inn in the small town of Glenaar, no more than half a day's ride to Vergren, according to the innkeeper.

On sixday, the group set out, once more through a cool and misty morning that would likely turn into another warm and moist day that would leave Beltur sweating heavily by midafternoon. He kept thinking about Relyn's words, and wondered if Relyn had stayed in Axalt because it really had been the most hospitable place. *Except we really didn't have that choice.*

He rode quietly for almost a glass, looking at the meadows, and the few fields that had been recently tilled and planted, and others showing sprouts of green. But he had said very little, when Jessyla drew her mount closer to him and asked, "You're wondering if coming to Montgren is such a good idea, aren't you?"

"Is it that obvious?"

"Yes, if you're looking, but I'm the only one doing that." She waited.

Finally, he said, "It's not as though we've had that many choices. To stay in Elparta we would have had to fight both the Council and Caradyn and most of the blacks. We'd have had to fight the Axalt Council. I can't help worrying about what we'll find out in Vergren."

"We might not find out a thing. Vaenturl didn't promise anything. He only said we'd be welcome."

"That's a promise of sorts. Besides, we have to start somewhere." But Beltur hadn't yet seen any place in Montgren that looked as though it needed healers or anything else he and the others could do, and that worried him as well.

Another glass or so passed. The mist burned off, and the warm spring sun beat down on Beltur. Then, ahead, he saw a keystone. As he rode closer, he made out the crisp letters cut in the square gray oblong rising from the green grass at the side of the road: VERGREN—5K.

"The innkeeper was actually right."

"You're getting even more skeptical," returned Jessyla.

"Not more," he replied with a slightly forced smile. *More like hot and impatient.*

He turned in the saddle and announced, "Just another five kays to Vergren."

"What if you can't find Vaenturl?" asked Lhadoraak.

"We find an inn and start looking for other possibilities," Beltur said with a cheerfulness he didn't feel, knowing that Jessyla could sense what he felt . . . and didn't, but that Lhadoraak might not.

Beyond the keystone, the road widened slightly, and while it was not paved, it was definitely heavily metaled, the gravel forming a relatively smooth and firm surface, the apparent result of years of careful upkeep.

About a kay farther along, Beltur saw a well-kept small house beside an orchard that was not only leafed out but with a hint of white flowers. More important, an older man stood not far off the road, replacing stones in the wall that bounded the trees. The man looked up as Beltur approached and then reined up.

"Will this road take us to the main market square in Vergren?" asked Beltur. "Without turning off it?"

"Aye, and all the way to Weevett and beyond, even Haven or Lydiar," replied the white-haired man.

"Thank you."

"My pleasure, Mage."

Beltur had thought about asking about Essek's Factorage, but had decided against it. The last thing he wanted was Lhadoraak and Tulya worrying even before there was something to worry about. There would be plenty of time to worry if he couldn't find Vaenturl.

As he eased Slowpoke forward, he overheard Tulya saying to Taelya, "You see. The people here are friendly."

Unfortunately, as Beltur well knew, friendliness didn't necessarily mean that they'd be permanently welcome, and he definitely didn't like the idea of forcing people to accept them.

With each few hundred yards that they rode, it became more obvious that they were nearing a more populated area. The land around each dwelling dwindled until the houses were side by side and extended back in each direction farther than Beltur could see. Unlike the houses of Axalt, those in Vergren appeared to be constructed of brick and timber, the brick being a rusty color, with massive timbered supports. *But then, we've ridden past a lot of oaks.*

Before that long the larger houses gave way to smaller houses crowded together, and then to shops and crafters' buildings. Up ahead Beltur saw an open space—or one without any buildings—that just might be the main market square. As they drew closer, he saw a number of vendors and some people browsing or shopping, if not as many as he might have expected. The square was about twice the size of the one in Axalt and less than half the size of the main market square in Elparta. As Beltur looked around, he wondered, far from the first time, if there was even an Essek's Factorage . . . and if he could find it.

Except that was scarcely difficult. On the east side, facing westward onto the square, was a large two-story structure. There was a name on the front set in large black letters—ESSEK. That made Beltur feel even more uneasy. Anyone who'd ever been in the square could scarcely have forgotten that name.

"There's the factorage!" said Jessyla.

"I see it. Anyone in the city would know that name."

"He didn't show chaos when he said it," Jessyla observed.

Beltur guided Slowpoke around the edge of the square, then reined up, dismounted, and handed Slowpoke's reins to Jessyla. "I don't even know if he'll be here."

She smiled encouragingly. "He wasn't lying. I could have told."

For all that, Beltur was still uncomfortable as he walked into the factorage. A great deal could have happened over the course of winter and early spring.

"Can I help you, ser?" asked a young man, stiffening slightly as he saw the blacks.

"You might be able to. I'm looking for a trader named Vaenturl. He said to ask for him here."

The youth looked surprised. After a moment, he said, "You'd best talk to my father, ser mage."

The factorage was even warmer than the square, and Beltur blotted his forehead as he followed the young man to the counter at the back.

"If you'd wait here, ser . . ." The youth turned away quickly, as if he might have offended Beltur in some fashion.

As he stood there, Beltur glanced around the space, twice as large as Barrynt's factorage, and with bolt after bolt of cloth in neat racks on one side, and with assortments of rope, twine, even what looked to be cables on the other.

"Ser . . ."

Beltur turned to see a man with a polite and warm smile, and receding sandy hair.

"My son said you had a question. Rather, that you were seeking someone. I'm Essek the younger. The factorage was named for my grandsire."

"I'm Beltur, and I've come from Axalt. Most recently, that is. I'm looking for a man who gave his name as Vaenturl."

Essek nodded. "Can you tell me more about this?"

"We traveled together from Elparta to Axalt in the last days of fall and the first day of winter. He told us that if we ever came to Vergren to ask for him at Essek's Factorage. I hadn't thought we'd be here any time soon, but certain matters . . . didn't turn out as we had hoped."

"Who might 'we' be, if I might ask?"

Beltur was getting the definite feeling that matters were not at all as he'd anticipated, but there was certainly no secret to the fact that Jessyla was with him. "My consort, Jessyla. She's a healer."

Abruptly, Essek smiled broadly, almost as if in relief. "I don't know that you've come to the right place, exactly, but you're more than welcome. I'll have to send word for . . . Vaenturl that you're here. He said you'd likely arrive in late spring, if you came at all."

"Where would you recommend that we stay?"

"I wouldn't wish to speak for . . . Vaenturl. I'm certain that, if you can wait a glass, he'll either be here or send word. I wouldn't want to speak for him," Essek repeated, "but where you decide to stay might depend on what he says. His word is always good. You're welcome in here, although I'm afraid we don't have much of interest except large lots of cloth, rope, twine, and the like."

"We can wait outside." *At least for a time.*

"I need to send word. If you'll excuse me . . ."

"Thank you. We'll be outside." Beltur turned and walked back out to where the others waited.

"Well?" inquired Lhadoraak anxiously.

"We're expected. The factor's sending word to Vaenturl, except that's apparently not his name. He'll either be here or send word about what we should do within the glass."

Jessyla nodded.

Tulya frowned. "Not his name? That doesn't sound promising."

"The factor—Essek the younger—said that his word was always good. He was telling the truth."

"A mysterious trader whose word is always good," mused Lhadoraak. "Who left word to expect you? I wonder what you've gotten us all into, Beltur."

Beltur shrugged. "We couldn't stay in Axalt, and even if we could have, Tulya wouldn't have been happy there." He turned to her. "Would you?"

"No . . . but this is . . ."

"A little frightening?" asked Beltur gently.

"Uncertain, anyway."

As they waited, Beltur studied the people who passed. Some nodded pleasantly. A few looked inquisitively, especially at Lhadoraak and Beltur, and even Jessyla. One small girl stopped and looked up at Taelya, who had decided to remain mounted, almost enviously, before her mother gently tugged her on her way.

Less than three quints later, Beltur caught sight of three men riding up the street on the same side of the square as the factorage. Two were heavily armed, both with blades in shoulder scabbards, and lance-like spears in saddle holders. They wore matching blue coats, and rode closely behind the third, who was clean-shaven, but dark-haired, and it took Beltur a moment to recognize him.

Vaenturl clearly recognized Beltur and Jessyla, most likely Jessyla, Beltur thought, because he smiled broadly as he reined up. "Beltur, Jessyla, I'm glad you're here."

Beltur sensed that Vaenturl, or whoever he really was, meant those words. "It took a moment to recognize you. You had a beard the last time I saw you."

"It works better that way . . ."

"And you're not Vaenturl . . . or rather that's a name you use when you're posing as a trader."

"Actually, when I'm using that name, I am a trader. It's not my birth name, though. You've gathered more people, I see."

"They're one of the reasons why we're here. Lhadoraak's also a black, but his daughter, Taelya, is a white, and she wasn't welcome in Axalt."

"She looks to be little more than a child."

"She's still a girl. She's only seven, but she can already do some magery. That made the Axalt Council uneasy."

For some reason, Vaenturl smiled. "So you have three mages and a healer?"

Beltur nodded.

"Five people . . . we can easily handle that many."

Beltur frowned. "Handle that many?"

"As guests. Maeyora and I. I already told her to expect company."

Beltur could sense Tulya's immediate relief. "According to Essek the younger, you've been expecting us, if a bit later than now. Might I ask why you thought we might be here?"

"I hoped as much as thought. Axalt is perfectly fine for the normal black mage. Neither you nor your consort fit, and I doubt that your consort is a normal healer."

"No, she's not." Beltur wasn't about to go into more detail, not until he understood much better exactly what was happening. He could sense that Vaenturl—for lack of a better name—was pleased, and wasn't harboring any chaos.

"Also, your friend is a black mage, and his daughter is a white. That, I suspect, is also not normal." Vaenturl offered an amused smile.

"By the way, since Vaenturl isn't your name, at least it isn't when you're not trading, what is it?"

"Oh . . . I'm sorry. You wouldn't know. My given name is Korsaen. Are you all up to a short ride? It's less than a quint." Korsaen looked to Taelya. "You certainly look ready, young woman."

"I am, ser." Taelya inclined her head politely.

A broad smile crossed Korsaen's face. "Then, we should ride . . ." He gestured.

As Beltur mounted up, he did notice something else. Several people were watching, and their eyes were not on Beltur or Lhadoraak, but on Korsaen. He also could see that Jessyla had made the same observation as they exchanged glances. *Korsaen is definitely someone, but who?*

Once Korsaen led the riders, and the mule and spare mount, away from the square, they headed north on a wider paved avenue for almost half a kay.

As they neared a lane that led off to the left, Beltur asked, "Where does the avenue go?"

"To the estate of the Duchess. Our modest grounds are at the end of that ridiculously long lane we're about to take."

That suggests he's not an immediate relation to the Duchess, but wealthy and powerful enough to be someone of import.

They rode along the lane, wider than most roads, with Beltur riding on one side of Vaenturl/Korsaen, and Jessyla on the other. Then came Lhadoraak and his family, with the two guards bringing up the rear.

After several hundred yards, the lane curved back to the north, and at the end of the curve were two tall brick gateposts. The two iron scrollworked gates were already swung open, and there was neither a guard nor a gatehouse. The lane continued, running through a meadow toward a long three-story stone-walled dwelling situated just below the crest of a rise some five yards higher than the meadow. A wall, little more than two yards high, enclosed an area perhaps three hundred yards on a side, and Beltur counted three substantial outbuildings, one of which looked to be a stable. There were gardens on both ends of the house. Beyond the open gates in the second wall, the lane was stone-paved and ran directly toward the center of the mansion, where it formed an oval around a small garden, with the north side of the oval going under the covered entrance. Off the rightmost curve in the oval another stone-paved lane led to the stable and to the outbuilding behind it.

Korsaen guided them onto the side lane to the stable, where he dismounted, and led his mount inside, turning the gelding over to a stableboy, while the two guards led their mounts into the stable and to stalls.

Beltur followed Korsaen's example, dismounting and leading Slow-poke into the stable, a good fifty yards long with stalls for over twenty horses, although Beltur only saw about ten.

"Most of our horses are in the north pasture, over the hill," said Korsaen. "Dallket, here, will show you the stalls and where the hay and grain are . . . and the water pump and buckets. I need to check with Maeyora about some things, but I'll be back likely before you've settled your horses."

Once Korsaen was walking back toward the mansion, Lhadoraak said quietly to Beltur, "Do you know what he is? He has to be powerful."

Beltur shook his head. "We traveled with him for close to an eightday. Jorhan thought he was a trader, and he never gave any indication he was more than that." He grinned. "It looks to me that it's better than an inn."

"And it might cost us more in the long run," said Tulya warily.

"He hasn't withheld or lied yet," said Lhadoraak.

"I like him," declared Taelya. "He's nice."

Tulya raised her eyebrows, but said nothing else.

"We're here. We might as well see to the horses," said Beltur, turning and wondering where he should stall Slowpoke.

"Ser," offered Dallket, returning from stalling Korsaen's gelding. "Your mount should have one of the bigger stalls. I'll show you. After that, I'll show the others where they can stall their mounts."

"Lead the way."

The youth turned and walked toward the north end of the stable, stopping some ten yards later and pointing to an open stall. When Beltur led the gelding into the stall, Dallket glanced from Slowpoke to Beltur and back again. "He's a warhorse, isn't he, ser? Your warhorse."

Beltur nodded.

"I've never met a war mage before."

"It wasn't my choice. The Prefect of Gallos attacked Elparta, and all the mages were required to beat back the invasion."

"Are you going to be a war mage for Lord Korsaen?"

Lord Korsaen? Lord of what? "We haven't talked about that," replied Beltur, managing a pleasant smile.

"I need to help the others, ser. There's a bucket in the stall. The water pump is just outside the door that's two stalls up, and I'll bring hay and grain to all the horses after you groom them."

"Thank you, Dallket."

"My pleasure, ser."

As the youth left, Beltur couldn't help wondering why Korsaen might be looking for a war mage. Was the Viscount threatening Montgren? Or was the Duke of Lydiar? Or did Korsaen have something else in mind?

All of those possibilities made him uneasy.

He wanted to say something to Jessyla about what Dallket had said, but he'd barely finished grooming and watering Slowpoke when Korsaen returned and promptly helped Taelya to groom her mount, although that meant that Korsaen did most of the work.

Then the lord said, "Maeyora has worked out what rooms you'll all be in. So follow me with whatever you need. The guest rooms are all on the second level of the east wing. That's because she thought our guests should appreciate the sunrises, since she does not."

Although Korsaen did not smile, Beltur sensed the humor in his voice.

The lord led them to an entry on the east end of the mansion and then up a stone staircase to the second level, stopping in the foyer at the top of the stairs. "There's another staircase at the other end of this wing that leads down to the center hallway, and the library, dining room, and all the other function rooms. The water taps in the washrooms only offer cold water," said Korsaen, "but one of the house porters will be up shortly with large kettles of boiling water for each washroom." He gestured to the first door on the left and then looked at Lhadoraak and Tulya. "I thought this room might be best for you. It shares a washroom with the adjoining room, and it seemed that would allow Taelya to have her own room while still being close to you."

"That is most thoughtful," said Tulya. "We thank you."

Korsaen opened the door and stepped back. "Dinner will be at fifth glass, but feel free to come down to the parlor any time after fourth glass."

Taelya immediately carried her small duffel into the room, and her parents followed, with Tulya closing the door behind herself.

Korsaen walked to the next door, across the hall and several yards farther along, and opened that door. "Maeyora thought this would suit you. It has an adjoining washroom and jakes." He paused, then said in a lower voice, "After you get washed up and ready for dinner, settled, I think we three should have a brief meeting so that we can go over some matters of interest to you, and perhaps all of your group. Perhaps at a quint past four downstairs in my study?"

After glancing at Jessyla, Beltur said, "We'd be pleased."

"Good. Oh . . . one other thing. If you'll leave anything you want washed outside your door this evening, we can take care of that as well. Please let Lhadoraak and his family know that as well."

"We can do that," said Jessyla. "That's most thoughtful."

"If you have any other questions about the room or the facilities, you can ask the porter when he arrives, or me when we meet." Korsaen smiled. "I had thought I might see you, and I'm very glad that you came. Until later this afternoon." With a nod, he turned and walked down the corridor to the center of the mansion.

When Beltur and Jessyla entered their room, for several moments she just looked around, taking in the bed, which was wide enough for three, covered with a cream and blue quilt, and four pillows with matching shams. The headboard and footposts were of a dark wood that Beltur didn't recognize, as were the two wooden armchairs with seats upholstered also in blue, and the small writing desk, and the armoire set against the wall.

"This is what I would think a room in a palace looks like," she finally said. "They must want you to do something very badly."

"He kept referring to both of us. I don't think that was just a courtesy."

"It might be a courtesy to me so that I'll be more amenable to what he has in mind."

That's very possible. But somehow Beltur hadn't gotten that feeling. "I didn't have a chance to tell you earlier. Dallket—the stableboy—he called Korsaen 'Lord Korsaen,' and said Korsaen was looking for a war mage. Well . . . he didn't say that. He asked whether I'd been a war mage, and when I said that I had been, very reluctantly, he asked if I was going to be a war mage for Lord Korsaen."

"Not if I have anything to say about it! Seeing you almost die twice was enough."

"I don't think that's quite what he has in mind. He's made a point to include you and not Lhadoraak."

"He wants me to persuade you to do what he wants."

"Or he thinks you'll be more sensible than I am."

"I doubt that."

At that point, there was a knock on the door. "Ser . . . Lady . . ."

Beltur opened the door to find two porters in dark blue livery outside, each carrying a large and steaming copper kettle.

"The hot water for you."

Beltur stepped back and watched as the two proceeded to the washroom, where one put a stopper in the bottom of the narrow tub, then turned on the single tap, waiting until the cold water in the bottom of the tub was several digits deep. Then he poured most of what was in the kettle into the tub and set the kettle on the rack next to the tub, beside the second kettle.

Without another word, the two porters left.

"I think that means you get to take the first bath," said Beltur. "You don't want to waste that hot water."

Somewhat more than a quint later, Beltur was bathed and fully dressed, wearing his mage-healer tunic, and watching Jessyla as she finished putting up her hair.

"It's still damp, and I can't do anything else with it."

Beltur wasn't about to argue about that. "You look wonderful."

"I look presentable. Mostly."

"Are you ready to see what Korsaen has to say?"

"I'll listen."

Beltur kept his wince to himself.

A few moments later, the two stepped out into the hallway, where, Beltur noticed, a small table had been placed by the door, and the door to Lhadoraak and Tulya's chambers.

Beltur gestured. "They meant it."

"I intend to take full advantage of their offer."

The staircase in the center of the mansion, which ran up a level and down to the main floor, was far more ornate than the one at the end of the east wing, and had creamy marble balustrades and banisters, and a dark blue carpeted runner over the marble steps. At the bottom of the steps was a wide hallway, also tiled in the creamy marble, that extended to the front entry and then back to a set of double doors.

Beltur was still looking around when Korsaen stepped out of a side door. "I thought I heard steps. If you'd join me here in the study. I just got back less than a quint ago."

The two followed Korsaen into the study, a comparatively small chamber perhaps four yards by five, paneled in the same dark wood as the desk and the circular table and chairs set in the middle of the maroon carpet. Korsaen moved to one of the chairs at the table and gestured for them to take a seat.

"As I recall," said the lord, looking to Jessyla, "you prefer smooth dark lager."

"Yes, thank you."

"And pale ale for you?"

Beltur nodded.

Korsaen did not appear to have spoken or signaled to anyone, but in moments, a server entered through the still-open door and placed the beverages on the table before each, as well as a pale ale before the unoccupied seat.

"Maeyora will be joining us in a moment."

Even as Korsaen spoke, the study door opened, then closed, and Beltur managed to keep his mouth in place as Korsaen's consort walked toward the table. While Korsaen was dark-haired, thin-faced, and about the same height as Beltur, Maeyora was a good head shorter than Jessyla, compact and wiry, with silver hair. Beltur had read about the silver hair of Nylan, but he'd never seen anyone with that kind of silver hair before. She also had a strong black aura, and wore healer greens.

At that, Beltur almost nodded.

Korsaen smiled. "As you can see, I am outnumbered."

"Outnumbered, but never deceived, I think," replied Beltur in what he hoped was a humorous tone. "I've read about silver hair, from the dark angels, but I've never seen someone with it."

"It comes from my mother's time with a bard who turned out to be a druid," replied Maeyora openly. "My mother worried about it when it showed up with me. How do you find your quarters?" That question was addressed to Jessyla.

"They're lovely, more like a palace. But then, this is a palace, isn't it?"

"I would hope not," replied Korsaen, with a laugh. He lifted his beaker. "To your safe arrival here."

The others lifted their beakers as well, then drank, although Beltur noticed that Maeyora only took a tiny sip.

"I'm sure you're wondering why I asked you to meet with us," said Korsaen as he set his beaker on the table. "As you must have guessed, I'm a bit more than a trader. I do trade, but I use the trading to look for people who have certain abilities and who would be happier in Montgren than where they are or have been. You and those with you are looking for a place where you can settle down and gain some control over your lives. We may be able to help you find a place from which you'll never have to move again and where you'll have the opportunity to arrange matters much more to your liking."

"There's a price to any offer like that," replied Beltur warily.

"I'll admit it. There is. I've been looking for people like you for several years. Not for myself, of course, but on behalf of someone else. I never hoped to see three mages . . ."

"Four," said Beltur. "Jessyla also has some skills there, and is improving daily."

"That's even better."

"And the price?" prompted Beltur.

"You'll be the one setting the price. That's something you'll have to bargain out. Are you interested? At worst, you can refuse. At best, it might benefit all of us."

"Just who are we going to be bargaining with?"

"My aunt."

"Who is she? The sister or cousin of the Duchess?"

"No. The Duchess herself. She was the only surviving heir, and in Montgren, women can rule. She did and still does. Her consort died two years ago, and she's not ready to turn the land over to her daughter."

Jessyla offered a faint smile and looked to Maeyora. "Are you . . . ?"

"No. I'm one of those people Korsaen found."

"It's more like she found me," admitted the lord.

Beltur sensed the absolute truth behind both their statements. "All of this is . . . rather vague. Could you be a bit more detailed?"

"My aunt is looking for someone, or a talented group, to whom she can give the charter to a small town, more like a large village."

"What sort of trouble is she having?" asked Jessyla.

"I think that should come from her. I can say that it once was a lovely town, and could be again, but it will require a firm hand, or set of hands."

"You two doubtless have firm sets of hands," observed Jessyla.

"We aren't mages," replied Maeyora, "and Korsaen has his hands full with his duties as the largely unseen protector of Montgren."

"Montgren really doesn't have that many people," said Korsaen. "It's said that we have more sheep than people. It's more like twenty times more sheep than people. We can barely afford to maintain a single battalion of armsmen. The dukes and duchesses have always tried to keep tariffs on their people low."

Jessyla glanced around the well-appointed study.

Maeyora smiled. "You're thinking about this house . . . or you should be. I used to travel with Korsaen, and we did do a great deal of trading then. That is how we could afford to build the house."

Again, Beltur could sense the truth, and it also made sense, because, if Maeyora could sense people as well as Herrara or Jessyla could . . .

"You see why Korsaen wanted you two and me here?" asked the silver-haired woman.

Beltur did. "That's why you have a white mage as a border guard at the post outside of Bortaan?"

"Exactly. He fled from Hydlen some ten years ago. He wanted to live in whatever part of Montgren was farthest from Hydolar."

"You recruit mages from everywhere so that you don't have to pay armsmen?"

Korsaen shook his head. "Not just mages. People. We may only have one battalion of armsmen, but they're paid twice as much as any battalion anywhere, and they're probably three times as good."

"So why aren't you the one making whatever this offer is?" asked Beltur.

"The Duchess is the only one empowered to make the offer, and for something this important, she wouldn't delegate the decision. Maeyora and I will be at the meeting, of course."

Of course.

"Are you interested?"

"We're interested," replied Beltur, adding after looking at Jessyla, "but cautious."

"As you should be."

"We'll meet," added Jessyla. "Then we'll decide."

"And if you want Lhadoraak, he and Tulya should be there as well," added Beltur.

Korsaen nodded. "Before we adjourn to the parlor to wait for the others, is there anything else of concern?"

"There is one thing. We're going to need a farrier sooner or later."

Korsaen smiled broadly. "That is something that is easy to provide. I can have one here in the morning. For all the horses?"

"I'd like him to check all of them, but from what I can see, the mule is fine, and so is the mount that Lhadoraak's riding. Slowpoke—that's my big gelding—definitely needs reshoeing, and probably the others do as well."

"Now . . . I think we should enjoy our drinks, and then dinner." Korsaen rose, lifting his beaker and moving to the study door, which he opened. "I trust you won't mind if the children join us, since they seldom get to eat with company, and especially not with someone close to their own age."

"How old are they?" asked Jessyla.

"Korwaen is nine, and Maenya is six," replied Maeyora.

Two children who had been sitting on a settee in the parlor immediately rose as the four adults entered. Korwaen had light brown hair and his mother's wiry build, although it appeared he would be taller, while

Maenya had the silver hair and a narrower face. Both wore dark blue tunics and trousers.

"Korwaen, Maenya," said Maeyora. "I'd like you to meet Mage Beltur and Healer Jessyla. They've recently ridden all the way from Axalt."

Both children offered a polite head bow, then straightened, and said, almost simultaneously, "I'm honored to meet you."

"And we're pleased to meet you," replied Beltur and Jessyla.

Maenya looked questioningly at her mother.

Before Maeyora could answer, Beltur said, "Taelya is just a year older than you, and she's coming down with her parents in a few moments." Then he looked to Maeyora. "Your consort may have told you, but if he has not, Taelya is a white, and can do some magery already."

Maenya's eyes widened.

"Like you," said Beltur, "Taelya is very well-mannered."

The six had barely seated themselves in the parlor when Lhadoraak, Tulya, and Taelya entered from the hallway.

Lhadoraak and Tulya inclined their heads as they entered, but Beltur could sense that both were uneasy. Taelya smiled at Maenya, who offered a tentative smile in return.

"Welcome to Montgren," offered Maeyora warmly. "You've had a very long ride."

"It was very long," agreed Tulya.

Lhadoraak nodded agreement.

In moments, the server had returned and supplied Lhadoraak with lager, Tulya with pale ale, and all three children with pearapple juice.

"You've arrived just in time to see everything flower," said Korwaen. "Spring and early fall are the loveliest and most temperate times of the year in Montgren."

From that single sentence, Beltur knew that nothing of import would be discussed in the parlor or at dinner.

Nor was he wrong.

A filling dinner was served—excellent mutton chops, laced potatoes, served with a piquant cream sauce, pickled and seasoned turnips, followed by a fried sweet pastry that Beltur had never seen—accompanied by light conversation about the trip, the various cheeses and foods for which Montgren was known, and other informative and humorous tidbits.

Almost two glasses later, the five travelers made their way up the steps and toward their rooms. Taelya hung on to her mother's hand, more asleep than awake.

"That was quite a dinner," said Lhadoraak. "I didn't expect something quite so lavish."

"They must want something," said Tulya.

"They do," replied Beltur. "The Duchess is going to make an offer tomorrow. It may be difficult to refuse."

Lhadoraak frowned. "What sort of offer?"

"I don't know exactly. It has something to do with granting us a charter to a lovely town in return for our services. Korsaen wouldn't or couldn't tell us the scope of those services, but he wants all four of us."

"Has he said who he is?" asked Tulya.

"His consort called him the largely unseen protector of Montgren, and his official title is Lord Korsaen," said Jessyla. "He and Maeyora used to be traders. They made enough at it to be able to build this mansion. He's also the nephew of the Duchess."

Lhadoraak and Tulya exchanged glances.

"Beltur . . ." began Lhadoraak.

"You don't have to accept anything. All I'm asking is that you and Tulya come with us and listen."

"We can do that."

"Also, put any laundry you want washed on that little table there tonight. They'll take care of that as well."

"Beltur . . ." After a moment, Lhadoraak went on. "Is he telling you the truth?"

"He's telling the truth," said Jessyla. "There's not a single hint of withholding, evasion, or untruth. He also expects us to be equally truthful. That's why his consort is his partner. She can tell. She's also got druid blood. She told us that when Beltur commented on her silver hair."

Again, Lhadoraak and Tulya exchanged glances.

"Lhadoraak . . . we've been too many places where people didn't want us," said Beltur gently. "Someone here wants us badly enough to make quite an effort. It's at least worth hearing out."

Slowly, Tulya nodded.

Then she and Lhadoraak turned toward the door to their rooms.

Once Beltur and Jessyla were alone in their chambers, she turned and said, "As far as I could tell, they never lied or avoided answering—except about what the Duchess will say or offer. That frightens me, just a little."

"I worry about just how much she might want. And what the price is . . . and whether it's wise to accept."

"We won't know until she makes an offer." Jessyla paused. "But there are some things that come to mind. Most people here seem to smile. Korsaen rode into Montgren with just two guards, and neither was a mage. His gates are open. The factor knew who he was and said that his word was good. Has it been anything like that anywhere else we've been?"

Beltur smiled wryly. "Those are good points." *But are they enough?*

XCIX

At breakfast on sevenday, Korsaen told everyone that they would be meeting with the Duchess at the first glass of the afternoon, that the farrier would arrive by eighth glass, and that they would have clean laundry by the end of the day, and if they wanted what they wore washed as well, to set it out after dinner that evening.

After breakfast, Beltur checked all the horses, and the mule, again, and waited for the farrier to arrive. When the man did, Beltur escorted him to meet Slowpoke.

"This isn't necessary, ser mage."

Beltur smiled. "It is. I feared that one of his shoes might break, and I eased some extra order into binding his hoof and shoe, and I need to remove that . . . and explain how he got this far with the shoe in the shape it was."

The farrier took one look and said, "I see. He would have thrown that shoe."

"I know. That's why you're here."

Then Beltur went back to find Taelya, whom Tulya was getting ready to spend the day with Korwaen and Maenya.

He found them in the hallway. "I need a moment to talk to Taelya."

"Yes, Uncle Beltur?"

"Taelya," said Beltur, "you'll be spending time with Korwaen and Maenya. Korwaen is a boy, and boys don't always know their own strength. He's also bigger than you. If . . . if he tries to hit you or hurt you, the only magery you can use is your shield. He may not, but that is the only magery you may use. Is that clear?"

"Yes, Uncle Beltur. If he looks like he wants to hit me, can I use the shield first?"

"Yes, you may, but you can't touch him with the shield. You have to let him hit the shield."

"I won't. I promise."

Tulya voiced the words "Thank you" without actually speaking them.

Beltur watched the two as they walked toward the center staircase, hoping Taelya wouldn't need to use her shield. He still worried. Korwaen was clearly a child of power and privilege, well-mannered as he appeared to be, and he didn't want the combination of a strong-willed boy and a strong-willed girl who was also a mage to turn out badly.

At two quints past noon, the six who would meet with the Duchess gathered in the stable.

"Since the farrier is still working, I thought you could ride some of my horses," said Korsaen. "That way, they'll get some exercise, and we won't get in Ducont's way."

That was fine with Beltur, since Slowpoke and the other mounts could also use the rest.

Before long, all six were riding south on the lane and then north on the avenue leading to the palace of the Duchess of Montgren. The palace sat on a low hill, with a wall around the base of the hill and a single set of gates—open and guarded by two men in the light blue of Montgren. They inclined their heads as Korsaen rode past, but did not speak.

The palace proper was little more than twice the size of Korsaen's mansion, which was imposing, but would have easily fit inside the main courtyard of the palace of the Prefect of Gallos, and the outbuildings were also roughly twice the size of those at Korsaen's estate.

"We can just tie the horses at the rails by the main entry," said Korsaen as he reined up short of the pair of guards. "This shouldn't take that long, one way or the other. The Duchess isn't one for indirection or inane small talk."

"She's not one for any sort of inanity," said Maeyora dryly.

"Good afternoon, Lord Korsaen," offered one guard.

"The same to you, Rhaas."

"The Duchess sent word to you that she'd be in the large study."

"Then that's where we'll go."

Once they dismounted and were inside the circular entry hall, Beltur looked to the lord. "How does one address a duchess?"

"Just call her Duchess until she tells you otherwise," replied Korsaen with a laugh.

The palace was older and much darker than Korsaen's mansion, with wood paneling so dark, partly from age, that its polished surface looked almost black. Their boots echoed on the stone floor as they took the main corridor almost thirty yards before coming to a stop outside a door with a single guard, the first Beltur had seen since they entered the palace.

"If you'd announce us, Phaltyn."

"Yes, ser." The guard turned, rapped on the door, then opened it slightly and called, "Lord Korsaen and Healer Maeyora with the mages and the healer!"

"Have them come in. We're not to be disturbed."

*   *   *

The white-haired woman who sat behind the wide table desk closed the ledger she had been perusing and set it aside, gesturing to six chairs arranged in an arc. "Sit where you like, except for you, Korsaen. You sit on one end or the other."

Beltur and Jessyla found themselves in the middle with Lhadoraak and Tulya to Jessyla's right, and Maeyora and Korsaen to Beltur's left.

The Duchess looked directly at Beltur. "My nephew tells me that you four are looking for a place that's friendly to you and where you can settle. He also claims that you, Beltur, are the most powerful black he knows of. How true is that?"

"I have stronger shields and containments than any other black I've met. So far I haven't encountered a white who could break them. If I had, I wouldn't likely be here."

The Duchess looked to Maeyora, who nodded. Then she looked to Lhadoraak. "How strong a black are you, and do you agree with what Beltur said?"

"I'm moderately strong. I'm nowhere close to as powerful as Beltur. He may be one of the most powerful mages in Candar."

Maeyora again nodded.

"How good a healer are you?" The Duchess studied Jessyla.

"I'm better than many. I still am not as good as I'd like."

"Are you a mage as well?"

"I have some magely abilities, and I'm getting better. I have moderate shields, and I'm working on containments."

"You're a healer, too, aren't you?" The Duchess's pale green eyes fixed on Beltur. "How good?"

"In the more usual healing, I'm not as good as Jessyla, but I can remove small bits of wound and other chaos, and I can immobilize parts of a wounded person's body so that another healer can more easily set bones or do surgery."

"Do you have any problems with killing people who have killed others and terrorized villagers and other innocents?"

"If that is indeed the case, Duchess—"

"It's very much the case."

"If it is," repeated Beltur, "then I don't."

An amused smile crossed the Duchess's face. "You're skeptical of rulers, aren't you?"

"Until they prove I shouldn't be."

"How many have you stood up to?"

"Not as many as I should have."

"Such as?"

"I wasn't strong enough to stand up to the Prefect of Gallos. So I escaped because my uncle insisted. I stood up to the highest black mages in Spidlar, but never actually faced the Traders' Council. I stood up to the Council of Axalt."

"That will do." After a slight pause, the Duchess said, "I have a problem, actually two. So do you. You're a powerful black, but the nature of your power doesn't lend itself to conquest, which means you don't fit in lands such as Certis, Gallos, Lydiar, or Hydlen. You're male, which rules out Westwind or Sarronnyn. You have some degree of ethics, and that makes you a danger to most rulers or councils in lands such as Spidlar, Sligo, Suthya, or Axalt. My larger problem is that Montgren lies between Certis, Lydiar, and a tiny piece of Hydlen, and is not wealthy enough to support a large force of armsmen. That is not a problem either of us can resolve immediately. But I also have a smaller problem that the four of you could resolve. There is a town in the south of Montgren that lies on the trading route to Hydolar, which is also sometimes used by traders who wish to go to Jellico but who find Weevett, shall I say, too confining. Those traders are slowly destroying Haven. The town council no longer exists because no councilor would stand up to these renegade traders. Tariffs have not been collected in two seasons. I debated sending in a company of armsmen, but merely sending armsmen would be pointless. The remaining townspeople have no coins to speak of, and the traders will simply leave and not return until the armsmen leave before resuming their activities. If I create a fort there and permanently station armsmen at that post, I risk conflicts with Hydlen, Certis, or Lydiar, depending on whose traders bribe their rulers the most."

"I can see your problems," replied Beltur carefully, "but you are far more familiar with the situation than we are. With what you've said, I'm not certain how we might resolve this problem, since you've said that using force—"

"I didn't say that I could not use force. I said that I could not use armsmen by themselves, and the remaining townspeople neither have the will nor the ability to improve matters. If the Council of Haven, through its own abilities, resolves the situation in Haven without resort to a permanent use of armsmen by Montgren, neither the Viscount nor the dukes of Hydlen or Lydiar will be able to use their armsmen without risking involvement by the others."

"That makes sense," replied Beltur, "but exactly what role would we play?"

"It's very simple. I think you know generally what I'm going to say, but I don't blame you for wanting me to spell it out."

Beltur was afraid he might know what she was going to propose.

"Since the Council of Haven no longer exists, the town charter is void. I will issue a new charter naming the four of you as the Council of Haven with all powers and duties necessary to maintain a free town. You will appoint at least one and no more than three other councilors, from those resident in Haven *after* you have reestablished order. You will have full authority from me to do whatever is necessary to reestablish Haven."

"Even if you grant us such a formal charter," Beltur pointed out, "who will believe us if we ride in and announce it?"

"You'd have trouble that way," admitted the Duchess. "That's why you'll be escorted by a full company of my armsmen. They'll stay for an eightday, longer if necessary. I'll also provide fifty golds to each family to purchase or build lodgings, and a hundred golds for expenses for the first year." She smiled coolly. "If you're the Council, the Council can't run you out. Of course, that does mean you have to run Haven well enough that the people are satisfied and that the traders who pass through behave."

"There's one other small problem," Beltur said. "That's the question of how we make a living. Jessyla and I got by in Axalt by working as healers. I doubt Haven even has a healing house. Lhadoraak inspected flatboats and other boats and detected those who tried to evade tariffs. You don't levy tariffs, I understand."

"I'll pay you for the first year. That should enable you to put the Council on a sound basis. Once it is, you can pay yourselves a modest stipend as councilors. While we don't tariff goods passing through Montgren, every shop, crafter, inn, or public house pays a tariff each season. For small crafters, that may be as little as a copper a season. A fourth part of those tariffs come to the palace. Most of them are used to repair or build roads and bridges or to pay armsmen. If you choose to become the Council of Haven, Korsaen will supply you with a copy of the rules and procedures."

"What's to keep you from pushing us out once we get things in order?" asked Lhadoraak, his tone skeptical.

"Two things. First, it wouldn't be in my interest in the slightest. We haven't received tariff payments from Haven in almost a year. Second, do you really think I'd risk sending armsmen against two mages like you and Beltur?"

"How much pay for the first year?" asked Jessyla.

"What do you think is fair?" countered the Duchess.

Jessyla looked to Beltur, who leaned over and murmured, "You got a silver an eightday in Elparta and would have gotten that in Axalt by now. Five for the two of us?"

She nodded, then said, "Five silvers an eightday for each couple."

"That's more than fair." The Duchess smiled. "If tariffs are back to where they were in a year, or even close, I'll give each couple an additional twenty-five golds as a reward. That's if you decide to take on the task, but it won't be easy. I'll also include in the charter a provision that so long as the tariff payments to the duchy are made, Haven shall be open to all mages of good character."

"Black and white?" asked Lhadoraak.

"Black and white," affirmed the Duchess.

There was a silence of several moments before the Duchess asked, "Do you have any more questions?"

"What about the laws of Montgren?" asked Beltur. "If we decide to do this, is our council responsible for enforcing and carrying out the laws? Can we make any additional town laws? Can you override us?"

"I don't foresee that as a problem," replied the Duchess. "You'll also get a copy of the existing laws. How you enforce them is up to you. My interest is restoring Haven. It's to your interest as well."

In short, enforce the laws, but don't be idiots.

Beltur turned toward Lhadoraak. "This could be as bad as the invasion, in a less brutal way, and it's going to take longer. But it's likely the only chance we'll get with a duchess behind us. What do you think?" Beltur offered a wry smile. "I take that back. Don't think. What do you both feel? Deep inside?"

"Scared," blurted Tulya.

"I don't see any better choices anywhere," said Lhadoraak.

"I've seen much worse choices." Jessyla's words were sharp. "We're doing it."

"That sounds like someone else I know," said Korsaen quietly, with a look at Maeyora.

Beltur looked to Lhadoraak.

"I have to agree with Jessyla."

Beltur looked to the Duchess. "Then we're agreed."

"No further caveats?" She raised her eyebrows.

"If there are problems we haven't foreseen, it's to both our interests to work them out."

The Duchess nodded. "Then it's settled. It will take a few days to gather everything together. Since tomorrow is eightday, you won't be able to leave until threeday morning. You'll be working with Korsaen on the details." Her eyes went to her nephew.

Korsaen stood. "Since we're finished here . . ." He gestured toward the door.

Beltur noticed that the Duchess was already reaching for the ledger she had put aside.

Once they were all outside the study, he said quietly to Korsaen, "She's very direct."

"She always has been."

"I take it that Haven has become a smugglers' den with no law and less order and that all the people who could flee already did so."

"Many of them, but not all."

No one spoke as they left the palace and mounted up, then headed south out of the palace grounds and onto the avenue leading into Vergren, before turning onto the lane.

"Beltur," said Jessyla, "can we really do this?"

"We can." *The real question is what it will cost whom.* "We've been in five countries. I don't see a better opportunity. Do you?"

"No. That's part of what worries me."

"It worries me, too. But we've seen what works and what doesn't, and now it's our turn." Beltur couldn't help but wonder if Relyn had felt that way when he reached Axalt.

C

After returning to Korsaen's estate, Beltur suggested, after asking the lord, that the "council" of Haven meet in Korsaen's parlor to talk over matters, largely because he wanted to hear any and all concerns that Lhadoraak and Tulya might have.

Once everyone was seated, Beltur just said, "What are your thoughts, good, bad, and otherwise?"

"Do we really want to do this?" asked Lhadoraak.

"If we want the chance to be in control of our own lives, is there any alternative?" countered Beltur.

"Are you sure there isn't?" asked Tulya.

"In every place else we've been, whoever rules controls mages," Beltur replied. "If we want to always answer to others, there are alternatives. If we want more control over our lives, I don't see another alternative."

"We could be attacked by any one of three lands," said Lhadoraak.

"That's why Haven's still a part of Montgren, I suspect," replied Beltur. "None of those three want another to have it. What the Duchess didn't say was that our job will be to keep the town and the road open to all traders without favoring any."

"I don't like the idea of collecting tariffs," added Tulya.

"Do you have a better idea?" asked Jessyla.

"No."

"We'll have to look at how tariffs are charged," said Beltur. "Remember, Montgren doesn't tariff goods entering or leaving. They have to get silvers somehow."

"She wants arms-mages without paying for them," said Tulya.

"She's agreed to pay twice what we got in Spidlar," said Lhadoraak. "We only have to deal with townspeople and traders."

"That will likely be more frustrating, but not as dangerous," said Beltur. *At least most of the time.* "We also get golds for housing."

"Why us?" asked Tulya. "Aren't there other mages . . ."

"Where?" asked Beltur dryly. "Any mages in Gallos belong to the Prefect, or they're dead. The same seems to be true in Certis. None of the blacks in Spidlar would be interested, and I'd wager what few mages there are in

Montgren are already being used at the border posts. The Duchess isn't quite desperate, but she doesn't have any other real choices, either, and she's paying well."

"You're right on both counts," said Korsaen, standing in the doorway. "We were passing by, and I couldn't help hearing the last."

"If we didn't accept her offer, then what?" asked Lhadoraak.

"She might have offered you a position at a border post. They don't pay as well, a silver and a half an eightday."

"You were just passing by?" asked Tulya.

"Actually," said Maeyora, "we were coming to tell you that Jolika—the governess—would be coming down with Taelya in just a bit. We also wanted to let you know that your daughter is very good at politely taking care of herself."

Beltur found himself tensing.

"Oh?" said Tulya.

"Korwaen told her that she couldn't do something because she was a girl. She told him that there were many things he couldn't do because he was a boy. Before Jolika could stop him, he tried to push her over, but he discovered he couldn't touch her."

Beltur half relaxed.

"Maenya laughed at him. He wasn't too happy about that, and he said something like he could make her unhappy, even if he couldn't touch Taelya, but your daughter stepped in front of him with her shield up and told him it was cruel to hit his sister." Maeyora's voice hardened. "He knows better. He won't be eating with us this evening."

Beltur had the feeling that wasn't the only punishment Korwaen had suffered. He also had the feeling that Taelya would do just fine in Haven.

"Jolika said that Taelya was very polite the whole time," added Korsaen.

"That's Beltur's doing," said Tulya. "He's been very firm about what she is allowed to do with magery and what is not allowed."

Maeyora looked to Beltur.

"Taelya's the youngest white I've ever known or heard about," he explained, "and I worried about how she could hurt someone without meaning to. That's why almost everything she knows is to protect herself and not to attack."

"Beltur," said Maeyora, more warmly, "we're not angry, except at Korwaen. It was a very good lesson for him."

"Very good." Korsaen paused. "Do you have any more questions? Anything."

"Were you looking for us in Elparta?" asked Beltur.

"Not for you in particular. I knew about the invasion, and often, after a war, or so I've heard, there are those who discover they don't fit in. I'd been looking in Elparta and doing some trading as well, but . . . well . . . I wasn't impressed. Then, when I heard Jorhan was looking to accompany a trader, and he said that there might be a possibility of a young strong mage accompanying him . . ." Korsaen shrugged.

"And?" prompted Jessyla.

"After what you did to those brigands, I was even more interested. I stayed with the trading name because I wanted any decisions you made to be because you wanted to come to Montgren on your own, not because a lord offered something."

"How long have you known about how bad things are in Haven?" asked Beltur.

"I didn't know that tariffs hadn't been collected until I got back to Vergren. I knew things were bad and that we needed someone to right them."

"So you were really scouting us out," said Jessyla. "Did you scout out Maeyora as well? She can't be from Montgren."

Korsaen flushed. "I wouldn't have put it—"

"He did," interjected Maeyora. "He was very tactful and gentle about it."

Jessyla looked to Maeyora. "I suppose he proposed to you without saying who he was?"

"He did. I could sense he was more than a trader, but he simply said that he was attracted to me, and that he could offer me a good life. I made him wait two years. He had to make several trips to Ouesthyd before I accepted."

"You're from there?"

Maeyora shook her head. "I was born in Clynya. Mother persuaded my father to escort her to Ouesthyd before he returned to his homeland. I grew up there. She consorted a grower who had a great ability with pearapples. She still sends us kegs of juice every harvest."

"And some pearapple brandy occasionally," added Korsaen.

After a long pause, Beltur said, "What questions should I have asked that I likely don't know enough to ask?"

"You've asked all the questions I would have in your position," replied Korsaen.

"I have a question," said Jessyla. "Why didn't you and the Duchess do something about Haven earlier?"

"Because we couldn't find anyone like the four of you any sooner. We needed people who will be in Haven almost all the time and who can stand up to some rather tough and violent individuals on a personal basis. That requires people who want to make the town into what it could be. In return for the backing of the Duchess and a free hand in governing Haven under the laws of Montgren, you have the opportunity to shape Haven into a place where you, and those like you, will be comfortable."

"What if we can't?" asked Jessyla.

"I have great confidence in you. I also suspect that all of you feel that you could make things work if you were in charge. This is likely the only opportunity you'll get. Life doesn't give that many real choices. Most of what we see as choices are nothing of the sort. I doubt that you really had a choice to stay in either Elparta or Axalt." Korsaen paused. "Or am I wrong?"

After a moment, Jessyla said, "I don't think so."

"No," murmured Tulya.

"Haven's been a problem for some time," said Beltur. "Everything shows that. Why is the Duchess so interested now?"

"She's always been interested. It's a question of both golds and people. All the golds in the world wouldn't help without the right people. Frankly, Montgren doesn't have that many golds, and we're a land of herders, timbermen, and farmers. Almost all of our handful of mages come from elsewhere, as do most of our armsmen."

Beltur thought that over. "Are you afraid Hydolar will take over the town and the lands around it?" he finally asked.

"That's a possibility if you don't succeed. Neither Certis nor Lydiar would let the other have that area. They might allow the Duke of Hydlen to keep it if he restored order."

"So it's our job not only to restore order but keep three dukes at bay?"

"Restoring order will keep Certis and Lydiar at bay, and a strong council will keep Hydlen at bay. That area isn't that good for much except for pasture and hunting wild boar, and as a trading stop. An honest trader could do well there. Oh, there's some fertile bottomland in places, but that's only useful if there's order in Haven."

Beltur finally said, "So we're a gamble to keep Haven as part of Montgren?"

"Isn't everything in life a gamble?" returned Korsaen quietly.

"I've heard that before." Beltur wondered if Korsaen had played plaques with the gambler who'd had his hands broken, or if the words were just a coincidence.

"Sayings that get repeated often have truth behind them. The trick is knowing when."

"What do you really expect from us?" asked Beltur.

"To make Haven a safe place for yourselves. If you do that, then nothing else matters."

Beltur stiffened. There was no equivocation, no reservation, and nothing hidden.

"And it will likely be the hardest task you've ever undertaken," added Maeyora, gently.

Beltur had no doubts that Maeyora's statement was absolutely true . . . and that what he and Jessyla faced was the biggest gamble of their lives.

He looked at Jessyla.

They both smiled.